FOR THE HEART

LAVYRLE SPENCER
HEATHER GRAHAM POZZESSERE
CATHERINE COULTER

Silhouette Books

Published by Silhouette Books
America's Publisher of Contemporary Romance

SILHOUETTE BOOKS

FOR THE HEART

Copyright © 1997 by Harlequin Books S.A.

ISBN 0-373-48359-7

The publisher acknowledges the copyright holders of the individual works as follows:
SWEET MEMORIES
Copyright © 1984 by LaVyrle Spencer
A MATTER OF CIRCUMSTANCE
Copyright © 1987 by Heather Graham Pozzessere
AFTERGLOW
Copyright © 1987 by Catherine Coulter

Printed in U.S.A.

Sweet Memories

With love to
the Huebners:
Jeannie
George
Jason
Tracy
and
Duke
And for my "other daughter,"
Theresa Schaeffer

Chapter One

At last, Jeff was coming home, but he wasn't alone. Watching the big-bellied jet taxiing to a stop, Theresa Brubaker felt two conflicting emotions—excitement that her "baby brother" would be here for two whole weeks, and annoyance that he'd dragged along some stranger to interfere with their family holiday. Theresa never liked meeting strangers, and at the thought of meeting one now, especially a *man,* a nervous ache grabbed her between the shoulder blades. She worked her head in a circle, flexed her shoulders and tried to shrug away the annoyance.

Through the soles of her knee-high snow boots she felt the shudder and rumble of the engines as they wheezed a last inflated breath, then whistled through a dying decrescendo and sighed into silence. The accordion pleats of the jetway eased forward, its mouth molded against the curve of the plane, and Theresa riveted her eyes on the doorway set in the wall of glass. As the first footsteps of disembarking passengers thudded down the tunnel, she self-consciously glanced down and made sure her heavy gray wool coat was buttoned up completely. She clutched a small black leather purse against her left side in a way that partially concealed her breast and gave her reason to cross her arms.

Her heart tripped out a staccato beat of anticipation—*Jeff. My crazy clown of a brother, the life of the family, coming home to make Christmas what all the songs said it should be. Oh, there's no place like home for the holidays.* Jeff—how she'd missed him. She bit her lower lip and trained her eyes on the door as the first passengers debarked: a young mother carrying a squalling baby, a businessman with a topcoat and briefcase, a bearded, blue-jeaned ski bum hefting a blue satchel boasting the word Vail, two long-legged military men clad in dress blues and garrison caps with visors set squarely across their eyebrows. *Two long-legged military men!*

"Jeff!" Her arm flew up joyously.

He caught sight of Theresa at the same moment she saw his lips form her name. But sister and brother were separated by a fifteen-foot-long ramp and handrail, and what seemed to be one-quarter of the population of Minneapolis greeting incoming arrivals. Jeff pointed her out while she read his lips again—"There she is"—and shouldered through the crowd toward the crown of the ramp.

She was scarcely conscious of her brother's companion as she flew into Jeff's arms, lifting her own around his neck while he scooped her off the floor and whirled her in a circle. His shoulders were broad and hard, his neck smelled of lime, and her eyes were suddenly swimming with tears while he laughed against her temple.

He plopped her onto her feet, smiled down into her joyous face and said gruffly, "Hiya, Treat."

"Hiya, snot-nose," she choked, then tried to laugh, but it came out a chugging gulp before she abashedly buried her face against him again, suddenly conscious of the other man looking on. Beside her ear, she heard the smile in Jeff's voice as he spoke to his friend.

"Didn't I tell you?"

"Yup, you did," came the stranger's voice, rich and deep.

She backed up. "Tell him what?"

Jeff grinned down teasingly. "That you're a sentimental fool. Look at you, tears flooding everything, and all over my dress blues." He examined his crisp lapel where a dark blotch showed.

"Oh, I'm sorry," she wailed, "I'm just so glad to see you." She dabbed at the tear spot on his jacket while he touched her just beneath an eye.

"You'd be sorrier if you could see how those tears make the freckles you hate so much stand out like new pennies."

She slapped his finger away and dabbed at her eyes self-consciously.

"Don't worry about it, Theresa. Come on, meet Brian." Jeff clapped an arm around her shoulders and turned her to face his friend. "This is the light o' my life, who never let me chase women, smoke pot or drive when I drank." At this last, Jeff winked broadly. "So let's not tell her what we did last night, okay, Scanlon?" He squeezed her shoulder, grinned down fondly while his teasing did absolutely nothing to disguise the deeper note of pride in his voice. "My big sister, Theresa. Theresa, this is Brian Scanlon."

She saw his hand first, with long, tapered fingers, extended in greeting. But she was afraid to look up and see where his eyes rested. Thankfully, the way Jeff had commandeered her shoulders, she was able to half hide behind him with one arm about his waist while extending her own hand.

"Hello, Theresa."

She could no longer avoid it. She raised her eyes to his face, but he looked straight into her eyes, smiling. And what a smile!

"Hello, Brian."

"I've heard a lot about you."

I've heard a lot about you, too, she thought, but answered gaily, "I'll just bet you have. My brother could never keep anything to himself."

Brian Scanlon laughed—a pleasant baritone rumble like a soft roll on a timpani—and held her hand in a hard grip, smiling at her from beneath the horizontal visor of his military hat that made her suddenly understand why some women shamelessly chase soldiers.

"Don't worry, he only told me the nice stuff."

Her glance fluttered away from his translucent green eyes that were far more attractive than in the photographs Jeff had sent, then Brian released her hand and moved to flank her other side as they headed away from the gate area toward the green concourse, still talking.

"All except for a couple of stories about our nasty childhood pranks, like the time you stole a handful of Grandpa Deering's pipe tobacco and taught me how to roll it up in those white papers that come with home permanents, and we both got sick from the chemicals in the paper when it got in our lungs, and the time—"

"Jeffrey Brubaker, I did not steal that tobacco. You did!"

"Well, who found the leftover papers in the bathroom vanity?"

"But who put the idea in my head?"

"I was two years younger. You should have tried to talk me out of it."

"I did!"

"But that was after we got sick and learned our lesson."

All three of them dissolved into laughter. Jeff squeezed her shoulder once more, looked across the top of her head at Brian and set things straight. "I'll be honest. After we got greener than a pair of garter snakes she'd never let me smoke again. I tried it more than once when I was in junior high, but she squealed on me every time and managed to get me grounded more than once. But in the end, she saved me from myself."

To Theresa's left, Brian's laugh rolled like faraway thunder. She noted its full, mellow tone, and now, when she spoke, that tone became every fuller, richer.

"He did tell me about another incident with home permanents when you gave him one against your mother's orders and forgot to set the timer." While he teased, he studied her hair. Jeff had said it was red, but Brian hadn't expected it to be the hue of a poppy!

"Oh, that," she wailed, hiding a cheek behind a palm. "Jeff, did you have to blab that to him? I could have died when I took those curlers out and saw what I'd done to you."

"*You* could have died? Mother was the one who could have died. That time it was *you* who should've gotten grounded, and I think you would have if you hadn't been eighteen already and going to college."

"Let's finish the story, little brother. In spite of the fact that you looked like an explosion in a silo, it got you that spot in the band, didn't it? They took one look at that ball of frizz and decided you'd fit right in."

"Which also put you beyond mother's good graces for the remainder of the summer, until I could prove I wasn't going to start sniffing cocaine and popping uppers every night before we played a gig.''

They had reached the escalator to the lower level where the luggage return was located, so were forced to break rank while riding down.

Studying the backs of the two heads below him, Brian Scanlon couldn't help envying the easy camaraderie between sister and brother. They hadn't seen each other for twelve months, yet they fell into a familiar groove of affectionate bantering as if they were good friends who saw each other daily. *They don't know how lucky they are,* he thought.

The revolving luggage carousels were surrounded, for holiday travel was at its heaviest with only a couple days left till Christmas. As they waited, Brian stood back and listened while the two of them filled in each other on family news.

"Mom and dad wanted to come and pick you up, but I got nominated instead because today was the last day of school before vacation. I got out at two, right after the Christmas program was over, but they both have to work till five, as usual.''

"How are they?''

"Do you have to ask? Absolutely giddy. Mom's been baking pies and putting them in the freezer, and worrying about whether pumpkin is still your favorite and dad kept asking her, 'Margaret, did you buy some of those poppy-seed rolls Jeff always liked?' And mom would lose patience and say, 'Willard, that's the third time you've asked me that, and this is the third time I'm answering. Yes, of course I bought poppy-seed rolls.' Yesterday she baked a German chocolate cake, and after all that fussing, came out and found dad had taken a slice from it. Boy, did the fur fly then. When she scolded him and informed him she'd baked the cake for dessert tonight, dad slunk off and took the car to the car wash and filled it up with gas for you. I don't think either one of them slept a wink last night. Mother was absolutely grumpy this morning, but you know how she gets when she's excited—the minute she sees you it'll dissolve like magic. Mostly she was upset because she had to work today when she'd rather have stayed home and gotten things ready, then come to the airport herself.''

It was plain to Brian that this homecoming had taken on premiere proportions in his family's hearts, even before Theresa went on.

"And just guess what dad did?''

Jeff only smiled a query. Theresa tipped him a smile with hidden meaning. "Get ready for this one, Jeff. He took your old Stella up to Viking Music and had new strings put on it and polished it all up and brought it out to the corner of the living room where you always used to leave it.''

"You're kidding!''

"God's truth."

"Do you know how many times he threatened to turn both me and my fifteen-dollar Stella out of the house if the two of us didn't quit bruising his eardrums with all our racket?"

Just then a duffel bag came circling toward them, and Jeff shouldered forward to grab it. No sooner had he set it behind him than a guitar case followed. As he leaned to snag it, Theresa exclaimed, "Your guitar! You brought your guitar?"

"Guitars. Both of ours."

She glanced up at Brian Scanlon, remembering he, too, played. She caught him studying her instead of the luggage return, his eyes the hue of rich summer moss, and Theresa quickly dropped her gaze.

"Can't let those calluses get soft," Jeff explained, "and anyway, two weeks without pickin' would be more than we could stand, right, Scan?"

"Right."

"But I promise I'll pick a few on the old Stella, just for dad."

A second guitar came bumping down the conveyor belt, followed by another duffel bag, and Theresa watched Brian's shoulders stretch his blue uniform jacket taut as he leaned to retrieve them. A young woman just behind Brian was giving him the once-over as he straightened and turned. The end of the guitar case caught her on the hip, and Brian immediately apologized.

The blonde flashed him a smile, and said, "Anytime, soldier boy."

For a moment he paused, then politely murmured, "Excuse me," and shouldered his duffel, glancing up to meet Theresa's eyes, which slid away shyly.

"All set?" She directed her question at her brother, because Brian made her uncomfortably aware of how inordinately pretty his eyes were for a man, and ever aware that they never dropped lower than her coat collar.

"Yup."

"Homeward bound. Let's go."

They stepped beyond the sliding doors of Minneapolis—St. Paul International into the crisp bite of December cold. Theresa walked between them again as they entered the cavernous concrete parking lot. But when they approached the correct row, she announced, "Dad and I traded cars for the day. I have his wagon, he has my Toyota."

"Hand me the keys. I'm dying to get behind a wheel again," her brother declared.

They loaded guitars and duffel bags into the rear and clambered inside. Through the fifteen-minute ride to the nearby suburb of Apple Valley, while Jeff and Theresa exchanged pleasantries, she tried to overcome her resentment of Brian Scanlon. She had nothing against him personally.

How could she? She'd never met him before today. It was strangers in general—more particularly *male* strangers—she tried to avoid. Somehow she'd always thought Jeff guessed and understood. But apparently she was wrong, for when he'd called and enthusiastically asked if he could bring his buddy home to spend the Christmas holidays, then explained that Brian Scanlon had no family, there'd been no hesitation from Margaret Brubaker.

"Why, of course. Bring him. It would be just plain unchristian to make a man spend Christmas in some miserable barracks in North Dakota when there are beds to spare and enough food for an army."

Listening on the extension phone, Theresa had felt her heart fall. She'd wanted to interrupt her mother and say, Just a minute! Don't the rest of us have any say about it? It's *our* Christmas, too.

There were frustrations involved with living at home at age twenty-five, and though sometimes Theresa longed to live elsewhere, the certain loneliness she'd suffer if she made the move always gave her second thoughts. Yes, the house belonged to her mother and father. They could invite whom they chose. And even while Brian Scanlon's intrusion rankled, she realized how selfish her thoughts were. What kind of woman would deny the sharing of Christmas bounty with someone who had no home and family?

But as they drove through the late-afternoon traffic, Theresa's apprehension grew.

They'd be home in less than five minutes, and she'd have to take her coat off, and once she did, it would happen again, as it always did. And she'd want to slink off to her room and cry...as she often did.

Even as the thoughts flashed through her mind, Brian said in his well-modulated voice, "I certainly want to thank you for letting me come along with Jeff and horn in on your holidays."

Theresa felt a flush of guilt working its way past her high gray coat collar, and hoped he wasn't looking at her as she politely lied. "Don't be silly. There's an extra bed in the basement and never a shortage of food. We're all very happy that Jeff thought of inviting you. Since you two started up the band together you're all we hear about when he calls or writes. Brian this and Brian that. Mother's been dying to get an eye on you and make sure her *little boy* has been traveling in good company. But don't pay any attention to her. She used to practically make his girlfriends fill out an application blank with three references."

Just then they drew into the driveway of a very run-of-the-mill L-shaped rambler on a tree-lined street where the houses were enough alike as to be almost indistinguishable from one another.

"Looks like mom and dad haven't gotten home yet," Theresa noted. A fresh film of snow dusted the driveway. Only one set of tire tracks led from the garage, but a single pair of footprints led up to the back door. "But Amy must be here."

The doors of the station wagon swung open, and Jeff Brubaker stood motionless beside the car for a moment, scanning the house in the way of a man seeking reassurance that none of the familiar things had altered. "God, it's good to be home," he breathed, sucking in a great gulp of the cold, pure Minnesota air. Then he became suddenly effervescent, almost jogging around to the tailgate of the wagon. "Come on you two, let's get this junk unloaded."

Thinking ahead to the next five minutes, Theresa appropriated a guitar case to carry inside. She didn't know how she'd manage it, but if worse came to worst, she might be able to hide behind it.

At the sound of the tailgate slamming, a gangly fourteen-year-old girl came flying out the back door. "Jeffy, you're home!" Smiling with a flash of tooth braces, Amy Brubaker threw her arms wide with an open gesture Theresa envied. Not a day went by that Theresa didn't pray her sister be granted the blessing of growing normally.

"Hey, dumpling, how are ya?"

"I'm too big for you to call me dumpling anymore."

They embraced with sibling exuberance before Jeff plopped a direct kiss on Amy's mouth.

"Ouch!" She jerked back and made a face, then bared her teeth for inspection. "Look out when you do that. It hurts!"

"Oh, I forgot about the new hardware. Let's see." He tipped her chin up while she continued curling her lips back as if not in the least daunted by her unattractive braces. Looking on, Theresa wondered how it was her little sister had managed to remain so uninhibited and charmingly self-assured.

"I tell everybody I got 'em decorated just in time for Christmas," Amy declared. "After all, they do look a little like tinsel."

Jeff leaned back from the waist and laughed, then quirked a smile at his friend. "Brian, it's time you met the rambunctious part of the Brubaker family. This is Amy. Amy, here he is at last—Brian Scanlon. And as you can see, I've talked him into bringing his guitar so we can play a couple hot ones for you and your friends, just as ordered."

For the first time, Amy lost her loquaciousness. She jammed her hands as far as they'd go into the tight front pockets of her blue jeans and carefully kept her lips covering the new braces as she smiled and said almost shyly, "Hi."

"Hi, Amy. Whaddya say?" He extended his hand and smiled at Amy with as charming a grin as any of the rock stars beaming from the postered walls of her bedroom. Amy glanced at Brian's hand, made an embarrassed half shrug and finally dragged one hand from the blue denim and let Brian shake it. When he released it, the hand hung in the air between them for a full fifteen seconds while her smile grew and grew, until a reflection flashed from the bars of metal spanning her teeth.

Watching, Theresa thought, *oh, to be fourteen again, with a shape like Amy's, and the total lack of guile that allows her to gaze point-blank in unconcealed admiration, just as she's doing now!*

"Hey, it's cold out here!" Jeff gave an exaggerated shiver. "Let's go in and dig into mom's cake."

They carried duffel bags and guitar cases into the cheery front-facing kitchen of the simple house. The room was papered in an orange- and gold-flowered pattern that was repeated in the fabric inserts of the shutters on the windows flanking the eating area, which looked out on the front yard. An ordinary house on a street with others just like it, the Brubaker home had nothing exceptional to set it apart, except a sense of familial love that Brian Scanlon sensed even before the mother and father arrived to complete the circle.

On the kitchen table was a crocheted doily of white, and in the center sat a pedestal plate bearing a mouth-watering German chocolate cake under a domed lid. When Jeff lifted the lid, the gaping hole came into view. In the hollow wedge was a slip of folded paper. He took it out to reveal a recipe card from which he read aloud: "Jeff, it looked too good for me to resist. See you soon. Dad."

The four of them shared a laugh, but all the while Theresa stood with the broad end of Jeff's guitar case resting on the floor at her toes, and the narrow end shielding the front of her coat. She was the delegate hostess. She should ask for Brian's jacket and hat and make a move toward the hall closet.

"Come on, Brian," Jeff invited, "see the rest of the place." They moved to the living room and immediately four raucous, jarring chords sounded from the piano. Theresa grimaced and glanced at Amy who rolled her eyeballs. It was "Jeff's Outer Space Concerto."

They drew deep breaths in unison, signaled with nods and bellowed simultaneously, "Je-e-e-eff, knock it off!" While the sisters giggled, Jeff explained to Brian, "I composed that when I was thirteen...before I became an impresario."

Theresa quickly hung up her coat in the front-hall closet and hustled down the hall to her bedroom. She found a pale blue cardigan sweater and whisked it across her shoulders without slipping her arms into the sleeves, then buttoned the top button at her throat. She glanced critically in the mirror, realigned the button-and-buttonhole panels so the sweater covered as much of her as possible, but found to her dismay it did little to disguise her problem. *Oh God, will I ever learn to live with it?*

Her usual, end-of-the-day backache plagued again, and she sighed, straightening her shoulders, but to no avail.

The house tour had stopped in the living room where Jeff had found his Stella. He was twanging out some metallic chords and singing an offbeat melody while Theresa tried to bolster her courage and walk out there. Undoubtedly it would be the same as it always was when she met a man. Brian Scanlon would scarcely glance at her face before his eyes would drop to her breasts and he would become transfixed by them. Since puberty she had relived those awful moments too many times to count, but Theresa had never become inured. That horrifying instant when a man's eyebrows twitched up in surprise, and his lips dropped open while he stared at the outsized mammary glands that had, through some unfortunate freak of nature, grown to proportions resembling volleyballs. They rode out before Theresa like a flagship before a fleet, their double-D circumference made the more pronounced by her delicately boned size-nine frame.

The last time she'd been introduced to a strange man he was the father of one of her second-grade pupils. Even as a parent, the poor man hadn't been able to remember protocol in his shock at glimpsing her enormous breasts. His eyes had riveted on them even while he was shaking Theresa's hand, and after that there'd been such awful tension between them the conference had been a disaster.

If she had carved a notch on her bedroom dresser every time that had happened down through the years, there'd be nothing before her now but a pile of wood chips. Now meeting the apprehensive eyes of the woman reflected in the mirror, Theresa quailed with all the familiar misgivings. Red hair and freckles! As if it wasn't enough that she'd been cursed with these mountainous breasts, she'd landed hair the color of paprika and skin that refused to tan. Instead it broke out in brilliant orange heat spots, as if she had an incurable rash, each time the sun grazed her skin. And this hair—oh, how she hated it! Coarse, springy ringlets that clung to her scalp like a Brillo pad if cut short, or if allowed to grow long, developed untamable waves reminiscent of those disastrous messes fried onto women's heads in the early days of the century before hot permanents had been perfected. Detesting it either way, she'd chosen a middle-of-the-road length and as innocuous a style as she could manage, brushing it straight back from her face and clasping it at her nape with a wide barrette, below which the "tail" erupted like a ball of fire from a volcano.

And what about eyelashes? Didn't every woman deserve to have eyelashes that could at least be seen? Theresa's were the same hue as her hair—pale threads that made the rims of her eyelids look pink and sickly while framing eyes that were almost the identical color of her freckles, a pale tea-brown. She thought of the dark spiky lashes and the stunning green of Brian Scanlon's eyes, and her own drooped to check her sweater once again, and tug it close together, as Theresa realized she could no longer avoid confronting him. She must return to the living room. And if he stared at her breasts with lascivious speculation she'd think of the strains of her favorite Chopin Nocturne, which always had a calming effect upon her.

Amy and Jeff were sitting on the davenport while Brian faced them from the seat of the piano bench. When Jeff caught sight of her, he thwacked the guitar strings dramatically, and let the chord reverberate in fanfare. "There she is!"

So much for slipping quietly into their midst.

Brian was no more than five feet away, still wearing his formal garrison cap. She was conscious of a wink of silver on the large eagle medallion centered above the black leather visor as his eyes swerved her way, directly on a level with the objects of Theresa's despair. Her pale brown eyes met his of sea green. The certainty of what would happen next seemed to lodge in her throat like a pill taken without water. *Now!* she thought. *Now it will happen!* She steeled herself for the sickening embarrassment that was certain to follow.

But Brian Scanlon relaxedly stretched six feet of blue-clad anatomy to its feet and smiled into Theresa's eyes, his own never wavering downward for even a fraction of a second or giving the impression that it even crossed his mind.

"Jeff's been demonstrating the old Stella. She doesn't sound too bad."

Aren't you going to gawk like everybody else? She felt the blush begin to tint her face because he *hadn't* looked, and to cover her fluster grabbed onto the first words that entered her mind.

"As usual, my brother thinks of nothing but music." Theresa strove to keep her voice steady, for her heart was knocking crazily. "And here you sit with your hat and jacket still on. I'll show you where you'll sleep, since neither one of these two had the courtesy to do it."

"I hope I'm not putting anybody out of their bed."

"Not at all. We're putting you on a hideaway bed in the family room downstairs. I just hope nobody puts you out of yours, because it'll be in front of the TV and fireplace, and dad likes to stay up at least until after the ten o'clock news."

He didn't look! He didn't look! The exaltation pounded through her brain as Theresa led the way back through the kitchen to the basement door that opened into the room just behind the stove wall. Oddly enough, she seemed more aware of Brian Scanlon because of the fact that he'd assiduously remained polite and refrained from dropping his eyes. She took his guitar and he his duffel bag, and she led him downstairs into a large basement area with a set of sliding glass doors facing the rear yard.

The room was paneled in warm pecan and carpeted in burnt orange that burst into a glow as Theresa switched on a table lamp.

Brian watched her hair light up as she paused above the lamp, then scanned the room, which contained a country pine coffee table, a cushioned davenport and pillowed rockers in the Colonial style. A fireplace was flanked by a television set, and at the end of the room where Brian stood, a thick-legged kitchen set of glossy pine was centered before the sliding glass door.

"Mmm...I like this room. Very homey." His eyes came back to settle upon Theresa as he spoke.

He seemed the type who'd prefer art deco or chrome and glass, but an appreciative reaction riffled through Theresa, for her mother had largely let her choose the colors and textures of the furnishings when they'd redecorated two years ago. It wasn't her own house, but it gave Theresa a taste of home planning, making her eager for the day when she could exercise her own tastes through an entire house.

Brian noted her tightly crossed arms beneath the baby blue sweater and the nervousness that was absent only while her sister and brother were close by.

"I'm sorry it has no closet, but you can hang your things up here." She opened a door leading to an unfinished portion of the basement where the laundry facilities were housed.

He crossed toward her, and she stepped well back as he popped his head around the laundry-room doorway, one foot off the floor behind him. There was a rolling laundry rack with empty hangers tinging in the air currents from the opening of the door. "There's no bath down here, but feel free to use the upstairs tub or shower any time you want."

When he turned to her, his eyes again rested directly on hers as he noted, "It sure beats the BOQ on base, especially at Christmas time." She was conscious of how crisp and correctly knotted his formal navy blue tie was, how smoothly the dark blue military "blouse" contoured his chest and shoulders over the paler blue of his shirt, of how flattering the square-set cap was to the equally square-cut lines of his jaw.

"BOQ?" she questioned.

"Bachelor Officers' Quarters."

"Oh." She waited for his eyes to rove downward, but they didn't. Instead, he began freeing the four silver buttons bearing the eagle-and-shield U.S. Air Force insignia, turning his back on her and taking a stroll around the room while freeing the "blouse" and shrugging out of it. He slipped his hat off the back of his head with a slow, relaxed movement, and she saw his hair for the first time. It was a rich chestnut color, trimmed—according to military regulations—far too short for her taste, and bearing a ridge across the back from the band of his cap. He turned toward Theresa again, and she noted that around his face the chestnut hair held the suggestion of waves, but was cut too short to allow them free rein. It would be much more attractive an inch and a half longer, she decided.

"It feels good to get out of these things."

"Oh, here! Let me hang them up."

"Just the blouse—I mean the jacket. We get in trouble if we hang up our caps."

As she came forward to take his jacket, he extended his cap, too, and its inner band was still warm from his head. As she scuttled away around the laundry-room doorway again, that warmth seemed to singe her palm. When she tipped the cap upside down to lay it on the rack above the clothes bar, a spicy scent of some hair preparation found its way to her nostrils. It seemed to cling to the jacket, too, as she threaded its shoulders over a hanger and hooked it on the rack.

When she returned to the family room, Brian was standing in front of the sliding glass doors with his hands in his trousers pockets, feet wide-spread, gazing out at the snowy yard where twilight was falling. For a long moment Theresa studied the back of his sky blue shirt where three crisp laundry creases gave him that clean-cut appearance of a model on a recruiting poster. The creases rose up out of the belted waistline of his trousers but disappeared across his shoulders where the blue fabric stretched taut as the head of a drum.

She crossed the room silently and flipped on an outside spotlight that flooded her father's bird feeder. Brian started at the snap of the light, glancing aside at her as she crossed her arms beneath the sweater and joined him at the wide window, studying the scene beyond.

"Every winter dad tries to entice cardinals, but so far this year we haven't had any. This is his favorite spot in the house. He brings his coffee down here in the mornings and sits at the table with his binoculars close at hand. He spends hours here."

"I can see why." Scanlon's eyes moved once more to the view outside where sparrows, caught in the beam of light that lit the snow to glimmering crystals, twittered and searched for fallen seed at the base of the feeder pole. The far edge of the property was delineated by a line of evergreens that appeared almost black in the waning light. Their limbs were laden with white. Suddenly a blue jay darted from them, squawking in the crass, impertinent note of superiority only a blue jay can muster, scattering the sparrows as he landed among them, then cocking his head and disdaining the seeds he jealously guarded.

"I wasn't sure if I should come with Jeff. I felt a little like I was horning in, you know?"

His hands were still buried in his trousers pockets, but she felt his eyes turn her way and hoped she wouldn't blush while attempting to lie convincingly. "Don't be silly, you're not horning in."

"Any stranger in the house at this time of the year is like a fifth wheel. I know that, but I couldn't resist Jeff's invitation when I thought about spending two weeks with nothing to do but stare at the bare walls of the quarters and talk to myself."

"I'm glad you didn't. Why, mother didn't hesitate a minute when Jeff called and suggested bringing you home. Besides, we've all heard so much about you in Jeff's letters, you hardly seem like a stranger. As a matter of fact, I believe *one* of us had a tiny bit of a crush on you even before you stepped out of the car in the driveway."

He laughed good-naturedly and shook his head at the floor as if slightly embarrassed, then rocked back on his heels. "It's a good thing she isn't six years older. She's going to be a real knockout at twenty."

"Yes, I know. Everybody says so."

Brian heard no note of rancor in Theresa's words, only a warm, sisterly pride. And he need not lower his eyes to her chest to see that as she spoke, her forearms unconsciously guarded her breasts more closely.

Thanks for warning me, Brubaker, he thought, recalling all that Jeff had told him about his sister. *But apparently Jeff told his family as much about my background as he told me about them,* he thought, as Theresa went on in a sympathetic note.

"Jeff told us about your mother. I'm sorry. It must have been terrible to get the news about the plane crash."

He studied the snow again and shrugged. "In a way it was, in a way it wasn't. We were never close after my dad died, and once she'd remarried, we didn't get along at all. Her second husband thought I was a drug addict because I played rock music, and he didn't waste any more time on me than was absolutely necessary."

She evaluated her own family, so warm, supporting, so full of love, and resisted the urge to lay a comforting hand on Brian's arm. She felt guilty for the many times she'd wished Jeff wouldn't bring him home. It had been thoroughly selfish, she chided herself, guarding her family's Christmas from outsiders just as the jay guarded the seeds he didn't want to eat.

This time when she said the words, Theresa found they were utterly sincere. "We're glad to have you here, Brian."

Chapter Two

"They're home!" shouted Jeff overhead, then he stuck his head around the basement doorway and ordered, "Hey, you two, get up here!"

As an outside observer, Brian couldn't help envying Jeff Brubaker his family, for the greeting his friend received in the arms of his mother and father was an emotional display of honest love. Margaret Brubaker was hiking her rotund body out of the deep bucket seat of the low-slung Celica when Jeff swooped down on her. The grocery bag in her arms was unceremoniously dropped onto the snowy driveway in favor of hugs and kisses interspersed with tears, hellos and general exuberance while Willard Brubaker came around the car and took his turn—albeit with far fewer tears than his wife, but there was an undeniable glitter in his eye as he backed off and assessed Jeff.

"Good to have you home, son."

"I'll say it is," put in his mother, then the trio shared an enormous three-way hug. Margaret stepped back, crushing a loaf of bread. "Land! Would you look at what I've done with these groceries. Willard, help me pick 'em up."

Jeff waylaid them both. "Forget the groceries for now. I'll come back and get 'em in a minute. Come and meet Brian." With an arm around each of his parents' shoulders, Jeff shepherded them into the kitchen where Brian waited with the two girls. "These are the two who had the courage to have a kid like me—my mom and dad. And this is Brian Scanlon."

Willard Brubaker pumped Brian's hand. "Glad to have you with us, Brian."

Margaret's greeting was, "So this is Jeff's Brian."

"I'm afraid so, for all of two weeks. I really appreciate your invitation, Mrs. Brubaker."

"There are two things we have to get settled right now," Margaret stated without prelude, pointing an accusatory finger. "The first is that you don't call me Mrs. Brubaker, like I'm some commanding officer. Call me Margaret. And the other is...you don't smoke pot, do you?"

Amy rolled her eyeballs in undisguised chagrin, but the rest of them shared a good-natured laugh that managed to break the ice even before Brian answered frankly, "No, ma'am. Not anymore." There was a moment of surprised silence, then everyone burst into laughter again. And Theresa looked at Brian in a new light.

To Brian it seemed the Brubaker house was never quiet. Immediately after the introductions, Margaret was flinging orders for "you two boys" to pick up the groceries she'd dropped in the driveway. Supper preparations set up the next clatter as fried potatoes started splattering in a frying pan, and dishes were clinked against silverware at the table. In the living room, Jeff picked up his old guitar, but after a few minutes, shouted, "Amy, will you go shut off your damn stereo! It's thumping through the wall loud enough to drive a man crazy!" The only quiet one of the group appeared to be Willard, who calmly settled himself into a living-room chair and read the evening newspaper as if the chaos around him didn't even register. Within ten minutes it was evident to Brian who ruled the Brubaker roost. Margaret issued orders like a drill sergeant whether she wanted to be called Margaret or not. But she controlled her brood with a sharp tongue that wielded as much humor as hauteur.

"Theresa, now don't fry those potatoes till they're tougher than horsehide the way you like 'em. Don't forget your father's false teeth. Jeff, would you play something else in there? You know how I've always hated that song! What ever happened to the good old standards like 'Moonlight Bay'? Amy, get two folding chairs out of the front closet and keep your fingers off that coconut frosting till dessert time. Willard, keep that dirty newsprint off the arms of the chair!"

To Brian's surprise, Willard Brubaker peered over the top of his glasses, muttered too softly for his wife to hear, "Yes, my little turtledove," then caught Jeff's eye, and the two exchanged grins of amused male tolerance. Willard's gaze caught Brian's next, and the older man gave a quick wink, then buried himself behind his paper again, resting it on the arms of the chair.

Supper was plentiful and plain: Polish sausage, fried potatoes, baked beans and toast—Jeff's favorite meal. Willard sat at the head of the table, Margaret at the foot, the two "girls" on one side and the two "boys" across from them.

While they ate, Brian observed Margaret's buxom proportions and realized from whom Theresa had inherited her shape. Throughout the pleasant meal Theresa kept her blue sweater over her shoulders, though there were times when it plainly got in her way. Occasionally, Brian glanced up to find Amy gazing at him with an expression warning of imminent puppy love, though Theresa never seemed to look at him at all.

Midway through the meal the phone rang, and Amy popped up to get it.

"Hello," she said, then covered the mouthpiece and looked disgusted. "It's for you, Jeffy. It sounds like dumb old Glue Eyes."

"Watch your mouth, little sister, or I'll wire your top braces to your bottom ones." Jeff took the phone and Amy returned to the table.

"Glue Eyes?" Brian glanced at Theresa.

"Patricia Gluek," she answered, "his old girlfriend. Amy never liked the way Patricia used to put on her makeup back in high school, so she started calling her Glue Eyes."

Amy plopped into her chair with a grunt of exasperation. "Well, she plastered it on so thick it looked like her eyelashes were glued together, not to mention how thick she used to plaster Jeff with all those purrs and coos. She makes me sick."

"Amy!" snapped Margaret, and Amy had the grace to desist.

Brian curled an eyebrow at Theresa, and again she enlightened him. "Amy worships Jeff. She'd like to keep him all to herself for two solid weeks."

Just then Jeff dropped the receiver against his thigh and asked, "Hey, you two, want to pick up Patricia after supper and go to a movie or something?"

Brian craned around to look over his shoulder at Jeff.

Theresa gulped. "Who, me?"

Jeff flashed an indulgent smile. "Yeah, you and Bry."

Already Theresa could feel the color creeping up her neck. She never went on dates, and most certainly not with her brother's friends, who were all younger than herself.

Brian turned back to Theresa. "It sounds fine with me, if it's all right with Theresa."

"Whaddya say, Treat?" Jeff was jiggling the phone impatiently, and the eyes of everyone at the table turned to the blushing redhead. A bevy of excuses flashed through her mind, all of them as phony as those she'd dreamed up on the rare occasions when single male teachers from school asked her out. At her elbow she sensed Amy gaping in undisguised envy.

Brian realized the house was totally silent for the first time since he'd entered it and wished the rock music was still throbbing from Amy's room. It was obvious Theresa was caught in a sticky situation where refusal would be rude, yet he could tell she didn't want to say yes.

"Sure, that sounds fun."

She avoided Brian's eyes, but felt them hesitate on her for a minute while Jeff finalized the plans, and she withdrew from center stage by going to get dessert plates for the German chocolate cake.

When the meal was finished and Theresa was helping with dishes, she cornered Jeff for a moment as he passed through the kitchen.

"Jeffrey Brubaker, what on earth you were thinking of, to suggest such a thing?" she whispered angrily. "I'll pick my own dates, thank you."

"Lighten up, sis. Brian's not a date."

"You bet he's not. Why, he must be four years younger than I am!"

"Two."

"Two! That's even worse! Why, it makes it look like—"

"All right, all right! What are you so upset about?"

"I'm not upset. You just put me on the spot, that's all."

"Did you have other plans for tonight?"

"On your first night home?" she asked pointedly. "Of course not."

"Great. Then the least you'll get out of the deal is a free movie."

Oh no! the peeved Theresa vowed. *I'll pay my own way!*

Getting ready to go, Theresa couldn't help but admire how carefully Brian had concealed his reluctance. After all, who'd want to be saddled with a *big* sister? And worse yet, a freckle-head like her? She scowled at the copper dots in the mirror and despised each one with renewed intensity. She tried to yank a brush through her disgusting hair, but it was like a frayed sisal rope, only not nearly as pleasing in color. *Damn you, Jeffrey Brubaker, don't you ever do this to me again.* She drew the hair to the nape of her neck, tied it with a navy blue ribbon and considered makeup. But she owned none except lipstick, which she slashed onto her surly lips as if scrawling graffiti on a rest room wall. *I'll get you for this, Jeff.* Little thought was given to the clothing she chose, beyond the certainty that she'd put on her gray coat and leave it buttoned until they got back home.

She wasn't, however, planning on running into Brian in the front hall by the coat closet. When she did, she came up short, caught without a sweater or guitar or table to hide behind. Instinctively, one hand went up to finger her blouse collar—it was the best she could do.

"Jeff went out to start the car," Brian announced.

"Oh." The word was barely out of her mouth before Theresa realized Brian had shed military attire in favor of brown tennis shoes, bone-colored corduroys and a polo-style shirt of wide horizontal stripes in red and beige. He'd been carrying a brown leather waist-length jacket, and shrugged it on while she watched, transfixed. If Brian had subjected Theresa to the blatant inspection she gave him, she'd have ended up in her room in tears. She hadn't even realized how pointedly she'd been staring until her eyes traveled back up to his. She felt utterly foolish.

But if he noticed, he gave not the slightest clue beyond the hint of a smile that disappeared as quickly as it had come. "All ready?"

"Yes." She reached for her gray coat, but he took it from her hands without asking and held it for her. Even as Theresa felt the flush coloring her cheek at the unfamiliar gesture of good manners, she could do nothing but slip her arms into the coat, exposing the front of her so there was no hiding her proportions.

They called good-night to her parents and Amy and stepped out into the biting winter night. Theresa had gone on few enough dates in her life that it was difficult not to feel seduced into believing this was one, for he held the door of the station wagon while she slid in next to Jeff, then slipped his arm across the back of the seat as he settled in, too. She caught the drift of the same scent she'd detected when he handed her his cap earlier, and since Theresa wasn't a woman given to using perfumes herself, his faint hint of...sandalwood, that was it, came through all the clearer.

Jeff had the radio on—there was always a radio on—and he turned it louder as the gravelly voice of Bob Seger came on. Jeff's own voice had the grating earthiness of Seger's, and he picked up the refrain and sang along.

"We've got to learn this one, Bry."

"Mmm...it's smooth. Nice harmony on the chorus."

When the chorus came around again, the three sang along with it, their harmony resonant and true. "Ooo, shame on the moon...." Beside her, Theresa heard Brian's voice for the first time—straightforward, mellow, the antithesis of Jeff's. It sent shivers up her arms.

When they reached Patricia Gluek's house, Jeff went inside while Theresa and Brian transferred to the back seat, leaving a respectable distance between them. The radio was still playing and the lights from the dashboard lent an ethereal glow to the space beyond the front seat.

"How long have you and Jeff been playing and singing together?"

"Over three years now. We met when we were stationed at Zweibrücken together and started up a band there, and luckily we both landed at Minot Air Force Base, so we decided to look for a new drummer and bass player and keep a good thing rolling."

"I'd love to hear the band sometime."

"Maybe you will."

"I doubt it. I don't have many chances to swing by Minot, North Dakota."

"We'd like to get a new group started when we get out next summer, and hire an agent and make it a regular thing. Hasn't Jeff mentioned it?"

"Why, no, but I think it's a great idea, at least for Jeff. He's wanted to be a musician since he spent that first fifteen dollars on his Stella and started picking up chords from anybody who'd teach him."

"Same with me. I've been playing since I was twelve, but I want to do more than just play."

"What else?"

"I'd like to try writing, arranging. And I've always had the urge to be a disc jockey."

"You have the voice for it." He certainly did. She remembered her first appreciative surprise upon hearing it earlier. But it went on now, turning attention away from himself.

"Enough about me. I hear you're into music, too."

"Grades one through six, Sky Oaks Elementary."

"Do you like it?"

"I love it, with the rare exceptions like yesterday during the Christmas program when Keri Helling and Dawn Gafkjen got into a fight over who was going to be the pink ornament and who was going to be the blue one and ended up crying and getting the crepe-paper costumes all soggy." She chuckled. "No, seriously, I love teaching the younger kids. They're guileless, and open, and..." *And they don't gawk.* "And accepting," she finished.

Just then Jeff returned with Patricia, and introductions were made as Brian and Patricia shook hands over the front seat. Theresa had known the girl for years. She was a vivacious brunette, now in her second year at Normandale Community College. She was waiting to step into her former status as Jeff's girlfriend the moment he got out of the service, though they'd agreed to date others during their four years apart. So far, though, the attraction had not faded, for each of the three times Jeff had been home, he and Patricia had been inseparable.

When the pretty brunette turned toward the front, Theresa was chagrined to see her and Jeff share a more intimate hello than they'd apparently exchanged inside the house. Jeff's arms went around Patricia, and her head drifted to his shoulder while they kissed in a way that sent the blood filling up the space between Theresa's freckles. Beside her, Brian sat unmoving, watching the kiss that was taking place in such a forthright manner it was hard to ignore.

Goodness, would they never stop? The seconds ticked away while the music from the radio didn't quite conceal the soft murmurs from the front seat. Theresa wanted to crawl into a hole and pull the earth over her head.

Brian laced his fingers over his belly, slumped low in the seat, dropped his head back lazily and politely turned to gaze out his side window.

I am twenty-five years old, thought Theresa, *and I've never known before exactly what was implied by "double date."* She, too, gazed out her dark window.

There was a faint rustle, and, thankfully, it was Jeff's arm lifting from around Patricia's shoulders. The wagon chunked into gear, and they were moving at last.

At the theater, Theresa made a move toward her purse, but Brian stepped between her and the counter, announcing unceremoniously, "I'll get it." So, rather than make an issue of the four-dollar expenditure, she politely backed off.

When he turned, she said, "Thank you."

But he made no reply, only tipped his shoulders aslant while slipping his billfold into a back pocket where the beige wales of the corduroy were slightly worn in a matching square that captured Theresa's eyes and made her mouth go dry. He turned around, caught her gaze, and she wished she'd never come.

Things got worse when they'd settled into their seats and the movie began, for it had an "R" rating, and exposed enough skin to create sympathetic sexual reactions in a sworn celibate! Halfway through the film the camera zoomed in on a bare spine, curved hips and a naked feminine back over which two masculine hands played, their long, blunt fingers feathered with traces of dark hair. A naked hirsute chest rolled into view, and the side of an apple-sized breast, then—horror of horrors!—an upthrust nipple, controlled by the broad, dark hand. A bearded jaw eased into the frame, and a mouth closed over the distended nipple.

In her seat beside Brian, Theresa wanted more than ever to simply, blessedly, *die.* His elbows rested on the armrests, and his fingers were laced together, the outer edges of his index fingers absently stroking his lips as he slumped rather low in the seat.

Why didn't I consider something like this happening? Why didn't I ask what was playing? Why didn't I wisely stay home in the first place?

Theresa tolerated the remainder of the love scene, and as it progressed a queer reaction threaded through her body. Saliva pooled beneath her tongue. She could feel her pulse throbbing in the place where her purse was pressed tightly against her lap. And a quicksilver liquid sensation trickled through her innards, setting her alive with sensations she'd never experienced before. But outwardly, she sat as if a sorcerer had cast a spell upon her. Not so much as a pale eyelash blinked. Not a muscle twitched. She stared spellbound as the climax was enacted, reflected in the facial expressions of the man and woman on the screen and the animal sounds of fulfillment.

And not until those climaxes ended did Theresa realize Brian's elbow had been skewering hers with pressure that grew, and grew, and grew....

The scene changed, and he wilted, pulling his elbow against his side as if only now realizing what he'd been doing. Her elbow actually hurt from the pressure he'd been applying. He shifted uncomfortably in his seat, crossed an ankle over a knee and negligently dropped his laced fingers over the zipper of his corduroy pants.

Considering what had happened within her own body, Theresa had little doubt the same had happened to Brian. The remainder of the film was lost on her. She was too aware of the man on her right, and she found herself wondering who he'd been thinking of while the pressure on her elbow increased. She found herself wondering things about the male anatomy that the screen had carefully hidden. She recalled pictures she'd seen in the bolder magazines, but they seemed as flat, cold and lifeless as the paper upon which they'd been printed. For the first time in her life, she ached to know what the real thing was like.

When the film ended, she took refuge in chattering with Patricia, making certain she walked far enough ahead of Brian that their elbows didn't touch or their eyes meet.

"Anybody hungry?" Jeff inquired when they were back in the station wagon.

Theresa felt slightly queasy, sitting once again with Brian only a foot away. If she tried eating anything, she wasn't sure it would stay down.

"No!" she exclaimed, before anybody else could agree.

"Yeah, I—" Brian spoke at the same time, then politely changed course. "I've been thinking about a piece of your mother's German chocolate cake all through the movie."

In a pig's eye, thought Theresa.

Oddly enough, nobody talked about the film as they drove back to Patricia's house. Nobody said much of anything. Patricia was snuggled up with her shoulder behind Jeff's. Now and then he'd turn and smile down at her with the dash lights clearly outlining the ardent expression on his face. Patricia's shoulder moved slightly, and Theresa conjured up the possibility of where her hand might be. Theresa gazed out her window and blushed for perhaps the tenth time that day.

When they pulled up in Patricia's driveway, Jeff turned off all the lights and gathered Patricia into his arms without a moment's hesitation. Behind the couple, another man and woman sat like two bumps on a log.

Kisses, Theresa discovered, have more sound than you'd think. From the front seat came the distinct rush of hastened breathing, the faint suggestive sounds of lips parting, positions changing, the rustle of hands moving softly. The rasp of a zipper sizzled through the dark confines of the car, and Theresa jumped, but immediately wished she hadn't, for it was only Jeff's jacket.

"Come on, Theresa, what do you say we go for a little walk?" Brian suggested. The overhead light flashed on, and she hustled out his door, so relieved she wanted to throw her arms around him and kiss him out of sheer gratitude.

When the door slammed behind them, Theresa surprised herself by releasing a pent-up breath and bursting out with the last words she expected to say. *"Thank you."*

He stuck his hands into his jacket pockets and chuckled. "No need to thank me. I was getting a little uncomfortable myself."

His admission surprised her, but the frankness definitely relieved some of the tension.

"I can see I'll have to talk with my little brother about decorum. I wasn't exactly sure what to do!"

"What did you used to do when that happened on double dates?"

She was embarrassed to have to admit, "I've never been on a double date bef—" She stopped herself just in time and amended, "I've never been on one."

"Aw, think nothing of it. They're both adults. He loves her—he's told me so more than once—and he intends to marry her soon after his hitch is done."

"You amaze me. I mean, you take it all in stride." *Heavens,* thought Theresa, *do couples do things like that in the same car with as little compunction as her brother showed and think nothing of it?* She realized suddenly how very, very naive she must seem to Brian Scanlon.

"He's my friend. I don't judge my friends."

"Well, he's my brother, and I'm afraid I do."

"Why? He's twenty-one years old."

"I know, I know." Theresa threw up her hands, exasperated with herself and uncomfortable with the subject.

"How old are you, Theresa? Twenty-five, right?"

"Yes."

"And I take it you haven't done a lot of that sort of thing."

"No." *Because every time I got in a car with a boy, he went after only the most obvious two things, never caring about the person behind them.* "I was busy studying when I was in high school and college, and since then...well, I don't go out much."

They were ambling down a snowy street, feet lifting lazily as the streetlights made the surface snow glitter. Her coat was still buttoned high, and her hands were buried in its pockets. Their breaths created white clouds, and their soles pressed brittle ice that crunched with each step.

"So, what did you think of the movie?" Brian asked.

"It embarrassed me," she admitted.

"I'm sorry."

"It's not your fault, it's Jeff's. He's the one who picked it."

"Next time we'll be sure to ask before we blindly follow him, okay?"

Next time? Theresa glanced up to find Brian smiling down at her with an easy laziness that was meant to put her at ease, but that lifted her heart in a strange, weightless way. She should have answered, "There won't be a next time," but instead smiled in return and concurred. "Agreed."

They turned around and were heading toward the Gluek driveway when Jeff backed the station wagon onto the street and its lights arced around, caught them in the glare, and he pulled up beside them.

"Would you two mind if we took you home?" Jeff asked when Theresa and Brian were settled in the back seat again.

"Not at all," Brian answered for both of them.

"Thanks for understanding, Bry. And Treat, you'll take good care of him, won't you?"

She wanted to smack her brother on the side of the head. Jeffrey Brubaker certainly took a lot for granted!

"Sure." What else could she have answered?

When they pulled up at home, Brian opened his door and the light flashed on. Patricia Gluek turned around and hooked an elbow over the back of the seat.

"Listen, a group of us are getting together at the Rusty Scupper on New Year's Eve, and you're both invited to join us. We plan to have dinner there and stay for the dancing afterward. It'll be a lot of the old gang—you've met them all before, Theresa—so what do you say?"

Damn it, does the whole world think it has to line up escorts for the wimpy little Theresa Brubaker who never gets asked out on dates? But she knew in her heart that Patricia was only being cordial and thinking about Brian, too, who was Jeff's houseguest and couldn't very well be excluded. He had one foot on the driveway, but this time instead of putting Theresa on the spot, he answered, "We'll talk it over and let you know, okay?"

"Some people from school are having a party in their home, and I told them I might go." The manufactured tale came glibly to Theresa's lips while she was still puzzling out where it had come from.

"Oh." Patricia sounded genuinely disappointed. "Well, in that case, you'll come, won't you, Brian? We have to make dinner reservations in advance."

"I'll think it over."

"Fine."

Brian swiveled toward the open door, but Jeff reached out and caught his arm. "Listen, Scan, thanks. I mean, I guess I ought to come in with you and play the host, but I'll see you in the morning at breakfast."

"Go on. Have a good time and don't worry about me."

When the car pulled away, Theresa and Brian stood on the back step while she dug in her purse for the house keys. When she found them and opened the door, they stepped into a dim kitchen where only a single bulb shone down on top of the white stove. It was silent—no stereo, no guitar, no voices.

They were both excruciatingly aware of what Jeff and Patricia were probably going off to do, and it created a corresponding sexual tension between them.

Seeking a diversion, Theresa whispered, "You said you were hungry for cake. There's plenty of it left."

He wasn't, really, but Brian wasn't at all averse to spending a little more time with Theresa, and the cake offered an excuse.

"I will if you will."

"It sounds good."

She moved toward the front hall, which was in total shadow, and made no move to turn on the light while removing her coat. Again, Brian was behind her to help her out of the garment, then hang it up. She left him there with a murmured thanks and returned to the kitchen to find two plates, forks and glasses of milk, taking them to the table where the cake still sat.

He joined her, choosing a chair at a right angle to hers, and they sat for a long time eating, saying nothing. The rafters of the house creaked in the December cold, and though it was very dark with only the small hood light illuminating the blotch of stove beneath it, she sensed Brian Scanlon studying her while he downed gulps of milk that sounded clearly in the silence.

"So, you're going to a party with someone from school on New Year's Eve?"

"No, I made that up."

His chin came up in surprise. "Oh?"

"Yes. I don't like people arranging dates for me, and furthermore, you don't need to be saddled with *me* on New Year's Eve. You go with Jeff and meet his friends. He's got some really nice—"

"*Saddled* with you?" he interrupted in that smooth, deep, unnerving voice that sent shivers up her nape.

"Yes."

"Did I give you the impression tonight that I resented being with you?"

"You know what I mean. You didn't come home with Jeff to have to haul me around every place you go."

"How do you know?"

She was stunned, she could only stammer. "You...I...."

"Would it surprise you to know that you're a big part of why I wanted to meet Jeff's family?"

"I...." But once again, she was struck dumb.

"He's told me a lot about you, Theresa. A lot."

Oh, Lord, how much? How much? Jeff, who knows my innermost fears. Jeff, who understands. Jeff, who can't keep anything to himself.

"What has he told you?" She tried to control the panic, but it crept into her voice, creating a vibrato that could not be disguised.

He made himself more comfortable, stretching his long legs somewhere beneath the table to find the seat of a chair as he leaned back to study her shadowed face speculatively. His eyes held points of light as he caught an elbow on the table edge and braced one jaw on his knuckles, tipping his head.

"About how you looked out for him when he was a kid. About your music. The violin and piano. How you used to sing duets for your family reunions and pass the hat for nickels afterward, then, as soon as you had enough, go to the store to buy your favorite forty-fives." His lips lifted in a slow half smile, and his free hand moved the milk glass in circles against the tabletop.

"Oh, is that all?" Her shoulders wilted with relief, but in the dimness she had crossed her elbows on the tabletop and took refuge behind them as best she could.

"You always sounded as if you'd be someone I could get along with. And maybe I liked you even before I met you because he likes you so much, and you're his sister and I also like him very much."

Theresa was unused to being told she was liked. In her lifetime a few of the opposite sex had overtly tried to demonstrate what they "liked" about her, in the groping, insulting way she'd come to despise. But Brian seemed to have come to admire something deeper, her little-exposed self, her musicality, her familial relations. All this before he had ever laid eyes on her.

But those eyes were on her now, and though she could not make out their color in the veiling shadows, she caught the sparkle as he continued perusing her freely, the tip of his little finger now resting in the hollow beneath his full lower lip. She seemed unable to draw her eyes away from it as he went on quietly.

"I'd love to go to that party with you on New Year's Eve."

Their eyes met, hers wide with surprise, his carefully unflirtatious.

"But you're...you're two years younger than I am." Once she'd said it, she wanted to eat the words.

But he asked undauntedly, "Does that bother you?"

"Yes, I...." She blew out a huge breath of air and leaned her forehead on the heel of one hand. "I can't believe this conversation."

"It doesn't bother me in the least. And I sure as hell don't want to go to that kind of a thing alone. Everybody'll be paired off, and I won't have anybody to dance with."

"I don't dance." *That* was the understatement of the night. Dancing was a pleasure she'd abandoned when her breasts grew too large to make fast dancing comfortable, their sway and bob not only hurting, but making Theresa feel sure they must appear obscene from the sidelines. And chest-to-chest dancing was even worse—being that close to men, she'd found, only gave them ideas.

"A musical woman like you?"

"Music and dancing are two different things. I've just never cared for—"

"There's time before New Year's Eve to learn. Maybe we can change your mind."

"Let me think about it, okay?"

"Sure." He got to his feet, and the chair scraped back, then he carried their two plates across the room and set them in the sink with a soft chink.

She opened the basement door and snapped on the light above the steps. "Well, I'm not sure if mother made your bed down here or not."

She heard his steps following her down the carpeted incline, and prayed she'd find his bed all decked out, ready for him, so she could simply wish him good-night and escape to her own room upstairs.

Unfortunately, the davenport wasn't either opened or made up, so Theresa had little choice but to cross the room and begin the chore. She tossed the cushions aside, conscious now that Brian had snapped on the lamp, and it flooded the area with mellow light that revealed her clearly while she tugged on the folded mattress and brought it springing out into the room.

"I'll get the bedding," she explained, and hustled into the laundry room to find clean sheets and blankets on a shelf there. He had turned on the television set when she came back out to the family room, and a late movie was glimmering on the screen in black and white. The volume was only a murmur as she shook out a mattress pad, concentrating fully on it when Brian stepped to the opposite side of the davenport to help her.

His long fingers smoothed the quilted surface with the expertise of a soldier who's been trained to keep his bunk in inspection-ready order. A sheet snapped and billowed in the air between them, and above it their glances met, then dropped. Images of the movie's love scene came back to titillate Theresa, while they tucked the corners of the sheets in, and Brian's hands pulled it far more expertly than hers, for hers were shaking and seemed nearly inept.

"Tight enough to bounce a coin," he approved.

She glanced up to find him looking at her instead of the sheet, and wondering what this man was doing to her. She had never in her life been as sexually aware of a male as she was of him. Men had brought her nothing but shame and intimidation, and she'd avoided them. Yet here she stood, gazing into the green eyes of Brian Scanlon over his half-prepared bed, wondering what it would be like to do with him the things she'd seen on a movie screen.

Redheads look ugly when they blush, she thought.

"The other sheet," he reminded her, and abashed, she turned to find it.

When the bed was finally done, she found her pulses leaping like Mexican jumping beans. But there still remained one duty she, as hostess, must perform.

"If you'll come upstairs, I'll give you clean towels and washcloths, and show you where the bathroom is."

"Jeff showed me after supper."

"Oh. Oh...good. Well, feel free to shower or...or whatever, anytime. You can hang your wet towels over the sink in the laundry room."

"Thank you."

They stood one on either side of the bed, and she suddenly realized she was facing him fully for the first time without shielding her breasts. Not once since she'd met him had she noticed him looking at them. His eyes were fastened on the freckled cheeks, then they moved up to her detestable red hair, and she realized she'd been standing without moving for a full thirty seconds.

"Well...good night then." Her voice was soft and shaky.

"Good night, Theresa." His was deep and quiet.

She scuttled away, racing up the stairs as if he were chasing her with ill intent. When she was settled into bed with the lights out, she heard him come upstairs and use the bathroom.

Put a pillow over your ears, Theresa Brubaker! But she listened to all the sounds coming from beyond her bedroom wall, and two closed doors, and envisioned Brian Scanlon performing his bedtime rituals and wondered for the first time in her life how a husband and wife ever made it through the intimacies of the first week of marriage.

The following morning, Theresa was awakened by the thump-thump-thump of Amy's stereo reverberating through the floor. Rolling over, she squinted at the alarm clock, then shot out of bed as if it was on fire. Ten o'clock! She should have been up two hours ago to fix breakfast for Brian and Jeff!

Within minutes she was washed, combed, dressed in blue jeans and a loose white blouse with a black cardigan slung across her shoulders and buttoned beneath the blouse collar.

Her parents had gone to work long ago. Jeff's door was closed, and the sound of his snoring came from beyond. It appeared Amy was still in her room, torturing her hair with a curling iron while Theresa tried to tame her springing curls by smoothing a hand over the infamous tail that bounced on her shoulders.

She crept down the hall to the kitchen but found it empty. The basement door was open—it appeared Brian was up. She was filling the coffeepot when he slipped silently to the doorway leading directly to the kitchen from one side of the living room.

"Good morning."

She spun around, sending water flying everywhere, pressing a hand to her heart.

"Oh! I didn't know you were there! I thought you were still downstairs."

"I've been awake for a long time. Routine is hard to break."

"Have you been sitting in there all by yourself?"

"No." He grinned engagingly. "With Stella."

She grinned back. "And how did you two get along?" She put coffee in the percolator basket and set the pot on the stove burner.

"She's a brassy old girl, but I talked sweet to her and she responded like a lady."

It wasn't what he said, but how he said it that made Theresa's cheeks pink. There was an undertone of teasing, though the words were totally polite. She wasn't used to such a tone of voice when speaking with men, but it, combined with his lazy half smile while he leaned one shoulder against the doorway, gave her the feeling she imagined a cat must have when its fur was slowly stroked the wrong way.

"I didn't hear you playing."

"We were whispering to each other."

Again, she couldn't resist smiling.

"I...I'm sorry nobody was up to fix breakfast for you. It's my first day of Christmas vacation, and I guess my body decided to take advantage of it. I never even wiggled at the usual wake-up time. I heard Jeff still snoring. He must have come in late."

"It was around three."

So—he hadn't been able to sleep. Neither had she.

"Three!"

He shrugged, his shoulder still braced on the doorway. He was wearing tight, faded blue jeans and a white football jersey that hugged his ribs just enough to make them tantalizing.

She recalled how long it had taken her to get to sleep after the curious way he'd managed to stir her senses last night, and wondered what had really kept him awake. Had he lain in the dark thinking of the movie as she had? Thinking of Jeff and Patricia in the car? Himself and her having cake and milk in the dusky kitchen?

His slow perusal was beginning to make Theresa's nerves jump, so she shrugged. "Why don't you sit down, and I'll pour you a glass of juice?"

He obliged, though she still wasn't rid of his gaze, even after she gave him a glass of orange juice. His eyes followed her lazily as she turned the bacon, scrambled eggs and dropped bread into the toaster.

"What do you and Jeff have planned for today?"

"I don't know, but whatever it is, I was hoping you could come along."

Her heart skipped, and she was disappointed at what she had to reply. "Oh, no, I have too much to do to help mother for tomorrow night, and I have to get ready for the concert I'm playing in tonight."

"Oh, that's right. Jeff told me. Civic orchestra, isn't it?"

"Uh-huh. I've been in it for three years and I really enjoy—"

"Well, good morning, you two." It was Amy, barely giving her sister a glance, aiming her greeting primarily at Brian. To his credit, he didn't flinch even slightly at the sight of Amy, decked out in crisp blue jeans that fit her like a shadow, a skinny little sweater that fit nearly as close, craftily styled hair with its shoulder-length auburn feather cut blown and curled back from her face in that dewy-fresh style so stunningly right for teenage girls. Her makeup application could have taught "Glue Eyes" a thing or two several years ago.

"I thought teenagers spent their vacations flopping around in baggy overalls these days," Brian noted, managing to compliment Amy without encouraging any excess hope.

"Mmm..." Amy simpered. "That just goes to show what you know."

But Theresa was fully aware that had Brian not been under the roof, that's exactly how Amy would have spent her day, only she wouldn't have poked her nose out of her burrow until one o'clock in the afternoon.

Amy stepped delicately to the stove and lifted a piece of cooling bacon, nibbled it with a provocative daintiness that quite surprised her sister. Where in the world had Amy learned to act this way? When? Just since Brian Scanlon had walked into the house?

"Amy, if you want bacon and eggs, get yourself a plate," Theresa scolded, suddenly annoyed by her sister's flirtatiousness. Even though she realized how small it was to feel a twinge of irritation at this new side Amy was displaying, Theresa was undeniably piqued. Perhaps because the fourteen-year-old had the remarkably freckle-free skin, hair the color of most Kentucky Derby winners and a trim, tiny shape that must be the envy of half the girls in her freshman class at school. Theresa suddenly felt like a gaudy neon sign beside an engraved invitation, in spite of the fact that it was Amy who wore the makeup. Theresa held her sweater over her elbow as she reached to turn off a burner.

From the table, Brian observed it all—the quick flash of irritation the older sister hadn't quite been able to hide, the guarded movements behind the camouflaging sweater and even the guilt that flashed across her face for the twinge of envy she could not quite control in moments such as these.

He rose, moved to her side and smiled down into her startled eyes. "Here, let me pour the coffee, at least. I feel like a parasite sitting there and doing nothing while you slave over a hot stove." He reached for the pot while she shifted her eyes to the eggs she was removing from the pan.

"The cups are...." She half turned to find Amy watching them from just behind their shoulders. "Amy will show you where the cups are."

They had just begun eating when Jeff came slogging out of his room in bare feet and faded Levi's, scratching his chest and head simultaneously.

"I thought I smelled bacon."

"And I thought I smelled a rat," returned Theresa. "Jeff Brubaker, you should be ashamed of yourself. Bringing Brian here as your houseguest, then abandoning him that way."

Jeff shambled to a chair and strung himself upon it, more lying then sitting. "Aw hell, Brian didn't mind, did you, Bry?"

"Nope. Theresa and I had a nice long talk, and I got to bed early."

"What did you think of old Glue Eyes?" put in Amy.

"She's just as cute as I expected from Jeff's descriptions and the pictures I've seen," replied Brian.

"Humph!"

Jeff leaned his elbows on the table and closely scrutinized his younger sister. "Well, lookee here now," he sing-songed. "If the twerp hasn't taken a few lessons from old Glue Eyes herself."

Amy's mouth puckered up as if it was full of alum. She glared at her brother and snapped, "I'm fourteen years old, Jeffrey, in case you hadn't noticed! And I've been wearing makeup for over a year now."

"Oh." Jeff lounged back in his chair once again. "I beg your pardon, Irma la douce."

She lurched to her feet and would have stormed out of the room, but Jeff caught her by the elbow and swung her around till she landed on his lap, where she sat stiffly with her arms crossed obstinately over her ribs, an expression of strained tolerance on her face.

"Wanna come along with Brian and me to shop for mom and dad today? I'm gonna need some help deciding what to get for them."

Her irritation dissolved like a mist before a wind. *"Reeeally?* You mean it, Jeff?"

"Sure I mean it." He pushed her off his lap, swatted her on the backside and sent her on her way again. "Get your room cleaned up, and we'll go right after we eat." When she was gone he looked at the spot from which she'd disappeared around the hallway wall. "Her jeans are too tight. Mother ought to talk to her about that."

Left behind, Theresa recalled the breakfast conversation with something less than good humor. Why was it so irritating that Jeff had noticed Amy's burgeoning maturity? Why did she herself feel lonely and left out and—*oh, admit it, Brubaker!*—jealous, because her sister of fourteen was accompanying Brian Scanlon, age twenty-three, on an innocent Christmas-shopping spree?

With the house to herself, Theresa put on her classical favorites, and spent the remainder of the morning boiling potatoes and eggs for the enormous pot of potato salad they'd take to the family gathering scheduled for the following night, Christmas Eve. In the afternoon she washed her hair, took a bath, filed her nails and rummaged in Amy's room for some polish with a little more pizzazz than the colorless stuff she usually wore. She came up with something called "Mocha Magic" and grimaced as she painted the first stripe down a nail. *I'm simply not a "Mocha Magic" girl,* she thought, but completed the single nail, held it aloft and assessed it stringently. She fluttered her fingers and watched the light dance across the pearlescent surface and decided—thinking in Amy's current teenage vernacular—what the heck, go for it!

When all ten nails were finished she wasn't sure she'd done the right thing. She imagined them glistening, catching the lights while she fingered the neck of her violin. *I'm a conservative person trapped inside the body of a Kewpie doll,* she decided, and left the polish on.

She put on a beef roast for supper and pressed her long, black gabardine skirt and the collar of the basic long-sleeved white blouse that completed the orchestra "uniform" worn by its female members. The blouse was made of a slick knit jersey, and there'd be no sweaters to hide behind, no bulkiness to disguise the way the slippery fabric conformed to her frame.

She was at the piano, limbering up her fingers with chromatic scales, when the shopping trio returned.

Jeff was bellowing her name as he opened the door and followed his ears to the living room. He reached over her shoulder and tapped out the melody line to "Jingle Bells," then sashayed on through the living room with two crackling sacks on his arm, followed by Amy, also bearing packages. By the time the pair exited to hide their booty, Brian stood in the opposite doorway, his cheeks slightly brightened by the winter air outside, jacket unzipped and pulling open as he paused with one hand in his back pocket, the other surrounding a brown paper sack. His eyes were startlingly attractive as the dark lashes dropped, and he glanced at Theresa's hands on the keyboard.

"Play something," he requested.

Immediately she folded her palms between her knees. "Oh, I was only limbering up for tonight."

He moved a step closer. "Limber up some more, then."

"I'm limbered enough."

He crossed behind her toward the davenport, and her eyes followed over her shoulder. "Good, then play a song."

"I don't know rock."

"I know. You're a classy person." He grinned, set his package down on the davenport and drew off his jacket, all the while keeping his eyes on her. She pinched her knees tighter against her palms. "I meant to say, you're a classical person," he amended with a lazy grin. "So play me a classic."

She played without sheet music, at times allowing her eyelids to drift closed while her head tipped back, and he caught glimpses of her enraptured eloquent face. When her eyelids opened she focused on nothing, letting her gaze drift with seeming unawareness. He had little doubt that while she played, Theresa forgot he stood behind her. He dropped his eyes again to her hands—fragile, long-fingered, with delicate bones at wrist and knuckle. How supplely they moved, those wrists arching gracefully, then dropping as she weaved backward, then forward. Once she smiled, and her head tipped to one side as the pianissimo chords tinkled from her fingertips while she inhabited that captivating world he knew and understood so well.

Watching the language of her hands, her body, was like having the song not only put into words but illustrated as well. He sensed that within Theresa the music acted as bellows to embers and saw what passions lay hidden within the woman whose normally shy demeanor never hinted at such smoldering fires.

By the time the song ended and Theresa's hands poised motionless above the keys, he was certain her heart must be pounding as heavily as his own.

He laid a hand on her shoulder and she jerked, as if waking up.

"That's very nice," he praised softly, and she became conscious of that warm hand resting where the strap of her bra cut a deep, painful groove into her flesh. "I seem to remember an old movie that used that as its theme song."

"The Eddy Duchin Story."

The hand slipped away, making her wish it had stayed. "Yes, that was it. Tyrone Power and...." She heard his fingers fillip beside her ear and swung around on the bench to face him, again tucking her palms between her knees.

"Kim Novak."

"That's it. Kim Novak." He noted her pose, the way she rounded her shoulders to minimize the prominence of her breasts, and it took an effort for him to keep his eyes on her face.

"It's Chopin. One of my favorites."

"I'll remember that. Chopin. Do you play Chopin tonight, too?"

He stood very close to her, and Theresa raised her eyes to meet his gaze. From this angle, the shoulder-to-shoulder seam across his white jersey made his torso appear inordinately broad and tapered. His voice was honey smooth and soft. Most of the time he spoke that way, which was a balm to her ears after the affectionate grate of Jeff's clamorousness and her mother's usual bawling forte.

"No, tonight we do all Christmas music. I believe we're starting with 'Joy to the World' and then a little-known French carol. We follow that with...." She realized he probably couldn't care less what they were playing tonight, and buttoned her lip.

"With?"

"Nothing. Just the usual Christmas stuff."

She was becoming rattled by his nearness and the studied way he seemed to be itemizing her features, as if listing them selectively in credit and debit columns within his head. She suddenly wished she knew how to apply makeup as cleverly as Amy, picturing her colorless eyelashes, and her too-colorful cheeks, knowing Brian could detect her many shortcomings altogether too clearly at such close range.

"I have to peel potatoes for supper." Having dredged up that excuse, she slid off the bench and escaped to the kitchen, where she donned a cobbler's apron to protect her white blouse as she worked.

A short time later her mother and father returned from work, and in the suppertime confusion, the quiet moment with Brian slipped to the back of Theresa's mind. But as she prepared to flee the house with violin case under the arm of her gray coat, she came to a halt in the middle of the kitchen. There stood Brian with a dish towel in his hands, and Amy, with her arms buried in suds, having uttered not a word of her usual complaints at having the job foisted on her.

"I'm sorry I had to eat and run, but we have to be in our chairs ready to tune up by six forty-five."

Jeff was on the phone, talking with Patricia. "Just a minute—" He broke off, and lowered the receiver. "Hey, sis, do good, okay?"

She gave him a thumbs-up sign with one fat, red mitten as she headed toward the door, found it held open by Brian, his other hand buried inside a dish towel and glass he'd been wiping.

"Good luck," he said softly, his green eyes lingering upon her in a way that resurrected the closeness she'd shared at the piano earlier. The cold air rushed about their ankles, but neither seemed to notice as they gazed at each other, and Theresa felt as if Chopin's music was playing within her heart.

"Thanks," she said at last. "And thanks for taking over for me with the dishes."

"Anytime." He smiled, grazed her chin with a touch so light she wondered if she'd imagined it as she turned into the brisk night that cooled her heated cheeks.

The annual Christmas concert of the Burnsville Civic Orchestra was held each year at the Burnsville Senior High School auditorium. The risers were set up and the curtains left open and the musicians made their way to their places amid the metallic premusic of clanking stands and metal folding chairs. The conductor arrived and tuning began. The incessant drone of the A-note filled the vaulted space of the auditorium, and gradually, the room hummed with voices as the seats slowly filled. The footlights were still off, and from her position at first chair Theresa had a clear view of the aisles.

She was running her bow over the honey-colored chunk of resin when her hand stopped sawing, and her lips fell open in surprise. There, filing in, came her whole family, plus Patricia Gluek, and of course, Brian Scanlon. They shuffled into the fourth row center and began removing jackets and gloves while Theresa's palms went damp. She had played the violin since sixth grade and had stopped having stage fright years ago, but her stomach drew up now into an unexpected coil of apprehension.

Amy waggled two fingers in a clandestine hello, and Theresa answered with a barely discernible waggle of her own. Then her eyes scanned the seat next to Amy and found Brian waggling two fingers back at her. *Oh, Lord, did he think I waved at him?* Twenty-five years old and waving like her giggling first graders did when they spotted their mommies and daddies in the audience.

But before she could become any further unnerved by the thought, the footlights came up, and the conductor tapped his baton on the edge of the music stand. She stiffened her spine and pulled away from the backrest of the chair, snapped her violin into place at the lift of the black-clad arms and hit the opening note of "Joy to the World."

Midway through the song Theresa realized she had never played the violin so well in her life, not that she could remember. She attacked the powerful notes of "Joy to the World" with robust precision. She nursed the stunning dissonants of "The Christmas Song" with loving care until the tension eased from the chords with their familiar resolutions. As lead violinist, she performed a solo on the compelling "I Wonder As I Wander," and the instrument seemed to come alive beneath her mocha-colored fingernails.

She began by playing for him. But she ended playing for herself, which is the true essence of the real musician. She forgot Brian sat in the audience and lost the inhibitions that claimed her whenever there was no instrument beneath her fingers or no children to direct.

From the darkened house, he watched her—nobody but her. The red hair and freckles that had been so distracting in their brilliance when he'd first met her took on an appropriateness lent by her fiery zeal as she dissolved into the music. Again, there were times when her eyelids drifted shut. Other times she smiled against the chin rest, and he was somehow certain she had no idea she was smiling. Her sleeves draped as she bowed the instrument, her wrist arched daintily as she occasionally plucked it, and the hem of her black skirt lifted and fell as she tapped her toe to the sprightlier songs.

The concert ended with a reprise of "Joy to the World," and the final thunder of applause brought the orchestra members to their feet for a mass bow.

When the house lights came up, Theresa's eyes scanned the line of familiar faces in row four, but returned to settle and stay on Brian, who had lifted his hands to praise her in the traditional way, and was wearing a smile as proud as any on the other faces. She braved a wide smile in return and hoped he knew it was not for the others but just for him. He stopped clapping and gave her the thumbs-up signal, and she felt a holiday glow such as she'd never known as she sat to tuck her instrument back into its case.

* * *

They were waiting in the hall when she came from the music room with her coat and mitts on, her case beneath an arm.

Everybody babbled at once, but Theresa finally had a chance to croon appreciatively, "Why didn't you *tell* me you were coming?"

"We wanted to surprise you. Besides, we thought it might make you nervous."

"Well, it did! No, it didn't! Oh, I don't know what I'm saying, except it really made the concert special, knowing you were all out there listening. Thanks, all of you, for coming."

Jeff looped an elbow around Theresa's neck, faked a headlock and a punch to the jaw and grunted, "You did good, sis."

Margaret took command then. "We have a tree to decorate yet tonight, and you know how your father always has trouble with those lights. Let's get this party moving home!"

They headed toward the parking lot, and Theresa invited, "Does anybody want to ride with me?" She could sense Amy reserving her reply until she heard what Brian answered.

"I will," he said, moving to Theresa's side and taking the violin case from her hands.

"I will too—" Amy began, but Margaret cut her off in midsentence.

"Amy, you come with us. I want you to run into the store for a carton of milk on our way home."

"Jeff? Patricia?" Theresa appealed, suddenly feeling as if she'd coerced Brian into saying yes, since nobody else had.

"Patricia left her purse in the station wagon, so we might as well ride with them."

The two groups parted, and as she walked toward her little gray Toyota, Theresa suddenly suspected that Patricia had had her purse with her all along.

In the car she and Brian settled into the low bucket seats and Theresa put a tape in the deck. Rachmaninoff seemed to envelope them. "Sorry," she offered, and immediately pushed the eject button. Without hesitation, he reseated the tape against the heads and the dynamic Concerto in C-sharp Minor returned.

"I get the idea you think I'm some hard-rock freak. Music is music. If it's good, I like it."

They drove through the moonlit night with the power and might of Rachmaninoff ushering them home, followed by the much mellower poignance of Listz's "Liebestraum." As its flowing sweetness touched her ears, Theresa thought of its English translation, "Dream of Love." But she kept her eyes squarely on the road, thinking herself fanciful because of the residual ebullience of the performance and the occasional scarlet, blue and gold lights that glittered from housefronts as they passed. In living-room windows Christmas trees winked cheerfully, but it wasn't just the trees, it wasn't just the lights, it wasn't just the concert and not even Jeff's being home that made this Christmas more special than most. It was Brian Scanlon.

"I saw your foot tapping," he teased now.

"Oh?"

"Sure sign of a dancer."

"I'm still thinking about it."

"Good. Because I never get to dance much anymore. I'm always providing the music."

"Never fear. If I don't go, there'll be plenty of others."

"That's what I'm afraid of. Rhythmless clods who'll abuse my toes and talk, talk, talk in my ear."

"You don't like to talk when you dance?" Somehow she'd always imagined dancers using the close proximity to exchange intimacies.

"Not particularly."

"I've been led to believe that's when men and women whisper...well, what's known as *sweet nothings.*"

Brian turned to study her face, smiling at the old-fashioned phrase, wondering if he knew another woman who'd use it. *"Sweet nothings?"*

She heard the grin in his voice, but kept her eyes on the street. "I have no personal knowledge of them myself, you understand." She gave him a quarter glance and lifted one eyebrow.

"I understand. Neither do I."

"But I'll give it some thought."

"I already have. Sounds like not a half-bad idea."

She felt as if her face would light up the interior of the car, for it struck Theresa that while she had no knowledge of sweet nothings, she and Brian were exchanging them at that very moment.

They made it home before the others, and Theresa excused herself to go to her room and change into jeans, blouse and loose-thrown sweater again. From the living room she heard the soft, exploratory notes of the piano as a melody line from a current Air Supply hit was picked out with one finger. She came down the hall and paused in the living-room doorway. Brian stood before the piano, one thumb hooked in the back pocket of his pants while he lackadaisically pressed the keys with a single forefinger. He looked up. She crossed her arms. The piano strings vibrated into silence. She noticed things about him that she liked—the shape of his eyebrows, the way his expression said *smile* when there really was none there, his easy unhurried way of speaking, moving, shifting his eyes, that put her much more at ease the longer she was with him.

"I enjoyed the concert."

"I'm glad."

"My first live orchestra."

"It's nothing compared to the Minneapolis Orchestra. You should hear them."

"Maybe I will sometime. Do they play Chopin?"

"Oh, they play everything! And Orchestra Hall is positively sensational. The acoustics are world acclaimed. The ceiling is made of big white cubes of all sizes that look like they've been thrown up there and stuck at odd angles. The notes come bouncing off the cubes and—" She had looked up, as if expecting the living-room ceiling to be composed of the same cubes she described, not realizing that she looked very girlish and appealing in her animation, or that she had thrown her arms wide.

When her eyes drifted down, she found Brian grinning in amusement.

The kitchen door burst open and the noise began again.

When the Brubaker family decorated their Christmas tree, the scene was like a three-ring circus, with Margaret its ringmaster. She doled out commands about everything: which side of the tree should face front, who should pick up the trail of needles left scattered across the carpet, who should fill the tree stand with water. Poor Willard had trouble with the tree lights, all right, but his biggest trouble was his wife. "Willard, I want you to move that red light so it's underneath that branch instead of on top of it. There's a big hole here."

Jeff caught his mother by the waist, swung her around playfully and circled her arms so she couldn't move, then plopped a silencing kiss on her mouth. "Yes, his little turtledove. Shut up, his little turtledove," Margaret's tall son teased, gaining a smile in return.

"You're not too big to spank yet, Jeffrey. Talking to your mother like that." But her grin was as wide as a watermelon slice. "Patricia, get this boy off my back." Patricia made a lunge at Jeff and the two ended up in a heap on the sofa, teasing and tickling.

Margaret had turned on the living-room stereo, but while it played Christmas music, Amy's bedroom was thumping with rock, and though the door was closed, the sound came through to confuse the issue. Jeff sang with one or the other in his deep, gravelly voice, and before they got to the tinsel, the phone had rung no less than four times—all for Amy.

Brian might have felt out of place but for Patricia's being an outsider, too. When it was time to distribute the tinsel, she was given a handful, just as he was, and protesting that it was *their* tree would have sounded ungracious, so he found himself beside Theresa, hanging shimmering silver icicles on the high branches while she worked on the lower ones. Jeff and Patricia had taken over the other half of the tree while the two elder Brubakers sat back and watched this part of the decorations, and Amy talked on the phone, interrupting herself to offer some sage bit of direction now and then.

They ended the evening with hot apple cider and cinnamon rolls around the kitchen table. By the time they finished, it was nearing eleven o'clock. Margaret stood up and began stacking the dirty cups and saucers.

"Well, I guess it's time I get Patricia back home," Jeff announced. "Do you two want to ride along?"

Brian and Theresa both looked up and spoke simultaneously.

"No, I'll stay here and clean up the mess."

"I don't feel like going out in the cold again."

Theresa took over the task her mother had begun. "You're tired, mom. I'll do that."

Margaret desisted thankfully and went off to bed with Willard, ordering Amy to retire also. When the door closed behind Jeff and Patricia, the kitchen was left to Theresa and Brian. She carried the dishes to the counter and filled the sink with sudsy water and began washing them.

"I'll dry them for you."

"You don't have to. There are just a few."

Overruling her protest, he found the dish towel and stood beside her at the sink. She was conscious that he was comfortable with silence, unlike most people. He could go through long stretches of it without searching for ways to fill it. The stereos were off. Jeff's teasing was gone, and Margaret's incessant orders. Only the swish of water and the clink of glassware could be heard. It took them less than five minutes to wash and dry the cups and saucers and put the room in order. But while five minutes of silence beside the wrong person can be devastating, that same five beside the right man can be totally wonderful.

When she'd hung up the wet cloths and switched out all the lights except the small one over the stove, she found a bottle of lotion beneath the sink and squirted a dollop in her palm, aware of Brian watching silently as she worked the cherry-scented cream into her hands.

"Let's sit in the living room for a while," he suggested.

She led the way and sat down on one end of the davenport while he sat at the other, leaning back and draping his palms across his abdomen, much as he had in the theater. Again silence fell. Again it was sustaining rather than draining. The tree lights made Theresa feel as if she was on the inside of a rainbow looking out.

"You have a wonderful family," he said at last.

"I know."

"But I begin to see why your dad needs to spend some quiet time with the birds."

Theresa chuckled softly. "It gets a little raucous at times. Mostly when Jeff's around."

"I like it though. I don't ever remember any happy noise around my house."

"Don't you have any brothers and sisters?"

"Yeah, one sister, but she's eight years older than me, and she lives in Jamaica. Her husband's in exporting. We were never very close."

"And what about your mom and dad? I mean, your real dad. Were you close to them?"

He stared at the tree lights and ruminated at length. She liked that. No impulsive answers to a question that was important. "A little with my dad, but never with my mother."

"Why?"

He rolled his head and studied her. "I don't know. Why are some families like yours and some like mine? If I knew the answer and could bottle it, I could stop wars."

His answer made her turn to meet his eyes directly—such stunning, spiky-lashed beauties. She was struck again by the fact that such pretty eyes somehow managed to make him even more handsome. In them the tree lights were reflected—dots of red and gold and green and blue shining from beneath chestnut eyebrows and lashes, studying her without a smile.

His steady gaze made Theresa short of breath.

There were things inside this man that spoke of a depth of character she was growing surely to admire. Though he was really Jeff's senior by only two years, he seemed much older than Jeff—much older than her, too, she thought. Perhaps losing one's family does that to a person. It suddenly struck Theresa how awesome it must be to have no place to call home. She herself had clung to home far longer than was advisable. But she was a different matter. Brian would leave the Air Force next summer, and there would be no mother waiting with pumpkin pies in the freezer. No familiar bedroom where he could lie on his back and consider what lay ahead, while the familiar lair secured him to the past. No siblings to tease or go Christmas shopping with. No old girlfriend waiting with open arms....

But how did she know? The thought was sobering. She suddenly wanted to ask if there was a woman somewhere who was special to him, but didn't want to sound forward, so she veiled the question somewhat.

"Isn't there anyone left behind in Chicago?"

The smile was absent, but why did it feel as if he was charming her with the twinkle in his eye? "Since we've already eliminated parents and sisters and brothers, you must mean girlfriends." She dropped her eyes and hoped the red tree lights camouflaged the heat she felt creeping up her neck. "No, there are no girlfriends waiting in Chicago."

"I didn't mean—"

"Whether you did or not doesn't matter. Maybe I just wanted you to know."

The silence that followed was scarcely comfortable, quite unlike that which had passed earlier. It was filled with a new, tingling two-way awareness and a thousand other unasked questions.

"I think I'll say good-night now," he announced quietly, surprising Theresa. She wasn't *totally* naive. She'd sat on living-room davenports with those of the opposite sex before, and after a lead-in like Brian's, the groping always followed.

But he rose, stretched and stood with his fingers in his hip pockets while he studied the tree a minute longer. Then he studied her an equal length of time before raising a palm and murmuring softly, "Good night, Theresa."

Chapter Four

Brian Scanlon lay in bed, thinking about Theresa Brubaker, considering what it was that attracted him to her. He'd never cared much for redheads. Yet her hair was as orange as that of a Raggedy Ann doll, and her freckles were the color of overripe fruit. When she blushed—and she blushed often—she tended to glow like the Christmas tree.

Brian had been playing in a band since high school. In every dance crowd there were women who couldn't resist a guitar man when he stepped down from the stage at break time. They flocked around like chickens to scattered corn. He'd had his share. But he'd always gone for the blondes and brunettes, the prettiest ones with artful makeup and hair down to the middle of their backs, swinging like silk—women who knew their way around men.

But Theresa Brubaker was totally different from them. Not only did she look different, she acted different. She was honest and interesting, intelligent and loving. And totally naive, Brian was sure.

Yet so much heart lay beneath that naivety. It surfaced whenever she was around her family, particularly Jeff, and whenever she was around music. Brian recalled her voice, when the three of them had been harmonizing in the car, and the verve she radiated when playing the violin and the piano. Why, she even had him listening to classical music with a new, tolerant ear. The poignant strains of the Chopin Nocturne came back to him as he crossed his wrists behind his head in the dark and thought of how she'd looked in the long black skirt and white blouse. The blouse had, for once, been covered by no sweater.

He wondered how a man ever got up the nerve to touch breasts like hers. When they were that big, they weren't really...sexy. Just intimidating. He'd been scared to death the first time he'd felt a girl's breasts, but since then he'd touched countless others, and still the idea of caressing Theresa's breasts gave him serious qualms. There'd been times when he'd managed to study them covertly, but Theresa allowed few such opportunities, covered as she usually was with her cardigans. But when she'd been playing the piano, he'd stood behind her and looked down at the mountainous orbs beneath her blouse, and his mouth had gone dry instead of watering.

Forget it, Scanlon. She's not your type.

* * *

The next morning, when Brian arose at his usual wake-up hour and crept barefoot upstairs to the bathroom, he came face to face with Theresa in the hall.

They both stopped short and stared at each other. He wore a pair of blue denim jeans, nothing else. She wore a mint green bathrobe, nothing else. There wasn't a sound in the house. Everyone else was still asleep, for it was Christmas Eve day so neither of her parents had to go to work.

"Good morning," she whispered. The bathroom door was right beside them.

"Good morning," he whispered back. Her feet were bare, and it was obvious even without a glance that her breasts were untethered beneath the velour robe, for they drooped nearly to her waist while she lifted her arms and pretended the zipper needed closing at her throat.

"You can go first," she offered, gesturing toward the doorway.

"No, no, you go ahead. I'll wait."

"No, I...really, I was just going to put on a pot of coffee first."

He was about to raise another objection when she swept past him toward the kitchen, so he hurried into the bathroom, taking care of necessities without wasting time, then heading for the kitchen to tell her the room was free. She was standing before the stove waiting for the coffee to start perking when he padded up silently beside her.

The sun wasn't up yet, but it had lightened the sky to an opalescent gray that lifted over the east windowsills of the kitchen, providing enough light for Theresa to see very clearly the dark hair springing from Brian's bare chest and diving into his waistline like an arrow. His nipples were like twin raspberries, shriveled up in the centers of squarely defined muscles. The only bare chests she'd ever seen in this house had been Jeff's and her father's. But this one was nothing like either of theirs, and the sight of him brought to mind vivid scenes from the movie they'd seen two nights ago. She dropped her eyes after the briefest glance, but down below she encountered more hair—dark wisps on his big toes. And suddenly she couldn't stand there beside him a moment longer, with him only half dressed and herself coming totally unstrung inside her mint green robe.

"Would you mind watching the coffee till it starts perking, then turn it down to low?"

In the bathroom she switched on the light above the vanity and checked her reflection in the mirror. Sure enough, beet red! That horribly unflattering red that made her look as if she was going to go off like a Fourth of July rocket. She pressed her palms to her cheeks, closed her eyes and wondered how it felt to be *normal* and come up against a half-naked man like Brian Scanlon in your kitchen.

Lordy, he flustered her so.

What do other women do? How do they handle the first attraction they feel? It must be so much easier when you're fourteen, like Amy, and you go at the natural pace: a first exchange of glances, a first touch of hands, a first kiss, then nubility taking over as boy and girl together begin exploring their awakening sexuality.

But I was thwarted at square one, Theresa thought miserably, looking at her awful freckles and hair, which by themselves would have been enough to overcome without the other even greater obstacles. *I was cheated by nature out of those first kittenish glances that might have led to all the rest, because all the first glances I ever received contained no more than shock or lasciviousness. And now here I am, midway through my twenties, and I don't know how to handle my very first sexual attraction to a man.*

She took a bath, washed her hair and didn't reenter the kitchen until she was properly dressed in a color she wore defiantly—cranberry. She loved it, but when it got anywhere near her hair, the two hues went to war and made her look like beets and carrots mixed in the same bowl. She had to keep the cranberry corduroy slacks separated from her flaming hair by a band of neutral color across her torso. When she explored her closet, she came upon a wonderful white sweat shirt Amy had given her for Christmas last year, which Theresa had never worn, no matter how many times she'd been tempted. To the average woman the sweat shirt would have been absolutely dishwater plain. It had hand-warmer pockets on the belly, zipper up the front and two sport stripes running down the sleeves: one of navy, the other of cranberry.

She took it from the hanger, slipped her arms into it and stepped before her mirror while she zipped it up. But the reflection that met her eyes made her want to cry. It looked like two dirigibles had been inflated beneath the garment. There was no power on earth that could make her wear this thing out to the kitchen and face Brian.

Angrily, she jerked it off and tossed it aside, replacing it with a prim oxford-cloth shirt in off-white with long sleeves and a button-down collar, over which she draped the everlasting, hated cardigan.

She was saved from encountering Brian's bare chest again, when she heard him take over the bathroom while she was arranging her hair in a round mound just above her collar. When it was confined, at least it didn't look as if it was going to carry her away into the wild blue yonder if a stiff wind came up.

In the bathroom, Brian, too, assessed himself in the mirror. *She's scared of you, Scanlon, so the issue is settled. You don't have to think about the possibilities of falling for her.*

But the room was scented with feminine things—the flowery essence of soap left behind in the damp air. There was a wet washcloth over the shower-curtain rod, and when he grabbed it down to close the curtains, he found himself staring at it for a long moment while he rubbed a thumb across the cold, damp terry cloth. With an effort, he put her from his mind and folded the cloth very carefully, then laid it on a corner of the tub. But while he stood beneath the hot spray, soaping his body, he thought of her again, and of the movie, and couldn't help wondering what it would be like in bed with that freckled body, the generous breasts and red hair.

Scanlon, it's Christmas, you pervert! What the hell are you doing standing here thinking about your best friend's sister like some practiced lecher?

But that's not the only reason I can't get her off my mind, his other self argued honestly. *She's a beautiful* person. *Inside, where it counts.*

He intentionally kept things light and breezy when he met Theresa in the kitchen again. But it was easier, for the rest of her family was beginning to rouse, and one by one they padded out to have coffee or juice. By the time they all sat down to breakfast together, the day had changed mood.

It was set aside for preparations. There was a family gathering planned at Grandma and Grandpa Deering's house, and everybody would take something for the supper buffet. Then tomorrow, the pack would descend upon the Brubaker house for Christmas dinner, so Margaret, Theresa and Amy were busy all day in the kitchen.

Margaret was at her dictatorial best, issuing orders like a drill-team sergeant again while her daughters carried them out. Willard spent part of the day watching for cardinals, while Jeff and Brian broke out their guitars at last, and from the kitchen Theresa heard her first of Brian's guitar playing. She dropped what she was doing and moved to the living-room doorway, pausing there to observe him tuning, then fingering an augmented chord of quietly vibrating quality, bending his head low over the instrument, listening intently as the six notes shimmered into silence. He sat at the piano bench, but had swung to face the davenport where Jeff sat, and didn't know Theresa stood behind him.

Jeff, too, strummed random chords, the two guitars quietly clashing in that presong dissonance that can be as musical in its own off-harmonic way as cleanly arranged songs.

Jeff played lead, Brian rhythm, and from the moment the discordant warmup crystalized into the intro to a song, Theresa recognized a marvelous communion of kindred musicians. No signal had been spoken, none exchanged by eye, hand or tongue. The inharmonious gibberish of tuning had simply resolved into the concord of one single silently agreed-upon song.

Between musicians there can be a connection, just as between friends who somehow single each other out, recognizing empathy from the moment of introduction, just as a man and woman sometimes attract each other at first glimpse. It's something that cannot be prompted or dictated. Among members of a band this connection makes the difference between simply playing notes at the same time and creating an affinity of sound.

They had it, these two. There was almost a mystical quality about it, and as Theresa looked on and listened from the kitchen doorway, shivers ran up her arms and down her legs. They had picked up on "Georgia on My Mind." Where was the clashing rock? Where were the occasional sour chords she used to hear from Jeff's guitar? When had he gotten so *good?*

Neither Brian nor Jeff looked at each other while they played. Their heads were cocked lazily, eyes blankly turned to the waists of their guitars in that indolent, concentrative pose Theresa recognized well. How many times had she stood before Jeff and asked him a question when he was in such a trance, only to be separated from him by the wall of music until the song finished and he looked startled to find her standing there?

Jeff began to sing, his softly grating voice evocative of Ray Charles's immortal rendition of this song. A lump formed in Theresa's throat. Amy had come up silently behind her, and they stood as motionless as the hands of a sundial. Jeff "took a ride" at the break, and Theresa stared at his supple fingers running along the frets with an agility she'd never seen before. Pride blossomed in her heart. *Oh, Jeff, Jeff, my little brother, who started on that fifteen-dollar Stella in the corner, just listen to you now.* He vocalized the last verse, then together he and Brian "rode it home," and as the last poignant notes ebbed to fade-out, Theresa looked back over her shoulder into Amy's wide, amazed eyes. The room was silent.

Jeff's eyes met Brian's, and they exchanged smiles before they concurred, in their two deep voices, "All ri-i-ight."

"Jeffrey," Theresa said softly at last.

He glanced up in surprise. "Hey, Treat, how long have you been standing there?"

Brian swung around on the piano seat, and she gave him a passing smile of approval but moved to her brother, bending across his guitar to give him a hug. "When did you get so good?"

"You haven't heard me for over a year, closer to a year and a half. Brian and I have been hittin' it hard."

"Obviously."

She turned back to Brian. "Don't take me wrong, but I think you two were made for each other."

They all laughed, then Brian agreed, "Yeah, we kind of thought so the first time we picked a song together. It just happened, you know?"

"I know. And it shows."

Amy, with her hands jammed in her jeans pockets, inched closer to Brian's shoulders. "Gol, wait'll the kids hear this!"

Theresa couldn't resist the temptation to tease. "Is this Amy Brubaker speaking? The same Amy Brubaker who inundates us with AC/DC and scorns anything mellower than Rod Stewart?"

Amy shrugged, showed a flash of braces behind a half-sheepish grin, and returned, "Yeah, but these guys are really *excellent,* I mean, *wow.* And anyway, Jeff promised they'd do some rock, too. Didn't you, Jeffy?"

Instead of answering, Jeff struck a straight D chord, hard and heavy, with a dramatic flourish, and after letting it sizzle for a prolonged moment he met Brian's eye, and the next chord bit the air with the brashness of unvarnished rock. How they both knew the chosen song was a mystery. But one minute only Jeff's chord hung in the air, and the next they were hammering away at the song as if by divine design. Amy stood between them, getting into the beat with her hips. "Yeah..." she half growled, and Brian gave her a nonchalant quasi smile, then turned that same smile on Theresa, who shrugged in reply, a proud smile on her face while she enjoyed every note, rock or not, and each sideward thrust of Amy's hips.

When the song ended, Margaret and Willard were standing in the doorway, applauding. Amy rushed for the telephone, undoubtedly to rave on about the good tidings to as many friends as possible, and Theresa reluctantly returned to the kitchen to listen from there while she worked.

In the late afternoon, they all went to their respective rooms to change and get ready for the trip across town to Grandpa and Grandma Deerings'. When they rendezvoused in the kitchen to load the car, it was Margaret who suggested, "Why don't you bring your guitars? We'll do some caroling. You know how your grandparents enjoy it."

So the station wagon was packed with potato salad and cranberry Jell-O, a vintage Gibson hollow-body 335 and a classic Epiphone Riviera, a rented amp, a stack of Christmas presents and six bodies.

Willard drove. Theresa found herself in the back seat sandwiched between Jeff and Brian. His hip was warm, even through her bulky coat, and when he and Jeff exchanged comments, she was served up tantalizing whiffs of his sandalwoody after-shave, for he'd slung an arm across the back of the seat and repeatedly leaned forward to peer around her.

If Brian thought he'd feel out of place at the family gathering, the delusion was put to rout within minutes of arriving. The tiny house of mid-forties' vintage was popping at the seams with relatives of all ages and sizes. Grandpa Deering was deaf, and when Jeff took Brian over to introduce him to the shriveled little man, he shouted for his grandfather's benefit. "Grandpa, this is my friend, Brian, the one who's in the Air Force with me."

The old man nodded.

"I brought him home to spend Christmas with us," Jeff bawled at the top of his lungs.

Mr. Deering nodded again.

"We play in a band together, and we brought our guitars along tonight to do a few carols."

The bald head nodded still once more. Grandpa Deering raised a crooked forefinger in the air as if in approval, but said not a word until the two were turning away. Then he questioned in his reedy old quake, "This y'r friend who fiddles with you?"

It was all Brian could do to keep a straight face. Jeff turned back to his grandfather, leaning closer. "Guitar, grandpa, guitar."

The old man nodded and said no more, replaced his arthritic palms one on top of the other atop a black, rubber-tipped cane and seemed to drift into a reverie.

When Brian and Jeff turned away, Brian whispered in his friend's ear. "Doesn't his hearing aid work?"

"He turns it down whenever it's convenient. When the music starts he'll hear every note."

The thirty-odd aunts, uncles and cousins ate from a table containing more food than Brian had ever seen in one place, and after the buffet supper, opened gifts, having exchanged names at Thanksgiving. When it was time for the music, everyone found a spot as best he could on the floor, the kitchen cabinets, end tables, arms of furniture, and the entire group sang the old standard carols while Theresa was cajoled into playing along with the guitars on an ancient oak organ whose bellows were filled by foot pedals. She complied good-naturedly and pulled out the old stops from whose faces the mother-of-pearl inserts had long ago fallen. For the benefit of the small children in the group, Brian and Jeff were enticed into doing a run-through of "Here Comes Santa Claus," which evolved into a jazz rendition that would have shocked its composer, Gene Autry. Jeff took an impromptu ride, taking outrageous liberties with the melody line, ad-libbing arpeggios while Brian modified the chords to smooth, fluid jazz. When it was over, the house burst into whistles and clapping, and the youngsters called for "Jingle Bells." When that was finished, someone called, "Where's Margaret? Margaret, it's your turn. Get up there."

To Brian's surprise, the hefty-chested dictatorial Margaret stepped center front, and while her daughter played an accompaniment on the wheezy organ, she belted out a stunning "Oh Holy Night." When the song ended, and Theresa spun around on the seat of the claw-foot organ stool to face Brian's eyebrows raised in surprise, she leaned near his ear and whispered, "Mother was a mezzo-soprano with a touring opera company before she married daddy."

"That leaves only Amy. What about her?"

From his far side, Amy spoke up. "I only got the beat, I didn't get the voice, so I play drums in the school band."

Brian smiled. "And dance, I'll bet."

"Yeah. Just wait and see."

Theresa knew a kind of keen envy. Amy could dance the socks off any three partners who tried to keep up with her. The sample she'd given earlier today in the living room had been only a hint of the rhythm contained in her svelte, teenage limbs. Theresa had always been extremely proud of Amy's dancing ability, and more so, her sister's lack of inhibition whenever any music started. While Theresa herself had felt a lifelong urge to dance, she'd never yielded to it.

She should have grown inured to giving up enjoyments such as dancing. By now, she shouldn't miss them, but she did. She transferred all her emotions into her music and took from it the satisfaction she was denied in other modes of self-expression, as she did now on this Christmas Eve.

She shunned the petty envy that she'd come to hate in herself and lauded, "Amy is the best dancer I know. It's too bad she isn't old enough to go with you on New Year's Eve."

Brian only smiled from one sister to the other, hoping the older of the two would agree to go with him, after all.

On the way home they dropped Jeff off at Patricia's house, where another family celebration was winding down. Jeff would get in on the end of it. When the remainder of the group reached the Brubaker house, the two older ones toddled off to bed while the remaining three turned on the tree lights and sat in the cozy living room exchanging anecdotes about past Christmases, music, the Air Force, school dances, Grandpa Deering and a myriad of subjects that kept them up well past midnight. Jeff joined them then, announcing that he'd just flown in on his jet-propelled sleigh and was looking for a plate of cookies and glass of milk before he filled any stockings.

When Theresa went to sleep that night, it was not to visions of sugar plums dancing in her head, but to visions of Brian Scanlon's long, dexterous fingers moving along the fingerboard of an Epiphone Riviera, picking out the chords to a love song whose words she strove to catch.

On Christmas morning Theresa was awakened by Amy, pouncing on her bed, giggling. "Hey, come on! Let's make it to those prezzies!"

"Amy, it's blacker than the ace of spades outside."

"It's seven o'clock already!"

"Ohh!" Theresa groaned and rolled over.

"Come on, get your buns out of here and let's go get the boys and mom and dad."

From down the hall came a hoarse call. "Who's doin' all that giggling out there?" Jeff. "Come in here and try that!"

Amy sprang off Theresa's bed and went to wage an attack on her brother, and the squealing that followed told clearly of a bout of tickling which soon awakened Margaret and Willard. The thumping on the floor aroused their houseguest downstairs, and within ten minutes they had all gathered in the living room and snuggled around the Christmas tree, dressed in hastily thrown-on robes, jeans, half-buttoned shirts, bare feet and bedroom slippers, sipping juice and coffee while gifts were distributed.

Brian was sharing a Christmas unlike any he'd ever experienced. This boisterous, loving family was showing him depths he'd never known. The gifts exchanged among them underscored that love again, for they were not many but well chosen.

For Willard, his children had decided on a telescope that would take its place before the sliding glass door downstairs; for Margaret, a mother's ring that would take its place proudly on her right hand, and which prompted a listing of the three birthdays. Brian carefully marked in his memory the date of Theresa's. To Margaret and Willard together the children gave a gift certificate for a weekend at the quiet, quaint Schumaker's Country Inn in the tiny town of New Prague, an hour's ride from the Twin Cities.

From their parents, Jeff, Amy and Theresa received, respectively, a plane ticket home for Easter, a pair of tickets to an upcoming rock concert by Journey and a season ticket to Orchestra Hall.

To Brian's surprise, each of the Brubakers had bought a gift for him. From Margaret and Willard, a billfold; from Amy, blank tapes—obviously she knew he and the other band members learned new songs by taping cuts from the radio; from Jeff, a Hohner harmonica—they'd been fooling around on one at a music store, and Brian had said he'd always wanted to play one; and from Theresa, an LP of classical music, including Chopin's Nocturne in E-flat.

When he opened the last gift, he looked up in surprise. "How did you have time to find it on such short notice?"

"Secret." But her eyes danced to her father's, and Brian remembered Willard's leaving the house for "last-minute items" yesterday.

To Brian's relief, he, too, had brought gifts. For Mr. and Mrs. Brubaker, a selection of cheese and bottle of Chianti wine; for Amy, a pair of headphones, which brought a round of good-natured applause from the rest of the group; for Jeff, a wide leather guitar strap tooled with his name; and for Theresa, a tiny pewter figurine—a smiling frog on a lily pad, playing the violin.

She smiled, placed it on her palm and met Brian's irresistible green eyes across the living room.

"How did you know I collect pewter instruments?"

"Secret."

"My darling brother, who can't keep anything to himself. And for once, I'm happy he can't. Thank you, Brian."

"Thank you, too. You'll make a silk purse of this sow's ear yet." Which was ironic, for Brian was far, far from a sow's ear.

She studied the frog with its bulging pewter eyes and self-satisfied smile and lifted a similar smile to Brian. "I'll call him 'The Maestro.'"

The fiddling frog became one of Theresa's most cherished possessions, and took his place at the forefront of the collection shelved on a wall in her bedroom. It was the first gift she'd ever received from any male other than a family member.

That Christmas Day, filled with noise, food and family, passed in a blur for both Brian and Theresa. They were more conscious of each other than of any of the others in the house. The family ate and got lazy, ate again, and eventually their numbers began thinning. That lazy wind-down prompted dozing and eventually, an evening revival of energy. As most days did in this house where music reigned supreme, this one would have seemed incomplete without it. It was eight o'clock in the evening, and the crowd had dwindled to a mere dozen or so when out came the instruments, and it became apparent the family had their favorites, which they asked Jeff and Theresa to play. Margaret and Willard were nestled like a pair of teenagers on the davenport, and applauded and chose another and another song. Eventually, Brian and Jeff branched off into a rousing medley of rock songs, during which Theresa joined in, Elton John-style, on the piano. Then Jeff had the sudden inspiration, "Hey, Theresa, go get your fiddle!"

"Fiddle!" she spouted. "Jeffrey Brubaker, how dare you call great-grandmother's expensive Storioni a *fiddle*. Why, it's probably cringing in its case!"

Jeff explained to Brian. "She inherited her fiddle from one of our more talented progenitors, who bought it in 1906. It's modeled after a Faratti, so Theresa is rather overzealous about the piece."

"Fiddle!" Theresa teased with a saucy twitch of the hip as she left the room. "I'll show you *fiddle*, Brian Scanlon!"

When the beautiful classic violin came back with Theresa, Brian was amazed to hear the sister and brother strike into an engaging, foot-stomping rendition of "Lou'siana Saturday Night," along with which he himself provided background rhythm, while he wondered in bewilderment how Theresa happened to know the song, so different from her classics. After that, the hayseed in all of them seemed to have stuck to their overalls, and Jeff tried a little flat picking on "Wildwood Flower," and by that time, the entire group had gotten rather punchy. The usually reserved Willard captured Margaret and executed an impromptu hoe-down step in the middle of the room, which brought laughter and applause, to say nothing of the sweat to Margaret's brow as she plopped into a chair, breathless and fanning her red face but totally exhilarated.

"Give us 'Turkey In The Straw'!" someone shouted.

Again Brian was shown a new facet of Theresa Brubaker, a first-chair violinist of the Burnsville Civic Orchestra, as she sawed away on her 1906 classic Storioni, scraping out a raucous version of the old barn-dance tune, in the middle of which she lowered the violin and tapped the air with the bow, the carpet with her toe and watched her mother and father circling and clapping in the small space provided, while in a voice as clear as daybreak, Theresa sang out:

Oh, I had a little chicken
And it wouldn't lay an egg
So I poured hot water up and down her leg
Then the little chicken hollered
And the little chicken begged
And the damn little chicken
Laid a hard-boiled egg.

She was joined by the entire entourage as they finished by bellowing in unison, "Boom-tee-dee-a-da...*slick chick!*"

Brian joined in the rousing round of applause and shrill whistles that followed. As he laughed with the others, he saw again the hidden Theresa who seemed able to escape only when wooed by music and those she loved most. She covered her pink-tinged cheeks with both hands, while the "fiddle" and bow still hung from her fingers and her laughter flowed, sweet and fresh as spring water.

She was unique. She was untainted. She was as refreshing as the unexpected burst of hayseed music that had just erupted from her grandmother's invaluable 1906 Storioni.

He watched Theresa bestowing hugs of goodbye on her aunts and uncles. She had forgotten herself and impulsively lifted her arms in farewell embraces. Already Brian knew how rare these moments of forgetfulness were with Theresa. Music made the difference. It took her to a plane of unselfconsciousness nothing else could quite achieve.

He turned away, wandered back to the deserted living room, wondering what it would take to make her feel such ease with him. He sat down on the piano bench and picked out a haunting melody, one of his favorites, with a single finger, then softly began adding harmony notes. Soon he was engrossed in the quiet melody as his hands moved over the keyboard.

The house quieted. Amy was in her room with the new headphones glued to her ears. Willard was downstairs setting up his new telescope. Margaret had gone to bed, exhausted.

There were only three left in the room where the tree lights glowed.

"What are you playing?" Theresa asked, pausing behind Brian's shoulder, watching his long fingers on the piano.

"An old favorite, 'Sweet Memories.'"

"I don't think I know it."

Jeff wandered in. "Play it for her." He swung the old Stella up by its neck, extending it toward Brian, who looked back over his shoulder, with a noncommittal smile. "Do old Stella a favor," Jeff requested whimsically.

Brian seemed to consider for a long moment, then nodded once, turned on the bench to face the room and reached for the scarred, old guitar. The first soft note sent a shudder up Theresa's spine.

Jeff sat on the edge of the davenport, learning forward, elbows to knees, for one of those rare times when he didn't have a guitar in his hands. He simply sat and paid homage. To the song. His friend. And a voice that turned Theresa's nerve-endings to satin.

She realized she had not heard Brian sing before. Not alone. Not... not....

It was a song whose eloquent simplicity brought tears to her eyes and a knot to her throat, tremors to her stomach and goose bumps to the undersides of her thighs as she sat on the floor before him.

My world is like a river
As dark as it is deep.
Night after night the past slips in
And gathers all my sleep.
My days are just an endless string
Of emptiness to me.
Filled only by the fleeting moments
Of her memory.

Sweet memories...
Sweet memories...

He hummed a compelling melody line at the end of the verse, and she watched his beautiful fingers, the tendons of his left thumb grown powerful from years of barring chords, the square-cut nails of his right hand plucking or strumming the steel strings.

She watched his eyes, which had somehow come to rest on her own as the words of the last verse came somberly from his sensitive lips.

> She slipped into the darkness
> Of my dreams last night.
> Wandering from room to room
> She's turning on each light.
> Her laughter spills like water
> From the river to the sea
> Lord, I'm swept away from sadness
> Clinging to her memory.

The haunting notes of the chorus came again, and Theresa softly hummed in harmony.

> Sweet memories...
> Sweet memories...

She had crossed her calves, hooked them with her forearms and drawn her knees up, raising her eyes to his. And as he looked deeply into the brown depths, grown limpid with emotion, Brian realized she was not some soulful groupie, gazing up in adulation. She was something more, much more. And as the song quietly ended, he realized he'd found the way to break down Theresa's barriers.

The room rang with silence.

There were tears on Theresa's face.

Neither she nor Brian seemed to remember her brother was there beside them.

"Who wrote it?" she asked in a reverent whisper.

"Mickey Newbury."

She was stricken to think there existed a man named Mickey Newbury whose poignant music she had missed, whose words and melodies spoke to the soul and whispered to the heart.

Since she could not thank the composer, she thanked the performer who had gifted her with an offering superseding any that could be found wrapped in gay ribbons beneath a Christmas tree.

"Thank you, Brian."

He nodded and handed the Stella back to Jeff. But Jeff had quietly slipped from the room. Brian's gaze returned to Theresa, still curled up at his feet. Her hair picked up the holiday colors from the lights behind her, and only the rim of her lips and nose was visible in the semidarkened room.

He slipped from the piano bench onto one knee, bracing the guitar on the carpet, his hand sliding down to curl around its neck. He could not make out the expression in her eyes, though he sensed the time was right...for both of them. Her breathing was fast and shallow, and the scent he'd detected in the steamy bathroom seemed to drift from her skin and hair—a clean, fresh essence so different from the girls in smoky night spots. Bracing elbow to knee, he bent to touch her soft, unspoiled lips with his own. Her face was uplifted as their breaths mingled, then he heard her catch her own and hold it. The kiss was as innocent and uncomplicated as the Chopin Prelude, but the instant Brian withdrew, Theresa shyly inclined her head. He wanted a fuller kiss, yet this one of green, untutored innocence was oddly satisfying. And she wasn't the kind of woman a man rushed. She seemed scarcely woman at all, but girl, far less accomplished at the art of kissing than at the art of playing the violin and the piano. Her unpracticed kiss was suddenly more refreshing than any he'd ever shared.

He pushed back, straightened and intoned quietly, "Merry Christmas, Theresa."

Her eyes lifted to his face. Her voice trembled. "Merry Christmas, Brian."

Chapter Five

The week that followed was one of the happiest of Theresa's life. They had few scheduled duties, the city at their feet and money with which to enjoy it. She and Brian enjoyed being together, though they were rarely alone. Everywhere they went the group numbered four, with Jeff and Patricia along, or five, if Amy came, too, which she often did.

They spent an entire day at the new zoo, which was practically at their doorstep, located less than two miles away, on the east side of Burnsville. There they enjoyed the animals in their natural winter habitat, rode the monorail part of the time, then walked, ate hot dogs and drank hot coffee.

It was a sunless day, but bright, glittery with hoarfrost upon the surface of the snow. The world was a study in black and white. The oak branches startled the eye, so onyx-black against the backdrop of pristine landscape. The animals were sluggish, posed against the winter setting, their breaths rising in nebulous vapors, white on white. But the polar bears were up and about, looking like great shaggy pears with legs. Before their den, Theresa and Brian paused, arms on the rail, side by side. The bears lumbered about, coats pure and as colorless as the day. A giant male lifted his nose to the air, a single black blot against all that white.

"Look at him," Brian said, pointing. "The only things that are black are his eyes, lips, nose and toenails. On an arctic ice floe he becomes practically invisible. But he's smart enough to know how that nose shows. I once saw a film of a polar bear sneaking up on an unsuspecting seal with one paw over his nose and mouth."

It was a new side of Brian Scanlon: nature lover. She was intrigued and turned to study his profile. "Did it work?"

His eyes left the bears and settled on her. "Of course it worked. The poor seal never knew what hit her." Their eyes clung. Theresa grew conscious of the contact of Brian's elbow on the rail beside hers—warm, even through their jackets. His eyes made a quick check across her shoulder where the others stood, then returned to her lips before he began to close the space between them. But Theresa was too shy to kiss in public and quickly turned to study the bears. Her cheeks felt hot against the crisp air as Brian's gaze lingered for a moment before he straightened and said softly, "Another time."

It happened before the habitat of another animal whose coat had turned winter white. They were watching the ermine coats of the minks when Theresa turned toward Brian saying, "I don't think I could wear—"

He was only three inches away, encroaching, with a hand covering his nose and mouth, eyes gleaming with amused intent.

She smiled and pulled back. "What in the world are you doing?"

From underneath his glove came a muffled voice. "I'm trying the polar bear's sneaky tactics."

She was laughing when his glove slipped aside and swept around her, his two hands now holding her captive against a black railing. The quick kiss fell on her open lips. It was a failure of a kiss, as far as contact goes, for two cold noses bumped, and laughter mingled between their mouths. After the brief contact, he remained as he was, arms and body forming a welcome prison while she leaned backward from the waist, the rail pressed against her back and her hands resting on the front of his jacket.

"There, you see," she claimed breathily, "it didn't work. I saw you coming anyway."

"Next time you won't," he promised.

And she hoped he was right.

Patricia took them on a guided tour of Normandale College campus, beaming with pride at its rolling, wooded acres. They were walking along a curving sidewalk between two buildings with Patricia and Jeff in the lead, when Jeff's elbow hooked Patricia's neck and he hauled her close, kissing her as they continued ambling. Brian's eyes swerved to Theresa's, questioning. But Amy walked with them, and the moment went unfulfilled.

The following night they went to St. Paul's famed Science Omnitheater and lay back in steeply tilted seats, surrounded by an entire hemisphere of projected images that took them soaring through outer space, whizzing past stars and planets with tummy-tickling reality. But the dizzying sense of vertigo caused by the 180-degree curved screen seemed nothing compared to that created by Brian when he found Theresa's hand in the dark, eased close and reached his free hand to the far side of her jaw, turning her face toward his. The angle of the seats was severe, as if they were at a carnival, riding the bullet on its ascent before the spinning downward plunge. For a moment he didn't move, but lay back against his seat with the lights from the screen lining his face in flickering silver. His eyes appeared deep black, like those of the polar bear, and Theresa was conscious of the vast force of gravity pressing her into her chair and of the fact that Brian could not lift his head without extreme effort.

His forehead touched hers. Again their noses met. But their eyes remained open as warm lips touched, brushed, then gently explored this newfound anxiety within them both. There was a queer elation to the sense of helplessness caused by their positions. She wished they were upright so she could turn fully into his arms. But instead she settled for the straining of their bodies toward each other, and again, the unfulfilled wishes that grew stronger with each foray he initiated.

The elementary kiss ended with three teasing nibbles that caught, caught, caught her mouth and tugged sensuously before he lay back in his seat again, watching her face for reaction.

"No fair making me dizzy," she whispered.

They were still holding hands. His thumb made forceful circles against her palm. "You sure it's not the movie?"

"I thought it was at first, but I'm much dizzier now."

He smiled, kept his eyes locked with hers as he lifted her hand and placed its palm against his mouth, wetting it with his tongue as he kissed it.

"Me too," he breathed, then carried the hand to his lap and held it against his stomach, folded between his palms before he began stroking its soft skin with the tips of his callused fingers while he turned his attention back to the broad screen. She tried to do likewise, but with little success. For the interstellar space flight happening on the screen was vapid when compared to the nova created by Brian Scanlon's simplest kiss.

One evening Brian and Jeff provided the music for the promised rock session, to which Amy invited a mob of her friends. The house was inundated with noisy teenagers who gave their approval by way of prompt, rapt silence the moment the music began.

Theresa was cajoled into joining the two on piano, and before ten minutes were up, the boys and girls were dancing on the hard kitchen floor, after Margaret came through the living room decreeing, "No dancing on my carpet!" She seemed to forget she and her husband had danced a hoedown on it within the past week.

Still, the evening was an unqualified success, and at its end, Amy was basking in the reflected glow of "stardom," for all her friends went away assured that Jeff and Brian would be cutting a record in Nashville soon.

The day following the party there were no plans made. All five of them were together in the living room, lounging and visiting. The stereo was tuned to a radio station, and when a familiar song come on, Brian unexpectedly lunged to his feet, announcing, "The perfect song to learn to dance to!" He exaggerated a courtly bow before Theresa and extended his hand. "We've got to teach this woman before Saturday night."

"What's Saturday night?" Amy asked.

"New Year's Eve," answered Patricia. "I've invited these two to join Jeff and me and a group of our friends."

Jeff added, "But your sister claims ignorance and has declined to go."

Theresa dropped her eyes from the hand Brian still held out in invitation. "Oh no, please. I can't...." She felt utterly foolish, not knowing how to dance at age twenty-five.

"No excuses. It's time you learned."

She replied with the most convenient red herring she could dream up on short notice. "No dancing on the carpet!"

"Oh, go ahead," Amy said, then admitted, "the girls and I dance on the carpet all the time when mother's at work. I won't tell."

"There!" Theresa looked up at Brian, feeling her face had grown red. "Dance with Amy."

To Theresa's relief, Brian willingly complied. "All right." He directed his courtly gesture to the younger girl. "Amy, may I have this dance? We'll demonstrate for your reluctant sibling."

Amy's braces caught a flash of afternoon sun from the window as she beamed in unabashed delight. "I thought you'd never ask," she replied cheekily.

Looking on, Theresa felt years younger than Amy, who, at fourteen, could bound to her feet, come back with a coquettish response, then present her slim body for leading. Theresa wished she could be as uninhibited and self-confident as her younger sister. Jeff and Patricia joined in the demonstration, Jeff holding his partner stiffly and frowning. "Watch carefully now...a-one...a-two...."

As he always could, Jeff made Theresa laugh with his proficient clowning, for he held Patricia in a prim, stiff-backed, wide-apart mime of the traditional dance position, until the girl threw up her hands and declared laughingly, "You're a hopeless case, Brubaker. Find yourself another partner."

Jeff didn't ask, he commandeered. One minute Theresa was watching from the piano bench, the next she was on her feet, being sashayed around in Jeff's arms. Askance, she saw Brian watching her progress. In all honesty, Theresa had no delusions about being able to dance and dance gracefully. Now, with her brother, her natural rhythm couldn't be denied. Theresa's feet took over where her self-consciousness left off. Within a dozen bars, she was moving smoothly to the music.

She'd been hoodwinked—she realized it later—by Jeff and Brian, who'd probably been in cahoots the entire time—for she'd been following Jeff's lead no more than a minute when her hand was captured by Brian's. "I'm cutting in, Brubaker. Snowball time."

After that there seemed no question about New Year's Eve. And when

Theresa surreptitiously took Patricia aside to ask what she was wearing, the issue seemed settled.

On Friday, Theresa knocked on Amy's door, but when she got no answer, she peeped inside to find her sister lying in a trancelike state, arms thrown wide, ankle draped over updrawn knee, eyes shut, with the black vinyl headset clamped around her skull.

Theresa went in, closed the door behind herself and touched Amy's knee.

Amy's eyes came open, and she lifted one earpiece from her head. "Hmm?"

"Would you take that thing off for a minute?"

"Sure." Amy flung it aside, braced up on both elbows. "What's up?"

"Hon, I have a really big favor to ask you."

"Anything—name it."

"I need you to come shopping with me."

Amy mused for a minute, then rolled to one hip, reaching for the controls of the stereo to stop the music that was still filtering through the headphones. Then she sat up. "Shopping for what?"

Even before she asked, Theresa realized how ironic it was that she, the older, should be seeking the advice of a sister eleven years her junior. "Something to wear tomorrow night."

"You goin' to the dance?"

For a moment Theresa feared Amy might display an adolescent jealousy and wasn't sure how she'd deal with it. But when Theresa nodded, Amy bounded off the bed exuberantly. "Great! It's about time! When we goin'?"

An hour later the sisters found themselves in the Burnsville Shopping Center, scouring three levels of stores. In the first dressing room, Theresa slipped on a black crepe evening dress that gave her shivers of longing. But it was scarcely over her head before her perennial problem became all too evident: her bottom half was a size nine, but her top half would have required a size sixteen to girth her circumference.

Theresa looked up and met Amy's eyes in the mirror. They'd never before exchanged a single word about Theresa's problem. But, distraught, the older sister suddenly became glum and depressed. Her gaiety evaporated, and her expression wilted. "Oh, Amy, I'll never find a dress. Not with these damn, disgusting...*dirigibles* of mine!"

Amy's expression became sympathetic. "They make it tough, huh?"

Theresa's shoulders slumped. "Tough isn't the word. Do you know that I haven't been able to buy one single dress without altering it since I was the age you are now?"

"Yeah, I know. I...well, I asked mom about it one time...I mean, if it's hard for you and stuff, and if...well, if I might get as big as you."

Theresa turned and placed her hands on Amy's shoulders. "Oh, Amy, I hope you never do. I worry about it, too. I wouldn't wish a shape like mine on a pregnant elephant. It's horrible—not being able to buy clothes and being scared to dance with a man and—"

"You mean, *that's* why you wouldn't dance with Brian?"

"That's the only reason. I just...." Theresa considered a moment, then went on. "You're old enough to understand, Amy. You're fourteen. You've been growing. You know how the boys look at you funny as soon as you have a pair of goose bumps on your chest. Only when mine started growing they just kept right on until they got to the size of watermelons, and the boys were merciless. And when the boys were no longer boys, but men, well...." Theresa shrugged.

"I figured that was why you wear those ugly sweaters all the time."

"Oh, Amy, are they ugly?"

Amy looked penitent. "Gol, Theresa, I didn't mean it that way, I just meant...well, I know you never wore that neat sweat shirt I gave you last Christmas. It was way more *in* than anything you had—that's why I bought it for you."

"I've tried it on at least a dozen times, but I'm always scared to step out of my bedroom in it."

"Gol...." The word was a breathy lament as Amy stood pondering the everyday dilemmas her sister had to face. "Well, we could pick out something nice for tomorrow night if we got separate pieces, like a skirt and sweater or something."

"Not a sweater, Amy. I wouldn't be comfortable."

"Well, you can't go out for New Year's Eve in corduroy slacks and a white blouse with an old granny cardigan over your shoulders!"

"Do you think I *want* to?"

"Well...." Amy threw up her palms in the air. "*Horse poop,* there's got to be something in this entire shopping center that's better than *that.*" She cast a scathing look at the fashionless shirt Theresa had discarded.

Theresa found her sense of humor again. "Horse *poop?* I suppose mother doesn't know you say things like that, just like she doesn't suspect you dance on the living-room carpet?" Theresa knew perfectly well that at fourteen, Amy experimented with a gamut of profanity much worse than what she'd just uttered—she was at the age where such experiments were to be expected.

Suddenly the gleam in Amy's eyes duplicated the one from her dental hardware. "Listen, what about the sweater? Don't say no until you try, okay?" She splayed her fingers in the air and gazed toward heaven, theatrically. "I have *theee* perfect one. *Theee* most *excellent* sweater ever created by sheep or test tube! I've had my eye on it since before Christmas, but I was outa bucks, so I couldn't get it for myself. But if they have one left in large, you're gonna love it!''

A quarter hour later, Theresa stood before a different mirror, in a different shop, in a different garment that solved all her problems while remaining perfectly in vogue.

It was a lightweight bulky acrylic of rich, deep plum. The neckline sported a generous cowl collar that seemed to become one with wide dolman sleeves. Because it draped rather than clung, it seemed to partially conceal Theresa's overly generous silhouette.

"Oh, Amy, it's perfect!''

"I told you!''

"But what about slacks?''

Amy nabbed a pair of finely tailored gabardine trousers of indefinable color: soft, subtle, as if tinted by the smoke from burning violets. She stood back to assess her older sister and proclaimed in the most overused word of her teenage vernacular, *"Excellent.''*

Theresa whirled around and grabbed her sister in a compulsive hug. "It is! It is excellent.''

Amy beamed with pride, then took command again. "Shoes next. He's got a good six inches on you, so you could stand a little extra height. Some classy heels. Whaddya say?''

"Shoes...right!''

Theresa was pulling her head from beneath the sweater when she thought of the one last thing she'd need help with. "Amy, do you think I'd look too conspicuous if I tried a little bit of makeup?''

Amy's lips were covering her braces as Theresa asked, but her smile grew crooked, and wide, then winked in the glow of the dressing-room's overhead light fixture. "Well, it's about time!'' she declared.

"Now, just a minute, Amy,'' Theresa said as she noted the gleam in her sister's eye. "I haven't decided for sure....''

But that evening, something happened that crystallized the decision. She was in her room, the door open as she was examining the new sweater, when she felt someone's eyes on her. She looked up to find Brian in the doorway, studying her. It was the first time he'd seen her bedroom, and his eyes made a lazy circle, pausing on the shelf holding her pewter figurine collection, then dropping to the bed, neatly made, and finally returning to Theresa, who had quickly replaced the sweater in the closet.

"Have I managed to change your mind about the dance yet?'' He crossed his arms and nonchalantly leaned one shoulder against the door-frame.

Theresa had never been honorably pursued before; it took some getting used to. It was disconcerting, having him peruse her bedroom, which seemed an intimate place to come face to face with a man. She'd turned toward him, and he remained very still, one hip cocked as he lounged comfortably and kept his eye on her. *Do I look him in the eye? Or in the middle of his chest? Or at some spot beyond his shoulder? Twenty-five years old and acting less self-confident than I'm sure Amy would act in this situation.* She chose the middle of his chest.

"Yes, you have, but don't expect me to dance as well as Amy."

"All I'll expect is that at some point during the evening, you'll at least look me in the eye."

Her unsettled gaze flew up to his, caught a teasing grin there and dropped again, flustered.

"So this is where you hide away." As he moved farther into the room, he nodded toward the shelf. "I see The Maestro has joined the others. I envy him his spot, looking down on your pillow." He stopped close before her.

She searched but could find not a single reply and swallowed hard, feeling the blush creep up.

"Jeff was right, you know?" Brian teased softly.

She raised questioning eyes to his teasing brown ones.

"R...right? About what?"

"The blush camouflages the freckles. But don't ever stop." With a gentle fingertip he brushed her right cheek. "It's completely irresistible." Then he turned and sauntered off down the hall, leaving Theresa with her fingertips grazing the spot of skin he'd so lightly touched. It seemed to tingle yet. The touch had been petal light, but she'd felt the calluses on his fingertips. Both the sensation and his teasing had left her with a light head and a fluttering heart.

That night, late, Theresa tapped softly at Amy's door, then went in to announce, "I'm going to need your help learning how to put on makeup, and I'll have to borrow some of yours, if you don't mind."

Amy's only answer was a beam of approval as she dragged Theresa farther into the room and shut the door with a decisive click.

They did a trial run that lasted till the wee hours. Sitting before a lighted makeup mirror in Amy's room, Theresa experienced the full range of giddy adolescent give-and-take she'd missed out on when she'd been at the age of puberty. The makeup session brought a twofold benefit: not only did it free the butterfly from the chrysalis, it also brought the two sisters closer. Given the disparity in their ages, they'd had little chance to share experiences of this kind.

Amy began by experimenting with foundation colors, trying a rainbow of skin tones on various sections of Theresa's face until the redhead declared, "I look like a Grandma Moses painting!"

Assessing, Amy corrected, "No, more like her palette, I think." They shared a laugh, then went to work finding the right hue that skillfully camouflaged the freckles and gave Theresa a new, subdued radiance.

Next came the eyes, but as Amy bent over Theresa's shoulder and peered critically in the mirror at the blue grease they'd smeared on one freckled eyelid, they burst out laughing once more.

"Yukk! Get it off! It feels like lard and looks like I took a beating."

"Agreed!"

Next they tried a green powder-base eyeshadow, but it made Theresa look like a stop-and-go light, so off it went, too. They settled on an almost translucent mauve that had so little color it couldn't clash with the skin and hair tones that needed to be catered to.

The first time Theresa tried to use the eyelash curler, she pinched her eyelid and yelped in pain.

"This is like trying to curl the hair on a caterpillar's back!" she despaired. "There's nothing there. I hate my eyelashes anyway. They have as much color as a glass of water."

"We'll fix that."

But the tears rolled from beneath her abused lids, and it took several long, painful minutes before Theresa got the hang of the curler, then learned how to brush her lashes with a mascara wand. The results, however, surprised even herself.

"Why, I never knew my lashes were so long!"

"That's 'cause you never saw the ends of 'em before."

They were a total wonder—quite spiky and alluring and made her whole face look bright and...and sexy!

The powdered blush proved an absolute disaster. They swabbed it off faster than they'd brushed it on, deciding Theresa's natural coloring couldn't compete with added highlighting, and decided to stick with the foundation hue only.

Theresa had always worn lipgloss, but now they tried several new shades, and Amy demonstrated how to skillfully blend two colors and accent the pretty bowed shape of her sister's upper lip with a highlighter stick.

With the makeup complete, Theresa appeared transformed. It was a drastic change but one that made her smile at Amy in the mirror.

Yet, Amy wasn't totally pleased. "That hair," Amy grunted in disgust.

"Well, I can't change the color, and I can't keep it from pinging all over like it was shot out of a frosting decorator."

"No, but you could go to the beauty shop and let somebody else figure out what to do with it."

"The beauty shop?"

"Why not?"

"But I'm going to look conspicuous enough with all this makeup on. What would he think if I showed up with a different hairdo, too?"

"Oh, horse poop!" Amy pronounced belligerently, jamming her hands onto her trim hips. "He'll think it's super."

"But I don't want to look like…well, it's a date."

"But it *is* a date!"

"No, it's not. He's two years younger than I am. I'm just filling in, that's all."

But in spite of her protests, Theresa recalled Brian's teasing earlier this evening and admitted he'd seemed fully amenable to being her escort.

Several minutes later, standing before the wide mirror at the bathroom vanity, she caught her glistening lower lip between her teeth in an effort to contain the smile of approval that wanted to wing across her features. Then her lip escaped her teeth, and she smiled widely at what she saw. She liked her face! For the first time in her life she genuinely liked it. It seemed a desecration to have to cleanse the skin and remove the radiance from the creature who looked so happy and pleased with herself.

As she forced herself to turn on the water and pick up the bar of soap, it seemed as if tomorrow night would never get there.

But New Year's Eve day arrived at last, and Theresa managed to get an eleventh-hour appointment on this busiest day of the year in the beauty shops. In the late afternoon, she returned home the proud possessor of a new haircut and of the simple tool required to achieve the natural bounce of ringlets on her own: a hairpick.

The beautician's suggestion had been to simply shape the hair and stop trying to subdue it but to soften it with a cream rinse and let it bounce free, with just a few flicks of the wrist and pick to guide it into a halo of color about her head. Even the redness seemed less offensive, for with the light filtering through it, it looked less brash.

While she hung up her coat in the entry closet, Brian called from the living room, "Hi."

But she avoided a direct confrontation with him and hurried down the hall to her room with no more than a "Hi" in return.

And now everyone was scuttling around, getting ready. The bathroom had a steady stream of traffic. Theresa took a quick shower, then went to her room and was applying a new after-bath talc she'd ventured to buy. It had a light, petally fragrance reminiscent of the potpourri used by women in days of old. Subtle, feminine.

She paused with the puff in her hand and cocked her head. On the other side of her bedroom wall was the bathroom, so sounds carried through. She heard a masculine cough and recognized it as Brian's. The shower ran for several minutes during which there were two thumps, like an elbow hitting the wall, while images went skittering through her mind. There followed the whine of a blow dryer, then a long silence—shaving—after which he started humming "Sweet Memories." Theresa smiled and realized she'd been standing naked for some time, dwelling on what was going on in the bathroom.

Crossing to the mirror, she assessed her devastatingly enormous breasts and wished for the thousandth time in as many days that she'd been in the other line when mammary glands were handed out. She turned away in disgust and found a clean brassiere. Donning it, she had to lean forward to let the pendulous weights drop into the cups before straightening to hook the back clasp of the hideous garment. It had all the feminine allure of a hernia truss! The wide straps had shoulder guards, meant to keep the weight from cutting into her flesh, but the deep grooves dented her shoulders just the same. The bra's utilitarian white fabric was styled for "extra support." How she hated the words! And how she hated the lingerie industry. They owed an apology to thousands of women across America for offering not a single large-size brassiere in any of the feminine pastels of orchid, peach or powder blue. Apparently women of her proportions weren't supposed to have a sense of color when it came to underwear! No wistful longing to clothe themselves in anything except antiseptic, commonsense, white!

Just once—oh, just once!—how she'd love to browse along the counters of feminine underthings with tiny bikini panties and bras to match and consider buying a foolishly extravagant teddy, only to see what it felt like to have such a piece of feminine frippery against her skin.

But she wasn't given the chance, for a teddy with size double-D cups would look as if it were two lace circus tents.

White undergarments in place, Theresa covered the full-figure white cotton bra with the new sweater and immediately felt more benevolent toward both herself and the clothing industry. The sweater was stylish and attractive and helped restore her excitement. The smoke-hued trousers fit smoothly, flatteringly, over her small hips, and the strappy high-heeled sandals she'd chosen added just the right touch of frivolity. Theresa had never been fond of jewelry, particularly earrings, for they only drew attention to a woman's face. But as she slipped a wristwatch beneath the cuff of the sweater, she decided her new mocha nail treatment deserved setting off, so clipped a delicate gold chain bracelet around her left wrist. Finally, into the draped cowl neck of the sweater, she inserted a tiny gold stick pin shaped like a treble clef.

Then she went across the hall to Amy's room to reproduce the makeup magic created in last night's secret session. But Theresa's hands were so shaky she couldn't seem to manage the applicators and wands.

Amy noticed and couldn't help teasing. "Considering this is *not* a date, you're in a pretty twittery state."

Theresa's brown eyes widened in dismay. "Oh, does it show?"

"You might want to stop wiping your palms on your thighs every thirty seconds. Pretty soon your new slacks are going to look like a plumber's coveralls."

"It's silly, I know. I wish I could be more like you, Amy. You're always bright and witty, and even around boys you always seem to know the right things to say and how to act. Oh, this must sound ridiculous coming from a woman my age."

Somehow Amy's next comment was again just the perfect choice to calm Theresa's nerves somewhat. "He's going to love your new hairdo and your makeup and your outfit, too, so quit worrying. Here, give me that eyeshadow and shut your eyes."

But as Theresa tipped her head back and did as ordered, her sister was given the difficult job of applying makeup to trembling lids. Yet, she managed to produce the same magical effect as the night before, and when Theresa looked into Amy's lighted makeup mirror, all complete, dewy and lashy, she unconsciously pressed a palm to her chest in astonishment.

Smiling, Amy encouraged, "See? I told you."

And for that precious moment, Theresa believed it. She swung around to give Amy an impulsive hug, thinking how happy she suddenly was that none of this had ever happened before. It was wonderful experiencing these first Cinderella feelings at age twenty-five.

"Good luck, huh?" Amy's smile was sincere as she stood back and stuck her hands in the pockets of her jeans.

In answer, Theresa blew an affectionate kiss from the doorway. As she turned to leave, Amy added, "Oh, and put on some perfume, huh?"

"Oh, perfume. But I haven't got any. I got some new bath powder, but you must not be able to smell it."

"Here, try this."

They chose a subtle, understated fragrance from the bottles cluttering Amy's dresser top, leaving nothing more for Theresa to do but face Brian Scanlon. That, however, was going to be the most difficult moment of all.

Back in her room, Theresa puttered around, putting away stray pieces of clothing, checking her watch several times. She heard the voices of Jeff and Brian from the other end of the house, joined by Amy's and her parents'. Everyone was waiting for her, and she suddenly wished she'd been ready first so she wouldn't have had to make a grand entrance. But it was too late now. She didn't care if she soiled her new trousers or not, she gave one last swipe of her palms along the gabardine, took a deep breath and went out to face the music.

They were all in the kitchen. Her mother and father were sitting at the table over cups of coffee. Amy stood with her hands in her front pockets telling Jeff she was going babysitting tonight. Brian was at the sink, running himself a glass of water.

Theresa stepped into the room with her heart tripping out sixteenth notes. Jeff caught sight of her, and his smiling response was instantaneous. "Well, would you lookit here...I think I asked the wrong girl to go out with me tonight." He swooped Theresa into his arms and took her on a Ginger Rogers-Fred Astaire swirl while grinning wickedly into her eyes, then affecting a convincing Bogart drawl, "Hiya, doll, whaddya say we get it on tonight?"

Brian looked back over his shoulder, and the water glass stopped half way to his lips.

As Jeff brought his sister to a breathless halt, she was laughing, aware that Brian had spilled out the water without drinking any. He turned away from the sink and crossed to clap a hand on Jeff's shoulder.

"Just your tough luck, Brubaker. I asked her first." His approving gaze settled on Theresa, creating a glow about her heart.

"Isn't her new hairdo great?" piped up Amy. "And she bought the outfit especially for tonight."

Amy Brubaker, I could strangle you. Jeff lightened his hold and settled Theresa against his hip. "She did, huh?"

Brian's eyes made a quick trip down to her knees, then back up to her makeup and hair. To the best of Theresa's recollection, it was the first time his eyes had ever scanned anything below her neck.

Margaret spoke up then. "Jeffrey, turn your sister around. I haven't had a look at what that beauty operator did to her yet."

Does everybody in the house have to blurt out everything? Beneath her fresh, translucent makeup Theresa could feel the pink ruining the entire effect and hoped that for once it didn't show. Jeff swung her around for her mother and father's approval, but at her shoulder she felt Brian's eyes following.

To Theresa's further chagrin, her mother's verdict was, "You should have done that years ago."

"You look pretty as a picture, dear," added Willard.

Unaccustomed to being the center of attention like this, Theresa could think only of escape.

"It's time to leave."

Jeff released her to check his watch. "Yup. You can head out. Patricia should be here any minute. She's picking me up in her car."

Theresa whirled around in surprise. "Aren't we all going together?"

"No, she's afraid I might overindulge tonight, and since she claims she's always levelheaded, she thought it would be best if she drove her car and dropped me off at home instead of the other way around."

"Oh." Once she grunted the monosyllable, Theresa felt conspicuous, for nobody said anything more. She realized she sounded rather dubious and ill at ease about being left alone with Brian. But he went to get her coat from the front-hall closet, and Jeff nudged her in the back. She followed and let Brian ease the coat over her shoulders, then she found herself doing something she'd never done before: helping Brian with his. He was dressed in form-fitting designer blue jeans, and a corduroy sport coat of cocoa brown under which showed a neutral tweed rag-knit sweater with the collar of a white shirt peeking from under its crew neck. As he struggled to thread his arms into a hip-length wool coat, she reacted as politeness dictated, reaching to assist him when the shoulder of his jacket caught. Theresa experienced an unexpected thrill of pleasure, performing the insignificant service.

"Thanks." He lifted the outer garment and shrugged his shoulders in a peculiarly masculine adjustment that made her knees feel weak. He smelled good, too. And suddenly all she could think of was getting out of the house and into the car where darkness would mask the feelings she was certain were alternately making her blush and blanch.

She kissed her mother and father good-night. "Happy New Year, both of you." They were spending it at home, watching the celebration in Times Square on television. "Amy...." Theresa turned to find her sister's eyes following her wistfully. "Thanks, honey."

"Sure." Amy leaned her hips back against the edge of the kitchen counter and followed their progress as Brian opened the door for Theresa and saw her out. "Hey, you're both knockouts!" she called just before the door closed.

They smiled goodbye, and a moment later were engulfed by the cold silence outside. Theresa's car waited in the driveway where she'd left it as she'd rushed in from the hair appointment. Brian found her elbow while they crossed the icy blacktop, but she suddenly didn't want to drive. It would take some of the magic away. "Would you mind driving, Brian?"

He stopped. They were at the front of the car, heading around toward the driver's side. "Not at all." Instead of leaving her there, he guided her to the passenger side, opened her door and waited while she settled herself inside.

When his door slammed, they found themselves laughing at his knees digging into the dashboard.

"Sorry," Theresa offered, "my legs are shorter than yours."

He fumbled in the dark, found the proper lever, and the seat went sliding back while he let out a whoof of breath. "Whoo! Are they ever!"

She handed him the keys and he fumbled again, groping for the ignition. "Here." In the blackness, their knuckles brushed as she reached to point out the right spot. The brief touch set off a tingle in her hand, then the key clicked home and the engine came to life.

"Thanks for letting me drive. A person misses it." He adjusted the mirror, shifted into reverse, and they were rolling.

The quiet was disarming. The scent she remembered emanated from his hair and clothing and mingled with her own borrowed perfume. The dash lights lit his face from below, and she wanted to turn and study him, but faced front, resisting the urge.

"So that's where you went this afternoon—to the beauty shop. I wondered."

"Amy and her big mouth." But Theresa grinned in the dark.

He laughed indulgently. "I like it. It looks good on you."

She glanced left and found his eyes on her dimly lit hair and quickly looked away.

"Thank you." *What is a woman expected to reply at a time like this?* Theresa wanted to say she loved his hair, too, but she really preferred a man's hair longer than the Air Force allowed, though she loved the smell of his, and the color of it. She heartily approved of the clothing he'd chosen tonight, but before she could decide whether or not to say so, Brian suggested, "Why don't you put on something classical? We'll have our fill of rock before the night is over."

The music filled the uncomfortable transition period while they rode, with Theresa giving occasional directions. Within fifteen minutes they reached the Rusty Scupper, a night spot frequented by a young adult crowd, many of them singles. They helped each other with coats, left them at the coat check and were shown to a long table set up for a large group. Theresa recognized some of Jeff's friends and performed introductions, watching as Brian shook hands with the men and was ogled by some of the women, whose eyes lingered on him with that inquisitive approval of the single female presented with an attractive male novelty. She watched their eyes drop down his torso and realized with a start that some women checked out men in much the same way men checked out women. She was totally abashed when an attractive sable-haired beauty named Felice returned her eyes to Brian's and smiled with a blatant glint of sexual approval. "Keep a dance free from me later, okay, Brian? And make sure it's a slow one."

"I'll do that," he replied politely, withdrawing his hand from the one that had retained his longer than was usual. He returned to Theresa's side, pulled out her chair and settled himself beside her.

In a voice low enough for only her ears, he questioned, "Who's she?"

Theresa felt dreadfully deflated that he should ask. "Felice Durand is one of the crowd. She's hung around with Jeff and his bunch since high school."

"Remind me to be monopolized by you during the slow dances," he returned wryly, filling Theresa with a soaring sense of relief. She herself had little experience on the boy-girl social scene, and Felice's bold assessment of Brian's body, followed by her forward invitation, was unnerving. But apparently not all men were hooked by bait as obvious as that dangled by Felice Durand. Theresa's respect for Brian slid up another notch.

Jeff and Patricia arrived then, and the table filled with lively chatter, laughter and orders for cocktails. Soon thereafter menus arrived, and Theresa was astounded at the inflated New Year's prices that had been substituted but told herself an evening with Brian would be worth it.

Carafes of wine were delivered, glasses filled and toasts proposed. Touching his glass to Jeff's, Brian intoned, "To old friends...." And with a touch of the rim upon Patricia's glass, and finally upon Theresa's, he added, "and to new."

His eyes held a steady green spark of approval as they sought hers and lingered after she self-consciously dropped her gaze to the ruby liquid, then drank.

Dinner was noisy and exuberant, and for the most part Theresa and Brian listened to the banter without taking part. She felt relieved that he, like her, was rather an outsider. She felt drawn to him, in a welcome semiexclusion.

Over tiny stem glasses of crème de menthe, they relaxed, sat back in their chairs and waited for the dancing to begin.

The dancing. Just the thought of it filled Theresa with a mixture of apprehension and eagerness. It hadn't been so difficult turning into Brian's arms that day in the living room. Here, the dance floor would be crowded; nobody would notice them among all the others. It should be easy to submit to the embrace of an attractive man like Brian, yet at the thought, Theresa felt a tremor tumble through her lower belly. *He's been stuck with me.*

Just then the waitress approached and spoke to the group at their general end of the table. "As soon as the dancing starts, it's a cash bar only, so if you wouldn't mind, we'd like to get the dinner bill settled up now."

Automatically, Theresa reached for her purse, just as Brian lifted one hip from the chair, pushed back his sport coat and sought his hip pocket. As he came up with a billfold, she produced the purse and was reaching to unzip it when his fingers closed over hers.

"You're with me," he ordered simply. Her eyes flew to his. They were steady, insistent. His cool fingers still rested upon her tense ones while her heart sent out a crazy stutter step.

Yes, I am, she thought. *I'm really with you.*

"Thank you, Brian."

He squeezed her fingers, then his slipped away, and for the first time she truly felt like his date.

Chapter Six

The band had a lot of talent wrapped up in five members, plus a female singer. They played a mix of mid- to easy rock, ranging from The Eagles to Ronstadt to The Commodores to Stevie Wonder, but all their music had a hard, sure beat to encourage dancers onto the floor, then once they were warmed up, back to the tables to cool down with another round of drinks. When half the group deserted their table in favor of the dance floor, Brian and Theresa remained behind in companionable silence, watching the dancers.

The band slammed into the driving beat of a recent Journey hit, and Theresa found herself mesmerized by the back view of Felice Durand's gyrating hips. She was wearing a fire engine red dress that slithered on her derriere with so much resistance that Theresa was certain the friction would soon send up a trail of smoke. But she was good. She moved with feline seductiveness, never missing a beat, incorporating hands, arms, shoulders and pelvis in a provocative invitation to naughtiness. Watching, Theresa felt a twinge of jealousy.

Suddenly Felice spun in a half circle, her back now to her partner as she sent an open-mouthed look of innuendo over her shoulder at him. Two more shakes and her eyes spied Brian. His chair was half turned toward the dance floor while one elbow hung on the table edge. A quick glance told Theresa he'd been watching Felice for some time.

Without missing a beat, the woman somehow managed to shift all her attention to Brian. Her hips traced corkscrews, her mouth puckered in a glistening pout, and her hands with their glossy bloodred nails conveyed come-hither messages. Theresa's eyes moved back to Brian, and she saw his gaze drop from Felice's face to her breasts to her hips and stay there.

A moment later, Felice spun adroitly to face her partner, then maneuvered herself into the crowd where she couldn't be seen, as if to say, you want more, boy, come and get it.

Brian glanced at Theresa and caught her watching him. She quickly dropped her eyes to a plastic stir stick she'd been playing with. She felt herself coloring and felt suddenly very much out of place. This young, brash crowd wasn't for her. Jeff fit in here, maybe even Brian, but she didn't.

Just then the music changed. The keyboard player chimed the distinctive intro to "The Rose"—slow, moody, romantic.

From the corner of her eye, Theresa caught a flash of fire engine red zeroing in on Brian, but before it quite registered, he'd lunged to his feet, captured Theresa's hand and was towing her toward the dance floor. They'd barely left their chairs when they were intercepted by Felice and her partner returning to the table.

The sable-haired beauty looked attractively flushed and sheeny from her exertions as she stopped Brian's progress with a hand on his chest. "I thought this one might be mine."

"Sorry, Felice. This is our song, isn't it, Theresa?" Too astounded to answer, she let herself be pulled through the crowd onto the dance floor, where she was swung loosely into Brian's arms.

"Is it?" She peered up at him with a gamine grin.

"It is now." His own conspiratorial grin eased the discomfiture Theresa had been feeling while watching him observe Felice.

"It occurs to me that in less than two short weeks we've gathered enough of *our songs* to fill a concert program."

"Imagine what a mixed-up concert it would be. Chopin's Nocturne and Newbury's 'Sweet Memories.'"

"And 'The Rose,'" Theresa added.

"And don't forget 'Oh, I had a little chicken and he wouldn't lay an egg....'"

"*She* wouldn't lay an egg."

"What's the dif—"

"*He* chickens don't lay eggs, not even when you pour hot water up and down their legs."

Brian laughed, a melodic tenor sound that sent ripples of response through his dance partner. Something wonderful had happened. During their foolishness their feet had been unconsciously moving to the music. Theresa's natural musicality had taken over of its own accord. With her guard down, and distracted by both Felice and their conversation, she'd forgotten to bring her shy reservations along with her onto the dance floor. She was following Brian's graceful, expert lead with a joyous freedom. He was a superb dancer. Moving with him was effortless and fluid, though he kept a respectable distance between their bodies.

When had their laughter died? Brian's green eyes hadn't left Theresa's but gazed down into her uplifted face, while both of them fell silent.

"Brian," she said softly. "I don't care if you dance with Felice."

"I don't want to dance with Felice."

"I saw you watching her."

"It was rather unavoidable." His dark eyebrows drew together with a brief flicker of annoyance. "Listen, Felice is like the countless groupies who hang around at the foot of the stage and shake it for the guitar man, whichever one is playing that night, hoping to score after the dance. They're a dime a dozen, but that's not what I want tonight, okay? Not when I have something so much better.''

At his last words his arms tightened and hauled her against him, that place she'd so often wondered about with half dread, half fascination. Her breasts were gently flattened against the corduroy panels of his sport coat, and her thighs felt the soft nudges of his steps. Upon her waist pressed a firm, secure palm, while hers found his solid shoulder muscle, his cool, extended palm. Against her temple his jaw rested.

I'm dancing. Breast to breast and thigh to thigh with a man. And it's wonderful. Theresa felt released and loose and altogether unselfconscious. Perhaps it was because, in spite of the fact that their bodies brushed, Brian retained a hold only possessive enough to guide her. His hips remained a discreet space apart while the other spots where Theresa's body touched his seemed alive and warmed.

He hummed quietly, the notes sure and true. The gentle vibrations of his voice trembled through his chest, and she felt it vaguely through her breasts. He smelled clean and slightly spicy, and she thought, *look at me, world. I'm falling in love with Brian Scanlon, and it's absolutely heavenly.*

The song ended, and he retreated but still held her lightly. His smile was as miraculous as the revelation she'd just experienced. Her own smile was timorous.

"You're a good dancer, Theresa."

"So are you."

The band eased into "Evergreen" without a pause, and as the notes began, it became understood Brian and Theresa would dance again. He took her against his body, dipping his head down a little lower this time, while she raised hers a fraction higher. And somehow it seemed portentous that the first word of the song was, "Love...."

"Theresa, you look as pretty tonight as I imagined you when Jeff first told me about you."

"Oh, Brian..." she began to protest.

"When I turned around and saw you standing in the kitchen I couldn't believe it."

"Amy helped me. I...well, I'm not too experienced at getting ready for dances."

He lifted his head, gazed into her eyes, folded her right palm against his heart and whispered, "I'm glad."

And the next thing she knew, her eyes and nose and forehead were riding within the warm, fragrant curve of his neck. Her cheek felt the textures of corduroy, wool and cotton and freshly shaved masculine skin.

She drifted in his spicy scent that grew more pronounced as the heat of their joined skins released it from his jaw and neck. Somehow—some magical somehow—their hips had nestled together, and she felt for the first time the contour of his stomach against hers, of his warm flesh within the tight blue jeans, seeking to find hers as his forearm held her securely about her waist, pressing her and keeping her close.

She tried closing her eyes but found she was already dizzy from the emotions his nearness stirred in her, and the slow turns he executed increased her vertigo. She opened her eyes and saw through her own lacy lashes the outline of his Adam's apple only an inch away. She watched his thumb as it rubbed the backs of her knuckles in rhythm with the music. He had captured her hand by cupping its backside, and her palm lay flat, pressed against his chest. She felt the steady thump of his heart, then became aware of how callused his fingers were as they stroked her hand. She recalled that long-fingered left hand upon the neck of the guitar as he'd been singing to her. Her eyes drifted closed again as she basked in the new feeling of wonder at where she was, who she was with and what kind of man he was.

This time when the song ended, neither of them moved immediately. He squeezed the back of her hand harder and tightened his right arm until his elbow dug into the hollow of her spine.

Brian, she thought. *Brian.*

He eased back, never releasing her hand as he led the way to their table, and the band announced a break.

At their places, Theresa sat in a private cloud with nobody but him. Their chairs were side by side, turned slightly outward from the table, and when Brian sat, he crossed an ankle over a knee in such a way that the knee brushed the side of her thigh. He left it there intentionally, she thought, a thread of contact still bonding them together while they had to forgo dancing.

"So, tell me about what it's like to teach music to elementary-school kids."

She told him. More than she'd ever shared with any other man.

And while she talked, Brian studied her face, with its shifting expressions of laughter, thoughtfulness and something utterly pure and wholesome. *Yes, wholesome,* he thought. *This woman is wholesome in a way I've never encountered in another woman. Certainly in none of the Felices whose offers I've taken up whenever the mood struck me.*

Women like Felice, in their siren-red dresses, with their sleek hair and slithery hips—women like that are one-nighters. This woman is a lifetimer. What would she be like in bed? Naive and unsure and very likely a virgin, he thought. *Totally opposite to the practiced felines who could purr deep in their throats and press themselves against a man with skilled teasing, which somehow always managed to repel even as it allured. No, Theresa Brubaker would be as honest and fresh as...as the Chopin Nocturne,* he thought.

"So, tell me what it's like to be on a Strategic Air Command base during the day and playing at the officer's club in the evenings."

He told her.

And while he talked, Theresa pictured the Felices, the "townies" who gazed up at the guitar man from the foot of the stage, for his and Jeff's band also played gigs in the canteens where enlisted men were allowed to bring civilian dates. Theresa thought about what he'd said—something about countless groupies hanging around the stage and *shaking it* for the guitar man, hoping to score after the dance. But he'd added, that's not what he wanted tonight. *Tonight?* The implication was clear. Back at their air base there would doubtless be others who'd capture Brian's attention, others in fire engine red dresses with faces and bodies like Felice Durand's. A man like him wouldn't be content for long with a wallflower like herself.

She imagined Brian stepping off the stage, taking up the offer of some groupie, tumbling into bed with her for the night.

And if Brian had ample opportunity, she supposed her brother did, too. The thought was sobering.

She came from her musing to find Brian's eyes steady on her face as he spoke in a sober voice. "Theresa, next June, when Jeff and I get out, I'm thinking about settling around Minneapolis some place so he and I can get another band going here."

"You are?" Crazy commotion started in the vicinity of her heart. Brian, returning here to live permanently? "But what about Chicago?"

"I've got no ties there anymore. None that matter. The people I knew will practically be strangers after four years."

"Jeff has mentioned that you two talked about staying together, but what about the rest of the band?"

"We'll audition a drummer and a bass player here, and maybe a female singer, too. We'd like to get into private parties, but it'll take a couple of years of playing night spots and bars before we can manage that."

He seemed to be waiting for her approval, but she was speechless. "Well...." She gestured vaguely, smiled brightly into his eyes and tried to comprehend what this could mean to her future relationship with him.

"That's not exactly the reaction I'd hoped for." She dropped her eyes to her lap and needlessly smoothed the gabardine over her left knee as he went on. "I told you before, what I really want to be—ultimately— is a disc jockey. I want to enter Brown Institute and go to school days and play gigs nights. Jeff is all for it. What about you?"

"Me?" She lifted startled brown eyes and felt her heartbeat tripping in gay expectation. "Why do you need my approval?"

Not a muscle moved on Brian for a full fifteen seconds. He skewered Theresa with his dazzling green eyes, but they were filled with unsaid things.

"I think you know why," he told her at last, his voice coming from low in his throat.

A resounding chord announced the beginning of the next set, and Theresa was saved from replying by the booming sound that filled the house. She and Brian were still staring into each other's eyes when the undauntable Felice appeared out of nowhere and commandeered Brian's left arm, hauling him out of his chair while his eyes still lingered on Theresa.

"Come on, Brian, let's see what you've got, honey!"

He seemed to shake himself back to the present. "All right, just one."

But Theresa was subjected to the prolonged torture of watching Felice appropriate her date for three throbbing, upbeat songs. It took no more than sixty seconds of observation for Theresa's mouth to go dry. And in another sixty, wet.

Brian moved his body with the understated liquidity of a professional stage dancer. But he did it with a seemingly total lack of guile. When he rotated his hips, the movement was so subtle, so sexy, Theresa's lips unconsciously dropped open. The supple twisting of his pelvis appeared to come as naturally to Brian as walking. His face wore a pleasant expression of enjoyment as he occasionally maintained eye contact with Felice. She circumnavigated him in a sultry trip that ended when she almost touched him with her breasts, shimmying her shoulders while the suspended offerings swayed, unfettered, within the folds of her halter-style dress. Felice said something, and Brian laughed.

The song ended and he placed a hand at the small of her back as if to guide her off the floor, but she swung to face him, pressing both hands on his chest, looking up into his face. He glanced briefly toward the table, and Theresa looked quickly away. The music gushed out in another jungle rhythm, and when Theresa's eyes returned to the dance floor she was stung with jealousy. Watching the lurch and roll, the toss and pitch of Brian's lean, oscillating body set up queer yearnings in her own, and it occurred to Theresa that she was as human as some of the men who ogled her when she walked into a room.

Felice managed to link her arm with Brian's at the end of the song and introduce him to somebody on the floor, thereby commandeering him for a third dance. But as Theresa looked on, she saw him put up no resistance.

When the pair arrived at the table, Felice cooed to Theresa. "Ooo, if I were you, I'd hang on to this one. He's a live one." Then, to Brian, "Thanks for the dance, honey."

Jealousy was something new for Theresa. So was the feeling of sexual attraction. Although Theresa no longer spoke in the teenager vernacular, a phrase of Amy's came to her now: *strung out*. She suddenly knew what it meant to be strung out on a man. It had to be this hollow, gutless, wonderful awareness of his masculinity and her own femininity; this sensation that your pulses had somehow found their way to the surface of your skin and hovered there just beneath the outermost layer, as if ready to explode; this supersensitivity to each shift of muscle, each facial expression, even each movement of his clothing upon his body. She watched in a new acute fascination as Brian shrugged out of his corduroy jacket and hung it on the back of his chair. It seemed each of his motions was peculiar to him alone, as if no other man had ever performed this incidental task in as attractive a way. Was this common? Did others who found themselves falling in love feel such out-of-proportion pride and possessiveness? Did they all find their chosen one flawless, superlative and sexy while performing the most mundane movements, such as sitting on a chair and crossing his ankle over a knee?

"I'm sorry," Brian muttered, taking his full attention back to Theresa.

"You didn't look very sorry. You looked like you were enjoying every minute of it."

"She's a good dancer."

Theresa's lips thinned in disapproval.

"Listen, I said I was sorry I left you sitting here for three dances."

She glanced away, finding it difficult to deal with her new-found feelings. Brian wiped his brow on the sleeve of his sweater, reached for a glass with some partially melted ice cubes and slipped one into his mouth. Theresa watched his lips purse around it as he turned to study the dance floor. The ice cube made his cheek pop out, then she watched his attractive jaw as he chewed and swallowed it.

When his eyes roved back to hers, she quickly glanced away. Her forearm rested on the table, and his warm palm fell across the sleeve of her sweater.

Their eyes met. He squeezed her arm once, gently. Her heart lifted. Though not another word was said about Felice, the issue was set aside.

A powerful force, this jealousy, thought Theresa, loving the feel of his hand on her arm.

When the tempo of the music slowed, Brian rose without asking her and reached for her hand. On the dance floor, wrapped close to his ragknit sweater, she could feel how the exertion had released both heat and scent from his skin. The moist warmth radiated onto her breasts. His palm, too, was warmer than before. The keen scent of his after-shave and deodorant was stronger than ever since he'd danced with Felice, and with

a secret smile against his shoulder, Theresa thanked the bold temptress
for warming Brian up.

Jeff and Patricia danced past, and Jeff leaned toward Brian to ask,
"Hey, man, wanna change partners on the next dance?"

"No offense, Patricia, but not a chance."

He resumed his intimate hold on Theresa, who peered over Brian's
shoulder at her brother to receive a lopsided smile and a broad wink.

Several times during the remainder of the evening Felice tried to snare
Brian for a slow dance, but he refused to be appropriated again. He and
Theresa sat out the up-tempo songs together and danced only the slow
ones. She was growing increasingly aware of the approach of midnight.
When they were at their table she surreptitiously checked her watch as
Brian slipped his jacket back on. The discreet time check proved that
she'd been consulting her watch at the rate of once every two minutes or
less.

They were on the dance floor when a song ended, and Theresa turned
toward their table to be waylaid by Brian's hand on her forearm. "Not
so fast there, young lady." When she turned back to him, he lifted a
wrist, tugged his corduroy sleeve up over his watch. "Only five minutes
to go. Let's stay out here until the big moment, okay?"

A flush of sexual awareness radiated through Theresa. Without realizing where her eyes were headed, they centered on Brian's lips. His
mouth was very beautiful, very sensual, the lower lip slightly fuller than
the upper, those lips slightly parted now, glistening enticingly as if he'd
just passed his tongue along them. She remembered the brief times they'd
touched her own, and the maelstrom of emotions his fleeting kisses had
created within her heart. The same reaction began again, just from her
gazing at his lips.

Her eyes raised to find his upon her own mouth. The lingering gaze
held sensual promise she'd never dreamed of finding in a man. She had
kissed relatively few men in her life, and all of them in private. The idea
of doing so in public heightened Theresa's inhibitions. She glanced
around the dance floor: there was a certain amount of anonymity when
so many people were pressed almost shoulder to shoulder in a throng of
this size and density.

Just then someone nudged Theresa from behind. She turned to find a
waitress elbowing through the dancers, passing out hats and noisemakers,
confetti and streamers. Brian got a green foil top hat that would have
done Fred Astaire proud. He perched it on his head, then adjusted its
brim to a rakish angle and pulled it low over the left side of his forehead.
He touched the brim, looking as though he wished his hands were encased
in formal white gloves, and cocked an eyebrow at Theresa. "How do I
look?"

"Like Abraham Lincoln gone Irish."

He laughed. "A little respectable and a little roguish?"

"Exactly." The green hat set off his dark, handsome face and hair in a way that made it difficult for Theresa to draw her eyes away.

"Aren't you going to put yours on?"

"Oh!" She lifted the tiara and turned up her nose in disgust. It was covered with horrible, shocking pink glitter that would clash abominably with her red hair. But she lifted her hands and gamely settled the circlet atop her head. As she felt with her fingertips to determine if it was on straight, Brian took over.

"Here, let me."

He brushed her fingertips aside, then adjusted the gaudy headpiece on Theresa's bouncy curls. His touch seemed to send fire straight down each hair follicle into her scalp. Just being near the man did the most devilish things to her senses.

"How do *I* look?" she asked, trying to get command of herself, keeping spirits light.

"Like the angels sprinkled you with stardust." He touched a fingertip to her left eyebrow. It felt as if she'd received a 110-volt shock. "But there's nothing wrong with a little stardust. Guess I'll put it back." Again he touched her, replacing the flake of pink glitter, this time on the crest of her left cheek, then running the finger slowly down to her chin before dropping his hand between them and capturing both of her hands without looking away from her astounded eyes. His own were penetrating, admiring and seemed to be radiating messages much like those she was unable to hide.

"You'd better close your eyes, Brian, or all this color will give you a headache," Theresa warned, realizing how garish she must look in the gaudy vermilion tiara, with hot pink glitter highlighting her freckle-splattered cheeks.

The drummer began a drum roll. It seemed to both Brian and Theresa the sound came from the opposite side of the universe, so wrapped up in each other had they become.

"Gladly," Brian agreed, "but not because anything gives me a headache." He was clutching her hands so tightly she completely forgot about everything except his eyes, reaching toward hers with a deep, probing knowledge of something she'd yearned to see in the eyes of one special man, a man just like the one before her now. Around them the crowd bellowed the countdown to midnight. "Five...four...three...two...one!" The band hit the opening chord of "Auld Lang Syne," and neither Theresa nor Brian moved for the duration of several heartbeats.

Then she was being enfolded in strong, warm arms and dragged against his hard chest, against his belly, against his hips and his warm, seeking mouth.

A coil of pink paper came flying through the air and drifted across the brim of Brian's green top hat, trailing down over his ear and jaw, but he was totally unaware of it. A shower of confetti settled onto Theresa's hair and shoulders and drifted down the bridge of Brian's nose, but they were lost in each other, aware only of the closeness they'd at last achieved. Their eyes were closed as they kissed with a full, lush introduction of tongues that sent shock waves skittering down Theresa's spine. Her arms were threaded beneath his, and her palms rested on the center of his back while one of his pressed between her shoulder blades, and the other slipped up into the warm secret place at her nape, under the cloud of soft hair.

The interior of his mouth was warm, wet and compelling. The shifting exploration of his tongue brought hers against it in answer, as a river of longing coursed through Theresa's body.

Brian started moving as if unable to be drawn from a deep spell—slowly, seductively—carrying her with him to the nostalgic rhythm and words of the song. Their hips joined, pressed and swayed together, but their feet scarcely shuffled on the crowded floor. He moved his head in a sensuous invitation to deepen the kiss and opened his mouth wider over hers. Her response was as natural as the evocative dance movements they shared: her own mouth opened more fully. She felt the sensuous drawing of his lips and tongue, and the moist heat of his mouth seemed to burn its way down the length of her body.

In her entire life, nothing like this had ever happened to Theresa. The kisses of her past had been accompanied either by timidity or groping, and sometimes by both in rapid succession. She let Brian rub her hips with his own, lightly at first, then with growing pressure until the side-to-side motion evoked images of further intimacies. Finally, he drew her against him with a possessiveness that made her ribs ache sweetly. And still the kiss continued....

He began humming into her open mouth, and auld acquaintances were indeed forgotten by both of them while she answered by humming too. Before the song was half through, before the new year had been completely ushered in, before she could quite capture the realization that it was really happening to her, Theresa felt Brian's body go hard within the blue jeans. But she remained against him, marveling that someone at last had unlocked her to the wondrous side of physical contact.

"Auld Lang Syne" drifted to an end, and somewhere in the reaches of her consciousness Theresa knew the song had changed into another as Brian lifted his head but not his hands. He held her in a warm embrace while they rocked, remaining hip to hip, breast to chest, gazing into each other's eyes.

"Theresa." He lifted his eyes to her hair, let them skim back to her enraptured face, which reflected amazement, arousal and perhaps a touch of apprehension. "This started before I ever met you. You know that, don't you?" His voice was rich with passion. Her lips dropped open, and she found it very difficult to breathe.

"B...before you met me?"

"Jeff told me things that used to make me lie in bed at night and wonder what you'd be like when I met you. I would have been the most disappointed man in the world if you hadn't turned out to be exactly as you are."

She dropped her eyes to the dusting of confetti on his shoulders. "But, I'm—"

"You're perfect," he murmured, lowering his head until his mouth cut off further words. Then, to her astonishment, he did something utterly provocative, and distractingly sexy. He loosened his hold momentarily and opened his corduroy jacket so that its bulk no longer disguised the state of his body—not in the least. Then he took her back where she belonged, inside the open jacket, with her hands between it and her sweater while they danced the remainder of the song.

When it ended, he backed away, but kept his arms looped behind her waist as their hips rested tightly together.

"Let's get out of here," he suggested in a low, throaty voice.

"B...but it's only midnight," she stammered, awed by the suddenness of the sexual urgings she felt. He lifted his eyes to her hair. It was peppered with confetti. The glittered crown had tipped awry, and he plucked it from her hair, then smiled down at her open lips.

"Let's go home."

"What about Jeff and—"

"Are you scared, Theresa?"

She felt the press of blood staining her neck and pushing upward, but he lifted her chin and forced her to meet his eyes. "Theresa, are you scared of me? Don't be. I want to be alone with you, just once before I leave."

But, Brian, I don't do things like that. I'm not like your groupies. The words crossed her mind, but not her lips. She'd look like a complete idiot if she said them and his intentions were honorable all along. Yet he'd opened his jacket and made his sexual state unquestionably clear! And she was a twenty-five-year-old virgin who was both tormented and compelled by the traumatic first that might very well happen if she agreed to leave early with him.

Instead of waiting for her answer, he turned her toward the edge of the dance floor, his palm riding the hollow of her spine while she led the way to the table, found her purse and couldn't quite meet Jeff's eyes as she and Brian said good-night.

He drove again, by tacit agreement. Inside her warm woolen coat, Theresa was shuddering throughout most of the ride home, even after the heater was blowing warm air. In the familiar driveway, he pulled the car to a stop, killed the engine and handed her the keys in the dark. She began pivoting toward her door when his strong grip on her wrist brought her up short.

"Come here." His command was soft-spoken, but tinged with gruff emotion. "It's been a long time since I kissed a girl in a car. I'd like to take the memory back to Minot Air Force Base with me."

It had been easier on the crowded dance floor when proximity took care of logistics. Now Theresa had to willingly lean her half of the way across the console that separated them. She hesitated, wondering how women ever learned to perform their part in these rites that seemed to inhibit her at every turn.

He exerted a light pressure on her wrist, pulling her slowly toward him, and tipped his head aside to meet her lips with a new kind of kiss that, though lacking in demand, was no less sensitizing. It was a tease of a kiss, a falling rose petal of a kiss. And it made her long for more.

"Your nose is cold. Let's go in and warm it up."

Chapter Seven

Inside, the house was quiet. The light above the stove was on again, and she hurried past its cone of brightness to the shadows of the hallway, knowing that if Brian got a look at her face, he'd see how uncertain and scared she'd suddenly become. She felt his hands taking the coat from her shoulders, though she hadn't known he'd followed her so closely. A myriad of conversational subjects jumped into her mind, but scattered into pieces like the colors in a kaleidoscope. Unable to believe she'd sound anything less than petrified if she introduced any of them, she was preparing to wish him a fast good-night and skitter off to bed, when he turned from the closet and lazily took her hand in one of his.

"It sounds like your mom and dad are in bed already."

"Yes...yes, it's awfully quiet."

"Come downstairs with me."

Trepidation stiffened her spine. She tried to dredge up a reply, but both yes and no stuck in her throat. He threaded his fingers through hers as if they were setting out to stroll hand in hand through a meadow and turned them both toward the basement stairs.

She allowed herself to be led, for it was the only way she could approach the seduction she knew was in the offing.

At the top of the basement stairs she snapped on the light, but once downstairs, he released her hand, crossed to the ruffled lamp and substituted its mellower glow, then unconcernedly switched off the garish overhead beacon.

Theresa hovered by the sliding glass door, staring out at the black rectangle of night, while she chafed her upper arms.

Behind her, Brian noted, "It looks like your folks had a fire. The coals are still hot."

"Oh," she squeaked, knowing what he wanted, but unwilling to abet it.

"Do you mind if I add a log?"

"No."

She heard the glass doors of the fireplace being opened, then the metallic tinkle of the wire-mesh curtains being pushed aside. The charcoal broke with a crunching sound as he settled a new log, and the metal fire screen slid closed again. And still Theresa cowered by the door, hugging herself while her knees trembled.

She was staring out so intently that she jumped and spun to face Brian when he reappeared beside her and began closing the draperies. He was watching her instead of the drapery pulls while he worked the cord, hand over hand. She licked her lips and swallowed. Behind him, the fresh log flared with a *whoosh* and she jumped again as if the puff had announced the leaping arrival of Lucifer.

The draperies drew to a close. Silence bore down. Brian kept his disconcerting gaze riveted on Theresa as he came two steps closer, then extended his hand in invitation.

She stared at it but only hugged herself tighter.

The hand remained, palm up, steady. "Why are you so scared of me?" His deep, flawlessly modulated voice delivered the question in the softest of tones.

"I...I...." She felt her jaw working but seemed unable to close it, to answer, or to go to him.

He leaned forward, balancing on one foot while capturing one of her hands and tugging her along after him toward the far side of the room where the sofa faced the hearth. The fire glowed brightly now; passing the lamp he switched it off, leaving the room dressed in soft, flickering orange. He sat, gently towed her down beside him, and resolutely kept his right arm around her shoulders while he himself slunk rather low, catching the nape of her neck on the cushion, and crossing his calves on the shiny maple coffee table before them.

Beneath his arms, Brian could feel Theresa's shoulders tensed and curled. Everything had changed during their ride home. She'd had time to consider what she was getting into. Her withdrawal gave him a corresponding sense of hesitation, which he hoped he was hiding well. One skittish partner in such a situation was enough. He had misgivings about kissing her again in an effort to break down her reserve. She was pinched up as tightly as a newly wound watch, and he knew she hadn't done anything like this very often in her life. Jeff had told him she was spooked by men, that she turned down most invitations or advances that came her way. And Jeff had told Brian, too, the reason why. That knowledge hovered above him like a wall of water about to curl in upon his head. He felt as if he was savoring his last lungful of air in anticipation of being sucked under when the tidal wave hit.

Brian Scanlon was scared.

But Theresa Brubaker didn't know it.

She rested against the side of his ribs, with her head cradled on his shoulder and the crown of her hair against his cheek. But her arms remained crossed as tightly as if she wore a straitjacket.

With the hand that circled her shoulders, he gently rubbed her resilient upper arm. Her hair smelled flowery and created a warm patch of closeness where it pressed beneath his cheek. He pinched the knit sleeve of her sweater between thumb and forefinger and drew it away from her flesh.

"Is it true that you bought this whole new outfit just for tonight?"

"Amy's worse than Jeff. She can't keep *any* secrets."

His hand fell lightly upon her arm again. "I like the new clothes. The color goes great with your hair."

"Don't mention the color of my hair, please." She clasped an open hand over the top of her head, burying her face against his chest.

He smiled. "Why? What's the matter with it?"

"I hate it. I've always hated it."

The arm that had been circling her shoulders lifted, and what he'd done with the sweater, he did with her hair, lifting a single strand, rubbing, testing it between his fingers while studying it lazily. "It's the color of sunrise."

"It's the color of vegetables."

"It's the color of flowers—lots of different kinds of flowers."

"It's the color of a chicken's eye."

Beneath her cheek she felt his chest heave as he laughed silently, but when he spoke, it was seriously. "It's the color of the Grand Canyon as the sun slips down beyond the purple side of the mountains."

"It's the color of my freckles. You can hardly tell where one stops and the others start."

His index finger curled beneath her chin and forced her to lift her face. "I can." The way he lounged, his chin was tucked against his chest, and she gazed up across his corduroy lapel, feeling its raised wales digging into her cheek as she met his slumberous green eyes. "And anyway, what's wrong with freckles?" he teased, running the callused tip of his left index finger across the bridge of her nose and the crest of one cheek. "Angel kisses," he whispered, while the finger moved down the tip-tilted nose and the rim of her lips, over the pointed chin and on to her soft throat where a pulse thrummed in rapid tempo.

She tried to say, "Heat spots," but nothing came out except shaky breath and a tiny croak.

His nape came away from the back of the sofa in slow motion while his sea-green eyes locked with hers. "Angel kisses," he whispered, closing her eyes with his warm lips—first touching the left, then the right eyelid. "Have you been kissed by angels, Theresa?" he murmured. The tip of his tongue touched and wet the high curve of her left cheek, and the end of her nose, then her right cheek.

"Nobody but you, Brian."

"I know," came his final murmur before his soft mouth possessed hers. His kiss plucked at her reserve, encouraging a foray into the unknowns of sensuality, but her crossed arms still maintained a barrier between them. His tongue sought nooks and crannies of her mouth that it seemed her own tongue had never discovered before. It swept across warm, moist valleys from where tiny explosions of sensation burst upon her senses. He eased the pressure, catching her upper lip between his teeth, sucking it, releasing it, sensitizing the lower one next in the same seductive way.

Framing the contours of her open lips with his, he eased her back firmly against the sofa, twisting at the waist until his chest pressed her crossed wrists.

"Put your arms around me like you did when you were dancing."

He waited with his lips near her ear, measuring her hesitation by the number of thundering heartbeats that issued the pounding blood through her body and raised a delicate pulsepoint at her temple, just beside her hairline. Just when he thought it was hopeless, she at last moved the first hesitant hand, and he lingered above her until finally her arms curved about his shoulders.

"Theresa, don't be afraid. I'd never hurt you."

She began to say, "Brian, don't!" just as his mouth stopped the words from forming, and she felt herself flipping sideways beneath the force of his chest and hands. He shifted and adjusted her without moving his mouth from hers, until she lay beneath him, stretched out on the long sofa, with one foot clinging to the floor for security. Panic and sexuality seemed to be pulling her in opposite directions. *Let him kiss me, let him lie on me, but please, please, don't let him touch my breasts.*

His body was warm and hard, and when he'd tucked her beneath him, Brian opened his knees wide, lifting one to press it over her left thigh, while the other flanked the outside of her right leg all the way to the floor. His belt buckle and zipper pressed hard into her thigh, biting through the thin gabardine of her slacks and bringing to mind images from the movie that was her chief frame of reference to a man's physique. This was more than she had ever willingly let a man do with her. She remembered watching Brian on the dance floor, and his hips took up the same rhythmic tempo that had stirred her earlier. It worked an identical magic on her now, releasing a flood of inner enticement that answered the dance of his body on hers.

"Theresa, I've thought of you for months and months, long before I ever met you." His eyes, as he pulled away only far enough to look into hers, held neither smile nor twinkle. To Theresa's awe-struck wonder, they held what seemed to be a look of near reverence.

"But why?" she whispered.

His left hand contoured her neck underneath her hair, while his right meandered across her brow as he traced her bone structure with two fingertips. "I knew more about you than any man has a right to know about a woman he's never met. Sometimes I felt almost guilty about it, but at the same time it drew me to you as if I'd been hypnotized."

"So Jeff told you more than you let on before."

His parted lips pressed against the side of her nose, then he looked into her eyes again. "Jeff loves you as much as any brother could love a sister. He understands what makes you tick...and what doesn't. I had a picture of you as a sweet-natured little music teacher, directing freckle-faced kids for their mommies and daddies, but until I met you, I had no idea you'd look quite so much like one of them yourself."

She tried to turn aside.

"No." He captured her chin, rubbed his index finger along her jaw-bone. "Don't turn away from me. I told you, I like your freckles, and your hair, and...and everything about you, just because they're you."

She stiffened involuntarily as his hand left her nape and slid between her shoulder blade and the cushion of the sofa. He felt her rigidity, so instead of slipping the hand around to the front of her ribs, he moved it to her shoulder, then down the length of her arm to entwine Theresa's fingers with his. He forced their joined hands up between his chest and her breasts, his forearm now pressing against one of the warm, generous orbs.

Brian thought of the hours he and Jeff had lain in their bunks and talked about this woman. He knew about the times she'd come home in tears over the teasing of some boy, as long ago as when she was only fourteen years old. He knew about the time Jeff had beaten one of her persecutors and been kicked out of school on probation. He knew about the time she'd gone to the high-school prom but came home in tears after her date had proved he was only after two handfuls of the most obvious thing. He knew why she hid in an elementary school where she had to deal mostly with children who were too young and innocent to care about her accursed size; and why she hid inside dark, unattractive clothes; and behind sweaters; and beneath the chin rest of a violin. He knew he was in a spot where, to the best of Jeff's knowledge, no man had ever been allowed before. And he understood that by making the wrong move, he could cause her interminable hurt, and himself as well.

He sought to relax her with soothing endearments, all of them genuinely from the heart. "You smell better than any girl I've ever danced with." He nuzzled her neck, stringing kisses along her jaw like pearls upon a waxed thread. "And you dance just the way I like a girl to dance." He dropped a kiss on the corner of her mouth. "I love your music..." On her nose. "And your innocence..." On her eye. "Your Nocturnes..."

On her temple. "And your long, beautiful fingers on the piano keys...."
He kissed five knuckles in turn. "And being with you at midnight on
New Year's Eve." At last he kissed her mouth, lingering there to dip his
tongue between her soft, innocent lips, to join her in a celebration of a
new year, a new discovery, a new awareness of how right they seemed
for each other.

Theresa felt lifted, transported above herself, as if this must certainly
be someone other than herself in Brian Scanlon's arms, hearing his murmured words of admiration. Perhaps she was an understudy having
stepped in at curtain time when the star performer fell ill. Perhaps these
words were meant for that other woman, the one with the silhouette of a
sylph, with mink-brown hair and golden, flawless skin. That other woman
had performed this part so many times she knew instinctively how to
react to this man's voice and movements.

But Theresa was not that practiced artiste. She was a hesitant ingenue
to whom the part did not come naturally. She wanted to lift her arms
around Brian's shoulders and return the string of kisses he'd just bestowed upon her, but relinquishing the guard she'd maintained for years
was no easy thing. Experience had taught her only too clearly that to
believe she could attract someone because of her hidden attributes was a
pipe dream. Each time she had done so, the man upon whom she'd pinned
her hopes had proved himself no more honorable than the boy who'd
made one blossom-kissed May prom night eight years earlier not a mem-
orable celebration of the end of a school year but an ugly memory of
shame and disgust she'd made sure had never been repeated since.

Brian's forearm rested across her right breast, depressing it in an almost
lackadaisical fashion that felt natural and acceptable to Theresa, until he
began moving his wrist back and forth as if something had tickled it and
he was relieving the itch by rubbing the skin across her sweater. His
fingers were still interlaced with Theresa, and he carried her own hand
atop his, turning it now so that the back of only his hand came into
contact with her breasts.

*Don't panic. Don't resist. Let him. Let him touch you and see if it
makes you react like the woman reacted in the movie.* Theresa swallowed,
and Brian's tongue did sensuous things to the inside of her mouth.

He pulled back, teased the rim of her mouth with a butterfly's touch
of his lips. "Theresa, don't be scared." She tried not to be, telling her
muscles to relax as he released her tense fingers and rested his warm
palm upon the ribbed waist of her sweater. *No. Don't let him be like all
the others. Don't let him want me for only that. Not Brian, who's been
so careful not to even look at me there during all these wonderful days
while he grew dearer.*

Beside them the fire danced, sending warmth radiating against the sides of their faces and bodies. But she pinched her eyelids shut, unaware of the troubled expression on Brian's face as he gazed down at her. She lay beneath him with the stillness of fallen snow, pale and motionless, and breathing with great difficulty. But her breath was not drawn through lips fallen open in passion, rather through nostrils distended in apprehension.

Her flesh was warm beneath the sweater, and her ribs surprisingly fine-boned, the skin over them taut and toned. Her frame, Brian now realized, was built for bearing much smaller breasts than those with which she'd been endowed. *Trust me, Theresa. It's you, your heart, your uncomplicated simple soul that I'm learning to love. But loving the soul of you means loving the body of you as well. And we must start with that. Sometime, we must start.*

He moved his hand up her ribs, his warm palm molding itself to the arch of her rib cage, finally placing four fingertips in the warm hollow just beneath one breast. Gently he brushed back and forth, giving her time to accept the idea of his imminent intrusion. Beneath the heel of his hand he felt an unnatural tremor, as if she were holding her breath to keep from crying. Against his belly her midsection was arched up off the cushions, not in enthusiastic acquiescence, but in fortification as if steeling herself to defend at a second's notice.

He covered her lips with his in forewarning, then rolled aside just enough to allow freedom of access to the warm, soft globe of flesh that brushed his fingernails and moved toward it with as much gentleness as he could muster. Seeking not to violate or to trespass, he breached the remaining space, playing her the first time with as fluttering a touch as he might have used to chime the strings of a guitar instead of strumming them. Beneath his mouth, hers quivered. *Easy, love, easy,* he thought.

His first touch brushed scarcely more than the seam of the stiff cotton garment that covered her, as he ran his fingertips along its deep curve, from the center of her chest across her breast to the warm, secret place beneath her arm.

She shuddered and tensed further.

He lightened his hold on her lips until their kiss became more of a commingling of breath than of flesh, a foretoken of the gentleness he was preparing for her. *Trust me, Theresa.* Once more he nudged her lips with a blandishment so weightless it might have been the gossamer approach of nothing more than the shadow cast by his head bending over hers.

But caution cracked through Theresa's nerves and kept her from mellowing and melting beneath him. She waited, instead, like a martyr at the stake, until at last he enfolded her breast, firmly, fully, running his thumb along the horizontal seam of her bra. She acquiesced for the moment, allowing him to discover the breadth, resilience and warmth of her breast.

As his hand caressed and explored, Theresa waited in agony, wanting so much more than what she was able to allow herself to feel in the way of response. She wanted to stretch and loll, to utter some thick sound in her throat as the woman had in the movie. She wanted to know the pleasure other women seemed to derive from having their breasts caressed and petted. But her breasts had never been objects of pleasure, only of pain, and she found herself recalling the hurt of countless callous insults, feeling diminished by those recollections, even while Brian bestowed a touch of utmost honor and respect. But as he pushed her sweater up to her breastbone, she was like a hummingbird poised for flight.

He sensed it, yet steeled himself and moved the next step further along the road toward mutuality, inching down until his hips rested on the sofa between her open legs, and his head dipped down, his open mouth replacing his hand, kissing her through the cotton fabric that separated her flesh from his.

Brian's breath was warm, then hot, and it sent waves of sensation shimmying up her ribs and along the outer perimeter of her breasts, cresting in a tightening sensation that drew her nipples up into a pair of hard knots, shriveling them like rosebuds that refuse to open. Through her bra he gently bit, and the sweet ache it caused made her hands fly into the air behind him, palms pushing at nothing.

He lifted his head. She heard him whisper, "Shh..." but she could not open her eyes and meet his gaze, for behind her lids was the vivid image of her nipples. She saw again the tiny, demure nipples of other girls in shower scenes from years ago, envying them their delicacy, their femininity, and her terror grew. If she could be assured he'd go no further, she might have relaxed and enjoyed the shivering sensation his kiss sent through her. But she knew, as surely as she knew the shape of her own bovine proportions, that the next step was one she could not suffer. She could not bare herself to the eyes of any man. Her breasts were freckled, unattractive and when released fell aside like two obscene mounds of dough.

Oh, please, Brian, I don't want you to see me that way. You'll never want to look at me again.

The fireplay illuminated their bodies, and she knew if she opened her eyes she would see too clearly how visible she was by its light. His mouth bestowed a breath-stealing warmth to her opposite breast, and, as with the first, it was a seductive nip through stiff cotton whose very scratch seemed to beguile her flesh to succumb.

But when Brian braced himself above her and slipped his hands behind her back to free the catch of her brassiere, no power on earth could allow Theresa to let him see her naked.

"Don't!" she whispered fiercely.

"Theresa, I—"

"Don't!" She pushed against the hollows of his elbows, her eyes wide with trepidation. "I...please...."

"All I'm going to do—"

"No! You're not going to do anything!" She flattened her shoulder blades to prevent his captured hands from doing what they'd been reaching behind her to do. "Please, just get off."

"You haven't given me a ch—"

"I'm not that kind of woman, Brian!"

"What kind?" Relentlessly he held her where she was.

"Loose, and...and easy." She struggled, unable to free her writhing limbs from the weight of his.

"Do you really believe I could ever think of you that way?"

Tears of mortification stung her eyes. "Isn't that what all men think?"

She saw the hurt flash across his green eyes, the line of his jaw harden momentarily. "I'm not *all men*. I thought maybe you'd come to realize that since I've been here. I didn't start this to see how much I could get out of you."

"Oh, no? Considering where your hands are right now, I'd say I have cause to doubt that."

He closed his eyes, let his head droop forward and shook it in a slow gesture of exasperation while emitting an annoyed puff of breath. He withdrew his hands and dragged himself away, rolling to sit on the edge of the sofa. But their limbs were still half tangled, and she was caught in a vulnerable, splayed pose, with one knee hooked beneath his, the other updrawn behind his back.

She arched up and tugged her sweater down to her waist while he heaved a frustrated sigh and ran a hand through his hair, then slouched forward, elbows to knees, letting his hands dangle limply while he stared absently into the fire, a deep frown upon his face.

"Let me up," she whispered.

He moved as if only now realizing he had her pinned in a less than modest sprawl. She disentangled herself and curled into the corner of the sofa, not quite cowering, but withdrawn behind her familiar shield of crossed arms.

"You really are an uptight woman, you know?" he said angrily. "Just what the hell did you think I was going to do?"

"Exactly what you tried!"

"So what does that make me?" He flung up both palms. "A pervert? Theresa, for God's sake, we're adults. It's hardly considered perverted to do a little petting."

She found the word distasteful. Her expression soured. "I don't want to be gawked at like some freak in a sideshow."

"Oh, come on, aren't you being a little dramatic?"

"To you it's dramatic, to me it's...it's traumatic."

"Are you saying you've never let a guy take off your bra before?"

She only puckered her mouth and refused to look at him.

He pondered her silently for several seconds before asking, "Had you considered that's not exactly normal—or healthy—for a twenty-five-year-old woman?"

Now her eyes met his, but they shot sparks. "Oh, and I suppose you're volunteering to break me in for my own good, is that it?"

"You'll have to admit, it might be good for you."

She snorted quietly and cast her eyes aside while he grew increasingly upset with her. "You know, I'm getting awfully damn tired of you crossing your arms like I'm Jack the Ripper...*and* of having my motives questioned when the way I look at it, I'm the one with the normal impulses here."

"Well, I've had plenty of lessons on the *normal impulses* of the American male!" she shot back.

They sat stonily for several long, strained minutes, staring straight ahead, disappointed that this night that had started so magically was ending this way.

Finally Brian sighed and turned to study her. "Theresa, I'm sorry, all right? But I feel something for you, and I thought you felt the same about me. Everything between us was right tonight, and I thought it led to this quite naturally."

"Not every woman in the world agrees with you!" she shot back.

"Would you look at me...please?" His voice was low, caring, hurt. She pulled her gaze away from the fire, feeling as if its hue had been drawn to the skin of her face, which was flooded with a heat of a very different kind. Theresa confronted his eyes to find a wounded expression there that disconcerted her. He rested an elbow along the back of the davenport, his fingertips very near her shoulder. "I don't have much time, Theresa. Two more days and I'll be gone. If I had weeks, or months to woo you, things would be different, but I don't have. So I used the accepted approach, because I didn't want to go back to Minot and wonder for the next six months about your feelings." His fingertips brushed the shoulder of her sweater very lightly, sending a shudder down her spine.

"I like you Theresa, do you believe that?" She bit the soft inside of her lip and stared at him, becoming undone by his words, his sincerity. "*You.* You, the person. The sister of my friend, the musician who shares a love of music with me, the girl who kept her brother straight, and who laughs while she fiddles a hayseed hoedown on her classic 1906 Faretti and understands what I feel when I play Newbury's songs. I like the you that never knew how to put on makeup before tonight and had to learn how from her fourteen-year-old sister, and the you that walked into the kitchen with the refreshing shyness of a fawn. I like the fact that you wouldn't know the first thing about dancing the way Felice does. As a matter of fact, there's not much about you I don't like. I thought you understood all that. I thought you understood the reason why I tried to express my feelings the way I just did.''

Her heart felt swollen, her throat thick, and her eyes and nose stung. Words like these, she'd always thought, were always spoken only in love stories, to the other girls, the pretty ones with miniature figures and silken hair.

''I do.'' She wanted very much to reach out and touch his cheek, but her inhibitions were long nurtured and would take time to crumble. So she attempted to tell Brian with the wistful, downturned corners of her lips, with the aching expression in her tear-bright eyes how remorseful she was at that moment. ''Oh, Brian, I'm sorry I said that. And it wasn't true. I said it because I was scared, and I...I just got panicky at the last minute. I said the first thing I could think of to stop you, but I didn't mean it. Not about you.''

His fingertips still brushed her shoulder. ''Did you think I didn't know you were scared?''

''I....'' She swallowed and dropped her eyes.

''I've known it since before I met you. I've watched you hiding behind sweaters and purses and even your violin ever since I first got here, but I thought if I took it slow, if I showed you that other things came first with me, you'd....'' He made a gesture with his palms, then his hands went limp. She felt her face heating up again, radiating with the embarrassment she felt at confronting this issue. It seemed impossible that she was actually talking about it...and with a *man*.

''Theresa, don't look away from me, damn it. I'm not some pervert who took a bead on you and came here to see if he could make another score, and you know it.''

Her tears grew plump and then spilled over, and at the moment of her discomposure, she drew her knees up tightly, circled them with her arms, dropped her forehead and emitted a single sob.

''B...but you don't know wh...what's it's like.''

''I understand that when you feel something as strong as I feel for you, it's natural to express it like I tried to.''

''Maybe for you its n...natural, but for me it's awful.''

''*Awful?* You find being touched by me *awful?*''

''No, not by *you*, just...*there*. On my breasts, I...kn...knew you were going to and I was so...so....'' She couldn't finish but kept her face hidden from him.

''My God, Theresa, do you think I don't know that? The village idiot couldn't miss seeing how you hide them. So what should I have done?

Bypassed them and touched you someplace else? What would you have thought of me then? I told you, I wanted—'' he stopped abruptly, glowered at the fire, ran his hands down the length of his face and grunted, almost as if to himself, "Oh, damn." He seemed to gather his thoughts for a minute, then faced her again and gripped her shoulder to force her to meet his eyes. Her own were still streaming, and his were angry. Or perhaps frustrated. "Listen, I knew about your hangup before I stepped off that plane. I've been trying to come to grips with it myself ever since I've been here, but I like you, damn it! And part of it is physical, but that's how it is. Your breasts are part of you, and you like me, too, but if you're going to shy away every time I try to touch you, we've got a real problem.''

She was surprised with his directness in stating the issue. Even the word *breasts* had inhibited her all her life. Now here he was, pronouncing it with the candor of a health teacher. But she could see he didn't understand how difficult it was for her to cast off her mantle of self-consciousness. It was seated in too many painful memories from her teenage years. And he, Brian Scanlon, long, lean, perfect, the target of admiration of countless enamored females, could hardly be expected to fathom what it was like to be shaped the way she was.

"You just don't understand," she said expressionlessly.

"You keep saying that. Give me a chance, will you?"

"Well, it's true. You're…you're one of the lucky ones. Look at you, all lean and trim and handsome and…well, you take for granted being… being *normal* and shaped like everyone else."

"Normal?" he frowned. "You don't think you're normal, just because you're built like you are?"

"No!" She glared at him defiantly, then dashed away a tear with an angry lash of her hand. "You couldn't possibly understand what it's like to be…to be gawked at like a…a freak in a sideshow. They started growing when I was thirteen, and at first the girls were jealous that I was the first one to need a bra. But by the time I was fourteen the girls stopped being jealous and were only…amazed."

Oddly Brian had never considered how girls had treated her. This was a secret hurt even Jeff hadn't known. He felt Theresa's remembered pain keenly as she went on.

"In school when we had to take showers the girls gaped at me as if I was the ninth wonder of the world. Gym class was one of the greatest horrors of my life." A faraway look stole over her face, and her eyes closed wearily. "Running." She laughed ruefully, the sound seeming to stick in her throat as her lids lifted again. "Running wasn't only embarrassing, it hurt. So I…I gave up running at an age when it's a natural part of a teenager's life." She blinked once, slowly, staring at a distant point while wrapping her arms around her knees. Brian gently closed a hand over her forearm, urging her to meet his gaze.

"And you resent it? You feel cheated?"

He understood! He understood! The knowledge freed her to admit it at last. "Yes! I couldn't...." She choked and tears came to her eyes. "I gave up so many th...things I wanted. Trading clothes w...with my friends. B...bathing suits. Sports. Dancing." She took a deeper gulp. "Boys," she finished softly.

He rubbed her arm. "Tell me," he encouraged.

Her gaze shifted to his face. "Boys," she repeated, and again stared at the patterns in the fire. "Boys came in two categories then. The gawkers and the gropers. The gawkers were the ones who went into a near catatonic state just being in the same room with me. The gropers were...well...." Her voice trailed away and she looked aside.

Brian understood how difficult this was for her. But it had to be said to clear the air between them. He touched her jaw. "The gropers were...."

She turned and met his eyes, then hers dropped as she went on. "The gropers were the ones who ogled and leered and liked to talk dirty."

A shaft of heat and anger speared through Brian, and he wondered guiltily if there were times in his youth when he might have tormented a girl like Theresa. Again she continued.

"I went on a couple of dates, but that was enough. Their side of the front seat hardly got warm before they were over on my side to see if they could get a feel of the...the notorious Theresa Brubaker." She turned and asked sadly, "Do you know what they called me, Brian?"

He did, but he let her admit it so the catharsis might be complete.

"Theresa Boob-Acres. Acres of boobs, that's what they said I had." She laughed ruefully, but tears like sad diamonds shot with orange from the fireglow dropped down her cheeks. She seemed unaware they had fallen. "Or sometimes they called me Tits Boobaker. Jugs. Udders—oh, there are a hundred insulting words for them and I know every one."

Brian's heart hurt for her. So much of this he'd learned from Jeff, but it was far more wrenching, hearing it from Theresa herself.

"The gropers..." she repeated, as if steeling herself to face one memory worse than the rest. Brian sat without moving, one hand along the back of the sofa, the other still lightly resting on her arm. Her voice was thick and uneven. "When I was in the ninth grade a bunch of boys caught me in the hall after school one day. I can remember exactly what I was wearing b...because I came home and b...buried it in the bottom of the g...garbage can." Her eyelids slid closed, and he watched her throat working. He'd heard it before and wished he could prevent her from going on, but if she shared it all it meant she trusted him, and this he wanted very badly. "It was a white blouse with little pearl buttons down the front and a tiny round collar edged with pink lace. I'd always l...loved it because it was a C...Christmas present from Grandma Deering." A tear plunged over her eyelid and she dashed it away, then gripped her own sleeves again. "Anyway, I had an armful of books when they—they caught me. I re...remember the books skittering along the floor when they...p...pushed me back against the lockers, and how...c...cold the lockers were." She shivered and rubbed her arms. "Two of the boys held my arms straight out while the other two f...felt me up." Her eyes closed, lips and chin quivered. Brian's hand squeezed the back of her neck, but she was lost to all but the memory and the hurt it revived. She drew a deep, shaking breath and her lips dropped open. "I was too sc...scared to tell mother, but they'd torn the b...buttonholes of my blouse, and I d...." She shrugged helplessly. "I didn't know how I'd answer questions about it, so I...I threw the blouse away where I was sure she wouldn't find it." A sob erupted at last, but she immediately firmed her lips and lifted her chin.

He could bear it no longer and gently forced her close, circling her neck with one arm, urging her into the curve of his body until her up-drawn knees pressed his chest and her feet slipped beneath his thigh. She was trembling terribly. He rested his cheek against her hair and felt a devastating sting at the back of his eyes. He closed them and uttered, "Theresa, I'm sorry," and kissed her hair and made futile wishes that he could change her memories to happier ones. She remained tightly curled in the circle of his arms. Again her voice went on tremulously, and she unconsciously plucked at the fibres of his sweater.

"In eleventh grade there was a boy I liked a lot. He was nothing like those other boys. He was quiet and musical and he...he liked me a lot. I could tell. Prom time came, and I'd catch him staring at me across the orchestra room—not at my breasts, but at my face. I knew he wanted to ask me to the prom, but in the end he chickened out. I knew he was scared of my...my enormous proportions.

"But s...somebody else asked me. A boy named Greg Palovich. He seemed nice enough, and he was handsome and really polite... until...until the end of the evening when we were in the c...car." All was silent for a long, tense moment. Her voice was sorrowful as she finished. "He didn't t...tear my dress. He was very careful not to." She turned her face sharply against Brian's chest. "Oh, B...Brian, it was so humiliating, s...so degrading. I still cringe every t...time I hear the word prom."

Brian's hand found her head and smoothed her hair, holding her face protectively against the aching thud of his heart. Again he experienced the deep wish to be sixteen, to be able to invite her to the prom himself and give her a glowing memory to carry away with her. He tipped her face up and ran a thumb beneath her eye, wiping the wetness aside. "If we were in school now, I'd see to it you had some happy memories."

Her heart swelled with gratitude. She watched the fire light the planes and curves of his face. "Oh, Brian," she said softly, "I believe you would." She sat up regretfully and resumed her former pose, feeling his eyes on the side of her face as she again stared at the fire and hugged her knees. "But nobody can change what's past. And neither can you change the nature of man."

"It's still happening?" he questioned quietly. When she only gazed ahead absently without answering, he caught her chin with a finger and forced her to look at him. "Look at me Theresa. Tell me the rest so we can put it behind us. It's still happening?"

She shifted her chin aside and dropped her eyes to her crossed arms. "It happens each time I walk into a room where there's a strange man I've never met before. I tell myself this time it won't happen. This time it'll be different. When we're introduced, his eyes will stay on my face." Theresa's voice was nearly a whisper now, filled with chagrin and an edge of shame. "But no man ever meets my eyes when he meets me. Their eyes always drop straight down to my chest." She fell silent, sensing his frowning scrutiny. His hand was gone from the back of her neck. Only his gaze touched her. When he spoke, his voice was firm.

"Mine didn't."

No, his didn't. And that was why she'd begun liking him almost immediately. But she knew why.

"You were forewarned."

He couldn't deny it, or the fact that if he hadn't been, his eyes very likely would have widened and dropped. "Yes, I'll admit it. I was."

She stared at a spurting blue flame that gathered a sudden surge of life, even as the fire dwindled. The shadows in the room were deep fingers of gray.

"I've never talked about this with anyone else before in my life."

"What about your mother?"

She turned her troubled eyes to his, and each of them saw the glint of the dying flames reflected beneath unsmiling eyebrows. "My mother?" Theresa gave a soft, rueful chuckle deep in her throat, closed her eyes and dropped her head back against the sofa cushion. Brian watched the curved line of her throat as she spoke. "My mother's answer to the problem was to tell me all I needed was a heavy-duty bra. Oh God, how I hate them. Wearing pretty underclothes is just another one of the things I had to give up. They don't make pretty ones for girls like me, and when you tried to...." She lifted her head but wouldn't meet his eyes. "Well, *before,* I couldn't bear the thought of you seeing me either with my bra or without it. I'm not a very pretty sight either way.''

"Theresa, don't say that." He eased closer and laid a hand on the top of her head and stroked her hair, then let his palm lie lightly on her bright, airy curls.

"Well, it's true. But it was never anything I could talk about with my mother. She's generously endowed herself, and once when I was around fourteen and came to her crying over how big I was getting, she treated the problem like it was something I'd get over when I got older. After all, she said, *she did.* When I asked if I could talk to somebody else about it, like our doctor or a counselor, she said, 'Don't be foolish, Theresa. There's nothing you can do about it but accept it.' I don't think she ever realized she's got a totally different personality than mine. She's...well, brazen and domineering. A person like that *can* overcome their hangups more easily than someone like me."

They sat in silence for several long minutes. She heard Brian draw a deep breath and let it out slowly. "So how do you feel about it now, now that you've talked about it with me?"

"I...." She glanced up to find him watching her closely. His hand had fallen from her head, but those knowing eyes held her prisoner. "Surprised that I really managed to tell you everything like I did."

"I'm glad you confided in me, Theresa. Somehow I think it'll help you in more ways than just...well, letting go."

She studied him now as carefully as he studied her. "Brian, tell me something." Her forearms were crossed atop her updrawn knees, and she picked at a thread of her knit sleeve, thoughtful for a moment, before turning to catch his eyes again. "Tonight at the dance you said that Felice reminded you of the groupies who hang around the stage and hope to...to score with the guitar man after the dance. You said...." She swallowed, amazed at her own temerity, but somehow finding herself unleashed in a new way. "Well, you said they were a dime a dozen, but that wasn't what you wanted...*tonight.*" Again she swallowed, but he refused to help her along. He was going to make her voice her question if she wanted an answer. "Does that mean you've...indulged with lots of girls like this...on other nights?"

"Some." The word was quiet, truthful.

"Then why...I mean, I'm not...experienced like those girls. Why would you want to be with me instead of them?"

He moved closer, his right elbow hooked on the back of the sofa, his hand gently stroking her arm. "Because bodies are not what love is about. Souls are."

"Love?" Her eyes widened and met his in surprise.

"You don't have to look so threatened by the word."

"I'm not threatened by it."

"Yes you are."

"No I'm not."

"If you fell in love, you'd have to face the inevitable sooner or later."

"But I haven't fallen in love, so I'm not threatened." She'd had to deny it—after all, he hadn't actually said he loved her.

"Fair enough. I answered your question, now you answer one of mine. And I want an honest answer."

But she refused to agree until she knew what he was going to ask.

"Why did you go through all the trouble of buying new clothes, learning how to put on makeup and fingernail polish and going to the beauty shop before our date tonight?"

"I...I thought it was time I learned."

He smiled, a slow grin that appeared briefly, then was gone, replaced by his too-intense study. He moved nearer, until she had to lift her face to meet his eyes above her. "You're a liar, Theresa Brubaker," he stated in a disarmingly quiet tone. "And if you didn't feel threatened, we wouldn't have had the discussion we just had. But you've got nothing to fear from me."

"Brian...." Her breath caught in her throat as he moved unhesitatingly to encircle her in his arms.

"Put your damn knees down and quit hiding from me. I'm not Greg Palovich, all right?"

But she was too stunned to move. He wouldn't! He wouldn't! Not again. Her muscles were tensing tighter, and she'd just begun to tighten her hold around her knees when with one swift sweep of his hand, Brian knocked her feet off the edge of the davenport. His strong hands closed around her shoulders, and he jerked her forward with deadly accuracy, pulling her up against his chest with their arms around each other. "I'm getting damn sick of seeing you with your arms crossed over your chest. And I'm starting back at the beginning, where you should have started when you were fourteen. Let's pretend that's how old you are, and all I want is a good-night kiss from the girl I took to the dance."

Before Theresa's astonishment could find voice, she was neatly enfolded against the strong, hard chest of the guitar man who'd had plenty of experience at seduction. His warm, moist, open mouth slanted across hers while one warm hand slipped up her neck and got lost in her hair. His tongue tutored hers in the ways of one far beyond fourteen years of age, slipping erotically to points of secrecy that started sensual urges coursing through her limbs and spearing down her belly. He lifted the pressure of his lips only enough to be heard while their tongues still touched. "I'm going to be so damn good for you, Theresa Brubaker. You'll see. Now touch me the way you've been wanting to since we left the dance floor.'' His tongue returned fully to her mouth, teasing, stroking hers with promises of delight. But he kept one arm around her ribs, the other hooked over the side of her neck, and his hands played only over her back, caressing it slowly but thoroughly while she let hers do the same upon him. Her hand wandered up his neck, to the soft, short hair that still retained the vestige of masculine toiletries she'd first smelled when she'd taken his cap. She thought of a line from the Newbury song: ''Wandering from room to room, he's turning on each light....'' And it felt as if Brian was showing her the light, one small room at a time. Their kiss grew more intimate as he murmured wordless sounds of approval, and she wanted to respond in kind, to give voice to the new explosive feelings she was experiencing. But just at that moment, he pushed her back gently.

''I'll see you tomorrow, okay, sweets? I can only be honorable up to a point.''

He got to his feet and tugged her along behind him. Looping a lazy arm around her shoulders, he sauntered with her to the stairway. There he stopped her just as she'd gained the first step. He stood on the floor so their eyes were now on the same level. In the deep shadows, his palms held her hips and he turned her to face him before he enclosed her in a warm embrace once again, found her lips for a last, lingering kiss, then turned her away with a soft, ''Good night.''

Chapter Eight

Theresa and Brian were not alone long enough during that day to speak of anything that had happened the night before, or to exchange touches or insight as to what the other was thinking of all that had passed between them. It was a lazy day. They'd all been up late and took turns napping, sprawled in chairs, on floors before the New Year's Day football games that flickered on the television screen or tucked into their own rooms. It seemed to take until nearly suppertime for everyone to come fully alive, and even then, it was a subdued group, for with only one more day before Brian and Jeff would be gone, they all felt an impending sense of loss.

The following morning, Theresa awakened shortly after dawn and lay staring at the pewter frog Brian had given her. She recalled everything that had happened between them since the first night when they'd sat side by side with his elbow pressing hers throughout that extremely sensuous love scene.

Who was she trying to fool? It had almost been predestined, this feeling she had for Brian Scanlon. She was falling in love with him, with a man two years her junior who admitted he'd had sexual encounters with any number of admiring fans. The idea that he was fully experienced and worldly made her feel inadequate and puerile. Again she wondered why he'd want an introverted, frightened virgin like her. She was daunted by his physical beauty, for it seemed to dazzle when compared to her ordinary-to-homely features, making her believe he couldn't possibly be attracted to her, as he'd said he was. How could he possibly be? With women like Felice fawning over him, pursuing him, eager to share more than just a bump-and-grind dance with him, why would Brian Scanlon possibly pursue Theresa Brubaker?

She sighed, closed her eyes and tried to imagine lying naked with him but found it impossible to picture herself in that context. She was too inhibited, too freckled, too redheaded to fit the part. She wished she were shaped like a pencil and had russet skin and sleek, auburn hair. She wished she'd found at least one boy or man sometime during her life who'd have been able to break through the barriers of self-consciousness to give her some sense of what to expect if she allowed Brian more sexual liberties.

The pewter frog sat on the shelf, caught in a still life, fiddling his silent note and smiling. *I'm like that frog. My life is like a silent note; I play, but I haven't felt the music of the heart.*

It was seven-thirty. She heard her parents leave for work, but the rest of the house was silent. She dragged herself from bed, dressed and made coffee, and still nobody else roused. Tomorrow Brian and Jeff would leave, and the house would seem abandoned. The mere thought of it filled her with loneliness. How would she make it from day to day when Brian was gone? How unfair that he should be snatched away just when they discovered their attraction for each other. She wandered to the bathroom, collected the dirty towels from the rack, hung up fresh ones, went to her room and added her own soiled laundry to the pile. She wondered how long she should wait before starting the washing machine to launder Jeff's clothes so he could take them back clean and save a laundry bill.

They had been running free all week, the whole bunch of them, and nobody had bothered much with homemaking chores. The pile of dirty clothes at the bottom of the laundry chute would be mountainous.

She waited until ten o'clock before creeping down the basement stairs like a burglar, sneaking onto each tread, afraid the step would creak and awaken Brian, who lay on his belly with both arms flung up, his ear pressed to one biceps. She halted in her tracks, gazing across the dim room at his bare back, at the outline of his hips and legs beneath the green blanket. His right leg was extended, his left bent with the tip of its knee peeking from under the covers. The only men she'd ever seen in bed were her father and Jeff. But seeing Brian there, listening to the light snuffle of his regular breathing, had a decidedly sensual effect upon Theresa.

She clutched her armload of dirty laundry and tiptoed to the laundry-room door, turned the knob soundlessly and latched it behind her with equally little noise.

She sorted out six piles of colors, dropped the first stack into the machine and grimaced at how loud the selector dial sounded when she spun it to its starting position—the clicks erupted through the silence like a tommy gun. When she pushed the knob to start the water flowing, it sounded like Niagara Falls had just rerouted through the basement. Soap, softener, then she picked her way across the floor between hills of fabric and opened the door to the family room.

She had just managed to get it closed silently again when Brian—still on his belly—lifted his head, emitted a snort and scratched his nose with the back of one hand. She stood transfixed, watching the light from the sliding glass door find its way across the ridges of his shoulder blades and the individual ones of his spinal column to the spot where the sheet divided his body in half. He cleared his throat, lifted his head again and intuitively glanced back over his shoulder.

Theresa stood rooted to the spot, holding onto the doorknob behind her, feeling the blood raddle her cheeks at being discovered there, watching him awaken.

His hair was standing up at odd angles. His cheek and jaw wore the shadow of a night's growth. His eyes were still swollen from sleep. "Good morning," he managed in a voice raspy from disuse. The greeting was accompanied by a slow over-the-shoulder smile that drew up one side of his mouth engagingly. Lazily, he rolled over, crooking one arm behind his head, presenting an armpit shadowed by dark hair and a chest sprinkled with a liberal portion of the same.

"Good morning." Her voice came out a whisper.

"What time is it?"

"After ten." She flapped an apologetic palm at the laundry-room door. "I'm sorry I woke you up with the washer, but I wanted to get the laundry started. Jeff's clothes...are...he...." To Theresa's dismay the words chugged away into silence, and she stood staring at half of a naked man, one who made everything inside her body go as watery as the sounds emanating from the other side of the wall.

"Come here." He didn't move; nothing more than the beguiling lips formed the invitation. His right arm cradled the back of his head. His left lay flat on his belly, the thumb resting in his navel, which was exposed above the blanket. One knee was straight, the other one bent so that its outline formed a triangle beneath the blankets. "Come here, Theresa," he repeated, more softly than before, lifting a hand toward her.

Her startled expression warned him she'd dreamed up an excuse, even before she began to voice it. "I have to—"

"Come." He rolled to one hip, and for a horrifying moment she thought he was going to get up and come to get her. But he only braced up one elbow and extended a hand, palm up.

She wiped her own palms on her thighs and advanced slowly across the room but stopped two feet from the edge of his mattress. His hand remained open, waiting. Upon it she could see the calluses on each of its four fingertips from playing the guitar. He had very, very long fingers. And he slept with his watch on.

It was so still just then she thought she could hear its electronic hum.

He moved himself up just high enough and strained forward across the remaining two feet to capture her hand and drag her toward him. Her kneecaps struck the frame of the bed, and she toppled down, twisting at the last minute to land half on one hip but coming to rest at an awkward angle, half across his bare chest.

"Good morning." His smile was thorough, teasing and warming places inside Theresa that she'd never realized hadn't known complete warmth before. He slipped one arm between her and the mattress and rolled to his hip facing her, managing to maneuver her stomach flush against his. She recalled in bemused fascination that she'd read that men often wake up fully aroused, but she was too ignorant to know if it was true of Brian this morning. He brushed her cheek with the backs of his knuckles, and his voice was charmingly gruff. "I find it hard to believe there's one woman left in this world who still blushes at age twenty-five." He dipped his head to touch her lips with a nibbling kiss. "And you know what?" He ran the tip of an exploring index finger across the juncture of her lips, causing them to fall open as she caught a breath in her throat. "Some day I'm going to see you wearing only that." He dipped his head again, but when their mouths joined, he rolled her over on her back and lay half across her body. His back was warm, firm, and beneath her palm she felt each taut muscle across his shoulders, then explored his ribs, like a warm, living vibraphone upon which her fingers played.

His naked chest was pressed against her breasts, flattening them in a way that felt wholly wonderful. She was wearing a thick wool hunter's shirt of gold and black squares, buttoned up the front, its deep tails flapping loose about her hips, which were squeezed tightly into a pair of washed-out denim Levi's. The shirt left her totally accessible—she realized that just as his weight bore down on her, and he lifted one knee across her thighs, rubbing up and down repeatedly, slowly inching higher until the inner bend of knee softly chafed the feminine mound at the juncture of her legs. Still kissing her, he found the arm with which she was protecting her breast and forced it up over his shoulder. Then his hand skimmed down the scratchy wool shirt, up under its tails and onto the bare band of skin between her jeans and bra. He drew a valentine on her ribs, then cupped her breast with unyielding authority, pushing on it so hard it caused a queer but welcome ache in the hollow of her throat. She felt the nerves begin to jump deep in her stomach, but controlled the urge to fight him off. The caress was brief, almost as if he was testing her, telling her, get used to it, try it, just this much, a little at a time. But, to Theresa's surprise, when his fingers left her breast, they skimmed straight down the center of her belly, along the hard zipper of her jeans and cupped the very warm, throbbing spot at the base of the zipper. Within the constricting blue denim her flesh immediately responded with a heat so awesome it caught her by surprise. She sucked in a quick, delighted breath, and her eyelids slammed closed. Her back arched up off the mattress and fire shot from the spot he caressed down to her toes. He clutched her with a hard, forceful palm, pushing upward until she was certain he could feel the pulsebeat throbbing through the hard, flat-felled seams of the Levi's. He stroked her through the tight, binding denim—once, twice, almost as if marking her with his stamp of possession.

Before she could decide whether to fight or yield, his hand was gone.

She lay looking up at his stormy green eyes while he braced on both elbows, and their labored breathing pounded out the message of mutual arousal.

"Theresa, I'm going to miss you. But six months and I'll be back. Okay?" His voice had gone even huskier with desire. What was he asking? The answer to the ambiguous question stuck in her throat.

"Brian, I...I'm not sure." She didn't think she could make such a promise, if he meant what she thought he did.

"Just think about it then, will you? And when June comes, we'll see."

"A lot can happen between now and June."

"I know. Just don't...." His troubled eyes traveled up to her hair. He soothed it back almost roughly, then returned his gaze to her amazed brown eyes, sending a message of fierce possession as absolute as that he'd delivered in his startling caress of a moment ago. "Don't find somebody else. I want to be first, Theresa, because I understand you, and I'll be good for you. That's a promise."

Just then Jeff's voice boomed from above; the washing machine had brought the house to life at last. "Hey, where is everybody? Brian, you awake?"

"Yeah, just dressing. I'll be right up."

Theresa nudged Brian aside and leaped off the bed. But before she could scamper away he captured her wrist and pulled her back down. She landed with a soft plop, sitting on the edge of the bed. He braced on one elbow, half curling his body around her to look up into her face.

"Theresa, will you kiss me just once, without looking like you're scared to death?"

"I'm not very good at any of this, Brian. I think you'd be a lot happier if you gave up on me," she whispered.

He frowned, released the hand she'd been tugging in an effort to regain her freedom. But when it was released, it lay on the mattress beside her hip with the fingers curled tightly underneath. He studied it, then with a single finger stroked the backs of the freckled knuckles. Looking up into her uncertain eyes, he said, "Never. I'll never give up on you. I'll be back in June, and we'll see if we can't get you past age fifteen."

How does a person grow to be so self-assured at twenty-three, she wondered, meeting his unsmiling gaze with her own somber eyes.

His weight shifted. He kissed her fleetingly and ordered, "You go on up first. I'll make my bed and wait a few minutes before I follow."

That night they spent quietly at home. Patricia came over to be with Jeff. Margaret and Willard sat side by side on the sofa while Jeff sat Indian fashion on the floor and Brian took the piano bench, and the two played their guitars and sang. Theresa was curled up in one armchair, Amy in another, and Patricia sat just behind Jeff, sometimes resting her forehead on his upper arm, sometimes stroking his shoulder blade, sometimes humming along. But Theresa sat wrapped up with feet beneath her, and palms tucked between her thighs, watching Brian only when his eyes dropped to the fingerboard of his guitar or veered away to some other spot in the room.

She waited for the song she was certain would come sooner or later, and when Jeff suggested it, her heartbeat quickened, and she felt hollow and hot and sad.

Brian was playing his own guitar this time, a classic Epiphone Riviera, with a smooth, mellow sound and a thin body. She stared at the guitar cradled against Brian's belly, and imagined how warm the mahogany must be from his skin.

My world is like a river
As dark as it is deep
Night after night the past slips in
And gathers all my sleep....

The poignant words affirmed the melody, speaking directly to Theresa's heart. Long before the song reached its second verse, her eyes had locked with Brian's.

She slipped into the silence
Of my dreams last night
Wandering from room to room
She's turning on each light.
Her laughter spills like water
From the river to the sea
I'm swept away from sadness
Clinging to her memory.

Theresa's eyes dropped to Brian's lips. They seemed to tremble slightly as they formed the next words.

Sweet memories...
Sweet memories...

His lips closed as he softly hummed the last eight notes of the song, and Theresa didn't realize Jeff's voice had fallen silent, leaving her to hum the harmony notes with Brian.

When the final chord diminished into silence, she became aware that everyone in the room was watching the two of them, adding up what seemed to be passing between them.

Jeff broke the spell. "Well, I've got packing to do." He began settling his guitar into its velvet-lined case. "I'd better get Patricia home. We'll have to get up and rolling by 8:30 in the morning."

The guitar cases were snapped shut. Jeff and Patricia left, and within twenty minutes the rest of the household had all retired to their respective beds.

Theresa lay in the dark, not at all sleepy. The words of the song came back to beguile with their poignant message.... "Night after night the past slips in and gathers all my sleep." She knew now what true desire felt like. It was tingling through each cell of her body, made all the more tempting by the fact that he lay in the room directly below hers, probably just as wide awake as she was, and for the same reason. But desire and abandon were two difference things, and Theresa Brubaker would no more have gone down those stairs and lain with Brian Scanlon beneath her parents' roof than she would have at age fourteen. Along with desire came an awareness of immorality, and she was a very moral woman who retained the age-old precepts taught her throughout her growing years. Knowing she would be disdained as "Victorian" in this age of promiscuity, she nevertheless had deeply ingrained feelings about right and wrong and realized she would never be able to have a sexual relationship with a man unless there was a full commitment between them first.

But the tingling, pulsing sensations still coursed through her virgin body when she thought of lying on the bed with Brian that morning, of his intimate touches. She groaned, rolled onto her belly and hugged a pillow. But it was hours before sleep overcame her.

They had a last breakfast together the next morning, then there were goodbye kisses for Margaret and Willard, who went to work with tears in their eyes, waving even as the car moved off up the street.

Theresa was driving to the airport again, but this time Amy was coming along. All the way, the car had a curious, sad feeling of loneliness, as if the plane had already departed. By unspoken agreement, Brian had taken the front seat with Theresa, and she occasionally felt his eyes resting on her. It was a sunny, snowy morning, its brightness revealing every colorful freckle, every strand of carroty hair she possessed. There was no place to hide, and she wished he wouldn't study her so carefully.

At the airport, they each carried a duffel bag or a guitar case to the baggage check, then entered the green concourse through the security check and walked four abreast down the long, slanting floor that echoed their footsteps. Their gate number loomed ahead, but just before they reached it, Brian grabbed Theresa's hand, tugged her to a halt and told the others, "You two go on ahead. We'll be right there." Without hesitation, he dragged her after him into a deserted gate area where rows of empty blue chairs faced the walls of windows. He took the guitar case from her hand and set it on the floor beside his own duffel bag, then backed her into the only private corner available: wedged beside a tall vending machine. His hands gripped her shoulders and his face looked pained. He studied her eyes as if to memorize every detail.

"I'm going to miss you, Theresa. God, you don't know how much."

"I'll miss you, too. I've loved...I...." To her chagrin, she began to cry.

The next instant she was bound against his hard chest, Brian's arms holding her with a fierce, possessive hug. "Say it, Theresa, say it, so I can remember it for six months." His voice was rough beside her ear.

"I've l-loved being w...with you...."

She clung to him. Tears were streaming everywhere, and she had started to sob. His mouth found hers. Theresa's lips were soft, parted and pliant. She lifted her face to be kissed, knowing a willingness and wonder as fresh and billowing as only first love can be—no matter at what age. She tasted salt from her own eyes and smelled again the masculine scent she'd come to recognize so well during the past two weeks. She clung harder. He rocked her, and their mouths could not end the bittersweet goodbye.

When at last he lifted his head, he circled her neck with both hands, rubbing his thumbs along the bone structure of her chin and jaws, searching her eyes. "Will you write to me?"

"Yes." She grasped one of his hands and held it fast against her face, his fingertips resting upon her closed eyelid before she pulled them down and kissed them, feeling beneath her sensitive lips the tough calluses caused by the music that bound Brian to her, made him someone so very, very right for her.

She raised her eyes at last, to find his etched with as much dread of parting as she herself felt. Oddly she had never thought men to be as affected by sentiment as women, yet Brian looked as if his very soul ached at having to leave her.

"All right. No promises. No commitments. But when June comes...." He let his eyes say the rest, then scooped her close for one last long kiss, during which their bodies knew a renewed craving such as neither had experienced before.

"Brian, I'm twenty-five years old, and I've never felt like this before in my life."

"You can stop reminding me you're two years older, because it doesn't matter in the least. And if I've made you happy, I'm happy. Keep thinking it, and don't change one thing about yourself until June. I want to come back and find you just like you are now."

She raised up on tiptoe, taking a last heart-sweeping kiss she couldn't resist. It was the first time in her life she had ever kissed a man instead of the other way around. She laid a hand on his cheek then, backing away to study him and imprint the memory of his beloved face into her mind.

"Send me your picture."

He nodded. "And you send me yours."

She nodded. "You have to go. They must be boarding by now."

They were. As Brian and Theresa rounded the wall toward their gate area, Jeff was nervously waiting by the ramp. He noted Theresa's tear-stained face and exchanged a knowing glance with Amy, but neither said anything.

Jeff hugged Theresa. And Brian hugged Amy. Then they were gone, swallowed up by the jetway. And Theresa didn't know whether to cry or rejoice. He was gone. But, oh, she had found him. At last!

At home the house seemed as haunted as an empty theater. He was there in each room. Downstairs she found the hideaway bed converted back to a davenport, and his sheets neatly folded atop a stack of blankets and pillows. She picked up the folded, wrinkled white cotton and stared at it disconsolately. She lifted it to her nose, seeking the remembered scent of him, pressing her face against the sheet while she dropped to the sofa and indulged in another bout of tears. *Brian, Brian. You're so good for me. How will I bear six months without you?* She dried her eyes on his sheet, brought his pillow into her arms and hugged it to her belly, burying her face against it, wondering how she would fill 176 days. She experienced the profound feeling that seemed to be the true measure of love—the belief that no one had ever loved so before her, and that no one would ever love in the same way after her.

So this was how it felt.

And it felt the same during the days that followed. School began and she was happy to get out of the house with its memories of him, happy to be back with the children, schedules, the familiar faces of the other faculty members she worked with. It took her mind off Brian.

But never for long. The moment she was idle, he returned. The moment she got into her car or walked into the house, he was there, beckoning. The way in which she missed him was more intense than she'd ever imagined loneliness could be. She cried in her bed that first night he was gone. She found smiling difficult during the first days back at school. Brooding came easily, and dreaminess, once so foreign to her, became constant.

On the first day after he'd left, Theresa returned home from school to find a note pinned to the back door: "Bachman's Florist delivered something to my house when they couldn't find anyone here at home. Ruth."

Ruth Reed, the next-door neighbor, answered Theresa's knock with a cheery greeting and wide smile. "Somebody loves somebody at your house. It's a huge package."

It was encased in orchid-colored paper to which was stapled a small rectangle of paper bearing the terse delivery order: "Brubaker...3234 Johnnycake Lane."

"Thank you, Ruth."

"No need for thanks. This is the kind of delivery I'm happy to take part in."

Carrying the flowers home, Theresa's heart skipped in gay anticipation. *It's from him. It's from him.* She jogged the last ten feet up the driveway and catapulted into the kitchen, not even stopping to take off her coat before ripping aside the crackling lavender paper to find a sumptuous arrangement of multicolored carnations, daisies, baby's breath and statice, interlaced with fresh ivy, all billowing from a footed green goblet. Theresa's hand shook as she reached for the tiny envelope attached to a heart-shaped card holder among the greenery.

Her smile grew, along with the giddy impatience to see his name on the gift card.

His name was there all right, but hers wasn't. The card read, "To Margaret and Willard. With many thanks for your hospitality. Brian."

Instead of being disappointed, Theresa was more delighted than ever. *So he's thoughtful, too.* She studied the handwriting, realizing it was written not by Brian but by some stranger in a florist shop someplace across town. But it didn't matter; the sentiment was his.

Brian's first letter came on the third day after he'd left. She found it in the mailbox herself, for she was always the first one home. When she flipped through the envelopes and found the one with the blue wings in the upper left-hand corner and the red and blue jets on the lower right, her heart skittered and leaped. She took the letter to her room, got the fiddling frog from his perch on the shelf and held him in her hand while she sat cross-legged on the bed, reading Brian's words.

But his picture was the first thing that fell out of the envelope, and she dropped the pewter frog the moment Brian's face appeared. He was clothed in his dress blues, his tie crisply knotted, the visor of his garrison cap pulled to the proper horizontal level over his brow. He was unsmiling, but the green eyes looked directly into hers from beneath their familiar, sculptured brows. Dear face. Dear man. She turned the picture over. "Love, Brian," he'd written on the back. Theresa's heartbeat accelerated, and warmth stole over her body. She closed her eyes, took a deep breath and pressed the picture against her breast, against the crazy upbeat rhythm his image had invoked, then laid the picture face up on her knee and began reading.

Dear Theresa,

I miss you, I miss you, I miss you. Everything has suddenly changed. I used to be pretty happy here, but now it feels like prison. I used to be able to pick up my guitar and unwind at the end of a day, but now when I touch it I think of you and it makes me blue, so I haven't been playing much. What have you done to me? At night I lie awake, thinking of New Year's Eve and how you looked when you came out into the kitchen dressed in your new sweater and makeup and hairdo, all for me, and then I wish I could get the picture out of my head because it just makes me miserable. God, this is hell. Theresa, I want to apologize for what happened that morning on my bed. I shouldn't have, but I couldn't help it, and now I can't stop thinking about it. Listen, sweets, when I come home I'm not going to put the pressure on for that kind of stuff. After everything we talked about, I shouldn't have done it that day, okay? But I can't stop thinking about it, and that's mostly what makes me miserable. I wish I'd been more patient with you, but on the other hand, I wish I'd gone further. Man, do I sound mixed up. This place is driving me crazy. All I can think about is your house, and you sitting on the piano bench. Last night I put the Chopin record on but I couldn't stand it, so I shut off the stereo. When I can handle it again I'll make a tape of "Sweet Memories," and send it to you, okay, sweets? It says it all. Just how I'm feeling every minute. You, slipping into the darkness of my dreams at night, and wandering from room to room, turnin' on each light. I don't think I can make it till June without seeing you. I'll probably go AWOL and show up at your door. Do you get Easter vacation? Could you come up here then? Listen, sweets, I gotta go. Jeff and I play a gig this Saturday night, but no girls afterward. That's a promise.

I miss you,
Brian

She read the letter nonstop for half an hour. Though each line thrilled her, Theresa returned time and again to his offhand question about Easter vacation. What would her parents say if she went? The thought rankled and made her chafe against having to tell them at all, at her age. The house seemed restrictive after that, and she felt increasingly hemmed in.

She had put off writing to Brian, feeling that to write too soon would seem...what? Brazen? Overstimulated? Yet his words were thrillingly emotional. His impatience and glumness were a surprise. She'd never dreamed men wrote such letters, holding back nothing of their feelings.

She didn't want to send her picture. But now that she knew what heart's ease there was to be found in having Brian's picture to bring him near, she realized he'd probably feel the same. She got out one of her annual elementary-school pictures, but for a moment wavered. It was a full-color shot: black and white would have pleased her more. The camera had recorded each copper-colored freckle, each terrible red uncontrollable hair and the breadth of her breasts. Yet this was just how she'd looked when he first met her, and still he'd found something that pleased him. Along with the photograph, Theresa sent the first love letter of her life.

Dear Brian,
The house is so lonely since you've been gone. School helps, but as soon as I step into the kitchen, everything sweeps back and I suddenly wish I lived somewhere else so I wouldn't have to see you in every room. The flowers you sent are just beautiful. I wish you could've seen the look on mom's face when she first saw them (and on mine when I opened the package and found they weren't for me). Naturally, mom got on the phone right away and called everyone in the family to tell them what "that thoughtful boy" had sent.

I really wasn't disappointed to find the flowers weren't for me, because what I got two days later was dearer to me than any of nature's beauties.

Thank you for your picture. It's sitting on the shelf in my room beside The Maestro, who's guarding it carefully. When your letter came I was really surprised to read how you were feeling, because everything you said was just what's happened to me. Playing the piano is just awful. My fingers want to find the notes of the Nocturne, but once I start it, I can't seem to finish. Songs on the radio we listened to together do the same thing to me. I seem to have withdrawn from mom and dad and Amy, even though I'm miserable when I sit in my room alone in the evenings. But if I can't be with you, somehow I just don't want to be with anyone.

It's really hard for me to talk about this subject, but I want to set the record straight. I know I'm really naive and inexperienced, and when I think of how uptight I get about the really quite innocent things we did together, I realize I'm paranoid about...well, you know. I really want to be different for you, so I've decided to talk to the school counselor about my "problem."

Did you really mean it about Easter? I've read that part of your letter a hundred times, and each time my heart goes all sideways and thumpy. If I came I'm afraid you'd expect things I'm not sure I'm prepared for yet. I know I sound mixed up, saying in one breath I'm going to see the counselor and in the next I'm still old-fashioned. I'm sure mother and dad would have a fit if their little Theresa announced she was going up to spend Easter with Brian. Some days mother drives me crazy as it is.

Here's my awful picture, taken in October with the rest of the Sky Oaks Elementary student body and faculty. You say it's the color of flowers. I still say vegetables, but here I am anyway. I miss you so much.

Affectionately,
Theresa

P.S. Hi to Jeff
P.P.S. I like the names "sweets."

Dear Sweets,
I can't believe you didn't say no, flat out. Now I'm living on dreams of Easter. If you come, I promise you'll set the rules. Just being with you would be enough to tide me over. You'll probably think I'm speaking out of turn, but I think somebody twenty-five years old shouldn't even be living with their parents anymore, much less having to get their okay to go off for a weekend. Maybe you're still hiding behind your mother's skirts so you won't have to face the world. God, you'll probably think I'm an opinionated sex maniac now, and that all I want is to get you up here so I can act like Greg What's-His-Name. Don't be mad, sweets, okay? Ask the counselor about it and see what she says. Your picture is getting curled at the edges from too much handling. I've been thinking, I wouldn't mind getting away from this place for a while. Instead of coming up here, maybe we could meet halfway in Fargo. Let me know what you think. Please decide to come. I miss you.

Love,
Brian

The counselor's name was Catherine McDonald. She was in her mid-thirties, always dressed in casual yet extremely up-to-date clothes and always wore a smile. Although they hadn't had many occasions to work together, Theresa and Catherine had shared many friendly visits in the teachers' lunch room, and Theresa had come to respect the woman's inherent poise, objectivity and deep understanding of the human psyche. There were school counselors whom Theresa thought more qualified to be truck drivers. But Catherine McDonald suited her role and was immensely respected by those with whom she worked.

Rather than meet in school, Theresa requested that they get together over cups of tea at the Good Earth Restaurant at four o'clock one Thursday afternoon. Potted greenery and bright carpeting gave the place a cheerful atmosphere. Theresa was led past the Danish tables and chairs on the main floor to a raised tier of booths overlooking it. Each booth was situated beside a tall window, and it was in one of these where Catherine was already waiting. The older woman immediately stood and extended a hand with a firm grip. Perhaps the thing Theresa had first admired about Catherine was the way the woman's eyes met those of the person to whom she spoke, giving an undivided attention that prompted one to confide in her and believe she cared deeply about the problems others unloaded upon her. Catherine's intelligent, wide-set blue eyes remained unwaveringly on Theresa's as the two greeted each other, settled down and ordered herbal tea and pita-bread sandwiches, then got down to the crux of the meeting.

"Catherine, thank you for taking time to meet me," Theresa opened, as soon as their waitress left them alone. Catherine waved a hand dismissively.

"I'm happy to do it. Anytime. I only hope I can help with whatever it is."

"It's personal. Nothing to do with school. That's why I asked you to meet me here instead of in the office."

"Herbal tea has a mellowing influence anyway. This is much much nicer than school. I'm glad you chose it."

Catherine stirred unrefined sugar into her tea, laid down the spoon and looked up with a laserlike attention in her blue eyes. "Shoot," she ordered tersely.

"My problem, Catherine, is sexual." Theresa had rehearsed that opening line for two weeks, thinking once the last word fell from her mouth the barriers might be broken, and it would be easier to talk about the subject that so easily made her blush and feel adolescent.

"Go ahead, tell me." Again the blue eyes held, while Catherine leaned her head with prematurely silver hair against the tall back of the booth in a relaxed attitude that somehow encouraged Theresa to relax, too.

"It has to do mostly with my breasts."

Amazingly, this woman still kept her eyes on Theresa's. "Am I correct in assuming it's because of their size?"

"Yes, they're...I've...." Theresa swallowed and was suddenly overcome by embarrassment. She braced her forehead on the heel of a hand. Catherine McDonald reached across the table and circled Theresa's wrist with cool, competent fingers, letting her thumb stroke the soft skin in reassurance before gently lowering the hand and continuing to hold it for a full thirty seconds. The contact was something strange and new to Theresa. She had not held a woman's hand before. But the firm squeeze of the counselor's fingers again inspired confidence, and soon Theresa went on speaking.

"I've been this size since I was fifteen years or so. I suffered all the usual persecution, the kind you might expect during adolescent years...the teasing from the boys, the awed stares from the girls, the labels males somehow can't help putting on that part of a woman's anatomy, and even the misplaced jealousy of certain other girls. I asked my mother at the time if I could talk to a doctor or counselor about it, but she's almost as big as I am, and her answer was that there was nothing that could be done about it, so I'd better learn to live with it...and start buying heavy-duty bras—"

Here Catherine interrupted with a single brief question. "You still live with your mother and father, don't you, Theresa?"

"Yes."

"I'm sorry. Go on."

"My normal sexual growth was...impaired by my abnormal size. Every time I found a boy I liked, he was scared by the size of them. And every time I settled for a date with somebody else, he was out for nothing but a groping session. I heard rumors at one time in high school that there was a bet among the boys that anybody who could produce my bra would win a pot worth twenty-five dollars." Theresa looked into her teacup, reliving the painful memory. Then she swept it from her mind and squared herself in her booth. "Well, you don't want to hear all the sordid details, and they're not really as important anymore as they once were." Theresa's eyes grew softly expressive, and she tipped her head slightly to one side. "You see, I've met a man who...who seems to...to look beyond the exterior and find something else that attracts him to me." Theresa sipped her almond tea.

"And?" Catherine encouraged quietly. This was the hard part.

"And...and...." Theresa looked up pleadingly. "And I'm a virgin at twenty-five, and scared to death to do anything with him!"

To Theresa's amazement, Catherine's response was a softly exclaimed, "Wonderful!"

"Wonderful?"

"That you've come right out and unloaded it at last. It was hard to say, I could tell."

"Yes, it was." But already Theresa found herself smiling, loosening up and feeling more and more eager to talk.

"All right, now let's get down to specifics. Tell me why."

"Oh, Catherine, I've been living with this oversize pair of pumpkins for so many years, and they've caused me so much pain, I hate them. The last thing on earth I want to do is let a man I think I love see them naked. To me they're ugly. I thought when he...if he saw them, he'd never want to look at me without my clothes on again. So I...I...."

"You held him off?" Catherine's eyes were steady as Theresa nodded. "And you denied your own sexuality."

"I...I hadn't thought about it that way."

"Well, start."

"Start?" Theresa was astounded by the advice.

"Exactly. Work up a good healthy anger at what you've been robbed of. It's the best way to realize what you deserve. But first, let me back up a square and ask about this man."

"Brian."

"Brian. Did his reaction to your size offend you?"

"Oh no! Just the opposite! Brian was the first man I've ever met who *didn't* stare at my breasts when we were introduced. He looked me straight in the eye, and if you knew how rare that was, you'd understand what it meant to me."

"And when he tried to make sexual contact and you put him off, was he angry?"

"No, not really. He told me he'd come to like other things about me that went deeper than superficialities."

"He sounds like a wonderful man."

"I think he is, but I have such an odd feeling about...well, he's two years younger than I am—"

"Maturity has nothing to do with chronological age."

"I know. It's silly of me to bring it up."

"Not at all. If it's a concern, you're right to introduce it. Now go on, because I interrupted again."

For the next hour and fifteen minutes Theresa expounded on all her secret hurts gathered up, stored through the years. She expressed her dismay over the things she'd had to forgo because of her problem, and the reluctance she'd always felt to discuss it with her mother, once Margaret had expressed her opinion on the subject all those years ago. She admitted she'd gone into elementary music because it allowed her to work with children who were less discerning than adults. She confessed that Brian had accused her of hiding in various ways. It all came out, and when Theresa had spilled every thought she'd harbored for so many years, Catherine pushed her teacup away, crossed her forearms on the table edge and studied Theresa intently.

"I'm going to suggest something, Theresa, but I want you to remember it's only a suggestion, and one you should think about for a while and mull over. There *is* an answer for you that you may never have considered before. I believe in time you and Brian will come to work out your self-consciousness, because he sounds like a man willing to go slowly at building your self-confidence. But even when you achieve sexual ease with this man, the other problems will not go away. You'll still feel angry about the clothes you're forced to wear, about your Rubenesque proportions, about the stares of strange men. What I'm suggesting you inquire about is a surgical procedure called mammoplasty—commonly called breast-reduction surgery.''

Theresa's eyes widened unblinkingly. Her lips fell open in surprise.

"I can see it never entered your mind."

"No, it...breast-reduction surgery?" The words came out on a breathy note of suspicion. "But that's *vanity* surgery."

"Not anymore. The surgery is becoming an accepted treatment for more than just bruised egos, and the idea that it's prompted only by self-indulgence is antiquated. It's my guess that you have more physical discomfort than you even attribute to breast size, and the surgery is being used to eliminate many physical ailments."

"I don't know. I'd have to think about it."

"Of course you would. It's not the kind of thing you jump into on a night's consideration. And it may not be the answer for you, but dammit, Theresa! Why should you live your life with backaches and rashes and without the amenities of a woman of more modest proportions comes to take as her due? Don't you deserve them, too?"

Yes, came the immediate, silent answer. *Yes, I do. But what would people think? Mother, dad, the people I work with.*

Brian.

"The yellow pages still list the surgeons under Surgeons—Cosmetic. The term has come to have negative connotations in some circles, but don't let it deter you if you decide to look into the possibility. Better yet, I know a woman who's had the surgery, and I know she'd give you the name of her surgeon and be willing to share her feelings with you. She spent her life suffering all the same ignominies as you, and the surgery has made a profound change not only in her self-image but in her general health. Let me give you her name." Catherine extracted a note pad and pencil from her purse and wrote down the name, then reached out to touch the back of Theresa's hand. "For now, just consider it, let the idea settle in, with all its constituent possibilities. And if you're worried about facing people, don't be. It's your life, not theirs. Not your mother's or your father's or those you work with." The sharp blue eyes brightened further. "Aha! I can see I've struck a nerve already. People be damned, Theresa. This decision is one you make for yourself, not for anyone else."

As they left the restaurant, the silver-haired woman turned toward the redhead. "Whenever you want to talk again, let me know. I'm always available."

That night in bed, Theresa considered the rather stupendous possibilities of "Life After Surgery." She thought of what it would be like to walk proudly, with shoulders back, wearing a slim size-nine sundress. She considered how it would feel to lift her arms and direct the children without the drogueish weights pulling at her shoulders. She dreamed of having no more painful shoulder grooves from the slicing bra straps that marred her flesh. She thought of summer without rash beneath her breasts where the two surfaces rubbed together constantly now. She imagined the sheer joy of buying the sexiest underwear on the rack, and of having Brian see her in it, then without it.

Brian. What would he think if she did such a thing?

In the dark, beneath the covers, Theresa ran her hands over her breasts, feeling their enormity, hating them afresh, but suddenly smitten by a hundred unasked questions about what it would entail to have them reduced in size. It was heady simply knowing she had the option!

She tried to imagine the freedom of having only half as much where all this flesh was now, and it seemed almost unbelievable that it could happen for her. But it was too important a decision to make on one night's consideration, and without all the facts, as Catherine had pointed out.

And there was her mother to consider. Somehow, she knew her mother would disapprove—her fatalistic attitudes already having been voiced. And the people at work—what would they think? How many times in her life had women—ignorant of the attendant miseries of having massive breasts—told her she should be happy she was endowed as she was? Their attitude was programmed by a cultural bias toward large breast size, so she shouldn't blame them for their uninformed opinions.

But with the new seed of suggestion planted, those countless comments and hurts from the past had already ceased to hurt as much.

But what if Brian objected? Always her thoughts went back to Brian, Brian, Brian. What would it feel like to have him see her naked if she was proud of her body instead of ashamed of it?

_____ *Chapter Nine*

Theresa didn't mention it in any of her letters to Brian, though their correspondence continued weekly, and more often semiweekly. He sent the tape of "Sweet Memories," and the first time she played it Theresa knew an aching loneliness. She closed her eyes and pictured Brian playing his guitar and singing the poignant song, felt again his kisses, yearned to see him, touch him. She still hadn't given him her answer about meeting him in Fargo. She wanted to—oh, how she wanted to—but she trembled to think of telling her parents about her plan. And no matter what Brian had said in his letters, she was sure if she went he'd expect a sexual commitment before the weekend was over.

In early March, Theresa was crossing the parking lot at school, picking her way across the ice-encrusted blacktop when one of her two-inch heels went skittering sideways and dumped her flat onto her back. Books flew, scattering across the pitted ice while she lay looking at the leaden sky with the wind knocked out of her.

Joanne Kerny, a fellow teacher, saw Theresa go down and hurried to help her sit up, a worried frown on her pretty face. "Theresa, what happened? Are you hurt? Should I get help?"

"N...no." But Theresa felt shaky. "No, I think I'm all right. My heel slipped, and I went down so fast I didn't realize I was falling until my head hit the ice."

"Listen, stay right here and I'll go get somebody to help you inside, right away."

The fall had made Theresa's head hurt, but she managed to stay on the job through the remainder of the day. She worked the following day, also, but by the third day she was forced to call for a substitute teacher: her back was in spasm. She went to the doctor, and his examination turned up no broken bones, but some very painfully bruised muscles, for which he prescribed a relaxant. But in the course of his examination and questioning, Dr. Delancy asked some questions he'd never asked before.

"Tell me, Theresa, do you have back pain regularly?"

"Not exactly regularly. Rather *ir*regularly and more so in my shoulders than my back."

He probed further. How often? Where? What seems to bring it on? Does it bother you to wear high heels? Are you on your feet all day? At what age did the back irritation start? And when he stopped at the door on his way out, his next order sounded dire enough to strike a bolt of fear through Theresa: "When you're dressed I'd like to talk to you in my office."

Five minutes later Dr. Delancy informed her without preamble, "I believe, young lady, that you're in for increasing back problems unless something is done about the cause of these aches, which, if I diagnose them correctly, are happening with increasing frequency the older you get. They can only be expected to get worse if untreated." At her startled expression he rushed on. "Oh no, this fall is only a temporary inconvenience. It'll heal and cause nothing permanent. What I'm speaking of is the strain on your back, knees and chest by the extreme weight of your breasts. The back and shoulder aches you've had, which started in your teen years, are undoubtedly being caused by a bone structure too small to support all that weight. I'm going to recommend a good specialist for you to talk to about it, because there is a solution to the problem, one that's far less critical, less risky, and less painful than the back surgery you may eventually have to undergo if you ignore the problem."

She knew what Dr. Delancy was talking about even before she put the question to him. "Are you talking about breast-reduction surgery?"

"Oh, so someone's suggested it to you before?"

She left the doctor's office with an odd feeling of predestination, as if the fall in the parking lot had happened to lend her a further and more valid reason for considering the surgery. Certainly if she were to bring up the subject to her mother and tell Margaret what Dr. Delancy's prognosis was, her mother would accept the idea of breast reduction far more readily than if Theresa suggested having it only to relieve herself of sexual hangups, and so she could wear the clothing of her choice.

Dear Brian,
I've done the most foolish thing. I slipped and fell down in the parking lot at school. We'd had rain on top of ice and I was wearing shoes with little heels, and down I went. I'm staying home for a couple of days, on doctor's orders, but he says it's just bruised muscles and they'll fix themselves. But meanwhile, I have another vacation (sort of), but I wish you were here to spend it with me.

The pen fell still. Theresa's gaze wandered off to the dismal gray day beyond the window. The clouds scuttled low while sleet pelted down to run in rivulets along the pane.

What would he think if she wrote, I've been thinking about having my breasts made smaller?

She hadn't realized, up to that point, she *was* considering it. But there were many questions yet to be answered before she could make her decision. And somehow, it seemed too intimate a revelation to make to Brian yet.

She pulled herself from her musing and touched the pen to the paper again.

I've been thinking a lot about Easter. I want to come, but you're right. I'm afraid to tell my folks....

Two days later the phone rang at four in the afternoon.

"Hello?"

"Hello, sweets."

It seemed the winds and rain of March dissolved, and the world erupted in flowers of spring. Theresa's free hand clutched the receiver and joy spiraled up through her limbs.

"B...Brian?"

"Do any other men call you sweets?"

"Oh, Brian," she wailed, and the tears suddenly burned her eyes. Her back still hurt. She was depressed. She missed him. Hearing his voice was the sweetest medicine of all. "Oh, Brian, it's really you."

He laughed, a brief dissatisfied sound ending with a gulp. His voice sounded shaky. "How are you? How's your back?"

"Suddenly it's much better." Through her tears she smiled at the phone cord, picturing his face. "Much, much better."

"Your letter just came."

"And yours just came."

"But I didn't know about your accident when I wrote. Oh, babe, I got so worried, I—"

"I'm fine, Brian, really. All except...." All except her life was none of the things she wanted it to be. She was afraid to have the surgery. Afraid not to have it. Afraid to tell her parents about it. Afraid to meet Brian in Fargo. Afraid her parents would disapprove. Angry that she had to seek their approval at all.

"Except what?"

"Oh, I d...don't know. It's s...silly. I...I just...."

"Theresa, are you crying?"

"N...no. Yes!" She placed a hand over both eyes, squeezing. "Oh, Brian, I don't know why. What's wrong with me?" She tried to hold back the sobs so he couldn't hear.

"Sweetheart, don't cry," he pleaded. His voice sounded muffled, as if his lips were touching the phone. But his plea brought the tears on in force.

"No one's ever c...called me sweetheart bef...before."

"You'd better get used to it."

The tender note in his voice reverberated through her pounding heart. She dashed the tears from beneath her eyes with the back of a hand and clung to the phone. So much to say, yet neither of them spoke. Their trembling feelings seemed to sing along the wire. She was unused to having emotions of this magnitude. Voicing them the first time was terrifying. Essential. She could not live with the sweet pain in her chest.

"I've m...missed you more than I ever th...thought human beings missed one another."

A throaty sound, much like a groan, touched her ear. Then his breath was indrawn with a half hiss and expelled in a way that made her picture him with eyelids clenched tightly. Silence swam between them again, rife with unsaid things. Her body was warm and liquid with sudden need of him.

When he spoke again his words sounded tortured, almost guttural. "You're all I think of." Tears were trailing freely over her cheeks, and she felt weighted and sick. Scintillating, silent moments slipped by, while the unspoken took on greater meaning than the spoken. If the house had not been totally silent she might have missed his next throaty words. "You and Easter."

Still he did not ask. Still she did not answer. Her heart trembled. "Brian, nothing like this...." She stopped to swallow a sob that threatened.

"What? I can't hear you, Theresa." In her entire life of painful shyness, no teasing, no taunts had ever hurt like this shattering longing.

"N...nothing like this has ever hap...happened to me before."

"To me either," he said thickly. "It's awful, isn't it?"

At last she released a sniffly laugh that was much sadder than tears, meant to allay the tension, but failing miserably. "Yes, it's awful. I don't know what to do with myself anymore. I walk around unaware."

"I forget what I'm supposed to be doing."

"I h...hate this house."

"I think about going AWOL."

"Oh, no, Brian, you mustn't."

"I know...I know." She listened to the sound of his labored breathing. Was he running a hand through his hair? Again stillness fell. "Theresa?" he said very, very softly. Her eyes slid closed. She touched the phone with parted lips. "I think I'm falling."

Her soul soared. Her body was outreaching, yearning, denied.

Again came his ragged breath, seeking control. "Listen, kiddo, I've got to go, all right?" The gaiety was decidedly forced. "Now you go rest and take care of your back for me, okay? There'll be a letter from me day after tomorrow or so. And I promise I won't go AWOL. Tell everybody there hello." At last he fell quiet. His voice dropped to a husky timbre. "I can't take this anymore. I have to go. But I won't say goodbye. Only...sweet memories."

Don't go! Don't hang up! Brian...wait! I love you! I want to meet you at Easter. We'll....

The phone clicked dead in her ear. She wilted against the wall, sobbing. *Why didn't you tell him you'd come? What are you afraid of? A man as gentle and caring as Brian? Do all who love suffer this way?*

Perhaps it was the bleakness and unhappiness that finally prompted Theresa to call the woman whose name had been given her by Catherine McDonald. She desperately needed to talk to somebody who understood what she was going through.

As she dialed the number several days later, her stomach went taut, and she wasn't sure she could voice the questions she'd rehearsed so often during the days she'd lain in bed under doctor's orders.

But from the moment Diane DeFreize answered the phone and greeted warmly, "Oh yes, Catherine told me you might call," the outlook in Theresa's life began to change. Their conversation was encouraging. Diane DeFreize radiated praise for the change wrought upon her life by the surgery she'd had. In little time at all she'd made Theresa eager to take the first step.

It was a day in the third week of March when she met Dr. Armand Schaum. He was a lean, lanky surgeon, one of the growing number of people she'd met lately who maintained eye contact on introduction. Dr. Schaum had the blackest hair she'd ever seen and a piercing look of intelligence in his nut-brown eyes. She liked him immediately. Obviously, Dr. Schaum was used to skittish women coming in with diffident attitudes and uncertain body language, as well as with the slumped shoulders caused by their condition. Theresa, like most, huddled in her chair at first, as if she'd come to his pleasant office asking him to perform some perverted act upon her.

Within five minutes, her attitude changed drastically, and she was struck by a sense of how very ignorant and misinformed she'd been all these years. She'd maintained the same outdated viewpoint as the rest of society: that breast-reduction surgery was vain and unnecessary.

Dr. Schaum explained the probable physical ailments Theresa could expect in the future if her breasts remained as they were now: not only backaches but also a bent spine; leg and knee troubles as well as varicose veins; breathing problems later in life when the chest wall responded to the excessive weight; recurrent rashes on the undersides of her breasts; an increase in breast size and its related discomforts if and when she chose the pill, pregnancy or nursing.

Vanity surgery? How few people understood.

But there were two negative factors Dr. Schaum was careful to point out. His long, angular face took on an expression of somber, businesslike concern.

"In mammoplasty, an incision is made around the entire areola—the brightly colored circle surrounding the nipple. The past method of surgery was to remove the nipple completely before replacing it in a higher position. But with a new method we called the inferior pedicle technique, we can now perform the surgery without severing the nerve connection completely. Now, the nipple remains attached by a slender stalk of tissue called the pedicle. With this technique we aren't able to reduce the breast size quite as radically, but the chance of retaining nipple sensitivity is greatly increased. With *all* breast surgery, that sensitivity is lost at least temporarily. And though we can never guarantee it will return, if the nerve connection is preserved, it's very likely. But it's important that you understand there's always the remote possibility of losing the erogenous zone permanently."

Dr. Schaum leaned forward in his chair. "The other consideration you have to make is whether or not you ever want to breast-feed a baby. Although there have been rare cases in which the pedicle technique was used, where mothers *were* able to nurse afterward, the possibility is highly unlikely.

"So having the surgery means accepting the fact that two important things are at stake: the breast's ability to produce milk and to respond to sexual stimulation. It means that you'll almost certainly have to give up the one, and there's the remote possibility of having to give up the other."

So that was the risk. Theresa was devastated. She lay in bed that night wide-eyed, more uncertain than ever. The idea of having all sensation irreversibly numbed was terribly frightening and very disheartening. Suppose the feeling never returned? She recalled those tingles, the feminine prickles of sexuality brought to her breasts by Brian's briefest touch, by nothing more than dancing close enough to lightly rub the front of his corduroy jacket, and she wondered what he'd think if she robbed *him* of the ability to arouse her in that particular way and herself of the ability to respond.

She cupped her breasts in her palms. They remained unstimulated. She moved her pajamas flutteringly across the nipples. Little happened. She thought of Brian's mouth...and it began.

Sweet yearning filled her, made her curl, wanting, wondering. What if this powerful feminine reaction was severed before she'd ever known the sweet evocative tug of a man's lips here? He had said, "You'll set the rules." Would he think her a tease if she asked for that much and then pulled back? Could she ask for that, then pull back herself?

She only knew that once...just once she must know the wonder before she wagered it.

He answered the phone in a crisp, military fashion. "Lieutenant Scanlon here."

"Brian, it's Theresa."

All was silent while she sensed his great surprise. She wasn't sure she should have called him in the middle of the day.

"Yes, can I help you?"

His brusqueness was a dash of cold water. Then she understood—there was someone nearby.

"Yes, you can help me by telling me you haven't given up on me yet, and that it's not too late for me to say yes to your invitation."

"I...." He cleared his throat roughly. "We can proceed with those plans, as discussed."

Her heart was going wild. She imagined how difficult it was for him to remain stern and unemotional-sounding. "Good Friday?"

"Right."

"The Doublewood Inn in Fargo?"

"Affirmative. At 1200 hours."

"D...does that mean noon, Brian?"

"Yessir. Have the proper people been notified?"

"I plan to tell them tonight. Wish me luck, Brian."

"You have it."

"Whoever's with you, turn your face away from him because I think you're going to smile." She paused, taking a deep breath, picturing him as he'd been that first day, with his back to her while he looked out the sliding glass door at the snowy yard, wearing dress blues, his too-short hair showing only slightly beneath the stern visor of his garrison cap. She clearly recalled the warmth and scent lingering in that cap when he'd handed it to her. "Lieutenant Scanlon, I think I'm falling in love with you." Silence. Shocked silence. "And I think it's time I did something about it."

After a short pause, he cleared his throat. "Affirmative. Leave it all to me."

"Not quite all. It's time I took my life into my own hands. Thank you for being so patient while I grew up."

"If there's anything we can do at this end to implement matters—"

"I'll see you in two and a half weeks."

"Agreed."

"Goodbye, dear Lieutenant Scanlon."

Again he cleared his throat. But still the last word came out brokenly. "Good...goodbye."

Theresa tackled her mother and father that night, before she could lose her nerve. As it happened, Margaret provided the perfect lead-in.

"Easter dinner will be at Aunt Nora's this year," Margaret informed them at the supper table. The meal was over. Amy had zipped off to do homework with a friend. "Arthur and his family will be coming from California on vacation. Land sakes, it must be seven years since we've all been together. Grandpa Deering will be celebrating his sixty-ninth birthday that Saturday, too, so I promised I'd make the cake and you'd play the organ, Theresa, while we—"

"I won't be here at Easter," Theresa interrupted quietly.

Margaret's expression said, don't be ridiculous, dear, where else could you possibly be. "Won't be here? Why, of course you'll—"

"I'm spending Easter in Fargo...with Brian."

Margaret's mouth dropped open. Then it pursed as a chalky line appeared around it. Her eyes darted to Willard's, then snapped back to her daughter. "With Brian?" she repeated tartly. "What do you mean, *with* Brian."

"I mean exactly that. We've agreed to meet in Fargo and spend three days together."

"Oh, you have, have you?" Margaret bit out. "Just like that. Off to Fargo without benefit of a wedding license!"

Theresa felt herself blushing, and along with it rose indignation. "Mother, I'm twenty-five years old."

"And unmarried!"

"Had you stopped to think you might be assuming things?" Theresa accused angrily.

But Margaret had ruled her roost too long to be deterred by any one of them when *she knew she was right!* Her face was pink as a peony by this time, the double chin quivering as she claimed distastefully, "When a man and woman go off, *overnight,* alone, what else is to be done but *assume?*"

Theresa glanced to her father, but his face, too, was slightly red, and he was studying his knuckles. Suddenly she was angered by his spinelessness. She wished he'd say something one way or the other instead of being bulldozed by his outspoken wife all the time. Theresa faced her mother again. Though her stomach was churning, her voice remained relatively calm. "You might have asked, mother."

Margaret snorted and looked aside disdainfully.

"If you're going to assume, there's nothing I can do about it. And at my age I don't feel I have to justify myself to you. I'm going and that's all—''

"Over my dead body, you're going!" Margaret lurched from her chair, but at that moment, unbelievably, Willard intervened.

"Sit down, Margaret," he ordered, gripping her arm. Margaret turned her fury on him.

"If she lives in our house, she lives by rules of decency!"

Tears stung Theresa's eyes. It was as she'd known it would be. With her mother there was no discussing things. There hadn't been when Theresa was fourteen and sought consolation over her changing body, and there wasn't now.

"Margaret, she's twenty-five years old," Willard reasoned, "closer to twenty-six."

Margaret pushed his hand off her arm. "And some sterling example for Amy to follow."

The words sliced deeply in their unfairness. "I've always been—"

But again, Willard interceded. "Amy's values are pretty much in place, don't you think, Margaret? Just like Theresa's were when she was that age."

Margaret's eyes were rapiers as she glared at her husband. It was the first time in Theresa's life she'd ever seen him stand up to her. And certainly, she'd never seen or heard them fight.

"Willard, how can you say such a thing? Why, when you and I were—"

"When you and I were her age it was 1955, and we'd already been married for a couple of years and had a house of our own without your mother telling you or me what to do."

Theresa could have kissed her father's flushed cheeks. It was like discovering some hidden person, much like herself, who'd been hiding inside Willard Brubaker all these years. What a revelation to see that person assert himself at last.

"Willard, how in the world can you as much as give permission to your own daughter to go off—"

"That's enough, Margaret!" He rose to his feet and turned her quite forcefully toward the doorway. "I've let you steamroll me for a lot of years, but now I think it's time we discussed this in the bedroom!"

"Willard, if you...she can't...."

He led her, sputtering, down the hall until the sound of his voice drifted back. "I think it's time you rememb—" Then the closing bedroom door cut off his words.

Theresa didn't know they were in the kitchen later that night when she roamed restlessly from her room thinking, she'd get something to drink, then maybe she'd be able to fall asleep.

They were standing in the shadows of the sparsely lit room when Theresa came up short in the dark entry, realizing she was intruding. She could see little of her mother, who stood in front of Willard. Their backs were to Theresa, their feet bare, and they wore tired old robes she'd seen around the house for years. But from the movement of her father's elbows, she suspected his hands were pleasantly occupied. A soft moan came from the throat of the woman who was so glib at issuing orders. "Will...oh, Will..." she whispered.

As Theresa unobtrusively dissolved into the shadow of the hall and crept back to her room, she heard the murmur of her father's very young-sounding chuckle.

In the morning the word Fargo didn't come up, nor did the name Brian Scanlon. Margaret was as mellow as a softly plucked harp, wishing Theresa good morning before humming her way toward the bathroom with a cup of coffee. The sound of Willard's shaver buzzed louder as the door opened. Then, from far way, she heard laughter.

It was Willard who sought out Theresa in her bedroom at the end of that day and questioned quietly from the doorway, "Are you planning to drive up to Fargo?"

Theresa looked up in surprise. "Yes, I am."

He scratched his chin contemplatively. "Well, then I'd better take a look at that car of yours, in case anything needs tunin' up." He began to turn away.

"Daddy?"

He stopped and turned. Her arms opened as she came across the soft pink carpet on bare feet. "Oh, daddy, I love you," she said against his less-than-firm jowl as his arms tightened around her. A hand came up to pet her head with heavy, loving strokes. Rough, then gentling a bit. "But I think I love him, too."

"I know, pet. I know."

And so it was, from Willard, the quiet one, the unassertive one, Theresa learned a lesson about the power of love.

Chapter Ten

The five-hour drive from Minneapolis to Fargo was the longest Theresa had ever made alone. She'd worried about getting drowsy while driving but found her mind too active to get sleepy behind the wheel. Pictures of Brian, memories of last Christmas and anticipation of the next three days filled her thoughts. At times she'd find herself smiling widely, realizing a rich appreciation for the rolling farmland through which she drove, as if her newly expanded emotions had opened her senses to things she'd never noticed before: how truly beautiful tilled black soil can be, how vibrant the green of new grass. She passed a pasture where newborn calves suckled their mothers, and for a moment her thoughts turned dour, but she wouldn't allow herself to think of anything except the thrill of seeing Brian again.

The sapphire lakes of the Alexandria area gave way to the undulating farmland of Fergus Falls, then the earth gradually flattened as the vast deltaland of the Red River of the North spread as far as the eye could see: wheat and potato fields stretching endlessly on either side of the highway. Moorhead, Minnesota, appeared on the horizon, and as Theresa crossed the Red River that divided it from its sister city, Fargo, on the Dakota side, her hands were clammy, clutching the wheel.

She pulled the car into the parking space before the Doublewood Inn, then sat staring at the place for a full minute. It was the first time in her life that Theresa was checking in to a motel by herself.

You're only having last-minute jitters, Theresa. Just because the sign says Motel doesn't mean you're doing anything prurient by checking in to the place.

The lobby was beautiful, carpeted in deep, rich green, decorated with Scandinavian furniture of butcher-block coloring and a plethora of live green plants that seemed to bring the golden spring day inside.

"Good morning," greeted the desk clerk.

"Good morning. I have a reservation." She felt conspicuous and suddenly wished the clerk were a woman instead of a man—a woman would sense her honorable intentions, she thought irrationally. "My name is Theresa Brubaker."

"Brubaker," he repeated checking his records, handing her a card to sign. In no time at all she had a key in her hand, and to her surprise the clerk told her brightly, "Oh, Miss Brubaker, your other party has already arrived. Mr. Scanlon is in Room 108, right next to yours." She glanced at her key: 106. Suddenly it was all real. She felt her face coloring and thanked the clerk, then turned away before he could see her discomposure.

She drove around to the back of the motel, wondering if their rooms faced this side, if Brian was watching her from one of the windows above. She found herself unable to glance up and peruse the spaces on which the draperies were drawn back. If he was watching her, she didn't want to know it. Inside, she stopped before room 108. Staring at the number on his door, her heart thudded. The suitcases grew heavy and threatened to slip from her sweating palms. *He's in there. I'm standing no more than twenty feet from him right now.* It was odd, but now that she was here she was suddenly reluctant to face him. What if either of them had changed in some way since Christmas? What if the attraction had somehow faded? *What will I say to him? What if it's awkward? What if... what if....*

Her own door was only one foot away from his. She opened it and stepped into a room carpeted in tarnished gold with a queen-size bed, a dresser, console, mirror and television. Nothing extraordinary, but to Theresa, experiencing independence for the first time, the room seemed sumptuous. She set her luggage down, sat on the end of the bed, bounced once, walked into the tiled bathroom, turned on the light, switched it off, crossed the long main room to open the draperies, switched on the TV, then switched it off again at the first hint of sound and color, unzipped her suitcase, hung up some garments near the door, then looked around uncertainly.

You're only delaying the inevitable, Theresa Brubaker. She stared at the wall, wondering what he was doing on the other side of it. *Just a minute more and my nerves will calm. I'd better check my makeup.* The mirror revealed everything fresh and unsmudged except her lips, which needed color. She dug out her lipstick and applied it with a shaking hand. It tasted faintly peachy and contained flecks of gold that glistened beneath the light when she moved. *You don't put on fresh lipstick when you want a man to kiss you, Brubaker, you dolt.* She jerked a white tissue from the dispenser on the wall and swiped it swiftly across her lips, removing all but a faint smudge of remaining color. The tissues was rough and left her lips looking faintly red and chapped around the edge. Nervously she uncapped the silver tube and reapplied the peachy gloss. She met her own eyes in the mirror. They were wide and bright with anticipation. But they were not smiling. She glanced at her breasts beneath the baby blue blouse she'd bought new for this occasion. She wore no sweater today, but felt naked without it, though the tiny blue heart-shaped buttons went from the waist of her white skirt up to the tight mandarin collar that was edged with a blue ruffle. The short gathered sleeves of the blouse had a matching miniature ruffle around their cuffs. Suddenly the puffy sleeves seemed to accentuate the size of her breasts but she forced herself to look instead at her very tiny waistband into which the blouse was securely tucked.

All it takes is a knock on his door, and this uncertainty will be over.

A minute later she rapped on 108 twice, but at the third flick of her wrist her knuckles struck air, for the door was already being flung open.

He stood motionless for a long moment, one hand on the doorknob. She, with her knuckles in the air, stared at him wordlessly. Theresa saw nothing but Brian's face, the searching green eyes with their dark spiky lashes, the lips open slightly, the familiar nose, short hair, cheeks shaven so recently they still shone. Then she became aware of how accentuated his breathing was. The form-fitting baby blue knit shirt fit his chest like liquid, hiding no trace of the swiftly rising and falling muscle beneath it.

Her body felt warm, thrumming, yet uncertain. She wanted to smile but stood immobile, staring at the face before her as if he were an apparition.

"Theresa," was all he said, then he reached out a hand and caught hers, drawing her into the room with firm certainty. And still he didn't smile, but only found her free hand, gripping both palms with viselike tenacity while gazing unwaveringly into her eyes. He swung her around, then turned his back to the door and closed it with his hips. "You're really here," he said hoarsely.

"I'm really here." What had happened to all the charming greetings she'd rehearsed for days? What had happened to the smooth entrance with all its urbane chic, meant to put them both on a strictly friendly basis from the first moment? Why wouldn't her lips smile? Her voice work? Her knees stop trembling?

Suddenly she was catapulted into his arms as he thrust forward, hugging her body full against his and taking her mouth with a slanting, wide, possessive kiss. Nothing gentle. Nothing hinting at easing into old familiarities, but the familiarity arising magically between them with all its stomach-lifting force. She found her arms around his trunk, hands pressed against his warm back. And, wonder of wonders, his heart was slamming against her so vibrantly she could feel the very difference between its beats. Her own heart seemed to lift each cell of her skin, sealing off her throat with its solid hammering. His hands at first forced her close, as if he couldn't get close enough, but then as their tongues joined in sleek reunion, Brian's palms roved in wide circles on her back, and as if it were the most natural thing in the world, he drew them up both her sides simultaneously, pressing her breasts, reaching inward with two long thumbs to seek her nipples briefly. His left arm returned to her back and he angled away from her slightly, cupping one breast fully, then exploring it through her blouse and brassiere while his tongue gentled within her mouth. Shudders climbed her vertebrae and raised the hairs along the back of her thighs while the pressure on her nipples continued in faint, sensuous, circular movements. It was so natural. So right. Theresa had no thoughts of stopping his explorations. They seemed as much a valid part of this reunion as the looks of reaffirmation they'd exchanged when she first stood before him.

The kiss went on unbrokenly as his hands clasped her narrow hipbones and pulled her pelvis securely against his. He rocked against her, undulating, weaving from side to side, pressing his most masculine muscles against her acquiescent stomach. Without realizing it, she found herself meeting each stroke of his hips, pressing against him, lifting up on tiptoe because he was so much taller and she yearned to feel his hardness closer to her point of desire.

Still clasping her hips, Brian ended the kiss. His warm palms pushed downward until her heels again touched the floor, then he held her firmly, so she couldn't move. He rested his forehead against hers while their strident breaths mingled, and their moist lips hovered close, swollen and still open.

Her hands were still on his back. She felt the muscles grow taut with resolution as he pressed firmly on her hipbones. It suddenly struck her how easily these things happen, how readily she had lifted against him, how opportune was the hand of Nature in making a body thrust and ebb when the circumstances called for it.

She was chagrined to think that now he might believe she'd come here with sex in mind. She hadn't, not at all. But how fast her body had dictated its wishes.

"I was so scared to knock on that door," she admitted. He lifted his forehead from hers, bracketed her cheeks with his palms and studied her at close range.

"Why?"

"Because I thought...." His eyes were as stunning as she remembered. They wore an expression of ardency that surprised her. "I thought, what if things aren't the same between us? What if we imagined...this?"

His thumbs brushed the corners of her mouth. His lips were parted and glittered with fragments of gloss from her lipstick. "Silly girl," he whispered, before pulling her face upward to meet his descending one. Again she raised on tiptoe, but this time their bodies barely brushed. The peach-flavored kiss was bestowed by his tongue and lips in a testing circle around her mouth, tugging, wetting once again while his hands drew upon her jaws, first lifting her, then letting her recede as if she were drifting in the surf, mastered by its rush and release. "Oh, Theresa," he murmured while her eyes fell closed. "Nothing's changed for me. Nothing at all." He pressed her away only far enough to gaze into her eyes. "Has it for you?"

How incredible that he should ask. He, who emerged so flawless in her loving eyes. When she studied him again, reality sccmcd to buckle her lungs and knees. The expression in his eyes said he'd been as uncertain as she had. Theresa ran her hands from his elbows along his hard arms to the wrists. "Nothing," she whispered, allowing her eyelids to close once more while pulling first his left hand from her jaw to kiss its palm, then doing likewise with his right. "Nothing." She looked into his somber eyes and watched them change, grow light, relieved. Her gaze dropped to his mouth. "You have more of my lipstick on than I do."

He smiled and hauled her close, speaking against her mouth so that she could scarcely discern the words. "So clean me up." Her tongue seemed drawn to his by some magical attraction, and she learned a new delight in taking command during a kiss.

"Mmm...you taste good," she ventured, backing away only slightly. She ran her nose along his jaw. "And you smell good, just like I remember, only stronger." She backed away and ran a fingertip over his jaw. "You just shaved."

He grinned, his hands now on her back, holding her against him, but undemandingly. "Just like a teenager getting ready for his first date."

"How long have you been here?"

"Twenty minutes or so. How long have you?"

"About ten minutes. I was in my room, putting on fresh lipstick, then wiping it off, then putting it on again and wondering which was the right thing to do. I was so nervous."

Suddenly it struck them how funny it was that they'd been so apprehensive. They laughed together, then gazed into each other's eyes, and without warning simultaneously answered the compulsion to hug. Their arms went about each other—tight, tight—reaffirming. His hands roved her back. Hers touched his hair. When he backed away, he looped his hands around her hips until she rested against his again.

"What do you want to do first?" he asked.

"I don't know. Just...." Her heart pulsed crazily. "Just look at you some more." She shrugged shyly. "I don't know."

He moved not a muscle for a long, silent moment. Then he nudged her backward with his thighs, directing her shoulders with his hands. "Come here then. Let's indulge ourselves for a while." He lifted a knee to the bed, then fell, tugging her along till they lay on their sides, each with an elbow folded beneath an ear. He rested a hand on her hip. Their eyes locked, their feet trailed off the end of the mattress.

Incredible. She had been in his room less than five minutes and already she was lying on the bed with him. But she had no desire to get up or to protest at his taking her there. His head lifted slowly. His mouth covered hers, urging her lips open once again, his tongue delving into the soft recesses, tickling the skin of her inner cheeks then threading its tip along her teeth, as if counting each. Her body came alive with desire, and her breathing grew fast and harsh, as did his. But when he'd explored to his satisfaction, he lay as before, head upon elbow, his hand still resting on her hip, but undemandingly.

It seemed best to set things straight immediately. Timidity brought color rushing to Theresa's face and made her voice unnatural. "Brian, I...." His eyes were so close, so intense, burning into hers. "I didn't come here because I was ready to go all the way with you."

His hand left her hip and fell to the hollow of her waist. "I know. And I didn't come here to force you to. But I want to. You know that, don't you?"

"I'm not ready for that, Brian, no matter what I...well, I might have led you to believe something else when we first kissed."

"I think we're both in for a hell of a weekend then. It's not going to be easy. Obviously your conscience and your libido are at odds." His hands left her waist, squeezed her upper arm gently, then caressed its length until his hand rested on the back of hers. "And my libido...well, there's no hiding it, is there?" Then, unceremoniously, he carried her hand to the zipper placket of his white brushed cotton slacks. It happened so unexpectedly she had neither the time nor inclination to pull away. One moment her hand rested on his hip, the next it was flattened along his zipper, and he'd raised his upper knee as he gently forced her fingers to conform to the ridge of hot, hard flesh within. His hand disappeared from atop hers and he rolled closer, letting his eyes drift closed as he spoke gruffly against the hollow of her throat. "I'm sorry if I'm too direct, but I want you to know...whatever you choose is what we'll do, as much or as little as you want. I'd be a damned liar if I said I wasn't thinking about making love to you ever since last January when I left you crying in that airport."

While he spoke, his body undulated against her palm, then she reluctantly slipped her hand up his shirtfront and pressed it against his chest. Beneath her palm his heart thudded crazily.

"Shh...Brian, don't say that."

He backed away, pinning her with a distracting, direct gaze. "Why? Because it's true of you, too?"

"Shh." She rested an index finger on his lips. He stared at her silently until at last the fires in his eyes seemed to subside. He clasped the back of the hand at his mouth, kissed its palm, then threaded its fingers through his own. "All right. Are you hungry?"

She smiled. "Ravenous."

"Should we go and find something to eat, then hit all the highlights of Fargo, North Dakota?"

"Let's."

With one lithe motion he was at the foot of the bed, one foot on the floor, the other knee on the mattress. He hauled her up against him and she landed on her knees with her arms around his neck, and his hands on her buttocks. He kissed her fleetingly, then rubbed the end of her nose with his own. "God, it's good to be with you again. Let's get out of here before I change my mind." With a squeeze and a pat he turned her loose.

They were walking hand in hand along the Broadway Mall in downtown Fargo when they suddenly stopped and stared each other up and down, then burst out laughing.

"You're wearing—"

"Do you realize—" they said in unison, then laughed again, standing back, assessing each other's clothing. They were both wearing white slacks, and the baby blue of her ruffle-necked blouse closely matched that of his knit pullover. She wore white tennis shoes on her feet and he white leather sport shoes with a Velcro-closed strap across the arch of his foot.

"If we dressed to please each other, I think we both did a good job," he said with a smile. "I like your blouse."

"And I like your shirt." Again they laughed, then caught hands as they moved on, exploring the entire three-block length of the mall from Main to Second Avenues. At its south end they studied the Luis Jimenez sculpture depicting a prairie farmer behind a pair of oxen, breaking sod for the first time. Sauntering northward they discovered that the curving mall was designed to represent the pathway of the Red River, and that carved granite markers of red, gray and brown had been set into the concrete on either side of the street to represent the cities flanking the great river as it coursed the length of North Dakota from Wahpeton to Pembina. As they sauntered, they read the names of the towns on the North Dakota side and the dates of their founding: Hunter, 1881; Grandin, 1881; Arthur, 1880. The stones were set varying distances from the street to depict the setback between the actual towns and the great life-giving river that fed the area.

The sun was warm on their backs, the sky overhead flawless cerulean. They had a sense of calm and an even greater one of delight in being together, swinging hands, watching their white-clad legs matching strides. The mall was dotted with redwood planters in which geraniums and petunias had been set out, and all along the mall's length ash trees were beginning to break into first leaf. At the Old Broadway Café, they peered into the twin oval windows on the front doors and decided to give the old landmark a try. Inside, the booths were the high private cubicles of another era, dark-varnished and set with stained-glass panels. The floor was ancient oiled hardwood that creaked and croaked as the waitress delivered their plate dinners of thick-slicked beef, potatoes and gravy and golden, buttered carrots.

"You haven't mentioned your mom and dad," Brian said, studying Theresa across the booth. "What did they say when you told them you were coming up here to meet me?"

She met his serious green eyes and decided to tell him the truth. "Mother assumed the worst. It wasn't a very pleasant scene." She dropped her eyes to her plate, drawing circles on it with a piece of beef.

Beneath the table his calf found hers and rubbed it reassuringly. He closed his ankles around one of hers and stopped the hand that had been pushing her fork in circles. She looked up at him.

"I'm sorry."

She laid her hand atop his. "Don't be. Something quite wonderful came about because of it." Wonder showed in her face. "Daddy. Would you believe he finally stood up to mother?"

"Willard?" Brian asked in surprise.

"Willard," she confirmed, still with the amazed expression on her face. "He shouted 'Margaret, that's enough' and...and...." Theresa had great difficulty not smirking. "And hauled her off to the bedroom, slammed the door, and the next time I saw them she was calling him Will, and the two of them were cooing like mourning doves. That was the end of Mother's resistance."

Brian dropped his fork with a clatter, threw his hands in the air and praised, "Hallelujah!"

They were still chuckling about it when they returned to the mall. They continued their stroll past The Classic Jewelers, stock-brokerage houses, Straus Drugs and so to the far north end where they discovered the Fargo Theater with its vintage art deco marquee announcing that Charlie Chaplin was playing tonight in *The Bank*.

"Do you like silent movies?" Brian asked hopefully.

"Love 'em." She grinned up at him.

"Whaddya say, should we give old Charlie a try tonight?"

"Oh, I'd love to."

"It's a date." He squeezed her hand, then led her across the street and they started back along the "Minnesota" side of the mall, reading the town names, peering in store windows. In one called Mr. T's, a bridal gown was displayed. Without realizing it, Theresa's feet stopped moving, and she stared at the mannequin. The sight of the white gown and veil, symbols of purity, brought to mind the coming night, the choice she had to make. She thought about other men she might meet in her life, the one she might possibly marry, and what he would think if she did not come to him as a virgin. But she found it impossible to imagine herself being intimate with any man but Brian.

While Theresa gazed at the bridal gown, two young men passed along the sidewalk. Brian watched their eyes assess her breasts—blatantly, neither of them trying to disguise their fascination. Their heads swiveled, gazes lingering as they drew alongside, then passed her. When they moved on, one of them must have made a lewd comment, for he did a little hip-swinging jive step while patting his thighs, then his companion laughed.

Brian was at first angry. Then he found himself assessing her breasts as a stranger would, and found, to his chagrin, that he was slightly embarrassed. Guilt followed immediately. He fought to submerge it, studying the back of Theresa's head as she gazed up innocently at the window display. But as they moved on up the mall, he was conscious of the eyes of each man they met. Without exception, they all dropped to Theresa's breasts, and Brian's discomfort grew.

Scanlon, you're a hypocrite. The thought was distinctly nettlesome, so he hooked an arm around Theresa's neck, settled her against his hip as they ambled back to the car, and when they reached it, he gave her a tender kiss of apology. Her hands rested on his chest. When she opened her eyes they held a dreamy expression, and he felt small and unworthy for a moment, realizing how hurt she'd be if she suspected he'd been embarrassed over her generous endowment. He traced the outline of her lips with a single finger and said softly, "What do you say we get away from people for a while?"

"I thought you'd never ask."

He smiled, kissed her nose, settled her inside, then started the engine. They crossed the river into Moorhead, drove out onto the blacktop highway heading east, then left it behind to wander the back roads between green woods, brown fields and blue ponds where ducks and blackbirds nested. Spring was burgeoning all around them. They felt it in the renewed warmth of the sun, smelled it in the damp earth, heard it as the sound of wildlife lifted through the air.

They discovered the lush wilds of the Buffalo River where it surged under a culvert beneath their gravel road. Brian pulled to the side, turned off the engine and invited, "Let's walk." She slipped her hand into his with a glad heart, letting him lead her down the steep bank to the dappled woods, where they picked their way aimlessly along the surging spring-swelled waters that rumbled southward. The river sang to them. The tangled roots of a long-fallen tree stood silver in their path. Brian led the way along the massive trunk to a spot where he could mount it, then reached down and helped Theresa up beside him. He walked the weathered trunk to its highest point, with her right behind him. Now the river flowed at their feet. A fish leaped. A trio of sparrows darted from the underbrush to the tangled roots of their tree. From far away a crow scolded. Everything smelled fecund, growing, renewed. From behind, Theresa lightly rested her hands on Brian's hips. He remained as before, unmoving, imbibing, gathering sweet memories. His hands covered hers, drew them firmly around his belt, and his arms covered hers while she pressed her cheek and breasts against his firm, warm back. A blue jay carped from a loblolly pine, and the sun shimmered on the forest floor through the partially sprouted leaves of the surrounding trees. Against Brian's back Theresa's heart thrummed steadily. His palms rubbed her arms, which were warm with gathered sunshine.

"Ahh..." he sighed, tilted his head back, said no more.

She kissed the center of his back. It was enough.

In time they moved on through the gold-and-green afternoon. As they ambled, they caught up on the past three months. Brian had stories about Jeff and air-force rigors, the band, the music they'd been working on. Theresa had anecdotes about life with a teenage sister, incidents from school, plans for spring concerts.

But none of it mattered. Only being together had meaning for them.

They found a nest with three speckled eggs, built in the reeds where the river backwashed and bent. They turned back as the afternoon waned and hunger imposed its demands. They kissed in a basswood grove, then climbed the pebbled bank again and settled into the car for the ride back to town. At their doors in the motel Brian said, "I'll pick you up at your place in half an hour." A quick kiss and they parted.

Chapter Eleven

The knock at her door announced a freshly showered and shaved Brian dressed in tight tan jeans, an open-collared shirt of pale tan-blue-white plaid, and a lightweight sport coat the color of an almond shell. She took one look and felt her mouth watering.

"Wow," she breathed.

He smiled guilelessly, looking down at himself and said, "Oh yeah?" Then he closed the door, eased his hips back against it, crossed his arms and grinned. "Come over here and say that, Brubaker."

She felt herself blushing, but swung away teasingly. "I'm not one of your groupies, Scanlon."

She was securing the latch of a trim gold bracelet when his strong hands closed over her wrists, dragging them around his neck. His eyes, ardent and determined, blazed into hers. "God, there are times when I wish you were." His mouth was warm, open and moist as it marauded hers. He swirled his tongue around her freshly applied lipstick, then delved brashly inside to stroke her teeth until they opened at his command. His tongue probed rhythmically in and out of her mouth, suggesting what was on his mind. He tasted of freshly brushed teeth and smelled like chrysanthemums and sage—not flowery, but spicy clean. He pulled back suddenly, leaving no question about the price he was paying for control. His stormy eyes sought and held hers. Then the storm cleared, he relaxed. His thumbs, still at her wrists, stroked lightly. Now it was his turn to declare breathily, "Wow."

Theresa's heart proved what a healthy, red-blooded twenty-five-year-old virgin she was. She was certain he could see it lifting the bodice of her blouse. She whispered thickly, "Let's go see what Charlie's up to."

At the Fargo Theater they were treated to a sensational performance by a local member of the American Theater Organ Society on an immense and wondrous pipe organ that rose out of the floor on a pneumatic lift. They sat in the balcony, because it was a dying species they'd have few more chances to experience. Theresa learned how readily Brian laughed at slapstick. While the organist tickled out an accompaniment, Charlie Chaplin duckwalked down a city street in his oversize shoes and baggy pants, went three times around a revolving door, then spent arduous moments whirling the dials of an imposing-looking vault. Brian snickered, slunk low in his seat. The vault door swung open and the lovable Charlie disappeared inside to return with his precious deposit: a scrub pail, mop and janitor's uniform. Brian rolled his head backward and hooted with full throat while Theresa's heart warmed more to the man beside her than to the one on the screen.

The organ created a musical echo of Charlie's misfortunes in leaving flowers for the black-eyed Edna Purviance, only to have the damsel believe they were a gift from the bank clerk named Charlie. When skulduggery started, the organ rumbled dramatically, creating vibrations through the theater seats. Beside her, Brian slumped low in his seat, trembling melodramatically, tossing his popcorn in the air when the heroine was tied and gagged, stamping and cheering when Chaplin came to her rescue, boo-hooing when the poor unfortunate bank custodian was left awakening from a dream, petting the rags of his floor mop instead of the waves of the damsel's head.

When the film ended and they returned to the street, Brian performed a superb imitation of Chaplin, knees crooked outward, shoulders rolling with his peculiar gait while he scratched his head with stiff fingers and made a vain attempt to open the door of the wrong car. He gave a Chaplinesque flap of the hands, looked around, dismayed, sad-eyed.

How easy it was for Theresa to gasp and clasp her hands before her, distraught at misfortune. She ran jerkily to her car, flung the door open, then stood on the pavement with eyes rolled heavenward in invitation.

Charlie Scanlon duckwalked to her, shyly studied his feet, swept into a clumsy bow, then waved her inside. She interlaced her fingers, simpered, then got in.

Brian made a swipe at the open door, missed, spun in a circle, missed again, spun another circle and finally connected with the difficult door and managed to slam it.

When he climbed in beside her and squeezed the invisible bulb of a horn and made a flatulent-sounding "T-o-o-t" out the side of his mouth, they wilted with laughter. In time they grew too weak to continue. Then they looked at each other in silent discovery.

They ate an Italian supper at a place chosen at random, reminiscing about old movies, but always thinking about the end of the evening ahead. Would it bring *good night* or *good morning*?

Laughter was gone when they walked slowly, slowly down the hall to their doors. They stopped dead center between 106 and 108.

"Can I come in?" he asked quietly at last.

She met his searching eyes, feeling the awesome tugs of carnality and denial warping her heart. She remembered her mother's words, the bridal gown in the window. She touched his chest lightly. "Will you understand how hard it is for me that I have to answer no?"

His hands hung loosely at his sides. He sucked in a huge gulp of air, dropped his head down as his eyes closed, then braced both hands tiredly on his hips and studied the toes of his brown boots.

She felt childish and unworthy. Tears began to burn her eyelids.

He saw and pulled her close, resting his chin against her hair. Though his body rested only lightly against hers, she was close enough to know that her nearness and this compulsion they both controlled so closely had aroused him. "I'm sorry, sweets," he whispered. "You're right and I'm wrong. But that doesn't make it any easier."

"Kiss me, Brian," she begged.

He took her head in both hands and tipped her face up for a deep, hungering kiss. But the pressure of his hands on her jaw and ears told of where he wanted those hands to be. And she clung to his wrists—the safest place—feeling beneath one thumb the surging rhythm of his pulse. They drew apart, troubled eyes clinging.

"Good night," he said raggedly.

"Good night," came her unsure reply.

Neither of them slept well, they confessed over breakfast. The day lolled before them; its hours would be too short, no matter how they were spent. Yet when considered in the light of their denial, those same hours seemed infinite. They browsed through West Acres Shopping Center, ate lunch in a McDonald's because their stomachs demanded filling, but neither of them cared the least about food. They roamed the green hills of Island Park and sat in its gazebo watching a group of children playing softball across the expanse of green grass. They had supper in the motel dining room, and afterward wandered into the casino where new laws allowed gambling with a two-dollar limit. But while Brian sat at a table playing blackjack, a man with sleek black hair, wearing an expensive silk suit, sidled up to Theresa, gave her a blatant visual assessment, slipped his hands to her hips and whispered in her ear, "You alone, baby?"

It happened so fast Theresa hadn't time to react until the cloying scent of his after-shave seemed to plug her nostrils, and his wandering hands registered their insult.

Suddenly Brian interceded. "Get your hands off her, buddy," he growled, jerking the man's arm, spinning him away from Theresa, whose stunned eyes were wide and alarmed.

The man's eyes narrowed dangerously, then eased as lascivious speculation crossed his features. He pulled free of Brian's hand, shrugged his shoulder to right the expensive suit jacket, and his eyes roved once over Theresa's breasts. "Can't say I blame you, fella. If those were mine for the night, I wouldn't be too quick to share 'em either."

Theresa saw the muscles bunch in Brian's jaw. His fists clenched.

"Don't, Brian!" She stepped between the two men, facing Brian, gripping his arm in an effort to turn him away. "He's not worth it," she pleaded. His arm remained steeled. "Please!" she whispered.

But Brian's livid face scarcely registered if he'd heard. He moved with mechanical deliberation, reaching down without looking to grasp Theresa's hand and remove it from his jacket. Then slowly, menacingly he clutched the man's lapels, lifting until his toes scarcely touched the carpet.

"You will apologize to the lady right now," Brian ground out, "or your teeth will be biting your own ass, from the inside out." Brian's voice was chilling as he held the stranger aloft, nose to nose.

"Okay, okay. Sorry lady, I didn't know—"

Brian jerked him up another inch. Stitches popped on the expensive jacket. "You call that an apology, sucker? See if you can't do better."

The man's eyes were bugging. Sweat erupted on his sheeny forehead and beneath his lizardlike nose. "I...I'm really sorry, m...miss. I'd like to b...buy you both a drink if you'd let me."

Brian slammed him back down to the floor, released his lapels distastefully while shoving the unpalatable intruder back until he stumbled against a table. "Pour your goddamn drinks in your pants, buddy. Maybe it'll cool you off." He turned. "Let's get out of here, Theresa." His fingers were like brands as he led her by an arm to the casino door, then out into the carpeted hall. She felt his hand trembling on her elbow and had to run to keep up with him. Wordlessly he turned down the hall to their rooms and was fishing in his trousers pockets for the key even before they reached their destination. When he leaned to insert the key into 108, there was no question of where he expected her to go. The door swung back and he found her hand, leading her inside. There followed a solid thud, then they were ensconced in a world of unbroken black. His arms closed convulsively around her, his body pressed close, sheltering, rocking her as he spoke gruffly against her hair. "I'm sorry, sweets, God, I'm so sorry."

"Brian, it's all right." But she was still shaken and vulnerable and, now that it was over, felt like crying. But his protection eradicated the sudden need for tears. His arms had strength she'd never suspected. They clamped her so hard her back hurt as he bent it in a bow.

"God, I wanted to kill him!" Brian's fingers dug into her flesh, just below and behind her armpits, and she winced, lifting her hands instinctively to press against his chest.

"Brian, it doesn't matter...please, you're hurting me."

The pressure fell away. He jerked as if shot. "I'm sorry...I'm sorry... sorry...." The voice was pained in the darkness, then his hands were gentle on her, finding her face in the inkiness, fingertips caressing her temples, then sliding into her hair as his mouth sought hers. "Theresa...Theresa..." he muttered, then circled her again with his arms. "I'd never hurt you, but I want you, you know that. God, I'm no better than him,'' Brian finished miserably, then took her mouth with an abandon that sent tongues of fire licking down her stomach. His hands left her back and roamed up her sides, pressing hard, too hard, as if it were compulsion he was trying to fight. She clung, unwilling to stop him yet, blessing the darkness.

His caress trailed down over her small waist, took measure of her hipbones, then traveled with uniform pressure down her buttocks, cupping them, pulling her up and inward against his tormented body. Along her sides his warm hands moved, compressing the swelling sides of her breasts until all else ceased to matter but that she know more of the treasured warmth of his palms upon them.

In the dense blackness she felt herself swept off the floor. Her arms instinctively encircled Brian's neck. In four steps he reached the bed and set her upon it, then joined her.

"Brian, we should stop..." she whispered against his mouth.

His tongue drove deep once more, then he softly nipped her lips. "We'll stop whenever you say." His kiss made dissent impossible, and then so did his touch. He covered her breasts with both wide palms, pressing down hard and flat and firm, for she lay with her torso precisely aligned with his. He found her hand in the dark, clamped his fingers over the back of it, carried it to his mouth and bit the outer edge, then turned its palm against her own breast. "Feel," he whispered fiercely, rolling aside. The nipple was distended. Even through her bra and summer sweater she could feel it. "Let me touch it too." Again he kissed her hand, then placed it on his ribs. "Let me teach you how good it can feel."

She could see nothing in the infinite darkness, but as she was devoid of sight, her other senses sharpened. His spicy smell, his brandy taste, the slight tremor in his voice were all magnified in their appeal. But above all, her body seemed finely honed to the sense of touch. His breath was like the whisk of a feather upon her face, the dampness his kiss had left felt cool on her lips, the hard contours of his masculinity took on nearly visible form, the seeking conviction of his hands moving toward the clasp of her bra was felt as if from another supremely sensitive dimension.

She whimpered softly, lifting a shoulder. The clasp parted and her breasts were free. But Brian's elbows remained at her sides, bracing him above her. Across her face he took soft, teasing nips with his teeth: chin, cheek, nostril, lip, jaw, even eyebrow—bone and all. The bites grew more evocative, tightening the coil of tension in her stomach. His hands splayed over her bare back. "Theresa...so soft," he murmured, knowing the full length and width of that vulnerably soft skin, then kneading it gently. "So innocent." In one smooth motion his hands skimmed her circumference while his hips pinned hers securely. Sweater and bra were eased up by his hands. Then the objects of her long despair became those of her awakening sexuality as they were enveloped in his palms—skin on skin, warm on warm, man on woman.

It was so good, so right, and made her yearn for the forbidden.

The callused fingers that knew a guitar's strings so intimately now plucked upon her, as one might surround and pluck the fragile seeds of a dandelion from its stalk, the span of his fingertips widening, narrowing, drawing upward, encouraging her nipples to follow and reach when his touch disappeared. And they did. Repeatedly her shoulders strained to follow, as if to say, please don't leave me yet.

His hips lay still upon hers, but his flesh was at its fullest, thick and solid between their bodies. At the moment she scarcely gave it a thought, so taken was she by the sweet swellings of these first caresses on her breasts. He turned his head aside and gently rubbed his hair across the naked nipples. "Ohh..." she sang softly, in delight, entwining her fingers in the hair at the crest of his skull, guiding his head, experiencing the silken texture upon her aroused flesh. A turn of that head, and now it was his cheek where his hair had been. Her hands neither commanded nor discouraged, but rested idly in his hair while she waited...waited....

And then it happened, the first wonder of his mouth upon her breast, a passing kiss of introduction—vague, soft—on her left nipple first, then upon her right. And she thought, *hello at last, my love.* Gradually, as he nuzzled, his lips parted until their sleek inner skin touched her. She felt the texture of teeth, closed yet, making her yearn for them to open, allowing entry. So still she lay, as still as a butterfly poised on a windless day—feeling, feeling, feeling. His silken tongue came to introduce her flesh into his mouth and lead her within where all was wet, warm and slippery soft.

"Ohhh...Bri...." His name drifted into silence, lost to the grander passion now building.

"Mmm..." he murmured, a sound of praise, while the warm breath from his nostrils dampened the swell of skin beyond reach of his mouth. "Mmm...." He was tugging now, sucking more powerfully until she twisted slightly in satisfaction. To each of her breasts he brought adulation, until it felt the threads of femininity seemed drawn from deeper within her...up, up, and into the man whose mouth taught her pleasure.

Combing his hair with limp fingers she charted the movements of his head. "Oh, Brian, it's so good..." she murmured. "All these years I've wasted...."

He lunged up, dragging his hips along her thighs, joining swollen lips to hers. "We'll make up for them," he promised into her open mouth. "Shh...just feel...feel...."

When his mouth took her breast again, it was with acute knowledge of her need, and just how far he could go to send her senses soaring without hurting her. He caressed with his palms while capturing a taut nipple between the sharp edges of his teeth, scissoring until a keen, welcome sting made her gasp. Then there came a point beyond which the arousal of her breasts alone would no longer suffice. It was painful in its yearning. It made her lift to him, made him press to her. He found her mouth in the dark; it had fallen slack in the throes of desire. His was hotter now, and as they kissed he undulated above her until her knees parted of their own accord, creating a lee into which his body arched, rocking against her.

No more difficult words had she ever spoken. "Brian, please...I can't do this."

"I know...I know," came his rough whisper, but his mouth covered hers as he continued the sinuous rhythm along her body, bringing desire knocking upon her heart's door, seeking entry, just as his body sought entry to hers.

"Brian, please don't...or soon I won't be able to stop you." Her hands clenched in his hair, pulling his head back. "But I must, don't you see?"

He stilled. Stiffened.

"Don't move," he ordered gruffly. "Not a muscle." They lay with their breathing falling hard against each other until with a soft curse he rolled from the bed and in the black void she heard him make his way into the bathroom. A line of light spilled, casting his shadow against the wall as he grasped the edge of the sink and leaned against it, his head hanging down.

She lay utterly still. Her pulse throbbed throughout her body. She closed her eyes until Brian returned and sank down on the foot of the bed, leaning his elbows on his knees while running both hands through his hair. Then, with a groan he fell backward, hands flopped palms up.

She laid a hand in his, and at her touch his fingers clasped hers tightly. He rolled toward her, pressing his face against her hip. When he spoke his words were muffled against her.

"I'm sorry."

"And I'm sorry if I led you on and made you expect more."

"You didn't lead me on. You told me from the start that you weren't coming here with sex on your mind. It was me who pushed the issue after promising not to. I thought I had enough control to settle for kisses." He gave a soft, rueful laugh and flung an arm over his eyes.

But she *had* come into his room with sex on her mind, with at least as much as she'd experienced. She had wanted those precious moments because if she decided to have the surgery she might forfeit them forever. She felt a pang of guilt, for it seemed she'd used Brian for her own ends, and now he lay beside her apologizing for his very natural desire. She considered explaining to him, telling him about the surgery. But now that she'd known the rapture to be found beneath his lips, she was doubly unsure about proceeding with it. And furthermore, it was difficult for her to believe that when June came and he was freed to the civilian world, there would not be countless other women he'd find more attractive than herself. June was a key word often mentioned in their letters, but Theresa realized how easy it was for a lonely man to make plans for the future, but when that future came, how easily those plans could be changed. The thought hurt, but it was best to be honest with herself.

There were no promises made between them. And until there were, she must avoid situations such as this.

"Brian, it's late. I should go back to my room."

He rolled onto his back again, but his fingers remained laced with hers. "You could stay if you want to, and all we'll do is sleep side by side."

"No, I don't think I have that much willpower." When she sat up to straighten her clothing she felt him watching and wished the bathroom light was off, dim though it was. Her hair was tousled, her hands shaky.

"Theresa...." He reached for her with the plaintive word.

Softly she begged, "Let me go now without persuasion...please. I'm only one step away from changing my mind, but if I did I think we'd both be unhappy with ourselves."

His hand fell. He eased off the bed, helped her up and they walked silently to the door. It yawned open, and they stood studying the carpet.

He looped an elbow around her neck and drew her temple to his lips. "I'm not disappointed in you." The words rattled quietly in his throat.

Relief flooded Theresa and left her weak. She sagged against him. "You're so honest, Brian. I love that in you."

His eyes met hers, earnest yet troubled, and still with a flicker of desire in their depths. "Tomorrow will be hard enough, saying goodbye after being together like this. It would only have been harder if we'd given in."

She raised up on tiptoe, brushed his lips with hers, then touched them fleetingly with her fingertips.

"I had begun to think I'd never find you in this big old world, Brian Scanlon...." But she could say no more without crying, so slipped into the loneliness of her own room and closed the door between them.

Chapter Twelve

Their last day together was bittersweet. They wasted precious hours silently pondering the lonesomeness they'd feel at parting. They suffered recriminations about the night before. They counted the weeks of separation ahead. Laughter was rare, and forced, and followed by long gazing silences that left them more unfulfilled than ever.

They checked out at eleven and drove aimlessly until 1:00 p.m. Brian was flying standby on his return flight, so she took him to the airport where they sat in the coffee shop at a table by the window, unable to be cheered or consoled.

"You have a long drive ahead of you. I think you should go."

She lifted startled eyes to his. "No. I'll wait with you."

"But I may not catch a plane until late afternoon."

"But...I...." Her lips started quivering, so she clamped them together tightly.

"I know," he said softly. "But will it be any easier if you stay to watch my plane take off?"

Dismally she shook her head and stared at her coffee cup through distorting tears. His hand covered the back of hers, squeezing it hurting-hard, his thumb stroking hers upon the handle of the cup. "I want you to go," he claimed, yet the unsteady words laced his request with depression. "And I want you to do it smiling." The tears swelled fuller. He tilted her chin up with a finger. "Promise?"

She nodded, and the motion jarred the tears loose and sent them spilling down her freckled cheeks. Frantically she wiped them away and pasted on the smile he'd requested. "You're right. It's a five-hour drive...." She reached for her purse, babbling inanities, making her hands look busy with important stuff, foolish words pouring from her lips while Brian sat across the table smiling sadly. She fell silent in midsentence, folded her lower lip between her teeth and swallowed an enormous lump in her throat.

"Walk me to the car?" she asked so low he could hardly hear.

Without a word he dropped some change on the table and rose. She moved a step ahead of him, but felt his hand at her elbow then sliding down to capture her fingers and hold them tighter. Then tighter.

At the car they stopped. Both of them stared at the metal strip around the driver's door. A truck pulled up beside them, someone got out and walked toward the terminal. Brian lifted Theresa's hand and studied its palm while scratching at it repeatedly with his thumbnail.

"Thank you for coming, Treece."

She felt as if she were suffocating. "I had a g...good...." But she couldn't finish, and when the sob broke, he jerked her roughly into his arms. A hand clamped the back of her head. Her fingers clenched the back of his shirt. His scent was thick and nostalgic where her nose was pushed flat against his chest.

"Drive safely." His voice rumbled a full octave lower than usual.

"Say h...hi to J...Jeff."

"June will be here before we know it." But she was afraid to think of June. What if he didn't come back to her after all? He was holding her so close all she could make out through her tears was the soft gray of his shirt. "Now I'm going to kiss you, then you get in that car and drive, do you understand?"

She nodded, her cheek rubbing a wide damp spot on the gray cloth.

"Don't think of today. Think of June."

"I...w...will."

He jerked her up. Their mouths joined for a salty goodbye. His hand clamped the back of her neck as he pressed his warm lips to her wet cheeks, as if to keep something of her—something—within his body.

He put her away from him with a sturdy push, opened the car door, then waited until the engine fired. Resolutely she put the car into reverse, backed from her parking spot, then hung her arm out the window as she pulled forward. Their fingertips brushed as she drove away, and a moment later a turn of the wheel whisked his reflection from her rearview mirror.

Theresa had expected her mother to be inquisitive, but oddly, Margaret only asked the most impersonal questions. How is Brian? Did he mention Jeff? Was there a lot of traffic? Both Margaret and Willard seemed to sympathize with their twenty-five-year-old daughter who mooned around the house as if she were fifteen. Even Amy, sensing Theresa's despondency, steered clear.

On her calendar, Theresa numbered the days backward from June 24 and grew more and more irritable as she remained indecisive about the surgery.

May arrived, and with it hot weather and uncontrollable children at school. The kids were so antsy they could hardly be contained in the stuffy schoolroom.

Spring was concert season, and Theresa busily prepared for the last two weeks of school, when teas were held for the mothers of the younger children and a combined evening performance of the choir, band and orchestra was scheduled. After-school meetings were necessary to coordinate the programs with the directors of the other two groups. It was a hectic time of year, but at the same time sad. She was sorry to have to say goodbye to some sixth graders as they moved into junior high and a new building and three of these managed to find out about Theresa's twenty-sixth birthday, presenting her with a birthday cake in class that day. The tenseness of the past days fled as she felt her heart brimming with special feelings for the three.

And the glow still lingered when she arrived home to find flowers and a note from Brian: "With love, until June 24th, when I can tell you in person." The flowers created a stir within the family. Amy was awed and perhaps a trifle envious. Margaret insisted the flowers be left in the center of the supper table, though it was impossible to see around the enormous long-stemmed red roses. Willard smiled more than usual, and patted Theresa's shoulder every time their paths crossed. "What's all this about June?" he asked. She gave him a kiss on the jaw, but had no reply, for she wasn't sure herself what June would bring. Especially if she decided to have the surgery.

At nine-thirty that night the phone rang. Amy answered it, as usual. "It's for you, Theresa!" Amy's eyes were bright with excitement. She anxiously shoved the receiver into Theresa's hand and mouthed, "It's him!"

Theresa's heart pattered. Only inadequate letters had passed between them since Fargo. This was the first phone call. Amy stood close, watching with keen interest while Theresa placed the phone to her ear and answered breathlessly, "Hello?"

"Hello, sweets. Happy birthday."

Theresa placed a hand over her heart and said not a word. It felt as if she'd been supping on sweet, sweet rose petals, and they'd all stuck in her throat.

"Are you there, Theresa?"

"Yes...yes! Oh, Brian, the flowers are just beautiful. Thank you." It was him! It was really him!

"God, it's good to hear your voice."

Amy was still three feet away. "Just a minute, Brian." Theresa shifted her weight to one hip, lowered the receiver and shot a piercing look of strained patience. Amy made a disgruntled face, shrugged, slipped her hands into her jeans pockets and grumbled all the way to her bedroom.

"Brian, I'm back. Had to get rid of a nuisance."

His laugh lilted across the wire, and she pictured him with chin raised, green eyes dancing in delight. "The kid, huh?"

"Exactly."

"I'm picturing you in the kitchen, standing beside the cupboard, and

LaVyrle Spencer

Amy beside you, all ears. I've been living on memories just like those ever since I left you."

Love talk was foreign to Theresa. She reacted with a blush that seemed to heat her belly and burn its way up to her breasts and neck to her temples. Her heart raced, and her palms grew damp.

"Oh, Brian..." she said softly, and closed her eyes, picturing his face again.

"I've missed you," he said quietly.

"I've missed you, too."

"I wish I could be there. I'd take you to dinner and then out dancing."

The memory of being wrapped in his arms, with her breasts crushed against his corduroy jacket came back in vivid detail and made her body ache with renewed longing to see him again.

"Brian, nobody's ever sent me flowers before."

"That just goes to show the world is filled with fools."

She smiled, closed her eyes and leaned her forehead against the cool kitchen wall. "And nobody's ever plied me with flattery before either. Don't stop now."

"Your teeth are like stars...." He paused expectantly, and her smile grew broader.

"Yes, I know—they come out every night." She could hear his humor blossoming as he went on to the next line of the time-weary joke.

"And your eyes are like limpid pools."

"Yes, I know—cesspools."

"And your hair is like moonbeams."

"Oh-oh! I never heard that one." But by this time they were both laughing. Then his voice became serious once more.

"What were you doing when I called?"

She watched her fingertips absently smoothing the kitchen wall. "I was in my bedroom, writing a thank-you letter to you for the roses."

"Were you really?"

"Yes, really."

It was quiet for a long time. His voice was gruff and slightly pained when he spoke again. "God, I miss you. I wish I was there."

"I wish you were, too, but it won't be long now."

"It seems like six years instead of six weeks."

"I know, but school will be out by then, and we'll be able to spend lots of time together...if you want."

"If I want?" After a meaningful pause, he added, sexily, "Silly girl."

She thought her heart might very well erupt, for it seemed to fill her ears and head with a wild, sweet thrumming. To her amazement, his next words made it beat even harder.

"I wish you could feel what's happening to my heart right now."

"I think I know. The same thing is going on in mine."

"Put your hand on it."

Only a faraway musical bleep sounded across the telephone line as Theresa digested his order.

"Is it there?" he asked.

"N...no."

"Put it there, for me."

Timidly, slowly, she placed her hand upon her throbbing heart.

"Is it there now?"

"Yes," she whispered.

"Tell me what you feel."

"I feel like...like I've been running as hard as I can—it's like there's a piston driving in there. My hand seems to be lifting and falling with the force of it."

After a long moment of silence he said rather shakily, "That's where I want to be, in your heart."

"Oh, Brian, you are," she replied breathily.

"Theresa?" She waited, breathlessly. "Now slide your hand down."

Her lips dropped open. Her skin prickled.

"Slide it down," he repeated, more softly. The tremor was gone from his voice now. It was controlled and very certain. Her hand dropped to her breast. "And that's where I want to kiss you...again. And do everything that follows. I'm sorry now that we didn't do it in Fargo. But when I get back, we will. I'm giving you fair warning, Theresa."

The line went positively silent. Theresa's eyes were closed, her breathing labored. Turning, she pressed her shoulder blades and the back of her head to the wall. His face came clearly to mind. She moved her hand back to her breast and riffled her fingers softly up and down. The tiny movements sent shudders of sensation down the backs of her thighs. The thought of the surgery sizzled through her mind, and she opened her mouth to ask him what he would think if he came back and found her with beautifully average breasts, but ones that might not be able to show response.

"Theresa," he almost whispered, again sounding pained. "I have to go. You finish your letter to me, and tell me all the things you're feeling right now, okay, sweets? And I'll see you in six weeks. Till then, here's a kiss. Put it wherever you want it." A pause followed, then his emotional, "Goodbye, Treece."

"Brian, wait!" She clutched the phone almost frantically.

"I'm still here."

"Brian, I...." Her throat worked, but not another sound came out.

"I know, Theresa. I feel the same."

She would have known he'd hang up without warning. He was a man who never said goodbye.

"I'm giving you fair warning, Theresa."

His words stayed with her during the following days while she continued weighing the possibility of undergoing breast surgery. She had a second talk with Dr. Schaum. He told her the time would be perfect, just when school ended for summer vacation, a time of low stress and less social contact—both desirable. She had learned that her insurance *would* cover the cost of the surgery because of the prognosis for late-life back troubles. She'd received a brochure from Dr. Schaum explaining the surgical procedure, what to expect beforehand and afterward. The discomforts could be expected to be minimal, but they were the least of Theresa's concerns. Neither was she especially bothered by the idea of giving up nursing—babies seemed so far in the future. But the possibility of losing an erogenous zone made her reluctant, and at times depressed, especially when remembering Brian's lips upon her, and the wonder of her own feminine response.

She grew short-tempered with her family and also with her students as the weather warmed. The children's temperaments grew feisty, too. Fights broke out on the playground, and tears were often in need of swabbing. While she performed the duty, Theresa often wished she had someone to swab her own tears, shed in secret at night, as the decision time came closer and closer. If she was going to have the surgery, the choice must be made and made soon. In two weeks summer vacation would start, and three weeks after that, Brian would come home.

She thought of greeting him in a cool, cotton T-shirt—green, maybe— with a new trim profile of her choosing. How amazing to think she could actually choose the contour of breast she preferred! The surgeons didn't even make both breasts the same size anymore, but made the right larger than the left if the woman was right-handed, and vice versa, just as nature would have done. When nipples were replaced, they were lifted to a new, perky, uptilted angle that would remain attractive for the rest of her life.

The idea beguiled.

The idea horrified.

I want to do it.

I can't do it. What would Brian say?

It's your body, not his.

But I want to share it with him. To the fullest.

You still can, even if the sensation doesn't come back.

I should at least discuss it with him.

On the basis of one weekend in Fargo that ended unfulfilled, a bouquet of roses and a seductive phone call?

But he said he wanted me to be exactly the same when he came back!
Supposing you're even better?
Dear God, they'd cut my nipples off.
Not totally.
I'll have scars.
That will disappear almost completely.
But I loved being kissed there—suppose I lose the feeling?
Chances are you won't.
I'm scared.
You're a woman—the choice is yours.

A week before vacation she made her decision. When she told her parents, Margaret's face registered immediate shock and disapproval, her father's a gray disappointment that the body he'd bequeathed his daughter had turned out to be less than suitable.

As Theresa had expected, Margaret was the outspoken one. "I don't understand why you'd want to...to fool around with the body you've been given, as if it isn't good enough."

"Because it can be better, mother."

"But it's so *unnecessary* and such an expense!"

"Unnecessary!" These were all the arguments she'd been expecting, yet Theresa was deeply disappointed in her mother's lack of understanding. "You think it's unnecessary?"

Margaret colored and pursed her lips slightly. "I should know. I've lived with a shape like yours all my life, and I've gotten along just fine."

Theresa wondered about all the hidden slights her mother had suffered and never disclosed. She knew for a fact there were backaches and shoulder aches. Very quietly the young woman asked, "Have you, mother?"

Margaret discovered something important needing attention behind her and presented her back. "What a ridiculous question. Movie stars and playgirls tamper with their shapes, not nice girls like you." She swung around again. "What will people say?"

Theresa felt wounded that her mother, with typical lack of tact, could choose such a time to voice the fear uppermost in her mind—which was how it would affect herself. She cared so much about the opinion of outsiders that she let its importance overshadow the reason her daughter had come to this decision. With a sigh, Theresa sank to a chair. "Please, mom, dad, I want to explain...." She did. She went back to age fourteen and described all her disenchantment with her elephantine growth, and explained all that Dr. Schaum had predicted for her future. She omitted the details about her sexual hang-ups, but explained why she'd worn the sweaters, hidden beneath the violin, chosen to work with children and disliked meeting strange men.

When she finished, Margaret's eyes moved to Willard's. She mulled silently for a minute, sighed and shrugged. "I don't know," she said to the tabletop. "I don't know."

But Theresa knew. She had gained confidence by confronting her parents about the trip to Fargo, and she was very certain the surgery was the right thing for her. She sensed her mother softening and realized her own self-assurance was changing Margaret's opinion.

"There's just one more thing," Theresa went on. She met Margaret's questioning eyes directly. "Could you get the day off that Monday of the surgery and be there at the hospital, mother?"

Perhaps it was the realization that the young woman who was slowly but surely snipping the apron strings still needed Margaret's maternal understanding. Perhaps it was because there'd been times in Margaret's life when she'd wished for the courage her daughter now displayed. She squelched her misgivings, forced the squeamishness from her thoughts and answered, "If you're bound to go through with it, yes, I'll be there."

But when she was alone, Margaret leaned weakly against the bathroom door, compressing her own bulbous breasts with her palms, overcome by pangs of empathetic transference. She opened her eyes and dropped her hands, breathing deeply, admitting what courage it took for her daughter to make the decision she had.

On Memorial Day, Theresa washed her hair by herself for the last time for at least two weeks; she wouldn't be able to lift her arms for a while after the surgery. She packed a suitcase with one very generously sized nightgown, and three brand-new pairs of pajamas, size medium. She harnessed herself into her size 34DD utilitarian white bra, but packed several of size 34C—not blue, not pink, not even lacy; those would have to wait. She'd be wearing the smaller, sturdy white bra day and night for a month. She dressed in a size extralarge spring top, but packed a brand-new one, again size medium, that looked to Theresa as if it had been made for a doll instead of a woman.

The following morning, Margaret was there when they rolled Theresa into surgery on the gurney. She kissed her daughter's cheek, held her hand in both of her own, and said, "See you in a little while."

Three and a half hours later, Theresa was taken to the recovery room, and an hour after that she opened her eyes and lifted a bleary smile to Margaret, who leaned close and brushed the thick, coppery hair back from Theresa's forehead.

"Mom...." The word was an airy whisper. Theresa's eyelids fluttered open twice, but her eyes remained unfocused.

"Baby, everything went just fine. Rest now. I'll be here."

But a limp, freckled hand lifted and dreamily explored the sheets across her breast. "Mom, am...I...beautiful?" came the sleepy question.

Gently restraining Theresa's hand, Margaret felt tears sting her eyes. "Yes, baby, you're beautiful. But you've always been. Shh...." A drugged smile lifted the corner of Theresa's soft lips.

"Brian...doesn't...know...yet...." The lethargic voice hushed into silence, and Theresa drifted away into the webbed world of sleep.

Later Theresa was lucid and alone in her hospital room for the first time. She'd been warned to limit all arm movement, but could not resist gingerly exploring the mysteries sheathed beneath the white sheets and contained within the new, stiff, confining bra. She stared at the ceiling while moving her hands hesitantly upward. As they came into contact with the greatly reduced mounds of flesh, Theresa's eyelids drifted closed. She explored as a sightless person reads braille. She knew the exact pattern of the incisions and found them covered with dressing inside the bra, thus she imagined more than felt their outline. The stitches ran beneath the curves of both breasts, contouring them like the arcs of an underwire bra. That incision was bisected on each breast by another leading straight upward to encircle the nipple.

She felt no pain, for she was still under the influence of the anaesthetic. Instead, she knew only a soaring jubilation. There was so little there! She lightly grazed the upper hemispheres of both breasts, to find them unbelievably reduced in breadth. And from what she could tell, blind this way, it seemed her nipples were going to be as tip-tilted as the end of a water ski. She felt a surge of overwhelming impatience to see the revised, improved shape she'd been given.

I want to see. I want to see.

But beneath her armpits tiny tubes were inserted to drain the pleural cavity and prevent internal bleeding and pneumonia. For now, Theresa had to be content with imagination.

Amy came to that night, filled with smiles and flip teenage acceptance of the momentous move Theresa had made. She produced a letter bearing familiar handwriting, but teased her sister by holding it beyond reach. "Mmm...just a piece of junk mail, I think."

"Gimme!"

"Gimme?" Amy looked disgusted. "Is that the kind of manners you teach your students? *Gimme?"*

"Hand it over, snot. I'm incapacitated and can't indulge in mortal combat until these tubes are removed and the stitches dissolve."

Truthfully, as the day wore on, Theresa's discomfort had been growing, but the letter from Brian made her forget them temporarily.

Dear Theresa,

Less than four weeks and we're out. And guess how we'll be coming home? I bought a van! A class act, for sure. It's a Chevy, kind of the color of your eyes, not brown and not hazel, with smoked windows, white pinstriping and enough room to carry all the guitars, amps and speakers for an entire band. You're gonna love it! I'll take you out for a spin the minute I get there, and maybe you can help me look for an apartment, huh? God, sweets, I can't wait. For any of it—civilian life, school, the new band, and you. Most of all *you.* (Theresa smiled at the three slashes underlining the last word.) Jeff and I leave here on the morning of the 24th. Should be pulling in there by suppertime. Jeff says to tell your mother he wants pigs in the blanket for supper, whatever that is. And me? I want Theresa-in-the-blankets after supper. Just teasing, darlin'...or am I?

Love,
Brian

Theresa refolded the letter, but instead of putting it on her bedside table, tucked it beneath the covers by her hip. She looked up to find Amy sprawled, unladylike, in the visitor's chair.

"Brian bought a van. He and Jeff are going to be driving it home."

"A van!" Amy's eyes lit up like flashing strobes, and she sat up straighter in the chair. "All ri-i-ight."

"And Jeff says to tell mom he wants pigs-in-the-blanket for supper when they get here."

"Boy, I can't wait!"

"*You* can't wait? Every day seems like an eternity to me."

"Yeah." Amy glanced at the sheet beneath which the letter was concealed. "You and Brian, well...looks like you two got a thing goin', I mean, since you went up and met him and everything, you two must really be gettin' it on."

"Not exactly. But..." Theresa mused with a winsome smile. Beneath the covers she touched the envelope hopefully.

"But you've been writing to each other for five months, and he sent you the roses and called and everything. I guess things are startin' to torque between you two, huh?"

Theresa laughed unexpectedly. It hurt terribly, and she pressed a hand to her rib cage. "Oh, don't do that, Amy. It hurts like heck."

"Oh, gol...sorry. Didn't mean to blow your seams."

Theresa laughed again, but this time when she pressed the sheets against herself, she caught Amy's eyes assessing her new shape inquisitively.

"Have you...well, I mean...have you seen yourself yet?" Amy's eyes were wide, her voice hesitant.

"No, but I've felt."

"Well...how...." Amy shrugged, grinned sheepishly. "Oh, you know what I mcan."

"They feel like I'm wearing somebody else's body. Somebody who's shaped like I always wished I could be shaped."

"They look a lot smaller, even under the blankets."

Theresa turned the top of the sheet down to her waist. "They are. I'll show you when we're both back home."

Amy jumped up suddenly, pushed her palms into her rear jeans pockets, flat against her backside. She looked ill at ease, but after taking a turn around the bed, stopped beside her older sister and asked directly, "Have you told him?"

"Brian?"

Amy nodded.

"No, I haven't."

"Gol, I probably shouldn't have asked." Amy colored to a becoming shade of pink.

"It's okay, Amy. Brian and I...really like each other, but I didn't feel our relationship had gone far enough for me to consult him about having the surgery. And I'm scared of facing him again because he doesn't know."

"Yeah...." Amy's voice trailed away uncertainly. She grew morose, then speculative and glanced at Theresa askance. "You could still tell him. I mean before he comes home."

"I know. I've been considering it, but I'm kind of dreading it. I...oh, I don't know what to do."

Amy suddenly brightened, putting on a jack-in-the-box smile and bubbling, "Well, one thing's for sure. As soon as we spring you from this joint, you and I are going shopping for all those sexy, cute, *tiny* size nines you've been dying to shimmy into, okay?"

"Okay. You've got a date. Soon as I can put my arms up over my head to get into them."

The following day on his rounds, Dr. Schaum breezed around the corner into Theresa's room, the tails of his lab coat flaring out behind his knees. "So how is our miniaturized Theresa today? Have you seen yourself in a mirror yet?"

"No...." Theresa was taken by surprise at his abrupt, swooping entry and his first question.

"No! Well, why not? You haven't gone through all this to lie there wondering what the new Theresa Brubaker looks like. Come on, young lady, we'll change that right now.''

And so Theresa saw her reshaped breasts for the first time, with Dr. Schaum holding a wide mirror against his belly, studying her over the top of it, awaiting her verdict.

The stitches were still red and raw looking, but the shape was delightful, the perky angle of the upturned nipples an utter surprise. Somehow, she was not prepared for the reality of it. She was...*normal*. And in time, when the stitches healed and the scars faded, there would undoubtedly be times when she'd wonder if she'd ever been shaped any differently.

But for now, a wide-eyed Theresa stared at herself in the mirror and beamed, speechless.

Dr. Schaum tipped his head to one side. ''Do I take that charming smile to mean you approve?''

''Oh...'' was all Theresa breathed while continuing to stare and beam at her reflection. But when she reached to touch, Dr. Schaum warned, ''Uh-uh! Don't investigate just yet. Leave that until the tubes and sutures are removed.'' Only the internal stitches were the dissolving type. The external ones would be removed by Dr. Schaum within a few days.

Theresa returned home on the fourth day, the drainage tubes gone from beneath her arms, but the sutures still in place. Amy washed her sister's hair and waited on her hand and foot with a solicitude that warmed Theresa's heart. Forbidden to even reach above her to get a coffee cup from the kitchen shelf, Theresa found herself often in need of Amy's helping hand, and during the next few days the bond between the sisters grew.

They were given the go-ahead for the long-awaited shopping spree at the end of the second week, when Theresa saw Dr. Schaum for a postop checkup.

That golden day in mid-June was like a fairy tale come true for the woman who surveyed the realm of ladies' fashions with eyes as excited as those of a child who spies the lights of a carnival on the horizon. ''T-shirts! T-shirts! T-shirts!'' Theresa sang exuberantly. ''I feel like I want to wear them for at least one solid year!''

Amy giggled and hauled Theresa to a Shirt Shack and picked out a hot pink item that boasted the words, ''Knockers Up!'' across the chest. They laughed exuberantly and hung the ugly garment back with its mates and went off to get serious.

Standing before the full-length mirror in the first item she tried on—a darling sleeveless V-neck knit shirt of fresh summer green, held up by ties on each shoulder—Theresa wondered if she'd ever been this happy. The sporty top was nothing extraordinary, not expensive, not even sexy really, only feminine, tiny, attractive—and utterly flattering. It was the kind of garment she'd never been able to even consider before. Theresa couldn't resist preening just a little. "Oh, Amy, look!"

Amy did, standing back, smiling at her sister's happy expression in the mirror. Suddenly Amy's shoulders straightened as she made a remarkable discovery. "Hey, Theresa, you look taller!"

"I do?" Theresa turned to the left, appraised herself. "You know, that was something Diane DeFreize told me people would say afterward. And you're the second one who has." Theresa realized it was partly because her posture was straighter since her self-image had improved so heartily. Also, the absence of bulk up front carried the eyes upward rather than horizontally, creating the illusion of added height. She stood square to the mirror again, gave her reflection a self-satisfied look of approval and seconded, "Yes, I do."

"Wait'll Brian sees you in that."

Theresa's eyes widened and glittered at the thought. She ran a hand over her bustline, wondering what he'd say. She still hadn't told him.

"Do you think he'll like it?"

"You're a knockout in green."

"You can't see my strap marks, can you?" The wide, ugly indentations in Theresa's shoulders hadn't been erased yet, but Dr. Schaum said they would disappear in time. The shoulder ties of the top were fairly narrow, but wide enough to conceal the depressions in her skin.

"No, the ties cover them up. I think you should make it your first purchase. *And* be wearing it when Brian gets here."

The thought was so dizzying, Theresa pressed a hand to her tummy. *When Brian gets here. Only one more week.*

"I'll take it. And next I want to look for a dress—no, eight dresses! The last time I bought one that didn't need alteration was when I was younger than you are now. Dr. Schaum says I should be a perfect size nine."

And she was. A swirly-skirted summer sundress of pink was followed by another of navy, red-and-white flowers, then by a classic off-white sheath with jewelry neckline and belt of burnished brown leather. They bought tube tops and V-neck T-shirts (no crew necks for Theresa Brubaker this trip!) and even one blouse that tied just beneath the bustline and left her midriff bare. Jewelry, something Theresa had never wanted to hang around her neck before for fear it would draw attention to her breast size, was as exciting to buy as her first pair of panty hose had been, years ago. She chose a delicate gold chain with a tiny puffed heart, and it looked delectable, even against the red freckles on her chest. But somehow even those freckles seemed less brash to Theresa. Her choice of garment colors was no longer limited by available size, thus she could select hues that minimized her redness.

When the day ended, Theresa sat in her room among mountains of crackling sacks and marvelous clothes. She felt like a bride with a new trousseau. Holding up her favorite—the green shoulder-tie top—she fitted it against her front, danced a swirling pattern across the floor, then closed her eyes and breathed deeply.

Hurry, Brian, hurry. I'm ready for you at last.

Chapter Thirteen

It was a stunning June day, with the temperature in the low eighties and Minnesota's faultless sky the perfect, clear blue of the delphiniums that bloomed in gardens along Johnnycake Lane. Across the street, a group of teenagers were waxing a four-year-old Trans Am. Next door, Ruth Reed was standing beside her garden, checking to see if there were blossoms on her green beans yet. Two houses down, the neighborhood four- and five-year-olds were churning their chubby legs on the pedals of low-slung plastic motorcycles, making engine noises with their lips. Up and down the street the smell of cooking suppers drifted out to mingle with that of fresh-cut grass as men just home from work tried to get a start on the mowing before mealtime. In the Brubakers' front yard, an oscillating sprinkler swayed and sprayed, twinkling in the sun like the sequined ostrich fan of a Busby Berkeley girl.

It was a scene of everyday Americana, a slice of ordinary life, on an ordinary street, at the end of an ordinary workday.

But in the Brubaker house, excitement pulsated. Cabbage rolls stuffed with hamburger-rice filling were cooking in a roaster. The bathroom fixtures gleamed and fresh towels hung on the racks. In the freshly cleaned room a bouquet of garden flowers sat on the piano—marigolds, cosmos, zinnias and snapdragons. The kitchen table was set for six, and centered upon it waited a slightly lopsided two-layer cake, rather ineptly decorated with some quite flat-looking pink frosting sweetpeas and the words, "Welcome home, Jeff and Brian." Amy adjusted the cake plate one more time and turned it just a little in an effort to make it appear more balanced than it was, then stood back, shrugged and muttered, "Oh, horse poop. It's good enough."

"Amy, watch your mouth!" warned Margaret, then added, "There's not a thing wrong with that cake, so I want you to stop fussing about it."

Outside, Willard had a hedge trimmer in his hands as he moved along the precision-trimmed alpine current hedge, taking a nip here, a nip there, though not a leaf was out of place. Periodically, he shaded his eyes and scanned the street to the west, gazing into the spray of diamond droplets that lifted and fell, lifted and fell across the emerald carpet of lawn—his pride and joy. The kitchen windows were cranked open above his head, and he checked his wrist, then called inside, "What time is it, Margaret? I think my watch stopped."

"It's five forty-five, and there's not a thing wrong with your watch, Willard. It was working seven minutes ago when you asked."

In her bedroom at the end of the hall, Theresa put the final touches on the makeup that by now she was adept at applying. She buckled a pair of flat, strappy white sandals onto her feet, inspecting the coral polish on her toenails—they'd never been painted before this summer. Next, she slipped into a brand-new pair of sleek white jeans, snapped and zipped them up, ran a smoothing palm down her thighs, and watched herself in the mirror as she worked the kelly green top over her head, covering her white bra. She adjusted the knot upon her left shoulder, stood back and assessed her reflection. *You don't look like a Christmas tree, Theresa, but you look like*—she searched her mind for a simile Brian had used—*like a poppy blossom.* She smiled in satisfaction and flicked the lifter through her freshly cut and styled hair, fluffing it around her temples and forehead until it suited perfectly. Around her neck she fastened the new chain with the tiny puffed heart. At her wrist went a simple gold bangle bracelet. She inserted tiny gold studs in her ears and was reaching for the perfume when she heard her father's voice calling through the screened windows at the other end of the house.

"I think it's them. It's a van, but I can't tell what color it is."

Theresa pressed a hand to her heart. The hand wasn't yet used to feeling the diminished contour it encountered in making this gesture. Her wide eyes raked down her torso in the mirror, then back up. *What will he think?*

"Yup, it's them!" she heard in her father's voice, before Amy bellowed, "Theresa, come on, they're here!"

A nerve jittered in her stomach, and the buildup of anticipation that had been expanding as each day passed, thickened the thud of her heart and made her knees quake. She turned and ran through the house and slammed out the back door, then waited behind the others as the cinnamon-colored Chevy van purred up the street, with Jeff's arm and head dangling out the window as he waved and hollered hello. But Theresa's eyes were drawn to the opposite side of the van as she tried to make out the face of the driver. But the windshield caught and reflected the bowl of blue sky, and she saw only it and the branches of the elm trees flashing across the glass as the vehicle turned and eased up the drive, then stopped.

Jeff's door flew open, and he scooped up the first body he encountered—Amy—lifting her off her feet and swirling her around before doing likewise with Margaret, who whooped and demanded to be set on her feet, but meant not a word of it. Willard got a rough hug, and Theresa was next. She found herself swept up from the ground before she could issue the warning to her brother not to suspend her. But the slight twinge of discomfort where her stitches had been was worth it.

Yet while all this happened, Theresa was primarily conscious of Brian slipping from the driver's seat, removing a pair of sunglasses, stretching with his elbows in the air and rounding the front of the van to watch the greetings, then be included in them himself. Theresa hung back, observing the faded blue jeans slung low on his lean hips, buckling at the knees from a long day of driving; the loose, off-white gauze shirt with three buttons open; the naked V of skin at his throat; his dark, military-cut hair and eyes the color of summer grasses that smiled while Amy gave him a smack on the cheek, Margaret a motherly hug and Willard a handshake and affectionate pat on the shoulder.

Then there was nobody left but Theresa.

Her heart pounded in her chest, and she felt as if her feet were not on the blacktop driveway but levitated an inch above it. The sensuous shock of recognition sent the color sweeping to her face, but she didn't care. He was here. He was as good to look at as she remembered. And his presence made her feel impatient, and nervous, and exhilarated.

They faced each other with six feet of space between them.

"Hello," he greeted simply, and it might have been a verse from the great love poets of decades ago.

"Hello." Her voice was soft and uncertain and quavery.

They were the only two who hadn't hugged or touched. Her tremulous lips were softly opened. The corners of his mouth lifted in a slow crescent of a smile. He reached his hands out to her, calluses up, and as she extended her fingertips and rested them upon his palms, she watched the summer-green eyes that last December had so assiduously avoided dropping to her breasts. Those eyes dropped now, directly, unerringly, down to the freckled throat and the V-neck of her new knit shirt, and then lower, to the two gentle rises within. Brian's mouth went slightly lax as he stared in undisguised amazement.

His puzzled gaze darted back up to her eyes, while Theresa felt her face suffuse with brighter color.

"How are you?" she managed, the question sounding foolishly mundane, even in her own ears.

"Fine." He released her fingers and stepped back, replacing the sunglasses on his nose while she felt him studying her from behind the dark lenses. "And you?"

They were conversing like robots, both extremely self-conscious all of a sudden, both trying in vain to regain calm footing.

"Same as ever." They were scarcely out of Theresa's mouth before she regretted her choice of words. She wasn't the same at all. "How was your trip?"

"Good, but tiring. We drove straight through."

The others had preceded them up the back steps, and Theresa and Brian trailed along. Though he walked just behind her shoulder, she felt his eyes burning into her, questioning, wondering. But she couldn't tell his true reaction yet. Was he pleased? Shocked for sure, and taken aback, but beyond that, Theresa could only guess.

Inside, the Brubaker house was as noisy as ever. Jeff—exultant, roaring, fun loving—stood in the middle of the kitchen with his arms extended wide and gave a jungle call like Tarzan, while from somewhere at the far end of the house The Stray Cats sang rock, and at the near end The Gatlins crooned in three-part harmony. Margaret tended something on the stove, and Jeff surrounded her from behind with both arms, his chin digging into her shoulder, making her wriggle and giggle. "Dammit, ma, but that smells rank! Must be my pigs-in-the-blanket."

"Listen to that boy, calling my cabbage rolls rank." She lifted a lid off a steaming roaster, and Jeff snitched a pinch of something from inside. "Didn't that Air Force teach you any manners?" his mother teased happily. "Wash your hands before you come snitching."

Jeff grinned over his shoulder at Brian. "I thought we were done with C.O.'s when we got our walking papers, but it looks like I was wrong." He patted his mother's bottom. "But this one's all bluff, I think."

Margaret whirled and whacked at his hand with a spoon, but missed. "Oh, get away with you and your teasing, you brat. You're not too old for me to take the yardstick to." But Jeff had leaped safely out of reach. He spied the cake, and gave an undulating whistle of appreciation, like that of a construction worker eyeing a passing woman in high heels. "Wow, would y' look at this, Brian. Somebody's been busy."

"Amy," put in Willard proudly.

Amy beamed, her braces flashing. "The dumb thing is listing to the starboard," Amy despaired, but Jeff wrapped an arm around her shoulders, squeezed and declared, "Well, it won't list for long cause it won't last for long. I'd say about twenty minutes at the outside." Then a thought seemed to occur to him. "Is it chocolate?"

"What else?"

"Then I'd say less than twenty minutes. Shh! Don't tell ma." He picked up a knife from one of the place settings and whacked into the high side of the cake, took a slice out and lifted it to his mouth before anybody could stop him.

Everyone in the room was laughing as Margaret swooped toward the table with the steaming roaster clutched in a pair of pot holders. "Jeffrey Brubaker," she scolded, "put that cake down this minute or you'll ruin your appetite! And for heaven's sake, everybody sit down before that child forces me to get the yardstick out after all!"

Brian took it all in with a sense of homecoming almost as familial as if he were, indeed, part of the Brubaker clan. And it was easy to see Jeff was their mood-setter, the one who stirred them all and generated both gaiety and teasing. It was so easy being with them. Brian felt like a cog slipping into the notches of a gear. Until he sat across from Theresa and was forced to consider the change in her.

"Take your old place," Willard invited Brian, pulling a chair out while they all shuffled and scraped and settled down for the meal. During the next half hour while they gobbled cabbage rolls and crusty buns and whipped potatoes oozing with parsley butter, then during the hour following while they ate cake and leisurely sipped glasses of iced tea and caught up with news of each other, Brian covertly studied Theresa's breasts as often as he could.

Once she looked up unexpectedly while passing him the sugar bowl and caught his gaze on her green shirtfront. Their eyes met, then abruptly shifted apart.

How? Brian wondered. *And when? And why didn't she tell me? Did Jeff know? And if so, why didn't he warn me?*

The kitchen was hot, and Margaret suggested they all take glasses of iced tea and sit on the small concrete patio between the house and the garage. Immediately they all got to their feet and did a cursory scraping of plates but left the stacked dishes on the cupboard, then filed out to the side of the house where webbed lawn chairs waited.

While they relaxed and visited, Theresa was ever aware of Brian's perusal. He had slipped his sunglasses on again, even though the patio was in full shade now as the sun dipped behind the peak of the roof. But occasionally, as he lifted his sweating glass and drank, she felt his gaze riveted on her chest. But when she looked up and smiled at him, she could not be sure, for she saw only the suggestion of dark eyes behind the tinted aviator lenses, and though his lips returned the smile, she sensed it did not reach those inscrutable eyes.

"Oh yeah!" Amy suddenly remembered. "Glue Eyes called and said you should be sure to call her as soon as you got home."

Jeff pointed an accusatory finger at his playful sibling. "Listen, brat, if you don't can it with that Glue Eyes business, I'll have ma take the yardstick to *you.*"

"Aw, Jeff, you know I don't mean it. Not anymore. She's really okay, I guess. I got to like her a lot last Christmas. But I've called her Glue Eyes for so long it kinda falls outa me, ya know?"

"Well, someday it's gonna fall out when you're standing right beside her, then what will you do?"

"Apologize and explain and tell her that when I was learning to wear makeup I tried to put it on exactly like she does."

Jeff gave her a mock punch on the chin, then bounded into the house to make the phone call, and returned a few minutes later, announcing, "I'm going to run over and pick up Patricia and bring her back here. Anybody want to ride along with me?"

Theresa was torn, recalling the ardent reunion embraces she and Brian had witnessed last time, yet not wanting to stay behind if Brian said yes. He seemed to be waiting for her to answer, so she had to make a choice.

"I'll help Amy and mother with the dishes while you're gone," she decided.

"I'll drive you, Jeff," Brian offered, stretching to his feet, adjusting his glasses and turning to follow Jeff to the van. Theresa watched him walk away, studying the back of his too-short hair, the places where the gauze shirt stuck to his back in a tic-tac-toe design from the webs of the lawn chair, his hands moving to his hips to give an unconscious tug at the waistband of his jeans. His back pockets had worn white patches where he carried his billfold, and his backside was so streamlined the sight of it created a hollow longing in the pit of Theresa's stomach.

He's upset. I should have told him.

No, you had no obligation to confide in him. It was your choice.

In the van, the two men rode down the street where evening shadows stretched long tendrils across green lawns. Brian drove deliberately slow. He pondered, wondering how to introduce the subject, and finally attacked it head on.

"Okay, Brubaker, why didn't you tell me?"

Jeff gave a crooked smile. "She looks great, huh?"

"Damn right she looks great, but my eyeballs nearly dropped onto the goddamn driveway when I saw her standing there with her...without her...aw hell, *they're gone.*"

"Yup," Jeff slouched low in the seat and grinned out the windshield. "I always knew there lurked a proud beauty inside my Treat."

"Quit beatin' around the bush, Brubaker. You knew, didn't you?"

"Yeah, I knew."

"Did she write and tell you and ask you not to tell me?"

"No, Amy did. Amy thought I should know, so I could warn you if I thought that was best."

"Well, why the hell didn't you?"

"Because I didn't think it was any of my business. Your relationship with Theresa's got nothing to do with me, beyond the fact that I'm lucky enough to be her brother. If she'd wanted you to know beforehand, she'd have told you herself. I figured, what business was it of mine to go stickin' my two cents worth in?"

"But...." Brian gripped the steering wheel. "But...*how?*"

"Breast-reduction surgery."

Brian's shaded brown lenses flashed toward Jeff. "Breast re—" He sounded flabbergasted. "I never heard of such a thing."

"To tell you the truth, neither had I, but Amy told me all about it in her letter. She had it done three weeks ago, right after school got out for summer vacation. Listen, man—" Jeff turned to watch his friend guide the van onto a broader double-lane avenue "—she's...I don't want to see her get hurt, okay?"

"Hurt?" Brian turned sharply toward Jeff, then back to his driving. "You think I'd hurt her?"

"Well, I don't know. You're kind of...well, you act kind of pissed off or something. I don't know and I'm not asking what went on between you and Theresa, but go easy on her, huh? If you're thinking she should have confided in you for some reason, just understand that she's a pretty timid creature. It'd be pretty damn hard for a girl like Theresa to even have the surgery, much less write and discuss it with a man—I don't care *how* close you'd been."

"All right, I'll remember that. And I'll cool it around her. I guess I backed off pretty suddenlike when we said hello, but Christ, it was a shock."

"Yeah, I imagine it was." They rode in silence for some minutes, then just as they approached Patricia's house, Jeff turned to Brian and asked in a concerned voice, "Could I ask just one question, Bry?"

"Yeah, shoot."

"Just exactly what *do* you think of Theresa?"

Brian pulled the van up at the curb before Patricia's house, killed the engine, removed his sunglasses and half turned toward Jeff, draping his left elbow over the steering wheel. "I love her," he answered point-blank.

Jeff let his smile seep up the muscles of his face, made a fist and socked the air. "Hot damn!" he exclaimed, then opened his door and jumped down to cross the yard on the run.

Brian watched Jeff and Patricia meet in the center of the open stretch of lawn. Jeff flung his arms around the young woman, who lifted her arms around his shoulders, and they kissed, pressed tightly against each other. It was just the way he'd been planning to greet Theresa.

Patricia's parents stepped out the front door and called, "Hi, Jeff. Welcome home. Are you gonna stay this time?"

"Damn right, I am. And I'm gonna steal your daughter!"

"Somehow, I don't think she minds one bit," Mrs. Gluek called back.

Patricia clambered up into the high van, scooted over and gave Brian a peck on the cheek. "Hiya, bud. Long time, no see."

Jeff was right behind Patricia. "Come here, woman, and put your little butt where it belongs, right on my lap." There were only two bucket seats up front. Jeff pulled Patricia down on his lap, and she laughed happily, flung her arms around his neck and kissed him while the van started rolling.

The dishes were done when the van lumbered up the street a second time, pulled into the driveway and began disgorging its passengers. They meandered to the patio, where Margaret, Willard and Amy joined them. When Theresa came out of the kitchen onto the back step, she found Brian standing below her, waiting.

Her heart did a flip-flop, and everything inside her went warm and springing. He reached up a hand to take hers, and she felt a wash of relief that he was touching her at last.

"Come here, I want to talk to you." He pulled her down the steps to his side, and asked softly, "Do you think your folks would mind if we went for a walk?"

"Not at all."

"Tell them, then. I want to be alone with you, even if it's in the middle of a city street where people are sitting on their doorsteps watching us pass by."

Her heart swelled with joy, and she stepped to the edge of the patio, made their excuses and returned to Brian. He captured her hand, and their joined knuckles brushed between their hips as they ambled down the driveway and onto the blacktop street that was still warm beneath Theresa's sandals after the heat of the summer day. The shadows were falling as evening settled in. The sun rested on the rim of the horizon like a golden, liquid ball. They passed between yards where other sprinklers played the hushed vespers of water droplets spraying greenery.

"Is there someplace we can go?" he asked.

"There's a park about two blocks away."

"Good."

Nothing more was said as they sauntered hand in hand down the center of the street.

"Hi, Theresa," called a woman who was sitting on her front steps.

"Hi, Mrs. Anderson." Theresa raised a hand in greeting, then explained quietly, "I used to babysit for the Andersons when I was Amy's age."

Brian made no reply, lifting a hand in silent greeting, too, then continuing on at Theresa's side, stealing glances at her breasts when she dropped her chin and watched the toes of her white sandals. He wondered what secrets her clothing concealed, what she'd been through, if she hurt, if she was healed. But mostly, he wondered why she hadn't trusted him enough to tell him.

The eastern sky turned a rich periwinkle blue as the sun slipped and plunged into oblivion, leaving the western horizon a blaze of orange that faded to yellow, then violet as they approached a small neighborhood park where a silent baseball diamond was surrounded by a grove of trees. Deserted playground equipment hovered in the stillness of dusk. Great, aged oaks were scattered across the expanse of open recreation area, creating blots of darker shadows beneath their widespread arms, while picnic tables made smaller dots between the trees. Brian led the way from the street onto a crunchy gravel footpath, taking Theresa beneath the shadow of an oak before he finally stopped, squeezed her fingers almost painfully, then turned her to face him.

She looked up into the twin black dots of his sunglasses. "You've still got your glasses on."

Without a word he removed them, and slipped a bow inside the waist of his blue jeans so the glasses hung on his right hip.

"I guess you're a little upset with me, aren't you?" she ventured in a perilously shaky voice.

"Yes, I am," he admitted, "but could we deal with that later?" His long fingers closed over both of her shoulders, drawing her close to his wide-spraddled feet, close to the length of his faded Levi's, close to the naked V of skin above his shirt where dark hair sprigged. Her heart was hammering under her newly reshaped breasts. Her body moved willingly against his, then their arms sought to hold, to reaffirm, to answer the question, Is this person all that I remembered?

Brian's lips opened slightly as he lowered them to hers, which waited with warm, breathless expectancy. Tears bit the back of Theresa's eyes, and she was swept with a feeling of relief so overwhelming her body seemed to wilt as the apprehension eased away into the twilight. Then the waiting ended. They clung with the newly revived reassurance that what they'd found in each other twice before was still as appealing and had been magnified by their time apart.

His mouth was June warm. Indeed, he even seemed to taste of summer, of all things she loved—flowers, music, lazy sprinklers and somewhere, the remembered scent of something he put on his hair. But he had ridden nine hours in a warm van, had crossed miles of rolling prairie in the wrinkled clothing he wore now, and from that clothing emanated a scent she had never quite known before—the scent of Brian Scanlon, male, inviting, a little dusty, a little soiled, but all man.

The kiss was as lusty as some of the rock songs she'd heard him sing, a swift succession of strokes, tugs and head movements that seemed to elicit the threads of feelings from the very tips of her toes and send them sizzling up her body. She poured her feelings into the kiss, meeting his mouth with an equal ardor. With his feet widespread, his midsection was flush against hers, and it felt good, hard, sexy. Theresa was vaguely aware of a difference in the feeling of her breasts pressed against his chest—

the smallness, the new tightness, the ability to be closer as his forearm slipped down across her spine and reeled her even more securely against his hips.

"Theresa...." His lips were at her ear, kissing her temple while his beautiful voice lost its mild note and took on a foreign huskiness. "I had to do that first. I just had to."

"First?"

He released a rather shaky breath and backed away from her, searching her upturned face in the deep shadow of the oaks. "It occurs to me we've got some talking to do, wouldn't you say?"

"Yes." She dropped her eyes, blushing already.

"Come on." Capturing her hand, he led her to the nearby area where the swings hung as still as the silence over the park that in daytime rang with children's voices. A steel slide angled down, casting its shadow on the grass as the moon slipped up into the eastern sky and the first stars came out. Brian tugged her along to the side of a large steel merry-go-round and sat down, pulling her to sit beside him, then dropping her hand.

"So..." he began, following the word with a sigh, then leaned his elbows on his thighs. "There've been some changes."

"Yes."

He pondered silently, made an impatient, breathy sound, then burst out, "God, I don't know where to begin, what to say."

"Neither do I."

"Theresa, why didn't you tell me?"

She shrugged very childishly for a twenty-six-year-old woman. "I was afraid to. And...and I didn't know what...well, I mean, we're not...."

"What you're trying to say is that you didn't know my intentions, is that it?"

"Yes, I guess so."

"After what we shared in Fargo, and our letters, you doubted my intentions?"

"No, not *doubted.* I just didn't think we'd had enough time together to get our relationship on its feet." *I wasn't even sure you would come....*

"With me, Theresa, it's not the *amount* of time, but the *quality* of it, and our weekend in Fargo was quality for me. I thought it was for you, too."

"It was, but...but, Brian, we hadn't done much more than just...well, you know what I'm saying. What we did together didn't really mean a commitment or...." Her voice trailed away. This was the most difficult conversation she'd ever had.

Brian suddenly sprang to his feet, walked three paces away from the merry-go-around and swung to face her. "Couldn't you trust me enough to tell me, Theresa?" he accused.

"I wanted to, but I was scared."

"Of what?"

"I don't know."

"Maybe you thought I was some lecher who was only after you because you had big knockers, is that it? Did you think if you told me you didn't have them anymore, I'd brush you off? Is that what you thought?"

She was horrified. It had never entered her mind that he might consider such a thing. Tears blurred her eyes. "No, Brian, I never thought that... never!"

"Then why the hell couldn't you have trusted me enough to confide in me and tell me what you were planning, give me time to get accustomed to it before I walked into your yard totally unsuspecting? Christ, do you know what a shock it was?"

"I knew you'd be surprised, but I thought you'd be pleasantly surprised."

"I am, I was...." He threw his hands into the air exasperatedly and whirled, presenting his rigid back. "But, God, Theresa, do you know what I've been thinking about for six months? Do you know how many nights I've lain awake thinking about your...*problem* and figuring out ways to finesse you into losing your inhibitions, telling myself I had to be the world's most patient lover when I took you to bed for the first time, so I didn't put some irreversible phobia into you or make your hangup worse than it already was?" Again he spun on her. "We may not have had time to share much, but what we did share was a pretty damn intimate baring of souls, and I think it gave me the right to be in on your decision with you, to share it. But you didn't even give me the chance."

"Now just a minute!" She leaped to her feet and faced him in the flood of moonlight that was growing brighter by the minute. "You've got no claim on me, no right to—"

"The hell I don't!"

"The hell you do!" Theresa had never fought or sworn in her life and was surprised at herself.

"The hell I don't! I love you, dammit!" he shouted.

"Well, that's some way to tell me, shouting at the top of your lungs! How was I supposed to know?"

"I signed all my letters that way, didn't I?"

"Well yes, but that's just a...a formal closing on a letter."

"Is that all you took it for?"

"No!"

"Well, if you knew I loved you, why couldn't you trust me? Had you ever stopped to think it might have been something I'd have welcomed sharing? Something that might have brought us even closer? Something I would have felt *honored* to share? But you didn't give me a chance, going ahead without a word like you did.''

"I resent your attitude, Brian. It's...it's possessive and uninformed."

"Uninformed?" He stood now belligerently, his hands on his hips. "Whose fault is that, mine or yours? If you'd bothered to *inform* me, I wouldn't be so damn mad right now."

"I discussed it with people who didn't lose their tempers, like you're doing. A counselor at school, a woman who'd had the surgery before and a cosmetic surgeon who eventually performed the operation. I got the emotional support I needed from them."

He felt shut out and hurt. During the past six months he'd felt a growing affinity with Theresa. He'd felt they were slowly becoming intimates, and he'd returned here thinking she was ready to pursue not only an emotional relationship but a physical one as well. He found himself intimidated by the changes in her body more than he'd been intimidated by her abundant breasts—they'd been only flesh, after all, and that he could approach and touch the same as he had other women's. The psychological preparations he'd made for approaching her again had been made at no little cost in both sleep and worry. Now that he found it all for naught, he felt cheated. Now that he knew she'd turned to others and implied they'd been more help than he could have been, he felt misunderstood. And now that he wasn't sure how long he'd have to wait to pursue her sexually, he felt angry—dammit, he'd wanted to make love to her, and soon!

"Brian," she said softly, sadly, "I didn't mean that the way it sounded. It wasn't that I didn't think you'd support my decision. But it seemed...presumptuous of me to involve you in something so personal without any commitments made between us." She touched his arm, but he remained stiff and scowling, so she returned to sit on the merry-go-round.

He was very upset. And hurt. And wondering if he had the right to be. He swung back to the merry-go-round, flopped down several feet away from her and fell back, draping his shoulders and outflung arms over the mound-shaped steel heart of the vehicle. As he flopped backward he gave a single nudge with his foot, setting the steel framework into motion. He lay brooding, looking up at the stars that circled slowly above him, getting a grip on his feelings.

Theresa sat with her shoulders slumped despondently, feeling the slight rumbling vibrations rising up through the tubular steel bars.

Oh, misery! She had thought this night of Brian's homecoming would see them close, loving, reveling in being together once again. She felt drained and depleted and unsure of how to deal with his anger. Perhaps he had a right to it; perhaps he didn't. She was no psychologist. She should have discussed it with Catherine McDonald and sought her advice regarding whether or not to tell Brian her intentions.

The merry-go-round was set off kilter, so centrifugal force kept it moving in what seemed a perpetual, lazy twirl. The tears gathered in Theresa's throat and then in her eyes. She brushed them away with the back of her wrist, turning away so he couldn't tell what she was doing.

But somehow he sensed it. A hand closed around her bare elbow and pulled her back and to one side. "Hey..." he cajoled softly. "Come here."

She draped backward across the domed center of the merry-go-round. The steel was icy beneath her bare arms as she angled toward him until only their shoulders touched, and the backs of their heads were pressed against the hard, hard metal as they studied the stars. Around and around. Dots of light on the blue-black sky twinkled like reflections of a revolving mirrored ball above a ballroom floor. Crickets had set up their endless chirping, and the night was growing damp, but it felt good against Theresa's hot face. The incandescent moon lit their draped bodies, the bars of the swing set and the crowns of the oak trees that passed slowly as Brian's foot kept nudging the beaten earth.

"I'm sorry, Theresa. I shouldn't have shouted."

"I am too." She sobbed once, and in an instant, he'd pulled her close.

"Listen, sweets, could I have a couple days to get used to it? Hell, I don't know whether I'm allowed to look at them or not. I do, and I feel guilty. I don't, and I feel guiltier. And your family, all avoiding the issue as if you'd never had any other shape. Anyway, I guess I built my hopes up too high, thinking about tonight and what it was going to be like, seeing you again."

"Me too. I certainly didn't want us to fight this way."

"Then let's not, not anymore. Let's go back and see if everybody else is as tired as I am. I've been awake since two a.m. I was too excited to sleep."

"You too?" She offered a shaky smile.

He smiled down at her in return, brushed a knuckle over the end of her nose and kissed her lightly.

He'd meant to give her only that single light kiss, but in the end, he couldn't let her go with just that. Slowly, deliberately, he returned his mouth to hers, dipping his tongue into the secret warmth of her lips, which opened in welcome. His body spurted to life, and his shoulders quivered as he pressed his elbows to the metal surface on either side of her head. God, the things he wanted to do to her, to feel with her, to have her do to him. How long would he have to wait? The kiss lingered and lengthened, growing more dizzying than the slow circling of their perch. The way Theresa lay, sprawled backward over the curved metal, the outline of her breasts was lined by moonlight as they jutted forward. It was as sexy a pose as he'd ever seen her in, and he knew it would take no more than a quick shift of his palm, and he'd feel the relief of touching her intimately. He needn't touch her breast about which he was so unsure—her stomach looked hollow and inviting, and her white slacks were very taut and alluring. He thought about running his hand down her ribs, exploring the warm inviting length of her zipper, and the sheltered spot between her legs as he'd done once before. But one thing might lead to another, and he had no idea if she was allowed to move, twist, thrust, if she had stitches, and where, and how many....

And once he started something, he had no intention of drawing back.

In the end, Brian pacified himself with the kiss alone. When it ended, he regretfully lurched to his feet, dragging Theresa with him, crossing the shadowy park toward the house where they could mingle with people and wouldn't have to confront the remaining issue...at least for a while.

Chapter Fourteen

The others had gone inside where they were visiting and having second pieces of cake when Brian and Theresa walked up the driveway. The kitchen lights slanted out across the darkened yard and back step in oblique slashes of creamy brightness. Mosquitoes hummed and buzzed against the back screen door, and a June bug threw its crusty shell at the light time and again. Frogs and crickets competed for first chair in the nighttime orchestra. The moon was a pristine ball of white.

From inside came the voice of the group Theresa and Brian could see as they walked up the driveway. They were clustered around the kitchen table, but outside it was peaceful and private. Just short of the back step, Brian stopped Theresa with a hand on her arm.

"Listen, there were a lot of things I wanted to talk about tonight but...." The thought remained unfinished.

"I know." Theresa recalled the many subjects she had stored up and was eager to share with him.

"And just because I didn't get into any of them doesn't mean I'm still mad, okay?"

She was studying the middle button on his shirt, which faced her and the moon. By its light the gauze appeared brilliant white while her own face was cast in shadow. He touched her beneath the chin with a single finger, forcing her to tilt her head up. "Okay?" he asked softly.

"Okay."

"And I probably won't see you for a while after tonight, because Jeff and I have a lot of running to do. I have to find an apartment and buy some furniture, and we want to start working on getting a band together right away. We have to renew our union cards and try to find a decent agent and audition the new drummer and bass guitarist and maybe a keyboard man, too. Anyway, I'm going to be jumping for a while. I just wanted you to know."

"Thanks for telling me." But her heart felt heavy with disappointment. Now that he was back, she wanted to be with him as much as possible. In his letters he'd suggested she could come along with him and help pick out furniture, but now he was eliminating her from that excursion. She could understand that he had a lot of mundane arrangements to make, just to get settled into an apartment, and that she'd only be in the way when they were auditioning new players, but somehow she'd thought they'd find time each day to see each other. But she smiled and hid the fact that she was crushed by his advance warning. Was this how fellows turned girls down gently? *No,* she reprimanded herself, *you're being unfair to Brian. He's not like that. He's honest and honorable. That's why he's warning you in the first place.*

The finger beneath her chin curled, and he brushed her jaw with his knuckles. "I'll call as soon as I've got my feet planted."

"Fine." She began turning toward the back step, but his hand detained her a second time.

"Wait a minute. You're not getting away without one more kiss."

She was swung around and encircled in warm, hard arms and pulled against his moonlit gauze shirt. While his lips closed over hers, the picture of the naked V of skin at his neck came into Theresa's mind, and she suddenly wanted to touch it. Hesitantly, she slipped her hand to find it, resting her palm on the sleek hair and warm flesh, then sliding it upward to rest at the side of his neck while her thumb touched the hollow of his throat. The thudding of his pulse there surprised her. Lightly, lightly, she stroked the warm, pliant depression. He made a soft, throaty sound, and his mouth moved over hers more hungrily. He clasped the back of her head and swept the interior of her mouth with lusty, intimate strokes of his tongue that sent liquid fire racing across her skin.

Some queer surge of latent feminine knowledge pulsed through Theresa. In her entire life, she'd never actively provoked a sexual response from a man. Instead, she'd always been too busy fighting off the bombardment of unwanted physical advances her partners seemed always too eager to display. Now, for the first time, *she* touched—a hesitant touch at best. But the response it kindled in Brian was at once surprising and telling. All she had done was stroke the hollow of his throat with her thumb, yet he reacted as if she'd done far more. The tenor of his kiss changed with a swift, swirling suddenness, and became totally sexual, not the insipid good-night gesture that it had begun to be.

It came as a surprise to think she, Theresa Brubaker, elementary music teacher, freckled redhead, inexperienced paramour, could generate such an immediate and passionate response by only the briefest of encouragements. Especially when she considered that he was a guitar man, a performer who had, admittedly, enjoyed all the adulation that went with his career. He must have known a great many very experienced women, far more experienced than her. Yet, he thrilled to her very inexperienced touch, and this in turn thrilled Theresa.

Realizing the power she possessed to stimulate this man, she suddenly grew impatient to test it further.

But she hadn't the chance, for as quickly as his ardor grew, he controlled it, lifting his head to suck in a great gulp of damp night air and push her gently away. "Lord, woman, do you know how good you are at that?"

"Me?" she asked, surprised.

"You."

"I'm not good at that at all. I've barely had any practice."

"Well, we'll remedy that when the time is right. But if practice makes perfect, I think you'll end up being more than I can handle."

She smiled and in the dark felt herself flush with pleasure at his words. "Hasn't anybody ever told you it's not nice to start things like that when you don't intend to finish them?" came Brian's husky teasing.

"I didn't start it. You did. I was heading into the house when you stopped me. But if you're done now, let's go in." Smiling, she turned toward the step again.

"Not so fast." Once more she was brought up short. "I can't go in just now."

"You can't?" She turned back to face him.

"Uh-uh. I'll need a couple of minutes."

"Oh!" Suddenly she understood and whirled around, presenting her shoulder blades. As she pressed her palms to embarrassed cheeks, he chuckled softly behind her shoulder, audaciously kissed the side of her neck and captured her hand. "Come on, let's go for a little walk through the backyard. That should cool me down. You can talk about school, and I'll talk about the Air Force. Those are two nice, safe, deflating subjects."

Brian treated sexuality with such frankness. Theresa wondered if she'd ever be as open about it as he was. Her body felt flushed with awareness, equally as charged as his. Thank heavens it didn't show on women!

They entered the kitchen five minutes later and pulled up chairs to join the others around the table, while Margaret sliced cake for them, and the conversation continued. When ten-thirty arrived, Jeff pushed his chair back, lifted his elbows toward the ceiling and gave a broad, shivering stretch while twisting at the waist.

"Well, I guess it's time I get Patricia home."

"Want to take the van?"

"Thanks, I'd love to."

Brian tossed Jeff the keys. "We'd better unload our suitcases first, cause I'm ready for the sack. I'll need my stuff."

While the unloading was being done, Theresa escaped to the lower level of the house to put out clean sheets and blankets for Brian's bed. She experienced a feeling of déjà vu, recalling the intimacies she and Brian had exchanged on this davenport, both on New Year's Eve and the following morning. Somehow, she realized it would be best not to have Brian encounter her here, with the mattress opened up and the bed between them, ready for use. So she left the bedding and the light on and said her good-night to him along with the rest of her family in the kitchen, before they each retired to their respective beds.

In the morning, Theresa was disappointed to discover both Brian and Jeff gone when she woke up. It was only a little before nine, so they must have been up early. The day stretched before her with an emptiness she hadn't anticipated. Many times she paused to wonder at how the absence of a single person could create a void this distracting. But it was true: knowing Brian was in town made it all the harder to be apart from him. It seemed he was never absent from her thoughts for more than an hour before his image popped up again, speaking, gesturing, sharing intimate caresses and kisses. And, too, angry.

It was the first time she'd seen his anger, and in the way of most lovers, Theresa found it now stimulating to remember how he'd looked and sounded when he was upset. Knowing this new facet of him seemed almost a relief. Everybody has his angry moments, and the way she was feeling about Brian, she thought it imperative to see both his best and worst sides, and the sooner the better. She had fallen totally in love with the man. If he asked her to make a commitment today, she'd do it without hesitation.

But the first day passed, and a second, and a third, and still she hadn't seen Brian again. Jeff reported he'd found a one-bedroom apartment in the nearby suburb of Bloomington. It was vacant, so Brian had paid his money and taken immediate occupancy. The two men had wasted no time going off to a furniture story to buy the single item that was essential: a bed. A water bed, Jeff said. The news brought Theresa's glance sharply up to her brother, but Jeff rambled on, relating the story of how the two of them had hauled the bed to Brian's apartment in the van, then borrowed a hose from the apartment caretaker to fill the thing. The heater hadn't had time to get the water warmed up the first night, so Brian had ended up spreading his new bedding on the carpeted living-room floor to sleep.

Theresa pictured him there, alone, while she lay in her bed alone, wondering if he thought of her as strongly as she thought of him each time she slipped between the sheets for the night. It was late June, the nights hot and muggy, and she blamed her restlessness on that. It seemed she never managed to sleep straight through a night anymore, but awakened several times and spent long, sleepless hours staring at the streetlight outside her window, thinking of Brian, and wondering when she'd see him again.

He called on the fourth day. Theresa could tell who it was by Amy's part of the conversation.

"Hello?... Oh, *hiiiii*...I hear you found an apartment... Must be kind of creepy without any furniture... Oh, a pool!... All riiiiight!... Can I really!... Can I bring a friend?... Sure she does... Sure she can... Yeah, she's right here, just a sec." Amy handed the receiver to Theresa who'd been listening and waiting in agony.

The smile on Theresa's face put the June sun to shame. Her heart was rapping out an I-missed-you tattoo that made her voice come out rather breathily and unnaturally high.

"Hello?"

"Hiya, sweets," he greeted, as if they'd never had a cross word between them. How absolutely absurd to blush when he was ten miles away, but the way he could pronounce that word always sent shafts of delight through her.

"Who's this?" she asked cheekily.

His laugh vibrated along the wires and made her smile all the more broadly and feel exceedingly clever for one of the first times in her life.

"This is the guitar man, you little redheaded tease. I just got my new phone installed and wanted to give you the number here."

"Oh." Disappointment deflated Theresa with a heavy *whump*. She'd thought he was calling to ask if he could see her. "Just a minute—let me get a pencil."

"It's 555-8732," he dictated. She wrote it down, then found herself tracing it repeatedly while the conversation went on. "I've got a nice apartment, but it's a little empty yet. I did get a bed though." Had he gone on, she might not have become so flustered. But he didn't. He let the silence ooze over her skin suggestively, lifting tiny goose bumps of arousal at the imagery that popped into her mind at the thought of his bed and him in it. Theresa glanced at Amy who stood by listening, and hoped she'd had the receiver plastered hard enough against her ear that Amy hadn't gotten a drift of what Brian said.

"Oh, that's nice!" Theresa replied brightly.

"Yes, it's very nice, but a little cold the first night."

Again, she came up against a blank wall. "Oh, that's too bad."

"I slept on the floor that night, but the water's all warmed up now."

Like a dolt, she went on speaking the most idiotic inanities. "Oh, that's nice."

"Very nice, indeed. Have you ever tried a water bed?"

"No," she attempted, but the word was a croak, hardly discernible. She cleared her throat and repeated, "No."

"I'll let you lie on it sometime and see how you like it."

Theresa was so red by this time that Amy's expression had grown puzzled. Theresa covered the mouthpiece, flapped an exasperated hand at her younger sister and hissed, "Will you go find something to do?"

Amy left, throwing a last inquisitive glance over her shoulder.

"I've got a pool, too," Brian was saying.

"Oh, I love to swim." It was one of the few sports in which she'd ever been able to participate fully.

"Can you?"

For a moment she was puzzled. "Can I?"

"Yes, I mean...are you allowed to...yet?"

"Oh." The light dawned. Was she healed enough to swim. "Oh, yes, I'm back to full activities. It's been four weeks."

"Why didn't you tell me that the other night?"

His question and the tone of his voice told her the reason for his pause. He'd been waiting for the go-ahead! The idea threw her into a semipanic, yet she was anxious to pursue her relationship with him, though she knew beyond a doubt there would be few days of total innocence once they began seeing each other regularly. Considering her old-fashioned sense of propriety, it naturally put Theresa in a vulnerable position, one in which she would soon be forced to make some very critical decisions.

"I...I didn't think about it."

"I did."

She realized it now—how lightly he'd held her when they caressed, as if she were breakable. Even when they'd kissed in the driveway near the back door, he'd pulled her head hard against him, but hadn't forced her body in any way.

Neither of them said anything for a full forty-five seconds. They were coming to grips with something unspoken. During that silence he told her his intentions as clearly as if he'd illustrated them by renting a highway billboard with a two-foot-high caption. He was ready for a physical relationship. Was she?

When the silence was broken, it was Brian who spoke. His voice was slightly deeper than usual, but quiet. "Theresa, I'd like us to spend next Saturday together...here. Bring your bathing suit, and I'll pick up some corned beef at the deli, and we'll make a day of it. We'll swim and catch some sun and talk, okay?"

"Yes," she agreed quietly.

"Okay, what time should I come and get you?"

She had missed him terribly. There was only one answer she could give. "Early."

"Ten in the morning?"

No, six in the morning, she thought, but answered, "Fine. I'll be ready."

"See you then. And, honey?"

Being called *honey* by Brian was something so precious it made her chest ache.

"Yes?"
"I miss you."
"I miss you too."

It was Friday. Theresa had spent a restless night, considering the possibilities that lay ahead for her with Brian. She thought not only of the sexual tension between them, but of the responsibilities it brought. She had thought herself totally opposed to sex beyond the framework of marriage, but her brief experience in Fargo warned that when bodies are aroused, moral attitudes tend to dissolve and disappear in the expanding joy of the moment.

Would I let him? Would I let myself?

The answer to both questions, Theresa found, was an unqualified *yes*.

The following day she went to the drugstore to buy suntan lotion, knowing she'd suffer if she didn't apply an effective sunscreen to her pale, freckled skin that seemed to get hot and prickly at the mere mention of the word *sun*. She chose the one whose label said it had ultraguard, then ambled to a revolving rack of sunglasses and spent an enjoyable twenty minutes trying on every pair at least twice before choosing a rather upbeat pair with graduated shading and large round lenses that seemed to make her mouth appear feminine and vulnerable when the oversize frames rested on her nose.

She wandered along the shelves, picking up odd items she needed: emery boards, deodorant, hair conditioner. Suddenly she came up short and stared at the array of products on an eye-level shelf. *Contraceptives.*

Brian's face seemed to emblazon itself across her subconscious as if projected on a movie screen. It seemed inevitable that he would become her lover. Yet why did it seem prurient to consider buying a contraceptive in advance? It somehow took the warm glow of love to a cooler temperature and made her feel cunning and deliberate.

Without realizing she'd done it, she slipped the dark glasses on, hiding behind them, though the price tag still dangled from the bow.

Theresa Brubaker, you're twenty-six years old! You're living in twentieth-century America, where most women face this decision in their mid-teens. What are you so afraid of?

Commitment? Not at all. Not commitment to Brian, only to the undeniable tug of sexuality, for once she surrendered to it, there was no turning back. It was such an irreversible decision.

Don't be stupid, Theresa. He may keep you out by the pool all afternoon and all this gnashing will have been for nothing.

Fat chance! With my skin! If he keeps me out there all afternoon I'll look like a brick somebody forgot in the kiln. He's already hinted he's going to take me into his bedroom to try out his bed.

So, buy something! At least you'll have it if you need it.

Buy what? I've never paid any attention to the articles about products like these.

So, pick one up and read the label.

But she checked the aisle in both directions first. Even the label instructions made her blush. How on earth could she ever confront the fact that she'd have to use this stuff while she was with a man? She'd die of embarrassment!

It's either that or end up pregnant, her unwanted-companion voice persecuted.

But I'm not that kind of girl. I've always said so.

Everybody's that kind of girl when the right man comes along.

Yes, things have changed so much since Brian came into my life.

She studied the products and finally decided on one. But on her way to the checkout stand, she bought a *Cosmopolitan* magazine and dropped it nonchalantly over her other selections when setting them on the counter. *Cosmopolitan,* she thought, how appropriate. But Helen Gurley Brown would scold me for not placing the contraceptive on top of the magazine instead of vice versa.

On her next stop at the Burnsville Shopping Center, she found it necessary to buy a new purse, one large enough to conceal her new purchase. She chuckled inwardly that it turned out to be her first purchase of a contraceptive that should lead the way to her buying something she'd wanted all her life: a shoulder bag. Her shoulders had carried more than their share of strain in years gone by. She'd never felt willing to hang a purse on them as well, though she'd often wanted to own one. Well, she did now.

But the chief reason she'd come to the clothing store was to shop for a bathing suit, another item that was expanding her clothing horizon, for the suits she'd worn in the past had had to be one-pieces, altered to fit.

Now, however, she tried everything from string bikinis to skirted one-piece jobs in the Hedy Lamarr tradition. She chose a very middle-of-the-road two-piece design that wasn't exactly tawdry, but fell just short of being totally modest. The fabric was the color of her father's well-kept lawn and looked like shiny wet leather when the light caught and reflected from it. The bright kelly green was a hue that in days of old she'd have said contrasted with her coloring too sharply—the old stop-and-go-light look. But somehow, since her surgery, Theresa's confidence had grown. And since the advent of Brian in her sphere, she had felt far less plain than she used to. This gift he'd given her was something Theresa meant to repay in some way someday.

* * *

The following morning she awakened shortly after five o'clock. The sun was peeking over the eastern horizon, turning the sky to a lustrous, pearly coral, sending streaks of brighter melon and pink radiating above the rim of the world. Closing her eyes and stretching, Theresa felt as if those shafts of hot pink were penetrating her body. She felt giddy, elated and as if she were on the brink of the most momentous day of her life.

The Maestro grinned down at her from the shelf, and it seemed as if he fiddled a gay, lilting love song to awaken her. She smiled at him, slithered lower in the bed, raised both arms above her head and rolled to her belly, savoring the keen satisfaction a simple act like that now brought into her life. It made her feel diminutive and catlike. Beneath her, the bulk was gone, in its place a body proportioned by a hand that had, in this case, improved upon Nature.

There were times when she still had difficulty realizing the change had happened and was permanent. Sometimes she found herself affecting mannerisms no longer necessary: crossing one arm and resting the opposite elbow on it to give momentary relief by boosting up her breasts, yet at the same time hiding behind her arms. Walking. Ah, but there simply hadn't been a chance to run yet. But she would, someday soon. Just to feel the ebullience and freedom of the act.

She threw herself onto her back, studied the ceiling and checked the clock. Was it broken? Or had only five minutes passed since she'd awakened? Would the rest of the morning go this slowly until Brian came to her?

It did.

In spite of the fact that she performed every grooming ritual with the pomp and time-consuming attention of a ceremony. She shaved her legs...all the way up, for the first time in her life. She filed her toenails into delicate rounded peaks and polished them with Chocolate Mocha polish. She gave herself a careful and complete manicure, painting her fingernails with three coats. She washed her hair and arranged it with care that was positively silly, considering she was going to leap into a swimming pool within minutes after she got there. But she spared no less care on her makeup. She ironed the aqua blue collar of a white terry beach coverup with matching lounging pants whose ribbed ankles had a matching aqua stripe that continued up the outsides of the legs, and up the arms of the loose sweat-shirt style jacket. She took a bath and put an astringent after-bath splash up her legs and down her arms, and finally, when only a half hour remained, she put her bedroom in order, then hung up her housecoat and picked up the green bathing suit. She slipped into the brief panties, easing them up her legs and turning to present her derriere to the mirror, checking the reflection to find it firm, shapely and nothing she would change, even if she could. The elasticized brief rode across the crest of each hipbone, and just below her navel, exposing both it and the tender hollow of her spine.

As she turned to face the mirror again, with the strappy suit top in her hand, she assessed her reflected breasts. The crescent-shaped scars beneath each had been the fastest to heal, and the circular ones about the nipples had all but vanished. The only ones that were still highly detectable were those running vertically from the bottom up to each nipple. Dr. Schaum had told her to expect them to take a good six months to fade completely, but had assured her they would, for the newer method of surgery allowed the skin to be draped instead of stretched back into place, thus taking stress off the suturing and allowing the tissue to heal almost invisibly. They did, however, itch. Theresa opened the jar of cocoa butter and gently massaged a dollop of the soothing balm along the length of each scar. But as she finished, her fingertips remained on her left breast. But it was not the scar she saw. She saw a woman changed. A woman whose horizons had expanded in thousands of definable and indefinable ways since her surgery. She saw a woman who no longer cared that her freckles ran down her chest and up her legs, a woman who no longer considered her hair carrot-colored, but merely "bright," a woman whose medium, orange-sized breasts appeared almost beautiful to her own eyes. The nipples seemed to have shrunk from the surgery, and their perky position, pointed upward instead of down, never ceased to be a source of amazement.

She raised her arms above her head experimentally. When she did this, her breasts lifted with her arms, as they'd never done before. She pirouetted swiftly to the left, watching, to be rewarded by the sight of her breasts coming right along with her instead of swaying pendulously several inches behind the movement of her trunk.

A marvelous, appreciative smile burst across her face.

I am female. I am as beautiful as I feel. And today I feel utterly beautiful.

She hooked the bathing suit top behind her back, then lifted her arms to tie the strings behind her neck, examining the way the concealing triangles of sheeny green covered her breasts. She ran her fingertips along the deep V, down the freckled skin to the spot where the two triangles met. There was scarcely any cleavage! The wonder of it was almost enough to make her high!

She hated to slip the white terry pants and jacket on and cover herself up. Oh, glorious, glorious liberation! How wonderful you feel!

She packed a drawstring bag with sunscreen, towels, hair lifter, makeup, cocoa butter, shampoo, a pair of jeans and a brand new bra made of scalloped blue lace. Her thirty days of wearing the firm support bra were over. This little wisp of femininity was what she'd long craved.

While stuffing her belongings in the bag, she realized even this was a new experience to be savored, for she'd never gone skipping off with boys to the beach when she was a girl. There was so much catching up to do!

By the time ten o'clock arrived, Theresa was not only ready, she was a totally self-satisfied ready.

The van turned into the driveway, and she stepped out onto the back step to await him. Through the windshield she saw him smile and raise a palm, then shut off the ignition, open the door and walk toward her.

He was wearing his aviator sunglasses, white, tight swimming trunks beneath an unbuttoned navy blue shirt with three zippered patch pockets, white buttons and epaulettes. The shirt's long sleeves were rolled up, exposing his arms from the elbow down, and its tails flapped in the light breeze as he approached. He moved around the front of the van in a loose-jointed amble, keeping his eyes on her face until he stood on the apron of the step below her, looking up. Lazily, he reached up to remove the glasses while every cell in her body became energized by his presence.

"Hello, sweets."

"Hello, Brian." She wanted very badly to call him an endearment, but the expressive way she spoke his name actually became an endearment in itself.

Was it she who reached first, or he? All Theresa knew later was that one moment she stood two steps above him, and the next, she was in his arms, sharing a hello kiss beneath the bright June sun at ten o'clock on a Saturday morning. She, the timid introvert who'd often wondered why some women were blessed with lives in which scenes like this were taken for granted, while others could only lie in their lonely beds at night and dream of such bliss.

It wasn't a passionate kiss. It wasn't even very intimate. But it swept her off the step and against his partially exposed chest while she circled his neck with both arms, captured in such a fashion that she was looking down at him. He lifted his lips, brushed them caressingly over hers, then dipped his head to bestow another such accolade to the triangle of freckles that showed above the zippered white terry coverup. "Mmm...you smell good." He released her enough to allow her breasts and belly to go sliding down his body until she stood before him, smiling up at his admiring, stunning, summer eyes.

"Mmm...you do too."

His hands rested on her hipbones. She was piercingly aware of it, even as they gazed, unmoving, into each other's faces and stood in broad daylight, for any of the neighbors to see.

"Are you ready?"

"I've been ready since six a.m."

He laughed, rode his hands up her ribs and turned her toward the door. "Then get your stuff and let's not waste a minute."

Chapter Fifteen

The Village Green Apartments were tudor-trimmed stucco buildings arranged in a horseshoe shape around a dazzling aqua-and-white swimming pool. The grounds were wooded with old elms whose leafy branches drooped in the still summer morning. Theresa caught a glimpse of the pool as Brian passed it, then pulled around the far side of the second building. Glancing up, she saw small decks flanking the length of the stucco walls, and an occasional splash of crimson from a potted geranium in a redwood tub.

Inside, the halls were carpeted, papered and silent. Padding along with Brian at her shoulder, Theresa found herself unable to keep from watching his bare toes curl into each step as he walked. There was something undeniably intimate about being with a barefoot man. Brian's feet were medium sized, shaded with hair on his big toes, and it struck her how much more angular a man's foot was than a woman's. His legs were muscular and sprinkled with a modicum of hair on all but the fronts and backs of his knees. He stopped before number 122, unlocked the door and stepped back.

"It's not much yet, but it will be."

She entered a living room with plush, bone-colored carpeting. Directly across from the door by which they'd entered was an eight-foot-wide sliding glass door decorated with an open-weave drapery that was drawn aside to give a view of the pool and surrounding grassy area. The room held one chocolate brown director's chair, a cork-based lamp sitting beside it on the floor and nothing else except musical equipment: guitars, amplifiers, speakers as tall as Theresa's shoulders, microphones, a reel-to-reel recorder, stereo, radio, tapes and records.

Forming an L in juxtaposition with the living room was a tiny galley kitchen with a Formica-topped peninsula counter dividing it from the rest of the open area. A short hall presumably led to the bathroom and bedroom beyond.

Theresa stopped in the middle of the carpeted expanse. It seemed very lonely and barren, and it made Theresa somehow sad to walk into the quiet emptiness and think about Brian here all alone, with no furniture, none of the comforts of home, nobody to talk to or to share music with. But she turned and smiled brightly.

"Home is where the heart is, they say."

He, too, smiled. "So I've heard. Still, you can see why I invited you over to swim. It's about all I'm equipped to offer."

Oh, I wouldn't say that, came the sudden impulsive thought. She shrugged, one thumb hooking the drawstring of the carryall bag that was slung over her shoulder. She glanced around his living room again. "Swimming is one of the few active pastimes I've enjoyed ever since I was little. I love it. Is all this equipment *yours?*" She ventured across to the impressive array of sound equipment, leaning forward to gaze into the smoked-glass doors of his component cabinet.

"Yup."

"Wow."

He watched her move from piece to piece, touching nothing until her eye was caught by a three-ring notebook lying open on the floor beside an old, beat-up-looking flat-top guitar. She knelt, examined the handwritten words, and looked up. "Your song-book?"

He nodded.

She turned the pages, riffling through them slowly, stopping here and there to hum a few bars. "It must have taken you years to collect all these."

She found herself drawn to the sheets simply because they contained his handwriting, with which she'd grown so familiar during the past half year. The songs were arranged alphabetically, so she couldn't resist turning to the *Ss. S-A, S-E, S-L, S-O*...and there it was: "Sweet Memories." Without realizing she'd done it, her fingers grazed the sheets feeling the slight indentation made by his ballpoint pen years ago.

Sweet memories of her own came flooding back. And for Brian, standing near, watching her, the same thing happened. He was transported back to New Year's Eve, dancing with her in his arms, then curling her against his chest before a slow, golden fire. But it was shortly after ten o'clock on a June morning, and he'd invited her here to swim. He brought himself back from his concentrated study of the woman kneeling before him to ask, "Would you like to change into your suit?"

Reluctantly she left her musings. "Oh, I have it on. All I have to do is jump out of these." She pinched the stretchy terry cloth and pulled it away from both thighs, while grinning up at him.

"Well, I'm ready if you are."

"Just a minute. I think I'll leave my sandals in here." She rolled to a sitting position with one knee updrawn and began unbuckling the ankle strap. While she tugged at it, he moved closer to stand beside her and study the top of her head. She was terribly conscious of his chestnut-colored legs, sprinkled with hair, just at her elbow, and of his bare toes close to her hip.

"I wouldn't have taken you for a woman who'd wear toenail polish." Her hands fell still for a second, then tugged again and the first sandal came free. As she reached for the second one, she raised her eyes to find him standing with arms akimbo, looking down at her, the front panels of his shirt held aside by his wrists. His bare chest drew her eyes almost magnetically.

"I'm trying a lot of new things these days that I've never had the nerve to try before. Why? Don't you like it?"

He suddenly hunkered down, captured her foot and began removing her sandal. "I love it. You have the prettiest toes of any violin player I've ever gone swimming with." The sandal dropped to the floor, and to Theresa's astonishment, he carried the bare foot to his lips and kissed the underside of her big toe, then the soft, vulnerable skin of her instep. Her eyes flew open, and the blush began creeping up. Brian grinned and unconcernedly retained possession of her foot, lazily stroking its arch with a thumb. "Well, you said you were trying new things you'd never tried before, and I thought this might be one to add to your list." This time, when his teeth gently nipped at the sensitive instep, her lips fell open and her eyes widened.

Theresa stared at him. Her throat had gone dry, and she was unable to move. When he'd lifted her foot, she'd lost her balance and teetered back, so sat now with elbows locked and both hands braced on the carpet behind her. Suddenly she realized her fingers were clutching the fibers. Though her eyes were riveted on Brian's face, she was arousingly aware of his pose. Balancing on the balls of his feet, his knees were widespread, but pointed at her so that it was all she could do to keep her eyes from dropping to the insides of his thighs. She knew by some magical telepathy, though she hadn't looked, that his inner thighs were smoothed of hair, just as his knees were. The muscles of his legs were bulged and taut, his insteps curved like those of Achilles running. His unbuttoned shirt fell loose and wide at his hips. The elasticized fabric of his white bathing trunks was molded to his thighs and conformed to the masculine rises and ridges between his legs.

Swallowing the lump in her throat, Theresa carefully withdrew her foot. "I think we'd better go out," she advised shakily.

"Right. Grab your bag." Straightening those alarmingly close knees, he reached a hand down and tugged her to her feet. He rolled the sliding screen back and she moved out into the sun ahead of him, her senses so fully awakened by his nearness that even the sound of the vinyl rollers gliding in the track made her feel as if they'd just wheeled smoothly up her spinal column. How odd to be stepping into the intense heat of the late June sun, yet be shivering and experiencing the titillating effect of goose bumps rising up her arms and thighs.

There was nobody else in the pool area this early in the day. Yellow and white striped umbrellas were still closed, and the tubular plastic chairs and recliners were all pushed neatly under the tables. The concrete rectangle was surrounded by a broad stretch of thick green grass on all sides, and as Theresa crossed it, the cool blades tickled her bare toes.

The pool was stunningly clear, its surface shimmering slightly. In the aqua depths an automatic cleaning device snaked back and forth, back and forth, sweeping the pool floor.

Brian dipped one knee and stuck his toe in the water.

"It's warm. Should we go in right away and work off our breakfasts?"

"I was too excited to eat breakfast." Realizing what she'd said, she sucked on her lower lip and chanced a quick peek at the man beside her to find him gazing down benignly at her pink cheeks.

"Oh, really?"

"I'll never succeed as a femme fatale, will I? I don't think I was supposed to admit that."

"A femme fatale would keep a man guessing. But one of the first things I liked about you was that you didn't. I could read you as easily as you just read the words to 'Sweet Memories' in there. That *is* what you were reading, isn't it?"

"Yes."

"I wonder how many times I played it and thought of you during the past six months."

He stood so near, Theresa thought she could feel nothing more than the auburn hairs on his arms entwined with the strawberry blond ones on her own. His eyes held a sincerity mixed with controlled desire, and she met it with an expression much the same. On the cool ceramic coping upon which they stood, his right foot eased over an inch until his toes covered hers, and Theresa wondered if a touch that innocent could release such a wellspring of response within her body, what must the carnal act inspire? His voice was deep and held a note of self-teasing. "There. Now we're even. Whatever the male equivalent of the femme fatale is, I'm not it. I don't want to hold any of my feelings back from you. I never wanted to, not since the first day I met you."

"Brian, let's go swimming. I'm dying of the heat...whatever's causing it."

"Good idea. Especially since we have the place to ourselves for now."

He moved to the end of the pool and cranked open one of the umbrellas, then angled its top toward the sun. She flung her tote bag on the tabletop, then unzipped her coverup, shrugged it off and tossed it over the back of a patio chair. With her back to Brian she shimmied the elastic waist of the matching terry pants down past her hips, then flung them, too, onto the chair.

She heard the buttons and zippers of his shirt hit the metal tabletop with a ping, and assumed he was standing behind her, studying her back. This was the moment about which she'd dreamed and fantasized for years. She, Theresa Brubaker, clad in a bathing suit that left just enough to the imagination, was about to turn and face the man she loved. And she didn't have to cross her arms over her chest, nor keep her towel draped around her neck, or hunch her shoulders to disguise the thrust of her feminine attributes.

She turned to find him staring, as she'd known he'd be. Neither of them moved for a long, silent stretch of time. His chest was bare, and the white trunks dipped just below his navel, leaving it surrounded by a thin line of hair leading from the wider dark mat above. His nipples looked like copper pennies in the shade of the umbrella. His ribs were lean. His lips were partially open. His eyes unabashedly scanned her from face to knees, then lingeringly moved back up again with the slow deliberation of an art critic.

"Wow," Brian breathed. And incredible as it seemed, even to herself, Theresa believed him. The airy word was all she needed to reaffirm her desirability. But she could imagine her damn freckles zinging to life on her blushing neck and cheeks, so she turned to open her bag and rummage through it for the sunscreen.

"You'll probably eat your word within an hour. You've never seen what happens to me when the sun hits my skin. I'm a living demonstration of why physicians refer to freckles as heat spots. And I burn to a brilliant neon pink." From the depths of her bag she retrieved the lotion and uncapped it, then squirted a generous curl into her palm. "Want some?"

"Thanks." He took the bottle, and they busied themselves applying the sweet-scented lotion to their arms, necks, faces and legs. When Theresa rubbed it along the edge of the V-neck on her suit, she felt his eyes following the movements of her palm and glanced up to find him putting lotion on his chest. Her eyes dropped to his long fingers that massaged the firm musculature, delving through crisp hair, leaving it glistening with oils. He took another squirt, handed the bottle to her, and they stared at each other's hands—his running across his hard belly and along the elastic waist of his trunks; hers traversing delicate ribs, and the horizontal line along the bottom of her bikini top before curving into the depression of her navel, then around her exposed hipbones.

The lotion was slick and fragrant. It smelled of coconut, citrus and a hint of berry, filling the air around them like ambrosia. Watching his hands gliding over his skin, Theresa conjured up the thought of them gliding over hers. She dropped to the chair and began doing her legs, stretching first one, then the other out before her, sensing his eyes fol-

lowing again as she stroked the tender flesh of her inner thighs. She kept
her eyes averted but saw peripherally how he lifted one leg to hook his
toes over the edge of a lawn chair and massage fruit-scented magic along
the length of his leg. He'd turned to the side, and she had a chance to
study him without being studied herself.

Her eyes traversed his curving back, the buttock, the raised thigh and
the junction of his legs where secrets waited. It suddenly flashed across
Theresa's mind why in Victorian times men and women were never allowed to go ocean bathing together. It was a decidedly sensual thing,
studying a man in swim trunks.

She dragged her eyes away, wondering if she was supposed to feel
guilty at this new and unexpected curiosity she harbored. She didn't. Not
at all. She was twenty-six years old—it occurred to her it was high time
this curiosity surfaced and was appeased.

"Will you put some on my back?" he asked.

"Sure, turn around," she answered jauntily. But when she was squeezing the bottle, her outstretched palm trembled. His back was smooth and
had several brown moles. He had wide shoulders that tapered to trim
hips, the skin taut and healthy. When her hand touched his shoulder he
twitched, as if he, too, were keyed up with awareness, and had been
awaiting that first touch with as great a sense of anticipation as she. When
her fingers curved around his ribs to his sides, he lifted his arms slightly
away from his body to allow her access. For a moment, she was tempted
to run both hands all the way around his trunks and press her face to the
hollow between his shoulder blades. Instead she squirted a coil of white
into her palm and worked both hands unilaterally across the crests of his
hard shoulders and up the sides and back of his neck, even into the hair
at its nape. Already the hair was longer, which pleased her. She had never
been crazy about his Air Force haircuts, for she'd imagined that if allowed
to grow to collar length, his would curve gently in thick, free swoops.
As her fingers massaged his neck, he tipped his head backward and a
guttural sound escaped his throat. Her palms, as well as the nerve endings
along the rest of her body, felt as if they were instantly on fire.

It grew worse—or better—when he turned and took the bottle from
her slippery fingers, ordering quietly, "Turn around."

She spun from the ardor in his eyes, then felt his long palms pressing
a cold mound of lotion against her bare flesh, then begin turning it warm
with the friction and contact of skin upon skin. His touch made it extremely difficult to breathe, and impossible to control the tempo of her
heart, which seemed to rise up and search out the spots his hand grazed,
pounding right through the walls of her back. His fingers curved over her
shoulder, up beneath her hair, forcing her chin to drop forward, spreading
the essence of wondrous exotic delicacies all about her. He massaged the

breadth of her shoulder blades, skipped over the elasticized back strip of her suit, and after taking another liberal amount of sunscreen, his finger-tips eased up beneath the strap, running left to right beneath it, from just beneath her left armpit to the same spot under her right. Lower they went, down the delicate hollow of her back, and along the elastic of her emerald green briefs, curving upon the sculptured hipbone, teasing at the taut rubberized waistband that cinched tightly against her flesh. The oils made his hands glide sensuously across her skin, and she shuddered beneath them.

His touch disappeared. She heard the faint sound of the cap being replaced on the bottle, then of the bottle meeting the aluminum tabletop. But she didn't move. She couldn't. She felt as if she'd never move again as long as she lived, not unless this fire in her veins was cooled and put out. If it wasn't, she'd stand there and burn into a cinder.

"Last one in's a moldy worm," came the heavy, aroused voice from behind her. Then she was sprinting to the end of the pool—running at last!—hitting the water stretched out full length, just at the instant Brian hit it. The shock was breathtaking. From the heat of a second ago her body dropped what seemed a full fifty degrees. She swam furiously, a powerful, controlled crawl to the far end of the pool, her body temperature stabilizing by the time she reached her goal.

Side by side they swam eight laps, and in the middle of the ninth, Theresa spluttered, waved limply and declared, "Goodbye, I think I'm drowning," then went under. When her head surfaced, he was treading water, waiting.

"Woman, I'm not through with you yet. Sorry, no drowning till I am." And unceremoniously he disappeared, came up in the perfect position to command her body in an exemplary demonstration of a Senior Lifesaving hold, with his left arm angled across her chest while he hauled her to the far end of the pool beneath the overhanging diving board.

She let herself go limp and he pulled along in an unresisting state of breathlessness and sensuality. His elbow clamped down on her left breast, and it felt wonderful.

At the pool wall he released her, and they both crossed their arms on the sleek concrete, resting their cheeks on their wrists while facing each other, both panting, feet flapping lazily on the surface of the blue water behind them.

"You're melting," he announced with a grin, reaching out a fingertip and running it beneath her right eye.

"Oh, my makeup!" She slipped under the water again and scrubbed at her eyelids before emerging sparkly lashed, and asking if she was still discolored.

"Yes, but leave it. It's very Greta Garbo."

"You're a very good swimmer."

"So are you."

"As I said before, it was about the only physical exercise that was easy for me when I was growing up. But I kind of gave it up too, when I was in my late teens, because I was afraid it would...well, build up the muscles all the more, if you know what I mean."

He was studying her wet face carefully. "It seems like there are a lot of things you had to give up that I'd never have suspected."

"Yes, well that's all over now. I'm a new person."

"Theresa, is it...well, are you sure you aren't overdoing it, swimming so hard? It worries me, even though you said you're a hundred percent again."

As if to reaffirm her full recovery, she caught the edge of the pool and boosted herself up, twisting to a sitting position above him with her feet dangling in the water. "One hundred percent, Brian."

He joined her on the edge of the pool. She flung her hair back, feeling his eyes following each movement as she wrung her hair out and sent rivulets running down her back and over her shoulder. Beneath them the concrete was sun-warmed, and the water soon joined their flesh to the sleek surface with a tepid slipperiness.

He ran his hands over his cheeks to clear them of excess water, then wove his fingers through his hair, running them toward the back of his head, and studying the umbrella at the far end of the pool as he asked quietly, "Theresa, would you feel self-conscious answering some questions about your operation?"

"Probably. But ask them anyway. I've been working very hard on my self-image and on trying to overcome self-consciousness. But if you don't mind, I'd better have a little lotion on my face and back. I feel like most of it washed off."

They got to their feet, leaving dark gray footprints along the concrete as they made their way toward the opposite end of the pool. Theresa dried her hair, then spread her towel out on the soft grass and sat down on it while applying lotion to her face once more. When she was done, she flipped over and stretched out full length on her stomach, thinking it would be infinitely easier to answer his questions if she wasn't looking at him.

His hands eased over her skin, spreading it with lotion once more while he asked quietly, "When did you decide to have it done?"

"Remember when I wrote and told you I slipped in the parking lot and fell down?"

"I remember."

"It was right after that. When the doctor examined my back he told me I should look into having the problem solved permanently."

"Your back?"

"There's a lot of back and shoulder discomfort that goes along with it. People don't know that. The shoulders are especially vulnerable. I thought probably you'd noticed the grooves—they still show a little bit."

"These?" His fingertips massaged one of her shoulders, and she felt a heavenly thrill ripple through her body before he went on, "I wasn't exactly looking at your shoulders before, but I see the marks now. What else? Tell me everything about it. Was it hard for you, psychologically, I mean?"

Belly down, on a beach towel, with her cheek on the back of her hand, with her eyes closed, she told Brian everything. All about her misgivings, her mother's and father's initial reactions to her decision, her fears and uncertainties, omitting the fact that the feeling had not yet returned to her nipples. She couldn't force herself to share that intimacy with him yet. If and when the time came, she'd be honest, but for now she glossed over that and the part about being unable to nurse a baby.

When her recital was finished, he was still sitting beside her with his arm circling one updrawn knee. His voice was soft and disarming.

"Theresa, I'm sorry for getting mad at you my first night back. I never understood about a lot of it."

"I know. And I'm sorry I didn't at least write and tell Jeff, and let him tell you what my plans were."

"No, you were right. You didn't owe me anything. That first night when we went for a walk, I'll admit part of my problem was I was scared. I thought maybe now that you'd taken the big step you'd be out for bigger fish than this underage guitar man whose past isn't quite as pure as you deserve."

His words brought her head up. Bracing on one elbow she twisted to look back over her shoulder at him. "I long ago stopped placing any importance on the differences in our ages. You're more mature than most of the thirty-year-old men I work with at school. Maybe that's why you were so...I don't know. Understanding, I guess. Right from the first, I sensed that you were different from all the others I'd ever met, that you really did look into me, the person, and judge me by my inner qualities or shortcomings."

"Shortcomings?" He flopped down on his back almost underneath her partially lifted chest and touched the tangled locks above her left ear. "You don't have any shortcomings, sweets."

"Oh, yes I do. Everybody does."

"Where they been hidin'?"

She smiled at his playfulness, glanced down at her forearm, and answered, "Several thousand of them have been lurking just below the surface of my skin and are just now coming out to introduce themselves."

Indeed, her "heat spots" were heating up. The freckles on her arms had already grown so fat their perimeters were dissolving into one another.

He rolled his cheek against the towel, pulled her soft inner arm to his lips, and declared quietly, "Angel kisses." He kissed her again, higher, almost at the bend of elbow. "Have you been kissing any angels lately, Miss Brubaker?"

She studied his green eyes, and let her feelings show in her own. "Not as often as I want to." She smiled and added impulsively, "Gabriel."

"Then what do you say we remedy that?" With a swift flexing of muscle, he was on his feet, reaching out a hand to tug her up. He gathered towels, togs and lotion and handed her the bag. She followed willingly, walking at his side while one light hand guided her shoulders as she crossed the grass toward the sliding door of his apartment.

She stepped inside where it was cool and shaded. She heard him snap the lock on the screen door, then step to the drapery cord and draw the curtain closed until the midday light was even more subdued through the open weave of the fabric. It threw gentle checkers across the thick carpet and her bare toes. She had the fleeting thought that her hair was probably plastered to her head in some places and flying at odd angles in others, and that her makeup was all washed away. Behind her she heard a metallic click, then the soft *shhh* of a needle settling onto a disc. She was frantically scrambling to find her comb in the bottom of the tote bag when a guitar introduction softly filled the room, and an insistent hand captured the drawstring bag and pulled it from her nervous fingers, as if Brian would brook no delays, no repairs, no excuses.

My world is like a river
As dark as it is deep....

As the poignant words met her ears, she was turned around by lean, hard fingers that closed over the sensitive spot where her neck met her shoulders. When his eyes delved into hers, he wordlessly searched out her palms and carried them up around his neck. His body was moving in rhythm to the music but so very slightly she scarcely felt the evocative sway of his shoulders beneath the soft flesh of her inner arms. But some magical force made her body answer the almost imperceptible beckoning as he swayed, drawing nearer and nearer until the fabric of her suit brushed the hair upon his chest. The invitation was wordless at first, as his warm palms found her naked back and pressed her lightly against him. Then he began humming softly, drawing away only far enough to continue searching her uplifted face while his palm gently caressed the hollow between her shoulder blades, then traced the depression down her spine. With only the slightest force he urged her hips closer, closer, until her bare stomach touched his—sleek to rough. He undulated slowly as if bidding her to join him. She responded with a first hesitant movement until she felt his hips and loins, confined by the taut piece of clothing that covered him, pressed firmly against her.

His breath was warm upon her mouth as he touched it first with the tip of his tongue, then lightly with the outermost surfaces of his lips. He was still humming. As her lips dropped open she felt the soft intonation tickling the crests of them. The sound, the feeling and his careful doling out of contact served only to tantalize, then he lifted his head and began singing the refrain that had been in her heart since she'd heard him sing the words with the battered old fifteen-dollar Stella in his lap.

> Sweet memories,
> Sweet memories....

When the voice on the record hummed the final notes and took the song home, she was settled securely against the full, hard length of Brian's body, feeling all its surfaces, ridges and textures as if she were on an elevated plane of sensory awareness.

In the thundering silence between songs, his hard body and soft voice combined in a message of latent passion. "Theresa, I love you, girl...so much...so much." It seemed too sweeping to take in. Their bodies no longer moved, but were pressed together until the naked skin of his thighs and belly seemed bonded to hers by the slightly oily, very fragrant suntan lotion whose aroma evoked images of tropical islands, warm sunlit shores and the calls of cockatoos. Her senses were filled with the smell of him, his warmth and firmness, but mostly with the sleek texture of his skin.

"Brian...my guitar man, I think I started loving you when you stepped off that plane and looked me square in the eye."

Another song had begun, but its rhythm went unheeded, for they were entwined in each other's arms, hearing only the beats of their hearts pressed together with nothing but two triangles of thin green material between them. The kiss lost all tentativeness and blossomed into a full complementary exchange of sleek tongues and throaty murmurs. His head moved sensuously above hers, wooing and winning her slow, sure acquiescences. Her inhibitions began dissolving until he felt her hips reaching toward a closer communion with his as she raised up on tiptoe to mold her curves more securely against his, all the while clinging to his sleek shoulders.

His palms moved down to learn the shape of her firm hipbones once more, then the solid flesh of her rounded buttocks, cupping them in both hands as he drew close.

He tore his mouth from hers, his eyes glowing with the fire of a passion too long denied. "Sweets, I promised I wouldn't come back here and force this issue. I said I'd take it slow, and give you time to—"

"I've had twenty-six years, Brian. That's long enough."

When he lifted his head she felt deprived at the loss of his warm lips and reached with her own, as if she suddenly couldn't get her fill of these long-delayed joys.

"Do you mean it, Theresa? Are you sure?"

"I'm sure. Oh, Brian, I'm so sure it hurts...right here." She took her palm and pressed it against her heart. "I thought I'd be afraid and uncertain when this moment came, but I'm not. Not at all. Somehow, when you love, you know." She gazed up at him in wonder, touching his lips with her fingertips. "You just know," she breathed.

"Yes, you know, darling."

Slowly he covered her shoulders with his hands and pressed her away from him to gaze into her ardent eyes while he spoke. "I want you to look around at this room." She felt herself turned until her bare back was pressed against his rough-textured chest. From behind he circled her ribs, his forearms resting just below her breasts, touching their undersides. "This room has no furniture because I wanted us to pick it out together. I thought about waiting to ask you until afterward, but I find I want to know first. Will you marry me, Theresa? Just as soon as it can be arranged? And we can fill this place with furniture and your piano and music and maybe a couple of kids, and make sweet memories for the rest of—"

"Yes!" She spun and looped her arms around his neck, cutting off his words with the kiss and muffled word before lifting her mouth from his and singing, "Yes, yes, yes! I didn't know whether I wanted you to ask me before or after but it's probably best before, 'cause I probably won't do so well...." His eyebrows drew into a puzzled frown. "I'm not experienced at this part," she explained diffidently.

The next minute she was scooped up into his arms and felt his hard belly against her hip while he carried her down the hall to his bedroom.

"Trust me. You will be, as soon as it can be arranged."

From the bedroom doorway where he paused, she saw her marriage bed for the first time. It looked like any other bed, covered with a quilted spread of brown-and-blue geometric design that matched the two sheets haphazardly thrown over the curtain rods to lend the room privacy.

"I never thought to ask you before I bought a waterbed if you like them or not."

"Can a person get seasick on it?"

"I hope not."

With her arms looped around his neck she drew his head down until his mouth joined hers. Muffled against his lips she muttered, "Well, I brought plenty of dramamine pills along, just in case."

The trip to the bed in Brian's arms was like crossing the bridge of a rainbow connecting the earth to heaven. When she was a girl, Theresa had wondered, as all girls do from the time they feel the first stirrings of maturity, what the man would be like when the moment came? And the setting—would it be dark? Winter or summer? Day or night? Inside or outside? And our first intimate encounter—would it be rushed or slow? Silent or vocal? Reckless or poignant? Would it leave me feeling more—or less?

The sheets rippled at the windows. The sun brought the blue-and-brown pattern alive, backlighting it until the entwined diamonds and parallellograms danced upon the shimmering fabric, while from outside came the faraway voices of children who clanged the gate to the pool area, then whooped gleefully as they took their first plunge.

From the living room came the strains of love songs, distant now, unintrusive, but mellow and wooing. Brian's bare feet moved soundlessly across the cocoa-colored carpet. His lips wore a faint smile, and his steady eyes rested upon Theresa's while he sat on the edge of the bed with her legs across his lap. She felt a faint surge of liquid motion lift them momentarily, then subside. Twisting at the hip he placed her the wrong way across the bed, across its width, lying on his side next to her with his knees slightly updrawn.

He braced up on one elbow, smiling down into her face, running the tip of an index finger along the rim of her lower lip. The smile had drifted from her face, and her lingering apprehensions were reflected in the wide brown eyes and the slightly parted lips.

"Are you scared?" he asked softly.

She swallowed and nodded. "A little."

"About anything in particular?"

"My lack of experience, among other things."

"Experience will take care of itself. What are the other things?" His fingers trailed along her jaw and began gently freeing the strands of hair from about her temples, absently arranging them in a bright corona about her head.

Already she felt the telltale blush climbing her chest. "I...." The words stuck, creating a tight knot in the center of her chest. "I don't...." His eyes left the hair he'd been toying with and met hers, but his fingers were still threaded through the red strands, resting upon the warm skull just above the left ear. "Oh, Brian." She covered her face with both hands. "This is so hard, and I know I'm blushing terribly, and there's noth- ing less becoming to a redhead than blushing, and I've never—"

"Theresa!" His gentle reprimand cut her off as he circled her wrists and forced her hands away from her face. She stared up at him in silence. The reprimand left his voice, and it became compelling. "I love you. Did you forget that? There's nothing you can't tell me. Whatever it is, we'll work it out together, all right? And, just to set the record straight, red-heads look darling when they blush. Now, would you like to start again?"

The muscles in her stomach were jumping. Her fists were clenched, the tendons tight beneath his grasp. She sucked in a huge, fortifying gulp of air and ran the words out so fast she wouldn't have a chance to change her mind. "I - don't - want - to - get - pregnant - and - I - went - to - the - drugstore - yesterday - and - bought - something - to - make - sure - I - wouldn't - but - the - instructions - said - I - had - to - use - it - half - an - hour - before - and - I - don't - know - before - *what* - or - how - long - anything - takes - because - I've - never - done - this - before - and - oh - please - Brian - let - my - hands - go - so - I - can - hide - behind - them!"

To Theresa's amazement, he laughed lovingly and wrapped her in both of his arms, falling to his side and taking her along until they lay almost nose to nose. "Is that all? Ah, sweet Theresa, what a joy you are." He kissed the tip of her very red nose, then lay back, running a finger along the crest of her cheek. His voice was quiet and calm. "I had the same thought myself, so I came prepared, too. That means you have a choice, sweetheart. You or me."

She tried to say me, but the word refused to come out, so she only nodded.

"Well, now's the time." He sat up and tugged her along after him, and she padded to the living room for her purse, then back down the hall toward the bathroom.

When she returned to the bedroom he was lying on his back across the bed, still in his swimtrunks, with his arm folded behind his head.

Through the open doorway he had watched the green bathing suit ap-pear as she opened the bathroom door, crossed the hall and approached the bed. Long before she reached it, he'd extended a palm in invitation.

"Come here, little one."

She lifted one knee to the edge of the bed, placing her palm in his, and let him tug her down until she fell into the hollow of his arm, partially across his chest. The water stirred beneath them, then went still. His right arm remained beneath his head, but even one-handed he eased her closer, tighter, until she hovered above him, and his eyes conveyed the remainder of the message. She bent her head to touch his lips with her own, and the kiss began with a meeting no heavier than the morning mist settling upon a lily. It expanded into the first brief touch of tongue tips—tentative, introductory, promising. He tasted slightly sweet, as if some of the tropical sunscreen still lingered on his lips. His tongue sought the deeper secrets of her mouth, and hers his. Seek, touch, stroke, chase, devour— they shared each advancing step of the intimate kiss. Longing sang through her veins, enlivening each of her senses until she perceived each touch, sound, taste, sight and smell with that new, exultant keenness she'd discovered for the first time today. His relaxed pose lifted the firm muscles of his chest and exposed them in a way that invited exploration.

She let her hand seek out his neck first, recalling the throaty sound he'd uttered when she'd stroked that soft hollow once before. She allowed her thumb to explore the hard knot of his Adam's apple, and beneath the soft pad, the masculine point jumped as he swallowed. When her thumb slid down to the shallow well at its base, she felt his pulse racing there, pressing against her finger like a knocking engine.

It had happened again, that response she could kindle so effortlessly in this man. She sensed it and experimented, a little bit more. Her hand left his neck and flattened upon the firm rise of his chest, experiencing the rough texture of hair, then the tiny point of his nipple, which she first fanned, then scissored between her fingers, while bracing over him, moving her lips downward to touch the warm skin on his chest. She tasted him. Sweet oil and salt and sun and chlorine and coconut and papaya. She had not dreamed he would have taste, yet he did, and it was heady and sensual. Beneath her tongue the rough hairs of his body felt magnified, yet silky. Upon her lips she felt the faint oily residue left behind by the sunscreen. He was warm and resilient and utterly male.

Lifting her head, she felt drugged by senses that had sprung to life from the shield behind which they'd been protected for so many years. Suddenly she was eager to know all, feel all, to glut herself on every texture, hue and scent his body possessed. Her eyes met his, then dropped to travel across the shadowed throat, his ear, his nipples, his jaw where a tiny, tiny scab remained from some incidental nick of razor, perhaps. She touched it with a single fingertip, then pressed the length of her palm along the underside of the biceps of the arm bent beneath his head. She ran the hand down to his armpit, awed that even the wiry hair there could be something she craved to know, simply because it was part of his physical makeup.

"Brian," she breathed, looking into his eyes. "I'm like a child tasting candy for the first time. I never knew all these things before. I have so much to catch up on!"

"Catch then. We have a good seventy years."

A flickering smile passed her features, but was gone again, wiped away by this new rapt interest in his body. He closed his eyes, and like an eager child she twisted onto one hip, bracing a palm on the bed to get a better overview of this delicacy called Brian Scanlon. Still it wasn't enough. Finally, she pulled both legs up beneath her and sat on her haunches at his hip—looking, touching, familiarizing.

"You're...exquisite!" she marveled. "I never thought a man could be exquisite, but you are." His belly was hard, his ribs tapering to the indentation of his waist, just above the spot where his trunks sliced his abdomen. Within the white trunks she saw the mysterious raised contours of his arousal and wondered if it hurt him to be bound up so tightly.

She lifted her eyes to his and found he'd been watching her. A charming, lopsided grin bent the corner of his mouth.

"Darling girl." He lazily lifted his hand and ran a finger along the path of one string of her tie top, starting at the side of her neck, traveling beside it to the point where it met the band beneath her breasts. She shuddered with delight. "I don't think I'm the one who's exquisite." The finger idled up the opposite strap. Her eyelids felt weighted and a coil of anticipation wound through her stomach. His four fingertips traced the line of her collarbone, then moved downward, drawing a quartet of invisible Ss along the freckled mound of her breast. The faint tickle lifted the fine hairs on her bare stomach. He gave the other breast equal attention, fingering her skin with the brush of a dragonfly's wings. Her eyelids slid closed, and her head drooped slightly backward, listing to one side while his callused fingertips followed the first strap again, but this time also moved over the shimmery green triangle of fabric to graze the hidden, uptilted nipple that gave an unexpected spurt of sensation down her arms, stomach and straight to the seat of her femininity.

Her eyelids flew open. "Brian!"

A troubled look crossed his features as he misread her exclamation and withdrew his hand.

"Brian! There's feeling there!"

"What?" His fingers poised in midair.

"There's feeling there! It happened, when you touched me just then, something slithery and fiery went...went whooshing down my body, and...oh, Brian, don't you see? The doctor said sometimes the sensation never returns, and I've been scared to death thinking it hadn't come back to me."

He braced up on one elbow and cupped her jaw. "You never told me before."

"I am now, but oh Brian, it doesn't matter anymore, oh please, do it again!'' she begged excitedly. ''I want to make sure I wasn't just imagining it.''

He toppled her over beside him, his lips joining hers to press her onto her back as his hand roamed across her ribs, and up, but stopped just short of her breast.

He lifted his head and she opened her eyes to find him gazing down intently into her eyes, his brows lowered in concern. ''I won't hurt you, will I?''

''No,'' she whispered.

His mouth and hand moved simultaneously, the one to bestow a kiss, the other a caress. He contoured the warm globe of flesh with his palm, gently at first, then with growing pressure, squeezing, fondling, finally seeking out the nipple, which he tenderly explored through the slip of sheeny, damp material.

Her lips went slack and she dropped her shoulders flat to the bed, lolling in the new feelings of arousal. It was slighter than before, but there just the same. She concentrated hard on grasping it, blindly guiding his hand to the exact spot she thought would revive the strong spurt of sensation as before.

Braced above her, he watched the feelings parade across her face, and at last he reached for the bow at the nape of her neck. Her eyes opened as she felt it slipping free, but just before he could lower the green triangle, she stopped his hand.

''Brian, I have scars, but please don't let them stop you. They'll be there for several months yet, but then they'll fade. And they don't hurt, they only itch sometimes.''

Some softening expression around his eyes told her he understood, and accepted. Then he peeled the first green tidbit of fabric down and laid it over her ribs, while she watched his eyes. They dropped to the vertical red scar, then flew back to her brown gaze. Wordlessly he stripped down the other half of the bathing suit top.

Where was the shame she had once known? Absent. Evaporated beneath the far greater impact of the loving concern that emanated from Brian's face.

He slipped his hands behind her back and came away with the suit top, then tossed it onto the pillows and rolled to give her his full attention again.

''How can it not hurt?'' Gently he cupped her right breast, riding his thumb up the scar, then lightly, lightly circling the nipple. ''Did they make an incision here?''

''Yes, but that scar is all healed.''

''And here, too.'' He traced the faded crescent beneath, to its inception just below her armpit. ''Oh God, it hurts me to think of them doing that to you." He lowered his head, trailing his lips along the lower contour scar.

"Brian, it's all over, and it wasn't nearly as bad as you'd think. If I hadn't done it, I might not have been able to overcome all my hangups and be here with you. I feel so different. So...."

He lifted his head and searched her with tortured eyes. "What do you feel? So...what?"

"Beautiful," she admitted, with a lingering note of shyness. "Feature that, would you?" She smiled and her voice became soft and accepting. "Theresa Brubaker with her red hair and freckles, feeling beautiful. But it's partly because of you. Because of how you treated me last Christmas. You made me believe I had the right to feel this way. You were all the things I'd ever hoped to find in a man."

"I love you." His voice was strange, throaty and deep, and not wholly steady. He dipped his head and touched his lips to the cinnamon-colored dots between her breasts. "Every freckle of you." He moved his mouth to the gentle swelling mound. "Every red hair of you." And finally to the crest. "Every square inch of you."

He adored her with the gentle strokes of his tongue, and she lay in a blaze of emotions that sprang more from her consummate love for him than from the part of her he tenderly kissed.

"What's happening?" he queried, running his tongue down along the underside of her breast.

She sucked in a breath as a sensual response shuddered down her backbone. "I'm falling in love with my body, and your body, and what they can do to each other. I'm plunging through space...freefalling. Only it's so strange...I'm falling up."

He ran his tongue up to her nipple again, and closed his lips and tongue around it, murmuring some wordless accolade deep in his throat, while both of his arms reached behind her and his hands slid down to cup her buttocks and roll her firmly against him, both of them now on their sides.

"Mmm...you taste like summer...."

"Tell me," she whispered, threading her fingers through his hair, knowing an insatiable appetite for his words, as well as for his arousing touches.

"Sandy beaches and suntan oil that tastes like Popsicles and the sweetest fruit in the jungle...." He lightly nipped the top of a breast with his teeth. "Berries and coconut..." He slipped lower, licking the sensitive skin on the rib. "Mangos and kiwi... Mmm...." His mouth pressed moistly upon the softest part of her abdomen, just above the navel. "There's something else here...wait, let me see...." He dipped his tongue into her navel and made several seductive circles around and within it. "Mmm...I think it's passion fruit."

She felt him smile against her belly and smiled in return.

His mouth was arousingly warm, and his breath heated the silky triangle of fabric still covering her. His chest weighted her legs, then he lightly bit her through the bathing suit—fabric, hair and a little skin. Her ribs lifted off the bedspread, and she gasped while desire welled and bubbled over in her feminine depths. His fingers found the sensitive skin at the back of her knee, then his mouth warmed the flesh that she'd thought could not possibly know a heat any greater than it had already experienced. She trembled and lifted her hips from the bed, offering herself as fully as he cared to partake. He kissed her through the silky bikini and worked his chin firmly against the throbbing flesh within until she found herself moving against the hardness, seeking something... something....

And when her desire had grown to its fullest, he moved back up to join his mouth to hers, running his palms along the elastic waist of her briefs, then down inside to cup her firm backside while rolling his weight fully on top of hers, his hips undulating against hers while their mouths locked in a bond of mutual desire.

His weight lifted. She felt the wisp of fabric leave the juncture of her legs and inch downward along her thighs, then pass lower still until his mouth was forced to leave hers, and he eased the garment down and off, then tossed it over his shoulder to join its mate on the pillows.

He pressed her back, back, against the bed and caressed her bare stomach with his musician's fingers that were capable, she learned, of much more than adroitly strumming love songs. They raised a kind of music in her flesh as he explored the soft skin of her inner thighs, then the most intimate part of her body.

She was eager, and open, and not in the least abashed by his touch that sought and entered her virgin flesh. Love, that gift of the gods, took away all insecurities, all timidity, all shame, and allowed her the freedom to express her newfound femininity in the way she had so long dreamed.

A soft, passionate sound issued from her throat. She stretched and allowed him total access to explore her as he would, trembling at times, smiling at others, her heart a wild thing in her breast.

But just short of taking her over the edge of bliss, he lay back. And then it was her turn to explore. "Experience will take care of itself," Brian had said. And she believed it as she embarked upon her half of this maiden voyage toward mutuality.

She found the tight waist of his trunks and slipped her palms inside, against the skin of his lower spine, finding it cool from the slightly damp fabric.

Her caresses were restricted by the taut garment, yet she thrilled at the firmness beneath her palms and the inviting rhythm her touch had set off in his hips. He reached behind his back, found her arm and carried it up out of the elastic and around to his front, pressing it against the flattened, hidden hills between his legs, moving against her palm to initiate it into the ways of sexual contact.

To Theresa's amazement, her own voice begged throatily, "Take it off, Brian, please."

The words were partially muffled by his lips, but when the request had been made, he lifted his head and smiled into her beseeching eyes, his breath beating warmly upon her face.

"Anything you say, love."

He slipped to the edge of the bed, and she rolled onto her side and curled her body up like a lazy caterpillar, watching as he reached inside the garment and found a hidden string against his belly, tugged it, then stood and skinned the trunks down, down, down, before dropping to sit on the edge of the bed again and kicking the suit away across the carpet as he rolled toward her, reaching.

He was beautiful, and somehow it seemed the most natural thing in the world to reach out and caress him.

"Oh, Brian, you're silky...and so hot."

"So are you. But I think that's how we're supposed to be." He reached again for the entrance to her womanhood, touching it with a sleek, knowing rhythm until sensation dazzled her nerve endings. She closed her eyes and undulated with the protracted and relentless stroking.

"Brian, something's happening!"

"Let it. Shh...."

"But...but...." It was too late to wonder if it was torture or treasure, for in the next instant the question was answered for Theresa. A burst of sensation lifted her limbs and sent liquid explosions rocketing outward. Then she was shuddering, feeling spasms from the deepest reaches of her body, until she fell back sated, exhausted, gasping.

"Oh, sweet, sweet woman. The first time," he said against her neck after a minute, still holding her tightly. "Do you know how rare that is?"

"No...I thought from the movies that it happens to everyone."

"Not women, not all the time. Usually just men. You must have been storing it all these years, waiting for the right one to come along and set it free."

"And he did."

He smiled lovingly into her eyes, then kissed each lid, then her nose, then her swollen lips. And while he strung the kisses upon her face, he raised his body over hers and pressed it firmly to her entire length.

"I love you, darling—keep remembering that in case it hurts."

"I love you, Br—"

She never finished the word, for in that instant he entered her and she knew the sleek ligature of their two joined bodies, but no pain, only texture and heightened sensations building once again as his hips moved above hers. She felt only pleasure as he began moving, reaching back to teach her how to lift her knees and create a nesting place of warm, firm flesh that buttressed his hips as he shared the consummation of their love.

When he clenched his fists and quivered, she opened her eyes to find his closed in ecstasy. He rode the crest of his climax while she watched the reaction expressed on his beloved features—the closed, trembling eyelids, the flaring nostrils and the lips that pulled back in a near grimace as sweat broke out on his back and the muscles rippled for an exhausted moment. Then he shivered a last interminable time, called out at the final peak, and relaxed.

So this is why I was born a woman and Brian Scanlon was born a man, why we were meant to seek and find each other in this world of strangers. She caressed his shoulder blades, coveting the dead weight of him pressing her into the resilient water-filled baffles beneath her.

"Oh, Brian it was so good...so good."

He rolled to his side and opened his eyes, lifting one hand that appeared too tired to quite succeed in the effort of caressing her face. It fell upon her cheek.

He chuckled—a rich, resonant sound from deep in his chest and closed his eyes and sighed, then lay unmoving.

She studied him in repose, smoothed the tousled hair above his temple. His eyes didn't open, and his palm didn't move. She knew an abiding sense of completion.

The noon sun lit the ceiling of the room by some magical twist of physics. The sheets at the window riffled lightly, and the sounds of the pool activity were constant now. From the living room came the repeated songs of the same record—she smiled, wondering how many times it had played.

"Do you know when I first became intrigued with you?"

She turned to find his eyes open, watching her. "When?"

They were still entwined, and he pulled her closer to keep possession of her while he went on. "It started when Jeff let me read a letter from you. In it you said you'd gone out on a date with somebody named Lyle, and he turned out to be Jack the Gripper."

She chuckled, recalling both the letter and the disastrous date.

"That long ago?"

"Uh-huh. Two years or more. Anyway, after we laughed about it, and I wondered what kind of woman had written it, I began asking questions about you. Little by little I learned everything. About your red hair." He threaded his fingers into it just where her widow's peak would have been, had she one. "And your freckles." He trailed a finger down her nose.

"And your endowment." He passed a palm down her breast. "And about the time Jeff defended you and punched out that kid, and about how you taught music in an elementary school and played violin, and how Jeff thought the sun rose and set in you, and how much he wanted you to be happy, to find some man who'd treat you honorably and wouldn't ogle and grope and grip."

"Two years ago?" she repeated, stunned.

"Longer than that. Closer to three now. Since Jeff and I were in Germany together. Anyway, when I saw your picture. It was one of your school pictures, and you were wearing a gray sweater buttoned around your shoulders, with a little white blouse collar showing from beneath. I asked Jeff a lot of questions then, and pieced together a picture of you and your hangup even before I knew you. There have been times when I even suspected that Jeff filled me in on all the details about you in hopes that when I met you I'd be the first man to treat you right, and end up doing exactly what I just did."

"Jeff?" she exclaimed, surprised.

"Jeff. Didn't you ever suspect that he engineered this whole thing from the start, feeding me tidbits about his marvelous, straight sister, who'd never had boyfriends, but who had so much to offer a man—the right man."

She braced up on one elbow and looked thoughtful. "Jeff! You really think so?"

"Yes, I do. As a matter of fact, he all but admitted it when we were on the plane back after Christmas. He suspected things had fired up between us and came right out and said it'd been on his mind a while that he wouldn't mind me as a brother-in-law."

She smirked and lifted a delicate jaw. "Remind me to give old Jeff a gigantic thank-you kiss next time I see him, huh?"

"And what about you? When did you start thinking of me as a potential lover?"

"The truth?" She peered up at him coquettishly.

"The truth."

"That night in the theater, when the love scene was on the screen. Your elbow was sharing the armrest with mine, and when the woman climaxed, your bones were almost cutting off my blood supply. Then when the man's face came on, showing him in the throes of rapture, your elbow nearly broke mine, and when it was over, *you* wilted."

"Me?" he yelped disbelievingly. "I did not!"

"You did too. I was practically dying of embarrassment, and then you dropped your hands down to cover your lap, and I wanted to crawl underneath the seats."

"Are you serious? Did I really do that?"

"Of course I'm serious. Would I lie about a thing like that? I was so turned on myself I hardly knew what to do about it. Part of it was the movie, but part of it was you and your arm. After that I couldn't help wondering what it would be like with you. Somehow I knew you'd be good...and gentle...and just what a freckled redhead needed to make her feel like Cinderella."

"Do I make you feel like Cinderella?"

She studied him for a long moment, traced his lips with an index finger and nodded.

He captured the finger, bit it, then as his eyes closed, he lay very still, pressing her four fingertips against his lips.

"What are you thinking?" she whispered.

His eyes opened, but for a moment he didn't answer. Instead he pressed his palm to hers and threaded their fingers together with slow deliberation. His fingers squeezed possessively. Hers answered. "About tomorrow. And the day after that and the day after that, and how we'll never have to be alone again. There'll always be each other...and babies." His fingers gripped more tightly. His eyes probed hers. "Do you want babies, Theresa?"

He felt her grip relax, then tug away. His stomach went light with warning, and he gripped her hand to keep it from escaping. "Theresa?"

She gazed at his face, wide-eyed, and when he saw the color begin to heighten between her freckles, he leaned above her on an elbow, frowning. "Theresa, what is it?"

She brushed his chest with her fingertips, dropping her eyes to follow the movement instead of meeting his frown. "Brian, there's something I haven't told you about my surgery."

In a split second a dozen fledgling fears spiraled through him, all dire: the surgery had somehow taken away more than met the eye, and they'd never have the babies he was dreaming of.

"Oh no, Brian, not that." She read his trepidation, soothingly bracketed his jaws. "I can have babies—all I want. And I *do* want them. But...." Again she dropped her eyes while her fingers rested against his chest. "But I'll never be able to nurse them. Not after the surgery."

For a moment he was still, waiting for the worst. Suddenly he crushed her tightly. "Is that all?" he sighed, relieved. She hadn't known he was holding his breath until it rushed out heavily upon her temple. Her lips were on his warm collarbone as he secured her fast and rocked her in his arms.

"It doesn't matter to me, but I thought you should know. I thought in case you had any feelings about it we should talk about it now. Some men might consider me only...well, half a woman or something."

He pulled back sharply. "Half a woman?" He sounded gruff as he squeezed her shoulders. "Never think it." Their eyes locked, and she read in his total love and approval. "Think about this." He drew her into the warm curve of his body as he rolled aside and snuggled her so near, his heartbeat was like a drum beneath her ear. "Think about everything we'll have some day—a house where there'll always be music and a gang of little redheaded rascals whose—"

"Brown-haired," she interrupted, smiling against his chest.

He went on with scarcely a missed beat. "Redheaded rascals whose freckles dance when—"

"Oh no! No freckles! If you give me freckled, redheaded babies, Brian Scanlon, I'll—"

The rest was smothered by his kiss before he grinned at her, continuing. "Redheaded rascals whose freckles dance when they play their violins—"

"Guitars. I won't have anybody hiding under any violins!"

"Mrs. Scanlon, will you kindly stop complaining about this family of ours? I said they'll be redheads and I meant it. And they'll play violin in the orchestra and—"

"Guitars," she insisted. "In a band. And their hair will be deep brown like their daddy's."

She threaded her fingers through it and their eyes met, heavy-lidded again with resurgent desire. Their bodies stirred against each other, their lips met, tongues sipped, and hearts clamored.

"Let's compromise," she suggested, scarcely aware of what she was saying, for already his hips were moving against hers.

He began speaking, but his voice was gruff and distracted. "Some redheads, some brown, some with freckles, some with guitars, some with vio—"

Her sweet seeking mouth interrupted. "Mmm-hmm..." she murmured against his lips. "But it'll take lots of practice to make all those babies." Her breasts pressed provocatively against his chest. She writhed once, experimentally, glorying in her newly discovered freedom. "Show me how we'll do it."

Their open mouths clung. His strong arm curved beneath her and rolled her atop him, then he settled her hips upon his, found the soft hollows behind her knees and drew them down until she straddled him in soft, feminine flesh. He pressed her hips away, and ordered thickly against her forehead, "Love me."

Her heart surged with shyness. Then love moved her hand. Hesitantly she reached, found, then surrounded.

Their smiles met, faltered, dissolved. Eyelids lowered as she settled firmly upon him. A guttural sound of satisfaction rumbled from his throat, answered by her softer, wordless reply. Experimentally she lifted, dropped, warming to his encouraging hands on her hips.

Drawing back, she found his eyes still shuttered, the lids trembling.

"Oh, Brian...Brian...I love you so much," she vowed with tears beginning to sting.

His eyes opened. For a moment his hands calmed the movement of her hips, then they reached to draw her face down as he kissed the outer corner of each eye. "And I love you, sweets...always," he whispered, drawing her mouth to his to complete the promise within it. "Always...always."

In the living room a forgotten record circled, circled, sending soft music down the hall. To its lazy rhythm their bodies moved. At the windows, sheets rippled, and beneath two lovers the soft swell of confined water rose up as an afterbeat to their rhythmic union. They would build a repertoire of sweet memories throughout their years as man and wife, but as they moved now, reaffirming their love, it seemed none would be so sweet as this moment that bound them in promise.

When their bodies were gifted with the manifest of that promise, when the sweet swelling peaked and the shudders ceased, they reaffirmed it once again.

"I love you," spoke the man.

"I love you," answered the woman.

It was enough. Together, they moved on toward forever.

A Matter of Circumstances

1

From one of the assorted ketches, catamarans, speedboats and yachts, a Jimmy Buffet tune was rising high on the air, tarnished by only a shade of static. The late afternoon was tempering the heat, and a breeze was flowing in from the water, cooling Sean Ramiro's sun-sizzled arms and chest. To all outward appearances he was as negligent and lackadaisical as the carefree Sunday loafers who laughed, teased, flirted and played around the docks. But when he raised his head for a moment, tilting back the brim of his Panama hat, a careful observer might have noted that he surveyed the scene with startlingly intense green eyes.

All seemed peaceful and pleasant. A lazy afternoon by the water. Girls in bikinis, guys in cutoffs, tourists with white cream on their noses, and old geezers in bright flowered shirts. Kids threw fish tails to the gulls that hovered nearby. Sean arched his shoulders back, grimacing at the feel of the wooden dock piling that grated through the thin material of his cotton shirt. He'd been sitting there a long time now.

Farther down the dock Sunday fisherman were cleaning their catches. A young sailor in tie-dyed cutoffs was hosing down his small Cigarette boat. A group of beer drinkers passed him, heading for the refreshment stand that was located where the rustic-looking wooden docks gave way to the cold reality of the concrete parking lot.

Sean heard a little titter of laughter and gazed sideways, annoyed to realize that he had become an object of fascination for two well-endowed teenagers in string bikinis. He tensed, swearing to himself. If something was going to happen after this long and futile day, it would surely happen now, while the kiddies were in the way.

He lowered his head, feigning a nap, hoping they would go away.

At his side, what looked like a credit-card-sized AM/FM receiver suddenly made a little buzzing sound. Sean picked it up and brought it to his ear.

"Hey, Latin lover!" Anderson teased. Sean looked up; he could see Harvey Anderson in the refreshment stand, chatting while he turned hot dogs on a grill. "You got a fan club going there, you know? I think you should be on grill duty. You're too pretty to blend into the woodwork."

Sean idly moved the radio in front of his mouth. "Anderson, it's not that I'm too pretty—you're just too damned ugly. You'd scare away the devil himself.''

Todd Bridges, unseen, but not far away in the parking lot, broke in on the conversation. "Must be those Irish eyes, Sean. Keep 'em lowered, eh?''

"Todd...''

"Hey, who said duty was a chore?'' Harvey interrupted. "Will you look at that? I am in love! Thunderstruck and all that junk. Now I really think you should be grilling the hot dogs, Ramiro! Ah, I'd like just a whiff of the air she breathes!''

Harvey was always falling in love with anything in a bikini. But Sean idly turned his head, tilting the brim of his hat just a shade. He arched a dark brow and was surprised to discover that his breath had caught in his chest.

This time Harvey was right on the mark.

She was coming in from the end of the dock. She walked slowly and casually, and with the most sensual grace Sean had ever witnessed. She wasn't wearing a bikini, but a one-piece thing cut high on the thighs, and man-oh-man, did those slim sexy thighs go on forever.

If someone were to have asked Sean Ramiro what he first noticed about a woman, he would have given it a little thought, then answered with honesty, "Her eyes.'' Eyes were the mirror of the soul, as the saying went. And so he looked first at her eyes.

He couldn't see their color, not from his position, not with the way he was forced to squint into the sun. He did see that they were sparkling like the sun, that they were large and exquisite, that they were framed with thick lashes...that they enchanted.

He didn't know why, but his eyes fell then to take in the whole of her. Her easy, idle movement. Her walk...

He was—even on duty—spellbound by that walk. The never-ending length of her golden tanned legs, the curve of her hips. He liked her waistline, too, smooth and sleek. Just like Harvey, he was instantly in love. Spaghetti straps held the yellow swimsuit in place. The top was straight cut, but she needed no help to display her cleavage. Her still-damp skintight bathing suit couldn't hide the fact that her breasts were firm, round, perfect. Sean realized that he felt a bit like a kid in a candy store, almost overwhelmed by the desire to reach out and touch.

"Will you look at those...eyes,'' Harvey breathed in awe.

"What is it?'' Todd demanded from the parking lot.

"Boy, did you draw the wrong straw!'' Harvey told him.

Sean looked back to her face.

It was a perfect oval. High boned. Classical. She could have posed for history's most famous artists, and not one of them could have found a flaw. Her mouth was generous, but elegantly defined. Sean could imagine her laughing; the sound would be as provocative as the curve of those lips. Her nose was long and straight, and her eyes—those wondrous eyes!—were framed by high brows that added to their captivating size and beauty. And her hair…

Her hair matched the coming of the sunset in glorious color. It wasn't blond, neither was it dark. It was a tawny color, like a lion's mane, with deeper highlights of shimmering red to match the streak of the sun against the sky.

"I am in love!" Harvey repeated.

"Oh, watch your hot dogs!" Todd grumbled from the parking lot.

Sean grimaced, jerking involuntarily as the radio suddenly gave out a burst of static. Then Todd's voice came back on the air.

"I just got a buzz from Captain Mallory. Someone pulled in faulty information. Blayne isn't here, and he isn't coming. He's got a reservation on a flight north at six."

For a moment Sean completely forgot the woman, as he closed his eyes in disgust. Damn that Blayne! The senator had received threats against his life, but he had lifted his naive nose to the police, who had bent over backward to protect him. Still, as public servants, it was their job to protect him.

They'd been tipped off today that Blayne, who had mysteriously disappeared, had ordered a catered lunch delivered to the docks this morning for a sailboat registered as the *Flash Point*. Meanwhile, another threat had been phoned in to the police. Of all the lousy details to draw, Sean had drawn this one. He'd had to spend the whole stinking day on the dock, waiting for Peter Blayne to make an appearance and to see that he got off the docks without mishap.

Now it seemed the fool had never been anywhere near the docks to begin with, nor intended to be. The boat had gone out earlier, but without the senator aboard.

Sean opened his eyes again. Not even his disgust at the wasted day could really have any effect on him—not when he was staring at *her*, and she was coming closer. A scuba mask and a pair of flippers dangled from one hand as she moved along, still at that lazy, no-hurry pace. Her face was tilted upward, and the smallest signs of a smile curved her lip, as if she was savoring that soft kiss of sun and breeze against her cheeks.

Just like some ancient goddess, Sean thought, and he could almost see her walking along at that slow confident pace, naked and assured, in some flower-strewn field, while a primitive drumbeat pulsed out the rhythm of her fluid motion and an ancient man bowed down before her.

"Hey!" Harvey's voice, quiet and tense, suddenly jolted Sean from his daydream.

"What?"

"It's back. The *Flash Point*. Way down the dock—she didn't berth where she should have!"

Sean stared down the dock. It was true. The *Flash Point* was in, and two kids—or young men—were securing her lines.

He stood, slowly, carefully, unaware that he grimaced as all the muscles in his six-foot-two frame complained. Absently he rubbed a shoulder and stared down at the ketch. Nice. It had three masts and probably slept a dozen in privacy and comfort.

It was Blayne's boat, and someone had gone out on it. But if Peter Blayne was really catching a six o'clock flight, they couldn't possibly have picked him up and brought him back on the ketch. It was six now.

Someone behind him began an excited conversation, half in Spanish, half in English. Two men cleaning fish were talking about a woman, trying to decide if it was "her" or not. Without thinking, Sean tuned in the words, then tuned them out, more concerned with the arrival of the *Flash Point* than he was with "that rat's old lady."

He supposed he should saunter down and ask a few questions. Pulling his open shirt across his chest to conceal the holster strapped underneath, he stared at his quarry, then started toward it. He rubbed his jaw and the dark stubble there, wondering if he didn't look more than a little like a bum. Good for sitting around on a dock idly, but a little scary, maybe, to the elite teenagers battening down the *Flash Point*.

He didn't realize how quickly he was moving until he suddenly plowed into somebody—and knocked them down. He started to bend down and offer a hand, then he noticed that he wasn't the only person racing toward the *Flash Point*.

From the end of the pier a slim, handsome young Latin with a grim look of purpose and something bunched in his arms was hurrying toward the ketch—or toward the end of the dock. Sean wasn't sure.

What he *was* sure about was the man's identity.

It was Garcia. Definitely. Julio Garcia, old Jorge's son. He had his father's flashing dark eyes and arresting, near-gaunt face.

Sean immediately felt tension riddle him. The police might have been wrong about Blayne's whereabouts, but if so, it seemed a strange coincidence that the people threatening him had received the same faulty information.

"You stupid ox!"

Momentarily startled, Sean stared in the direction of the feminine voice that had spat out the epithet. It was her. The sensually swaying woman with the never-ending legs and great eyes.

Eyes...

They were topaz. Not brown. Not green. Not hazel. They were the color of light, shimmering honey, sparkling now like liquid sunlight, like precious gems reflecting the last dying rays of the sun in a burst of rebellious glory.

And he'd just knocked her down flat, without a word of apology. He could reach out and touch her. He could...

He offered her a hand. She took it with delicate fingers, watching him warily.

If only Garcia wasn't just yards away...

"Hey!" The voice came from down the dock. Garcia was gripping the arm of one of the kids who had been working on the *Flash Point*. "I don't know what you're talking about!"

Even from this distance Sean could hear the kid's angry retort to whatever Garcia had said. Then the kid's voice lowered, and Garcia said something with a frightening vehemence.

Sean didn't know that he had dropped the woman's hand when she was halfway up until she thudded back to the wood with a furious oath. "You are the rudest person I have ever met!"

He barely heard her; he was too tense, watching Garcia.

"Don't you speak English? *Estúpido!*" the woman snapped.

Absently he offered a hand to her again.

"Don't touch me! Just move, please. Honest to God, I don't know what's wrong with people these days!"

Sean ignored her, anxious to reach Garcia. But even as he stepped past her, the kid with Garcia looked up and started yelling. "Hey, Mrs. Blayne! Can you do something with this guy? He insists that the senator is aboard and I keep telling him that he isn't!"

Blayne!

Sean swung around and stared at the beauty he'd just knocked over, then ignored. Mrs. Blayne? His wife? She couldn't be! Blayne was in his mid-forties or early fifties if he was a day; this woman was twenty-five, twenty-eight, tops!

She was impatiently dusting herself off after her fall on the sandy dock, but she smiled at the kid with a rueful shake of her head. "Tell him Peter had to be in Washington tonight. He isn't on the *Flash Point*—he probably isn't even in the state anymore."

The kid started speaking earnestly to Garcia. Sean was momentarily frozen, with two thoughts registering in his mind.

Blayne wasn't here; they had all been wrong, and it was probably for the best. Garcia hadn't identified himself during any of the threatening calls, but who else could be so violently angry with the senator except for some crackpot? And Garcia was definitely a crackpot.

The other thought, which interrupted his professional logic in a way that annoyed him, was about her. She was married to the man. And quite obviously for his money, since the age difference was definitely vast!

It was irritating, and somehow it hurt—for all that any feelings on his part were ridiculous. She was just a dream. The absolute, perfect dream you might see on the page of some magazine, then forget just as soon as the page was turned. Yet he wanted to shake her. To demand where her morals were—and her dignity and pride!—that she would marry an old guy like Blayne just for the sake of material possessions.

But even as he thought that, he smiled a little ruefully. Because the question that was really bothering him was, why him and not me? I'm thirty-three and as healthy as the "ox" you just called me. I'm the one who could show you what life was meant to be, just what you were built for, lady!

He reminded himself that he didn't like blondes. But any man, face-to-face with this particular blonde, would want her.

"Roberto, man, it is her! Julio, the old lady!"

Sean frowned, realizing then that the two fishermen were yelling to Garcia. He was halfway to the man himself, but paused.

The two fishermen jumped into a speedboat.

"Hey, wait—" he called to them. Where the hell was Harvey? Couldn't he tell something was happening? But how would he? Nothing illegal was going on. Two men had jumped into a speedboat, and Julio Garcia was talking to a kid. Nothing to get arrested for, but...

"Get out of the way! Get down!"

The heavily accented command came from Julio Garcia. Sean ducked, then fell flat as a whole barrage of bullets was suddenly spewed haphazardly in his direction. He tasted sand as he fell hard against the wood, reaching for his .38 caliber Smith & Wesson as a second barrage began.

Julio was fast; he kept firing as he raced down the dock. The shots rang out discordantly against the absolute and lazy peace of the afternoon, shocking everyone, causing chaos and so many screams that Sean didn't know where to look.

The woman!

He rolled just in time to see that the thing under Julio's arm had been potato sacking, and that Julio had looped it over her head, thrown her struggling but constrained figure over his shoulder and made a wild leap for the speedboat.

Sean didn't dare shoot; he would hit the woman.

He didn't think; he just reacted. He dove into the water, determined to reach the boat before it could jet out into open water and head for the endless nooks and crannies that the mangrove islands could provide.

2

He wasn't accustomed to making mistakes. A homicide detective simply couldn't make mistakes and expect to live.

But as he dove into the murky water his gun was swept from his hand by a stinging collision with the wood and instantly disappeared into a growth of seaweed. Still submerged, Sean could hear the motor of the speedboat revving up, and he knew he didn't have a spare second left. It seemed necessary at any cost to reach that boat and then come up with a plan of action, minus his gun.

His fingers grasped the edge of the boat while it was already in motion. Water splashed into his face, blinding him, gagging him. He held on, feeling the tremendous force of the pressure against him.

Ass! he accused himself, but too late. To give up now would be to risk the murderous blades of the propeller, so, thinking himself the greatest idiot ever to draw breath, he grated his teeth against the agony of his hold and tried to bring his body as close as possible to the side of the boat.

The motor was suddenly cut, and Sean remembered just in time to ditch his ID card and gun clip.

"*¿Qué pasa? ¿Qué pasa?*"

He heard the furious query, then a colorful spate of oaths in Spanish. Someone reached over the side of the boat to pull his half-drowned body over the edge.

He was dizzy; his head reeled as he lay soaked between two side-to-side seats. He gasped in a breath even as he heard the motor rev into motion again and felt the vibrations with his entire body.

The three men—Garcia and the two fishermen—were fighting away, screaming and gesticulating over the terrible hum of the motor, an occasional word of English slipping into the Spanish tirades.

"What happened? Who the hell is he?"

"I don't know. Why didn't you kill him?"

"We're not murderers!"

"We agreed if we had to—"

Something pounded viciously against his head, and Sean groaned despite himself. Twisting, he saw that the burlap sack containing the girl was stretched out over the seat so that her feet dangled right over his head, only the toes bared.

Of all things he noticed that her toenails were filed and manicured and glazed in a deep wine red. For some reason that irritated him. Maybe he realized he'd half killed himself over some mercenary socialite.

"Why did we take her?" one of the fishermen whined.

"She's twice as good as the old man! Hey, if he wants her back, he'll see that my father is set free!" Garcia proclaimed.

"So who the hell is this guy?" the second fisherman asked.

Sean, blinking furiously, more to clear his head than his eyes, pushed himself up to his elbows. If the stinking motor would just stop! He would need his wits to get out of this one. In the last few minutes the sun had decided to make a sharp fall. The boat was carrying no lights. Everything seemed to be a haze of darkness: the sea joining the sky, the men seated in the motorboat nothing more than macabre silhouettes. There weren't even any stars out. He was grateful that there didn't seem to be any other boats out, either.

He felt, though, that all the men were staring at him. Especially Garcia, who was seated next to the bundled, struggling figure in burlap.

Her toes crashed into his nose when he tried to elbow himself into a better position.

"*Me llamo* Miguel Ramiro," he began, yelling above the motor, but just as he started screeching, the motor was cut.

"*Cállate!*" Garcia snapped. Shut up.

Sean heard the water lapping against the side of the boat, then a woman's shout from nearby, and Garcia's quick answer. They came alongside a much bigger vessel, some kind of motorized, two-masted sailboat. A ladder was dropped down; Garcia motioned the two fishermen up first, then turned to stare down at Sean. Despite the poor light Sean could see the dark, wary glitter in his eyes.

"Who are you?"

"Miguel Ramiro."

"And who is Miguel Ramiro?"

The woman—Mrs. Blayne—could blow the whole thing in a matter of seconds, but he had to come up with something. He damn well couldn't introduce himself as a cop. He inclined his head toward the burlap. "She is mine," he replied in Spanish.

Garcia arched a dark brow, then leveled the gun at Sean. "Then you take her up the ladder—and then explain yourself."

Sean struggled to his feet between the wooden seats. He bent over the burlap, trying to figure out just where to grab her. He obviously made a mistake, because his hand encountered something nicely rounded, and the bundle let out an outraged shriek and began twisting and squirming all over again.

"Stop it!" he snapped in English. A recognizable piece of anatomy swung toward him, and in sudden exasperation he gave it a firm swat. Her outraged cry reached him again, and he tried to murmur convincingly, "It is Miguel. I am with you, my darling."

Garcia's brow arched higher; Sean figured he couldn't press his luck too far and decided it didn't matter in the least right now which part of her anatomy he came in contact with. He reached down, gripped her body and tossed her over his shoulder, wincing as she came in contact with a sore spot, right where he had hit the deck to avoid the gunfire.

"Up the ladder," Garcia said.

Sean nodded and started up. His squirming burden almost sent him catapulting back down.

For Garcia's benefit he swore heatedly in Spanish, then added contritely in English, "My love, please! It is me, Miguel!"

Her reply was inarticulate, but Sean knew what she was saying: who the hell was Miguel?

Maybe he would be better off if she remained wrapped in burlap for a while. He probably wouldn't have to carry this thing off for too long. Harry and Todd had been on the docks. Search boats and helicopters would be out soon.

Yeah, but the coastline was a maze of islands and shoals and shallows and roots.... The mangroves, the islets, the Everglades.... They had sheltered many a criminal throughout the years.

He couldn't think about it that way. He just had to play the whole thing moment by moment.

Starting now.

He crawled over the starboard side of the sailboat to find four people already studying him in the light of a single bulb projecting from the enclosure over the hull. There was a short, graying woman, plump and showing traces of past beauty, and a younger woman, somewhere in her early twenties, with huge almond eyes and a wealth of ink-dark hair. Then the two fishermen. They must have seen him on the dock all day, just as he had seen them. Well, he would just have to make that work to his advantage. They were both in their late twenties or early thirties, jeaned and sneakered, and dark. One wore a mustache; the other was slimmer and as wary as Garcia himself.

Garcia came up the ladder right behind Sean. They all stared at one another for a moment, then the older woman burst into a torrent of questions. What was going on here? Who was this man? Who was struggling in the sack? Where was Peter Blayne? Had they all gone loco?

Then she burst into tears.

Garcia took both her shoulders and held her against his chest. "Mama, Mama! It will be all right! We were wrong, you see. The senator was not on his boat. But his wife was—we've got his wife! And if he wants her back, we must get Papa back first. It's better than the senator."

The woman looked dubiously at the sack that twisted over Sean's shoulder, then pointed a finger in his direction. "Who is he?"

"That," Garcia said, rubbing his chin and looking keenly at Sean, "is something we're still trying to figure out."

Sean sighed deeply and spoke in heavily accented English. "I told you, *amigo*—I am Miguel Ramiro. And I am in love with her."

Garcia started to laugh, and the fishermen laughed with him.

"And she is in love with you, too, *amigo*?" Garcia asked skeptically.

Sean gave them a sheepish look, then gritted his teeth, because the girl in the burlap was screeching something and twisting with greater fury. He smiled grimly and gave her a firm swat once again, which shut her up for several well-needed moments.

"*Sí, sí!*" Sean cried passionately. He irritably muttered a few epithets in Spanish, then added, "But you know these *Americanas!* She's fond of the hot Latin blood in private, but when we are in public I am not good enough to clean her shoes!"

"She's a senator's wife and she's having an affair with you?" Garcia said.

"I told you—"

"I believe it, Julio," the younger woman suddenly interrupted him. Sean paused, gazing her way. She was looking him up and down with an obvious appreciation that was quite gratifying—he needed someone to believe him!

"Maria, I did not ask you."

But Maria put her hand on Julio Garcia's arm and gave him a sexy little smile, her almond eyes wide. "But I tell you, because I am a woman, too, yes?"

"Yes, you are all woman, little one," Julio said pleasantly to her, and she laughed delightedly.

"Latin men make the best lovers, yes, Julio?" She giggled. "I see it all well! She is married to some dull old man, but who can live like that? So she finds Miguel—"

"*Sí!* I was the gardener!" Sean said quickly.

"And he is *muy hombre*!" Maria laughed. "So she calls him in on the side, but pretends, Oh, no! Never!"

The fishermen started to laugh again, too. They were all grinning like the most amiable friends.

Except that Garcia was leveling his gun at Sean's chest.

"Juan!" Garcia said. "Start her up. We leave the motorboat right where it is. We go to the cove where we intended. Mama, Maria, you go below. Now!''

"But—'' Maria began.

"Now!'' Garcia snapped, and Maria, with one last sultry grin for Sean, obeyed.

Sean and Garcia stared at each other, both ignoring the grunts and oaths that came from the burlap bag.

Sean heard the crank as the anchor was pulled in and felt the motion as the sailboat began to move.

"Amigo,'' Garcia said softly, "do you know what is going on here?''

Sean shook his head vehemently and lied. "I only know that she is mine. You took her, and I followed.''

Garcia shrugged and stared at him a while longer.

"I mean you no harm. I mean no man any harm. All I seek is freedom for my father.''

Sean remained mute, thinking that this wasn't the time to explain to an impassioned man that spraying a populated dock with bullets and kidnapping a young woman were not sound means to reach the end he sought.

"I know nothing of your father. I am here for her.''

"So stay with her. But if her husband does not produce my father...''

"Then what?''

"Then we shall see. Justice should be equal.'' He waved the gun.

"Your father is not dead,'' Sean said.

Garcia shrugged again, then smiled. "But you will be, and the woman, if you cause trouble.''

Sean lowered his head. Where the hell was everyone? There didn't seem to be another boat in the water; he hadn't heard a single damned helicopter out searching....

Night had fallen. And the Atlantic was one hell of a big ocean!

"Put her down.''

Sean braced himself, then lowered her to the deck.

"Get the hood off her,'' Garcia continued.

His captors had spoken Spanish to one another, and Sean had spoken Spanish to them, but he was certain that Julio Garcia's English was completely fluent. Once she started to talk he could well be in serious trouble, despite his story.

"The hood!'' Garcia snapped.

Sean hunched down and moved to take the burlap from her—a difficult procedure, because she was struggling so wildly. At last it came free, and she stared at him—glared at him—with eyes so wild they might have been those of a lioness, and her hair in such a tangle it could have been a massive tawny mane. She was pale, and those fascinating tawny eyes of hers were as wide as saucers, but she'd lost absolutely none of her fight. She stared at him and recognized him as the long-haired, unshaven, rude Cubano who had knocked her down just before this mess had begun.

"You!" She hauled back and struck him hard on the chin.

His eyes narrowed, and he thought quickly. No self-respecting man in his invented position would accept such behavior.

He hauled off and slapped her back, bringing a startled gasp from her—and further fury. She tore at him, nails raking, fists flying. Grunting as her elbow caught his ribs and her nails his cheek, he managed to wrap his arms around her, bringing them both crashing down on the deck. Scrambling hastily, he straddled her, caught her wrists and pinned them.

That didn't calm her at all. She called him every name he'd ever heard and writhed beneath him.

Garcia, still holding his gun, suddenly caused her to go quiet with his laughter. "Miguel," he told Sean in Spanish. "You have yourself a tigress here. Maybe it is good you are along."

Sean saw that she was struggling to understand the words, but her knowledge of Spanish just wasn't good enough. Then she started to scream again. "What the hell is going on here? I warn you, I will prosecute you to the full degree of the law! You'll go to prison! Let me go this instant! What in God's—"

"Shut up!" Sean hissed at her. "I'm on your side!"

Garcia crouched down beside them. She surely realized that she was in trouble, but if she hadn't before, she must now, because Garcia leveled the gun at her temple.

"Mother of God, but you've got a mouth!" he said in English. "Don't threaten me. Think of your sins. If your husband doesn't get my father out of that prison, you will die." He grinned. "You and your lover will die together."

Her eyes reverted to Sean's again, registering shock. "He's not—"

Sean didn't really have any choice in the matter. His hands were occupied securing hers. He had to shut her up.

He leaned down and kissed her.

Her mouth had been open, and he came in contact with all the liquid warmth of her lips, exerting a certain pressure that he hoped would be a warning.

She struggled anyway.

He held his fingers so tightly around her wrists that she didn't dare cry out. Garcia, chuckling again, rose.

Sean tried to take that opportunity to warn her. He moved his lips just above hers and whispered, "Behave! Shut up and follow my lead. For God's sake, the man has a gun and is upset enough to use the damn thing! I'm—"

"Get off me!" she whispered vehemently in turn. "You...kidnapper!"

"I'm not with them! I'm—"

"Get off me!"

"Shut up, then!"

She clamped her lips together, staring at him with utter loathing. He sighed inwardly, wishing that he hadn't bothered to stick with her. The hell with her. Let them shoot her!

Then she was talking again, this time to Garcia. "Look, I still don't get this. If you'll just let me go now we'll forget all about it. I promise. You can't get any money through me. I just don't have any. And as for him—"

"Shush!" Sean interrupted, glaring at her. He wasn't about to be shot and thrown to the sharks for his above-and-beyond-the-call-of-duty attempt to save her.

She was going to try to interrupt him again. He tightened his hold on her, his eyes daring her to denounce him to Garcia. He tried to come up with his best and most abusive Spanish to keep Garcia entertained and drown her words.

She must have put on suntan oil sometime during the day, because one of her hands slipped from his grasp, and she used it to lash out at him. His patience was growing thin. He was even beginning to wish that he had decided to practice law, as his mother had suggested. So far he'd been half drowned, thoroughly abused and was surely bloody and bruised from her flying fists and nails. This couldn't go on much longer.

What had happened to terrified victims?

"Don't touch me! Let me go! Get your filthy paws off me! You son of a bitch! Who the hell—"

He had to do something before they both wound up shot and thrown back into the sea.

She just wasn't going to see reason. Sighing inwardly, Sean twisted her quickly to the side and brought the side of his hand down hard just at the base of her skull. With a little whimper she fell peacefully silent at last.

Mandy hadn't panicked at the sound of gunfire; it had come too suddenly. Nor had she really panicked when the burlap had been thrown over her. That, also, had been too sudden. She hadn't even really panicked when she found herself absurdly cast into battle with the rude, green-eyed, unshaven Latin hulk on deck.

But when she returned to awareness in a narrow bunk below deck she *did* panic, because what brought her to awareness was the terrible feel of rope chafing against her wrists.

She was tied to the headboard of the small bunk, tied so tightly that she couldn't begin to move her arms.

She almost screamed—almost—as a feeling of absolute helplessness overwhelmed her. Not only were her wrists tied, but her ankles, too. Someone had tossed a worn army blanket over her poorly clad figure, but it didn't cover her feet, and adding insult to injury, she could see the cheap, filthy rope that was attached to the same type of panel posts framing the foot of the bunk. Someone knew how to tie knots—good knots.

Oh, hell! Just like a Boy Scout! Did they have Boy Scouts in Cuba?

She closed her eyes and tried to swallow the awful scream that hovered in her throat; she tried to reason, but reasoning seemed to give her little help.

What the hell was going on?

Facts, facts…Peter always warned her to look to the facts. Okay, fact: she had gone out this morning with a few students to study coral markings. Pleasant day, easy day. Peter had seen that a lunch had been catered. They'd done some work; they'd partied and picnicked, and absolutely nothing had been wrong in the least. Mark Griffen had given an excellent dissertation on the shark's incredible survival from prehistory to the present, and Katie Langtree had found some exceptional examples of fossilized coral. Easy, fun, educational, pleasant…

Her only responsibility—her one big worry for the day!—had been to see that the *Flash Point* was returned in good shape: galley clean, equipment hosed. And even that had seemed like a breeze, because the kids had vowed to do all the work, and they were a dependable group. They also knew they would never use the yacht again if she wasn't returned shipshape.

So…facts! They'd come in, they'd docked. Mark had started rinsing the deck; Katie and Sue had been at work in the galley; Henry Fisher had been covering the furled sails. Everything in A-B-C order. She had stepped off the *Flash Point*, seen that the kids were hard at work at their tasks, then started lazily down the dock, looking forward to a cold canned soda from the refreshment stand.

Facts.…

Next thing she knew, she was out of breath and flat on her back, with a tall dark man standing over her and not paying the least attention to her—even though he had just knocked her down in the rudest fashion. She briefly pictured his face; unshaven; his hair a little long and near ebony in color; his nose as straight as a hawk's; his skin sun-darkened to a glistening bronze. And against all that darkness his eyes had been the brightest, most shocking green. If she lived to be a hundred she would never forget the impact of those kelly green eyes against the bronze of his skin.

Facts!

She had said something to him, something about his rudeness. He had barely paid attention. She'd realized then that he must be Latin—Cuban, Colombian, Nicarauguan. Spanish speaking, as were so many of the area's residents.

English or Spanish speaking, no one had the right to be so rude!

Rude! How the hell could she be worrying about rudeness right now! Fact: she was tied hand and foot to a bunk, and some wacko was running around with a gun. He'd already shot up half the docks; she could only pray he hadn't killed someone.

And she had been the target! Why? Why on earth would anyone kidnap her? She didn't have any money to speak of. She did okay, but paying one's electricity bill on time was tremendously different from coming up with hundreds of thousands of dollars to meet a ransom demand!

No, no...kidnappers demanded ransom from others, not the victim. Peter had money. Not tons of it, but he was certainly one of the affluent. Because of their deep friendship, Peter would surely pay to keep her from being—Don't think of it!

Murdered...

"Oh, God!"

The little breath of a prayer escaped and she fell into sheer panic once again, whimpering and tugging furiously at the ropes. All she managed to do was tighten the knots and chafe her flesh until it was raw.

"Oh, God!" she repeated, panting and lying still. Her wriggling had brought the blanket up to her nose; she was going to sneeze.

Why?

The question came back to haunt her again. There was a lot of money in south Florida. Tons of really rich people lived here. Why not abduct a banker's daughter, or a plastic surgeon's wife? Why her? Peter would pay for her, yes, but Peter just wasn't worth that much!

And who the hell was the green-eyed Cuban? Or Colombian, or whatever he was?

Involuntarily she moistened her lips with the tip of her tongue and squirmed uncomfortably. Panic was zooming in again. The young, intense, dark-haired man had been the one to shoot up the dock and throw the burlap over her. Then everything had been a blur; her strongest memory was of a motor screeching through the night, stopping long enough for her to hear a furious volley of Spanish, then starting up again. And then someone had touched her, and naturally she had tried to escape. The dark-eyed man had first imprisoned her. But once she had been freed from the burlap it had been that same rude, green-eyed man who had imprisoned her a second time. Rude! He was much more than rude! He was brutal. He'd slapped her, subdued her, kissed her—and knocked her out. And the other man had been saying something about Peter being her husband and the scruffy Latin being her lover!

"Oh, God!"

It seemed to be absolutely all she could think of to whisper, but then, the Almighty was surely the only one who could banish her absolute confusion and growing terror.

Once again panic, a sizzling sensation inside of her that grew and swelled and overwhelmed, seemed to be taking charge. She struggled some more and realized sickly that, once again, all she achieved was a greater misery. The knots grew tighter, and the coarse hem of the blanket tickled her nose.

She blew at it, trying to force it beneath her chin. Tears welled in her eyes, and she decided firmly that she wasn't going to cry.

And then she wondered why not. There was a group of crazy Latins outside who were intending to murder her—or worse. She'd already been mauled and bruised, and she didn't understand any of it, and she just very well might wind up shot, so why the hell shouldn't she cry?

For one minute she suddenly lay very, very still, her memory going back...back.

If it had been three years ago she wouldn't have cared in the least. They could have done anything, and she simply wouldn't have cared. She could remember standing over the coffins, Paul's and the baby's, and hurting so badly that she yearned to be dead, too, to be going with them, wherever that might be. She could even remember the thought; take me, God. Take me, too. There is nothing left for me, nothing at all....

She'd cried then. Cried until there were no more tears, cried until she'd been numb, the only thought in her mind that it was so unfair. But of course, no one on earth could explain why life cold be so horribly unfair, and in time, still baffled, she'd had to learn acceptance, because the only alternative was insanity.

Peter had been there for her.

Crushed and nearly broken himself, he had still been there for her. Peter, her parents, her brother. But despite her love for her own family, Peter had been the one who somehow gave her the greatest comfort. Perhaps because his loss had been as keen: his only son, his only grandchild.

Huge burning tears were forming behind her eyes. She blinked furiously, trying to think of Peter. He was so strong, so moral. He'd never wavered under fire; he always did what he thought was right. He always went by principle. She wasn't going to cry, and she wasn't going to break. Somehow, no matter what happened to her, she would rise above these people.

She tensed, aware that someone had come below. Twisting, she could see that she was in the stern of the old sailboat. Another bunk, identical to the one she lay on, was straight across from her, and two small closets at the end of the bunks stood at the stern. There was a slatted wooden door just past her head; her entire space of confinement couldn't have been much more than fifty square feet.

Two people were somewhere beyond that door. At least two people, laughing and talking in Spanish. She strained to make out the words, but they spoke too quickly.

Why the hell hadn't she paid more attention to Spanish in school? Why? Because the teacher had been a horrible nasty woman whom everyone in the entire school had thought was creepy. She'd had the most awful way of pointing her finger and saying, *"¡Repitan, por favor!"* in a sickeningly sweet voice, and no one had paid her the least attention.

Irrelevant! Totally irrelevant right now! She'd been hearing Spanish all her life; surely she could comprehend something of what was being said, she insisted to herself.

She did. At long last she did.

Cerveza.

Someone was asking someone else if he wanted a beer. Great! That bit of genius would surely help her vastly!

But then she stopped worrying about her comprehension or lack thereof. Foootsteps were approaching the door. Her muscles cramped with tension from head to toe, and panic sizzled through her once again.

She was helpless, absolutely helpless. Trussed like a pig on its way to the slaughterhouse. Totally, horribly vulnerable.

The door opened; she thought about closing her eyes, but too late.

One of the men ducked as he stepped through the door. He straightened too soon, cracked his head and swore beneath his breath. He turned to her and she found herself staring into his eyes.

Green eyes. Bright, startlingly...tense as they stared into hers.

He glanced over his shoulder quickly, then moved to kneel down beside her.

"Mrs. Blayne."

He said it in English, and she couldn't detect any hint of an accent.

"Mrs. Blayne, are you all right? Juan was assigned to watch me all night. I couldn't get back to you. Maybe he trusts me now. I'm not sure. This is important, please listen."

He was reaching toward her.

She couldn't help herself; she let out a small scream. Oh, God, what was going on? Who was he? How on earth could he be on her side when he seemed to be just like them?

The young man with the dark eyes suddenly appeared in the doorway, laughing, saying something about *amor.*

"Amor?" Mandy shook her head. Lover! "N—"

A hand clamped down over her mouth, stifling her words, stealing her breath. He twisted his head toward the man at the door and laughed, too, and when he spoke next there was an accent in his words.

"Amigo, you got a gag anywhere?"

The dark-eyed man chuckled and responded in Spanish, then turned away. Then the green-eyed stranger leaned his furious face so close to hers that she felt the whisper of his breath and the blaze of his body heat.

"Damn it! The next time I try to say something, you shut up and listen!"

There was no accent at all this time...

He straightened and slowly drew his hand away. Still terrified, and completely baffled, Mandy stared up at him in silence.

"Good," he murmured grimly. "Now—"

"Who the hell—" she began, then froze. He was leaning toward her again, tangling his fingers in the hair at her nape, bringing his mouth to hers....

The dark-eyed man was at the door again, she realized, staring at her. And at him. At the green-eyed stranger.

Who was kissing her again. Pressing his mouth to hers urgently, feverishly, heatedly. Stealing away any words she might have spoken.

3

Cerveza...

He tasted of beer, and though she stiffened and tried to twist away, she was in that horrible position of helplessness, chin caught by his powerful hand, mouth overpowered by his.

But beyond the terror, beyond the fury, beyond that awful helplessness, the kiss wasn't that bad.

Wasn't that bad!

Oh, Lord, she was getting hysterical. This was insane; she was going insane already. So much for inner strength. Not that bad! It was wretched; it was humiliating!

And it could get much, much worse, she reminded herself, and that was her last thought, because suddenly all the little sensations seemed to overwhelm her, and she felt as if she was nothing but burning kinetic energy. She felt the rasp of his bearded cheek and the warm texture of his lips, the moistness that seemed like lava, and the taut muscles of his chest, crushed hard against her breast. She felt the whisper of his breath and thought ridiculously that he smelled rather nice, and that the slight taste of beer wasn't so awful, either, and really, she could live through this, because what other choice did she have?

The man in the doorway chuckled again, saying something and addressing the green-eyed man as Miguel.

At last "Miguel" drew away from her, but those green eyes remained on hers, as bright as gems, sparkling out a warning so potent that it might have been written on the air.

He kept staring at her as he answered the other man. What he said she didn't know, she just kept staring back into those green eyes, wishing with all her heart that she was free, not trussed and tied here so ignominiously. Wishing that she could reach up, wrench out a thatch of that ebony hair and punch him through a wall!

And then she was afraid all over again. Deeply afraid. Because every man on the sailboat could come in at any time and do anything to her, and all she would be able to do in turn was fight until her wrists bled from the cruel chafing of the rope.

She averted her eyes from his at last and suddenly realized that it was day. Ugly old curtains were pulled over the tiny portholes, but light was filtering in nevertheless.

She'd slept here the night through, and of all the ridiculous things, while her life hung in the balance, she was suddenly and desperately the recipient of nature's call. They were still prattling away, so she burst out in interruption, "I have to go to the bathroom."

They both stopped speaking and stared at her.

"*¡Baño!*" she snapped. "I have to...go!"

Then they both stared at each other and started laughing again. Miguel said something; the other man, addressed as Julio, shrugged, then turned away.

She cringed as Miguel pushed aside her hips with his own so he could sit and lean over her. He gave a disgusted oath, granted her another sizzling glance and moved on to his objective: freeing one of her wrists.

She breathed a little more easily, closed her eyes and prayed for strength, and said carefully, "Who are you?"

He glanced back toward the door quickly, then whispered, "For God's sake, trust me! Go along with me!"

Julio was back; she couldn't say anything more. Actually, she could have, because she didn't trust Miguel in the least, but somehow she chose not to.

He kept working on her wrist. She gazed past his broad bare shoulder to Julio. "Señora Blayne," he told her, "we really do not wish to hurt you. If you can behave, you will be well. Miguel says he can handle you—"

She couldn't help but interrupt. "Oh, he does, does he?" she asked, flashing Miguel a glance of pure loathing.

"And for your sake, señora, I hope he speaks the truth."

Her right hand fell free. Miguel clutched it, inhaling with concern at the rope burns there. She tried to snatch it from him, but he held tight, warning her with his eyes once again.

She clenched her teeth against the tears that threatened. He started to free her other hand. When her left wrist was released he moved to her feet. Rubbing her wrists, she turned her head defiantly to stare at Julio.

"Why are you doing this? You're mistaken if you think that Peter Blayne is a wealthy man. He isn't. If you're asking a huge ransom for my return you won't get it."

"*Señora*, we do not want money. Money, bah, what is that? A man wants money, it is easy. He works for it."

A new fear settled over her; they didn't want money! Then...

Julio suddenly pounded his heart. "Freedom! You will be our ticket to freedom!"

"But..."

Her feet were free. Miguel was standing above her again, taking her hands.

"Let me go! I can stand by myself."

He looked as if he were going to argue with her, but he didn't. He released her, and she swung her long bare legs over the bunk and attempted to stand in a huff.

She keeled over instantly, right into his arms. And she felt those hated hands encircle her waist, holding her steady.

"Damn you!" She tried to slap him, but he ducked, and she cried out when he caught her wrists. They were so sore!

Julio laughed. "You and Miguel had better make up *señora*. Oh, you needn't worry—or pretend. We will say nothing to the senator about your affair. He might not think an unfaithful wife worth much."

"I'm not—"

"You said you had to go to the head!" Miguel snapped, his English heavily accented again.

She was certain that this ordeal had cost her her mind.

He muttered something to Julio in Spanish, then reached for her arm and wrenched her to her feet. Julio moved out of the way, and Miguel led her roughly through the little door and three feet down a narrow hallway to another door.

"The head!" he snapped, shoving her in.

Face flaming, she slammed the door.

And then she didn't even have to go anymore. She pressed her palms to her temples, dizzy, nauseated—and scared. He'd said she should trust him. How the hell could she, and who was he, anyway?

She tried to take deep breaths, and at last she felt that at least she wasn't going to be sick. She noticed then that the facilities were quite clean, and managed to use them. The water that ran into the sink was sporadic, but clear and clean, and she splashed a lot of it over her face, thinking how good it was to rinse the salty stickiness away. She stared into the mirror over the sink and saw that her eyes were as wide as gold doubloons; her cheeks appeared far too pale beneath her tan.

Feeling dizzy again, she gripped the small sink. At last she opened her eyes and stared longingly out the circular porthole. The sailboat's outer rail hid any view of the water, but she could see the sky, and it was a beautiful blue, with just a few puffs of cottonlike clouds.

What a glorious day! Monday. She should have been at work by now, joining her colleagues at the site. White-smocked and gloved, she should have been up to her wrists in dirt, seeking the treasures beneath it.

Where was help? The whole dock had been chaos. Surely the police had been called. Surely someone—everyone!—knew that she was missing by now. They would have known it as soon as she had been taken; there had been witnesses all over the place!

"Señora Blayne!"

Her name, snapped out in a feminine voice, was followed by a rough pounding at the door.

"What?" she yelled back.

"Open the door! I will give you a robe, and you can take a shower."

Mandy gazed instantly at the tiny shower cubicle; the longing to feel clean was a strong one. She didn't know how many hours they had been at sea. She had no idea of where she was, or what the chances were that she would ever get back to civilization alive. It just didn't make any sense to turn down a shower.

Mandy threw open the door to find a young woman standing before her, a very young woman, somewhere between eighteen and twenty-one.

What she lacked in age, though, she made up for in manner. She was beautiful in an exotic way, with flashing dark eyes and a voluptuous figure, well defined in tight jeans and a red sweater, and with a head of richly curling, near-black hair.

She was shorter than Mandy's five-feet-eight inches, which for some odd reason—she was clutching at straws!—made Mandy feel just a little bit better.

The Latin girl lifted her chin, eyeing Mandy regally, then stuffed something made of dull gray terry into Mandy's hands.

"I am Maria. Here, take this. The bathing suit is not much covering, eh?" the girl said, and once again swept Mandy with a disdainful glare. She chuckled, displaying a fine set of small white teeth beneath her generous rose-tinted lips. "Not that you have much to cover!" She shook her head. "What Miguel sees in you...but then, maybe he has not had enough to distract him!"

Mandy was about to tell her that she really didn't give a damn what Miguel saw in anyone. All she wanted to do was get away from the whole stinking lot of them. She decided to keep silent, though she wasn't sure why, because she certainly didn't trust Miguel.

"Thanks for the robe," she said flatly, and closed the door, smiling bitterly as she heard the girl burst into an outraged spate of Spanish. Maria was no part of the power here, that much was obvious. She was nothing more than a young girl—uncertain, insecure, and perhaps idolizing the handsome well-built Miguel.

Mandy turned on the water; it came out cold, but she hadn't been expecting anything better. Stepping beneath the weak spray even as she peeled away her bathing suit, she started shivering vehemently—and not from the cold. Fear swept through her again as she wondered just what was going on. Who was Miguel? Who was Julio? And, for that matter, just who the hell was Maria? And if they were after "freedom" instead of money, just how did they think she could supply it?

She swallowed convulsively and found a fairly new bar of soap. She let the water run over it as she stood there behind the strangely new pink plastic curtain in a state of something akin to numbness. She didn't want to use anything of theirs, but she decided that the soap would be okay if she let the water rinse away layer after layer in a pool of suds.

And then suddenly she began to feel better—angrier, but better. She really did have to fight them; she couldn't allow herself to be so victimized. Fight them...and use any means that she had. Maria's very childlike insecurity was a weapon she must remember and use.

She would get to the bottom of this! She would find out exactly what they wanted—and see that they never got it! There would be a chance for escape somewhere along the line. There would have to be!

She closed her eyes and ducked her head beneath the trickling water to rinse her hair, shaking and shivering still, but now just a bit calmer, a bit more in control. It was amazing what a cold shower could do.

But just then—just when she had convinced herself that she could survive!—she heard her name spoken again, and spoken much too close!

"Mrs. Blayne..."

She let out a shriek of horror, aware that the husky, low-timbred, unaccented tone belonged to green-eyed Miguel.

"Damn you!" he swore next, and she shrieked again, because his arms were suddenly around her, wrapping her in the pink plastic curtain. She dragged in a breath to scream again, but that massive tanned hand of his was suddenly over her mouth, and to her absolute horror he was standing behind her, touching her, in the tiny confines of the shower stall.

He pulled her hard against him. All the naked length of her back was against his chest and hips; he wore only a pair of cutoffs, and she could feel with painful clarity all the rippling muscle that composed his shoulders and arms, all the short dark hair that ran riot over his chest. She squirmed, near hysteria, but she managed only to wedge her bare buttocks more intimately against him.

"Stop it, please, will you?" he begged her in a whisper, dipping his mouth near her ear. "I'll explain if you'll just—"

His hold had loosened. With a burst of strength she wriggled away from him and opened her mouth to inhale again for a frenzied scream, too frightened to realize that her scream could do nothing but bring her other captors running.

"Damn it, you're worse than a greased pig!" he rasped out, and then his hands were on her again, but far worse. Because this time, in his attempt to restrain her, his fingers closed over her breast before finding a hold against her ribs again, and he'd already regained a smothering hold over her mouth.

Still swearing beneath his breath, he manipulated her around to face him, and that, too, was far worse, because then her breasts were pressed against his chest and her hips were horribly level with his, and she had never been forced to realize so staggeringly that a man was a man, and this one was made of iron. She almost passed out, but the water, cold and beating against her back, revived her, and she found herself tilting her head to stare into those incredibly green eyes. She realized a little belatedly that he was angry and aggravated, but intense and serious and not—apparently—about to molest her. Not any more than he already had, that was!

"Listen! I'm not going to hurt you! I had to come in here because I had to talk to you without the others hearing. Mrs. Blayne, please, promise me that you won't scream again and I'll move my hand."

Promise that she wouldn't scream....

She wasn't sure that she could. The screams just kept building inside of her. She was standing naked in a two-by-two cubicle, crushed against a near-naked stranger with the muscled build of a prizefighter. Screaming was instinctive!

"Please!" he urged her again.

She didn't know why she nodded at last. Perhaps because she didn't have any choice. And perhaps because she wanted to believe him, because she wanted to trust someone. Perhaps it was something in his eyes that promised pride and integrity and sincerity. Perhaps it was because she would pass out and pitch helplessly against him, if she didn't breathe soon....

Slowly he eased his hand from her mouth. His eyes slipped from hers for just a moment, traveling downward, then upward once again, locking with hers.

"Mrs. Blayne," he whispered, "I'm a cop. If you want to come out of this, play along with me. I'm all that can stand between you and—"

"A cop!" she gasped incredulously. A cop? The hell he was! Where was his badge? Where was his gun? Cops didn't help kidnappers. They didn't assault the victims!

"Mrs. Blayne, I'm with—"

"If you're a cop," she demanded, shaking, realizing all over again that she was naked with him in a tiny space, "where's your badge?"

"I dumped it. I lost my gun coming after—"

"Get out of here!" she snapped suddenly, aware that hysteria was rising in her again. "Cops don't crawl into the shower with kidnap victims! They don't—"

She hadn't realized how her voice was rising until his hand fell over her face again, shutting her up.

"*Shh!* Are you trying to get us both killed? If they even get a whiff of who I am, I'll become shark bait, lady. And I'll be damned if I think you're worth it!"

Her eyes widened. Could it possibly be true? His Spanish had been perfect; his English, when he spoke to her alone, had no accent whatsoever. Yet when he spoke to Julio, he sounded as if he was barely comfortable with the language. Like a chameleon, he could change in the wink of an eye....

"Eh? Miguel?"

They both froze as someone rapped on the door again and called out to Miguel. A barrage of Spanish followed. Miguel held still for a moment, then called something back, something that she didn't understand a single word of.

Footsteps moved away from the door. Mandy was crushed so tightly to his chest that she felt the expulsion of his breath and the rapid beating of his heart.

He stared down at her then with absolute dislike and fury. Still holding her to him, he reached around and turned off the water; it seemed that his striking eyes became razors that sliced right through her.

"Listen to me, lady. Listen good. I'm a cop—whether you believe it or not. Go along with me. I'm only going to warn you once, because, honey, I can bail out of this thing real easy by myself. I spent all night talking my heart out to convince them that I'm a refugee, too, that I was your gardener, that you're married to a man twice your age, and therefore became involved with me hot and heavy. They didn't take you to kill you or rape you. Julio Garcia is a desperate man, but fairly ethical, for a kidnapper. I don't trust his companions all that far, however. Julio decided to keep me around because he thinks I can keep you under control. Blow that, and we could both be dead. Pull one more stunt against me and I swear I'll jump overboard and swim out of this thing. I don't mind sticking around to fulfill my job, but I'll be damned if I'll keep worrying about getting killed *because of* you instead of *for* you!"

She stared at him, shaken by his anger, shaken by the intensity of his words. Was he really a cop? Or was he one of *them*, just a little more educated, a far better actor? What a way to control a captive, to convince her that a cop was with her and on her side!

He shook her suddenly. "Do you understand?"

She lowered her eyes, then closed them quickly. All she saw when she looked down was his muscled and hairy male chest, slick and hard against her breasts. And of all things, she felt her nipples harden against him.

"Yes!" She gasped, trying to escape him, but he held her against him, and she shook in sudden horror and confusion. "Yes! No! I don't understand any of this. I—"

"Just go along with me now! Julio just said to get the hell out, lunch is ready. I don't have time to try to convince you any further."

He released her completely and stepped out of the shower stall, finding a towel to dry his slick shoulders and chest. He didn't look back at Mandy but stuffed the towel toward her, then found the gray terry robe and shoved that to her over his shoulder.

Quivering and confused, Mandy hurriedly accepted the towel, though she didn't bother to dry herself thoroughly, and fumbled into the robe. It was worn and fell to her feet, but it didn't make her feel especially secure. She wrapped it around herself as tightly as she could, then knotted the belt.

His back was still to her, but just inches away. Beneath his tan she noted a smattering of freckles across his shoulder and thought them curious, considering his coloring.

Oh, God! Who the hell was he really?

"Are you decent?" he asked her.

She started to laugh, but caught herself quickly, afraid that if she got started, she would never quit. "You didn't worry whether I was 'decent' or not when you charged into the shower!" she accused him.

"Shh! Damn you!" he said in a vehement whisper, whirling around, hands on hips, to face her.

Her lip started to tremble, but she didn't intend to let it. She tossed back her head and stared at him dubiously. "Do cops always run around in the pursuit of duty with no weapons, no ID and no shoes?"

He groaned impatiently. "I told you—"

"Oh, I know what you told me," she said. "I'm just not sure I believe a word of it."

He closed his eyes and sighed, then stared at her in exasperation. "Gamble, then. You're with me, or you're not. But if you're against me, remember, I'm gone."

"Gone? From where?" she demanded.

"From wherever we are. Near Cat Cay, I think. I'm a hell of a good swimmer. A dive overboard, that's all it would take. They don't watch me like they're going to watch you."

"And why the hell should they trust you?"

"Because I know how to play this game, lady," he said grimly.

"Either that, or you're one of them."

He smiled with a certain malicious humor and advanced those few inches to her, rounding his fingers over her shoulders so that she almost screamed again from the pure electricity of that touch.

Never had she seen anything as intense, as compelling, as frightening—

as dangerous!—as the kelly green blaze of his eyes. She couldn't speak; she couldn't have screamed even if it had been her most ardent desire. She could only stare at him in silence.

"Lady, place your bet quickly. We've got to go now, unless you want Julio in this head along with the two of us! If I were you, though, I'd change my tune—quickly. I'd admit to this ignoble affair and cling to me as if we'd been passionately involved for ages! Hey—" he cocked his head, daring her "—you might not like your other options. Julio is fairly ethical, but those other two have been talking about your *senos* all day."

"My—my what?" Mandy swallowed.

"Breasts, Mrs. Blayne. They're quite entranced with...them."

She started to jerk away, and he laughed without a trace of amusement. "Like I said, there's only so far I'll go for you if you won't cooperate. So have it your way. I'm a fugitive like the others, probably a murdering rapist. Take me—or leave me."

She swallowed again, lowering her eyes, desperately trying to decide whether to trust him or not. She didn't.... But what were her options?

He'd kissed her, struck her, abused her! But not done half of what he might have, she reminded herself.

He was already reaching for the door. She clutched his arm, and he turned back to her, arching a dark brow.

"If you're really a cop, why can't you overpower them? Why can't you arrest them?"

"Oh, God help me!" he breathed, looking heavenward. "Mrs. Blayne, should I really introduce myself as a police officer? And arrest them? Now that's a laugh. I'll say, 'Hey, let's go to jail.' I haven't got a weapon on me, but they'll just say, 'Sure, let's go, you want to put us in jail, fine.'"

Mandy flushed. "But you should be trying...."

"I *am* trying!" He swore heatedly. "I'm trying to keep you alive—and I'm trying to stay on top of you myself to keep these guys from deciding that, hey, they have you, so what the hell...if you catch my meaning, Mrs. Blayne. Although God knows you seem to be strange enough! Maybe you'd enjoy their attentions. Did you marry Peter Blayne for his money? Yeah, I could be way off. Maybe you'd enjoy the excitement."

"What?" Stunned, outraged, she shrieked the word.

She should have learned not to shriek by now. He slapped a hand over her mouth before she could blink and drew her against his hard length in a frightening manner, staring down at her with danger sparking from his eyes.

"Shut up!"

Shut up? She had no choice. So she blinked, realizing that this man—this cop?—thought she was the senator's wife, just as the others had assumed. He actually assumed that she'd married an older man for money. Oh, how dare he!

His hand moved from her mouth. She smiled very sweetly, narrowing her eyes. "No, Miguel. I married Peter Blayne because he's fabulous in bed, and I don't need any excitement! So lead on. Just keep your hands off me and I'll be as quiet as a mouse."

He grinned crookedly, and she was startled at the effect of his expression on her. He was a handsome man, really handsome. Dark, tall, broad, muscled, sexy and very physical. And fascinating, with those strange bright eyes. And when he looked at her in that dry, insinuating fashion she felt an involuntary sizzle sweep through her. One she instantly denied, vehemently denied. She was still in love with a memory, still convinced that only a deep and rich emotion could ever create such steaming awareness....

She closed her eyes, dizzy. What if he wasn't a cop? And what if he was?

It was insane. Was she cracking already? So weak that she was willing to cling to anyone—especially anyone male and muscled—because she was scared? She wasn't. She wasn't!

His scent was all around her, the roughness of his touch, that feel of steel in his arms. She wanted to trust him.

"Mrs. Blayne," he said softly, with a touch of amusement, "I won't touch you, but I suggest that you *do* touch me now and then. You were having a passionate affair with me, remember?"

"Why...why," she whispered, head lowered, "would they believe that? Why would they believe that you would risk your life to be with me?"

He chuckled dryly. "Because Latins are a passionate people, Mrs. Blayne. They usually love deeply, hate deeply—and possess their women as loyally and heatedly as they do their pride."

She stared at him, searching his features, seeking an answer, and she prayed that she wasn't a victim more of his arresting features and eyes than she was of the circumstances.

"Are you Latin?" she asked him.

"Half," he answered curtly.

"Miguel!"

The call came from very near the door. Had they been overheard? Mandy started to shiver all over again. If he *was* here to help her and she caused him to be murdered, she would never forgive herself in a thousand years—even if he was an SOB.

Damn him! She wouldn't tell him that she wasn't Peter's wife, either!

"Let's go!" he hissed.

She nodded. He took her hand, and she didn't resist him, but just before he opened the door he twisted his handsome head ruefully toward her and mouthed out a quick query.

"I almost forgot. What's your name?"

"Blayne! You know—"

"Your first name, stupid!"

"Amanda!"

"Mandy?"

"Only to friends," she said pointedly.

He smiled. "And lovers, Mrs. Blayne? Mandy, let's go!"

4

Lunch consisted of a salad and *arroz con pollo*, chicken and rice, served belligerently to Mandy and charmingly to Miguel by Maria and another woman, up on deck.

Mandy had tried her hardest to assimilate the layout of the craft during her quick walk through the hall to the steps leading topside. There hadn't been much to assimilate. The vessel was old, at least forty years, worn, but well-kept. There were another two sets of sleeping quarters past the head, then a shabby salon and a galley, and to the extreme aft, the captain's cabin.

The older woman had stared at Mandy with extreme disapproval as they moved through the galley. Mandy had ignored her, but she hadn't been able to ignore the smell of the food; the aroma was captivating, and she was forced to realize that she was starving.

The deck of the motorized two-masted sailboat was lined with old wooden seats, and that was where Miguel led her. Mandy kept her mouth shut for several minutes while she perused her surroundings and her curious party of abductors.

There was Julio, called Garcia by the others; the young woman, Maria; the older woman; and two more men, one a heavyset fellow with a swirling mustache, the other gaunt and hungry-looking. Mean, Mandy thought, and far different from Julio Garcia, who, strangely, had the look of a poet.

They all laughed and chatted in rapid Spanish, drinking Michelob out of bottles and eating off paper plates as if they were simply out for a picnic at sea.

Including Miguel. He laughed and chatted along with the others, tensing only slightly beside her when some apparently ribald comment was made about her by either the man with the mustache—Juan, she thought his name was—or Roberto, the gaunt man with the lascivious eyes.

If Miguel was on her side, he certainly knew how to enjoy himself in the interim. He ate with a hearty appetite, complimenting the two women on their cooking. So far Mandy hadn't been able to pick up more than a word or two of the conversation, but mannerisms were universal, and it was easy to tell that Miguel was managing to fit right in. There was only one difference between him and the other men: they were carrying large guns in shoulder holsters.

Miguel had none. He was still barefoot, bare chested, clad in his wet cutoffs, assuring her that he could not be hiding a weapon anywhere on his person.

She turned her gaze to the ocean surrounding them, wondering how far they had come, and in what direction. Miguel had told her that he thought they were near Cat Cay, which meant the Bahamas. She saw nothing around them right now but the sea and sky, and her heart sank in desolation. She might never be found, never be rescued! There might well be hundreds of uninhabited islands in this stretch of the ocean. She'd been taken away in a little speedboat, and now she was on an old sailboat. The police—if they could even look for her now that they were out of American waters!—wouldn't even know what they were looking for.

The police!

She twisted her head slightly and stared at Miguel, seated so casually beside her, idly holding his beer and laughing at one of Roberto's jokes. Was he really a cop? It was hard to believe at the moment! He was taller, stronger, tougher than the other men, muscled but trim, lean and mean-looking. If he was a cop, why the hell hadn't he done something?

She told herself that no amount of muscle could combat a bullet, that maybe he was doing his best just to keep them both alive. It was hard, though, even if she realized that half her problem was that she resented him heartily for assuming that she was Peter's wife and that, being younger, she had latched on to him for material reasons.

And maybe she also resented him out of sheer frustration. By God, he was physically beautiful. His stomach was taut, his legs long and hard, his shoulders those of an Atlas.

That dark hair; those flashing eyes, emerald in the sun; that handsome face, high boned with arching dark brows, teeth pearly white against the full sensual curve of his mouth.... Not even the thick shadow of beard detracted from his looks. He seemed like a bulwark of character and strength—and he wasn't doing a damn thing for her! Just chatting away in Spanish and drinking his *cerveza!*

Maria collected his empty plate, and he stretched his free arm around Mandy. She tried not to stiffen; it was a casual gesture, and she decided she would rather trust him than be left vulnerable to Roberto's naked ogling.

Maria took Mandy's plate less than graciously, eyeing her maliciously, and to Mandy's own surprise she returned that nasty glare and inched closer to Miguel.

"Mandy." He spoke softly and she jumped, turning to look up at him. "You want something to drink?"

The accent was back in his words.

"Ah, yes. A diet Pepsi, please."

He started to laugh. "What do you think this is? They've got beer, water, guava juice and Coca-Cola. 'Classic', I believe."

She recognized his dry humor and just barely held her temper in check. "A Coke!" she snapped.

He started to translate her request to Maria, but Maria snapped, "I heard her," then disappeared below.

Maria returned with the soda and sat staring pointedly at Mandy. The older woman said something to her, which she ignored; then Julio grated out something impatiently and the two women—along with Roberto, Mandy noticed gratefully—went below deck. Mandy sipped her Coke, thinking that a soda had never tasted so delicious before. She stared around again, tensing as she realized that there was a small island on the horizon, and that a pleasure boat was anchored just beyond its beach.

How far away was it? she wondered yearningly. Three miles—or five? And did it really matter? If she had to, she could manage a five-mile swim....

"So, Señora Blayne, you are resigned to our company, sí?"

She started, forced into an awareness that the oddly genteel Julio Garcia was watching her.

"Resigned?" she queried regally, ignoring the pinch of Miguel's fingers suddenly tightening around her shoulders. "Not in the least. Perhaps," she added sarcastically, "You'd be so kind as to explain to me just what you're after so that I may become...resigned!"

Julio gazed curiously at Miguel then returned his dark soulful eyes to hers. "Miguel has not explained it to you?"

"She gave me no chance, this one!" Miguel pulled her closer against him, irritating her beyond belief by playfully fluffing her hair. She stiffened against him, but his hold was a powerful one for all its casual appearance, and she had no recourse except to smile grimly at Julio Garcia.

"I haven't the faintest idea of what is going on."

Julio shrugged and grimaced. "Your husband betrayed me, Mrs. Blayne. He swore to have my father freed. Empty promises."

My husband is dead, she thought with fleeting pain, and he never betrayed anyone in his life.

"My fath—my husband," she amended quickly, "is a senator, not a warden! What are you talking about?

"He is still in prison! Jorge Garcia—statesman, poet, one of the finest, most courageous freedom fighters ever to live!—still rots in prison! Peter Blayne promised to have something done. He said to trust in the law! Well, I have tried his laws for years! Ever since the Mariel boatlift—"

"Wait a minute!" Mandy interrupted in a burst of passion. "Are you trying to tell me that your father was a prisoner—a criminal—in Cuba, but that we should let him roam free in the United States?"

"Idiota!" Julio shouted, then went on in an irate shouting spree.

"Julio, Julio! She does not understand!" Miguel said, trying to soothe him.

Mandy was more furious than ever. She couldn't believe that this whole thing was over another criminal! "Don't swear at me in Spanish! Say it in English. *No hablo español!* This is the United States of America—"

Suddenly that long-fingered sun-bronzed hand was over her mouth again, and brilliant green eyes were boring into hers. *"Quieta! Cerra la boca,* Amanda!" Miguel snapped. "You want English? Shut your mouth. You don't understand! Julio, I will take her forward and explain, eh?"

Julio exploded into rapid speech again, pulling his gun from his holster and waving it around. Mandy inhaled deeply in shock as Miguel dragged her to her feet, his hand still over her mouth, and half led, half dragged her to the few clear feet of space that surrounded the main mast.

"Damn you!" he grated out tensely, releasing her mouth at last, but only to grip her shoulders and stare down at her like the wrath of God while he spoke. "Are you trying to get us both killed?"

She tossed her hair back. "He's crazy! I won't—"

"Yes, he's crazy! And that's exactly why you'd better start paying a little heed. Don't you know this story? Doesn't your husband ever talk to you about his work?"

Her husband? Oh, Peter...

Yes, Peter talked to her. But she'd been so involved with her own work lately that she hadn't really seen him in a while. She shook her head stiffly. "I don't know anything about any of this! Except that if Peter has refused to let some murderer roam the streets, then—"

He took a deep breath, a bitter breath. "For your information, Mrs. Blayne—Mrs. Bigot!—not everyone who came in on the Mariel boatlift was a murderer!"

"I am not a bigot! But don't you dare try to tell me that Castro didn't empty his prisons on the U.S.!"

"Oh, great! So everyone who is Cuban—"

"I didn't say that!"

"But you meant it!"

"The hell I did!"

"What are you, the head of the DAR, Mrs. Blayne? Your impeccable bloodlines go back to the *Mayflower*, I take it!"

"As a matter of fact," Mandy lied coolly, "they do!" She suddenly felt as if she was going to burst into tears. She hadn't meant to offend him, but she'd be damned if she would be responsible for putting a criminal—be he Irish, German, Spanish or all-American—back on the streets.

Her lashes fell over her eyes; she didn't understand why this terrible antagonism had suddenly erupted between them. He was her lifeline, however tenuous. She was simply terrified, and trying not to be.

Frightened, but determined to be strong. And there were so many chinks in her armor!

He was still angry, but was holding his temper in check. He spoke flatly to her, still holding her shoulders, his voice very distant.

"Jorge Garcia was not a murderer, a rapist, or even a thief. He was a political prisoner, but the charges trumped up against him could have sent him before a firing squad. He was, once upon a time, a brilliant man. Rich and a philanthropist, a lawyer, a scientist. He still had a few friends in the Castro regime, but even so his enemies managed to have him labeled as dangerously insane. He was sent out on the Mariel boatlift and consequently wound up with dozens of other cases, waiting to be reviewed by the immigration board."

"You're trying to tell me that Julio's father is not just a good man but a great one?"

"From all I've heard, yes."

She shook her head, her temper growing. "So we're at fault! The Americans are at fault, and it's okay for Julio to attempt to assassinate Peter and kidnap me."

"I didn't say it was all right! Julio has obviously snapped. Yes, gone mad, in a way. Apparently he's been frustrated half to death. It doesn't make him right. It just explains his behavior. You can't do anything— your husband probably couldn't even have done anything, no matter how hard he tried, except speed up some paperwork."

"Then why are you yelling at me?"

"I'm not yelling!"

"You sure as hell are!"

He released her shoulders abruptly. "Excuse me, Madame DAR. It's my Latin temper, you know."

"You're stereotyping yourself—not me!" Mandy snapped.

"I'm not trying to do anything except get us both out of this. I'm a cop, not a lawmaker, and not a politician. I don't even know what I'm doing here myself! But, Mrs. Blayne, please, if you're at all interested in living, please don't get into moral fights with Julio Garcia!"

She stared at him, then tossed her head. From the corner of her eye she glimpsed the island she had seen before—and the massive pleasure craft anchored right before it.

"I, uh, won't argue with Garcia anymore," Mandy said absently.

"Good. I don't think he wants to harm anyone. I—"

He broke off, frowning, as excited shouts suddenly came from the aft deck.

"Let's see what's up," Miguel murmured, and he started back. Mandy didn't follow him. She stood dead still where she was, feeling the ocean breeze, feeling the sun on her face.

The boat wasn't far away. No more than three miles, she was certain. And she really was a good swimmer. Her captors were so excited about whatever was happening off their own craft that she could probably be halfway to that other vessel before anyone even noticed that she was gone.

She hesitated just a second longer, thinking of Miguel. She didn't want to worry about him, yet she did. She had the sneaking suspicion that his presence had saved her from sexual abuse by the leering Roberto, and she didn't want him harmed on her behalf.

But he had managed to make himself one of them. They wouldn't kill him. At least, she convinced herself in those moments that they wouldn't. And if he was a cop, he would know how to take care of himself. She had a chance to escape, she didn't dare risk losing it.

She moved at last, staring forward. They were all there now: the two women, Roberto, Juan, Julio—and Miguel.

"A bloodbath!" she thought she heard someone say. But she wasn't really listening—or thinking.

Quietly she moved portside, stepped to the rail and dove into the water.

It was a good clean dive. The gray robe bulked around her somewhat, but to obtain her water safety certification every three years she'd had to swim a mile in her clothes—shoes, too—so the robe shouldn't be that bad. And of course she could always ditch it. And arrive at a strange boat stark naked. What a thing to think of at a time like this! Swim...

She broke the surface and took a breath, stroking smoothly, aware that she would have to pace herself to make the distance. Stroke, breathe, stroke, breathe. The sun was high in the sky, warm; the water was almost as warm as that sun, and very blue here, where it was deep. It felt good to swim, to feel the salt against her face, to feel the promise of freedom....

She cocked her head, inhaling, stroking, and heard shouts distantly from behind her. She clenched her teeth in dismay, having hoped to gain more distance before they discovered her absence.

She paused for a second, treading the water, to see what was happening. She was shocked to see that they were all watching her—not angry, but pale as a troop of ghosts.

"Stop, Amanda! Stop!"

It was Miguel shouting, and as she turned to begin swimming again with stronger strokes, she swore inwardly. Damn him! He'd said he was on her side, but he was the one standing on the rail, ready to dive after her and recapture her.

The salt stung her eyes; she felt like crying as she heard the splash of his body entering the water. He was coming after her. She renewed her strokes, still hoping she could outdistance him. She was good, she reminded herself. She really was a good swimmer....

But so was he. And he was stronger. In a matter of seconds he was almost at her feet.

"Amanda! Get back!"

His hand slid around her ankle, a vise that jerked her under water, then into his arms. She choked and gagged and came up against his chest, gasping.

"Damn you! Damn you!" she shrieked, furious and ready to cry. She could have done it except for him. "I hope you rot in hell for all eternity. Liar! You son of a bitch. You—"

He still looked white and grim. He shook her. "Get back. *Now!*"

He gave her a strong shove back toward the boat. The terry robe seemed to be locked all around her now, hampering her movements. She couldn't seem to swim at all anymore; she couldn't untangle her arms.

And Juan and Julio had already climbed into a little dinghy with no motor. They reached furiously, desperately, for the oars, then began coming toward her.

Miguel gave her another shove.

"I can't!"

He jerked at her robe; she tried to hold the sodden material while struggling to stay afloat.

"Take it off!"

She'd never heard such a fervent command. The robe was suddenly gone. "Swim!" he bellowed, shoving her.

She didn't have to swim; the dinghy was right behind her, and Julio and Juan were bending over, grasping her arms. Naked and humiliated she was lifted from the water and cast to the rotting floorboards of the tiny dinghy.

Instinctively she brought her knees to her chest and locked her arms around them, and only then did she realize that they weren't paying her the least attention—they were pulling Miguel into the dinghy after her. He landed half on top of her, dripping wet. There was nowhere to move, and when she tried to shrink closer within herself, he opened his eyes and stared at her with such grim fury that it was as if his eyes had become a glittering inferno that meant to consume her.

He was still gasping for breath, but he threw the robe over her as he shook his head in disgust. "Stupid woman!" he muttered.

Julio muttered a few words to Juan, gesticulating with a sharp intake of breath, and it was then that she realized the awful danger she had almost encountered. Surrounding the little dinghy was an assortment of at least five fins. Shark fins...

And the creatures were still swimming about, thrashing, nearly upsetting the tiny dinghy.

"Sit!" Miguel snapped, and the other two men instantly obeyed.

Mandy shivered miserably beside him as he fumbled for the oars and slowly, carefully, rowed the dinghy toward the sailboat.

Oh, God! She'd nearly swum into the middle of a school of sharks! She would rather be shot ten times over than die such a gruesome death. This man had actually dived after her, pitting himself against the same danger....

"Up, and carefully!" he told her tensely when they reached the boat. Julio and Juan went up the rope ladder first. Julio looked very gray, and she thought that he might be a kidnapper, but he hadn't wanted to see her die—not that way! "Up!"

Somehow she was touching the wet rope ladder. Clinging to it. She didn't feel as if she had any strength at all.

He was behind her, using the force of his body to protect hers against its own weakness. She closed her eyes, fighting dizziness.

She could still hear the sharks thrashing in the water. She turned back and froze in renewed fear. The water was red now. Blood red. The others had turned on one of their own kind and were ripping it apart with their huge jaws and razor teeth....

"Amanda, go."

One foot after the other. Again and again. Julio was there to drag her over the rail. She pulled the robe about her shivering body and lay on the deck, spent, exhausted, and still in shock.

She saw the sun above her, slowly sinking into the west. She felt the chill of a night breeze coming on. The sky was becoming pink and crimson and beautifully gold, and the moon, pale but full, had risen even before the sun could set.

Twenty-four hours...it had been a full day, she thought numbly. A full day since she had been taken, and suddenly none of it mattered except for those last few minutes. She had always thought that she would never really be afraid to die, but she was. And she would have died. In her furious quest for escape she would have stirred up the water to such an extent that the mindless beasts would have found her—except for him.

She was dimly aware that he had come aboard the boat, dimly aware that tense Spanish was being spoken in bursts all around her.

She opened her eyes. Maria, her huge almond eyes ablaze, was staring down at her. She spat on the deck, then began speaking again.

Puta. That was one word Mandy recognized. Maria was screaming because Miguel had almost died to save his Anglo whore. She was trash; she was not worth it.

Julio said something curtly; Maria started to speak again, but he slapped her.

Mandy knew she had acquired a serious enemy. She couldn't even care about that. She felt totally exhausted and numb, and she shivered with spasms she could not halt.

She opened her eyes once again in startled surprise when someone leaned down to her, wrapping strong arms around her.

She met glowing orbs of green: Miguel's eyes. She was too entangled in the robe to fight him, nor did she even think that she should. She stared at him, unable to find the words for an apology, unable even to form a "thank you" on her trembling lips.

Spanish broke out all around her again, but she didn't worry about it. In absolute exhaustion she laid her head against his chest and closed her eyes again.

"I am taking her below," Miguel said determinedly, breaking into English.

"*Sí.* Do it then, *amigo*," Julio agreed.

"*Madre de Dios!*" Juan swore, but Julio interrupted him.

"She will do us no good dying of pneumonia!"

Miguel walked past them with Mandy in his arms. She opened her eyes just before they came to the steps.

Night had almost fallen. It seemed to come so quickly out here on the water. Only a few stretches of gold and crimson lay against the eternal sea and sky. And then, as if they had been a delusion, those colors faded to black.

They moved through the galley, through the salon, down the hall. He used his foot to kick open the door, then laid her on the narrow bunk, swathing her in the blanket, holding her, his eyes enigmatic, only the pulse in his throat displaying any emotion.

"I—I'm sorry—" Mandy began.

"I swear to you," he interrupted her, "I *am* a cop! If you trust me, I'll get you out of this!"

He had every right to be furious, she knew. He'd put his own life on the line—for her. She shivered all over again, knowing she would never have had the nerve to dive into the water if she had known about all those sharks.

Suddenly there was a rapping at the door. Miguel stood quickly and opened it.

The older, gray-haired woman was there, a wooden tray in her hand. She spoke Spanish softly and gazed down at Mandy with the closest thing to sympathy that she had yet seen.

The woman lifted the tray, offering it to Miguel.

"Gracias, gracias," he told her, then she asked him something, and he answered her, stepping aside to allow her to enter the room. She sat down by Mandy's side, touched her forehead and cheeks, offered a weak smile, then wagged a finger beneath Mandy's nose, giving her a motherly scolding. She touched Mandy's cheek once again, shivered and then left.

"What...?" Mandy began, struggling to sit.

Miguel stuffed a shot glass of amber liquid into her fingers. "Drink it—it's rum. It will stop the chill."

She couldn't drink it. "Miguel..."

"Señora Garcia," he told her, wrapping his fingers around a second shot glass and setting the tray on the opposite bunk, "is not at all happy that her son took you. They meant to take your husband. Drink that!"

"Miguel..."

"Mrs. Blayne, by tomorrow they plan to reach some remote and private island where they have a little cottage. Juan will then return to Miami with the ransom note. Obviously your husband won't have any real power to give the Garcias what they want, but negotiations will start. At that time they will also be one man short. They don't want to hurt you. If you would have just one bit of faith in me and give me a little time, I could manage to settle this thing without risking your life."

"Miguel..."

"Drink that!"

She brought the shot glass to her lips with still-trembling hands, then gasped at the potency of the liquor, choked and coughed. He sat beside her and patted her back, but with little mercy. He tilted the glass toward her lips again.

"All of it!"

On her next try she drained the glass. He took it from her hands as she wheezed for breath once again. He swallowed his own without a grimace, haphazardly returned both glasses to the tray, then turned back to her.

He touched her lip, her cheek. "Good," he said. "You've got a little color back."

She lowered her head, her fingers plucking at the blanket. "I'm sorry. I had to do it." She moistened her lips and stared at him again. "Thank you," she whispered stiffly. "You saved my life."

"Line of duty," he told her, his eyes narrowing peculiarly on her hand. He clutched it, looking at the raw marks that still surrounded her wrists. "Do they hurt?" he asked, staring into her eyes again.

She shook her head. It was only a little lie.

The door suddenly burst open to reveal Julio Garcia. He gave a curt order to Miguel. Miguel shook his head vehemently. Chills of fear crept over Mandy again; she knew that they were arguing about her. Her wrist was suddenly shoved up toward Julio's face. He hesitated, then said something back to Miguel. Miguel glanced her way curiously then nodded to Julio. Then Julio, too, was gone, snapping out the cabin light as he went.

Darkness fell all around them. Mandy knew that she was still shivering, that he was still staring at her in the darkness.

"What...what was that all about?" she asked faintly.

"He wanted me to tie you up again."

"You tied those knots?"

"Yes. I had to make them good."

She sniffed in the darkness. "They *were*."

He didn't reply at first. Then he merely said, "Move over."

"What?"

"Move over. I can tie you up, or sleep next to you."

Something rebelled inside her. She wanted to tell him to tie her up, that she would rather suffer through that again than have him sleep beside her.

But she didn't. She didn't ever want to experience that panicky feeling of being so helplessly bound again. She didn't want the rope chafing her flesh until it was raw. And she felt so horribly tired and exhausted.

She moved as close as she could to the paneling that rimmed the bunk, painfully aware of his length and heat as he crawled in beside her. He didn't say a word. In time her eyes adjusted to the darkness and she realized that he was lying there very stiffly, hair still damp from his dive into the water, his profile clean and fascinating as he stared upward into the night.

"Miguel?" she whispered softly.

"What?"

"I really am sorry. I felt that I had to try.... It isn't that I distrust you so much, it's just that the opportunity was there. Thank you. I mean it. And I'm terribly sorry about putting you in danger."

She felt him shrug. The narrow bunk was barely wide enough for one person; two would necessarily feel each other's slightest movement.

"It's okay," he returned in the darkness. And then he was silent again.

"I know you're angry—"

"I'm not angry." He rolled toward her and touched her cheek in the darkness, lightly, for the briefest moment. Then he jerked his hand away from her, as if remembering something.

"I know what it's like to run for freedom, Mrs. Blayne. To seek escape at any cost. Go to sleep. You'll need rest and awareness, should another opportunity come along."

She swallowed and nodded, but knew she would never sleep. Escape...freedom. They seemed like hollow empty echoes now. He knew what it was like. That was what he had said.

She wished fervently that he was not beside her. And yet she was fervently glad of him, too. Of the feel of heat and strength.

She might detest him for some of the things he had said and done, but he was on her side; she had to believe that. And even if she feared him just a little in the deepest recesses of her heart, she could not help but admire him and believe in him.

Only a fool—or a very brave man—would dive into water teeming with sharks to save a woman who had done nothing to deserve it of him.

Sleep was impossible. She lay there miserably for hours and hours, not daring to move, not daring to get any closer to him.

Memories drifted in and out of her mind, good ones, bad ones, some from the distant past, some more recent. She couldn't tell if the man beside her slept, or if he continued to stare into the darkness, lost in the recesses of his own mind.

Somewhere in the night exhaustion and nerves overwhelmed her and she fell into a restless sleep. But even there the memories plagued her. Her son's tiny coffin seemed to float in space, and then the larger one, Paul's. Then the coffins began to change. Darkness and shadow became red, dripping red, blood red, and she could hear and see the terrible gnashing teeth of the sharks....

"Shh, shh! It's over! I'm beside you...you're all right!"

She stiffened, unaware that she had cried out, biting her lip.

"Mandy, go back to sleep. Easy..."

His hand was on her hair; his body was like a heat lamp next to hers. His voice was like the soothing whisper of an ocean breeze.

And maybe because she was still half-lost in a shadow land herself, she allowed herself to listen to that whisper, to be soothed by that strong masculine touch.

She sighed softly.

"You're all right," he whispered again. "It was just a dream."

The tension fell away from her body, and she slept. And this time no dreams came to plague her, just the pleasant sensation of being held safely in strong arms.

5

In the morning she came awake with a curious sense of peace, followed by a haunting disillusionment.

The senses could play such tricks upon the mind! She'd awakened to so many brilliant mornings feeling the lapping of waves, the movement of the ocean beneath her, the coolness of the dawn, and salt-flavored air all around her. Awakened smiling, warm, secure, content, her husband's arm wrapped around her, the lazy tempo of a night's anchorage away from the bustle of the city like a blissful balm.

All the things that went with it came back to her: laughter from above; calls that the "sleepyheads" should awaken; the smell of sizzling bacon—and then whispers. Whispers because Peter would be telling Miranda that the kids should be up, and Miranda would be hushing him, lowering her voice still further, and reminding him that the "kids" were still newlyweds, and newlyweds didn't spring right up from bed; they liked to stay there a while.

And of course by then Mandy and Paul would both be awake, staring at each other, giggling and trying very hard to shush each other so that his concerned parents wouldn't hear them. Then they would shoot out of bed anyway, because Jonathan would have awakened by then, and they were both still so overawed at being parents that they sprang to attention the second he opened his tiny mouth and let out his earsplitting cry.

Then they would be grabbing for robes, because the older Blaynes would come bursting in, so overawed at being grandparents that they too sprang to instant attention.

And then the bacon would burn, and it would have to be started all over. But it wouldn't matter, because they would have all weekend to dive and snorkel and swim and fish and play, and the real world would be miles away. The *Flash Point* would be their fantasyland until they all returned to their responsibilities.

Mandy opened her eyes and felt a nearly overwhelming hopelessness sweep through her. Those times were gone, Miranda was gone, Jonathan was gone and Paul was gone. She blinked against the sudden agony of reality. She hadn't felt this way in ages; she'd learned to insulate herself, to remember the good times, to find other things in life. She could even laugh aboard the *Flash Point*, bring flowers to the cemetery and smile as she remembered her infant son's beautiful smile.

It was this boat; it was this stinking boat. It was so much the opposite of all that had been beautiful. She was a prisoner, not a beloved wife, not an adored daughter-in-law, doted upon by her husband's happy parents. This was a rotting hulk, not the graceful *Flash Point*. It was all a mockery. There wasn't a grain of truth in any of the sensations.

Except that, rotting hulk or not, this vessel rolled on the sea just like any ship. The sea, the sky, the salt air—they were never ending. No matter what came and went in life, they would remain the same. But the warmth...

Mandy rolled over quickly. Miguel had taken the sodden robe off her when he put her on the bunk. Now she was barely covered by the worn blanket he had bundled around her. She was still warm, still warm from his body heat, gone now, but haunting her as thoroughly as the dream.

Mandy pulled the blanket back to her chin, wondering at the anguished stream of emotions he could elicit from her. She felt drawn like the proverbial moth to the candle, but she felt a little ashamed, too. He'd dragged her around half-naked—completely naked actually—bound her, knocked her out, reviled her—and saved her life. She knew exactly what he thought of her; he had said it in so many words. He'd prejudged her as a mercenary bigot, and he deserved to pay for that. Yet in his absurd way he was going above and beyond the call of duty, and he was certainly the most extraordinary man she had ever met.

And that was the main reason she resented him, Mandy thought. In the past three years she had become very independent. She'd been friends with Peter; she hadn't leaned on him. They both had their own work, and work had kept them sane.

But last night...last night had taught her something that she hadn't wanted to learn. Paul was gone; love was gone. Oh, every minute hadn't been perfect. They'd fought; they'd yelled. Any two people did that. Neither one of them had been able to cook worth a whit; she'd wanted a puppy; he'd thought one child was enough. Little things, big things. That was life. You just couldn't zoom through agreeing on everything. But through all those things there had been love. She'd barely known two years of it, but it had been good and solid and real. She had known when she buried her heart and very nearly her existence with her husband and son that she could never settle for anything less—and also that she didn't ever want to know that kind of love again. The pain of loss was so unbearable, so like a set of knives that whittled and whittled away at the insides....

She closed her eyes, inhaling and exhaling.

No, she didn't want to love again. And she certainly wasn't in danger of falling in love with this stranger. But it was dismaying to learn that sensation remained; just like the endless sea and sky, the basic need remained. A need to be held, to feel strength when one was failing, security when all was darkness. To admire, to respect a man, to like the feel of rippling muscle beneath her fingers, the tangy scent of sea and man, the gentle touch of fingers against her cheek.

She gave herself a furious shake, hoping to clear her mind of fantasy. She had to learn to get through these days one by one. She needed some good common sense. If only she had paid attention yesterday she would have known that the sharks were in the water and she would have never made that ridiculous attempt to escape. She had to learn to be wary and alert—and to try to remember that this was a team effort.

She started suddenly, aware not of sound but of a presence at the door. It was open, and Miguel was standing there, watching her with a strange dark expression. She frowned, and the expression faded. He was once again the same enigmatic man she was coming to know.

"I was trying to let you sleep," he said, sauntering in. His hair was damp, and he smelled like soap, and though he was still clad in cutoffs, they were different ones, undoubtedly borrowed from one of the other men. He carried a towel-wrapped bundle, which he gave her, tossing it over the blanket to land in the vicinity of her middle.

"Clothes. They're Maria's. She wasn't very happy about lending them, but Señora Garcia told her that you couldn't run around naked."

Mandy couldn't keep a rueful smile from creeping across her lips as her lashes fell over her cheeks. "Thanks," she said softly. "And thank Señora Garcia. Is there any chance of coming up with a toothbrush?"

"Yes, as a matter of fact, there is. Check below the sink in the head, there's a nice supply. Seems Julio is a tooth fanatic. He told me his teeth were riddled with cavities when he first came to the States. He's been trying to preserve the rest ever since."

"What about you?" she murmured.

"What?"

She kept her lashes downcast, wondering why she was so curious about him. "When you left Cuba..."

"I wasn't born in Cuba."

"But you said—"

"Oh, I am Cuban. Half. I just wasn't born there."

"Here?" She gazed up at him.

He grinned at her, sudden amusement in his eyes. "Here? Was I born in a boat? No. I wasn't born in the water, or in the Bahamas, which is where I'm pretty sure we are."

"I meant—"

"I was born in Dublin, Mrs. Blayne."

"Dublin! Ireland?"

He quickly brought his finger to his lips. "Would you please shush! Are you that determined to hang me?"

"No! Really, I'm sorry!"

She sat up as she spoke, and the blanket dropped to her waist.

She reached for it again quickly, embarrassed, and dragged it back around her before looking at Miguel again.

That strange expression was back...dark, tense. And hungry. Suddenly she was aware of exactly what it meant. He might be a cop, but he was a man, too, a man who found her appealing. He might think very little of her as a human being, but as a woman he found her appealing. Sexually appealing.

And that fact was not something he realized with any great fondness.

She tossed her hair back, a little bit indignant, and a little bit shaken.

She suddenly felt like teasing him! It would provide revenge that seemed very sweet. After all, he thought she was a mercenary woman who had married an old man for his wealth and position. And he was thoroughly convinced that she was a complete bigot. He deserved any torture she could dish out, even if he had dived into the sharks.

"Oh!" she murmured, sweetly distressed, holding the blanket to her breasts but allowing it to fall from her back. Then she had to lower her head and smile discreetly, because she had drawn exactly the response she wanted from him. He had stiffened like a poker. His jaw had squared, and she had heard the grating of his teeth.

She cleared her throat. "Really!" she whispered softly. "I wouldn't want to hang you at all. I appreciate everything that you've done for me!"

"For you and your husband, right?" he asked her softly.

"Peter? Ah...yes, of course."

She lowered her eyes again, very aware that he was doing his best to keep his distance from her because she was—in his mind—a married woman. His own assumption! Poor baby! Compelled by a sense of duty to dive into sharks after her. Compelled to sleep beside her to keep her from being bound and tied.

A part of her appreciated that sense of duty. But she didn't at all appreciate his continual jumping to conclusions about her, nor any number of his macho techniques. She'd suffered at his hands; he could damn well suffer at hers. He had taken his own sweet time to inform her that he was a cop, and he'd grabbed her in the shower to do it.

She gave him another wide-eyed innocent stare. "Do you know what the island will be like? I mean, what will the, uh, sleeping arrangements be?"

"You're stuck with me again, Mrs. Blayne. They'd set up a room for your husband. It will be yours—and mine—now."

"Oh."

"Don't worry, Mandy, love. I'll be as safe to be with as a teddy bear. Married women aren't my style. Especially—"

"Bigots?" she inquired sweetly. "A young bigot married to an old man for his money?"

"Your words."

"Ah, but Miguel! Doesn't that scare you to pieces? What if the story were close to the truth? Poor young me, married to poor old Peter! I mean, after all, think about the situation! You half attacked me at first, but then I discovered that you're my savior." Dragging the blanket with her, she came up to him, still smiling sweetly. "And here you are... young...muscled like a panther. I could just lose my mind!" she told him, lightly stroking his cheek with the tips of her nails.

He didn't move. Not a muscle. Not until he grinned slowly and snaked an arm around her so swiftly that she wasn't even aware of his intent until it was complete. She was pulled against him, while his fingers brushed tantalizingly over the small of her back and her buttocks.

"Mrs. Blayne—Mandy, darling!" he drawled in a soft and perfect parody. "Aren't you forgetting that your husband is a wonderful, wonderful lover?"

"Let me go!" she snapped. He'd meant to call her bluff! He did, pushing her from him. "Like I said, *Mrs.* Blayne, I'll be as safe as a teddy bear."

She recovered somewhat and smiled coolly again. "Good." But she was bluffing again. Touching him had been dangerous. Coming too near him would always be like tempting fire. She had realized it too late.

"Dublin!" she muttered beneath her breath. "Like hell! Cop—I wonder."

"I am a cop."

"*Miami Vice*, I take it." She sighed elaborately. "Humph. Where is Sonny Crockett when you need him?"

"Metro Miami. Investigator, homicide. Homicide gets kidnappings and death threats. And I'm sorry about not being Sonny Crockett. Luck of the draw, what can I tell you?"

"The truth is always nice."

"That is the truth."

"You're a half-Cuban detective who was born in Dublin?"

He laughed. "I think I fascinate you, Mrs. Blayne."

"Egos like yours always fascinate." The words were out quickly; she suddenly regretted them, along with her foolish actions. "I'm sorry," she said for what felt like the thousandth time. "Really, I am. I'm alive. I'm grateful." She couldn't help looking back up at him and shrugging. "And you're a teddy bear, if you say so."

"I am."

He was still grinning, aware that he intrigued her. And if he was bitter about what he considered her bigotry, he was also amused. It was a mixture of feelings she didn't particularly appreciate, but what did it matter? They had been cast into this situation together, she by no choice at all, and he simply because he had become a little overinvolved in his job. Besides, he could laugh at her all he wanted. She had one on him, too. She wasn't Senator Peter Blayne's wife.

His smile faded suddenly as he watched her, and he sounded tense when he spoke next. "You can, uh, take a shower and get dressed now if you want. Breakfast is on, and then we're going on to the island."

Mandy nodded wearily, reminded that she was still a captive. She whispered her next words. "Do you really know where we are?"

"Yes, I think I do."

He stiffened suddenly, and she realized that someone had come up behind him in the hall. His next words carried the heavy Spanish accent again. "Now, my love! In the shower. We eat, we go!"

The door closed. She wrapped herself in the still-damp robe, collected the clothing he had given her and slipped from the cabin to the head.

She was delighted to find a stack of new toothbrushes beneath the sink, so pleased that she issued a little cry of sublime happiness. Then she paused, shivering to discover that joy could be found in such a little thing under these strange circumstances. But, she told herself wryly, it seemed that as long as she was breathing and alive there could be elation in little things, and she might do well to seek it out.

She was uninterrupted in the shower this time, though she didn't close the curtain completely but kept a wary eye on the door, determined to be prepared if someone did burst in on her. That thought made her shiver and burn all over again, and she wondered once more at the contradictory range of emotions Miguel could elicit from her. She clenched her teeth as she rinsed her face, reminding herself again that he was just a cop doing his duty as he saw it and that his opinion of her was a harsh one.

This wouldn't last long! It couldn't! If they'd met at a cocktail party she would have coolly accepted his hostile notions, shrugged, then forgotten him. It was nothing more than the situation and her fear that were creating this horrible tendency to lean on him, to care what he thought. She didn't know anything about him. Not even his whole name. Not whether he was married or not, maybe a father of four or five. Maybe...

She turned the water off and dried herself quickly, then dug into the clothing that Maria had so grudgingly lent to her. Well, pooh to Maria—Mandy didn't like the clothes. The shirt was some kind of a ridiculous halter top in bright red that should have been worn in the early seventies. The cutoff jeans had been tie-dyed with a total lack of artistry and were too big, but at least they came with a ribbon belt. The whole effect was ridiculous, and Mandy thought wryly that Maria had planned it that way. For God's sake, what was the girl jealous of? Mandy wondered irritably. Then she decided she was glad she wasn't eighteen anymore; it was a hard age, when it seemed that women, especially, struggled to find security.

And then she wondered why she cared what she wore as long as she was wearing something, and why she cared one way or another about Maria's psyche, when the girl was doing everything in her limited power to be miserable.

Chin up, kiddo, she told herself. This whole thing boiled down to attitude. The sharks had stripped away her courage yesterday; she was going to dredge it back up for today. She was caught in a nightmare vortex, but even nightmares came to an end. This, like all things, would pass.

Thus determined, she swung open the door—only to have her head-high attitude quickly lowered a peg in confusion, because it wasn't Miguel waiting for her when she emerged, but Roberto. She didn't like the way he looked at her, and she didn't like the way he reached for her arm, sliding his hand along her ribs. She jerked away from him, saying that she was quite able to walk by herself, and hurried topside with him at her heels.

The first thing Mandy saw was the island—if one could call it that. It was really nothing more than a large growth of mangroves with a few handfuls of sand creating a spit of beach. Straining her eyes against the sun and the foliage, she could see some sort of ramshackle structure.

Roberto shoved her in the back. "Move."

She did so, quickly taking a place beside Miguel, who was already eating. The food smelled wonderful. It appeared that they were eating omelets. Even the coffee smelled rich and strong.

Maria, pouring more coffee for Julio, lowered her rich dark lashes and gave Mandy a narrow glance, sniffing delicately at her appearance. Julio barked out something to her, which brought on an immediate argument, with Maria stamping her foot and sullenly shouting and gesticulating. Julio gestured back, totally infuriated, and to her own irritation Mandy found herself inching closer to Miguel, barely aware of the arm that came around her shoulders, except that it gave her a sense of safety and security.

She didn't have the faintest idea what the argument was about, except that she was involved, and if Maria had been in control of the weapons Mandy would surely have been shot on the spot.

Señora Garcia stood up suddenly, clapping her hands over her ears and snapped out a single word. Julio and Maria both ceased their fighting instantly; Maria tossed her head in silence and stalked off below deck, while Julio slipped an arm around his mother's shoulder and spoke to her softly, apologetically.

Miguel took that opportunity to whisper to her, "Maria resents waiting on you. She thinks that you should be made to work. Julio says that you cannot be blamed for your husband's incompetence."

"Peter is not incompetent!" Mandy snapped indignantly.

He gave her a strange gaze, then looked away. "That's rather beside the point right now, isn't it? Here comes Maria. Take your food."

Maria, still sullen, was approaching Mandy, balancing a mug of coffee and a plate at the same time. Mandy accepted the coffee and set it down with a stiff, *"Gracias,"* then held up her hands to accept the plate.

Maria—purposely, Mandy was certain—let go of the plate just short of Mandy's hands.

The hot eggs spilled over her bare legs, burning. Mandy jumped to her feet to get the scorching food off her, while Maria jumped back, ostensibly in a startled fit of apology.

It was suddenly too much for Mandy to handle; she took two furious steps forward and caught the startled Maria by the shoulders and shook her.

"You little brat! Grow up! I didn't ask to be here, you idiot! You hurt me again and I'll find a way to hurt you back!"

Maria instantly started screaming as if Mandy had been trying to throttle her. Miguel leaped between the two, wrenching Mandy hard against his chest. Julio was shouting again in disgust, and Mandy suddenly realized with a little swallow that he was the only one who hadn't pulled out his gun. Both Roberto and a nervous Juan had their weapons aimed right at her.

She was wide-eyed with fright for a second, then she tossed her arms into the air. "You want me to behave? I'll behave! But keep that spoiled brat away from me!"

She spun around with such vengeance that she took even Miguel by surprise, returned to her seat and sipped her coffee while she wiped off her legs, looking for damage.

There was absolute silence for a moment. Then Mandy heard Julio say in English, "Clean it up, Maria."

"Me! The American whore dropped it. Julio, she half strangled me. *Me*—your cousin!—and you take her side!"

Mandy glanced up just in time to see Maria's huge almond eyes filling with tears. "Oh, for God's sake!" she snapped, and stood, doing her best to scoop up the eggs that lay on the deck onto the fallen plate. She shoved them at Miguel with a viciousness that caused him to raise one brow, but he gave her an amused grin and a little thumbs-up sign, then turned to give the plate to Maria.

Maria looked as if she would not accept it. She opened her mouth and closed it again, then finally snatched the debris and flounced away to discard it below.

Mandy hadn't seen Señora Garcia moving, but suddenly the dignified lady was standing before her, holding another plate. Mandy hesitated; Miguel sat down beside her. "Take it," he advised softly.

She did, thanking Julio's mother with another *"Gracias."* Señora Garcia smiled grimly in return and started into a soft monologue that left Mandy staring at her, quite lost.

"The *señora* apologizes to you for Maria's behavior," Miguel told her. "The girl is her niece, and not her daughter. If she had raised her, she would not be so rude. She would be much more a lady."

Mandy didn't know what to say; she merely nodded. She liked Mrs. Garcia, but she didn't know what she thought of her as a mother. After all, she had raised Julio, and Julio was definitely a kidnapper.

"Eat," Miguel warned her. "We are going to the island."

Mandy was startled to discover that she could eat with such an appetite; she was hungry, and the food was excellent. She finished one cup of coffee, then Señora Garcia came back over and offered her more. She asked Miguel something, and Miguel laughed.

"What?" Mandy asked.

"She asked if you wouldn't prefer Cuban coffee. I told her no."

"Did you?" Mandy asked him a little coolly. "As a matter of fact, I like Cuban coffee."

"Now and then, eh? Patronizing the locals?"

"Oh, God!" she muttered. "You're as bad as the rest of them! *You're* the damn bigot!"

"Shut up!" he told her suddenly.

"I will not—"

His fingers closed around her arm and he bent down to whisper to her tensely. "Mandy darling, we do not sound like a sweet pair of illicit lovers sitting here arguing about coffee!"

She glanced at Julio quickly and saw that he was gazing at the two of them suspiciously. She lowered her head quickly, then made a point of arguing back in a whisper that could be overheard.

"I'm sorry, Miguel, really!" She ran a finger delicately down his chest. "I'm just so afraid of everything! And Peter will certainly find out about the two of us now...." She let her voice trail away.

Miguel's eyes were on her in amazement—an amazement he quickly hid as he slipped an arm around her shoulders again. "You could always tell him the truth. You could get a divorce."

"Oh, but Miguel! I just love the money! Think what it does for us! I love making love in the Jacuzzi. I love the silk sheets, the champagne we sip—just touching one another—in the sunken garden...."

She heard him swallow sharply and, despite everything, she had to lower her head with a little shiver. What was wrong with her? She should be ashamed, but all she could think was that there were certain triumphs to be gleaned in any situation!

When she raised her head again she discovered that all the men were staring at her, and that she didn't like the look in their eyes at all.

She inched closer to Miguel again and heard him swallow sharply. This time she didn't take any great pleasure in the effect she had caused.

"Well," Julio said stiffly, rising. "Juan—supplies. Roberto—get the dinghy ready. Juan—you and I will take Señora Blayne first. You will come back for the others. Move quickly now. You'll need the day to get back." Juan rose, following orders like a trained puppy.

Mandy discovered then that she didn't want to leave Miguel's side; she was nervous, but also grateful that she would be with Juan and Julio, not Roberto. Small comfort, but all she had.

"Señora Blayne—come!" Julio had a hand extended to her; she hesitated, so Miguel prodded her slightly. She stood, but didn't take Julio's hand. He shrugged. "Starboard, Mrs. Blayne. The dinghy is ready. Mama, you come, too."

Mandy preceded him to the rope ladder and climbed over without looking back. Juan was there, ready to help her into the dinghy. She cringed at the feel of his hands on her waist, but he released her quickly, and once again she was grateful that he was not Roberto.

Señora Garcia followed her down; Juan helped her, too, with the greatest respect. Julio came next, then the dinghy moved away from the ship.

Mandy stared straight ahead, toward the island.

Sean couldn't believe his good fortune—just Roberto and Maria left aboard with him. If he could only assure himself that the two of them were occupied he could take a chance at the ship's old radio. He'd found it easily that first night, when he sat around with the three men drinking beer and telling them his woeful tale of being madly, passionately in love with a married woman, a rich American bitch, but oh, so sweet!

"Hey, Miguel, help me!" Roberto told him. He was pulling boxes of food from the galley cabinets to the deck.

"*Sí, sí,*" Sean said agreeably and ambled down to the galley.

Maria was there. She turned and leaned against the counter, giving him a broad, welcoming grin.

"Hello," she said in a soft, sultry voice.

He smiled, because she was such a pretty kid—with such a lot of growing up to do. Circumstances, though, hadn't been in her favor. Maria had grown up in a household of political protesters. Her father and mother had died; her uncle had been jailed in the old country and then the new.

Sean felt that he could understand her, and even Julio Garcia, in a way that Mrs. Peter Blayne never would. Julio didn't know that he was wrong; in his own way he had been at war all his life. Involved in a dying protest that knew no rules, all was fair. He was too young to remember the revolution when Castro had overthrown Batista. He only knew that suppression had given way to new suppression.

He wanted to be an American. He just didn't know how. Just like Maria. She wanted to be a woman. She wanted to be free and liberated. She didn't know how to go about fulfilling her wishes, either.

"Hi," he answered casually.

Julio had given her a little pistol, too. She had it tucked into the waistband of her very American designer blue jeans.

He was very tempted to reach for it. Maria would be incredibly easy to seduce and overpower.

But the timing was wrong. Julio and Juan had Amanda Blayne on the shore, and though Sean instinctively believed that Julio would never kill her on purpose, he just might panic and become dangerous because of his very nervousness. He hadn't quailed at all when he had riddled the dock with bullets.

Maria sauntered up to Sean and drew a bloodred nail over his naked chest. "You are stupid!" she told him huskily. "She is not for you. You will grow tired of her, yet you risk so much for her!"

He had to think about that one. She is not for you....

No, she wasn't. She was a married woman. And though he had acquired a reputation for his nightlife and the chain of broken hearts in his wake, he'd always stopped short when it came to married women.

He was supposed to be distant, professional. Yet she—far beyond the situation—was making him crazy. At the moment he wished with all his heart that he'd never lost his mind and gone diving after the speedboat. He wished he'd never thought of his story....

He wished that he'd never seen her face. Her perfect, beautiful, delicate Anglo face. Tawny eyes, tawny hair, tawny...flesh. Sun golden, sleek, curved, sensual. He wished he'd never seen her, touched her, known her, watched her, listened to her....

It made professionalism damn near impossible. He even hated the fact that he liked her. Liked her brand of determination, so wholehearted that she'd been ready to swim miles in the dusk for freedom. So heated that she refused to bow to anyone—not even with a trio of guns aimed at her.

He gave himself a shake, took both Maria's hands, smiled and placed them back by her sides. "*Chica*, I walk here by a slender thread already. You want your cousin to kill me for your honor?"

"Julio?" She sniffed indelicately. "If Julio were a real man we would not be in this fix. He would have taken the right man, not some *puta*."

"Maria! Bring the food!" Roberto ordered from above.

She grimaced, but decided not to disobey the order. It seemed that everyone knew Roberto had a streak of meanness in him.

Maria disappeared above deck. Sean reached beneath the cabinet and started gathering up supplies with one hand while he reached across to the radio with the other, keeping his eyes trained on the ladder and the hatch above it.

At first he could get nothing. He had to forget the supplies and give his entire attention to the ancient radio. Finally a voice came in—and to Sean's vast relief and amazement he realized that he'd reached the Coast Guard.

Quietly he tried to give his location and discovered with little surprise that search parties had been out since they disappeared. He warned the voice over the radio that he might have to cut out quickly. He advised the man as to the number of kidnappers and said that Juan would be coming back in to make their demands, then assured the man that the senator's wife was fine.

He was surprised by the silence that followed.

"Lieutenant Ramiro, the senator's wife has been dead over a year."

"What?" Sean shouted, then realized what he had done. He lowered his voice quickly. "She's here, with me. They nabbed her, and I came after her!"

"Oh, you've got a Mrs. Blayne all right, but she's not his wife. She's his son's widow. But he's tearing his heart out over her just the same. Just keep calm, lieutenant. It may take us some time to find you."

"I am calm," Sean retorted dryly. "I'm a ten-year vet with the force. Don't you come barging in. Garcia is as nervous as a cat."

"We'll tell the FBI. You keep a lookout. You're out of the U.S., but I'm sure they'll get complete cooperation from the Bahamian authorities. We'll advise the senator that his daughter-in-law is doing—"

Sean heard Roberto yelling at Maria as he approached the ladder. He flicked the radio off and turned back to stacking cans.

"That's enough!" Roberto snapped, holding his gun on Sean. Sean knew that Roberto didn't trust him. The man just wasn't the trusting sort. They were a strange alliance, Roberto and Julio. Julio the idealist; Roberto the thug.

Sean stood up, shrugging. Roberto waved the gun at him. "Go up. The boat is back."

Sean obediently went up to the deck. Juan was back with the dinghy, and Maria was handing the supplies over the rail to him.

"I'll help," Sean told her.

"*Gracias*, Miguel," she purred softly.

He took over her work, moving mechanically and grinning despite himself.

So she wasn't the senator's wife. He'd been torturing himself for nothing. She'd been intentionally driving him up a wall, but now...now it was his turn.

"Miguel! Come aboard!" Roberto ordered.

Juan was staying on the sailboat so he could return to Miami. He waved to Sean, who crawled down to the dinghy.

Sean looked at the island before him. It would still be dangerous getting out of this mess; Roberto was a danger all by himself.

And he was still a cop, and she was still one of the citizens he was sworn to protect. He just couldn't stop that damn grin.

Because she was going to pay.

6

It might have been a paradise, one of those quaint little outer islands where only those with their own boats might venture, a little piece of heavenly unaltered nature.

The island was beautiful, Mandy thought wryly, feeling the pressure of Julio's hand on her back as he urged her along. There was a stretch of beach so miraculously white it might have been snow rather than sand; to the left of the beach was an outcrop of coral and rock, fantastically entwined with the mangrove roots. To the right a stretch of rock and mangroves jutted out into the sea, creating a natural harbor. It was too small a spit of land to hold a hotel, just a dot on the ocean, but it was one of the loveliest little islands Mandy had ever seen.

"Señora Blayne, *por favor!*"

Julio prodded her once again, and she realized that she was stopping every few feet to look around. He was ushering her toward the structure she had seen between the trees, and she wondered why he should be so insistent. There was nowhere for her to go, and he certainly couldn't think that she intended to overpower him—especially since he was carrying a gun.

She shrugged wearily and continued walking. Señora Garcia had already entered the ramshackle place through a screen door; Mandy followed her, curiously surveying her surroundings.

It was an old frame house, with a kitchen being the first room, and something like a parlor behind it, and two doors at the rear of that parlor. Someone had cleaned the place, and Mandy could only assume that that someone had been Señora Garcia. Even clean, though, it was dismal. There was a double-sided fireplace between the kitchen and the parlor, a rickety old table in the kitchen, and an even more rickety sofa in the parlor. There were two mattresses on the floor lined up against the wall by the left rear door. And there were three pickle-barrel end tables, one by the sofa, one between the mattresses and one near the fireplace. There were no electrical wires—what had she been expecting?—and the only concession to contemporary standards seemed to be a battery-powered icebox next to the counter in the kitchen.

"Go through," Julio told her. His mother glanced at her unhappily and started to say something, but Julio interrupted her.

"She can be trouble! You have seen so!"

Mandy kept walking. Julio indicated the left door, and she opened it.

It was a bedroom, or at least it resembled a bedroom. There was a mattress on the floor. And there was another door at the rear.

"Is that a bathroom? Or am I allowed to ask?" Mandy asked bitterly.

Julio compressed his lips and nodded. Mandy found herself studying him curiously. He was a young man, handsome, with curling dark hair and a slim, sinewy build. But his dark eyes were full of such a feverish tension! She couldn't believe that he would really harm her; he seemed such a different type from Roberto.

A trickling of unease sped along her spine, and for all that she was usually ready to strangle Miguel, she suddenly wished desperately that he was with her.

"Yes, it is a bathroom. Old and faulty—and the water is brackish. Do not drink it. You understand?"

She nodded.

He smiled peculiarly, a little sadly. "This is it, Mrs. Blayne. Make yourself at home. I'm afraid it will take some time to reach your husband and have my demands met."

He turned to leave her.

"Wait a minute!" Mandy cried, not at all sure what she meant to do, but suddenly determined to make the young man with the nice mother go straight.

"Julio! Señor Garcia! Listen to me. You haven't harmed me. Not really. I feel that this is all a great misunderstanding. If you were to bring me back now—well, I wouldn't press charges. I guess you wouldn't get off scot-free, because you did fire bullets all over the docks. But I don't think you hit anyone, did you? Really, Julio, you don't want to be a criminal! You could go for an insanity plea—temporary insanity. Mental duress. Julio, they will straighten your father's situation out. It just takes time. You don't want him to be free while you're forced to be in jail, do you? You can't get away with this. Think about it. What good is it going to do when you do get hold of Peter? Julio, if we stop this whole thing right now, I'll do my best to help you. Peter will—"

"Mrs. Blayne," Julio interrupted laconically.

"Yes, Julio?"

"Shut up."

From sheer surprise, she did so. He gave her a rueful smile, turned and left her. When he closed the door she heard the sharp final sound of a bolt sliding home.

"Damn you!" Mandy muttered, threading her fingers through her hair in frustration. "Damn you, you idiot!"

Exasperated and desolate, she sank onto the mattress. For several moments she just sat there, pressing her temples between her palms. Then she lay back on the bed and stared around. There was nothing to see. Nothing but four walls and the door to her primitive bathroom. There was only one window in the room, and that had been boarded over. There was nothing but gloom.

She wished she could sleep. She wished that they had left her just a square inch of window to look through. Time hung so heavily! Each second seemed like an hour, and her imprisonment had only begun. All she could do was lie there in the gloom with her own thoughts—which were not particularly good company.

Every once in a while she heard voices from beyond the door. They were faint, and she couldn't make out a thing, because they were speaking in Spanish.

Where the hell was Miguel?

To her irritation, she was longing to see him. Longing desperately to see him, just because she couldn't stand the shadowed gloom and her own company anymore.

She tried to think about her work; she tried to think of all the little tedious things she had to do when she got back. She tried to think about the sea, serene and calm. She even tried to imagine sheep jumping over a fence so she could sleep and keep her mind from going a million frustrated miles an hour. Nothing worked. She had never imagined that simple confinement could be so frightening, so wearing. She thought that soon she would go mad; she would race for that bolted door and scream and cry and beat her head against it.

Just when she felt that she had reached that point, the door suddenly swung open. Mandy blinked against the sudden light, shielding her eyes.

For a moment she froze; it was Roberto. Roberto, giving her his lascivious white-toothed smile. She shivered inside, going as cold as ice. She was alone in this room with nothing but a white-sheeted mattress, no avenue of escape. No strength, no hope—and fully aware of the man's feelings regarding her.

No, no, Julio wouldn't allow it. Miguel wouldn't allow it. But where the hell *was* Miguel?

"Amanda?"

She took a deep breath and felt the blood move through her veins once again.

Miguel stepped past Roberto and stared at her, offering her his hand.

She didn't think anything then. She bolted from the mattress, straight toward him, grasping that hand and pressing herself against the strength of his naked chest, her head lowered.

She felt his free hand on her hair, hesitant, then soothing. He wrapped an arm around her and led her through the tacky parlor, Roberto at their heels.

Julio sat at the kitchen table, playing cards with Maria. Señora Garcia was standing over a frying pan set on a Sterno stove on the counter. She was cooking hamburgers; it might have been the great American barbecue.

Miguel started to move away from Mandy; she inched toward him with a little gasp, drawing a snicker from Maria. Mandy stiffened, while Miguel accepted two plates of food from Señora Garcia. He shoved them at Mandy with a curious expression, then turned back to accept two cans of Old Milwaukee.

"Two hours, no more," Julio warned Miguel without looking up from his game.

"Dos horas," Miguel agreed, and Julio did look up then, but not at them. He stared at Roberto, who insisted on keeping his gun out and trained on Miguel.

"I'll spell you soon, amigo," he said.

Roberto leered at Mandy and shrugged to Julio. Mandy thought she saw Julio shudder slightly, and she wondered again how these two had come together, an idealist and a...vulture.

"Come on," Miguel urged her with his Spanish accent. *"Dos horas!"*

She had no idea what he was talking about, but she eagerly followed him outdoors.

It was late afternoon again. The sea stretched out eternally before them, touched by the reflection of the dying sun, sparkling and rippling like something magical. Even the white beach seemed to shimmer with the colors of the coming evening, gold and pink, delicate mauve and diamond glitter.

Miguel walked beside her; Roberto followed at a distance. "This way," Miguel advised, walking toward the part of the beach where the rock and mangroves formed a secretive little haven, shadowed now in dusk.

She looked back. Roberto had paused. He was sitting on the beach, watching them, but giving them a certain distance. Mandy expelled a long sigh, which drew a sharp gaze from Miguel.

"He makes me nervous," she muttered.

If she'd expected reassurance, she didn't get it. "He doesn't thrill me, either," Miguel agreed. "But forget him for now. I spent hours arguing to get Julio to agree that you would go mad and be far more difficult to handle if you didn't get out a little."

He led her as far away from Roberto as possible, to the place where the roots met the rocks.

"Have a seat, Mrs. Blayne," he told her with a grin.

She sat on a stump, balancing both plates of hamburgers until he settled himself on the sand beside her. He opened both cans of beer, then handed her one as he took his own plate.

"Thanks," Mandy muttered, then lowered her head, because she was thinking about him, and she didn't want him to guess. She was on the stump; he was at her side, the breadth of his bare shoulders and back at her knee, his dark head angled toward her, his rich green eyes looking out to the sea.

She found herself liking everything about him; his height, his build, those eyes—even his scruffy jaw, strong beneath the beard. He was attractive—and she was attracted. She despised herself for it, because she considered herself sane and mature, and thought she knew enough about the human psyche to keep herself under control. She'd barely known him for forty-eight hours, yet she was desperately glad of his presence, ready to race to the sound of his voice, more than willing to trust herself to him.

Naturally. She sensed that he was all that stood between her and Roberto. But he was a cop—that was his job. There was no reason she should feel so ... quiveringly grateful. Especially when she knew what he really thought of her!

"Eat," he told her, and she saw that he was looking at her then, rather than the sea. And that there was a peculiar glint of amusement in his eyes.

Mechanically and a little warily, she brought her hamburger to her mouth. It seemed to stick against the dryness of her throat, and she sipped the beer to force it down.

Miguel seemed to have no such problems. He ate his hamburger with a hearty appetite, then leaned back against her legs, very relaxed—like an idle beach bum—while he sipped his beer.

She stiffened, ready to jerk her legs away. She stopped herself only because she knew that Roberto watched them, not fifty feet away.

The water, stretching out before them, was magically beautiful, as were the white purity of the sand, the wild and primitive tangle of mangrove and coral, the eternal sky, the twilight....

And the two of them. He was touching her, relaxed and lazy, as if they were the only two people on earth, a man and a woman.

She set her half-eaten hamburger down and sipped the beer. She was so glad to be out of that room, away from her own thoughts.

Yet she was so nervous, so horribly aware of him: of his tanned flesh, so sleek over the rippling muscles of his back and shoulders; his hair, ebony with the coming of the night; his scent, as fresh and salty as the night air, and here, in this wild splendor, so masculine that she felt nearly consumed just by his presence....

It was all because she had to rely on him, she told herself furiously. Circumstance! At a cocktail party she would have walked away from him.

But here she couldn't walk away. Being with him was playing dangerous havoc with her emotions and her senses, and she knew it.

But what was she afraid of? He assumed that she was married to Peter, and he steered clear of married women; he had told her so with indisputable passion.

Maybe she should be glad, grateful to learn that her instincts and emotions still functioned. She worked, she laughed, she enjoyed people, but she hadn't really felt anything in so long. Maybe even the fear and the fury were good; she was reacting, and there had been times when she had felt that anything would be better than the horrible numbness. But this...

Even Peter had tried to introduce her to a string of young men. She'd never felt the least interest, just the numbness. And now she felt like a traitor, to Paul and—far worse—to herself. How could she possibly be attracted to a man who treated her so poorly?

He was there; he was a buffer. That was all, absolutely all. And she wasn't only attracted to him. She was also indignant and outraged by his methods. To top it all off, she still didn't even know if she should really believe him or not, because he was a fabulous actor, slipping from accent to accent with barely a thought.

"You really are absolutely beautiful, you know."

Mandy started, choking on her beer, staring involuntarily into the heavy-lidded sparkling green eyes that were now resting on her in the most sensual fashion. She swallowed warily. "Thank you," she muttered. Then she asked, "You really are a cop?"

He chuckled softly. "Yeah, I really am."

Mandy stared out to sea again while confusion overwhelmed her. His voice...the huskiness in his voice. What had happened to him suddenly? The cut-and-dried manner was gone—as was the hard and passionate man who had vowed he didn't touch married women, who despised her for marrying an old man.

"Uh..." She cleared her throat, searching for a safe topic of conversation. "What is Julio doing with Roberto? They don't seem a bit alike."

He shrugged. "They're not. Juan is with him because they're second cousins or something. I think Roberto is merely in it for the money."

"The money?"

"Mmm. The Garcias still have family in Spain, and a number of wealthy Colombian connections. If I've gotten things right, Roberto is a mercenary. He's been hired for his expertise. That's why I don't trust him. God, you're beautiful.''

"Would you stop that!" Mandy snapped after a moment. He'd changed his tone so quickly that it had taken her time to catch up, and now she knew that she was nearly as red as the twilight.

"I can't seem to help myself," he said, swallowing the last of his beer, then crushing the can in one hand while he continued to stare at her.

She swallowed the last of her beer, compelled to return his stare, fascinated, horrified.

He took her can from her hand, brushing her fingers with his own, rising to his knees, a breath away from her.

"You hate married women. Especially me. I married old Peter Blayne for his wealth and possessions, remember?" she told him quickly. Too quickly. Breathlessly...

"I know," he told her softly, his arm moving around her. His face wasn't an inch from hers. She felt the power of his chest and shoulders, saw the smoldering green fire in his eyes. "I know all that. But don't you feel it? The sea and the breeze and the night, you—and me?"

"No! No!" Mandy told him hastily. "I don't feel anything. Just that you hate me. Remember?"

He shook his head. "I don't hate you, Mandy, though I keep thinking of all the reasons why I should. I think and think of all the reasons why I should stay completely away from you. I tell myself over and over again that you're married. That I'm a cop. That you're completely off limits. But, Mandy...I tell you, I can't help myself. No matter what I think, I see you. I see those golden eyes of yours, that tawny lion's mane. I see your body—oh, God! Do I see your body! Naked and gold and glistening, lithe and curved—''

"Stop it!" Mandy shrieked, trying to edge away as his knuckles brushed over her cheek. She lost her balance instead and toppled over into the sand.

He was right behind her, stretching over her, bracing his weight on his hands, his palms beside her head. He seemed to cover her, his legs entangled with hers.

"Get up—" she began in panic.

"Oh, Mandy! I can't!" he vowed passionately, and she felt all the sexual quality of him, the power in his thighs, the brush of his hairy chest against her skin, the ridiculously sweet pressure of his hips on hers.

"Roberto! Roberto is watching us!" she protested.

"And I must convince him that we are lovers," Miguel whispered softly, shifting, bringing himself halfway to her side, cupping her jaw in his hand to bring her face to his.

"Amanda, I can't bear this. Being with you, night and day. Sleeping beside you. I'd sell my soul for you. I can't care that you're a married woman, I can't think of anything. I have to have you!"

Heat like liquid fire exploded through her—right along with a raging sense of panic. He was way too much male. She didn't know what to do with him; she didn't know how to escape him. She felt lost and overwhelmed and desperate!

"Wait. Wait!"

"Hold me, Mandy. Just hold me!"

Hold him? His arms were vise clamps around her, his body an inferno of steel. She was quivering like a cornered rabbit, straining against him with all her might—futilely.

"Miguel..."

"Oh, Lord, I was in agony, listening to you! I envisioned the two of us in a Jacuzzi, sipping champagne, just barely touching, coming nearer and nearer, until you were mine."

He shifted, touching her. Lightly. Fingertips against her cheek, stroking her throat, running over her collarbone, so near the neckline of her halter top. Fingertips...dancing dangerously over the mounds of her breasts, fascinated with the naked flesh of her midriff. Gentle, tender, erotic in their motion, in their very being. And she was powerless. Shivering and aware and powerless, and so keenly touched by the vibrant heat of his body, his weight, the rough feel of his legs.

"Champagne...you and me. The warm waters rushing around us. Mandy, you've got the most beautiful breasts I've ever seen."

"Miguel, don't you—"

"God, you're glorious...splendid. Champagne and pizza. Completely naked...us...together."

"Damn you! I'll strangle you once we're free."

"Remember when you touched me? This morning? Oh, Mandy, I felt desire in that touch. I know that Peter Blayne's an old man. I know that you're young and sensual and I can't see any reason why we shouldn't—"

"There are a million reasons!"

He smiled, totally disbelieving her. And then his fingertips were moving again. Just gently stroking her ribs...then moving higher, brushing her breasts. Her nipples were hard, and he could feel it, and that was making him grin even more widely.

"I'll report you. If we live I'll report you to all your superiors. Every one of them! They'll fire you."

"You're just saying that, Mandy. I can feel you. I knew this morning that you wanted me."

"I do not!"

"I don't care about anything! Report me. I'd give my job—my life— for one night with you."

Oh, no! What had she done this morning? Threats weren't working; they didn't mean a thing to him!

"Please..." she whispered, but even that did nothing.

"You've cast a spell on me," he told her huskily. "I can't let you go. It's all that I can think about—you, me, tangled together, hot, sweating, straining."

"Miguel, you're a cop! I'm a married woman!"

Suddenly he was laughing, staring down at her and laughing. Then he rolled away from her and sat up, wrapping his arms around his knees and staring out at the sea once again.

"Mrs. Blayne, you're the most ridiculous liar I've ever met," he told her with curt amusement.

"What?" Stunned, she scrambled to her feet and stared down at him, her hands on her hips. She felt relieved, furious—and bereft.

He gazed up at her, still smiling. "Amanda Blayne, you're Peter Blayne's daughter-in-law, not his wife."

"How do you know?"

"Because I managed to get through to the Coast Guard on the radio."

"What?"

"I keep telling you—I'm a cop. Sworn to protect and all that jazz. I'm sorry I haven't tried to stop a bullet for you yet, but I did get to the radio."

Her temper flared out of all proportion. She should be jumping up and down with joy that someone had been advised of the situation, but he'd just made such a fool of her! Without thought she suddenly leapt at him, pummeling his chest and shoulders.

"You bastard! You didn't bother to tell me! Instead you pulled this little act. I'll kill you! I'll wring your stupid neck!"

"Whoa!" he protested, stunned by her vehemence, falling backward into the sand at her assault. He collected himself quickly and caught her flailing fists, then rolled and cast a knee over her hips and stretched her arms over her head, where he held them while he leaned against her, panting.

"Don't touch me! I swear, I *will* report you! How dare you?"

"Roberto is looking!"

"I don't give a damn!"

"You'd better—unless you want Roberto in this position!"

"What diff—"

"A lot, Mrs. Blayne. I'm not going to rape you, but Roberto would give his eyeteeth to do just that!"

Mandy went dead still, clenching her teeth and staring up at him, trying to regain her breath.

"You son of—"

"Hey! You lied to me! I risked my neck to let you know that I was a police officer. You lied—"

"I did not! You assumed that I was Peter's wife! You judged me without a—"

"You could have corrected me!"

"And why should I have bothered?"

"Courtesy, Mrs. Blayne. Common courtesy. Especially in this situation!"

"Courtesy! Oh—"

"Shush!"

She grated her teeth together again. He was staring down at her with an emerald spark in his eyes. He was amused.

And she was far too aware of him all over again. His fingers, curled within hers. His thigh, cast over her hips. His warmth. Everything about him that was male, that called to something inside her despite herself. She was quivering from the effect of his touch....

"Let me go, please, Miguel," she whispered.

He stared at her a moment longer, his eyes growing dark, tension suddenly lining his face. He sighed and released her, but still lay at her side.

"You asked for it, you know," he told her.

"Men!" she snapped. "They say you're all alike, and I believe it! You came at me with all kinds of insinuations and I just played along because *you* were the one who deserved it!"

He laughed again, and she was aware once more that she liked his smile, liked it very much.

"The champagne in the Jacuzzi was a killer," he told her.

She stiffened. "I was acting for the benefit of our captors, and you know it."

He shrugged. "You're just such a good little actress!"

"Oh, stop, please." And don't stay so close, please don't stay so close! she added silently, cast into an agony of confusion. It was just the circumstances, she told herself.

She closed her eyes. "Thank God you got to the radio! When is help coming?"

"I don't know."

Her eyes flew open again, and she edged up on her elbows to frown at him. "What do you mean you don't know? You just told me—"

"I mean I don't know! I tried to tell them where we were, but I'm not positive. It only takes a day to reach Cat Cay—we were on that old scow for two nights. I think that they motored in circles, backtracking on purpose. I still think that we're somewhere near Cat Cay. But there must be hundreds of these little swamp islands around. It may take time. And this has to be handled carefully. The Coast Guard can't just zoom up. That's not the way you handle a hostage situation You could—''

"Get shot?"

He shrugged. "That's not going to happen, Mandy." Distracted, he called her by her given name, not by the acid "Mrs. Blayne."

She looked from his profile to the ocean, picking up a handful of sand, letting it fall through her fingers.

He stood up abruptly and reached a hand down to her. "Let's walk on the beach. Our two hours are almost up."

"How can you tell?" she asked him despondently.

"Because," he said softly, "I can read the sky. And Julio has come out to take Roberto's place as watchdog."

Mandy glanced over her shoulder. It was true; Julio was sitting where Roberto had been.

She looked back to the strong hand being offered to her. She hesitated a moment longer, then took it. He pulled her to her feet, cast an arm around her and started walking idly down the beach.

Mandy went along because she felt she had little choice. It did feel good to move; it felt wonderful to be outside, rather than in that dim stuffy room. It felt good to have his arm around her. To know that he was with her, even if she still wanted to strangle him. Yet at the same time she knew that she needed him. He was her security, her buffer against fear and madness. This would end; all things ended. But for now...the evening sky was beautiful; the breeze was delightful. He was at her side—far better than facing Roberto's leers alone.

They walked through the surf, and the cool water bathed her feet. If she closed her eyes she could pretend that she was just on an outing, away for the day, taken to a primitive paradise on the winged sails of the *Flash Point*.

She sniffed suddenly and managed to cast Miguel a wry smile. "I don't even know your last name."

He gazed at her, hesitated a minute, then said, "Ramiro."

"Miguel Ramiro," she said. Strangely, he hesitated once again.

"Not exactly."

"Not exactly?"

"Well, don't tell these guys. My name is Sean. Sean Michael Ramiro."

"What?" Mandy started laughing. Maybe it was hysteria. She stared at him incredulously.

"Sean Michael Ramiro?" She moved away from him, almost doubled over with laughter, so incredible did she find it all. "Now I know you're a liar!"

"I told you I was born in Dublin!" he retorted.

"You said you were Cuban—"

"I said *half*-Cuban! My father was Cuban, my mother is Irish."

She was still laughing. "What a combination!"

"Oh, yeah! I forgot! You're Miss DAR! Daughter of the old *May-flower*!"

She was still laughing so hard she couldn't even take offense.

"Sean?"

"Yeah. Want to make something of it?"

"No, no!" She held out a defensive hand, but too late. He splashed over to her, gripped her hands, slid a foot behind her ankle and sent her crashing into the surf, then dropped down beside her.

"I'm sorry! I'm sorry!" she shrieked when he made a move to dunk her.

But he didn't dunk her. He touched her cheek, his weight and warmth against her again, while the cool surf raced delicately around them both. She felt the power of his arms on either side of her, saw the tension in his eyes, and she might well have been spellbound.

His head lowered. His lips brushed hers.... Just brushed them. And then his eyes were on hers again. Like the sea around them, reflected by the sinking sun, touched by the coming moon. They quested and they sought...and she must have answered.

Because his lips met hers again, with a coercive hungry pressure. His kiss filled her with that same hunger, captured her with fascination. She tasted sea and salt and passion and heat, felt the sweep of his tongue over her teeth...deep into her mouth. Filling her, entering her with a spiraling heat that sent a searing wonder rippling through her. He wasn't really touching her, just his mouth. Just the tickle of that growth of beard against her flesh, the fire of his lips, the fever of his mouth...

"Hey! Your two hours are up! She goes back to her room!"

Startled, they broke apart at Julio's announcement, shaken from the moment.

Mandy stared at Sean Michael Ramiro in absolute horror. She didn't accept his hand, nor did she even notice Julio, standing on the beach.

She raced back toward the house, eager now for her prison, desperate to be alone.

7

When darkness came to her shuttered prison, it came completely.

Mandy was absolutely convinced that she would go mad. She couldn't see her own hand in front of her face. She hadn't known that she was afraid of the dark, but then, she'd never seen darkness so complete.

For hours she lay on the mattress, still soaked from the surf, shivering, then going deathly still before shivering all over again. Sometimes it seemed that her mind was blank; sometimes it was as if a cacophony of thoughts and ideas raced within it.

And always it came back to two things. The darkness. Haunting, suffocating, ebony darkness. And Miguel. No, not Miguel. Sean Michael Ramiro.

Her feelings, his touch. The strident need she was beginning to feel for him. The moral horror that she could be so vulnerable, so dependent...

And so hungry. To be held, touched, loved. To laugh, to play and enjoy the play.

She yearned for him now in a terrible aching way. She thought that she could endure the darkness, if only he was next to her. Here, in this hell within paradise, he had become her salvation, and more. It seemed ridiculously complex; the emotional and the physical; the desire, the need. It seemed so incredibly basic and primitive. She simply wanted to fit against him, as nature had intended, without thought, without words.

There was no way to escape her sense of disloyalty, no way to lie in this utter darkness and not think of Paul, not think of the baby. No way to do anything other than lie there in anguish and agony, suffering the ceaseless gnawing of a fear that came not just from circumstances now, but, like desire, from instinct.

She went still when the door opened at last. The streak of light that entered was painful, as blinding as the darkness. Mandy closed her eyes against it, casting her arm over her face.

The light was quickly gone. Her whole existence suddenly centered around her other senses.

Someone was in the room.

She could feel that presence so strongly! Logic warned her that it could be Julio or Maria or Señora Garcia. A trembling within warned that it could too easily be Roberto.

But her world now knew no logic. She didn't need to be afraid; it was Sean. She knew from the presence that filled the room; she knew from his salty scent, the sound of his breath.

He stood just within the doorway for several moments, his eyes adjusting to the darkness. Then, very slowly, he came toward the mattress. He reached it and fumbled along the edge, then smoothed his hand over the sheet.

She shifted, giving him room. He started suddenly, aware of her movement.

"You're awake?"

"I'm awake."

"My God, it's darker than a coal mine in here."

"I couldn't find the light switch," she said, trying to joke, but she had no idea what his reaction was, since she couldn't see his face.

He didn't answer as he stretched out beside her. She didn't dare touch him, but she knew his position. Hands laced behind his head, ankles crossed, feet probably dangling over the edge.

"You okay?" he whispered after a while.

"Of course. Why wouldn't I be?"

She imagined that he might have grinned. "I guess you're not afraid of the dark."

"Terrified. But what could I possibly do about it?"

"Ask for a lantern."

"Would I get one?"

"Probably." He hesitated. "I don't think Julio means to be cruel. He just doesn't know that it's as black as Hades in here. Not that it matters if you're sleeping, but you've been in here quite a while. I'll get a lantern tomorrow."

She didn't answer him. She wasn't sure what to say. She was excruciatingly glad of his presence; he was like a lantern against the darkness.

She was also excruciatingly aware of him—and the last moments they had shared. She was frightened, not of him, but of herself, and so keyed up that she would never sleep, so miserable that she longed for nothing except oblivion.

The silence seemed to grow in the darkness and become a black cloud above them, filled with the portent of wind and rain. They did not touch, though they were no more than an inch apart. Then suddenly Mandy sneezed, and that sneeze ended the silence.

"Bless you," he muttered, turning toward her. His hand brushed her arm, and suddenly she knew that he was above her, that his dark brows were furrowed with concern, and that his handsome features had hardened into a scowl. "You're shivering like a leaf, and you feel like an ice cube!"

"Do I?" Mandy murmured.

"Yes, you do." He quickly stood, pulling at the mattress, fumbling and swearing when he stubbed his toe against it.

"Get up—can you?"

"Of course I can," she murmured, confused. "But why?"

"There's a top sheet on this thing, and you need to get under it. Take your clothes off."

"What?"

"Oh, come on! I can't see a damn thing in here. Besides, I've already seen you. Your clothes are still all wet from the beach, and you'll get pneumonia if you sleep in them. And then, should the time come when you need to move quickly, you won't be able to. Take your clothes off."

"I think I'd rather risk pneumonia!"

"Than me?"

How could a voice do so much? Reach out through the air and darkness like a velvet brush, teasing, warming.

"Umm."

"Still don't trust me?"

"Not in the least."

"Well, that's okay. I don't trust *you*, either."

"I'm not asking you to take your clothes off."

"Not yet. You'll get to it, though. Women are all alike."

She rolled off the mattress, laughing, perplexed. Somehow he had brought light and warmth into the room. And also that sense of security that was so very easy to rely on, so very easy to need—and so very dangerous. More dangerous, perhaps, than Julio and his accomplices.

"Laugh at me, will you, Mrs. Blayne?" he charged softly, and she knew that he was walking around to her. He hunched down in front of her and felt for her. She didn't know what he was looking for, but he found her breast.

"Hey! And you're asking me to take my clothes off?"

"Sorry, I thought it was your face."

"Umm. You'll get yours one day."

"Promises, promises. Off with 'em, lady."

"I don't think this is proper police procedure."

"Off!"

"Well, move, then!"

He did. Feeling like a stripper in broad daylight, Mandy shed her soggy cutoffs and top, then groped with a fair amount of panic for the sheet.

It was there, in his hands, ready to be wrapped around her. She sensed that he was laughing at her.

"I've already slept with the...real...you, you know."

"Oh, shut up!"

She was still shivering, but she did feel much better; she hadn't realized how chilling her wet clothing had been. But even now, with the dry sheet wrapped around her, she was cold.

"Lie down now," he said huskily.

"What wonderful relationships you must have, Mr. Ramiro! Take off your clothes. Lie down."

He laughed softly in the darkness, and once again she felt touched by the sound, brushed by velvet.

"When it works, do it. Lie down."

Gritting her teeth, she did so, cocooning herself in the sheet. Then she tensed as he crawled over to her. He didn't keep his distance this time; he brought his chest to her back and wrapped an arm around her waist, pulling her close to absorb his heat.

She must have been as stiff and unyielding as concrete, though she made no protest, because he chuckled softly again. "Ease up. I'm just trying to make you warm."

She didn't know that she had held her breath until she released it in a long sigh.

"I'm not the big bad wolf."

"Are you sure?"

"Positive. Why do I make you so nervous?"

"I'm not nervous."

"You are."

"Well, I have a right to be! Since I've met you, you've knocked me down, thrown me around...."

"What's a lover for?" he teased. "Mandy—Mrs. Blayne—I do apologize for my rougher methods."

"And your gentler ones?" she murmured without thought.

His arm tightened slightly around her midriff. "Meaning?"

"Nothing!" she said quickly. What had caused her to say such a thing?

And even as she asked herself the question, she knew the answer. The kiss. The real one, in the salty foam of the surf, interrupted by Julio's appearance.

In the darkness she felt his every breath, knew his every movement, no matter how slight. Knew him, living and breathing beside her.

Silence spread again, total in the darkness. And in that silence she thought it would be the easiest thing in the world to turn to him, to give in to temptation under cover of darkness.

She'd always known that she was young, that she would make love again one day. But one day had always meant some indeterminate future. It was something she hadn't dwelled upon, had not imagined easily. It would be awkward and difficult, and she would be nervous and afraid and, certainly, making comparisons. She had even begun to imagine how difficult it would be to remove her clothing, or watch a man disrobe, knowing his intent.

She wore no clothing now, but it was dark. And in the darkness she would not have to see a man's face. Not have to know if she brought pleasure or ennui, nor bear visible witness that she found it not thrilling in the least, but actually distasteful....

But it *would* be thrilling. With him. For her. She knew from his eyes, from his laughter, from his words, from the hands that touched her so well, from the hard length of his body, taut and warm against hers.

It was easy to forget because of circumstance. Easy to imagine that the darkness could cover her, and she could hide from truth and light and thought. Easy...

She would never do it; not even the darkness could take away her memories. And it wasn't just Paul; it was Paul and the baby. If one of them had made it—just one of them—she wouldn't have felt as if she had been stripped of everything. Everything that mattered. She wouldn't have been so afraid of emotion, of reaching out. But she had learned that pleasure brought pain.

She hadn't known that she was crying; her tears were as silent as the night. Then suddenly she felt a thumb against her cheek, wiping away the moisture there.

"How long?" he asked her very softly.

And she knew exactly what he meant. "Three years ago."

"What happened?"

She had to breathe very deeply before she could whisper out her answer. "A drunk driver," she said flatly. "The baby was killed instantly. Paul lingered a few hours."

"And the driver?"

"He died, too. There wasn't even anybody left to hate."

He didn't say anything else to her; he just ran his fingers gently, idly against her cheek, then over her hair. And he stayed there, beside her, his warmth all around her.

And in time she slept.

She awoke to find his glittering green eyes upon her.

The absolute darkness was gone; hazy light filtered in, like a gray fog. She could see him now, and herself, too well.

In the night she had turned to him. Turned and twisted and left half of her sheet behind. Their legs were completely entangled, her left one beneath his, her right one thrown across his thigh. She'd made a pillow of his arm—which he couldn't possibly move without tearing out a handful of her hair. Thus his patient and amused stare as she opened her eyes wider and wider with the realization of her position.

"Oh! Get off me, you—"

"Hey, you're the one on top of me, Mrs. Blayne."

And of course she was. Clenching her teeth and emitting a soft oath, Mandy moved her legs away from his and wrenched furiously at the sheet. It wouldn't give, not until he laughed and shifted his weight. Groaning, she wrapped it around herself and stared disgustedly at the ceiling, drawing another soft chuckle from him.

"Can't you go somewhere, do something—get out of here? You're never around when I—" She broke off abruptly.

Naturally he pounced on her words, leaning on one elbow to watch her closely. "When you what?"

"I have no idea. I was just talking."

"You were not. You were about to say 'when I need you!'"

"I do not need you." She paused, lowering her lashes. "You're just better than some of the alternatives around here."

"Wow! What an endorsement!"

"Will you please go do whatever it is you do when you're not around?"

"Ah, jealousy becomes you."

Mandy sighed with exaggerated patience. "I'm not jealous." Then she turned suddenly, holding the sheet tightly to her breasts, surprised that it really did seem nice to wake up and find him there, smiling at her—even if she had been definitely disturbed at first.

"I'm curious," she murmured, remembering what she had intended to say. "Here I am, entirely harmless, and they keep me under lock and key. And there you are—at least two hundred pounds of you—and they let you run around. Why?"

"Because I'm madly in love with you. I'm allowed to be here to keep a lid on you. I'm a kindred spirit, a refugee, too, or so they believe. I'm one of them—a gardener—pulled into the bedroom. And you, Mrs. Blayne, are the farthest thing from harmless that I've ever come across."

"What?"

"You half killed me the other night."

"*I* half killed *you*?"

"Umm. Scratching, flailing, slapping—you're about as harmless as a basketful of vipers."

"Oh, really? Funny, you don't look much worse for wear!"

"But I am. You might well have cost me months of normal sexual activity."

"What?" she shrieked, astounded at his accusation.

"You must have learned your kicks from Bruce Lee. Honestly, I felt mortally wounded. My mother would never forgive you. She's expecting grandchildren one of these days.''

She saw the grin he couldn't keep hidden then. "Oh, will you please get out of here? Go join your fellow refugees!''

The humor instantly fled from his eyes. "A refugee, Mrs. Blayne,'' he said, "is one who seeks refuge. I was born in Dublin, but both my parents were American citizens. Therefore I never had any need to seek refuge.''

He rolled away from her and rose, leaving her feeling a strange remorse; she had been teasing him, and she wasn't sure what she had said to make him draw away from her with such disgust.

His back was to her, his hands on his hips. "It isn't a dirty word, you know,'' he said.

"What?''

"Refugee, Mrs. Blayne. Little Miss Mayflower Princess. This country was established because people sought a better life. The Irish have come, the English, Italians, Germans and so on forever. That's part of the reason we're so unique, Mrs. Blayne. What do I do out there? I talk with them—in Spanish. I try to watch which way the wind is blowing, I try to read people. For your safety, Mrs. Blayne. If you had bothered to learn some Spanish—''

"Why should I have?'' she snapped, simply because she needed some defense; he was definitely attacking. "It's an English-speaking country!''

He swung around then, and to her surprise he was suddenly on his knees on the mattress, green fire in his eyes and radiating enough tension to make her shiver. "Yes, Mrs. Blayne, yes! It's definitely an English-speaking country. And you're right—those who seek its shelter should learn its language! But what kind of an isolationist are you? Nine out of ten Europeans learn at least two languages. They have to. They have to be able to talk to their neighbors. Haven't you ever wanted to learn for the simple joy of learning. Relating? Are you so smug, so satisfied with what you are, that you feel no need to give?''

"What the hell is this?'' Mandy retorted. "A soapbox? I took another language, Mr. Ramiro—it just happens to have been German, not Spanish. And I'm not a linguistics whiz. I'm ever so sorry. And if you think that I'm a bigot, I'm sorry about that, too, but it's certainly your prerogative.'' Mandy was gaining steam as she continued her argument. Gripping the sheet, she rose to her knees to face him, as angry as he was. "You'd better face a few facts, Mr. Ramiro! We had a lot of real criminals dumped on us! As a police officer, you should know that! And I don't care if a murderer is German, French, English, Japanese or all-American mongrel—he shouldn't be walking the streets!''

"So what are you saying? The Cubans are all murderers?''

"I didn't say that and you damn well know it!''

His hands suddenly clamped down on her bare shoulders; she felt their leashed force and the blaze of emotion that seemed to leap from him to her. And then, just when she was certain that he would either shake her or scream at her again or both, he released her with an oath of disgust and scrambled back to his feet.

He strode straight toward the door without a backward look, opened it and slammed it behind himself.

"Oh, you stupid son of a bitch!" Mandy muttered after him. But then she realized that tears were stinging her eyes, and she didn't know why.

She hurried up, stumbling to grasp her clothing, racing for the bathroom. Brackish water, a little yellowed from rusting pipes, spewed from the spigot. She closed her eyes to ignore the color and splashed her face. Why did they keep getting into all this? Why didn't he understand...? And why the hell was she worrying about him when she was still a kidnap victim?

She sighed and realized that she wasn't really frightened. Not anymore. Julio seemed more like a misguided child than a menace. Except that he did know how to use a gun.

But she didn't believe that he would really hurt her. The only person she was afraid of—bone deep!—was Roberto, but she didn't have to worry about Roberto, because Julio seemed determined that no harm would come to her.

"This is insane!" she whispered aloud.

She had faith that this would end, and it was strange what that feeling did for her morale. Strange, but even her arguments with Sean made her feel stronger—impatient, but optimistic.

"Pain in the..."

Her cutoffs and top were still damp, but since she had no other choice, she took a brackish and slightly yellow shower, then donned them again. When she had finished, she noticed that a delicious aroma was reaching her from beyond the door of her prison.

Sean had simply walked out. Why shouldn't she do the same?

She stalked over to the door and wrenched at the knob. It didn't give; since Sean had left, someone had come to bolt the door.

"Probably did it himself!" she muttered.

"Hey!" She slammed a fist against the wood. To her surprise, the door opened. Julio was standing there, clean shaven, attractively dressed in a clean cotton shirt and jeans.

He looked just like a nice kid—except that he was still carrying the gun tucked into his boy-next-door blue jeans.

"Good morning, Señora Blayne. We expect to hear something from your husband by tonight."

He smiled at her as if Western Union was simply sending the money to get her out of a rather sorry jam.

"Great," she muttered.

"Coffee?"

"Please," she accepted, with just a trace of irony. He indicated that she should precede him into the kitchen. His mother was there, smiling at Mandy with her usual sympathetic apology as soon as she saw her. Eggs and bacon were cooking in a skillet, and two kinds of coffee were brewing: the thick sweet Cuban blend and what was—according to the nearby can—Maxwell House.

Julio noticed the direction of her gaze. "Mama brewed it specially just for you."

Marvelous, she thought. Cater to your kidnap victim. Except that that wasn't really true, and she knew it. Señora Garcia was very upset that Mandy had been taken; she had made both kinds of coffee in a sincere effort to do anything in her power for Mandy.

She went up to accept the cup the woman offered her, telling her thank you. Señora Garcia smiled, and Mandy glanced out the kitchen window to the beach beyond.

Maria, Roberto and Sean—Miguel! She had to remember that, no matter how mad she got!—were all sitting around, paper plates discarded, laughing and chatting while they drank coffee.

Maria, it seemed, was growing quite fond of Sean. She kept placing her red polished fingertips on his bare bronzed arms as she spoke to him, her dark eyes beautiful with laughter.

And Sean...well, he was laughing back.

Oh, nuts to you! Mandy decided belligerently.

"Señora, por favor..."

She turned around. Señora Garcia had pulled out a chair for her at the table, where she had set down a plate filled with bacon and eggs. Mandy thanked her again and sat down.

Julio was sipping his coffee by her side. She picked up her fork because she was hungry, but after a few minutes she turned to her captor and spoke to him. "You know, don't you, that what you're doing is very wrong?"

He gazed at her sharply. Then he lifted his hands and let them fall. "My father is getting old, and he is very ill. Too many years in a dank prison. He will not live long. Using any means that I can manage, I will see to it that he knows freedom before he dies."

"But—"

"Señora Blayne," he interrupted very softly, "I was three years old when Batista was overthrown. He was certainly not a prize, but we went from one dictator to another. In the States the exiles pray for another revolution. In Cuba, those who have not been indoctrinated into the new regime work for the next revolution. When I was a child gunfire raged, people bled, and people died. The needs create the means, don't they? Spying is fine—when it is for your country. A spy must be hanged when he is from the other side. This is life. Violence is an ugly thing, but it can also be a way of life. Secrets, trial and error, violence, abduction. They are all means to an end. I will see my father free. It is that simple."

"Not here it isn't!" Amanda protested, frustrated. "Julio, this is a huge country! Peter Blayne doesn't run it, he just plays his part. The courts can be slow, justice slower, but they're the best shot we've got! Julio..."

"I cannot go back," he said flatly, rising. "If you want some time away from your room, now is it. The day is beautiful, the surf is warm. Come out to the beach."

She rose along with him, ready to take her plate to the counter. Señora Garcia took it from her hands, smiling.

Mandy stepped outside with Julio. The others fell silent as they passed by. Mandy caught Sean's eyes on her, but they were filled with the sun's reflection, and she couldn't read their expression.

She gazed at him just as blandly, then walked on toward the surf with Julio.

"What happens," she asked softly, "if Peter Blayne doesn't respond to you? I'm telling you right now, he doesn't have the power to walk up to a federal penitentiary and demand that your father be released."

Julio stared at her. "He'd best find that power."

"You'd kill me?"

He sat down on the sand, letting the water rush over his bare toes. Mandy did the same. "I would have to send him a piece of you next."

"A...piece of me?"

"A finger, Mrs. Blayne."

She thought that she would keel over into the water. It wouldn't happen; the Coast Guard were on their way. Sean...

Sean was laughing away with the charmingly voluptuous Maria up at the house.

She lowered her head, thinking that no matter what he thought of her, Sean would never allow her to be...dismembered.

"I would not wish to harm you," Julio added.

"Thanks," Mandy breathed bitterly. She turned around, looking back to the house. Sean, with his guarded gaze, was still watching her.

And so was Roberto, in that fashion that sent horrible chills down her spine. There was something about his grim look that was like a rabid dog's. She felt that she could almost hear his teeth gnashing, as if he would devour her like a shark.

Shivering, she looked back to the water. To the sea. It stretched out endlessly, as if they were alone in the world. With nothing better to do and a yearning to move, Mandy stood and started walking out into the waves.

"Where are you going?" Julio demanded sharply.

She turned and stared back at him, laughing with real humor. "Where could I go, Señor Garcia? I'm going to swim, nothing more. I certainly don't expect to swim back to Miami, if that's what you're afraid of."

He had the grace to laugh sheepishly in return, and Mandy kept walking until the water came to her chest, then she began to swim.

The sharks were still fresh in her mind, so she didn't venture too far, but it felt so good to be moving. She swam against the current; she swam with the current. She floated on her back and felt the sun on her face.

When she got back to the beach, Julio was gone. He was sitting with the others nearer the house. They had switched from coffee to beer to cool them against the heat of the sun.

Mandy lay back in the sand for a while, resting, then headed for the water once again. She knew the physical exertion would help her to sleep, to keep from thinking.

When she came out again, she faltered. The others had gone into the house; only Roberto waited for her. Roberto, who liked to keep his gun out, smoothing it with his fingers while he stared at her. He stroked that gun like...like a man would stroke a woman.

Mandy kept her distance from him, tossing her hair back, squeezing the water from it. She realized from the direction of his eyes that the soaked shirt was tight and see-through against her breasts.

Sucking in her breath, she crossed her arms over her chest and strode past him, heading for the house. He didn't follow her—except with his eyes.

In the house she discovered that Maria was loudly playing a portable radio. The girl was sitting in the parlor, idly dangling one long leg over the arm of the sofa, listening to the music. She looked Mandy up and down and smirked at her. Mandy ignored her, aware that she was damp and that her hair looked like a mop. What did it matter?

In an annoying way, though, something did matter. Mandy was still itching to slap Maria. She didn't like having that scornful laughter directed her way, nor did she like the way the girl watched Sean. Exactly what Maria wanted was written all over her lovely face, expressed soundlessly in her sensual pouting lips.

Poor kid, the teenage years were rough. Poor kid hell!

Mandy returned Maria's stare with a shrug, then looked around the kitchen. Lunch was on the table. Julio and Sean were eating; Maria had apparently already finished.

Señora Garcia laid out a plate for her. It was fish, deliciously spiced.

Mandy sat and ate; Sean and Julio both glanced at her, then resumed their conversation.

She grew irritated again that Sean Ramiro—policeman *extraordinaire*—still did nothing. Then she noticed that even while he was eating, Julio carried his gun, one hand in his lap, ready to make a grab for it.

When Julio finished eating he went up to his mother, encircling her waist with his arms to say something. Sean leaned across the table to her. "Want to go back outside?"

She would never understand what possessed her to snap back at him, but she did. "No, thanks. We bigots like to be alone!"

He sat back, lashes shielding his eyes, his mouth tightened in a grim line.

Mandy stood up and waltzed past Maria and her radio, surprised to hear a voice with a beautiful Bahamian accent announce that it was almost four o'clock.

Swimming had done one thing for her; it had caused time to pass. But, like an idiot, she had resigned herself to a locked room when she might have known freedom.

With a sigh she sank down on her mattress, then realized with a bit of a start that there was a kerosene lantern on the floor, and a book of matches.

Sean had kept his word.

With shaking fingers she lit the lantern. It occurred to her that she could probably light a fire and burn down the entire place. It also occurred to her that they might let her burn to death, and she wasn't desperate enough—yet—to risk that.

She frowned suddenly as a little pool of light fell around her. There was a book beside the lantern. She picked it up and read the title; it was on Caribbean fish. It might not be compelling, but it was certainly better than nothing. It had probably been the only thing that Sean could find in the place.

Smiling slightly, she began to leaf through it. Then she began to yawn, and to her amazement she found that she was drifting off. She blew out the lantern and let sleep come.

Later, probably much later, because it had become dark, she awakened with a start. Puzzled, she rose up on her elbows, keenly attuned to the darkness, frightened to the core, but not sure why.

And then she knew. There was no sound, no movement—but she knew. Someone was in the room.

And it wasn't Sean.

Someone was in the room and moving swiftly. She opened her mouth to scream, but a hand came down over it. A heavy sinewy weight fell against her, and she heard a terse whisper in Spanish.

Madness catapulted through her. She couldn't scream, so she tried to bite. She tried to kick and flail and fight, but that wiry arm remained around her, firm and unrelenting.

She could feel his breath. She could see again that image of gnashing teeth, of brutal hunger.

She tried everything, but she couldn't dislodge the hand over her mouth nor the weight bearing down on her.

She heard the sudden tearing of fabric and realized that his free hand was on her halter top. She felt his palm on her flesh, hot, urgent.

That was when she managed to twist her mouth free at last in a spurt of desperate energy. She gasped for breath, then screamed as loud as she could, and long.

His open palm crashed against her cheek, and the world seemed to spin. But it didn't matter, not at all. Because the door had burst open, bringing help.

She needed no light, no sound, no movement. She recognized the presence filling the doorway, filling the room.

Sean.

8

One moment Roberto was above her; the next he was not.

Light streamed surreally into the room from the parlor beyond. Gasping for breath, Mandy clutched the torn halter top to her, scrambling to her feet.

The still ebony night was immediately shattered. She was suddenly surrounded by shadows and shouts, and between those bursts of staccato noise she heard the heavy sounds of fists landing against flesh.

There was a loud crash. Roberto and Sean had gone flying through the doorway together to land on the parlor floor, both grim, both bloodied—both still at it. Shaken, Mandy followed them. Julio was yelling; Maria was screaming; and Señora Garcia was watching the proceedings, white-faced.

Just then a gun went off. Mandy screamed again, but no one heard her that time. Sean and Roberto had both ceased fighting at that shot, twisting to stare at Julio.

Mandy didn't understand what followed. Everyone was speaking in Spanish. Roberto was obviously swearing vehemently and trying to make some point. Every bit as vehemently, Sean was arguing his side. Señora Garcia tried to say something, and Maria started up again, staring at Mandy, then spitting in her direction.

Julio shouted out a command, which everyone ignored, so he shot another bullet into the ceiling—which finally brought the silence he desired.

With everyone quiet once again he started to talk to Roberto, and then to Sean. Finally he paused to stare at Mandy who was standing, wide-eyed and ashen, in the doorway. He cocked his head with interest, then shrugged and spoke to the two men again. Roberto protested; Julio swore.

And then, whatever the argument had been, it was decided. Sean and Roberto both stood and walked grimly out the front door. Señora Garcia crossed herself and stepped into the second bedroom, slamming the door. Julio followed the two men outside.

"What is going on!" Mandy finally screamed, clenching her fists at her side.

Maria, elegantly decked out in a long gauzy nightgown that nicely displayed her attributes, gave Mandy another of her scornful looks and spoke disdainfully. "You—you are the problem! You will get him killed!"

"What?" Mandy demanded, startled and alarmed.

"It is all your fault."

She'd had it with Maria, and no one else was around. Mandy strode to her in a sudden fury and grabbed a handful of dark glistening hair. "You tell me this instant what is going on!"

"Oww! Let go!" Maria screeched, trying to free her hair. "Julio says they are welcome to fight it out over you! And Roberto is a killer, you stupid *puta*! You will get Miguel killed!"

"Julio is not going to let them kill one another!" Mandy snapped.

"Roberto will break Miguel's neck! And all because of you!"

"He tried to rape me, you stupid little witch!"

"You should have enjoyed him—"

"Enjoyed? Rape? If you like him so much, sweetie, you're welcome to him! Now get out of my way!"

Mandy shoved Maria aside, wondering just how much of a killer Roberto was. Any man could look tough with a gun, and that seemed to be the source of Roberto's strength. She tried to assure herself that he was nothing but hot air, and that Sean could take care of himself.

But she was frightened. Very frightened. If something did happen to him, she wouldn't be able to live with herself.

If she lived at all, she thought grimly, because she would fight Roberto herself until she had no breath left in her body.

Mandy swung open the front door. The natural coolness of the ocean breeze touched her cheeks soothingly, but she felt no ease as she paused and stared into the star-studded night. She could see the three of them down near the surf.

Julio's gun was in his hand; Sean and Roberto were wrestling on the sand, coming together, drawing apart, falling to roll on the beach together.

Mandy ran down to where Julio stood. He was watching the action with no apparent emotion.

"Why are you letting them do this!" she screamed at him. "You can make them stop."

"I cannot. No one can."

"You've got the gun—"

"Miguel says that you are his, only his. Robert says that you are no virgin to be returned untouched. If you've had one lover, he should have rights, too."

"You didn't kidnap me for that vulture's amusement, Julio! Come on, think! You're in charge of this thing, aren't you? Julio, you're wrong in what you're doing, but you're a man with morals and ideals. You—"

"I am not in this alone now! If Roberto loses, he loses!"

"And if he doesn't? Julio! I can't believe this of you!" She paused, swallowing, because there was a set expression on his handsome face. "Julio! I am a person, not the spoils of war! And you know that!"

"Roberto cannot shoot Miguel. They are evenly matched, no weapons. That is fair—and it's all that I can do."

"Fair..." Mandy paused in horror, because beyond Julio, the two men were on their feet once again, carefully circling each other.

Mandy caught her breath. There was a scratch on Sean's shoulder, and a smear of blood at the right corner of his mouth, but he looked all right otherwise. The shimmering fury of the fight was in his narrowed eyes; he appeared more than ready to keep up the battle.

Roberto was the one looking the worse for wear. He was wiry and strong, but he simply didn't have Sean's powerful shoulders or arms. Roberto had already accrued one black eye—which was puffing and turning an ugly green color right now—and his jaw was swollen, too. But he still had a look of blood lust about him, as if he was playing right now. As if he would win when he was ready.

Sean suddenly ducked his head and made a lunge for Roberto, throwing him to the ground. They rolled together, then split apart. Roberto didn't look so self-assured this time, but he smiled slowly at his opponent and reached into his pocket, drawing out a switchblade.

"Look out!" Mandy screamed.

Sean saw the blade. It made a rushing sound as Roberto brought it slicing through the night, and Sean ducked. Roberto struck nothing but air. The pattern was repeated. Sean was a second ahead of it every time.

Mandy spun on Julio. "You told me he had no weapons! You said that it would be fair. You said—"

"I cannot intercede! Don't you understand? He must beat Roberto, or Roberto will not respect him."

Mandy didn't think that Roberto would ever respect anyone. No matter how this ended, he would try to stab Sean—or anyone—in the back whenever it suited his purpose.

She started walking across the sand, but Julio caught her shoulders. "What are you doing?"

"Roberto has a knife. Miguel will have me!"

"Get back here! Do you want to wind up cut?"

"I'd rather be cut," Mandy retorted vehemently, "than handed over like a trophy!"

"No!" Julio said, but she wrenched herself away from him, ignoring his gun as if it didn't exist. She didn't believe that he would shoot her.

Sean saw her coming. "Get out of here, Mandy!"

Roberto laughed, thinking to take advantage of the distraction. He lunged; Sean escaped in the nick of time. Mandy instinctively reached down for a handful of sand to throw in Roberto's eyes.

She did throw the sand, but it didn't matter. In that split second Sean had kicked Roberto's wrist, sending the switchblade flying out into the night.

Then Sean was flying, too. He threw himself against Roberto, sending the man down on his back, with Sean on top of him. He rolled Roberto over, wrenched the man's arm behind his back, then straddled him.

Mandy gasped with relief and sank onto the sand herself. She watched as Julio walked over to the two men and spoke to them, clipping out orders in a soft but furious rush of Spanish.

Mandy's fingers dug into the sand. She realized suddenly that she was touching something metallic. Her eyes fell to her fingers, and she saw that she had the knife. Her fingers curled completely around it. While the men were occupied with one another she slipped it into the pocket of her cutoffs.

Sean got back to his feet then; Julio was still talking to Roberto in scathing tones as Sean walked over to Mandy. He threaded his fingers through his hair, grinning at her, and reached down to help her to her feet.

She accepted his assistance, staring at him. "Are you—are you okay?"

His grin deepened and he shrugged. "Yeah, Ma, you should see the other guy."

She lowered her head, smiling, then allowed him to pull her to her feet. He slipped an arm around her, and they returned to the house together.

Maria was waiting in the kitchen. When she saw Sean, she gave a little cry of ecstasy and raced toward him, ignoring Mandy. Maria leaned on his free shoulder, kissing the cut there between bursts of excited concern.

Amanda eyed her with tolerant patience, raising a brow to Sean and moving away.

He set Maria away from him, speaking softly but firmly. She touched his shoulder again. "I will take care of it—"

"There is no need, Maria. It is nothing. I..." He paused, pulling Mandy back to his side. "We are going to bed."

He started walking, leading Mandy with him. She glanced back to see Maria standing there, and despite everything she felt sorry for the girl.

She and Sean seemed to share an opinion of Maria: that she was still a child, a child trying to play in a grown-up's world, no matter how lovely her face or figure.

I could be jealous, Mandy thought, and it was a disturbing idea. It was...the circumstances, she told herself. But it was more, and she knew it. Their time together had been limited, but it had also been very intense.

She felt that she knew him better than people she had known for years and years. He angered her; he intrigued her. He absolutely fascinated her.

The other bedroom door opened before they reached their own. Señora Garcia, still ashen, came out. She spoke softly to Sean, and he replied in kind. She smiled at last, nodded, then returned to the bedroom she apparently shared with Maria.

Mandy glanced back once again. Julio and Roberto still had not come in. Maria remained where she had been, though, watching them. Watching them just as tragically as Scarlett O'Hara had watched Ashley Wilkes walk into a bedroom with his Melanie.

Then she couldn't see Maria, because Sean prodded her into the bedroom. He lit the lantern before shutting the door.

Mandy stood still, feeling a little rueful, a little shy—and more than a little confused.

Sean placed the lantern by the bed, then noticed her standing there. He frowned curiously. "What's with you?"

"Thank you."

"For what?"

"You saved my life."

He shrugged, casting himself back on the mattress, locking his fingers behind his head, then gazing at her with an amused grin. "I didn't save your life. He had no intention of killing you."

"But I'd have rather died," she said softly. "And—and he might have killed you."

"I should hope not!" Sean snorted.

She walked over to the mattress and sank down beside him on her knees, then lightly ran a finger over the red scratch on his shoulder. "Shouldn't you clean it?"

He gritted his teeth and caught her hand. "It's no big deal. Just leave it alone."

She snatched her hand away, reddening. But he didn't notice; he was suddenly sitting up, playing with her torn shirt, trying to find a way to make it stay completely where it belonged.

"It's all right. Just leave it!" she snapped.

He drew his hand away, scowling. "If you walk around like that tomorrow we'll be in trouble all over again. In fact, if you hadn't flounced around today, all this might not have happened!"

"What are you talking about?" Mandy demanded furiously.

"You—in the water! Making that stupid outfit look like something from a centerfold."

"It's not *my* stupid outfit! Nobody warned me to dress for a kidnapping. And Maria didn't exactly give me the best stuff she had!"

"You could have stayed out of the water!"

"Oh, yeah? I'd like to see you locked up for hours and hours on end without going completely mad!"

He didn't have a ready answer for that one. He closed his eyes and lay back down, sighing. "I am going mad, I think," he mumbled. He kept talking in a flat monotone. "If I'd stayed locked up with you, I would be mad. And I wouldn't know anything."

Mandy hesitated a second. "What do you know?"

"Not too much," he admitted. "Juan was supposed to be back by now, but he isn't."

"Is Julio worried?"

"Not yet. He will be by tomorrow night, though. But if we're lucky, by tomorrow night we may be able to spot the Coast Guard."

Mandy moistened her lips. "What happens if Juan never makes it back? What will Julio do then?"

"Nothing," he told her.

"Nothing?"

"Stop worrying, will you? Things will break soon."

She didn't answer.

"For God's sake, lie down, will you please? Get some rest. If things do move, you'll want to be alert."

She lay down beside him, not touching him, but all too aware that he was there. He didn't speak.

"He threatened to chop off one of my fingers," Mandy murmured at last. "Julio did. To send to Peter."

There was a soft sigh from beside her. "That was a threat, nothing more."

"It sounded real."

"What good is a threat if it doesn't sound real?" He sat up, leaning over to blow out the lantern.

"But—"

"Mandy, quit it! Trust me. Everything is going to work out all right. Please, go to sleep."

He flopped back down on the mattress, and the ebony darkness surrounded them once again.

There had been exasperation in his voice, and the harsh sound of his temper rising. Cast once again into a vortex of confusion, Mandy lay still and concentrated on each breath she took.

It wasn't fair; he was blaming her for things that were beyond her control. She'd tried to thank him for risking his life, but even that had annoyed him.

"I didn't ask to be here!" she snapped suddenly, whirling to face him, though she couldn't see him at all.

"I didn't say you did."

"You have an attitude about this whole thing! In fact, you're one great mass of attitudes! I have to thank you, because I couldn't have dealt with that weasel myself. But it's not my fault he's such scum, and it's not my fault I've been given such ridiculous clothes to wear."

"I—"

"You just shut up for a minute! Don't you dare blame me for anything! I didn't make you come along—that was your choice."

Silence followed her last emphatic words. He didn't move, and she wondered what his reaction would be to her sudden show of temper.

"Sean?"

He chuckled softly, and the sound touched her like a caress in the night. "Are you quite through?" he asked.

"Quite!"

"Good. I'm not blaming you for anything—except for the sleep I'm missing right now."

"Sorry," she said stiffly.

"Lie down."

"You're at it again."

"I'm not." She couldn't see his grin, but she could feel it. "I didn't tell you to take your clothes off, I just said to lie down."

"You—"

"You—" His movement was swift, startling, as he gently shushed her with a hand over her mouth. "*Querida*, go to sleep!"

Meekly she sank back onto the mattress, his touch, his voice, reducing her to quivers.

Querida...

He'd said it so softly. *Querida*...darling, loved one...sweetheart. It wasn't just the word; it was the way he had said it, in Spanish, as if there wasn't an English word that would do justice to his meaning.

He curled up beside her, his back to her. She tried breathing again, deeply, counting each breath. She was no longer irritated, or even hurt, but she was still confused, both by him and by her own feelings. And also by the yearnings she felt in the darkness.

She tried to sleep, but she felt as if she was in the center of a maelstrom. It was of her own making, but it was there nevertheless. She heard the beat of her heart, each breath she took. And each breath that he took. She imagined that despite the space he had left between them she could hear the beat of his heart.

She couldn't sleep; she couldn't even keep her eyes closed. She felt a restless energy that defied the night, and if she closed her eyes too long, she thought of Roberto. She remembered waking up, not being able to see, yet knowing he was the one above her. She remembered feeling his hands, knew again the horror of failing in her fight against him....

She took a deep breath, then exhaled. Sean wanted to sleep, but maybe she could sit with the lantern on the other side of the room. Maybe he wouldn't mind.

Sean. She felt awareness ripple through her again, and she couldn't begin to understand herself. She should have been thinking of the million reasons why she didn't want anything to do with him. She should have been burying herself in guilt—even in pain. But none of that mattered, not tonight.

She didn't even really want the light; she wanted *him*, awake. Whispering to her, talking to her, reassuring her. She wanted to run her fingers over the sun-browned sleekness of his chest, press soft kisses against his skin, taste the salt of the sea on his flesh....

It was dark, but she knew that she burned crimson. How could she be thinking this way? Feeling this way?

She sat up abruptly, determined to reach carefully across him for the lantern and matches. She would take the light to a corner of the room and read her book. That might distract her from the thoughts that were playing such havoc with her mind.

But when she groped her way over him the rounded curve of her breast fell against his arm, and her bare midriff collided with his naked chest. The short crisp hairs there seemed to tease her mercilessly, just as the contact of their bodies, hot despite the coolness of the night, seemed to create a kinetic energy so startling that she drew in her breath.

He caught her arm, holding her where she lay. "Mrs. Blayne, just what are you doing?"

"I was...just...I was—"

"Mrs. Blayne, please don't touch me unless you mean it."

He said it jokingly, lightly, but she knew that he wasn't teasing.

"I won't..." she began, but the words froze on her lips. "Don't touch me unless you mean it," he had said. And she had meant it with all her heart and soul and being...this night.

The midnight blackness left no room for reason or thought, for a past or for a future. All she knew was that she wanted him. Wanted to touch him. To be touched. To go wherever touching might lead them.

She leaned over him, pressing her lips against the hollow of his shoulder, holding them there for a fervent moment, then pushing the tip of her tongue between them, tasting his flesh, closing her eyes at the sleek salt sensation, savoring the elusive liquid quivering that burst and streaked through her like dancing stars. Savoring his gasp, the catch of his breath, the shudder that racked him.

"Hey!" He clutched her shoulders harshly, wrenching her high above him. Even in the night she could see the glitter of his eyes. His muscles were taut, his whisper harsh.

"I said—" he swallowed sharply and continued through clenched teeth "—not to touch me unless—"

"I mean it," she interrupted him abruptly, her voice as harsh as his. She didn't want to talk about it; she didn't want to be warned. She wanted to be held. She wanted to make love. To feel the world spiraling around her, to arch and writhe and roll in sensual splendor and temptation.

Still he only held her.

She tried to whisper to him, but sound eluded her.

And then it didn't really matter, because he lowered her against him, slowly, until their bodies touched completely, her length on his, legs tangling, her breasts hard against his chest, their mouths not an inch apart.

Then touching.

Perhaps he was still distrustful; perhaps he had a reason to be so. He held her shoulders when he first kissed her, just touching her lips, then pulling away. Then he touched them once again, curiously, questingly. He tasted them next, his tongue an exotic paintbrush that swirled across them like sable. He traced the shape of her mouth, then pressed his lips against her shoulder.

And then it was as if he gave up all thought of reason. Of sanity. Of the past. Of the future.

His arms wrapped strongly around her; his lips were hard against hers, almost bruising in their sudden passion. His tongue made an intimate invasion, demanding total entrance, total surrender, bending the night magic of her body solely to his will, throwing her heart to the four winds of chance.

He held her in his arms and rolled with her, sweeping her beneath him, and the magic continued. His body against hers felt incredibly good, right, as if they had been made not just as man and woman, but as this man meant specifically for this woman, this woman meant just for this man. His body seemed to meld to hers, a fusion of heat, of fire. Like flint to stone they sparked, drew away, then sparked again...and ignited. It was a blaze she never wanted to put out....

He drove his fingers through her hair, holding her still to meet his kiss. He cupped and massaged her skull, cherished the richness of her hair. She stroked his nape and then his back, skimming lightly over his spine with her nails. And she thrilled to the pressure of his hips against hers, his desire evident.

He broke the kiss, easing away from her, longing with all his heart to see her. To see the color of her hair. To watch her as he touched her, stripped her...slowly, relishing each new bit of golden flesh revealed to his gaze.

Rolling closer to her, he ran his fingers over her cheek, then kissed her again with slow fascination and let his hands roam, exploring the roundness of her breast, soft and yet firm, the nipples taut beneath the thin cotton material. Just thinking of them, he felt an inner combustion. Now. He had to have her now....

But he forced himself to stay under control. He stroked her naked ribs before seeking out the tie of the halter top, gently undoing it, letting the material fall aside. Urgency claimed him again, hot and strident, as her naked breasts fell freely into his hands, taunted his palms. He lowered his head to her, drawing a pattern with his tongue in the deep valley between her breasts, then feeling the splendor of imagination obliterated in the magic of truth as he savored her with his lips, the gentle tender grazing of his teeth.

He felt dizzy with desire. He moved his hands against her, fingers slipping beneath the waistband of her cutoffs, dipping low upon her abdomen, then nearly yanking at the snap and zipper. She issued a soft little cry, and he kissed her to silence her, the motion of his hands edging the cutoffs lower and lower.

And then it was he who cried out, an oath of impatience, and he moved away from her, grasping the tattered hems of the cutoffs, easing them down the wickedly lovely length of her legs.

He wanted the light. He wanted to see her: the glorious fan of sunlight and wheaten hair; the shimmering desire in her eyes; her features taut with passion. The rise of her breasts; the dip of her belly. Her back; the curves of her buttocks. He wanted to see all of her.

He started to move off the mattress, and she realized his intent. Crying out softly, she rose to meet him, grasping his shoulders, burying her head against his neck and seductively pressing her breasts against him.

"No! Please."

"I was just going to light the lamp."

"No. No light. Let it be darkness. Let it be magic."

He should refuse. He should tell her that there could be magic in the light. He should not allow her to make love in the darkness.

Done in the darkness, in the ebony night, it would not be real. It would not exist in the morning's light.

"Please, Sean. Please."

Her whisper, her breath against his flesh, stirred the blaze of his near-desperate passion once again. He couldn't refuse her anything.

Kneeling, they moved together. Kneeling, he felt the exquisite femininity of her body, touched so thoroughly by his own. He kissed her, explored her and forced her back at last, pressing her down upon her stomach.

He couldn't see her; he had to know her. He pressed his mouth against the small of her back, against her spine. Lust burned raw inside of him. It was torture; it was delicious.

All along her spine he kissed her, moving his hands down over her buttocks, down her legs, knowing their shape. Down to her feet, and even there he played, kissing her toes, stroking the soles of her feet, massaging them. She arched; she moaned softly; she made little inarticulate sounds. Dear God, he wanted to see her! He smiled a little grimly, even a little maliciously, for the movements of her body cried to his, though she choked back her cries of arousal, of readiness.

He had no intention of being had so easily.

When his fingers left her feet they stroked, slowly, excruciatingly slowly, to her inner thighs, urging them apart, finding she had no strength for denial.

He rolled her over. She was as pliable as a kitten, as passionate as a tigress as she reached for him, whispering incoherently for him to stop, to come to her.

"Not yet," he whispered against her lips. He waited there, above her, as his fingers played between her legs, as she gasped and arched against him, holding him, pushing him away, trying to touch him in turn.

Her nails scratched lightly over his chest, explored his back, tried to dip beneath the waistband of his cutoffs and met with frustration. She tugged at the button and the zipper with trembling fingers and found frustration again. They would not give for her. And again for him it was agony...and it was ecstasy.

He kissed her, his tongue delving deeply into her mouth. And then he whispered of the wonder of her body, and what it was doing, whispered with his lips just half an inch from her mouth until she thought she would go mad.

"Sean!"

"What?"

"Take—take your clothes off."

"Aha! I told you that you would get to it eventually. All women are alike!"

"Sean..."

"Mandy, I'd strip for you anytime. In private, of course."

She half giggled, half sobbed.

And he thought that if he waited any longer he would explode, and they would have to pick up the pieces of what had once been a man. In seconds he had obliged her, tossing his cutoffs somewhere into the magical black arena surrounding them, returning to her with the full strength of his desire evident.

She touched him, and his impatience soared. He held her face with his hands, spread her thighs with his knees, kissed her deeply and entered her deeply.

The black magic of the night swirled around them. At first the tempo of their loving was slow, then frenetic. Kisses, caresses and the spiraling maelstrom of desire set them apart from the world. This was passion, born in the darkness, bred by fear and sensation, gratitude and natural hunger. And something more....

He had to be mad. He was lost within her. Lost in the welcoming embrace of her body, shuddering with sensation, volatile, ecstatic, as he had never been before. Touching her inside and out, knowing her, caressing her, reaching the pinnacle together, holding each other, drifting.

It was passion only, he told himself.

Strange. When he touched her damp brow, when she curled against him, when the curve of her breast so comfortably touched his chest and her slender leg was cast so trustingly over his...

It was passion.

Yet it felt ridiculously as if he were falling in love.

9

When Sean awoke, it was barely dawn with just the palest filtering of pink light entering the room. He could make out Mandy's huddled form, curled so trustingly against him, lips slightly parted as she breathed, her lashes falling against her cheeks, her hair falling over her shoulders—and his own.

He eased away from her and carefully pulled the covers to her shoulders. He wanted to hold her, to glory in her all over again, but the shield of darkness was gone, and he knew innately that she had been his only because of that darkness.

Sean rose silently and donned his cutoffs. He needed to be alone. He crept quietly from the room, closing the door tightly behind him.

Julio, on a mat outside the door, was awake, watching him, the ever-present Magnum at his side.

"I'm just going down to the beach," Sean said.

Julio nodded and lay back down on the mat. Sean continued on out the kitchen door. No one was really awake yet. No one but him.

He was glad. There was no time here like the breaking of the dawn. No time when the heavens appeared more magenta, no time when the coming sun kissed the sand more gently. A breeze stirred the trees and the rippling water.

He walked over the soft dunes and neared the water, listening to the soft rush of the tide, gazing at the glittering droplets caught and dazzled by the coming sun. Again the irony of it all struck him. Here, in this incredible Eden, they were prisoners. It should have been a place of freedom. No crime should touch this shore, only laughter and tenderness and...passion.

They should have made love beneath the stars, not on a shabby mattress inside a primitive cabin in the dark. This was a place of exquisite loveliness; it should have remained unsoiled.

Sean sat down and wrapped his arms around his knees.

So many things in his life had been beautiful, he thought.

Havana had been beautiful. Once upon a time it had been a fantastic city, a playground for the rich and famous. There had been dancing and music, beautiful women, poets and musicians, artisans and scholars. The warm Caribbean breezes had touched the patios of homes and nightclubs; the palms had swayed; the air had been touched by perfume.

Once upon a time...

He had been only six the last time he had seen Havana, but as long as he lived he would never forget that night.

Revolution had been brewing for a long time. The old men at the cafés had talked about it; the young men had shouted about it. Batista had been a dictator, and it was very true that the poor had suffered beneath him. Yes, revolution had been brewing. His father simply had not seen it clearly enough.

As a six-year-old Sean had adored both his parents. They'd met in New York City, where his mother had been a model and his father had been selling superior Havana cigars. They had fiery tempers, but totally different cultural backgrounds. Love had always been the tie that bound the two of them. It had been imperative that they learn about each other's cultures to appreciate and understand each other. Consequently, Sean had been born in Dublin, beneath the benign eyes of his maternal grandparents.

And consequently they had been in Havana on the night the gunfire began.

He could remember it all so clearly. December, but a hot night. His father had been downstairs on the patio, talking with a few cronies. His mother had been in the kitchen, humming, fixing rum punches for their company. Sean had been sitting at the kitchen table, laboriously practicing his handwriting.

And then it had started, a rat-tat-tatting somewhere down the street, so soft that they had ignored it at first. But then there had been screams, and his father, such a handsome man with his flashing dark eyes and lean whipcord physique, had come dashing up the stairs.

He'd shouted that they must go, that they must get to the airport. Sean could remember his mother bursting into tears when it became clear that his father was not going to join them.

"You're an American, too! You're an American citizen! This is not your—"

"I am an American, but I am also Cuban. Siobhan, go, now, for my son's sake! I will meet you in the States. I will meet you!"

And so they ran. His father's friend, Xavier, got them through the streets. Streets littered here and there with bodies. With soldiers, with revolutionaries. With the injured, with the dying. Streets that seemed alive with screaming.

At one point, they'd been stopped—by a looter, of all things on such a night. His mother had been held while he, a child, had struggled ineffectually. That had been when he decided he would never be helpless again.

With the pure fury of a child he had escaped the man holding him and bitten the man attacking his mother, giving Xavier the chance to wrest the gun from the man. Xavier had killed him, and their mad dash for freedom had continued.

They'd reached the embassy—and they'd gotten out.

But he'd never seen his father again, nor Xavier. They'd settled in Miami, where his mother had spent the next ten years of her life waiting for news of his father. When it came, it was bad. He had been shot that night. He had died with the revolution.

Adjusting to life in Miami had been hard. Sean spoke Spanish fluently, but his English had an Irish accent, and all the kids had made fun of him. Nobody had cared much what you sounded like in New York, because New York had been full of all kinds of people. But not Miami—not then.

Cubans began entering the city in droves, escaping to freedom. The federal government helped them, which led to resentment. Sean's life became ever harder. No one could understand a Cuban boy named Sean who had an Irish mother.

Somewhere along the line—the third grade?—he'd created a new world for himself. He started telling his schoolmates that Ramiro was Castilian, that his mother had married his father in Madrid.

Then his mother found out about the story. She'd gone as white as paste and started to cry in a way that tore his insides all to pieces. "Sean! How could you? How could you deny your father?"

That had been the last time he had ever done so. He had gone to his mother, and they had cried together. When he went to bed that night all he could think about was his father, his laughter, his temper, his total devotion to his wife—and to his son. His love for the world at large and for his own heritage.

From that moment on he was proud of what he was. Irish, Cuban— and American. American all the way.

And naturally, as time passed, things evened out. In high school half his classmates were various forms of Anglo, half were various forms of Latino. He played football with a natural ability, and by his junior year that made him incredibly popular.

He went to college in Nebraska on a football scholarship. He liked Nebraska, but not as much as home. And though he earned a law degree, he didn't want to practice. He wanted to be a cop. He'd wanted to be one ever since that night in Havana, when he had learned that law and order were precious commodities.

Then, when he'd first come home, he'd fallen in love. Her name was Sandra Johnson, and she had been beautiful. Blond and blue-eyed and blue-blooded all the way. They'd met at a nightclub and fallen in love to a John Denver tune, slow dancing beneath the colored lights. All he'd really known about her was that she worked in her family's business as a receptionist. That seemed to be all he needed to know at the time. They met every night. They made love on what seemed like every beach in the state.

She was passionate, lovely, and everything he had ever desired.

But on a cool September night, when he was twenty-four and thought that he owned the world, he had received a blow that nearly destroyed him.

She met him that night, tremendously nervous, teary-eyed, anxious and excited. She blurted out instantly that she was pregnant, then awaited his reaction.

He was thrilled. A home and a family. He was ready for them both. A child, his father's grandchild, to hold and love and nurture—and to whom to give the world, just as his parents had given it to him. America, with all its merging fascinating cultures.

He'd held her tenderly, and they'd planned their life. They would look into the nice new town houses on Miller Road, and they would be married in St. Theresa's. His pay wasn't great, but it was sufficient.

Sandra had been starry-eyed then, as happy as a lark. They had to meet each other's parents, of course. Sean knew that his mother would love Sandra. And by this time in his life he could see no reason why the Johnsons wouldn't like him.

He arrived at their house neatly suited. He was somewhat stunned by the mansion on the water, but he hadn't come from poverty. His mother had done well modeling, and his father's investments had all been in the U.S. His mom had a wonderful old home in Miami Shores. And if anyone was "class," it was Siobhan Ramiro.

But not to the Johnsons.

When the maid led him into the elegant receiving room Sandra was nowhere in sight. Only her mother and father were there, greeting him politely but informing him that Sandra was gone.

Where? he had demanded, confused.

And then it had all come out. They were terribly sorry, but didn't he understand that they were "the" Lockwood Johnsons; they couldn't possibly allow their daughter to marry a—a refugee.

Lockwood Johnson went on to say coolly that the baby had already been aborted.

Well, he—a cop—had gotten arrested that night. His temper—Irish, Cuban or all-American—had soared to a point where he had seen nothing but red, and he'd charged Lockwood Johnson with all the fury he had learned on the football field.

Johnson had probably expected something along those lines. He'd whistled, and four bodyguards had come rushing in. Even then, it had taken them fifteen minutes to wrestle him down.

He could still remember Mrs. Johnson murmuring something about the behavior of "riffraff," but all he really knew was that he had woken up in a jail cell.

All he could think at the time was that the Johnsons were the ones who deserved to be in jail. They'd murdered his child; they'd taken a piece of his heart.

Logically, he had known that they represented an extreme. His friends, his best friends, his co-workers, all came in mixed nationalities. Half the Cuban girls he knew had married Anglo men, and vice versa. Of course there were still cultural differences. Some people resented those who spoke Spanish; some thought it was good to know two languages. Things didn't change that quickly. But people were people, and friendships formed where they would, as did love—when it was allowed.

He had decided then that he wouldn't fall in love again. Especially not with a blonde.

So what the hell was he doing now? It was ridiculous; it was impossible. He should be staying as far away as he could from Mrs. Amanda—Anglo—Blayne.

He closed his eyes tightly then opened them to the lightening sky. He realized that he was clenching his fists so tightly that his nails were cutting into his palms.

He wasn't in love, he told himself dully. This whole thing was nothing more than circumstance. He had known her only a few days, and she'd turned to him only because she was frightened and lonely. She'd turned to him in the dark, hiding.

He straightened his shoulders. God! If they could just get off of this damned island!

He tried to bring himself under control, but anger filled him. He reminded himself that under no circumstances could he risk her life, yet he was ready to run headfirst into Roberto, just to end it all. Last night had been ecstasy; this morning was hell.

"Sean?"

He turned around and saw her standing there. All blonde and all beautiful. Thin and lithe and curved, and yet suddenly so Anglo that he wanted to scream. Her face was so perfect: tawny eyes alive above the high Anglo cheekbones. He couldn't read her expression; she seemed a little pale beneath her tan. She carried two cups of coffee and pressed one toward him.

He accepted, and found himself staring at her legs. Long legs, slimly muscled. He thought about the way they had wrapped around him, and he felt dizzy once again.

Good God, he wanted her. With all the heat and tempest and passion inside him, he wanted her. Right here, on the beach. He wanted Julio and Roberto and even Mama Garcia and Maria to drop dead, to fall into a hole. He wanted her naked beneath him on the white sand, far away from society. Far from a nightmare that he had forgotten, far from a place where an unborn child could be killed because of his heritage.

She laughed softly, just a little bit nervously. "Aren't you going to ask me to sit down?"

"No. Thanks for the coffee. Go away. What are you doing out here, anyway?" He scowled, staring back toward the water. He felt her stiffen and knew it was for the best. He didn't have any difficulty being friends with beautiful Anglos, or with dating them, or with going to bed with them, for that matter.

Just falling in love with them.

"I just walked out with the coffee. No one stopped me."

"Well, walk somewhere else."

She told him exactly what he should do with himself and turned on her heel.

Where the hell was the damned FBI? he wondered. One lousy little kidnapping and they hadn't appeared yet! They had a lot of nerve calling the cops yokels!

She walked away, not back to the house, but down the beach. He felt as if part of him had frozen over.

He turned slightly. Roberto was outside now, sitting near the door, training his damn Magnum on Amanda.

Sean looked back in her direction. She had finished her coffee and thrown herself into the surf.

For a long while he just sat there, watching her swim. Then she stood, wringing her hair out. Her ribs were bare, gleaming with water. The torn halter she had somehow mended was clinging to her breasts like a second skin. The cutoffs were doing little better at her hips.

Sean twisted slightly to see Roberto watching her, leering. Sean stood and marched down the beach. With no thought whatsoever, his temper soaring toward red again, he strode through the shallows to reach her, then grasped her shoulders, shaking her.

"Let me go, you animal!" she snapped. Her beautiful tawny eyes were red-rimmed. From the salt water? Or had she been crying?

He started to soften.

"I mean it! Get your filthy hands off me!"

He released her. Just like that.

"You liked my filthy hands well enough last night," he sneered.

"That was last night," she said coolly.

"Good. Because if you keep on the way you're going, it's not going to be my filthy hands on you—it will be Roberto's. And if you think I'll battle it out for you again, lady, you'd better think again."

He turned around and walked away from her.

By the time he reached the house Señora Garcia and Maria were outside. Maria had on a cute-little-nothing bikini. Accomplice to a kidnapping or not, Maria knew how to dress. She headed down to the water.

And at that moment Sean felt like speaking Spanish. He noticed that Amanda had stretched out facedown on the sand, a good distance away from them all. He strode back into the surf. Maria was just a kid, but right now he felt like nothing so much as playing kids' games in the water with her.

It was the longest day Mandy had ever experienced in her life.

When she awoke she was glad of the solitude he had given her. Though she was bundled in the covers, she felt her nudity acutely. Her nudity, and her body. Muscles that had been unused for a long time were delightfully sore. She felt guilt and she felt shame, yet she felt like a cat at the same time, wonderfully stroked and petted and loved.

Tears came to her eyes because it had been so good. Because he had been so tender and gentle and so wonderfully savage at just the right moment. Because she couldn't remember lovemaking being such a vivid experience, and because that made her feel guilty all over again, because she had loved her husband so much.

Yet even then, amid the guilt and shame, she had been all too aware of the forbidden knowledge that he had the power to ease the past, if not erase it. He was so powerful and fascinating that she savored the thought of him, just as her body savored the memory of his. His scent was still with her, as were the memories of his arms, of the way he felt inside her.

They were captives on an island, forced together, she reminded herself. It was a nightmare, and please God, it would end, and they would go their separate ways, back to the lives they had led before this one. And yet...

She had to see him. To talk to him. To admit that she was afraid of the light, but that she wasn't denying anything. She needed to touch him again, to know that his arms were still there—for now, at least. She needed to tell him how much she cared about him, how much she appreciated him, how much...she was fascinated by him.

It was almost like falling in love.

And so she had dressed, only to find her halter still ripped. She had stepped out of the room holding the shirt in place. Señora Garcia had clucked disapprovingly, then given her a needle and thread, and she had mended the halter. Then Señora Garcia had given her coffee, and she had hurried out to the beach, anxious to see Sean again.

She had received only the most horrible slap in the face, and it had hurt so badly that she had found herself awash with pain and confusion. The only way to rid herself of them had been to dive into the water.

Then he had touched her again, and she had felt such waves of shimmering heat, of anger, wash over her that she had been stunned all over again.

What had she done but make love with him?

She spent the morning lying in the sun; he spent it playing with Maria. Damn him. Cradle robber. What the hell did she care? She had been an idiot, and that was that.

So why in God's name was it tearing her to pieces? She should be worrying about her physical well-being. Juan wasn't back yet. When was Julio going to start snipping off her fingers?

A feminine voice started to chide her in Spanish. Mandy rolled over to find Señora Garcia standing beside her with a plate of food. She shook her head; she wasn't hungry.

Señora Garcia sighed, unhappily plumped her full figure down on the sand and pressed the plate into Mandy's hands.

Mandy ate resignedly. Lunch was a thin steak with rice and black beans, deliciously cooked. She ate everything on the plate, while Señora Garcia smiled at her.

At one point the older woman disappeared, then returned with a Coca-Cola. Mandy thanked her again and enjoyed the soda. The next time Señora Garcia left her, she didn't return.

Bored, and increasingly anxious and upset despite her determination not to be, Mandy took off for the water again. She swam and swam—and suddenly bumped into another body. Hands righted her, and she found herself staring into Roberto's dark eyes.

He laughed and gave her a mocking sneer. She kicked away from him swimming strenuously in the opposite direction, only to collide with another body.

Sean.

He pulled her back against his chest, but he didn't look at her. Instead he stared over her head at Roberto, who shrugged, then swam away.

Still Sean didn't release her shoulders. The water was cool, but she could feel his body heat like an inferno. She could feel his body, every part of it, pressed against her.

She was furious; she wanted to jerk away from him. At the same time she felt as if all his heat was seeping into her, turning her muscles to liquid. Making her wish ridiculously that they were longtime friends and lovers. That they could laugh like guilty children, that under the cover of water they could shed their cutoffs and fit together....

Roberto swam toward Maria. Señora Garcia had gone back into the house. Only Julio was on the shore, leaning against the house.

It might have been a scene from a resort brochure—except for the Magnum that Julio was holding.

Mandy wanted to break the silence, to tell Sean that she hated him, that she wanted him to get away from her—now! But his whisper touched her ear, soft, silky, sensual. So raspy and exciting that her mind might have been swept completely clear of all thought, except for...except for that all-encompassing excitement. It raced through her; it took control of her.

"Don't move," he implored raggedly. "Don't move at all."

His arms tightened around her as he started backing into deeper water. She was weightless; her feet didn't touch the sand. She just drifted along with him, his arms around her keeping her hips level with his.

And then they were in deeper water. So cool, when they were so hot. She didn't move; she didn't try to speak. His hands moved slightly, cupping her breasts, his thumbs grazing her nipples. A sound caught in her throat as he pressed his lips against her neck.

Then he moved so deftly that she was filled all over again with a quaking desire that was so physical it overrode even the sensation of the sun. She felt his hand near her midriff, and then his fingers were sweeping beneath the waistband of her cutoffs before sliding the zipper down. The pressure of his palm against her abdomen made her breath come too quickly, made her heart race. She thought that she was mad, then she felt that she had reached the clouds, because his mind held the same thought as hers. That simple touch, body to body, had brought this. The need...the desire...despite all else... It seemed somehow illicit, and therefore all the more fascinating. She should have been shocked; she should have hated him; she should have turned him away—she should have been screaming bloody murder.

And instead she couldn't wait to feel him inside her.

Her cutoffs fell, but he caught them. Beneath the water she was nude. He wrapped one arm around her waist and let his free hand play over her buttocks. Then, swiftly, he lifted her until her legs locked around his hips.

She couldn't stare into his eyes, so she rested her head against his shoulder. She stifled the cry that rose to her lips when he thrust into her, pressing her teeth lightly into his flesh.

"Look at me!" he warned her harshly. "Laugh, as if we're talking."

"I—I can't!" she gasped.

He was filling her. She burned; she ached; she needed more.

"Mandy...do it. Oh, Mandy."

He jerked, forcing her head back, forcing her to lace her fingers behind his neck and stare into his eyes. His smile was so wicked that once again it was as if the fact that they could get caught made every motion more thrilling. The friction of the water, the wonder of him, the pulsing of tension rose in her swiftly. Wonderfully. Suddenly she knew that she was going to burst, and that she would scream with the joy of it all.

But she didn't. He caught her lips in a kiss, and her animal cry of awe and shuddering satiation was caught between them. He held her tight, moving hard against her one last time, a part of her. She went lax, incapable of movement in the aftermath. Thank God he held her. Thank God that he groaned softly, crushing her against him. She couldn't have stood; she might well have drowned in reality, rather than just drowning in his arms.

The water rippled around them and actually began to grow cold.

"You've got to get these back on," he told her huskily.

"I can't move."

"You have to."

"You got them off, you get them back on."

She was so drowsy; his answering chuckle was so husky. She wanted to forget everything. She wanted to remain against his shoulder and fall asleep.

"All right," he said agreeably.

And then he let her go and dove beneath the water. But what he did to her there had nothing to do with getting her pants back on, and everything to do with getting her excited again. She started to protest, swallowed water, then wrenched the cutoffs back from him and struggled back into them.

When she finished, he was still laughing. "Not fair!" she cried.

Suddenly he wasn't laughing anymore. He pulled her close to him, against his heart. His whisper touched her ear. "I'm sorry. Do you forgive me?"

"I guess I just did."

"No, that was sex, not forgiveness. Do you forgive me?"

She couldn't say anything. She didn't know if she did or didn't; she just knew that she didn't want him to let her go.

"Damn it, Julio is waving that stinking gun of his around. Come on. We've got to go in. Night must be coming."

It was. And with the night came a horrendous argument between Julio and Roberto.

Mandy didn't understand any of it; it was all in Spanish. She was in the kitchen when it began, eating a sausage sandwich for dinner. Señora Garcia decided that Mandy shouldn't be a part of it. She hurried Mandy into her room, made her wait, then returned with shampoo and soap. Mandy knew that though her suggestion that Mandy might want a shower seemed casual, the older woman was very upset.

It also frightened her that Sean had seemed upset by the argument. He hadn't protested at all when Señora Garcia led Mandy out. He had remained at the table, listening tensely.

Mandy ambled restlessly around the room for a while as the argument went on. Finally she decided that she would take a shower; it would kill time.

When she came back into the bedroom Sean was there, lying under the blanket on the mattress, eyes open, staring up at the ceiling. He turned to her quickly, though, and flashed her a smile in the lantern light.

"What—?" she began.

But he didn't let her finish. He sprang up and she saw that he was naked. He walked quickly to her, then began unwinding the towel from her body. And then he began to kiss her shoulders, breasts, ribs.

She caught his shoulders. "Sean, wait. What—what was that all about? What's going on?"

"Later," he murmured.

His hands were on her hips, his lips pressed to her belly. His breath was against her flesh, and her flesh was responding.

She dug her fingers into his hair. "Sean..."

He nudged her legs farther apart, and his mouth rubbed over her until she thought she would fall.

She forgot the question she had asked. She forgot everything. She gasped and hung on to his hair, because she had to remain standing.

She came near to weeping, so vital was the sensation. She twisted and whimpered and gave herself gloriously to him. And only then did he stand to collect her weak form, carry her to the mattress and find his own reward.

The wonderful heat of the night wrapped itself around Mandy so completely that the island might in truth have been their own. Yet finally, when they had lain quietly together for some time, Sean turned to her, smoothing back her still-damp hair.

"We have to do something—tomorrow morning."

Her heart pitched and thudded; reality cut her like a knife. "Why? What happened?"

"Juan hasn't returned. Roberto thinks that he's been caught. He wants to take the skiff out tomorrow and go back."

In the darkness Mandy frowned. "I don't understand."

Sean hesitated for a long time.

"He wants to take one of your fingers with him. He called Julio a coward with no convictions and told him that his father will die in prison.''

"Oh, God!'' Mandy gasped.

Sean's fingers grabbed painfully at her hair. "You are to do nothing! Do you understand? Stay in here when you find me gone. Don't move, and I mean it. I won't be able to follow through with my plan if I have to worry about you, too. I mean it! Now go to sleep.''

"Go to sleep?''

"Yes!''

She would never sleep. And that night she didn't.

10

Sean didn't sleep, either; he lay awake, forming his plan.

There were certain things he had learned, and certain things that he had been taught. Individual heroics were seldom a part of police work. Shoot-outs were not day-to-day occurrences; not even the narcotics department ran around with their guns constantly blazing.

The basics of the job were to do your damnedest to see that the victim wasn't hurt in a hostage situation. If this had been a normal kidnapping, if Amanda had been stashed somewhere in the city without a resident cop, he and his partner and the team set up to investigate would have worked with the FBI, since kidnapping was a federal offense. As it was, he hadn't done any of the normal things. No paperwork in triplicate. No hours in his cubicle on the fifth floor. No arguments with the FBI.

But then, this situation was one in a million. He'd gotten to swim in the surf with a beautiful blond bombshell. What a lark. He'd even made love to her. God, wouldn't the guys at the station be green with envy?

Yeah, oh, yeah. Except that, like some green idiot, he'd gone and gotten involved. It couldn't last; it couldn't be. He and Miss DAR just weren't cut out to make a go of things.

But face it, he had a chip on his shoulder. And she didn't deserve his anger. So until she was taken away from him, for more reasons than one, she was his, and they would touch one hair on her head only over his dead body.

No joke there, he warned himself. So far he'd played the lackey because every fool knew what one bullet from a .357 Magnum could do to the human body. If one entered his body, there wouldn't be a prayer in hell that he could ever do anything for her again. But now...

Damn the FBI! They should have been here by now.

Divide and conquer—the saying was as old as time, but as true. He had to surprise one of them, get the gun and, if necessary, shoot the other.

Despite it all, he didn't hate Julio Garcia. Julio was just a dreamer, out of sync with the times, believing that he could change the world. This wasn't the way to do it, but Julio was no desperado. Sean just didn't know how far he would go.

Still, Julio would be the one he had to disarm. It would be risky, but it had to be done. Roberto was a hard-core criminal. He would slice off Mandy's finger without a second thought. Given half an opportunity, he would have raped her until she was half-dead—with no thought whatsoever.

Sean didn't think that Señora Garcia would interfere. She seemed to know that her son was diving straight for jail. She would just wait stoically for him.

And Maria? Maria was the long shot. Given a chance, she might well be dangerous. But then, she wouldn't want any of her precious beauty destroyed, either.

"Sean?"

Mandy whispered his name softly with the coming of morning, touching his arm, well aware that he was awake.

He shook her hand off. The last thing he wanted now was her touch. He couldn't waver; he couldn't think of her. He touched a finger to her lips in the darkness. "No words, no movement, no sound! Do you hear me?"

"Hey, it's my finger they're after!"

"Shut up. I mean it! Do you want to get me killed?" he asked angrily.

He thought he saw her eyes flash, even in the darkness. "No! I'd rather kill you myself!"

He chuckled softly, squeezed her hand and groped for his cutoffs. Then he stood quickly before she could say anything else and headed for the door.

As he'd expected, both Julio and Roberto were sleeping on mats outside the door. Roberto stirred slightly, gazing at Sean with wary contempt. Then Julio roused himself, so Roberto went back to sleep.

It was curious that Julio followed Sean so quickly, but it was to his advantage, and Sean was glad. He didn't look back, just hunched his shoulders instinctively and walked out the kitchen door and toward the beach. He paused just before the surf.

"You're upset, my friend?" Julio inquired from behind.

Sean shrugged, needing to get him to come closer.

"She won't be hurt, not really. She'll survive. What is one little finger, eh? They must know that I mean business."

Sean kept looking out to sea. "One little finger? Julio, I ask you, what is one little finger to you? And think about this—what if they catch you? So far you haven't hurt her. Perhaps she'll testify in your defense. She likes you."

Julio made an ugly sound. "The Americana testify for me? No, I do not think so. Her husband will not let an innocent man go free. Why should she bother with a guilty one?"

"Don't maim her, Julio."

"What? Maim?" Julio asked with annoyance, moving closer. "Will I touch her eyes? Her hair? Her legs? The things you cherish? I will leave plenty to love. It will one day be a brand of her courage for her."

"She'll probably die out here!" Sean replied bitterly. "Your dirty knives will give her tetanus. She'll bleed to death."

"Men have survived far worse things."

Julio was there—right where Sean wanted him. He never got a chance to say anything more. Sean smashed his elbow into Julio's ribs with such force that the man doubled over, unable to do more than gasp for breath.

Sean couldn't afford to show him any mercy. He brought his knee up into Julio's chin, sending him keeling over backward.

The Magnum fell into the sand without a shot being fired, nothing but harmless metal.

Sean scooped it up and tucked it into his pants, then reached down to Julio. "Sorry, *amigo*, but you're not touching her finger."

Julio, his mouth bloodied, still unable to stand without clutching his middle, grasped Sean's hand and stared at him heatedly. "Roberto was right!" he gasped. "I should have killed you at the very beginning."

"I think you've got a few broken ribs," Sean said flatly.

"I will scream. I will shout that Roberto should kill her."

"You don't want her dead, and you know it. Nor do you want to face a murder charge. Besides, I don't think you could shout that loud right now."

Julio winced, and Sean knew that his ribs were hurting him. "Let's go," he said. "To the door. You will call to Roberto to come outside. You will not sound alarmed, or I will put a bullet through your eyes. Got it?"

Morosely, Julio let himself be dragged back to the door of the shack.

"Do it!" Sean demanded, shaking him.

"All right! All right!" He hesitated just a second longer, then called, "Roberto! Roberto! *Ven aquí!*"

They waited, Sean using Julio as his shield. He listened, and he heard footsteps. The door opened, and though Julio had not sounded alarmed, Roberto was wary. He looked around the corner of the door—and instantly took a shot at Sean.

Sean ducked his head without a second to spare. He fired a quick shot back; he had no other choice.

He winced as he heard Roberto scream. That was followed by another scream, then another. Maria was up, along with Señora Garcia, and everyone was screaming.

Sean shoved Julio ahead of him once again and entered the cabin, searching for Roberto.

The man was on the ground, slumped against the wall, a trail of blood trickling down the wood. Sean saw that only his arm had been hit, but blood was spouting everywhere.

Roberto was keening with pain. Maria was standing by the back door, arms up, shaking and screaming hysterically. Señora Garcia just stood there, white-faced.

Sean inclined his head toward the wounded man. "Tend to him," he said briefly, then he carefully reached over Roberto to retrieve the other gun.

He barely noticed when Maria disappeared back into her room. He ordered Julio to sit beside his wounded friend.

"You've killed him," Julio said reproachfully.

"I have not. He'll live."

"What are you?" Julio demanded, narrowing his eyes. "You're no gardener."

Sean sighed. "I'm Lieutenant Ramiro, Homicide Division."

"Eh, Roberto, his name was real at least, eh?" Julio tried to joke to the still-suffering man. Señora Garcia was bending over him by then, trying to do something with the wound.

"Drop it—*cop!*"

His eyes shot immediately to Maria, who was holding a small Smith & Wesson with a pearl handle. He trained the Magnum on her in return. "Sweetie, you're not going to use that. Drop it."

Maria smiled and raised the muzzle just above his head, letting off a shot that splintered wood.

"Don't bet on that, lieutenant," she said calmly, adding a very explicit threat in Spanish.

He was just about to call her bluff and fire back when the other bedroom door suddenly flew open, and there was Amanda Blayne, in all her blond glory and rage. To Sean's astonishment she was wielding a switchblade, which she instantly pressed into the small of Maria's back.

"You drop it, brat. I've just about had it with you!"

As meekly as a lamb, Maria dropped her gun.

"Get it!" Sean warned Amanda, and she instantly did so. "You two—Julio, Maria—into the bedroom. *Señora*, can you help Roberto?"

Señora Garcia looked imploringly at Sean. "He needs treatment. He needs medicine," she begged in Spanish.

"I'm sorry. He should have thought of that before he shot at me."

When they had all been hustled into the bedroom that he had shared with Mandy—Mrs. Blayne, he had to start thinking of her that way again—he stood in the doorway and formally placed them all under arrest, reciting their rights. Although, if this was the Bahamas, they would have to go through it all over again, since he didn't have any jurisdiction here. Still, he wanted to play it safe.

Just as he was locking and bolting the door, Amanda started speaking excitedly. "Sean! The boat—Julio's boat—it's returning!"

Sean raced back to her and stared out the window. He turned to look at her. "I thought I told you to stay in the bedroom and not make a sound?"

Her huge tawny eyes met his. "You needed me!"

"I had the situation under control."

"Hmph!" Amanda sniffed indelicately. "She wanted to shoot...a certain part of your anatomy off! I rather thought you might miss it."

"I thought you didn't understand Spanish?"

"I've picked up a few words here and there."

"All the good ones, huh?"

"Sean, the boat!"

"Ah, yes."

"Well?"

He shrugged. "It could be Juan. Or it could be Juan and the Bahamian authorities and the FBI." He stared at her thoughtfully for a minute. "One way or the other, Mrs. Blayne, you'll be able to go home. Aren't you glad?"

"Of course. Aren't you?"

"Absolutely. I've got tons of paperwork waiting for me." He watched her speculatively a second longer, then stared back out the window. "As I said, it could be Juan. Or it could be Juan and the authorities. We have to find out. I'm going out. He won't be surprised to see me on the beach. You stay here. If anyone puts their face out that door—though the bolt should hold—shoot. Don't ask questions—shoot. Got it?"

"Sean—"

"Got it?"

"Oh, yes, sir! Yes, sir, Lieutenant Ramiro!"

"Damn WASP!" he muttered, pulling open the kitchen door.

"Excuse me, lieutenant!"

"What?" he asked, pausing. He felt empty. Already a gulf was opening up between them.

"I'm Catholic."

He frowned, shaking his head in confusion. "Good for you, Mrs. Blayne. What in hell does that have to do with anything?"

She smiled bitterly. "You just called me a WASP. It stands for white Anglo-Saxon Protestant. You'll have to think of something else to call me."

"Oh, Lord!" he groaned softly and slipped through the door.

He sat on the beach and watched as the boat moved closer. He sat stiffly, the gun concealed in his lap, feeling a niggling apprehension. Actually, it had gone easily. Far better than he had ever expected. No one was dead. And among the ones who were not dead were himself and the victim, Mrs. Amanda Blayne. They hadn't even been scratched.

But he was worried now that this might just be Juan, or Juan with a few reinforcements. He felt excitement and anxiety—and, strangely, that same overwhelming emptiness.

He'd wanted it to be over, right? Sure, right. It had been a kidnapping; a woman had been in danger. The fantasy had never been real. Never. It had all occurred in the midst of a nightmare.

But now it was over, and he felt empty.

He kept his eyes trained on the boat. It was about to anchor, and he saw Juan on the deck.

And then—moving so quickly he almost missed him—he saw another man. A tall black man in a uniform.

He stood up without thinking, hailing the boat, rushing down to the shoreline. "Hey! It's all right! Come on in!"

The figure stopped trying to disappear and stood, then brought a megaphone to his mouth. "Lieutenant Ramiro?"

"Yeah, yeah! Come on in!"

"Where is Mrs. Blayne?"

"Inside! She's—she's fine!"

The old boat was suddenly teeming with people. Juan was cuffed and disappeared with someone. The dinghy was lowered, and five men boarded it. Two Bahamian officials, a man in a three-piece suit—and an older, dignified looking man with a sad gaunt face and salt-and-pepper hair. Sean recognized him from his pictures. Senator Peter Blayne.

Sean just stood there as the dinghy came in. He was barely aware that Amanda came out of the house, that she stood slightly behind him. He wasn't aware of anything but the breeze and the sand beneath his bare feet.

"Mandy! Mandy!" The older man didn't wait for the dinghy to reach the shore. He stepped out while it was still in shallow water, soaking his shoes and his pant legs. "Mandy!"

In seconds she was racing down to meet him, and then she was in his arms. It was almost painfully apparent that they meant the world to each other.

Sean suddenly found it difficult to breathe. The older man was speaking, barely coherently, saying how frightened he had been, and what a fool, and how he'd never, never risk her again.

Sean had been as irritated as hell when Blayne had turned up his nose at police protection, but as he watched the scene and the man's agony he felt as if he should insist that this mess wasn't Blayne's fault at all. And, as it happened, if he'd accepted protection, the Miami PD wouldn't have been at the dock when Amanda Blayne was taken by the kidnappers.

Blayne wouldn't want any assurances from him, though; Sean knew that. The older man was staring at his daughter-in-law as if he could devour her, and Mandy was lightly trying to tell him that it hadn't been so bad, that she was fine, that he certainly wasn't at fault, that she was so glad to see him.

Then Sean couldn't give the tender scene his undivided attention anymore; one of the men in the three-piece suits was approaching him.

"Ramiro? Farkel, FBI. What's the situation here?"

What was it about cops and the FBI? Farkel had only introduced himself, but Sean disliked him already. He was a thin reedy sort of man, with a narrow nose, brown eyes, brown hair and a colorless complexion. When he smiled it looked more like a grimace.

Sean indicated the shack. "Two men, two women. They're in the back left bedroom. One has a gunshot wound to his shoulder, he probably needs medical attention as soon as possible."

The FBI man frowned. "You had a gun battle here? You were probably out of line, Lieutenant. You should have waited for us to come in. You could have caused injury to a civilian."

Sean curled his lip stiffly. "Sorry, Farkel. You see, they were going to start hacking off her fingers this morning, and it just didn't sound real nice to me."

"A finger would have been better than her life," Farkel said stiffly.

"They're in the back, Mr. Farkel. And I believe they're your responsibility now. Hey, go gentle on the old lady. She wasn't too happy about having anything to do with this."

The FBI agent walked past him; his associate—a younger blond man—glanced apologetically at Sean, who grinned in return. Some of the federal guys were okay. In fact, he was willing to bet that this one shared his opinion of Farkel.

"Damn yokel cops," Farkel was muttering. "They all think they're TV heroes."

"What's his first name?" Sean asked the young guy curiously. The man chuckled. "Fred. His name is Fred Farkel."

"He looks like a Fred Farkel," Sean muttered.

The blonde extended a hand. "Bill Duffy, Lieutenant. Sorry, he's my superior, but I'll try to be the liaison on the case in the future."

Sean nodded. Then the two Bahamian policemen walked up and introduced themselves, questioning him about the situation, too. They didn't seem to be any fonder of Fred Farkel than anyone else, and Sean had a feeling the man had made a few attempts to usurp their authority as well.

It didn't matter; it was all over for him now. All over but the paperwork.

The taller Bahamian, a guy named Matt Haines, told Sean quietly that a cutter would be coming in to take them back to Miami. Sean thanked him, then he and Bill Duffy went inside to deal with the fugitives in the house.

He was able to glance back at Mandy at last. For a moment her eyes met his. And for just a moment he thought that he saw something in them. Something warm. Something caring. Something that went beyond circumstances.

Then it disappeared. Her father-in-law's arm was around her shoulder, and he was suddenly pulling her enthusiastically forward, determined to reach Sean.

The senator's hand was extended, his smile deep and warm and real, and Sean thought in that moment that he knew why the man was elected over and over again.

"Lieutenant Ramiro! If I had a hundred lifetimes, I could never thank you enough!"

Sean returned his handshake, trying to keep his eyes off Mandy. "Senator, my pleasure. I mean, I didn't do anything out of the ordinary. I mean—"

She was turning bright, bright red. He didn't seem to be able to say anything that came out right.

"Didn't do anything out of the ordinary!" Peter Blayne exclaimed. "Why, son, you were seen! Jumping off that dock, trying to board a moving motorboat. Sir, I call that above and beyond the call of duty. You're too modest."

"Oh, yes, he's modest! Terribly modest!" Mandy said—and she felt the same confusion she knew he was feeling, because they both knew, even if Peter didn't, that neither of them had been modest at all.

And this was her father-in-law! Paul's father! Oh, God, if he found out, what would he think?

She stiffened miserably. There were so many things that she wanted to say to Sean; but none of them could be said. Not here. Not now.

She stared into his eyes and felt as if her insides congealed as he stared back.

His eyes were bright, as green as emeralds, as hard as diamonds. She must have been insane to think that there had ever been anything gentle about him. Or tender. He wasn't the man she had known, not the man with whom she had made love. With whom she had lain, afraid, in the night. With whom she had triumphed in the end.

His stare reduced the warmth of the Caribbean day to winter's chill. He was once again the stranger who had ordered her away from him on the beach, the man who had loved her—then hated her.

She lifted her chin, feeling her eyes well with tears, willing herself not to shed them. She didn't know what went on inside this man, and she decided then that she didn't want to know, that she didn't give a damn.

Circumstances...were over. Peter was standing beside her. She must consider the past few days a dream, a fantasy, a nightmare.

She extended her hand to Sean then, as cool as the waves that washed the beach. "Lieutenant, I want to thank you, too."

With a wry smile he took her hand. He remembered how it had felt on his body. It seemed so slim and soft and elegant—and now so remote. "No problem, Mrs. Blayne," he drawled. "Anytime."

"Oh, you'll be seeing more of us!" Peter Blayne assured him. "I'll see to it!"

Sean smiled. That was life as a cop. People you arrested wanted to kill you. People you got out of a jam wanted to be your friend for life. Peter Blayne would forget his promise. People always did.

"Sure," he said agreeably.

"Sean—Lieutenant, what will happen now?" Mandy asked him stiffly.

Sean shrugged. "The feds will press a number of charges. I assume they'll want you to testify in court." He gave her a slightly malicious grin, then laughed. "Fred Farkel will answer all your questions now. It's his ball game, as they say."

Mandy nodded. A silence fell over the three of them that seemed to puzzle Peter Blayne. It didn't matter. Two cutters had appeared on the horizon.

Matt Haines came out of the house and walked toward them. "Lieutenant, Mrs. Blayne, we'll have to invite you for a brief stay in Nassau. I hope you won't mind. We just have to clear up a few things and arrange our extradition procedures. It will just be for tonight. I'm sorry. I know you're anxious to get home."

Then everyone was on the beach—Julio, in handcuffs, Roberto, Maria, Señora Garcia, the FBI men and the Bahamians. Julio stopped in front of Mandy and Peter.

"Señor Blayne, I never wished to hurt her. But now perhaps you will understand. I wish for my father's freedom, just as you wished for hers."

Peter Blayne smiled sadly. "Julio, I told you I was doing my best. Your father will be out in a matter of weeks. But now *you* will go to prison."

"That does not matter, if my father is free."

"C'mon, Garcia," Farkel said roughly.

They passed by. Mandy was glad to see that they would not be on the same boat. She felt sorry for Señora Garcia; she even felt sorry for Julio. But she didn't ever want to see Roberto again, not as long as she lived.

She had to sit next to Sean in the dinghy that took them out to the cutter. She had to feel his bare leg, feathered with the short dark hairs, next to her own. To feel his breath, inhale his scent.

She didn't look at him; she stared straight ahead.

The cutter provided some relief; she was given a small cabin where she could bathe, and a soft terry robe that was totally decent and comfortable.

Mandy showered forever, loathe to leave the clean water. And loathe to reappear on deck, although she knew that Peter was waiting anxiously for her. Naturally Peter would quiz her. And naturally Sean would be there. And...oh, God!

Eventually she went out on deck. To her vast surprise and relief Sean was nowhere in sight.

She was given a delicious rum drink and an equally good meal, and Peter sat next to her, as if he never wanted to leave her side. He told her that her parents had been wired about her safety, that he'd had a student feed her cat. He chattered like a magpie, totally out of character. Then he asked her at last, "Oh, Amanda! Are you really all right? My dear, you're all I have left!"

Guilt churned in her stomach. "I'm fine, Peter, honest."

"But how—"

She took a deep breath. "Sean—Lieutenant Ramiro—pretended to be your gardener."

"My gardener?"

She grimaced and lowered her lashes, staring at her drink. "His Spanish is perfect. He's, uh, half Cuban. He convinced them that he was your downtrodden gardener, and my...my lover, and that he could convince me to be a well-behaved hostage. Julio really isn't a murderer, although I think his associate—Roberto—might have been. Thanks to the lieutenant I, well, I was as safe as possible the entire time. And Señora Garcia really shouldn't be punished, Peter, if there's a way around it. She was against what happened, and she was good to me."

He patted her hand. "We'll see, dear. We'll see what can be done. I'm sure you'll be able to speak in her defense at the trial."

She nodded, and then she wondered where Sean was.

Peter's thoughts must have been running along the same lines. "Where is that young man?" he wondered aloud. "What an interesting fellow. I'd quite enjoy getting to know him. He seems fascinating, don't you think?"

"Uh...fascinating," Mandy agreed, swallowing.

She didn't see him again, though, not on the boat. They docked in Nassau harbor and were given rooms in a hotel at the end of Market Street. Mandy had barely entered her own before Peter returned to her with a suitcase of her clothing, packed for her as soon as he'd received permission to come with the authorities to take her home.

She barely had time to dress before she was taken to the Bahamian police station. The authorities were charming, though. They asked her a million questions, which she answered to the best of her abilities.

Then she was free—or she thought she was. The FBI man, Farkel, was there, warning her that once she returned to the States she would be called upon once again.

She had a pounding headache by then, and Farkel felt like the last straw. She thought she was about to explode and then he was interrupted by Sean.

He, too, had changed. He was wearing a lightweight three-piece gray suit, austere, but very handsome on him. He stepped out from one of the little cubicles and spoke not to her, but to Farkel. "Fred, lighten up, will you? You'd think that Mrs. Blayne was the criminal. She's had enough for today, don't you think?"

Farkel stiffened. "I was just—"

"Every dog has his day, Farkel. You'll get yours. She's free for tonight. Our plane leaves in the morning, and once she's on U.S. soil you get to give her the whole third degree."

"And tonight?" Mandy heard herself whisper.

Peter answered for her. "Tonight we're going out on the town! That nice young Bahamian officer suggested Paradise Island for dinner, a show, even gambling." He chuckled, encircling Mandy's shoulder, pulling her close to him. "Mandy, I think we owe Lieutenant Ramiro the best dinner we can find. You, me, the lieutenant—and Paradise Island."

No, paradise is lost! Mandy thought a little frantically. But what could she do? Her father-in-law was on one side of her; the man with whom she had betrayed his deceased son was on the other.

Sean bowed whimsically, watching her in a strange way. He didn't want to go, she thought. No, he wanted to, and he didn't want to. Again she wondered if he hated her...or cared about her?

"A night on the town sounds good, senator," he told Peter. "Mrs. Blayne?" He offered her his arm.

Farkel snorted derisively and turned away. "Damned if they don't all think they're Sonny Crockett these days."

"Damn!" Sean snapped his fingers. "I just wish I could afford his wardrobe, Farkel."

"Your suit's not so bad."

"Thanks—your partner lent it to me."

"Gentlemen..." Peter began, distressed.

But he needn't have bothered. Sean didn't wait for Mandy to take his arm; he took hers. And the cool Bahamian breeze touched her heated face as they moved out into the night....

11

Mandy didn't know why Sean had decided to come to dinner with them. The place was lovely, the food was wonderful, but he seemed stiff and uncomfortable. She wondered if she looked as rigid as he did.

Only Peter seemed to be having a good time. He delighted in the story that the kidnappers had assumed that Mandy was his wife, telling Sean, "Good Lord! What flattery, that I should have such a child bride!"

Then he and Sean went on to discuss the situation with the elder Garcia.

Mandy concentrated on her shrimp cocktail. It was amazing. Last night she had been in absolute terror, wondering how Sean would ever stand up to two guns. Staring at her fingers, she shivered. She glanced up and found Sean's eyes on her. He smiled. She looked down again quickly, hoping that Peter hadn't caught the exchange.

"Oh, Mandy! I forgot to tell you! The team from Colorado called the school. You've been invited to be a part of the new dig."

"Really? How wonderful," she murmured.

"Dig?" Sean inquired.

"Yes," Peter said proudly. "Mandy is a paleontologist."

Sean arched one dark brow. "Dinosaurs?"

Despite herself, she grinned. "Their bones, actually, lieutenant."

"She teaches at the state college these days, but this sounds like the perfect time for a leave of absence. You could still manage some skiing out in Colorado."

"Yes, I suppose I could."

Skiing. She loved to ski. But at the moment the prospect meant nothing to her. She closed her eyes briefly. The dig, though, the dig would be good. The painstaking exploration, the wonder of discovery. The piecing together of ancient puzzles. It would be far away and remote, and she could forget all about Julio and Roberto—and Sean Ramiro.

Their main course came, pompano, broiled and garnished and savory, but Mandy couldn't taste it. She could only feel Sean's eyes on her from across the table. She wanted to scream. She wanted to demand to know what he was trying to do to her, here, in front of Paul's father.

"Do you have a family, lieutenant?" Peter asked Sean.

Sean grinned, swallowed a piece of fish, then replied. "Well, sir, everyone has some kind of family. But am I married? No. No children. My father is deceased, my mother lives in Miami Shores, and I've got no brothers or sisters."

"Divorced?" Peter asked him, and Mandy was stunned. Peter was never this rude.

"No, sir. I've never been married."

"Never came close?"

"Oh, yeah. I came close. Once."

Peter's curiosity was quelled by the tone of that reply. No further questions in that direction would be answered.

They bypassed dessert and ordered liqueurs. Mandy found herself feeling amazed. Last night she had been wearing old dirty clothing and sleeping in a hovel. Tonight she was surrounded by opulence: plush velvet, twinkling chandeliers, marble and silver. How quickly the world could change.

As quickly as Sean Ramiro.

They left the restaurant and went into the casino. Peter chose a roulette table; Sean sat down to play blackjack. Nervous and wishing that the evening would end, Mandy restlessly decided to play the slots.

Her little buzzer went off instantly to announce a two hundred dollar jackpot, and two hundred silver coins came spilling out into the catch tray.

She just stared at the coins, then started. Sean wasn't playing blackjack anymore. He was leaning casually against her machine, staring at her mockingly, lashes low over his eyes, looking sensual and handsome despite his negligent stance.

He touched a trailing lock of her hair. "Everything you touch turns to gold, huh?"

She jerked away from his touch. "Silver dollars, Mr. Ramiro. And my hair is dirty blond."

"Oh, I don't think anything about you touches...dirt."

"I work in the dirt. I dig up bones, remember?"

"I wonder why that never cropped up in casual conversation."

"We've never had a casual conversation."

"That's right. We were always pretty intense, weren't we? Need some help with your money?"

"No thanks. I'll just play it back."

He moved closer to her, his dark head bending. "Mind if I watch."

"Yes, I do. What are you trying to do to me?"

"What are you talking about?"

"Peter is here!!"

He arched a cynical brow at her. "Peter is here?" he repeated. "And now that Peter is here you have to pretend that you don't know me? Funny, I don't see the senator as a snob.''

"He's not—I'm not. Just go away, will you, please? Look, it's over. I never understood you, you never understood me. You've got a chip on your shoulder the size of a cement block. And I've got a few—''

"Prejudices?''

"No! Damn you. Problems of my own!''

"And what are they, Mrs. Blayne?''

How dare he? she wondered furiously. Confusion joined the tempest in her heart, and she was afraid that she would burst into tears right there.

She didn't. She just inhaled deeply and spoke with a voice as sharp as a razor. "No one, Ramiro, will ever need to tell me that life can be rough. I don't care what's happened to you, there is nothing—*nothing* in life like losing a child!''

She turned around in a whirl, leaving her coins in the machine, fleeing the room.

Peter would be upset, of course. He would wonder what had sent her flying out. But she couldn't even care about Peter just then; she had to leave.

Mandy had no problem getting a taxi to take her back over the bridge to Nassau and her hotel. Once she got there she knew she had to leave a message for Peter. She did so, then started forlornly for the elevator. She didn't know why she felt so lost, so miserable. It was as if the past and the present had collided to bring her agony just when she should have been eternally grateful that she had been rescued and given a future.

She should have sensed that something was wrong the moment she entered the room, but she didn't. She didn't even bother to turn on the light; moonlight was drifting in through the parted curtains anyway. She just closed and bolted the door, tossed her handbag on the dresser and fell back on the plush double bed.

It was then that she heard the rustle of movement and saw the silhouette moving in the darkness.

She tensed and opened her mouth to scream, but a hand clamped tightly over it.

"Shut up. It's just me.''

"Just you!'' Furiously she twisted away from him, sitting up, wishing she could see him clearly enough to belt him a good one. "You scared me half to death! What are you doing in here? I'm getting so sick of your strong-arm tactics.''

"Take your clothes off, Mandy.''

"What?''

"Take your clothes off. It seems to be the only way we can communicate.''

"Get out of here! I'll call the co—"

"Cops? Honey, you've got one already."

"Sean..."

"Mandy?"

His fingers slid into the hair at her nape, his palm cradling her skull. He held her there while he came ever closer, his lips meeting hers at last, hesitating for just a breath, then coming alive. For an instant, she clenched her teeth against him, but the warm pressure of his tongue dissolved her resistance, and with a little sigh she fell into his arms.

Circumstances changed. People did not. And darkness had come again.

In seconds he was stretched out beside her. They were both fully clothed, but she felt as if she was touching him, all of him.

But it was not passion that goaded him, not that night. He brushed her cheek, and she felt his eyes, emerald flames that defied the darkness.

"I'm sorry, Mandy."

She couldn't answer him. She shrugged.

"I can't forget what happened."

"No one has asked you to forget."

"Mandy..."

"You're strange, Sean. I thought I was, but you're stranger. We make love at night, and in the morning you behave as if I'm a bee with a particularly annoying buzz. One second you're as charming as a prince, and then the next—"

"I had a few raw deals. I took it out on you."

"I can't help the color of my hair, or who my ancestors were."

"Wait a minute! Wait a minute! Get off my case. You were the one who didn't want to touch me with a ten-foot pole the second other people appeared on the scene!"

"You don't—oh, never mind. You just—"

"Mandy!"

"What?"

"Did you smell this bed? Did you touch it? Feel it. So soft, so fresh."

She didn't know why she obeyed the command, but she did, inhaling deeply. And it was true, of course. The bedding smelled wonderful.

"It's so clean," she murmured.

He ran his knuckles tenderly over her hair. "And you're so clean."

"I beg your pardon. I was always clean."

"Well, I wasn't so great."

"Really? For shame, Lieutenant Ramiro." She couldn't stop herself from grinning in the darkness. "I'd never thought your confidence could be so low. I always thought you were at least okay."

"I was...okay?"

"Oh, definitely."

"Hmm. Well..."

"Well?"

"I'm great now. Want to try me? Clean as a whistle. I even shaved, and you didn't even notice."

"Oh, but I did. I think. You looked so great in that suit."

"Aha! I told you I was great!"

"Bragging will get you nowhere."

"Okay. Take your clothes off. We'll go back to brute force."

"Sean..."

He stopped her words with a kiss that seemed the most natural thing in the world. It always seemed to be like that; the taunts and the bitterness, but then somehow the laughter, and the irresistible urge to touch.

She would probably never know which was real, the laughter or the pain. But in the darkness, even darkness kissed by moonlight, it didn't seem to matter. When she was with him she always felt as if she had a driving thirst, as if his touch was water that cascaded over her, a fountain that sparkled and rippled, soothing and delighting, sweeping her away to new heights.

His hands moved over her, frustrated by her dress. He groaned softly. "Take your clothes off."

"Is that the only line you know?" she whispered.

"It's a damn good one," he assured her. And she laughed, laughed until his fingers rode along her bare legs to her bikini panties and teased her flesh through the silky fabric. Then her breath caught and she could laugh no more, and she was suddenly thinking that surely this would be the last time that she had to drink in all of him; the bronze flesh and muscle and sinew; the dark hair that dusted his legs and chest; the powerful line of his profile....

"You take *your* clothes off," she told him huskily. "On second thought..."

She started working on the tiny pearl buttons of his vest. He took a deep breath, watching her, watching the tiny frown that furrowed her brow. He held his breath as she undid the vest and then his shirt, and then he expelled it with a heady groan as she brought her mouth against him, delicately touching him with the tip of her tongue. Then she grew bolder, grazing his skin with gentle teeth that sent streams of lavalike desire rippling through his body. She moved sinuously against him, her hands moving over his back, his chest, then to his shoulders to shove the annoying material from the form she was so eager to know.

There was nothing like this, she thought. Nothing like feeling his reactions to her kiss, her touch. He trembled beneath her, yet he was taut, and with each ragged breath he took she felt bolder, more feminine, more vibrantly aroused herself. He was right: he was clean; he was great; the fresh masculine scent of his body was an aphrodisiac in itself, and she wondered at the beauty of him as her head reeled. She slipped her fingers along the waistband of his pants, teasing his belly, finding his belt buckle and leisurely working it free.

Too leisurely, perhaps. His groan resounded like thunder, and he set her aside, destroying her illusion of power. He left her to feverishly shed the remainder of his clothing, then lay back beside her.

"What's this?" he whispered huskily.

"My dress."

"Get rid of it!"

She giggled breathlessly. "I thought you were going to do a striptease and then dance."

"I intend to dance, all right." He swore softly in Spanish, having a miserable time with the tiny hook at her nape. He paused, shrugged and snapped it, and she didn't care in the least. She was suddenly as anxious as he was to feel their bodies together.

As soon as her clothes were gone she stepped back to him, remembering their first time. She knelt down and let her hair fall over his feet as she massaged them, then dusted them with kisses. Her body was liquid as she moved against him, using the tip of her tongue at the backs of his knees and all along his thighs.

He held his breath again, as taut as wire. She waited, drawing out the moment, her hair spilling over him.

And then she took him with her touch, with her kiss.

She heard his words, sweet and reverent, in English and in Spanish, and they all meant the same thing. His fingers were tempered steel when they closed around her arms as he drew her to him, moving swiftly, stunning her with the electric force of his entry. The moment was so fulfilling that she cried out softly, only to have her words stolen once again by a kiss.

They moved together in the moonlight, until finally she lay panting in sweet splendor. She was so tired, so spent, yet each new touch awakened her anew, until she moaned softly, curling into his chest with the sweetest sigh.

He held her there for what seemed like forever.

She didn't know when the change came, only that he suddenly stiffened and then rose before padding naked to the window to stare out at the Bahamian night.

She was too drowsy to rouse herself, and she wondered bitterly why he had decided to do so at such a time.

"What's the matter?" she asked softly.

He whipped around, like a lethal predator, and moved back to the bed, perching at the foot of it.

"What are we going to do now?" he asked her harshly.

"Sleep," she responded.

"That's not what I mean, and you know it."

"Sean, don't..." She lifted an imploring hand to him, but he ignored it.

"I asked you a question."

"Sean, I'm so tired."

"Then wake up. What are we going to do?"

"We're—we're going to fly back to the U.S. in the morning!" she snapped at last. "I have to go back to work. I assume that you do, too."

"And?"

"And what?"

"What about us?"

She held her breath, wondering what he was so upset about. Was he afraid that she would think she had some kind of hold on him? What was it with him? She didn't understand him, and when he was like this he actually frightened her.

She cared too much. Way too much. And she had promised herself that she wouldn't risk caring that much ever again. Her career, her love of the past, would be her life. Nice safe dinosaurs that had been extinct for years and years and years....

"You don't have a thing in the world to worry about, lieutenant," she whispered wearily. "I have no intention of becoming involved with you. You're as free as a lark."

"Oh?" he said coldly.

Chills raced along her spine; she wanted to touch him and erase the tension from his face. But she had already reached out to him, and he had ignored her.

"So," he murmured, "it all came true in a way, didn't it? I might as well have been your gardener, dragged in when the odd occasion warranted it, huh?"

She was instantly furious with him—and with herself, for always falling prey to him so easily. "You stupid bastard!"

"Yeah, you're kind of right there, too, aren't you?"

He prowled over to the window once again. "I've got just one more question for you, Mrs. Blayne."

"Do ask, lieutenant."

"I'm curious as to what precautions you've been taking."

"Precautions?" Mandy echoed hollowly.

He turned so suddenly that she thought he was about to take the drapes with him. "I'll be blunt, Mrs. Blayne. I'm talking about birth control."

"Don't you dare stand there and yell at me! I wasn't planning on having an affair! I was kidnapped! I usually don't worry about birth control when maniacs are abducting me! There's an old saying that it takes two to tango, and I'm here to tell you that it's true!"

"That's irrelevant."

"The hell it is!"

"It's irrelevant," he repeated, bending over her so that his arms surrounded her like a cage. "Because any precautions I might have taken would have been evident. So we know that wasn't the case."

She felt that she really did hate him at that moment. He stood over her like some superior god, the epitome of masculine force, beautiful still, and more hateful for it.

She stiffened her spine, as heedless of her nudity as he was of his. "You have no problems whatsoever, lieutenant. I will never again have a child. Does that satisfy you?"

For an instant she thought that he was going to hurt her, he looked so fierce. He didn't. He pushed himself away from the bed in a fury, muttering something she didn't understand. She shivered because without his warmth the night had grown cold.

She closed her eyes tightly. "Sean," she said miserably, "get out of here. Please, go!"

Once more he came back to her. He took a strand of her hair, curling it around in his fingers. She'd never seen him quite like this, and it was all she could do to keep from tearing away from him, to keep from screaming out.

"Not again, Mrs. Blayne," he said softly. "Not again. Here's another expression for you—those who play sometimes pay. And if you're given a price, my love, you will pay it."

"What—?"

"You can expect to see me again. Quite frequently. For the next few months, at least."

A new wave of trembling swept over her, along with a rush of conflicting emotions. She understood him now; at least, she thought she did. She'd assumed at first that he had no desire to be saddled with a child from their affair; now she knew it was the opposite. And with that knowledge she experienced a blank and cold dread, terrifying, horrible. It was if she had gone back in time, gone back to the time when the young highway patrolman had stood on her doorstep, telling her that not only her husband but her infant had been killed in the collision, the baby mercifully quickly....

But for her there had been no mercy. There had been her breasts, filled with milk for a tiny life that could never draw from them again. There had been the emptiness in her arms, the rage, the despair....

"Get out of here," she repeated dully.

He reached for her cheek, but she pushed his hand away. "I'll be around, Mandy."

"No," she pleaded.

And then she knew that he had misunderstood her entirely, because he swore again, then said, "What is it, Amanda? You couldn't handle a child named Ramiro? Too ethnic for your ears?"

She pressed her palms over her eyes tightly. "Yes! Yes! That's it! I'm planning to move to Boca Raton, too. Away from Miami. Haven't you heard that saying? 'Will the last American out please remember to bring the flag?' Please! Get out of here."

But he didn't. Not then. He straddled her and pulled her hands away from her face, then stared into her eyes with a gaze that burned into her soul. "No!" he thundered harshly. "You can't run away. Not this time!"

And then, miraculously, he released her.

She closed her eyes. She heard him dress swiftly, and then she heard him leave even more swiftly.

For at least an hour after that she didn't move. Not a muscle. She just lay there, trying to breathe.

And praying that she wasn't pregnant.

In the morning she felt awful.

The flight back took less than an hour. Peter's car met them, and they reached her home in another thirty minutes.

Peter was worried and solicitous. She could only be grateful that Sean hadn't been on their plane. He must have altered his arrangements.

Peter had arranged for the police and the FBI to come to her; she spent the afternoon with a pleasant blond man and a sergeant from the Miami PD. Things weren't really difficult; all she had to do was repeat what had happened over and over again. It was a cut-and-dried situation, but the culprits still had to be prosecuted.

A twinge of conscience touched her, and Mandy remembered to tell them that in her opinion Mrs. Garcia had been an unhappy bystander. She hesitated, then even spoke up for Julio, saying that she didn't believe he was malicious, just misguided. She was told that if she would say so at the trial, she might lessen their sentences.

"But kidnapping is a federal offense, Mrs. Blayne. No one can walk away from it," the FBI man told her.

"I know." She paused, shivering. "And Roberto should be locked up, with the key thrown away." She lowered her lashes. She had told them, of course, that he had attempted to rape her. She told them, too, about Sean's fight to save her from him.

She hadn't mentioned what had happened after that, though.

They left her, and she was alone with Peter. He wanted to stay with her; he wanted her to drink warm milk and go to bed and get better, since her shadowed eyes and pale cheeks had convinced him that she was sick.

He was supposed to be in Washington, and she knew it. With a dozen assurances she finally got him to go home, convincing him that she was determined to get a good night's sleep and go back to work in the morning. "All I want is Koala," she told Peter lightly.

Koala was her cat, so named not because he was cute, but because he was so ugly. He'd come to her door one day and moved in without giving her much choice.

Peter hugged her, then turned to leave at last, a haggard-looking man. She loved him so much. "Peter."

"Yes?"

"Promise me that you'll get a good night's sleep, okay?"

He grimaced. "Promise."

She thought that now her day was over. She thought that she could sink into a warm bath and try to think about about the new dig. She wanted to do everything she could to create distance between herself and Sean, the things he had said to her—and the horrible things she had said to him.

But she couldn't forget him; all she could do was miss him.

She couldn't even get comfortable. She ran her bath, but before she could step into the water, the phone rang.

It was her mother, sobbing over the phone, and once again Mandy was cast into the depths of guilt, aware that any decent daughter would have called her own parents by then. She talked to her mother for half an hour, then to her father for another twenty minutes.

They both wanted to fly in immediately, but her father was just recovering from bypass surgery, and Mandy didn't think he should be traveling yet. She managed to persuade them to wait a few weeks, telling them that she was absolutely fine and planning on a trip to Colorado anyway. She talked about the dig with forced enthusiasm, and at last they seemed to believe that it would be all right to wait to see her until the end of the month.

Hanging up from her parents brought no relief. The phone rang again instantly, and this time it was a reporter. She spoke politely to him, but then the doorbell rang. Another reporter. She spoke politely to him, too.

But when a third reporter reached her over the phone she was ready to scream. She had a pounding headache; all she wanted to do was hide.

She got through the third interview, then hurried through her small house, pulling all the drapes shut. She finally got into the freshly filled bathtub, where she strenuously ignored the phone every time it rang.

She sat in the tub for a long time, feeling the heat ease some of her tension away. Again she tried to think about work, to plan for the trip.

The water began to cool, and suddenly she jumped out of it as if she had been scalded. It had suddenly reminded her...of Sean. Of a day in the surf when she had surfaced to face Roberto, when she had backed away from him, when Sean had been there—and their minds had functioned as one.

She grabbed a towel and wrapped it around herself, shaking. She closed her eyes.

She couldn't stop thinking about him. Everything, every little thing, was a reminder.

After a few seconds she groped blindly in the medicine chest for one of the tranquilizers the doctor had given her just after the accident. She swallowed it quickly.

She paused for a minute, breathing deeply. Then she walked into the living room and resolutely did the one thing that would convince her that she had been right not to try. That it was better, much better, to have him hate her than...than anything else.

She picked up the picture on the mantle. The picture of a happy family. Herself, Paul and the baby.

As she stared at the tears welled in her eyes, and the immediate past dimmed slowly away.

12

Sean was back in his cubicle on the fifth floor, sipping his coffee and reviewing his file on the McKinley murder case, when Harvey Anderson sauntered in, leaning against the divider, the daily paper in one hand, his styrofoam cup of coffee in the other.

There was such a grin on his face that Sean sat back, crossing his arms over his chest and arching a wary brow.

"Whew!" Harvey whistled. "Nice, man, nice! Damned if you don't get all the luck."

"All right, Harvey, what luck? So far the situation looks like hell to me. I'm gone for a week, and what did you guys do? You let the paperwork on my desk grow like the stinking yellow pages.

"Hey...!" Harvey lifted his shoulders innocently. "We missed you—what can I say?"

"Thanks. Thanks a lot."

The grin left Harvey's face. He indicated the top file on Sean's desk. "We just got the report back from ballistics. The murder weapon was a Smith & Wesson, fifteen shots. One bullet fired, the one that killed him."

"The same gun found in the house?"

Harvey nodded. "Looks like the wife to me, beyond doubt."

"We can't use 'looks like' with the D.A.'s office, Harvey. You know that. I think it was his wife, too. We're going to need a motive—especially since she's still claiming that it was a break-in. And we can't get anyone except her stepchildren to say that there might have been trouble in the marriage. Let's work on it from that angle."

"His money was motive enough," Harvey snorted.

"Yeah, well..."

"Viable proof in court, yeah, yeah. We'll get it. I've got a hunch on this one." He grinned once again, "They can't all be neat and clean and wrapped up in a bundle for the feds, with glowing praise and the word 'hero' in all the papers."

Sean's eyes narrowed. "Okay, Harvey, out with it."

"Out with what?" His face was all innocence beneath his shaggy brown hair. "What's with you? When did you stop reading the paper?"

"I overslept. Hand it over."

"Man, you get all the luck. A week in the Bahamas and the blonde to boot."

"The paper, Harvey!"

Sean snatched it from him. It was true. His name and the word 'hero' were splattered all over the front page—along with a picture of Amanda Blayne in her doorway.

It shouldn't have been a flattering picture; it was a grainy black-and-white snapshot, and she was in the process of trying to close the door. Even so, she looked beautiful. Distressed, her hair tumbling about her face. Even in black-and-white, you could almost see the color, feel it...smell its fragrance.

Sean glanced over the article and gritted his teeth. The article was mainly about him; she couldn't have commended him more highly.

"Damn her," he muttered, the world suddenly turning a shade of red. What was she trying to do? Buy him off?

He slammed the paper down on the desk.

"Hey! What's with you?" Harvey protested. "If she were gushing all over me, I'd be halfway to heaven. And the big boys down at city hall are thrilled. What with so much corruption going on in the police force these days, they're thrilled to have gotten some favorable publicity for a change."

Sean just shook his head. "If the PR is good for the department, great. I just don't like being all over the paper, that's all."

Harvey didn't leave. He sat down on the edge of Sean's desk. "What was she like, huh?"

"Polite," Sean said curtly. Then he softened. Harvey wasn't actually his partner; Todd Bridges was. But homicide worked in teams, usually on several cases at a time, and the three of them, along with Harvey's partner, Jill Santini, had worked together many times.

They were friends, and Harvey's tone had been more curious than anything else.

"She's a...nice lady. Lots of spunk, lots of spirit. Hey, you can be the liaison between the PD and the FBI. You'll probably get to meet her that way."

"Naw, Sean. You're the man on this one."

"We're a team, right? You take it."

"Really?"

"Really."

"Wow!"

Harvey walked away, leaving his newspaper behind. Sean stared at it for a moment longer, threw it down, then picked it back up. He drummed his fingers on his desk, then picked up the phone and dialed information. He glanced at his watch. It was just after seven.

The hell with it. He dialed her number.

A soft, sleepy, too-sultry voice said, "Hello?"

"What the hell did you think you were doing?"

"I beg your pardon? Oh—Sean."

"Yeah, Sean."

"I don't know what you're talking about."

"Don't you get the paper?"

"I don't read it until I'm awake. Why?" she asked, suddenly defensive. "What did I do? Insult you?"

"No, no, you were glowing."

"Then what's your problem?"

"Too glowing, Mrs. Blayne. It isn't going to change the way I feel about anything."

She was silent, then she laughed bitterly. "Actually, I don't begin to understand how you do feel about anything. If anything I said offended you, I'm sorry. It wasn't intended. Excuse me. If you're done yelling, I have a class in an hour."

She didn't give him a chance to say anything else. She hung up.

He was left staring at the phone.

Harvey came back into his cubicle, his jacket slung over his shoulder. "Ready?"

"For what?"

The other man sighed. "You called me last night—at midnight, I might add—to say you wanted to go over to forensics first thing this morning."

"Oh, yeah. Give me just a second, will you?"

Harvey nodded and disappeared.

Sean stared at the phone again. He picked it up, not at all sure what he really intended to do.

"Hello?" She sounded more alert this time.

"Want to go to a party Friday night?"

"Sean?" she inquired skeptically.

"Yeah, it's me."

"And you're calling to see if I want to go to a party?"

"Yeah, well, it might be a little dull. It's just a...ethnic sort of thing. You're, uh, welcome to invite Peter, too."

"He's out of the state," she answered, and then dead silence came over the wire. "I don't believe you," she said at last.

"Will you come?"

"I..."

"Please."

"You're crazy."

"Probably."

"I..."

"I'll pick you up at seven."

He hung up quickly. He didn't want to give her a chance to refuse him.

"Sean?" Harvey called. Todd was standing there, too, now.

Sean grabbed his jacket, grinning as he joined them. He hadn't slept a wink all night, but suddenly he felt as if he could work three shifts straight.

Todd commented dismally on the weather as they went down in the elevator.

Sean cut him off. "You all coming to the annual bash this Friday?"

"Wouldn't miss it," Todd said, perking up.

Sean grinned. "Good. Harvey, you'll get to meet her after all."

"The blonde? She's coming?"

"Uh, yeah, I think so."

Harvey grinned suddenly, rolling his eyes. "I think there's a whole lot more to this story than the papers know!"

"And it's going to stay that way," Sean declared warningly.

"Sure. Sure it will," Harvey vowed solemnly.

Harvey stared speculatively at Sean's back as they walked out to the parking lot. Sean had sounded serious, and Harvey was surprised.

He and Sean had gone through the academy together. He'd been around when...well, he'd been with Sean's lawyer when they pulled a few strings to get Sean out of jail. It just...didn't seem possible.

He wondered who was in for the worse time, the beautiful blonde, or Sean Ramiro.

Amanda was still partially in shock when she reached the campus. In shock because he had called her, yelling, when she had given him every compliment she could, though she had been ready to scream at the mere mention of his name. And in shock because he had called her back and asked her to a party—just like that.

And also because she hadn't said no.

After a few minutes she roused herself somewhat from her stupor; it was wonderful to be back. There was a giant coffee cake waiting in her office, along with a score of her students and half the faculty. Everybody wanted to hug her, to tell her how grateful they were that she was fine, and how happy they were to see her back.

It was nice to feel so loved, but in time the furor died down.

She had an introductory class that morning, and a second, more advanced class after that. Teaching was fun. She loved it as much as she loved the subject, and it was good to back at work. It was so...normal.

But when her classes were over her mind returned to Sean—and to her own idiocy. Why in God's name hadn't she just told him that he was crazy, that he was absolutely insane, and that no, she wouldn't go anywhere with him? She didn't want to get involved with anyone, and especially a man who was like Dr. Jekyll and Mr. Hyde!

She had barely sat down behind the desk in her office when Valerie Gonzales, one of the associate professors, came by. "How about lunch?" the other woman asked.

"I'm not really hungry," Mandy told her ruefully.

Valerie wrinkled her nose. "I'm not, either, but Ed Taylor came in with a decaying alligator that he's determined to preserve, and the smell of formaldehyde is driving me nuts. Let's get out of here."

Mandy leaned back and grinned. "All you want is the inside scoop."

"That's right. Are you going to give it to me?"

"No."

Valerie shrugged. "I'll buy you a Mai Tai. That ought to do it."

"Think so, huh?"

They went to one of the nearby malls, where one of the restaurants specialized in appetizers. They ordered two apiece. Amanda refused the Mai Tai that Valerie had been sure would make her open up, but she decided that a glass of Burgundy was just what she needed.

And though she certainly didn't open up, she found herself admitting that she was going out that Friday with the "way-out cop," as Valerie referred to Sean. Mandy decided that she needed a little advice, and that Valerie might be able to help her. "Val, all he said was that it's some ethnic thing. What do you think I should wear? Is there some kind of Cuban holiday coming up?"

Valerie sipped her beer and pondered the question. "Not that I know of, so go for something casual. If they're celebrating, they might roast a pig."

"So...?"

"Well, you roast them whole, in a pit in the ground. It's an all-day event. By night it's ready to eat."

"Can you teach me some Spanish? I think I'm going to feel like a fish out of water."

Valerie laughed. "I know you know some Spanish. I swear all the time and you always know what I'm saying."

"Yeah, well, I don't think that's party conversation."

"Okay." Valerie hesitated. *"Buenas noches."*

"Good evening? Good night?"

"Yeah, both. *Como está usted?* How are you? *Bien, gracias*—fine, thank you. Umm...*dónde está el baño?* That one is very important to every woman."

"Why?"

"It means, where is the bathroom." She chuckled softly. "Then there's *te amo.*"

"Which means?"

"I love you."

"Valerie!"

"Aren't you in love with him? Just a little bit?"

"No. I'm not in love with anyone."

"Then it's just sex."

"Of course it's not just sex."

"Wow! Then you have made love, huh?"

"Valerie, stuff some more food into your mouth, will you, please?"

"Sure, but I can't teach you much Spanish that way!"

Friday seemed to roll around very slowly. Mandy fluctuated between longing to see him so badly that she hurt and dreading it so thoroughly that she almost called to cancel.

He didn't call her. She even began to wonder whether he had been serious. He hadn't asked for her address, but then, she was certain he could get it easily enough.

At some point she realized that although he might be crazy, she was the one suffering a terrible illness. She didn't want an involvement, yet she was involved. And that made her dilemma all the worse. She knew that she shouldn't see him. Seeing him would only bring more arguments, more disaster. She still couldn't tell whether he liked her or hated her— or if he was using her.

But none of it mattered. She had to see him. And not even the memory of her tragic past could intrude on that basic desire.

The week was a slow one on campus, too. They were almost at spring break. She made her arrangements to leave for the dig in Colorado on the Monday when the vacation began. She wouldn't really be able to get too involved in the work—she wouldn't have the time—but it would be fascinating just to be a part of it.

As much as she was looking forward with dread and fascination to seeing Sean again, she was glad that she could hop aboard a plane and leave—run away—the Monday after.

Friday night did come, as things inevitably did. He had said seven; at five she was in the shower, shampooing her hair, taking a long luxurious bath. She couldn't help reminding herself that he had usually seen her at her grubbiest, and she wanted to be perfect—as perfect as she could be.

If he was really coming for her...

She had never experienced anything in her life like the emotions and physical agitation that came to her unbidden that night, growing worse and worse as seven o'clock approached. She was anxious and scared and nervous—and her fingers shook so badly that her first application of mascara was applied to her cheeks rather than her eyelashes. Her stomach felt as if fifty jugglers were tossing eight balls apiece inside it. Her palms were damp; her body felt on fire. And to her eternal shame, she seemed incapable of remembering what he looked like dressed, recalling instead every nuance of his naked body. She was trying to pour herself a glass of wine when the doorbell rang.

She dropped the glass and stupidly watched it shatter all over the tile floor. She swept it up in a mad rush, raced to the door—then stopped herself, smoothing back her hair before throwing open the door.

At her first sight of him all the nervous heat and energy and anticipation churned through her anew. He was tan and clean shaven, his hair still damp from the shower. He was wearing a light suit, tailored to fit his physique, enhancing the breadth of his shoulders and the trimness of his waistline. The most noticeable thing about him, as always, was his eyes. So green, so shocking, against the strong planes of his face. The look of character in them gave him his rugged appeal, raised him above such an undistinguished word as "handsome."

Then she realized with dismay that he was in a suit—and she was in jeans. "Oh," she said softly.

"Does that mean come in?" he asked.

"Yes, yes, of course. Come in." She backed away from the door awkwardly. He followed her. For several seconds he stared at nothing but her, then he looked around her house.

There wasn't much on the first floor, just a living room that led to the kitchen on the left, the sun porch in the rear and the staircase to the right. It was pretty, though, she thought. The carpeting was deep cream, the furniture French provincial. The screen that separated the dining area from the rest of the room was Oriental.

"Nice," he said. He meant "rich."

She shrugged. "Thank you. Uh, would you like a drink? I think I need to change."

He acted as if he was just noticing her clothing. Then he frowned. "Where did you think I was taking you?"

"A friend of mine suggested…never mind. Why don't you help yourself. The kitchen is all yours. I'll be right down."

She fled up the stairs, tripping on the last one, and hoped he hadn't noticed. She changed into a kelly green cocktail dress, almost ripping it in her haste to reclothe herself. It seemed very illicit, suddenly, just to be in the same house with him, half-clad. Especially half-clad, and trembling, and thinking that she would just as easily, just as gladly, crawl into a bed, onto a floor—anywhere—with him as she ever had.

Unwilling to consider such thoughts for long, she raced hurriedly and breathlessly back down the stairs.

He was sipping wine and had poured a glass for her. He handed it to her, watching her. She thanked him, then they fell silent.

"How, was, uh, getting back to work?" she asked at last.

"Fine. How about you?"

"Fine."

Silence again.

"I've got great students," she offered.

He nodded. Eventually he said, "We should get going."

"Yes."

She was somewhat surprised to discover that his car was a lemon-yellow Ferrari. He smiled at her look, leaning over her shoulder as he opened the door to whisper tauntingly, "No, I'm not on the take. My father was a cigar king once upon a time, and he left a trust fund, which I managed to invest rather decently."

"Did I say anything?"

"Your eyes did."

She didn't even know where they were going; he drove in silence. When they got onto the Dolphin Expressway, and then onto I-95, she finally asked him.

"Miami Shores," he said simply then lapsed back into silence again.

She decided to break it. "I've been taking a few Spanish lessons."

His eyes met hers briefly in the mirror. "Oh? Why?"

"I thought I should be able to say a few things tonight."

He smiled. "That's nice."

There was something about that smile she didn't like.

He flicked on the radio. Mandy gave up, closed her eyes and leaned back in the seat. It was better than watching his hands on the steering wheel and remembering other places where they had been.

Eventually they turned off the highway and drove through a series of side streets until they pulled into a circular drive fronting a beautiful old Deco residence. Mandy wanted to ask him whose house it was, but he didn't give her a chance. He helped her out, then hurried to the door so quickly that she nearly tripped as she followed him.

He didn't ring the bell; he just walked in. And then Mandy understood that smile.

It was a party all right. It was even ethnic. Half the people there were dressed in green, and on a beautiful rich oak bar at the back of the living room was a massive glass keg of green beer.

"St. Patrick's Day!" she gasped.

"It is the seventeenth," Sean murmured.

"You rat!" It was all she could think of.

"Sean! You made it! Come in, dear, and introduce me to Mrs. Blayne!"

She didn't need to be introduced to his mother; Mrs. Ramiro had apparently given her son the emerald green of her eyes. She was a tiny creature, no more than five-two, slim and graceful, with marvelous silver hair and a smile that could melt a glacier.

Mrs. Ramiro was charming. She had a soft brogue and an equally soft voice, and she was entirely entrancing. "I'm Siobhan, Mrs. Blayne. You come with me!" She winked and tucked Mandy's arm into her own. Then she walked her guest around, introducing her to various people—who seemed to come in all nationalities. Spanish was spoken by some of them, but it was always broken off politely when Mandy appeared, and she was impressed with the sincere interest shown by those who met her.

At last Mrs. Ramiro brought her to the bar, where she was given a green beer.

"You look shell-shocked, child. What's the matter?" Siobhan asked her.

Mandy found herself being perfectly honest. "I thought I was going to have roast pig," she admitted finally, and Siobhan laughed. "I spent all week practicing my Spanish."

"Well, I daresay you'll get to use it. A number of my guests are Cuban and Colombian."

"On St. Patrick's Day," Mandy murmured.

"Oh, everyone's Irish on St. Patrick's Day." Siobhan laughed. "Aren't you, just a smidgen?"

Over the rim of her glass, Mandy saw Sean coming toward them, and she said very clearly for his benefit, "Oh, honestly, I don't know, Siobhan. As far as I know I'm just an American mongrel. No one ever seemed to be able to trace my family."

Siobhan laughed softly again. "I'll warrant there's some Irish in you somewhere!"

Sean smiled down at his mother, helping himself to the green beer. "Maybe there is, Mother. I tried to call her WASP once, and she told me that she was Catholic. Could mean a good Irish priest was nestled in the family somewhere."

"You called her what? Sean!"

"Dreadful of me, wasn't it?"

"Certainly. I don't know how you stood him for all that time, Amanda!" Siobhan shook her head. "I must get back to my other guests. Please, Amanda, have a wonderful time. I'm so glad to meet you. And I promise," she added, her eyes sparkling, "we'll roast you a pig next time!"

Mandy was left to face Sean again. She sipped her beer, staring steadily at him. "You really are a rat."

"Why?"

"You knew what I assumed."

"I'm sorry about the lack of a pig. Well, actually, we do have a pig. Cabbage and bacon."

"Umm."

He set his beer down on the bar and swept hers from her hand, then looped his arms around her and brought her against him. She stiffened, but he seemed not to notice. "There's music out on the patio. People are dancing. Dance with me, Mandy."

She didn't really have a chance to refuse. He simply led her out to the back, where a trio was playing and people were indeed dancing beneath soft colored lights.

The music was slow, and she found herself in his arms. Dancing with him came as easily as making love.

"Why did you come with me tonight?" he asked her at length.

Her face was against his shoulder; her hand was clasped in his. She could feel all the rhythms of his body, and the softness of his dark hair brushing her forehead as he bent his head.

"I—I don't know."

"Are you glad you did?"

"I don't know."

"Do you hate me?"

"I...no."

"You smell great."

"Thank you."

"You feel great."

"Thank you."

"Do you know what I'm thinking?"

"Do I want to know?"

"I don't know." He waited a moment, then continued. "I was thinking that I wish a leprechaun would suddenly whisk all these people away so I could ravish you this very second."

She wondered how just his words could affect her so deeply, but they could. She was glad that she was clinging to him; she needed the balance.

She closed her eyes before she spoke. "I didn't mean what I said, you know," she told him, then hesitated. "About Latins. You know. The, uh, last American remembering the flag."

His arms tightened around her as they swayed.

"You'd marry a Ramiro?"

"That wasn't the question. You never mentioned marriage."

"I suppose I didn't. But if I had—hypothetically, of course—what would your hypothetical answer have been?"

"I—I don't think that I—"

His interruption was a whisper that swept her ear like velvet. "But you can handle an affair?"

She didn't answer him.

"You'll sleep with me, but that's it, huh?"

Suddenly she wasn't leaning on his shoulder any longer; she was being held away from him, and his eyes were searching hers.

And she was desperately wondering why she was here. Dr. Jekyll always turned into Mr. Hyde.

He started to say something, but before he could a slim dark-haired young man tapped his shoulder apologetically, smiled with rueful fascination at Mandy, then cleared his throat as he remembered his mission. "Sean, we've got an emergency call. And you promised to introduce me."

"Harvey Anderson, Amanda Blayne. What's the call?" he inquired, annoyed.

"Mrs. McKinley's being treated at Jackson. Suicide attempt. Sorry, Mrs. Blayne. They want us. Pronto."

Sean's shoulders fell as he stared at Amanda. She knew that he was really aggravated, he had wanted the discussion to go further.

So had she. He never understood her, and it was largely her fault. Still, maybe this was for the best.

"I've got to go," he said. "Mom will see that you get home. I'm sorry."

"It's all right."

"I'll call you."

She nodded, knowing that he wouldn't reach her. She was going to change her flight and leave for Colorado in the morning.

He looked as if he was going to say something else, as if he longed to. As if he longed to touch her one more time.

But he didn't. He just closed his eyes briefly, shook his head and left her.

And perhaps it *was* for the best. Because although Mandy insisted again and again that she could call a cab, Siobhan Ramiro was determined to drive her home. She kept up a pleasant stream of chatter from the north of the city to the south and, surprisingly enough, agreed to come in for coffee before driving home.

Mandy soon discovered why.

As Siobhan sipped her coffee she dropped all pretense of casual interest and stared at Mandy with her clear green eyes. "I think my son is in love with you."

Mandy couldn't pull her eyes away from that green stare. Nor could she give anything but a bitter, honest answer. "Sometimes I think he hates me."

Siobhan lowered her eyes, smiling slightly. "No, he just doesn't always handle himself very well. You see..." She hesitated briefly, then shrugged and continued. "I came here to tell you something. I hope I can trust you. I'm not supposed to know this. A friend of his told me about it, because I was beside myself, worrying about him. There was a spell a few years ago when he had a different woman every week. He almost seemed to—to delight in starting an affair. And ending it. And they were all...blond."

Siobhan sat back in her chair with a sigh. "He grew out of it quickly, though he never became really involved again. Cruelty really isn't a part of his nature. I should have known all along. You see, there was this particular girl...well, he'd been madly in love with her. He wanted to marry her. He was going to meet her parents, she was going to come and meet me. All of a sudden it was off. I found out later that she had been pregnant—and that her parents had forced her into an overseas boarding school after a quick abortion."

"Why?" Mandy gasped, stunned by the story.

Siobhan smiled with a trace of her son's bitterness. "They were very rich. And totally bigoted. The name Ramiro just didn't fit in with their idea of their daughter's future."

"Oh," Mandy said weakly.

Siobhan rose. "Well, that's it. I—I hope I've helped. I noticed the sparks flying at the bar tonight, and knowing him, well, I thought maybe you deserved an explanation."

Mandy bit her lip, rising to escort her visitor to the door. "Siobhan," she said impulsively, "It *has* helped. And I hope you believe that I would never feel that way. Sean...Sean thinks that I do, though. I've got a few problems that he doesn't understand."

"I know," Siobhan said softly. "I know about your husband and your child. And I'm so sorry. But you've got a long life ahead of you. Neither of them would have wished you to spend it in misery."

"I'm afraid," Mandy told her.

"To care again? We all are."

"Siobhan," Mandy said again impulsively, "I'm going away for a while. To work."

"And more than that, to think?"

"Yes."

"Well, whatever you decide, I wish you the best."

"Thank you."

Siobhan kissed her cheek, smiled encouragingly, then hurried down the walk to her car.

Mandy watched the taillights until they disappeared in the night, then thoughtfully closed her door.

13

The dig was a recent one; the site had only been discovered about a year before. A camper had found a piece of bone sticking out of the ground in a field near the mountains. Curious, he had asked another friend to look at it, and luckily, the professionals had been called in before anything could be destroyed.

Mandy's time had just about expired, and she wasn't sure if she was sad—or grateful. There was a yearning in her to go home. She had desperately wanted to get away to think, but she hadn't really thought at all. By day she had chiseled and wrapped and plastered; by night she had lain alone and wished that she was not alone. What frightened her was that, though Sean hadn't actually said so, she knew that he wanted a wholehearted commitment, and she cringed like a child from that thought.

But then, she had thought she couldn't possibly make love with him, and that had occurred easily, beautifully. Maybe all things would follow suit. Maybe all she had to do was take the plunge.

As the afternoon fell she was sitting in her little spot in front of the phalanges of a Tyrannosaurus rex, carefully dusting the last of the sand from them with a sable brush so that they could be prepared for removal.

There was gigantic oak behind her, and a pile of rocks before her, so although the site was filled with workers, she was virtually alone. The find had been magnificent: a dozen of these particular beasts, and then any number of other creatures they had fed upon. She was glad to be alone, yet when she did try to think she panicked and wished that she was in the middle of a crowd.

A shadow suddenly fell across her work. Instinctively she looked up.

She was so surprised that the breath was swept cleanly from her.

Sean was standing there, in a standard three-piece suit. Tall and dark and handsome, a stray lock of hair falling over his forehead, his eyes as green as the spring fields. He stood there silently, then smiled slowly.

"Hello, Mandy."

She eased back at last, just staring for several moments. She lowered her head, thinking that this wasn't exactly how she had wanted to see him. She was in overalls and a dusty lab coat, and half the dirt that had been on the bones was smudging her face.

She shook her head, frowning, before she managed to speak. "What—what are you doing here?"

"I have a paper that needs your signature."

She frowned again. She'd heard from the FBI sporadically throughout the week, and no one had mentioned anything that required her signature.

"You're here on business?"

He hesitated a second too long. "Yes."

She smiled, looking back to the bones, delighted to see him, but wishing she'd had just a little more time.

He reached into his coat pocket for an envelope, then crouched down across from her. "This is it. You said you wanted to testify for Señora Garcia. This is a document compiled from your conversations with the FBI and the Miami PD. I need to get it back to the D.A.'s office. They've set a trial date for late September."

"Oh," Mandy murmured.

She read the document over. It had been accurately compiled and said exactly what she thought. She started to scrawl her name on it. "Is Señora Garcia in jail?"

"No. She's out on bond." He hesitated, then shrugged. "Julio's father is out, too. Peter had been pulling strings for him."

"What about Julio?"

Sean shook his head. "He's in jail. It's probably for the best. He'll definitely get time, and this will count toward it."

Mandy nodded. "Roberto?" she asked.

Sean's mouth twitched grimly. "I don't know what the courts will decide. But he's been connected to everything—drugs, robberies, murder. If they manage the case correctly, he'll end up with a dozen life sentences."

She lowered her head, shivering a bit. She still couldn't help but feel that Roberto deserved whatever he got.

"I, uh, got a telegram from Peter."

She raised her head quickly, frowning. "You did? Why?"

He smiled and reached into his pocket again, then passed her the paper. There were only two words on it, other than the address and the signature: MARRY HER.

Her hand started to shake; she clasped it with the other one and pursed her lips. Finally she said, "I guess he knew something was going on."

"So it seems."

"And you were wrong. He doesn't mind."

"I'm sure he minds." He paused, then asked, "Do you mind what I do?"

She stared at him, then shrugged. "Police work isn't the safest profession."

"But I'm in homicide. I deal with people who are dead—and harmless."

"But the people who made them dead aren't harmless."

He sighed softly. "Mandy, narcotics is a little scary. Not homicide. The last time I pulled a gun before I was on those docks—except on a shooting range—was four years ago. You watch too many cop shows."

She grinned. "Actually, I don't watch any."

"Oh."

"Aren't you forgetting something?"

"What?"

She tilted her head back, determined that, no matter what followed, she would not be punished for anyone else's sins. "I'm a blonde. Daughter of the American Revolution all the way. Rich bitch."

"Yeah, I know. I'm willing to overlook that."

"Are you? And what made you decide that I might not be a bigot?"

He lowered his head. Lowered his head, and lifted his shoulders and hands a little helplessly. "Mandy—"

"Oh!" she cried suddenly.

"What?"

"You're on his hip!"

"What?"

"Move back! Move back quickly. You're on my bone!"

"Oh." Red-faced, Sean scrambled to his feet, quickly moving away. Mandy hurried back to the slightly protruding bone, checking it quickly for damage.

She sighed with relief.

"Er, uh, what is he?"

"Tyrannosaurus rex," she answered absently.

"The big bad guy? The one in all the Japanese horror films?"

"Uh-huh. Except that he wasn't really so bad. See, look."

She stood, skirting the area to show him the complete layout of the skeleton. "Look at his arms—there. See how tiny they were in comparison to his bulk? He couldn't really grab and rip and tear. He could barely get things to his mouth. We think now that he was a scavenger—a carnivore, but one who went in *after* the kill had already been made."

She glanced up and blushed, surprised by the softness in his eyes as he stared at her. "You like your work, don't you?"

"Yes, very much."

"I like it, too. You could teach—me."

She didn't know what to say. As the breeze lifted her hair and wafted it around her face, she knew she should say something but, at that moment, she couldn't.

And then the moment was gone, because Dr. Theo Winter, who was in charge, came around the oak tree with a group of workers behind him, ready to start the plastering process. Mandy introduced Sean, but Dr. Winter was understandably unimpressed with anything but the cache of bones. All he wanted was for Sean to get off the site.

It was a good thing Dr. Winter hadn't seen Sean standing on the protruding skeleton, she thought wryly.

"I guess I'd better go," he told her, surprising her. She wasn't sure whether she was relieved or disappointed.

One of the assistants was asking a question, and she knew she had no right to be standing there talking while everyone else was working. But she didn't seem to be able to move any more than she could talk.

Sean solved that dilemma. He saluted her with a rueful grin, then walked away. She simply stood there, feeling the breeze in her hair, watching him leave.

Why hadn't he asked her to dinner or something? she wondered over and over again as the day wore on. But it wasn't a question that took much pondering on her part. It was going to be all or nothing. They weren't going to date. They weren't going to go for dinner or cocktails, or to the movies, or for a picnic in the park.

They were either going to get married or not—and only if she did marry him would she get to go to dinner and the movies and for walks on the beach. Maybe after the way they had begun it would be impossible to date.

She was beginning to understand him now; maybe he even understood her. She didn't think he was insensitive to her reasons for holding back; he just felt that they could be overcome—and should be.

Mandy thought she might hear from him the next day, but she didn't. He didn't contact her hotel, and he didn't appear on the site. She wondered if he had returned to Miami already and was startled to find herself annoyed at the thought. So much for hot pursuit!

On her last night there was a dinner party for her, which she made it through by rote. She realized that she had actually been doing all of her living by rote—until she met Sean.

There were a million good reasons why she should marry him, two that were extremely important. One, she loved him. Two, if the test she had bought at the drugstore worked, she was expecting his child.

The only thing that stood against her was the panic she felt at the prospect of loving so deeply again.

And the problem, which Sean didn't understand, was that it wasn't just an emotional reaction. It was physical. Her hands would sweat, her heart would beat too loudly. Confusion overwhelmed her at the thought.

Thought... Once upon a time she had assumed that she would simply never have another child, because the horror of loss was so deep. Of course, if not for circumstances, she would have been responsible enough never to let such a thing happen.

And now...now she knew that nothing would keep her from having this child.

Her thoughts would not leave her alone, not even for an instant. Not even while she said her goodbyes, lingered over breakfast to thank everyone—and nearly missed her plane because she seemed so incapable of doing anything right. She groaned while she raced through the airport terminal and decided that she was either going to marry Sean—he *was* serious, wasn't he?—or move to an isolated village in Alaska.

She settled into the sparsely populated first-class section of her plane and picked up a magazine. She had been staring at the picture of an elegant dining-room set for several seconds before she realized that it looked odd because it was upside down. She sighed, then froze.

Because Sean was on the plane, blocking those trying to board behind him, staring down at her in dismay.

"You're in first class?"

"What?"

"Oh, damn!"

He moved on by to let the others pass. Mandy just stared at the seat ahead of her. In a few minutes the passengers were all boarded and belted. The stewardess made her speech on safety, and then they were airborne.

At last Mandy kicked off her shoes and curled her feet beneath her, determined to get comfortable for the duration of the trip, despite the fact that her heart refused to slow its frantic beat. She didn't know if she wanted to laugh or cry. He really meant to force the issue.

The stewardess offered her champagne; she took it, intending to sip it. Instead, she swallowed the contents with a toss of her head.

The stewardess, of course, came right back, thinly concealing a shocked expression—and offered her more champagne.

"There's really nothing to be afraid of," the attractive young blonde told her. "Honestly. Captain Hodges has been flying for twenty years. He's wonderful. You won't feel a bump the entire way."

Mandy shook her head, smiling. "I'm not afraid of flying. I love to fly."

"Oh." Confused, the woman smiled, then quickly walked away.

Mandy stared out the window. They were already high above the clouds. It seemed that they were standing still above a sea of pure white cotton. If only she could concentrate. If only she could think about anything besides the fact that Sean was on the plane.

Her stomach lurched. What was the matter with her? He really did care. He had to care, or he would never have gone so far.

She took a deep breath, shivering. Did she really want to spend the rest of her life alone? Life was full of risks, and, yes, loving was a risk. But what was life except for a lonely expanse of years without the loving?

And now that Sean had touched her life, it seem absurdly bleak without him.

But could she love again? Worry about him, day after day? Pray that he came home each night? And what about children? Could she hold a child again, always knowing how quickly that life could be snuffed out?

"Move your feet."

Mandy started at the sound of his voice, then gasped, spilled her champagne and stared up at him guiltily.

"C'mon, move your feet!"

She did so, and he slid in beside her.

"What are doing up here? You're supposed to be in economy class!" she demanded.

"I bribed the stewardess."

"Stewardesses don't take bribes."

"Everyone takes bribes."

As if on cue, the stewardess walked by, watching them with a curiously knowing eye.

"What did you tell her?" Mandy asked suddenly.

He shrugged.

"Sean?"

"Nothing major." He smiled. "I just said that you were a deranged criminal whom I was trailing from Miami. I said I didn't want to put cuffs on you and frighten the other passengers—I just wanted to keep an eye on you." He smiled pleasantly, reached for a magazine, and gazed idly around the first-class cabin. "Nice."

"Sean, you didn't—"

"I did."

"I'll kill you!" Mandy snapped angrily just as the stewardess walked by again. The woman's eyes, cornflower blue and already big, seemed to grow as wide as saucers.

"Now, now, calm down, Mrs. Blayne," he said in a professional soothing voice. He winked at the stewardess, giving her a thumbs-up sign of assurance.

"Sean Ramiro—"

"Maybe you can plea bargain, Mrs. Blayne. Just stay calm, and I'll be at your side."

"I'm not a criminal!"

"Tsk, tsk, Mrs. Blayne. I'm afraid the State believes that lacing your great-uncle's coffee with that arsenic was a criminal offense."

The stewardess, barely a row ahead of them, stiffened and swallowed, and almost poured champagne on a businessman's lap.

"Sean, I *will* kill you!"

"Please, Mrs. Blayne. I really don't want to have to use the hand-cuffs."

"Oh, Lord!" Mandy groaned, sinking back into her seat and giving up. "There's definitely Irish blood in you—I've never heard so much blarney in my life!"

"Behave," he said wickedly, "and I'll get us more champagne. I do like this," he observed casually. "First class. It's a pity the department is so cheap."

"You really got the department to send you out to Denver?"

"Of course. I had to talk to you about the trial."

Mandy groaned again and turned to face the window. She didn't see the clouds anymore; only the reflection of his face. And for all his dry humor, she thought she saw pain mirrored there.

Her heart began to beat faster. It was the strangest thing, the most awful emotion. There he was, and there it was, all the laughter, all the love. All she had to do was reach for it, but she was unable to, taking two steps backward for every step forward.

She closed her eyes, then jumped when she heard him call the stewardess back.

"Could we get some more champagne, please?" He lowered his voice to a whisper. "I can control her much more easily if I keep her a bit sloshed, you know?"

"Oh, yes, of course!"

"Ohh!" Mandy groaned. "Couldn't you just have paid the difference for a first-class ticket?"

He started to answer her, then paused, thanking the stewardess gravely as she poured Mandy more champagne and offered a glass to Sean.

"Cheers!" he said, clinking his glass against hers.

She pursed her lips stubbornly, refusing to respond.

"Come on, where's the Mandy I used to know?"

A twitch tugged at her lips. "Damned if I know. Last I heard, you were taking a criminal back to Miami."

He started to smile wryly at her, but the stewardess returned with their lunch trays. And then, to Mandy's surprise, he didn't pay any attention to her at all. He was watching the stewardess.

The pretty woman seemed exceptionally nervous, which Mandy thought was Sean's fault, since he had convinced her that Mandy was a criminal.

The stewardess almost dropped the trays, but recovered her poise. Sean continued to watch her as she moved down the aisle, then sat back in his seat, perplexed.

"What's wrong?"

"Hmm?"

"What's wrong?"

She didn't like the way he looked. She really did love to fly, but suddenly she thought of all sorts of disasters. Someone had forgotten a little pin or something, and their jumbo jet was about to fall apart in midair.

Except that the flight wasn't even bumpy. It was so incredibly smooth that it felt as if they were standing still.

She gripped his arm tensely. "Sean," she whispered, "do you think there's something wrong with the plane?"

He stared at her. "The plane? Something wrong?" He shook his head. "I've never felt a smoother flight."

"Then what—?"

"Are you going to eat that steak?"

"What?"

"Eat, will you?"

He didn't pay any attention to his own food. He ate it, but he was giving all his attention to the stewardess.

The woman still seemed a little shaky when she returned. She had poise, though. She smiled; she chattered. It was just that her manner was slightly different, and not only with the two of them.

Mandy tried to quiz Sean again as soon as they trays were removed, but he interrupted her first word, murmuring, "Excuse me for a minute, please."

"Sean!"

But he was already gone. He disappeared into the little kitchen area— right behind the stewardess. And he seemed to stay there a long, long time.

When he emerged, he returned to his seat beside her like a sleepwalker, totally remote.

"Sean..."

"I don't believe it," he murmured distractedly.

"You don't believe what?"

"Shh. You didn't finish your champagne. Drink it."

Drink it. As if she would need it.

"Sean!" She slammed a fist against his shoulder.

"Shh!"

"You said there wasn't anything wrong with the plane."

"There isn't. I swear it."

The stewardess came hurriedly toward them once again, then bent to speak softly in Sean's ear. "We need you now, lieutenant."

He nodded and stood, ready to follow her again. She paused suddenly, looking back at Mandy with dismay.

"Will she be all right?"

"What? Oh, yes, of course. As long as you don't have any arsenic on board."

They disappeared together toward the cockpit. Mandy was ready to scream.

It seemed an eternity before he returned, though it was only about twenty minutes.

"Sean, what the hell is going on?"

"Hey!" someone complained loudly from behind them. "I take this flight constantly. What's going on? They should have announced landing by now. And we should be over land—not water!"

"Damn you, Sean Ramiro!" Mandy whispered, alarmed. "What's going on?"

He turned to her at last. "I didn't want to alarm you—"

"You didn't want to alarm me?"

"Shh! There's nothing wrong with the plane. Honest. In fact, there's really nothing wrong at all. We're just taking a little side trip."

"Side trip?"

"Er, yes."

Just then the pilot came over the loudspeaker. He sounded marvelously, wonderfully calm. He started by explaining that obviously their seasoned passengers would realize that they were not flying their usual route. He assured them that nothing was wrong. It was just that they had a "gentleman" aboard who was insisting that they fly on to José Marti airport— in Havana.

Mandy gasped and stared at Sean. "We're being hijacked to Cuba!"

"Yes, I know," he said uncomfortably. "I tried to talk him out of it."

The pilot then turned the microphone over to the "gentleman" in question, who told the passengers in broken English that he didn't want to hurt anybody, certainly not Captain Hodges, but that he had been away from his homeland now for eight years and was determined to go back.

"I don't believe this!" Mandy breathed. She stared at Sean again. "Can't you do something?"

"I'm afraid not. He's got a Bowie knife at the captain's back and a hand grenade to boot."

"How'd he ever get on the plane?"

"How the hell should I know?"

Their conversation ended at that point, because the stewardess began calmly putting them through a crash-landing procedure just in case they had difficulty landing. There was no panic on plane, possibly because the pilot came on again, assuring them that they had been cleared to land at José Marti.

"I really don't believe this!" Mandy whispered nervously as she prepared for landing.

"I am sorry, Mandy. Really."

"You're sorry?"

"Yeah. I'm trying to convince you that we're a great people, and all you get to meet are the kidnappers and the hijackers."

She gripped his hand tightly. "That's not true. I got to meet one really great cop."

The plane jolted as the landing gear came down.

"Hey, you're admitting it at last. I told you I was really great."

The wheels touched the ground and the brakes came on with a little screech. Mandy prayed that the runway was long enough for the jet.

It was.

In seconds the plane came to a complete stop. And then, seconds later, it began filling with the Cuban military.

Mandy quickly lost Sean. The stewardess came back for him, desperate for a translator.

It seemed to Mandy that she sat there by herself forever. Nothing happened to her; nothing happened to anyone, but it seemed like absolute chaos. There were just too many people on the plane, and at some point, the air conditioning went out.

The heat was sweltering, and just when she thought she couldn't take it anymore an announcement was made that buses would be coming to take the passengers to the terminal, where they were welcome to exchange their money and buy food and souvenirs.

Mandy craned her neck to find Sean, but she couldn't see him. Unhappily, she started to leave along with the others.

She was stopped at the steps by a trim officer with a Clark Gable mustache. She couldn't understand him, and he couldn't understand her. All she could tell was that he was insisting she stay behind, and a case of the jitters assailed her again. Why her? Oh, God! Maybe *they* though she was a murderess, too!

But she merely found herself escorted back to the center of the plane, where Sean was in earnest conversation with several more mustachioed officers. The talking went on and on, with everyone gesticulating.

Finally the man who looked to be the ranking officer shrugged, and the others laughed, then stared at her, smirking.

Sean turned to her then and gripped her arm. "Quick!" he whispered into her ear. "Let's go. There will be a car at the foot of the steps. Get right into it, and act as if you love me to death!"

"What?"

"Shh! Just do it!"

"I—"

"Mandy! Please!"

He didn't give her any choice. He shoved her down the aisle, then hurried her down the stairs.

The car was there, just as he had said, a black stretch limo. She climbed into the back with Sean, and was surprised when the official with the Clark Gable mustache followed.

At last they reached an impressive building with emblems all over beautiful wrought-iron gates. She managed to whisper to Sean, "Where the hell are we, and what the hell is going on?"

"The Swiss embassy," he whispered back. "The pilot is around here somewhere, too. He has to make special arrangements for fuel to get home."

The car stopped. The Cuban official was greeted by a tall blond man, but though this might have been the Swiss embassy, they were still speaking Spanish, and she was lost.

"Sean, I don't care about the pilot. What are *we* doing here?"

"They're, uh, trying to keep me here," he said.

"What?"

He took both her hands earnestly. "Just help me, Mandy. Go along with me. They know who I am."

"Who are you?"

"Oh, it all goes way back. You wouldn't want me to be stuck here forever, would you?"

She gazed at him warily. "Go on."

"Marry me. If I marry an American citizen—"

"You are an American citizen."

"Ah, but I told you, they know me! My father was involved in some things that—"

"Uh-uh! This guy is acting like your long-lost friend."

"Actually, he is. I was in school with him until the night I fled the country."

"I thought you were born in Ireland."

"I was. It's a long story." He put his hands on her shoulders and pulled her anxiously to him. "Well? They've given me a chance. The Swiss will give us a license and a minister. Mandy! Come on! You've got to get me out of this one."

She stared at him for a long, long time. At the sun above them, at the flowers, at the sky, at the beautiful mountains in the distance.

This wasn't how she had expected things to go at all. The other passengers were busy buying trinkets as mementos of their incredible day, while she was here with Sean, listening to the most outrageous cock-and-bull story she had ever heard in her life.

She lowered her head, smiling slowly, and just a little painfully. After all these years, he had come back to his Cuban heritage, and it was his Irish blarney that was showing!

Her past flashed before her eyes. And she knew that although it would always be there, the time had come to gently close the door on it.

"If I don't do this, they'll keep you here, huh?"

"They could put me in prison."

"Oh."

"Well?"

"I don't suppose I could let that happen to you, could I?"

"It would be terribly mean, considering all I've done for you."

She was silent. He gazed at his watch impatiently. "Mandy! We have to do this before they make the fuel arrangements!"

She shrugged. "Then let's do it."

The Swiss were charming. Papers were secured, and they were ushered into a little chapel that adjoined the building. The ceremony was in French, and amazingly quick, because everyone was rushing.

Mandy smiled through it all, wondering how Sean had ever convinced the Cuban military authorities to let him get away with this nonsense.

But when her "I do" was followed by a very passionate kiss, she assumed it would be something they could talk about for ages.

They were whisked very quickly back to the airport. The fuel had been secured, and all the passengers had reboarded with the rum, cigars, and so forth.

They were in the air before Sean turned to her sheepishly at last. "I have a confession to make. I asked Captain Rotello for special permission to marry you. I lied, though I really did go to school with him. And he did know about my father. Our dads had been friends."

"Oh," Mandy said simply.

"Well, do you hate me?"

She looked at him regally, a superior smile playing on her lips. She saw the tension and passion in his wonderful green eyes.

"Actually, no, I have a confession to make myself."

"Oh, really?"

"I knew you were lying all along. I may not speak Spanish, but I'm not a fool."

"Oh," he said blankly.

"I did intend to learn the language, of course. Completely. I mean, I'll be damned if I'll have you and our son talking about me when I don't understand a single word you're saying!"

"Our son?"

"Or daughter."

374 Heather Graham Pozzessere

"We're—we're having one?"

"In December. Maybe November."

He swallowed then, a little stiffly. "You married me...because you're pregnant?"

"I swear I'll hit you! I married you because I love you! Not because of your ridiculous story, and not because I'm pregnant. Come to think of it, you did threaten me about that! But—"

He smiled, his arm coming around her as he interrupted her. "You love me, huh?"

"Yes, and you know it."

"Yeah, well, it just sounds real nice to hear the words now and then. You'd better start practicing, because I'd like to hear them more frequently from now on."

"Hey, what's good for the goose—"

"I love you, Mrs. Ramiro. Desperately. Passionately. I love you, I love you, I love you—"

Unfortunately, the stewardess made an appearance just then.

"She loves me! She married me!" Sean told the woman.

"But I thought she was—you just married a murderess?"

"Oh, well, that—"

"Lieutenant Ramiro, what a line you gave me! Get back where you're supposed to be—in economy!"

But she wasn't serious. After all, it had been a most unusual flight. She merely arranged for more champagne.

Mandy laughed with him while they sipped champagne, then sobered slightly. "Is this real?"

"It's real."

"Sean...I may need help sometimes."

"We all need help sometimes."

"I do love you. So much. I guess I did, even on the island. I wanted to be rescued, but I didn't want to go back. Not to a life without you."

"Mandy..."

His champagne glass clinked down on his tray. His arms swept around her, his fingers curling into her hair. And when his lips touched hers she was hungry for him, so hungry that it was easy to become swept up in his embrace and to forget that they were on a populated plane.

He broke away from her, groaning softly, excitingly, against her cheek. "Mrs. Ramiro, watch your hands."

"No one can see me."

"Well, they might see me! Oh, God, I can't wait till we get off this plane. Your place or mine?"

"Mine. I think we should sell yours."

"I think we should sell *yours*." He smiled. "Oh, hell! I don't care where we go—as long as we get there!"

It took them another two hours to get anywhere; in the end he went to her house, because it was closer to the airport. And though Mandy would have thought that such a feat was impossible, he managed to disrobe them both while climbing the stairs, strewing fabric down the length of the steps, then landing them on her bed in what was surely record time.

She was so happy. So amazed that she was his wife, that they were making love on the evening of their marriage. That they were both totally, completely committed.

It was fast; it was feverish—it had to be at first.

But the night stretched before them. Time for her to warn him that she owned one of the ugliest cats in the world, time for him to warn her that his partners could be a pain in the neck. Time to discuss things that hurt; time to talk about the past, and time to put it to rest.

And then time to make love all over again.

"*Te amo,*" Mandy told him carefully, practicing the Spanish she had learned.

He smiled, tenderness blazing in his eyes, and she murmured the strange words again, "*Te amo*—here," she said, meeting his eyes, then kissing his chest. "And *te amo*—here."

With each repetition she moved against him, finding more and more deliciously erogenous zones.

"And *te amo*—here."

He gripped her hair, breathless, ablaze. He groaned, and at last swept her beneath him, pausing just an instant to whisper, "Mrs. Ramiro. I have never, never heard Spanish more eloquently spoken."

"*Querido!*" she whispered, and contentedly locked her arms about him.

He found life in her arms. And he gave her a new life, all she would ever ask in the world.

"*Querida!* My love, my love."

He kissed her abdomen and smiled as she arched to him.

She knew that she could love again.

Love a child, love a husband.

Even if he was rather manipulating and most certainly strange—and, oh, passionate!—and...

"Sean..."

She simply couldn't ponder it any longer.

It was the...circumstances.

Epilogue

Sean hesitated momentarily after he opened the door, wondering what Mandy's reaction would be to the visitor he was bringing home.

"Amanda?"

He stepped into the entryway of the big old frame house they had bought and stared through the living room to the office. As he had expected, she was at her desk, her reading glasses at the tip of her nose as she pored over term papers.

Katie—a toddling and mischievous two now—was playing sedately with her locking plastic blocks, probably trying to recreate a dinosaur like the one her mother had made her the night before, Sean thought wryly.

"Mandy?" he called again.

She looked up, saw him, threw her glasses down and scooped Katie into her arms before coming to meet him excitedly, her words rushing out.

"Sean, believe it or not, I had the best time in the world today! I went into the market on Flagler because they have the best ham in the world. I have to admit I always resented going there before, because everyone spoke Spanish, but mine has gotten so good, and I got into this wonderful conversation with the clerk and I started to teach her English! I—oh!"

Her spiel came to an abrupt halt when she saw that her husband was not alone, and she stared at her visitor in dead surprise.

Sean slipped an arm around her. "Julio stepped into my office just when I was getting off for the day. He was just paroled, and he was anxious to see you."

"Oh," Mandy murmured.

Julio Garcia, gaunt-looking in a too-big suit, smiled hesitantly and offered his hand.

She took it, balancing her daughter in her other arm.

"I had to come," he told her softly. "The government has released me. But that is nothing. I must ask you to forgive me. I must hope that you understand and can believe that I did not ever wish to harm you. That—that I know now how wrong I was." His eyes were totally in earnest.

Mandy smiled at last, feeling the assurance of her husband's arm around her shoulders. "I forgive you, Julio. How...how are your parents?"

He gave her a smile that seemed to light up the room. "They are well. Even my father is well. The United States gave him a doctor who is good. And Mama, Mama is Mama."

Mandy nodded, then asked curiously, "And Maria?"

Julio laughed. "Mama married Maria off to a man with a will like iron. She is like you—one babe in her arms, one to come."

Mandy didn't ask about Juan or Roberto. Sean had assured her at the trial that Roberto faced so many charges that even if he lived to be an old, old man, he would probably never leave prison again.

Juan, too, would not come up for parole. He had been involved in a narcotics case before the kidnapping, and the judge hadn't shown him one bit of leniency.

"I am very happy for you, Mrs. Ramiro," Julio said. "Congratulations. Your daughter is beautiful."

Mandy discovered that she was able to laugh proudly. "Yes, she is. Thank you."

Katie was staring at Julio with her knuckles shoved into her mouth, but she really was beautiful. She had Sean's green eyes and a headful of ebony curls.

"You wish a son now, yes?" Julio asked.

It was Sean, lightly massaging his wife's nape, who answered. "Not necessarily. I'm awfully fond of girls. A son, a daughter, it doesn't matter. Mandy and I were both only children, and we both wished that we'd had a brother or a sister, so..."

He shrugged, and Mandy flushed, because though they'd both been quite happy about it, this baby was as completely unplanned as Katie had been.

"Well..." Julio cleared his throat and shifted his weight from foot to foot. "I must go now, I did not wish to impose. I just wanted you to know that I appreciate how you told them at the trial that you did not think I was cruel, but needed help. And that I wished so much for your forgiveness. I have a good job already, too. I am a mechanic. One day I will own my own garage."

"I'm sure you will," Mandy said softly.

"Goodbye, then, *señora*. I wish you and your husband and your lovely family all the best."

Sean walked him to the door. Mandy watched them, hugging Katie to her.

When Sean returned she was still smiling, so he arched one of his dark brows curiously. "Okay, out with it. What are you thinking?"

She laughed, managing to hug him and Katie at the same time. "I was just thinking that I really do forgive him with all my heart. Without him, I'd have never met this weird cop who stuck by me through thick and thin—and then married me, to boot.''

"Hey, duty called. And you were such a marvelous blond bombshell.''

"Yeah?''

"Yeah.''

He grinned, then kissed her warmly and deeply until Kate let out an outraged squawk that Mommy and Daddy were crushing her.

They laughed together again, and their eyes touched, full of promises.

Afterglow

Chapter 1

"Look, George, I'm not all that *bored*. And what do you do with a man, anyway?" Chelsea broke off abruptly at George's literal belly laugh.

George was eight months' pregnant.

"All right, so Elliot did do something."

"At the very least, *something*," George agreed. "Stop a minute, Chelsea, I've got to move around a bit. The kiddo is growing restless."

Chelsea watched her beautiful friend ease her way to the edge of the chair, shove off using the arms and achieve a less than dignified upright stance. "There! Goodness, another month of this! I'll tell you, Chelsea, I think it would do men some good if they had to go through this." She patted her stomach and began her slow trek around the living room. "I swear the kid's going to be a drummer."

"Have you and Elliot decided what to name it?"

"It? No, whatever it's going to be, it still has no name. I told him if he didn't come up with something soon that I could agree with, I'd leave the state, have the kid and name it Lance or Brigitte."

Chelsea laughed. "Perfect hero and heroine names," she said.

"Come now, Chels, you've never had a Lance in any of your novels, have you?"

"Well, no, not that outrageous. But my Alex and Delaney and Brent, not to mention my Anthony, are alive and well, at least in my imagination."

"Don't forget that medieval hunk Graelam of yours!"

"Wasn't he a marvelous MCP?"

"At least your heroine broke him in the end. And I'll just bet after you got him domesticated on page four hundred and fifty, he became a total bore."

"True enough," Chelsea said, and sighed. "There's not a man around today to compete with his sublime nastiness, but he did live in the thirteenth century, George. He could hardly have been into sensitivity training. Too bad, but we'll never know what happened to his eternal love for his wife after, say, ten years or so.''

"They probably both croaked from not bathing," George said.

"Not true. I did have them bathe regularly, and I'll tell you, I felt guilty about it. No more medieval novels for me, except, you know, there was this secondary male character, and my fans seem to like him quite a bit—''

"All right, I've got the picture," George said, grinning down at her friend. "Another macho medieval hero in the works."

"And like Graelam, he'll be great in bed."

"All your heroes are, Chelsea. Now, my dear, let's get back to the present, where men shower and shave every morning. There are good men out there, Chels. I found Elliot, didn't I?''

"He's a throwback," Chelsea said, "to the best of my heroes."

"Oh, come on, Chelsea! Here you are finished with a book and at loose ends for how long—a week?—before you hit the computer grindstone again."

"Yeah," Chelsea agreed. "I sent off an outline for the next one yesterday, and I need to do some historical medical research before I start this one. Tell Elliot the hero is a doctor, and if he's real nice to me, I'll let him provide the raw material."

"He'll love it. Now let's find you a neat guy before you begin total immersion again."

"Where? You know I'm not into singles' bars, George."

George smiled and said somewhat complacently, "Well, as a matter of fact, do you have anything against doctors?''

Chelsea groaned and clutched a sofa pillow over her face. "Oh, no, don't tell me that you've conscripted Elliot into this manhunt?''

"As a matter of fact, why don't you come over to dinner Friday night and just see? Consider it firsthand research. Maybe you won't end up using Elliot after all."

"Harrumph! If I used any man I'd ever met as a model for one of my heroes—other than Elliot, of course—my readers would have fits. They don't want beer-drinking, potbellied heroes, George. For heaven's sake, they live with reality! They want the closest thing to a perfect man I can come up with."

"I know. Masterful, gentle, tender, a great lover, arrogant, of course, to add flavor—''

"You got it. There ain't nothin' like that around nowadays, I promise you. Even Elliot snores, I'll bet, and gets nasty every now and again."

"Sometimes, and not yet. Chelsea, surely you—'' George broke off abruptly at the pain in her lower back. "Drat. Not again. I swear this kiddo is going to do me in."

Chelsea bounded up from the sofa, all concern. "You want me to rub your back?"

"No, I'll be fine in a minute. That's one of Elliot's favorite chores, Ben-Gaying my back. Now will you be here for dinner on Friday?"

"Oh, all right. I can't imagine what you're going to drag in here."

"Trust me," George said.

On Friday morning Elliot Mallory, chairman of radiology, made his way down to the emergency room, only to be told that Dr. David Winter was over at Mulberry Union, swimming.

It was a bit early for Elliot's daily laps, but he knew his duty and swiftly changed into his swim trunks and dove into the pool. He didn't stop David until after he'd completed ten laps.

"Elliot! I thought you were an afternooner."

"I am usually," Elliot said. "You got a minute, David?"

"Sure."

Both men swam to the side of the pool and hoisted themselves onto the tiled apron.

"What's up? You got a special case? A problem only I can handle?"

"Nope, and don't sound so hopeful." Damn, but this was embarrassing as hell. He still couldn't quite figure out how George had wrung the promise from him. Well, there was no hope for it. "You busy tonight, David?"

David grinned wryly. "I was going for drinks with a couple of colleagues. Bores, both of them. You have something better to offer?"

"As a matter of fact, I just might. You want to come over to dinner?"

David looked distinctly wary. "Do you mind me asking who's doing the cooking?"

Elliot laughed, remembering David's only venture into George's cooking. "Come on, so the chicken was a little dry and the peas a bit hard."

"Thank God you made the Irish coffee and the cheesecake."

"I guess I agree with you. Let me reassure you that tonight I'm going to be the chef. I promise you a feast to add two pounds."

"I don't mean to sound ungrateful, Elliot. Lord knows George is the most—hey, wait a minute." He studied Elliot's face for a long moment. "All right, who else is coming to dinner?"

"A friend of George's. A very nice woman. A very attractive woman."

David groaned. "All right, I'll bite. What's this attractive, very nice woman's name?"

"Chelsea Lattimer. She's around twenty-eight, never been married, tousled, curly black hair, blue eyes—maybe they're green—but in any case, she's okay, David, I swear." He didn't add that Chelsea Lattimer was occasionally quite outrageous and outspoken. He'd teased her once that he was going to send her to London so she could take the speaker's corner in Hyde Park.

"Well, it's not as if I'm out on the town every night. Lord, this has been a long year!"

And lonely as hell, I'll just bet, Elliot thought silently. David Winter had been seduced by the University Medical Center to come from Boston to become chief of the trauma section. They hadn't become particularly close friends until after Elliot's marriage to George only two months before. The previous six months had seen Elliot sunk in oceans of self-pity, when he wasn't being a snarling dictator to his staff and an arrogant ass to his colleagues.

"Seven o'clock?" Elliot asked.

"You got it. Want to do some more laps?"

"Let's go." He grinned as he slid into the water. "At least you're more of a challenge than George ever was."

Chelsea looked at her image in the mirror. You look like a crow, she told herself. Stop it, Chels! If you compare yourself to your heroines or to gorgeous George, you'll crawl in the closet and never come out.

Well, maybe I'm not too bad. She ran her brush through her thick hair once more, only to see the irrepressible black curls bounce up in different directions. Tangled glory, that's what I've got. Now how about that for an absurd title? Sure beats *Passion's Pulsing Pleasures*, or *Torpid Tender Trials*.

She laughed, gave herself a thumbs-up sign in the mirror and was out of her Sausalito condo in five minutes. It was only a twenty minute ride over the Golden Gate into the city. George and Elliot had moved to his old restored Victorian upon their marriage—only because his was larger, George had assured her. And, of course, George had added, it was so much less plastic and modern than her condo.

As Chelsea wove her way onto Lombard Street she remembered George's words. *Trust me*. Well, since Elliot was such a beautiful man, George certainly wouldn't stick her with a gnome. Would she? Maybe George had lost her objectivity, being eight months' pregnant and all.

She turned right onto Divisidero and headed up into Pacific Heights. This is where I'd live, she thought, if I ever moved out of Sausalito. The view from the top of the hill was breathtaking—all beautiful Bay, Alcatraz, Angel Island and, of course, her beloved Sausalito. She pulled into the Mallorys' driveway ten minutes early. She recognized George's Porsche, Esmerelda, and Elliot's Jaguar, whose unlikely appellation was Cock and Bull. No other cars. So the newest Don Juan doctor of San Francisco hadn't arrived yet. Just as well.

The splendid Mallorys, as she had termed them in her mind, met her with great enthusiasm and plunked her down on the sofa with a white wine, all within five minutes.

"Elliot's making his famous fresh garden bisque soup, Caesar salad, apricot basted ham—"

"Peach, George."

"Yes, peach basted ham—"

"That's all I need," Chelsea interrupted, waving her hand. "Can't you cut out the croutons from the salad, Elliot?"

"Croutons?" George asked. "What's that?"

Elliot laughed, tweaked his wife's perfect nose and said, "That's those little fried pieces of day-old French bread, love. Sorry, Chelsea, but you gotta eat it the way I serve it. What are you worried about? You're a skinny little twit."

"With computer derriere," Chelsea said.

"Oh, bother," George said. "Here I am looking like the proverbial spider and you're worried about having a rounded butt!"

"Exactly," Elliot said.

"If I could manage to heave myself out of this chair, you jerk, I'd make you eat your words!"

"You'd make me eat *exactly*?" Elliot asked, looking innocently bewildered.

"I think I will have a wine spritzer now, servant," George said.

"Don't get huffy, wife, or I won't Ben-Gay you tonight."

Elliot turned in the doorway. "A spider, huh? Maybe that's why I like to rub your back. My vision is limited."

George fell back in her chair, groaning. "Are you sure you want to get married, Chels? Just look at what I have to put up with."

But Chelsea was gazing wistfully after Elliot. "You're so lucky, George," she said with a sigh.

"Yes, I know, but it took the dratted man long enough to realize it. Ah, there's the doorbell, Chelsea. Would you get it? By the time I get myself out of this chair the poor man will think he's got the wrong house and leave."

"You're not George," the man said when Chelsea opened the front door.

"No," she said. "Neither are you." And thank God you're not a gnome.

He looked a bit taken aback, then smiled. "No, I'm David Winter. And you, I take it, are Chelsea Lattimer."

Chelsea nodded and stepped aside. Goodness, she thought, he's not bad-looking. No, not at all. She felt like a shrimp standing beside him, armpit height, she thought. He looked like a reasonable facsimile of a hero. His hair was a lovely chestnut color and his eyes a real hazel, nothing wishy-washy and in between.

"Good grief, George," she heard his deep voice boom from the living room, "I'm not a gynecologist! Please, don't do anything we'll regret this evening."

"Such a sweet-talking man," George said. "Hello, David. You've met Chelsea?"

"Yeah," Chelsea said. "He determined that I'm not you."

"Dear me, if you were, you'd be in deep trouble!"

George beamed at the two of them. A very nice couple, she thought, though David did look very proper in his three-piece suit, complete with white shirt and tie. And Chelsea, marvelous, of course, but very Marin casual in her dark blue corduroy jeans and white knit sweater. She cleared her throat. "I think I'll help Elliot in the kitchen."

To Chelsea's surprise David laughed deeply. "Please, George, don't! Just stay where you are. Trust Elliot, please."

Elliot emerged from the kitchen and greeted David. "A white wine?"

"Fine with me."

"I'll be with you guys in just a minute." He called over his shoulder, "Don't worry, Chelsea. I bought two bottles of Chablis just for you."

"Well," David said after a moment. "It's a pleasure to meet a friend of the Mallorys'. Do you live here in the city?"

"No, in Sausalito."

David's eyes brightened with interest. "It's a beautiful town. I've been looking around there for a house. What part?"

"On Bridgeway. In a condominium complex called Whiskey Springs."

"I've got my sailboat docked just across from you," David said. "We're practically neighbors. But I'm not interested in a condo."

"No, of course not," Chelsea agreed. Perfectly innocuous conversation, idiot. But he made a condo sound like something from the slums. Your turn. Men love to talk about themselves. "You're a doctor?"

"Yes. I've been out here less than a year, actually. I hail from Boston."

"I went to school in Boston," Chelsea said.

"There are so many. Which one?"

"The best one," Chelsea said, tilting her chin up just a bit. "Boston College."

"Oh. An excellent school."

"Did you go to school in Boston?"

"Just medical school. Harvard."

"Oh." A stuffed-shirt former preppie. She should have guessed. "And you were on staff at Mass General?"

"Why, yes. How did you know?"

It fits. "Just a guess. You did undergraduate at Princeton? Yale?"

"Princeton."

"Where did you go to prep school?"

"Andover."

Lord, did it all fit! Well, keep him talking. He was a joy to look at. "Why did you come West?"

"A great offer."

"It must have been a big change."

"Yes, a very big one," he said. He continued to George, "When's the baby due?"

"In four weeks exactly, thank God."

"Is Elliot driving you nuts?"

"No," George said in some disgust, "at least, not in the way you mean. I think he wonders why I'm not still jogging."

Elliot, who had just come into the living room bearing a tray with drinks on it, grinned and said, "I was thinking that I could build her something like a skateboard and she could make her way around on her stomach. She'd certainly be high enough off the sidewalk."

"That boggles the imagination, Elliot." Chelsea laughed.

David became quiet, his thoughts on the very happy couple. And Elliot won't be just a father, he was thinking, he'll be a parent. David had just realized in the past ten months how much he didn't know about his own two children. Sure, he thought, I'm a great father. Haven't I provided them with everything? He shook away his depressing thoughts and looked at Chelsea Lattimer. He felt as if she'd given him the third degree and he'd flunked. Well, he had a long evening ahead of him, and after all, didn't women like to talk about themselves?

"Well," George said brightly, taking away his chance to speak, "how's the beans, doc?"

"Actually, French green beans, George, with pearl onions and slivered almonds," Elliot said.

"Here I was hoping for hot dogs and chips."

There was a brief pause, and Chelsea blurted out, "What kind of a doctor are you?"

"Now I'm chief of the trauma section at the university. I hang out mostly in the emergency room when I'm not in the OR."

"It means," Elliot said, "that he's a damned fine surgeon and has an uncanny and much needed flair for organization."

"Oh," Chelsea said. She'd heard that surgeons, or blades, were normally an obnoxious breed, full of themselves and their great talent. Oh, well, it was just for one evening. Let him keep talking; it would make the time go more quickly. He sent her a smile at that moment that looked anything but obnoxious, and Chelsea found herself smiling back.

"Are you from California, Miss Lattimer?" David asked.

"Chelsea, and yes, from Santa Barbara. My folks still live there."

Aha, David thought. A native Californian and probably so laid back she'd sneer at anything or anyone from the pseudointellectual East Coast.

"Chelsea's dad is a dentist," George said.

"You've got brothers and sisters?"

"Nope, I'm their one and only. I think they gave me one look and decided not to press their luck."

"I'm an only child, too," David said. "My parents couldn't have more children, though I understand they wanted to."

It still fits, Chelsea thought. Produce a son whose first words were probably "conservative" and "rich," and of course they'd want to produce a veritable battalion.

"Naturally," Chelsea said aloud.

That earned her a raised, questioning eyebrow from David Winter. Elliot called them to order then, and they trooped to the table.

"I still can't figure out," George said after everyone was served, "how Elliot can time everything so it's all hot when it hits the table."

"Natural male superiority," Elliot said. "Don't you agree, David?"

"With the dirty look I just got from Chelsea, I think I'll keep my opinions to myself."

"I thought," Chelsea said, annoyed, "that surgeons especially, always gave their opinions, asked for or not."

"Surgeons are just men," David said.

"And women," Chelsea added quickly.

Elliot shot David a rueful look. "We're surrounded by career women, David. Guess we'd better watch our step."

"There are more and more women doctors," David said stiffly. "Most of them, however, still don't go into surgery."

"And why do you think that's the case?" Chelsea asked.

Never in his life had he been asked such a question by another person, much less by a woman he'd just met. Just who the hell did she think she was, anyway? A flaky California rich girl, probably. Sausalito wasn't a cheap place to live, after all. Still, it wouldn't be polite to put her soundly in her place. And his Boston Brahmin parents had taught him manners. He said easily, "Perhaps women don't like such a demanding schedule."

"Or perhaps," Chelsea said, "they aren't given the opportunity. I read an article last year that gave the appalling rate of suicide among women residents in surgery."

"It's a very difficult pace to maintain," David said, proud of himself for his display of patience. "And training takes a long time. I venture to say that most women would prefer doing other things than training for five years or so."

"You mean like having babies?"

"That, yes."

"Would you like some more Caesar salad, David?" George asked, shooting a look at her friend. Chelsea should realize that there would be time enough to infuriate him after she got to know him better.

He shook his head, even as Chelsea said, "Don't you see a place for a bit of compromise, doctor?"

"In medicine? There's been quite a bit already." His tone implied to Chelsea that there'd been far too much.

"But if women didn't compromise enough, men wouldn't be born and have the chance not to compromise."

Elliot laughed and rolled his eyes at his wife. "Your point is well taken, Chelsea, if I understand it."

"I'm certain that an intelligent, open-minded male of the species could," she said.

"Perhaps," David said, wanting to smooth things over, "women have different priorities. A family, children..."

"Men don't count family and children as a priority?"

"That isn't what I meant!" Damned pushy female! He thought with some fondness of drinking with the two boring colleagues. Both male. Neither with a big mouth.

Chelsea, receiving an agonized look from George, forced herself to retrench. But she didn't want to. She wanted to smack the righteous look off his handsome face. "Delicious dinner, Elliot," she said, sending him a dazzling smile.

Outrageous female! David thought. Probably never worked a day in her pampered life. What the hell did she know about priorities, responsibility and achievement?

Chelsea polished off another glass of white wine. She was inevitably feeling more mellow, and a bit guilty. David Winter still appeared as good-looking as he had when she first laid eyes on him, but he was a stuffed shirt, damn it. But, her thinking continued, she had antagonized him, challenged him, made things a bit uncomfortable. I'll back off a bit, she decided.

After the delicious meal George excused both herself and Chelsea and hauled her friend upstairs. George whirled on her friend the moment she'd closed the bedroom door. "You're being obnoxious, Chelsea, and you know it. You probably took a dislike to David on your drive over here, didn't you?"

"He's a stuffed shirt and a preppie," Chelsea said defensively.

"A bit, maybe, but you've been attacking him as if he were Hitler himself! For goodness' sake, give the poor fellow a chance!"

"You think I should change my stripes, huh?"

"You have so many to choose from!"

"You're right, George," Chelsea said, appearing much struck. She added thoughtfully, smiling impishly, "I think I'll try my fluffy, feminine, helpless stripes for the rest of the evening. Maybe it'll loosen up our three-piece-suited preppie doctor from Boston. It's probably exactly what he's used to from women."

"Don't go overboard," George warned as they made their way back downstairs. "He's not stupid."

They heard the men laughing in the living room. David, having added Irish coffee to his three glasses of wine, was feeling no pain. He was stretched out on the floor in front of the fireplace, laughing at one of Elliot's stories.

It took him a good ten minutes to realize that Chelsea Lattimer had ceased her obnoxious comments. Had she indeed been obnoxious? He wasn't so sure now. Indeed, she was laughing enthusiastically at every story and joke he told.

Over more Irish coffee Chelsea, at George's encouragement, waxed eloquent on her ill-fated experience with an interior decorator whose dearest love was to place Dresden shepherdesses on every available surface. Women, David thought, but without rancor this time. All they're interested in is spending money. But she was cute, a bit giddy after all that wine, but that just seemed to add to her burgeoning charm. He watched her dark blue eyes sparkle at a bout of repartee between George and Elliot and decided that this bit of female fluff would be quite nice in bed. Lord knew it had been a long time.

Elliot pulled out Trivial Pursuit and matched himself up with Chelsea. Chelsea, quite aware that Dr. David Winter was nearly as mellow as she, decided to continue her role as the cute lamebrain. She felt sorry for Elliot. They were trounced throughly. But no one really cared. Too much wine had passed down all their respective throats, except George, who had had only a wine spritzer.

"Lord, look at the time," Chelsea said, blinking owlishly down at her watch. "It's nearly one in the morning!"

As they'd all been lounging on the floor during the game, David had gotten quite a good look at Chelsea's legs. Very nice. Very nice, indeed.

"Yes, it is late," he agreed. "I think I'd like to follow you home, Chelsea, if that's okay with you."

He'd taken off his tie and coat, and Chelsea was looking fondly at his muscled forearms. "All right," she said. If he wanted to play masterful protector, it was just fine with her. Maybe he wasn't such a stuffed shirt after all.

They reached her condo some thirty minutes later. Chelsea was sober as a judge. George accused her of having a hollow leg, and she supposed it was true when it came to white wine. She wondered, looking at David as he came toward her from his car, if the same could be said about him. His very nice hazel eyes were a bit glazed.

He stopped about three inches from her and gave her what could only be called a scorching look. "Come here," he said, and drew her into his arms.

Merciful heavens, she thought, one of my heroes couldn't do it any better.

Chapter 2

His mouth was hard and aggressive, and his hands were quickly stroking down her back to curve around her hips.

Her heroes wouldn't do that! Oh, yes, they would, she amended to herself. Most of them were arrogant, conceited, masterful, out and out rakes, she supposed.

Well, this wasn't the eighteenth century!

His mouth suddenly gentled, and for an instant, but just an instant, she responded.

"You're such a sweet little thing," he said against her lips, and pulled her closer.

"Sweet little what?" Dear heavens, was that sterling bit of endearment his introduction to bed?

David raised his head, feeling a bit dazed. She squirmed away from him, and he reluctantly dropped his hands from her very nice bottom.

"I don't know," he said truthfully. "I guess I got a bit carried away."

"Do all preppie doctors from Boston act like they're God's gift to women?"

David's wits returned with some rapidity. He stared down at her. She was sounding like the woman he'd first met. He felt frustrated and a bit angry. "I don't think I'm mistaken, Miss Lattimer. You rather liked what I was doing until—" He broke off in amazement. "You're a tease," he said. "A damned tease. You led me on...."

"I'm not a tease! You're a conceited idiot. If you will remember, Dr. Winter, I didn't know you existed before five hours ago! Well, maybe it was six hours. And just because I was nice to you and listened to your stupid jokes, you believe I want to hop in the sack!"

"What I think is that you're weird," David gritted between clenched teeth. "I would think by the time a woman reached your age, she was through with game playing."

Had Chelsea been sitting in front of her computer, her fingers would have been drumming a wild tattoo on the keys. "You might look like a hero," she said, "but your character leaves a great deal to be desired. Now why don't you go to your precious hospital and fondle a patient!"

"Fondle a patient! Of all the ridiculous—"

"Good night, Dr. Winter." She slammed her key into the lock and was thankful when it turned on the first try. "Don't forget to fasten your seat belt!"

David stared a moment at the slammed door. Damn you, Elliot, he thought. How could you set me up with a nut case? And a probable schizophrenic. From obnoxious to fluff-head to tease.

"He's a no-conversation lecher!"

George looked thoughtfully at Chelsea, who was pacing ferociously about the Mallorys' living room the following Tuesday afternoon.

"I think David is rather amusing," George said. "Lord knows he's very nice to look at."

"What do you know about it?" Chelsea said in a nasty voice. "The only person you hear or see is your damned husband. How could you set me up with that—"

"That what, Chels? Talk about changing your stripes! You made the man feel like he was the most marvelous male specimen in the universe. What did you expect him to do? Kiss your hand at the front door and sweep you a courtly bow?"

Chelsea groused under her breath, finally admitting, "Well, maybe I did go just a bit overboard with the fluffy, air-head feminine act, but—"

"But what? I think you're being unfair. David may be just a bit reserved, but according to Elliot, he's an excellent doctor, has a good sense of humor and deals well with the emergency room staff, which I imagine, can't be a barrel of roses."

"Apples," Chelsea said. "Bed of roses. He called me a tease, the jerk!"

"He's a good kisser, huh?"

"I didn't hang around long enough to really check him out. Well, maybe just a little bit, to punish him for being such a nerd." That really hadn't been the case at all, but Chelsea wasn't about to change now. She was on a roll.

George burst into laughter. "Oh, Chels, I wish you could hear yourself! It's too much! Please, get yourself a glass of white wine. I can't bear all this useless energy."

Two glasses of white wine later, Chelsea was sitting cross-legged on the living room floor, looking thoughtfully at George. "You really think he deserves another chance?"

"I most certainly do," George said. "Why don't we try again, say this Friday night? And, Chels, why don't you wear your own stripes. You know, the natural, fun, loving ones, and no changing in the middle of the river."

"Stream," Chelsea said. "And it's horses, not stripes." She added, her voice glum, "Dr. Winter probably doesn't care for natural, fun, or loving."

"Just give it a shot."

"Look, David, it was all a mistake. George told me Chelsea had the flu. That's probably why you found her behavior a little weird. She was taking antihistamines and drinking, which isn't too bright, admittedly. That would make anyone odd. You did think she was okay, didn't you?"

"Look, Elliot, she's a conceited little rich girl, just like—well, just like some women I've known. She's probably never done an ounce of work in her life, and she's got the nicest bot—" He broke off as a resident approached. After a quick discussion the resident left.

"I've got to go, Elliot. A traffic accident."

"About Friday night?"

"All right. Seven o'clock."

Chelsea, lost in San Francisco in the year 1854, didn't hear the telephone until the fifth ring. Sarah Butler, her part-time housekeeper, companion, phone answerer and good friend, was across the street at the grocery store, buying radishes for some unlikely concoction that would have only ninety-five calories in it.

It was George. "Hi, Chels. Hope I didn't interrupt you, but everything is go for Friday."

"I can't believe David Winter ever wants to see me again."

"Well, he does, and he'll be here with bells on."

"More likely another three-piece charcoal gray suit with a pearl-colored silk tie and a starchy white shirt."

"My, what a memory you have for a man you didn't particularly like."

"All writers have excellent memories," Chelsea said with great, but instant, untruth.

"Sure, and all cats eat Alpo."

"Now that's bizarre, George."

"I know. Get back to the novel. I'll see you soon."

"Chelsea," David said stiffly as he trailed behind Elliot into the Mallorys' living room.

"Hello, David," Chelsea said, looking up from the sofa with a show of mild interest. Oddly enough, she felt a bit nervous, a very unusual state for her, and her voice sounded clipped as she said, "How have you been this past week?"

"Busy. Very busy."

"How interesting."

Yeah, you sound fascinated, David thought, but said nothing. "You feeling okay, George?" he asked, turning to his hostess.

George's back was throbbing more than usual, but she gave David her flawless smile. "Just fine, David."

"Are you over your flu, Chelsea?" he asked.

Chelsea looked at him blankly. George said in a very carrying voice, "Elliot! Where are you? We've got starving folk in here!"

"Ah," Elliot said, emerging with a tray of goodies from the kitchen, "a man's work is never done. At least I'm not barefoot or looking like a spider."

"Jerk," George said with high good humor. "Why," she asked, examining the tray, "is this cheese spread on crackers?"

"Wash out your mouth, woman!" Elliot added to David, "She does know the difference, I think. It's my special homemade cheese ragomontade, artfully set on gourmet wheat—"

George giggled. "Stop that, you're making it up. There's no such thing as ragomontade!"

"Delicious," Chelsea said, "whatever it is. Do you cook, Dr. Winter?"

He arched a brow at her. "Sorry, it's a skill I never acquired."

"Ah, you found a wife to drudge for you, huh?" As soon as the words were out of her mouth she cursed herself silently. Why did she react to him with instant sarcasm?

"Elliot," George sang out, "could you pour Chelsea some white wine?"

"Yes, I did find a wife," David said, "but she didn't cook, either." Take that, you lovely-bottomed, smart-mouthed woman! My God, he thought, looking at her closely, she was blushing!

Despite the reddened cheeks, David had to admit that Chelsea Lattimer looked quite lovely. He was sure he'd think so even if he weren't so horny. She was wearing a yellow silk dress with black doodles on it, and high-heeled black shoes. She'd probably come up to his Adam's apple, he thought. It occurred to him that she must want to make amends. She was certainly dressed to impress.

He discounted his own impeccable appearance.

Elliot shot his wife an "I'm going to get you for this" look, but George just smiled sweetly at him. How could he have fallen for that flu bit? "Chelsea was just telling us her latest plot when you arrived, David."

That drew a startled look. "Plot?" he asked, giving her his full attention. "I don't understand. You're a writer?"

"Yes."

"You're published?"

He didn't have to sound so bloody incredulous, Chelsea thought. "Why, yes." She added modestly, "I was very lucky. In the right place at the right time with the right manuscript, and all that."

"Oh, bosh, Chels," George said. "She never got even one rejection slip, David. The very first publishing house she went to signed her up immediately."

"Which hardcover house are you with?" David asked.

"I'm not. I'm original paperback."

"Oh. Mass market. Well, there are plenty of fine novels in paperback."

"Of course, and the distribution is so much greater. One would rather have two hundred thousand readers instead of just five thousand."

Two hundred thousand! Was that just a number she'd used for illustration? David blinked. Had she bought that condo in Sausalito with her own money, then, and not Daddy's? Why the hell hadn't Elliot told him she was a writer? He shot Elliot a look, which was blandly ignored.

"Perhaps I've read your work," he said. "What name do you use?"

"My own. Chelsea Lattimer."

"Sorry, but I'll keep an eye out. What do you write? Fiction? Nonfiction? Biographies?"

Chelsea looked him straight in the eye. "Fiction. I write long historical novels. The ones filled with adventure, intrigue, lots of romance—"

"And delicious sex," George added, rolling her eyes.

David blurted out before he could stop himself, his voice filled with incredulous distaste, "You write *romance* novels?"

"Yes, I do," Chelsea said. "May I have some more wine, George?" Time out, she thought. Oh, Lord, what should she do now?

"Certainly, Chels."

Chelsea forced herself to drink slowly from her newly filled glass.

David fidgeted with his whiskey for a moment. "Do you plan to switch to more...literary work in the future?"

"Exactly what do you mean, David?" Chelsea asked, not moving a muscle.

"Well, really, Chelsea, that stuff is drivel. It's pap for idiots and frustrated women—"

"I'm not a frustrated idiot, David," George said, winking at Chelsea.

"What do you read, David?" Chelsea asked. "Or perhaps I should say, do you read?"

Elliot seated himself on the arm of his wife's chair. He was grinning; he couldn't help it. He felt rather sorry for David, who was quickly digging a hole so deep he'd have to use a bullhorn to call someone to come to rescue him.

"Well, of course I read. Good literature, the classics, biographies and some bestsellers."

"Which bestsellers?"

"Well, you know, this and that. Whatever is on the *New York Times* Best Seller list, I suppose."

"Ah, you're led by what other people think," Chelsea said. "Don't you have any favorite authors? People you've picked yourself?"

He knew he was fitting himself for his own coffin, but her damned calm, patronizing attitude was too much. "Yes, I like to read Westerns, as a matter of fact. Westerns, of course, aren't exactly great literature, but they have value, good plots, historical insights—"

"My novels also have good plots, historical insights and accuracy."

"But it's tripe! Good grief, men and women never behaved the way those novels have them behave!"

"Have you ever read one?"

"Certainly not," he snapped.

"Why not? As a doctor, it would seem to me to be the epitome of idiocy to draw a conclusion based on not one shred of evidence, or, if you will, make a diagnosis without examining the patient."

"It's not the same thing," he said. He shot Elliot a look of sheer desperation, but Elliot only smiled at him blandly.

"I don't particularly care for Westerns, but at least I've given them a try," Chelsea went on. "At least half a dozen, I'd say. Why isn't it the same thing?"

"Men are better...no—" David plowed his fingers through his hair. "It's just that men's literature is more accurate, more entertaining—"

"Are you saying that women's literature has less entertainment value, less accuracy, than men's literature?"

"It's not true to life."

"You lived in the 1860s? Or shot up a town marshal?"

"Of course not," David said. "Look, Chelsea, can we drop this? I'm sorry if I've insulted the type of novel you write. All right?"

"Certainly," Chelsea said, giving him an "I just tromped you into the ground smile." She wanted to laugh when he practically ground his teeth. "I'll just bet you hated *Romeo and Juliet* and only go to the movies to see people get shot full of holes."

David, unwisely, didn't ignore that aside. "I loved the play and see all kinds of movies," he said, his voice very cool.

"Well, people need romance, all people. Even you, Dr. Winter, must have had those marvelous, romantic feelings with a woman you loved or were infatuated with. Unfortunately, for many people those intense feelings don't last. That's why they read books and go to movies. It fills a need, it presents an ideal, brings back their own memories. Life is sometimes too bereft of—"

"Bull," David said.

"I hope both of you have sharpened your appetites," Elliot said, rising. "Dinner's ready, if I don't mistake my nose. Come on, George, let me heave you out of that chair and into the dining room."

Over spaghetti that tasted like heaven come to earth, David asked George when she would be returning to modeling and TV.

"In November. I'll only be traveling one week a month, so my husband here can't get into too much trouble in my absence."

"You find modeling acceptable?" Chelsea couldn't resist asking David as she crunched into a delicious slice of garlic bread.

"For a woman," he said, grinning at her. "I meant to tell you," he continued to Chelsea, "you look gorgeous tonight. Silk becomes you."

"It's sixty percent polyester," Chelsea said.

"I like a woman who's cheap to keep."

Chelsea laughed. Perhaps he wasn't such a bigoted, intolerant stuffed shirt after all. Perhaps he had a modicum of wit.

Elliot asked George a question, and when she didn't answer, all eyes at the table turned toward her.

"Elliot," George said with great calm, "I think the kiddo is going to come soon."

Elliot turned perfectly white. "But it's three weeks too soon! How do you know, George?" He was out of his chair as he spoke.

"Contractions," George said. "At least we got through dinner," she added, giving her husband a tense smile.

"You love spaghetti," Elliot said wildly. "I was wondering why you were eating like a bird. Oh, God!"

"Who's your doctor, George?" David asked calmly.

"Maggie Smith, at the university."

"What's her number?"

George looked at him helplessly. "It's evening. I don't know. Oh, wait, it's in my address book. I forgot that Maggie insisted—"

"Where's the address book, George?"

She told him. David turned to Elliot. "Why don't you bundle George up and take her to the hospital? I'll call Dr. Smith and meet you there."

Twenty minutes later David pulled his Lancia into the parking garage at the hospital.

"The baby is three weeks early," Chelsea said.

"Probably just as well," David said as he helped her from the car. "She was getting awfully big, and her pelvis doesn't look all that accommodating."

"You never lost your cool. I couldn't think of a thing to say or do. I'm a disaster in an emergency."

"I have two children of my own, a great deal of training and George isn't my wife," David said.

Chelsea shot him a look, but said nothing. He had said that he'd been married. Two children? Were they in Boston with their mother? What had happened to their marriage? Whatever, thank God for his cool, matter-of-fact conduct.

When they reached the waiting room on the fifth floor, a nurse told them that Dr. Smith was with Elliot and George, and that Mrs. Mallory was doing nicely.

"Want a cup of coffee?" David asked.

"How can you be so calm about all this? Oh, yes, your training. I'm sorry. Yes, thank you."

"It's a natural process, Chelsea," he said patiently. "George is young and very healthy, and she doesn't drink white wine," he added.

He left her to get coffee.

"And I don't drink whiskey," she muttered to his retreating back.

Elliot came into the waiting room ten minutes later, looking less distracted. "All's well," he said. "Look, you guys don't have to hang around. Maggie thinks it's going to take a while."

"Both my children were born at the crack of dawn," David said.

"Does George hurt?" Chelsea asked, ignoring David's words.

"She's handling everything just fine. We did Lamaze."

"I think I'll stay around," Chelsea said.

"Me, too," David added.

"It's up to you," Elliot said, running his fingers through his thick dark hair. "I'll come out with progress reports when I can."

"I think," David said slowly, "that the birth process is just as hard on men as it is on women."

Chelsea could only stare at him. "You're kidding," she said finally.

"What I meant was that the waiting is wretched."

"That's true," Chelsea conceded. "If it were my choice, though, I'd rather do the waiting than the yelling."

David winced a bit at that.

"Did you do Lamaze with your wife?"

"No," he said, his voice suddenly terse and chilly. "Margaret didn't want to." He added, a touch of bitterness in his voice, "I didn't get to see my children born."

"I'm sorry," Chelsea said for want of anything better. Deep waters, she thought, and murky. "How old are your kids?"

"Mark is eight, and Taylor is six."

"Two boys, huh?"

"No, Taylor's my daughter. Taylor is an old family name."

"You must miss them very much."

"Yes, yes, I do," David said. He hadn't seen them in six months, since he'd gone back to Boston to visit. And he hadn't stayed all that long.

Margaret drove him bananas. He tried a smile. "I wish we had a deck of cards."

"What's your game?" Chelsea asked, a definite fleecing light in her blue eyes.

His smile widened. "Poker. Five-card stud."

"If you like," Chelsea said in an offhand manner, "you can come to our monthly poker game. This month—next week, in fact—it's at my house in Sausalito."

"Just who attends this poker game?"

"Don't sound so wary! I'll just bet you're picturing a bunch of giggling females, gossiping while they toss cards around."

"Something like that."

"How old are you, David?" she asked him abruptly.

"Thirty-six," he said. "Why?"

"I was just wondering how long it takes a man to develop so many ridiculous assumptions."

"I was always a quick study," he said, grinning at her.

Chapter 3

"George was reading about the Romanovs," Elliot said to David the next day in the hospital cafeteria. "Our son's name is Alexander Nicholas, which is close enough for jazz, I suppose. I guess it beats Lance or Stud."

David raised his cup of coffee. "Congratulations, and the name is quite a handle. George is feeling okay today?"

"She's got the energy of a tiger, which is frightening as hell. She was already out of bed this morning, staring in the nursery window."

"Is she breast-feeding?"

Elliot shook his head. "Her career prohibits it. Can't have a cover girl all filled with milk, you know."

"My wife breast-fed our kids," David said. "Her mother deemed it appropriate."

Elliot looked at David intently and felt a pang of concern. He sounded depressed as hell. "Your kids coming out for the Christmas holiday?"

"Yep. I can't imagine how they're going to adjust to laid back California."

"They'll have a blast, you'll see. Speaking of laid back, did you get Chelsea home all right last night? Rather, at dawn?"

"No, she had her own car. I assume she got home all right." David fiddled with his Styrofoam cup, shredding the rim. After all the interminable waiting during the previous night, they'd come to a truce, of sorts. She'd been almost mellow, and stone sober. He added, "She invited me over this Friday for her monthly poker game."

If Elliot hadn't been so tired and preoccupied, he would have said something to that, probably issued a red alert, but he didn't. He said only, "You'll have an interesting time, I'm sure."

"You look like hell, Elliot. Go home and get some sleep."

The PA system came alive suddenly. "Dr. Winter to ER, stat."

David rose immediately. "Give my love to George, and my blessing to the perfect baby."

Elsa Perkins was efficient, cute and coming on to him. She was a very young nurse, just out of training, but she had the fortitude and stomach of a seasoned trooper, which were necessary to serve in an emergency room. Their patient was a boy with second-degree burns, who, with his friends, had wanted to try some black magic in the family garage. The kids had hung black towels over the windows, lit candles around a crate cum altar—and promptly set the place on fire. The parents were having a fit in the waiting room.

"Okay, champ," David said, gently patting the boy's shoulder. "You're gonna be just fine, but you're not going to feel like slaying any dragons for a while, or burning any more candles. You just lie still while I talk to your folks. Do you hurt anymore?"

The boy had wide brown eyes that were beginning to glaze over from the painkiller. He shook his head.

"Good job, Elsa," David said. "Stay with him until he's out, all right?"

"Certainly, doctor," she replied.

He spoke soothingly to the parents, then talked briefly with the doctor from the burn unit upstairs. The boy was stable, thank the Lord, and with a couple of skin grafts on his legs, he'd be just fine.

Ten minutes later David went into the operating room for three hours, suturing up the belly of a man who'd had his riding lawn mower roll over on him.

Then there was a woman carried in by her white-faced husband, bleeding profusely from what turned out to be a miscarriage. David, an intern and a nurse were covered with her blood before they got her stabilized.

It was nearly ten o'clock in the evening when he finally stopped, drew a deep breath and realized that he was starving.

"I brought you a corned beef sandwich, doctor," said Elsa, giving him her special smile.

"You read my mind," he said, grinning. "Thank you."

"You work so hard." He recognized her tone as "just out of nursing school" doctor worship.

"So do you," he said in a crisp voice. "Sandwich is great. Thanks again."

Her look said clearly that she'd get him anything he wanted, and he carefully gave all his attention to his sandwich. When he was finished, she smiled again.

"Well," he said, standing up and stretching. "At least we didn't lose anyone today."

Elsa's smile fell away. "I'm sorry, Dr. Winter. The older woman who came in earlier with chest pains...she died."

"Damn," David said.

By the time Friday night arrived David didn't care whether or not Chelsea Lattimer's poker party was a group of gossiping women or a troupe of singing parrots. He realized as he drove over the Golden Gate Bridge toward Sausalito that he'd missed her, crazy woman that she doubtless was. He'd called her once, but had gotten her answering machine. He hated answering machines and hadn't left a message.

Chelsea showered, dressed and exchanged her small diamond stud earrings for some gold loops, all within fifteen minutes. The earrings took the longest. She'd just had the nerve to get her ears pierced three months before, and she was still chicken about changing earrings. She stared a moment at the small gold loops. Gives me a certain pizzazz, she decided, and shook her head to make them jingle a bit, which they didn't.

Another fifteen minutes and she was walking out of her small kitchen carrying two trays of goodies—guacamole, tortilla chips and onion dip. The onion dip was for Maurice, her gay interior decorator friend from the city who wouldn't touch anything that was *green*. Sarah, her housekeeper, made it especially for him each time he came over. His real name was Elvin, he'd told her once when he was more than eight sheets to the wind.

He's late, Chelsea thought forty-five minutes later. He probably won't be coming. She, Maurice, Delbert—an over-the-hill jockey who used to race at Golden Gate Fields—and Angelo—an exporter of Chinese oddities who had a shop on Union Street—had already settled down for serious play.

When the doorbell rang she jumped and dropped her cards. Maurice yelped. "Good God, Chels! A full house! Lord, guys, talk about being saved by the bell!"

"Stick it, Maurice. It's David Winter. Please, please be reasonable and not too crazy, all right?"

Why am I so nervous? she wondered, unconsciously pulling down her pink wool sweater. "Hi" was all she could think of to say when she opened her front door. Lord, he looked gorgeous. He was wearing casual corduroy jeans and a ribbed navy sweater.

"Sorry I'm late," David said, shoving a paper bag toward her, "but I stopped to buy some cookies and a bottle of white wine."

She smiled up at him, pleased. "That's all right," she said, dimpling at him. "My friends would kill for a cookie and I'd kill for the white wine."

If at first David thought he'd walked into bedlam, an hour later he was being fleeced by the inmates. Unmercifully, and with great good humor.

Between hands Maurice said to Chelsea, "My God, sweetie, the green stuff is turning black! Please cremate it."

"Oh," Chelsea said, staring at the remains. "I guess Sarah forgot to add lemon. It keeps it from turning, you know."

"Come on, Maurice," Delbert said, "it still tastes good. All you've got to do is close your eyes."

Angelo belched. "More beer, Chels?"

Chelsea got to her feet and headed for the kitchen. David rose to stretch his legs and stare a moment at his dwindled pile of poker chips. He followed Chelsea into her kitchen.

"This place should be raided," he said. "When I saw that gleam in your eyes at the hospital I should have known I'd be out of my league."

"You'll notice who the big winner is, of course," Chelsea said blandly.

"Yeah. You've gotten about twenty dollars off me."

"So far," said Chelsea. She patted his arm and said in a lowered voice, "I wanted to tell you, you're doing great. My friends, well, they're very—"

"California. Laid back. Cutthroats."

"Only three words and you got right to the heart of the matter," she said, grinning. "And you're not even a writer. I am impressed."

He found himself smiling back. She looked cute; that was the only word to describe her at the moment. Her hair was mussed, her lipstick long gone and one earring was hanging precariously off her ear. He touched it.

"I hope they're not too expensive," he said.

"Oh, dear. I haven't quite gotten the knack yet, I don't think. I just got my ears pierced a little while ago."

"Want me to fix it for you?" David didn't wait for an answer. He turned her around and straightened the hoop. "You smell good," he said. His hand strayed to her bare neck.

That feels good, Chelsea realized, and for a moment she closed her eyes and enjoyed his fingers lightly stroking her skin.

"How 'bout we call a halt to the poker game? I don't want to write out any IOUs. I just bet Angelo would send someone to break my legs if I didn't pay up soon enough."

She felt his lips lightly touch her neck. That felt good, too, and she didn't move until his arm came around her and his hand caressed her stomach.

"I thought doctors were rich," she said.

"Probably not nearly so rich as writers," he said, his warm breath against her neck, "and your hours must be a hell of a lot saner than mine."

"So you want me to get rid of Maurice, Delbert and Angelo so we can neck?"

He grinned and ran his fingers through her thick soft hair. "Doesn't sound like a bad idea to me. If you really want to, I suppose I could force myself."

"None of my heros ever has to force himself," she said, slowly easing and turning to face him. "They're always eager."

"Last time I was eager, I got called a jerk."

"Actually," Chelsea said, smiling at the memory, "I called you a nerd, but maybe that was just to George. Don't look so hurt. After all, you called me a tease."

"Hey, Chels, where's my beer?" Angelo's voice carried extremely well.

"Why don't you give Angelo the rest of the six-pack and send him home happy?"

"Stop making out with that poor man, Chels!" Maurice yelled out.

"Ah, come on, Maurice," Delbert said. "He hasn't lost more than twenty bucks."

"Come on out, Chels," Maurice demanded in a louder voice. "We haven't checked this guy out enough yet."

"Yeah, he could be a mad rapist!" Angelo hooted.

"Hell," David said, "I'm never angry."

"My family," Chelsea said. She picked up Angelo's beer and walked out of the kitchen.

Lord, David thought, his eyes following her, she's got the cutest bottom.

Two hours later, and fifty dollars poorer, David stood beside Chelsea as she bid good-night to the poker gang and listened to each of them tell her what to do if he got fresh.

"You go for the lowest moving parts," Maurice said.

"Naw," said Angelo, "you bite his neck. Go right for the jugular."

When she closed the door she turned to face David and, for a moment, was taken aback at the look in his lovely eyes. Hero's eyes, she thought. Brilliant hazel. Very nice, all of him.

"Are you sorry you came?" she asked, not moving from the door.

"Will you loan me enough money for the toll back across the bridge?"

"You could always sell your body on the streets of Sausalito."

"You think I'd only get a dollar?"

"It's Friday night. The toll's two dollars."

"So that's what you think I'm worth, huh?"

"Your worth, doctor," she said, moving toward the wrecked living room, "is still in doubt."

He helped her clean up, grimacing at the black dregs of the guacamole. "That stuff *does* look disgusting. Next time use lemon," he said.

"Is Elliot teaching you how to cook?" she asked, arching an amused brow at him.

"Nope. I was just agreeing with Maurice."

Chelsea stacked the dishes in the sink, then fidgeted a bit putting left-overs into the refrigerator, aware that David was standing in the kitchen doorway watching her every move.

"I suppose," she said in a challenging voice, turning to face him, "that you want to neck now."

"You've got a cute bottom."

"I said neck, not bottom."

"I expect I'd make my way south, eventually."

She eyed him silently for a moment. "I suppose men think that if they've spent money on a woman the next step is bed. Let me remind you that you didn't *spend* a dime. You *lost* fifty bucks through lack of skill and cunning."

"You won about forty of that fifty dollars. Wouldn't you believe me if I swore I lost that money to you on purpose?"

"And that's the same thing? Do you know something, David? I don't even know if I like you."

"You know something, Chelsea? I don't know if I like you, either."

"Then why do you want to neck?"

"Because I think you're sexy. Don't you think I'm sexy, too?"

"Let me tell you something, Dr. Winter. I'm really very used to having the last word."

"Do your heroines always best your heroes verbally?"

She frowned at that. "Sometimes. Well, it depends. If the hero is a Mark I, my heroine gives him all sorts of grief verbally—" She broke off at his puzzled look. "A Mark I hero is the strong, macho, arrogant type. A Mark II hero is the witty, sexy, understanding, neat type."

"Which do you prefer?"

"Both."

"You don't want much, do you, lady?"

"We're talking about broad character types, David."

"That's what I tried to tell you last week. The stuff you write just isn't real, any of it. Your hero's supposed to be a woman's prince, isn't that right? The ultimate man with no flaws, a man who doesn't belch like Angelo, doesn't wag his finger like Maurice and is at least a foot taller than Delbert the jockey. You write fairy tales. Admit it."

"I will admit one thing," Chelsea said. "I write books to entertain. Escapist literature, if you wish. My readers are for the most part women. I ask you, if the very hassled woman of today takes time to read, does she want to read about the trials and tribulations of a real woman and her real husband—real people have to worry about bills, taxes, kids and probably worst of all commuting and the car breaking down. And real life extends to the bedroom. Does a real woman want to read about a man who's too tired to give her pleasure, or even worse, doesn't care.

No, don't interrupt me! I did give you a chance. I write entertaining literature—yes, literature, David. It's not Proust or Stendhal. I have never wanted to write the great American novel. I just want to write what I enjoy reading, and I enjoy writing romance novels.''

"I suppose some women do need that sort of thing."

"If you make it sound like a hefty dose of castor oil one more time, I'm going to smear the black guacamole on your face! Every damned novel, even your ridiculous Westerns, has romance in it. If there were no romance in life, this would be an awfully grim place. Don't you believe in romance? Didn't you experience it when you were going out with your ex-wife? You know, loss of appetite, all your thoughts of that one person—''

David held up his hands and sighed deeply. "How did this happen again? If I recall correctly, we've been through all this in fine detail before. All I wanted to do was neck."

Chelsea, who'd learned from George how to expertly flick a towel, connected with David's thigh with a satisfying thwap. He yelped. She burst into laughter. "I've always said that if intelligent discussion fails, try pain."

David straightened and, without a word, stalked toward her.

"David!"

She flicked him again with the towel, but only got his thick sweater. "Drat!" She chose retreat and scurried around the kitchen table.

"It won't do you any good," David said. "You've now got a Mark I hero on your hands. The Mark II just expired quietly."

"How much do you weigh?"

That stopped him for a moment. "One-eighty. Why?"

Chelsea inched nearer the doorway. "How tall are you, David?"

"Six-one or thereabouts. Why?"

"Well," she said, cocking her head, "you've got the basic ingredients for a Mark I." She dashed toward the open doorway. She yelled over her shoulder, "But I just bet you're slow!" She felt a strong arm circle her stomach, and then she was lifted and carried like a sack of avocados into the living room.

"Put me down, you jerk!"

"Is a jerk better than a nerd?"

"They're both equally repulsive!"

David sat down on the sofa and dragged Chelsea facedown over his thighs. "You've got the nicest bottom," he said, wistfully eyeing her.

"You already said that," Chelsea said, squirming to look up at him. "Parts is parts, David. Now let me up."

"Only if you promise to turn civilized and kiss me."

"All right," she said with no hesitation at all.

He was grinning when he turned her over. "Time to pay up, lady."

She was out of his arms and standing in front of him in an instant. "Your question was in reality two. When I said yes, I was answering only the first. Behold, a calm, civilized person."

He said nothing for a long moment, merely stared at her thoughtfully.

Chelsea said nervously, "I got you fair and square. Why don't you just admit it?"

"I'm trying to figure out what a Mark I hero would do in this situation. How 'bout if I throw you on the floor and tickle you until you plead for mercy?"

Chelsea shook her head. "No, that's a definite Mark II reaction. Much too lighthearted for a Mark I."

"Hmm, how 'bout if I grab you, fling you over my shoulder and toss you in the shower? Lots of cold water."

"That's just punishment with no real satisfaction for the hero. Nope, won't cut it."

"I think I've got it." David rose quickly, grabbed her hand and tossed her down onto the sofa. He eased down on top of her and pulled her hands above her head.

Chelsea didn't struggle. She felt the hard length of him on top of her, but he wasn't too heavy. It had been such a long time since she'd felt anything even remotely close to the kind of warmth he was so easily building in her. He leaned down and very gently touched his lips to hers. "I'm glad you've got a seven-foot sofa," he said against her mouth.

"I can't even think of a raunchy pun to go with that," she said. He kissed her again. "Are we necking yet?" she asked with a Transylvanian accent, and nibbled at his throat.

"No," he said slowly, "I don't think so." He paused a moment, then asked in a very intense voice, "Chelsea, do you ever get serious?"

"You have very white teeth."

"I know. Do you? I mean, do you ever respond to things in an appropriately serious manner?"

"Of course, but *things* rarely call for seriousness. You, on the other hand, probably go overboard with seriousness."

He said stiffly, "I certainly never laugh my way into a woman's bed."

"I wasn't aware that we were in anyone's bed. Besides, I doubt you could laugh your way into the shower!"

"We are, nearly," he snapped, pulling back from her, "and the shower is probably just where you belong."

Chelsea could only stare at him. "You mean you want heavy breathing and perhaps readings from Shakespeare's sonnets?"

"You're really quite immature," he said. "Quite immature." He swung off the sofa and rose, standing over her.

She still couldn't believe he was serious. "Shall I go dress in black?" she asked him, pulling her sweater back into its demure place. "Or perhaps I could just stuff a stocking in my mouth so I wouldn't lacerate your serious sensibilities with my immature humor.''

He shoved his fingers through his thick hair. "Look, Chelsea, a sense of humor is all well and good, but when one is supposed to be serious...and involved, one doesn't want to make the other person feel that what he's doing is something to joke about.''

"I don't believe you," she gasped. "Let me add that that convoluted sentence you just managed to string together is neither a Mark I or a Mark II thing to say. That's a stuffed-shirt-Eastern-pseudointellectual bit of garbage! No wonder your wife divorced you! You are the most full-of-it man I've ever met! And you can't even play poker decently!''

David felt more frustrated than angry. Damn it, she was a frivolous, silly California twit, with no pretense to anything but a cute butt, and her big mouth certainly took the attraction away from that attribute.

"And I am not immature," Chelsea said, scrambling up from the couch. "Just because I don't swoon all over you and sigh when you make your stupid male pronouncements, or moan with great seriousness when you kiss me—''

He shook his head, cutting her off sharply with, "Damn it, you drive me crazier, in a shorter amount of time, than any female I've ever known. Good night, Chelsea. Since you're trying to find a man, I'll be glad to keep my eyes open for you—but I doubt there's any male silly enough to endure your biting his throat like a vampire when he just wants—''

"Vampire! You idiot! If I were looking for a man, you, Dr. Great, wouldn't have gotten a second glance. And just wait a minute," she hollered after him. "I didn't finish my sentence! My sentence before this one!''

"Put it in your next novel! I'm sure you can think up a sufficiently revolting male villain to say it to.''

"I'm going to kill you, George," Chelsea gritted, the slammed door rattling on its hinges. "I'd rather be bored than put up with that stuffed shirt.''

Chapter 4

"Damn it, Elliot, I even called her to apologize yesterday, and she had the nerve to hang up on me!"

"Then what did you do?" Elliot Mallory asked with great interest, although he knew full well what had transpired. Between taking care of Alex and visits from Chelsea, George was going nuts, and she had told him everything.

"I called her back. I asked her to go to dinner with me. And she told me she had a deadline and no time to *waste*! That fluff-headed woman needs a keeper!"

"I like the keeper part," Elliot said, unable to keep the grin off his face. "Usually, Sarah—her housekeeper—does a pretty decent job. What I don't understand, David, is why you're so heated up about all this. It sounds to me like you and Chelsea can't be together for five minutes without one of you going into a royal snit. This time you wanted to be serious and soulful and she wanted to play. Last time you treated George and me to a marvelous battle-of-the-sexes act. And, David, Chelsea isn't immature. She's very open and giving and witty. It's just the way she is."

"You're right. I was out of line, damn her eyes!"

Elliot blinked. He leaned back on his elbows and stared out over the pool. The minute he'd seen David, usually a morning swimmer, come in at one o'clock in the afternoon, he had known he was in for it. Just the night before he'd sworn to George that he wasn't going to get involved anymore—"No, damn it, George, that's it! Those two...keep your hands to yourself, no, stop it, I won't change my mind"—but none of it had done him any good. So much for swearing anything.

"She's so different, and I was very rude. What upsets me even more is that I don't know why I turned into a Mr. Hyde. She's so lovely, so warm, and I...well, I was an ass, damn it!''

"Did you ever hear about Chelsea's parents?" Elliot asked, mentally praying for absolution himself from the sin he was about to commit.

"No, why?''

"Well, if Chelsea acts a bit different sometimes, or flippant, perhaps, you might consider her relationship with her parents. They're really quite rich, you know. Her dad's a dentist, her mom a world traveler. Chelsea's been alone a good deal of her life. I know they don't help her financially, and I'm certain she's much too proud to ask." Not one single lie, he thought, congratulating himself. He was as good with words as Chelsea. Maybe he should take up writing, too. A medical thriller, maybe.

"But the condo in Sausalito. You know real estate prices around here, Elliot.''

"She probably rents it, a special deal, I think George told me once. I don't know how she makes ends meet, poor girl." He managed a commiserating sigh.

"She won forty dollars off me at poker," David muttered.

"Good. Now she'll be able to afford groceries.''

"She has a housekeeper!''

"I think Sarah gives her a break. Chelsea helped her husband get his mystery manuscript read at her publishing house.''

"But what about her writing? Surely the kinds of books she writes sell, don't they?''

Elliot shrugged, saying only, "I've heard that publishing houses don't always pay as promptly as they should. Maybe she's got a problem with advances and holdbacks and stuff like that." Deception was a wearing experience, he thought. Chelsea, to the best of his knowledge, made more money than David, and as for her parents, they were utter screwballs, true, but they loved their only daughter to distraction. Why the hell was George so set on getting these two disparate specimens together?

He heard David say under his breath, "Then she'd never accept money from me. She's so little...I want her to eat.''

"I've got an idea, David," Elliot said, rising and stretching. He felt pleasantly refreshed after his fifty laps. He also felt guilty for making David think Chelsea was a starving waif. "Why don't you wait a week, then give her another call?''

David looked alarmed, and Elliot said sharply, "She won't starve, David. Remember the forty dollars.''

When Elliot dutifully related the conversation to his wife that evening over dinner she burst into laughter. "You, Elliot Mallory, are a born intriguer! Now all I've got to do is work on Chelsea. I've got a week, you say?''

"Yeah, if David doesn't break down and have groceries delivered to her house."

"That was really a nice touch," she said, marveling at his abilities. "Now you just leave the rest to me." She paused a moment, and he knew she was listening. "That, if my radar isn't off today, is the sound of your son demanding his dinner."

Elliot rose, hugged her against him and said, "Let's go marvel over the little devil together, okay?"

Mrs. Cambrey, their live-in nurse, appeared at that moment. She smiled. "You heard him, I guess?"

"Oh, yes, Anna. Why don't you go relax? Papa and I are going to do the honors."

"You two do too many of the honors now," Anna said. "I'm getting lazy and fat."

"It'll be my turn tomorrow," George said. "I'm going to pig out at a Mexican restaurant with a very dear, starving friend of mine."

George eyed Chelsea speculatively as she sipped her spritzer. It was a beautiful clear day, and they were lunching at Chelsea's favorite Mexican restaurant in Mill Valley.

George had waxed eloquent about her perfect son for a good fifteen minutes, giving Chelsea time to down one glass of white wine.

"I understand you're working under a deadline," George said, finally changing the subject as she crunched on a tortilla chip. "Hmm, yummy hot sauce."

Chelsea blinked. "You know I'm not. Where did you ever get that idea? I'm in the middle of the third book of the San Francisco trilogy."

"Oh, dear," George said, looking guilty, "I forgot. Forgive me, Chels. Have you decided what to order yet?"

"George," Chelsea said, bending her patented stare on her friend, "come clean."

"I think I'll try the macho burrito, with beef, not chicken. Come clean? It's just a silly misunderstanding, I'm sure. It's just that David told Elliot he wanted so much to apologize to you, and you told him you didn't have the time for him."

"So I lied," Chelsea said, shrugging elaborately. "I told you how obnoxious he was, George. Apologize, beans! That eastern uptight idiot probably doesn't know the meaning of the word."

"What do you think, Chels? Do refried beans come with the lunches?"

"George," Chelsea said in her most menacing voice. She had to put her flame on simmer because the waitress came up with a big smile and her pencil poised over her order pad.

"Another white wine for my friend, please," George called after her a moment later, as she left with their orders.

"Now," George said, "let me tell you something maybe you don't know about David." Unlike her husband, George was a firm believer in Machiavellian means. After all, she'd taken good care of her brother, Tod. Well, maybe not completely, but...

"I don't want to hear anything about that jerk!"

"It seems that what he said, the way he reacted to your joking around, was all the result of his first wife. It seems that once, when he had just finished a thirty-six-hour shift as an intern, he wasn't able to...well, perform. His wife laughed at him." *Dear heavens, I should be an author! Brilliant!*

If Chelsea were wearing socks, she would have been startled out of them, George thought. Indeed, she seemed so upset that it didn't occur to her to think it unlikely that any man would admit to nonperformance, much less to a woman laughing at him about it.

"But...but I wasn't laughing at him! How could he have thought that? We were joking around, talking about necking and Mark I and Mark II heroes, and we ended up on the sofa. All I did was nibble on his neck— maybe not all that funny, but I was kind of nervous. I just did a tiny bit of my Dracula routine. George, for heaven's sake, I'm not used to lying around with a man on top of me."

I wasn't, either, until Elliot. She said in her most consoling voice—at least she hoped it was consoling—"Poor David, he's so lonely, you know. You must realize that he misses his kids something awful, and he works so hard. Sometimes eighteen hours a day, Elliot told me."

Chelsea sat back in her chair, her white wine in one hand, her chin propped up on the other. "You know, he did very well with my crazy friends that night. And he was amusing, and funny. I just never thought that...well..."

"Exactly," said George. "Ah, here's my macho burrito!"

Chelsea stared down at her nacho plate, but for one of the few times in her twenty-eight years she didn't have any appetite for her beloved Mexican food. "I've been a jerk," she said. "His wife *laughed* at him?"

"So sad," George said, shaking her head as she cut enthusiastically into her burrito.

Chelsea said in a glum voice, "I'll just bet he doesn't call me again."

"Well," George said brightly, "perhaps it's just as well. Maybe it's true that opposites don't attract, or shouldn't, in any case. Hand me the hot sauce, please, Chels."

Chelsea frowned at her, wondering how she could be so utterly insensitive. They weren't really opposites, after all.

"Hello. Chelsea?"

She gripped the phone tightly. "Yes. David?"

"Yes. I was wondering if maybe you were finished with your deadline."

"As a matter of fact I sent the manuscript off just this morning," she said with great untruth. "How are you, David?"

David blinked at the phone. He heard a man shouting at an intern in the emergency room and quickly kicked the door to the small lunchroom shut with his foot. She sounded happy to hear from him. "I, uh, would you like to have dinner with me? Now that you're not under any more pressure from your publisher."

"When?"

"Uh, well, how about tomorrow night? Do you have a favorite place?"

Elsa opened the door at that moment. "Dr. Winter, we've got a motorcycle accident."

"I'll be right there." To Chelsea, he said quickly, "Emergency, I'm sorry. I'll pick you up at seven o'clock, all right?"

"That would be grand," Chelsea said, and smiled, a sweet, tender, understanding smile, as she gently replaced the receiver. Poor man, she thought, looking with a bemused smile at the now silent phone. She'd been insensitive to him with all her joking around. But she had been nervous. She sighed. To be honest with herself, for once, her thinking continued on a rueful smile, she hadn't had that much experience with men, and the little experience she'd had, had left her lukewarm, if not cold. Only heroines in her novels enjoyed sex. Only heroes, spun from her optimistic imagination, were perfect lovers. And how was she to deal with a man whose wife had laughed at him when he couldn't "perform," as George had put it? She shuddered. Even her heroines—although never faced with such a circumstance—certainly wouldn't laugh! No, her heroines would be loving and caring and full of tender concern.

Oh, hell! Reality simply wasn't like what went on in her novels. David was right about that. But for that matter, reality wasn't what was portrayed in his damned Westerns. Stupid, pigheaded man!

Chelsea rose and walked out the front door, yelling back to Sarah, who was making a salad, that she was going for a walk. She crossed Bridgeway and walked down the road that led to the sailboat docks on Richardson Bay. San Francisco and Marin were the most beautiful spots in the United States, she decided. The day was perfectly clear, and when she walked out on the farthest dock she could see Alcatraz and San Francisco in all their glory. She wondered where David's sailboat was berthed.

After a few moments of indulging in the scenery Chelsea began to plot, something as natural to her as breathing. Why not, she thought, consider writing a follow-up trilogy using the children of her current heroes and heroines? She wasn't usually big on sequels because of all their pitfalls—such as heroines now in their forties or fifties still with eighteen-inch waists—but it was something to think about. She remembered how the trilogy had gotten started, all from the fan mail she'd received for one novel, touting the hero's brother. And he, bless his heart, was now the hero in the first of the trilogy.

Chelsea continued wandering, thinking about the young heroine in her current novel. Her name was Juliana—Jules, for short—and she was in for a tough time. Now what should I do once I have her married to the hero? How will he act toward her? Paternal? Benevolent? Yes, of course, that's obvious, but next she...

The blast of a car horn brought her out of her plotting fog.

"Watch where you're going, lady!"

She hadn't realized that she'd stepped off the curb into the oncoming traffic. She shouted out a "Sorry!" and scurried across the street. I know. She'll want her husband to love her, but doesn't know how to go about it. Then Byrony and Brent will get into the act, along with Chauncey and Delaney. Then there's the obsession Wilkes has with her. Ah, endless opportunities....

She stretched out on a blanket in her front yard and plotted away the afternoon.

"You look gorgeous," David said smiling down at Chelsea the following evening precisely at seven o'clock. "You haven't lost any weight, have you?"

She cocked her head. "That's always the least of my problems," she said. "How are you, David? Are you dreadfully tired?"

"No, not really. Today wasn't particularly slow, but it wasn't a madhouse, either."

She patted his arm. "I'm glad. You don't want to wear yourself out. You look very fine. I don't think we should waste your finery on the place I was thinking of. Have you ever been to the Alta Mira?"

He hadn't, and was duly impressed by the panoramic view from the hotel dining room windows.

David ordered a very expensive Chablis, looking briefly toward Chelsea to see if she approved. She did, and beamed at him.

Lord, he thought, forcing his eyes down to the ornate menu, she looked lovely tonight. He liked the clingy dress, but wondered how she managed to get around without stumbling and killing herself on the three-inch high heels she was wearing. Maybe, he thought, she wanted to come up to his chin. Her black hair was fluffy and soft-looking and framed her pixie face adorably.

"And the seafood salads are delicious," Chelsea said after a while. He'd had enough time to study the menu through three times!

David set down the menu and smiled at her. "Why don't you order for me? I'm a sucker for seafood, particularly shrimp or crab. Ah, and here's the wine. Why don't you taste it? You're the one with the expert taste buds.''

Chelsea tasted, approved and ordered for both of them. She sat back in her chair, feeling suddenly shy. She swallowed, then began her tour guide rundown on the sights they could see from their table.

"You keep your fingernails short. I like that," he said when she'd finally ground to a halt with Strawberry Point, just across Richardson Bay from them.

"Oh," Chelsea said, curling her fingers under. She hadn't filed her nails in an age. "Well, it's hard to type with long nails."

"It would be pretty hard on my patients if I didn't keep mine short, too," he said.

"I don't know," she said thoughtfully, a dimple appearing on her left cheek. "If the patient were particularly obnoxious, you could slip just a bit."

He thought of just such a particularly obnoxious man who'd come into the emergency room yesterday with bruised knuckles from a fight and complained because he'd had to wait for thirty minutes. He took another sip of wine, then said cautiously, "I understand that in your profession, your money doesn't come to you regularly."

"That's right," Chelsea agreed. "I call it a bolus of bucks when it does arrive."

"Bolus? Do you know what a bolus is?"

"Sure, it's a big shot of something you give to a patient who needs the something very quickly."

"You got that from Elliot, right?"

"Yep. I'll have to tell George that Elliot has indeed been good for something."

He didn't know what to make of that, but he was tenacious and wasn't to be sidetracked. "Are you expecting a bolus of bucks soon?"

"Why?" She cocked her head questioningly. "Do you need a loan?"

Her voice was teasing, but David, so concerned that she was only eating a salad for dinner, didn't catch it. "No. Wouldn't you like a steak or something more substantial to go with the salad?"

"You, David, haven't yet seen the Alta Mira salads! It's the kind of serving you have to take home and eat for three days."

Oh, God, that was why she'd ordered the salad. He closed his eyes for a moment, aware that he had to tread very carefully.

"When will you get to see your kids?" Chelsea asked, wanting to take his hand, perhaps to comfort him. He didn't look particularly miserable, as George had said he was, but some people hid their feelings very well. Her heroes especially, at least the Mark Is.

"My kids? At Christmas. They'll be coming out from Boston for a couple of weeks. Then, with any luck at all, they'll come out here again during the spring. Would you like a slice of bread, Chelsea? With butter? Here's some delicious-looking strawberry jam.''

She shook her head. "Why don't you have some? It's really wonderful. I bet you really miss them.''

"Yeah, I do. Why don't I order us some soup?''

"David, I'm not all that hungry.''

"All right,'' he said quickly, not wanting her to become suspicious. "You told me you were an only child. That must have been tough.''

"Tough? Not really, I've got a couple of zany parents. Didn't I tell you about them?''

He tried to remember, but only Elliot's words were clear in his mind. "No, not much, at any rate. What makes you say they're zany?''

Chelsea laughed, a clear, sweet sound. "Actually, I think the word was invented for them.'' She saw that he wanted to hear more and set out to making it amusing. "My dad, if you don't recall, is a dentist. Imagine if you can a man in his early fifties, as tanned as any surfer, with a gold chain around his neck. He's a health food freak and jogs five miles a day. All this, you understand, while my mother is either packing or unpacking for or from a trip to the Lord knows where. How about your folks? Are they a bit zany or...ultraconservative?''

"The latter,'' he said. She was so brave, he thought, no bitterness at all in her voice when she spoke of her parents. He couldn't help it. He pictured a lonely little girl—who somehow managed in his mind to have a cute bottom—who escaped her miserable existence in fantasy. "Is that why you started writing?'' he asked abruptly.

Chelsea blinked and took another drink of wine. "Writing? I started writing because, like many writers I know, I'm also a voracious reader, and one day I threw the novel I was reading across the room and said I could do better. That's how I started writing.''

"Oh.'' So she'd read a lot to escape her loneliness. He pictured a lonely little girl curled up in a corner with books piled around her, thick glasses on her nose....

"Do you wear glasses for reading?''

His mental leaps were most odd, but Chelsea didn't mind. She thought again that for a very lonely, overworked man, he was extremely charming. She had a fleeting memory of him lying on top of her on the sofa and felt a bit of warmth at the thought. Oh, well, she thought, it wouldn't have continued even if he hadn't turned weird on her. She probably would have frozen up on him and kicked him out of her condo. She sighed.

"Chelsea, do you wear glasses for reading?'' he repeated, wondering at the myriad expressions that had flitted across her expressive face. Oh, Lord, maybe she couldn't afford glasses. Just maybe...

"No, I've got perfect vision, just like my dad. Old Eagle Eye, I call him.''

Thank God, he thought.

"Do you wear reading glasses—or operating glasses, as the case may be?"

He shook his head. "You're very small," he said abruptly.

That brought forth a merry laugh, which was cut off with the arrival of their waiter, carrying two heaped plates.

"Do you think this will fill in all the cracks, doctor?"

"Most impressive," David said. Lots of shrimp, he thought. That was good.

He took a bite and nodded in approval. "How tall are you, Chelsea?"

"I'm afraid that, like the pink stuff on the plate, I'm also something of a shrimp. Five foot two and a half. My dad used to have me do stretching exercises, complained like mad that it was all my mother's fault, bad genes and all that."

Had Chelsea but known it, she was attaining near saintlike stature in David's eyes for her lighthearted treatment of what must have been an utterly miserable childhood. He saw that she wasn't eating and began talking, to give her time to attack her meal.

"And then there was this guy who came into the emergency room at Mass General with appendicitis. Now that's okay, but he also had a huge tattoo on his belly, in vivid color, of a lady on her back, her legs twined around his navel."

"You're putting me on!" Chelsea nearly choked on her wine. "Please tell me you took a picture?"

"Nope, but the intern who shaved him before the operation was very careful to leave lots of hair on the naked lady's feet. The surgical team nearly broke up."

Chelsea had a faraway look in her eyes, and the dimple was playing on her cheek.

"What are you thinking?"

"Oh, I was thinking about putting a scene in a book like that. The guy's name could be Jonathan, and he could be a minister, say, who'd suffered stomach pains for a long time because he was afraid that people would report his tattoo to the press and he'd be laughed at. You see, some friends talked him into the tattoo when he was very young and in the navy. Poor man. I suppose he'll survive and the surgeon, someone like you, David, would keep mum about it."

David stared at her for a long moment. "You're something else, you know that?"

"Not really," Chelsea said quickly, a bit embarrassed. "Did you like the salad? Would you like dessert? It's really quite obscene here, you know."

"Obscene? That sounds interesting. No, nothing for me. But you'd like something, wouldn't you, Chelsea?"

He'd handled it wrong, he thought when she shook her head. If he'd ordered something, maybe she would have, too. He could at least have talked her into taking bites of his. Well, next time he'd be brighter.

He had a sudden inspiration. "Let's stop and get some cookies, all right?"

"You're determined to add dignity to my derriere, aren't you?"

He gave her a beatific smile.

Chapter 5

Why are you so nervous, you silly twit? Chelsea grinned at her silent castigation. She loved to talk historical to herself. But she was nervous, she supposed, perhaps because David might turn weird on her again. Well, she decided, this time I will act very serious.

To her surprise, when they reached her condo he gently touched his hands to her arms, leaned down and very lightly kissed her. He didn't even give her a chance to show him the temporary depths of her seriousness.

"I'll speak to you soon, Chelsea. Thanks for a great evening." He waved once and disappeared into his car, a black Lancia named Nancy. The car's license plate was NANCY W. When she'd kidded him about having a vanity plate on the way back to her condo, he'd said that even Easterners occasionally had bouts of whimsy.

"Most odd," Chelsea said, walking into her living room a few moments later. She really wouldn't have minded a bit more than that sterile kiss. She jumped at the sound of the doorbell.

"Yes?" she asked, opening the door without unfastening the chain.

"It's David. You forgot your doggie bag."

Chelsea blinked, utterly bewildered. Was that an odd come-on? No, it couldn't be. He was serious. It hadn't been her idea in the first place to trot the rest of her salad home. Wilted lettuce wasn't her idea of gourmet dining. Oh, well, since he had been nice enough to bring it back... She opened the door, and David, smiling down at her, thrust the doggie bag into her hand. "Sleep well," he said, and was gone again.

"Most extraordinarily odd," she said, and tossed the doggie bag into the trash compactor. "Well, I've never known a man from Boston before. Maybe they're all like he is. Odd and cute, and an occasional touch of whimsy."

By the time she eased into bed an hour later she'd convinced herself that he was very tired—after all those long hours at the hospital—and needed his rest.

Next time, she thought, burrowing her head into her pillow, she'd get him to kiss her a bit more. An experiment.

To her surprise, the next morning she was yanked from the 1850s by the ringing phone beside her desk. Usually her agent, editor and friends didn't call her until afternoon, the hours from eight o'clock in the morning until noon being sacred. "Yes?"

"Chelsea? David."

She immediately shifted from her standoffish voice. "Oh, hello. How are you? Just a second, let me turn off my computer."

David heard some shuffling about, then her voice again. "Okay."

"Are you busy tonight?"

"Well, I—"

"I apologize for calling you so late, but I just managed to arrange coverage."

"That's all right," she assured him. "No, I'm not busy. How about I buy you dinner this evening? I know this great place and—"

There was dead silence on the line.

"David?"

He was thinking furiously. The last thing he wanted was for her to spend her meager supply of money on his dinner! "Yes, I'm here. Actually, I wanted to invite you to my apartment—I'll cook you dinner."

"I didn't think you cooked."

"I'm a quick study, don't you remember? Don't worry, I won't poison you."

And so it was that Chelsea, dressed casually in jeans, a pullover and new dangly earrings, drove into the city that evening. He probably invited me to his apartment so he could make out, she thought, cynical and interested all at the same time. But what was wrong with my apartment? Unanswerable.

David lived on Telegraph Hill near Coit Tower, and it took Chelsea thirty minutes to find a parking place. His apartment was more or less a penthouse in a four-flat building. The view was an unbelievable panorama of the Bay and the city. He was cooking the most enormous steaks she'd ever seen out on the covered deck.

"Are you sure you don't need to borrow some money from me?" she asked in a teasing voice after a brief tour of the luxurious apartment. "This is quite a setup, doctor. I'm beginning to think that I'm in the wrong profession."

He nodded and smiled and showed her his study.

"Ah, just look at all those Westerns! And is that Proust tucked back in there? But your collection is lacking, David. Tell you what, I'll autograph some of my books for you. Add some taste and color to your shelves.''

"I'd like that. But better, let me go buy some. You do get royalties, don't you?''

"About thirty-two cents a book. I foresee earning another dollar off you.''

Better than nothing, he thought. He didn't notice the designer jeans she was wearing, which cost a good thirty dollars a leg.

When they sat down at David's kitchen table a little while later David had his fingers crossed. Elliot had told him how long to cook the steak, what vegetable to buy and how long to keep it in the microwave, and what dressing to use on the salad. He'd also bought a huge bottle of white wine, her favorite Chablis, despite the red meat dinner.

"This is decadent,'' Chelsea said, eyeing the huge piled plate in front of her.

"I hope you like everything,'' David said.

She looked him straight in the eye. "Yes, I do. Like everything, that is,'' she added, giving him an impish smile. He looked better than the dinner, she thought. His hair was tousled from his stint of cooking the steaks on the windy deck. He was wearing a white shirt, rolled up to his elbows, with jeans. A nice combination, she decided. She liked the hint of curling hair she saw on his chest.

"Chelsea, eat,'' David said.

She took a bite of steak and made approving noises.

"Are you dreadfully tired, David?'' she asked after managing five bites of steak. She wasn't much of a red meat lover, but he looked so apprehensive she vowed to consume every bit.

"Tired?'' He blinked at that. "No, why would you ask?''

"You work such long hours. Elliot said something about eighteen hours a day.''

Elliot had said that? Why, for God's sake? He did, sometimes, but all of them did. But Chelsea was regarding him with such sweet concern that he hesitated to tell her the truth. He temporized. "Well, occasionally, but not all that often, really. Just sometimes.''

"Ah, very clear, Doctor. I, on the other hand, lead such a lazy life that I many times feel guilty.''

"But your writing—''

"I write about five hours a day, usually. I find that my creative brain cells give out at about one in the afternoon. Then I'm as free as the proverbial bird.''

"Aren't you ever lonely, Chelsea?''

"Sometimes,'' she agreed, forking down some quite well-prepared green beans. "But you see, I have a small group of friends, and I have all my characters, and Lord knows my poor brain is working all the time on their problems.''

"Friends' and characters' problems?''

"Primarily just my characters' problems. My friends do very well without my advice. I do have to watch myself with the plotting. It puts me in something of a fog. I nearly bit the bullet the other day crossing the street without my brain being there with my body.''

He looked alarmed. "You must be careful about that.''

"I was just joking, David. Not to worry.''

"More wine?''

"Certainly," she said, her eyes sparkling. "Sometimes I think I'm a wino in the making.''

"How much do you drink?''

He'd asked in his professional doctor's voice, and Chelsea began to laugh. "Now, David, enough of that. Next thing I know, you'll be sending me a bill for professional care.''

"Oh, no, I promise.''

He was treating her with kid gloves, she realized suddenly. Most odd, was her first thought. And on their last date he'd asked so many questions about her parents and her income. As if she were a mental patient or something. Disconcerting.

She shoved her plate back. "No more, not another bite, you've stuffed me royally.''

He started to urge her to eat more, then bit his tongue. He said easily, "I'll make you up a doggie bag, just like a restaurant.''

Warmed over steak? Surely he must be kidding.

But she only smiled. "Why don't you show me some photos of your kids? I'd love to see them. Do they look like you?''

"Okay, and yes, Taylor does.''

How, David wondered some fifteen minutes later, could he have ever believed her obnoxious or fluff headed? She was warm, caring and showed such interest in his children that he was a bit dazed. In fact, his thinking continued as he rifled through snapshots of a vacation in the Bahamas three years before, she was treating him almost too warmly, as if he were a shell-shocked soldier sent home from the battlefield. A bit bizarre.

As for Chelsea, she was gazing with avid interest at several photos of David in a swimsuit, sprawled on the white sand in Nassau. And the one of him standing, looking every bit as gorgeous as any of her heroes....
She particularly liked the sprinkling of hair on his chest, and the traditional thinner line of hair to his belly.

"Very nice," she managed, her voice a bit thin.

"What? Oh, the pictures? The Bahamas, as I said.''

"No, you. Your photos are very nice. You're an athlete, I suppose.''

"I jog and swim," David said. "And I try not to pig out too often."

"It shows. One thing that drives me crazy is novels where the hero is a businessman who probably sits on his derriere ten hours a day and has the most perfect body imaginable. I simply can't imagine how he could get such a bod, much less keep it." She added, beaming at him, "At least yours is justified."

He groaned. "Not back to Mark I and Mark II, are we?"

"No," Chelsea said firmly. "I don't want you to think I'm frivolous again."

"Look," David said, sliding his long fingers through his hair, "I really am sorry about that. I don't know what got into me."

You remembered your wife laughing at you for being impotent.

"And I have something of a snap temper, I suppose. Are we both forgiven?"

He nodded.

"Behold a very serious woman."

"Please, Chelsea, I didn't mean, that is...do whatever you want to."

"Well, I can't drink any more wine because I've got to drive home in a little while." She paused, seeing his eyes cloud at her words. Poor David, he was so lonely. "Do you like to dance?" she asked abruptly.

"As a matter of fact I do. I'm really quite good."

"Are you now?" She slanted him a challenging look.

"Yes, ma'am. Let's go to Union Street. There's a great place there, but noisy."

"You're on!"

They had a great time until David got beeped. "Damn," he said. Chelsea, fearing the worst, followed him as he immediately went to a phone and made a call.

"Damn," she heard him say again, and then he listened. "I'll be right there. Call Dr. Braidson and tell her what's happened. Ask her to come in right away." He set the phone down, looking at it for a moment as if it were an alien instrument. Why tonight? he was thinking.

He gave her a rueful look. "I'm sorry, but there's an emergency, and my coverage just collapsed under a heap of bodies."

"No problem. I can take a taxi back to my car."

He looked indecisive for a moment. "I'm afraid I've got to let you, but I don't want to, Chelsea. Look, can I see you this weekend? Maybe Saturday? We could go sailing if the weather's nice."

"Fine," Chelsea said, and looked at his mouth.

He quickly leaned down and kissed her lightly. He stroked his long fingers over her jaw, kissed the tip of her nose and left.

"You're not a bad dancer," she called after him. He turned briefly and smiled.

"You ain't, either, kiddo!"

* * *

The morning was sunny and warm a week before Thanksgiving, but Chelsea, as a native Californian, expected nothing else. She dropped down to retie the lace on her sneaker, then stood up, stretched a bit and breathed in the wonderful smell of the eucalyptus trees all around her in Golden Gate Park. She wished George could have been with her today, but Georgina, the cover girl, was off making a commercial in Boston, the first since Alex's birth, and wasn't due back until this evening. Okay, lazy buns, she told herself, let's go!

Chelsea enjoyed jogging. She wasn't as disciplined as George, nor did she have as much endurance, but she could go a couple of miles in the park before collapsing in a heap.

A few moments later her feet were working on maintaining a smooth pace and her brain was solidly in 1854 in San Francisco—before the park was even here, she realized with a smile. Back then she'd have been running on sand dunes and breathing in gritty sand.

Now, her plotting voice said, our hero Michael—nickname, Saint. Love it. I've got to find a couple of books on what doctors knew and did back then, and oh, yes, I've already established him as a great storyteller, so there's no reason not to use funny tidbits about medical history, if I can find them. And as for Jules, it's neat that she's from Maui, a great place then, with all the whalers and—

Chelsea heard the strangled whoosh of a motor right behind her, pulled herself back to the present and turned quickly. But it was too late. A guy was fighting with a moped, and losing. How weird-looking it was, she thought blankly in that split second, with all those tools and things tied to the bars.

The moped slammed into her, and she felt something sharp and cold against her stomach. The force of it sent her hurtling onto her back into a clump of azaleas. Her head struck a rock, and she gasped, a small, soft sound.

Chelsea came to her senses, aware that she was moving and that there was a loud noise dinning in her ears.

"Take it easy," a soothing voice said, and she felt a gentle hand on her shoulder. "Just lie still."

"Where am I?"

"In an ambulance. We'll be at the hospital in just a moment."

"What happened?" Her voice sounded odd, high and thin, almost like a child's. The siren made her head ache abominably.

"A moped hit you and knocked you down. I think the damned fool is stoned."

"My stomach," she gasped suddenly, trying to hug her arms about her and draw up her legs, but she felt hands holding her, and the soothing voice continued telling her to lie still.

It isn't *your* stomach that's on fire, she wanted to shout to that voice, but she didn't. She hurt too badly.

Her mind latched onto her doctor in 1854, Saint. But at the moment she couldn't find the humor in it. "I was on the side of the road, not in anyone's way," she said. Then her mind fizzled out, the pain damping everything.

"I know," the voice said, "just hang on."

What was that about the moped being stoned?

She moaned again, feeling tears sting her eyes.

Suddenly the movement stopped, and she was aware of being flat on her back on some sort of moving table. There were voices and faces peering down at her.

"In here," a woman's clear voice said.

The table stopped, and there was a man leaning over her. "Do you understand me, Miss?"

She licked her lower lip. "Yes," she said.

"Where does it hurt?"

"My stomach."

The face was gone, and suddenly she felt her clothes being pulled off.

"What the hell! Chelsea!"

It was David's voice, blank with surprise. He was leaning over her now, and the other man was gone. "What happened to you?"

"Stoned," she managed. "Moped."

She heard the first man tell him about her stomach.

Suddenly she felt cool air on her chest. Dear God, they were stripping her in front of David. She yelled, "Stop it! Don't you dare take my clothes!"

"Chelsea—" David's voice was low, soothing, immensely professional, and she hated it "—I've got to examine you, and I can't do it with your clothes on. Now, just hold still and relax. All right?"

"No!" She tried to get up, but strong hands were on her shoulders, pressing her down. "Get away from me!"

"I won't hurt you," David said, holding her as gently as he could. Damn it, he had to get her calmed down. "Please, Chelsea, hold still!"

She was panting, the pain jabbing at her, making her want to yell. "Get out, David! You're not going to see me with no clothes on! Get out!"

There were several moments of pandemonium.

David drew a sharp breath. He leaned over her and took her face between his hands. "Listen to me!" He held her head until her eyes focused on his face. "No more of this damned nonsense, do you hear me? I am a doctor and you are now a patient and you're hurt. If you don't hold still, I'm going to belt you. You got that, Chelsea?''

"I don't want you to," Chelsea said.

"I don't give a damn. Now, will you hold still and try to act like a reasonable adult?''

"I hate you.''

"Good, just hold still and try to cooperate.''

Oh, Lord, David thought, finally releasing her. "Your belly hurts?''

"Yes.''

"I'm going to check it out now. Don't move!''

David straightened and took a needle from Elsa, who was standing beside him. "Chelsea, you're going to feel a little prick. I'm just taking some blood.''

She didn't really feel anything, just a bit of odd pressure. "My stomach,'' she whispered. "It feels numb and hot at the same time.''

"I know. Just hold still.'' She heard him say something about crossing and typing, and something else about a crit.

Chelsea felt her shorts and panties being dragged over her hips and down her legs. Her sneakers made a silly thumping noise when they hit the floor. She closed her eyes, feeling more humiliated and embarrassed than she ever had in her entire life. And she hurt.

She gritted out, "The jerk was stoned! I was plotting, David, but it wasn't my fault. I was out of the way!''

"I know. Don't worry now.'' David saw the pool of blood on her belly and motioned quickly to Elsa. Gently he swabbed away the blood. He saw the puncture mark immediately. There had been something sharp on the moped and it had gone into her just as if she'd been stabbed. But how deep? That was the important question.

"Chelsea,'' he asked, "does this hurt?''

"Yes,'' she whispered, flinching away from his fingers.

She heard a woman's voice saying crisply, "Blood pressure 110/80, pulse 145.''

She saw David's head very close to her stomach. "Relax, Chelsea,'' he said, not looking at her. As gently as he could he probed the wound, trying to find the base. He hoped nothing vital had been penetrated. He didn't think so, but he wasn't certain. He said to the nurse, "Get an IV going now.''

His mind was sorting through options as he straightened and took out his stethoscope. He listened to her heart and lungs. Suddenly he heard her moan, and he flinched.

"Chelsea,'' he said, taking her face between his hands again, "something on the moped stabbed you. What we've got to do, now, is an exploratory laparotomy. I can't take the risk that something vital wasn't penetrated. In a moment I'll have you sign some papers. Then I'll give you a shot and there won't be any more pain. All right?''

"It hurts," Chelsea said. "So does my wretched head."

"I imagine it does. But you're going to be just fine, I promise. Now hold still, just another quick prick." He got the IV going and ordered antibiotics.

"I don't like this at all," Chelsea said, trying very hard not to sob. "I don't want you looking at me!"

"Now I'm just going to look at your head." She felt a sheet being pulled over her. It had taken them long enough, she thought angrily. "How many fingers, Chelsea?"

"Four."

"Good, now follow my finger."

She did. He started probing, and she tried to jerk away when he found the small lump behind her left ear. "Hold still," he said sharply. She felt him strike her lightly with something, and one elbow jumped, then the other. "Tell me if you feel this," he said.

"Ouch!"

David took the needle he'd been lightly pricking against her legs and gently scratched it up the bottom of her bare foot. "Feel that?"

"Yes."

He looked closely into her eyes with a silly-looking instrument. He said while he looked, "I don't think there's any doubt that you know who you are and who I am. Your brain is intact. Everything looks good here."

"I don't like lying here like a piece of meat," she said.

"I wouldn't, either. Now I've got to examine the rest of you. Just relax."

He gently turned her onto her stomach, and the pain in her stomach intensified. She stuffed her fist into her mouth.

David checked every inch of her back, bottom and legs. No other puncture wounds, no bruises. He stroked his hands over her ribs. "Any pain?"

She shook her head, not speaking.

He shifted her onto her back again and pulled the sheet over her. Her face was white with pain. He knew he was going to operate, and he also knew he should wait for the anesthesiologist, but he didn't wait. He told Elsa in a low voice to bring morphine.

Chelsea's eyes were closed, and her lashes only flickered slightly when he asked, "There's no pain anywhere but your belly?"

She managed to gasp out, "It's just my rotten stomach!"

"Okay, now I'm going to raise you a bit. Here's a pen. Sign right here."

"What is it? My will? I'm leaving you all my money?"

"No, you're giving me permission to do a laparotomy. That's all."

She wanted to ask what a laparotomy was, but she felt a sharp bolt of pain in her stomach and couldn't think straight. She signed the paper.

"Good," David said. He injected the morphine into her IV line and checked again to see that the tape holding the needle in her arm was secure.

"You're a damned lecher," she gritted out. "Don't you dare pull that sheet down again."

She thought she heard some laughter, but wasn't certain. David was leaning over her again. "Now just breathe normally. You're not going out yet, but the pain is going to all but go away. Then I'm going to take some very pretty pictures of your insides. Then the OR."

What the devil was the OR? she wondered vaguely. Operating room. "No!" she yelled, trying desperately to sit up. Everything was spinning. David's face flickered in and out.

"You look ridiculous in that dumb white coat," she said; then she felt incapable of doing or saying anything else.

She felt insensible, her brain like mush, but at least the pain was only a dull throbbing.

David was saying, "Get me Dr. Madson. I want him to do the surgery."

He took Chelsea's hand in his, and for the first time since he'd seen her sprawled on the gurney he smiled. "You're going to be all right, Chels. And when you wake up you won't be able to yell at me for operating on you." Dr. Madson was the finest abdominal surgeon on staff. He shook his head. She'd actually called him a lecher!

He held her hand while Dr. Corning, the anesthesiologist, asked her questions.

"What do you mean, do I take any drugs?" she asked, her voice slurred and slow. "Ask that idiot on the moped."

"Chelsea, are you on any antibiotics, prescribed stuff like that?"

"No," she said, "not even birth control pills."

Thorpe Corning smiled at David and said suavely, "Something for you to take care of, David. Now, Miss Lattimer, any allergies? Like to penicillin?"

"No, and please stop. I don't do anything except drink white wine."

"All right," Thorpe said, "now here's what's going to happen." Neither doctor was certain that she heard or understood.

"Take good care of her, Thorpe," David said.

"I always do, my man," Dr. Corning said, grinning as he rose. "And since she's a special interest, I'll sing to her while she's going under. I gather that's why you're not doing the surgery?"

"You got it," David said. "Besides, Dennis does pretty stitching."

* * *

Chelsea was aware of white, an endless expanse of white. She frowned, then gasped aloud at the throbbing pain in her stomach.

She heard a voice, a very gentle, firm voice, telling her to hold still.

Then David was saying insistently, "Chelsea. Open your eyes."

She could manage that, just barely. He was blurred at first, but she kept blinking until he was in focus.

David looked down at her, trying to smooth the lines of worry from his forehead. After all, the surgery had gone well. She just looked so small and lost, swathed in the white hospital gown, her face nearly as white as the sheets. Her black hair was tousled, her lips pale, devoid of her usual peach lipstick. She looked vulnerable, helpless, and he wished he could magically change this day into tomorrow. Even with painkiller, she would feel like the pits for a good eight more hours. He saw her bite her lower lip. He gently picked up her hand and held it.

"Chelsea," he said, "I know you hurt, but try not to fight it, all right? Just take shallow breaths. Abdominal surgery isn't pleasant, but the pain won't last all that long. I'll give you something for it in a little while."

"What are you doing here?" she asked, his words going through and over her head. She felt muddled and heavy and stupid. "I'm in bed, but my bedroom isn't white like this. I didn't invite you to spend the night, did I?"

"Not this time, no. You're in the hospital. Do you remember the moped?"

"I'm not stupid or senile." She flinched, remembering that odd sharp pain in her stomach. Now she remembered everything.

She heard him chuckle.

"You told me it wouldn't hurt anymore. What's wrong?"

He heard the fear in her voice and repeated what he'd already said. "You've had surgery. You were very lucky. The wound didn't penetrate anything important. You're going to be up and about in another week."

Surgery! Someone had cut her open! David!

But she couldn't work up the outrage to tell him that he'd had no right—no right at all—to cut her open; she felt too crummy. She swallowed the gasps of pain that threatened to erupt from her throat and turned her face away on the very hard pillow.

David straightened, releasing her hand. Dennis Madson had done a fine job. The incision was small, the stitches set beautifully, and he'd only given David an understanding smile when he'd said he didn't want to assist. David had paced the waiting room like an expectant father during the entire surgery, too scared out of his wits and much too worried to assist Dennis. It was only when it was over that Dennis had showed him the results.

He wished he could find something to say, but he couldn't. He knew she was upset, hurting and confused. He smoothed some black curls away from her forehead again, his touch featherlight. He thanked the good Lord that he'd been there in the emergency room to take care of her.

"You silly woman," he said very softly, smiling crookedly as he remembered her shouting at him, "You lecher!" He knew stories were already buzzing around the emergency room about Dr. Winter's lady friend coming in and yelling at him for taking off her clothes. He wondered how long he would have to endure the inevitable razzing.

Seeing that her face was white with pain, he shaved the time by thirty minutes. He said nothing to her, merely injected some more morphine into her IV. Not enough to put her under, just enough to take the edge off the pain.

To his chagrin he was called back to the emergency room. He spoke to her softly, but she didn't respond. He instructed a nurse to stay with her until he returned.

He closed his eyes for a moment when he heard a soft sob come from the narrow hospital bed.

Chapter 6

"Mercy, Chels, you look like a pale little Madonna!"

Chelsea looked up at gorgeous George smiling down at her, Elliot at her side.

"Why aren't you in Boston?" Chelsea asked, frowning.

"I got in last night. It's now today, morning to be exact. Never again will you go jogging without me. Was that head of yours in medieval England?"

"No, in San Francisco, in 1854, but it wasn't my fault."

"We know," Elliot said, gently squeezing Chelsea's hand. "You look good, Chelsea, a lot better than you did after your surgery."

"You saw me then? I don't remember you, Elliot."

"Well, I didn't get to see the pretty stitches on your belly, but David assured me that they were the best he'd ever seen."

Chelsea closed her eyes a moment against Elliot's wicked grin and her own dire embarrassment at her encounter with *Dr.* Winter, not just David Winter.

Elliot felt George's elbow in his ribs and said, "When you're feeling better, remind me to tell you about the time George came out of the anesthetic singing the French national anthem."

"I didn't know you'd had any surgery, George," Chelsea said, momentarily diverted from her thoughts, just as Elliot had hoped she'd be.

"She did, and scared the wits out of me. I remember finding her clutching her stomach, huddled against the refrigerator."

"Wearing your bathrobe," George added.

"At least yours was legitimate, George. There can be nothing more lowering than to be hit by a stoned moped," Chelsea said.

"She's speaking Georgette Heyer," George said. "She must be feeling better."

"You might know that the fellow didn't have a single injury," Elliot said. "Does that make you feel better?"

"I'm going to put a contract out on him."

"On who?" David asked, coming into the room. "Not me, I hope."

Chelsea felt every bone in her body shudder with embarrassment. She couldn't bring herself to look at him.

Chelsea didn't say a word, and David, put out by her ridiculous attitude, said, "You could thank me, Chelsea. I didn't let them shave you."

She gasped, and Elliot said quickly, shooting a quelling glance toward David, "Well, Chelsea, George and I brought you some obscenely fattening chocolates. George thought flowers would be a waste. She said you'd prefer stuffing your face."

"What I would prefer," Chelsea said, tight-lipped, "is to stuff them in David's face."

"No gratitude in this life," David said with a mock sigh.

"You operated on me!" Chelsea struggled to sit up, felt a terrible tugging pain in her stomach and flopped back down. "I know the law, Dr. Winter. You can't operate on anyone unless they sign consent forms!"

"You did," David said.

"I wouldn't! I didn't!"

"Would you care to see them?"

"Now, Chels," George began.

But Chelsea was now remembering signing something. "You tricked me," she said, lowering her eyebrows and indulging him with her most menacing stare. "It was something about my will—"

"No, that's what you said. I explained that it was a consent to do a laparotomy."

"Lapawhatamy? What the dickens is that? You didn't explain that, David. I am going to sue your socks off. I'm going to—"

"Just a moment, Chelsea," David said. "You have some visitors who gave me all the permission in the world to do whatever I wanted to."

"Cookie!"

"Comment ça va, mon petit chou?"

"Dad! Mother!" Chelsea gasped. "You were in Paris, Mother, you were...oh, I'm fine and I am not a little cabbage!"

Mrs. Mimi Lattimer, a very pretty woman in her early fifties with hair as black as her daughter's, leaned over Chelsea and pecked her lightly on her cheek. "I just flew back from Paris last evening, *ma chère.* Then we get this call from Elliot. *Et voilà! Ton père* got us on the first flight to San Francisco this morning."

Dr. Harold Lattimer, tanned, fit and with his daughter's vivid blue eyes, kissed her other cheek. "We'll be hearing fractured French for a while, Chels. You were plotting in the middle of the street, weren't you?"

"No, Daddy, really." She interrupted herself, saying abruptly, "Daddy, this *man* operated on me without telling me! I want you to smack him, sue him, send him back to Boston!"

"Now, Cookie," Dr. Lattimer said, "this man took very good care of you. He told me all about your injury and what was done. I approve. You were a bit of a pain in the butt, weren't you, in the emergency room? Caused a bit of commotion?"

Chelsea stared at her father. "There is no more loyalty toward offspring in this world," she said.

Dr. Lattimer laughed, revealing teeth as straight and white as his daughter's. "Cookie, don't be an idiot. Tell you what, all these folk are going to be getting you up soon. How about if I walk you around?"

Chelsea moaned, wrapping her arms about herself. "I don't want to move, not even for you, Daddy."

David, who had been watching this interplay, began to frown. He looked sharply at Elliot, and Elliot, understanding that look, just grinned and shrugged. If he was seeing an example of parents not caring about their only child, David thought, he would jump off the Golden Gate.

"Elliot," he said, his voice sharp, "I want to speak to you."

Saved by the dentist, Elliot thought, for before he could respond Dr. Lattimer said, "Tell us, Dr. Winter, when is this girl going to be released into her parents' custody?"

"Another three days. We'll want to build her strength back up before she goes home. Are you and Mrs. Lattimer staying?"

"*Bien sûr!*" said Mimi Lattimer, beaming at this very acceptable man. "Our little *chou* needs tender loving care." She paused a moment, her busy fingers twisting the beautiful pearls around her neck. "I wonder how the dear French would say that."

Chelsea moaned. Any port in a storm became a madhouse when her parents arrived. She didn't open her eyes when she felt David take her wrist. His fingers were long, she knew, the nails blunt.

"Why don't you go talk to your lawyer?" she asked when he released her hand.

He laughed softly, and without thinking, without realizing her parents were standing on one side of the bed, George and Elliot on the other, he gently rubbed his knuckles over her cheek. "Keep thinking nasty thoughts. It'll take your mind off your belly."

Harold Lattimer shot an interested look toward his wife.

"*L'amour*," Mimi announced.

David straightened like a shot. To Elliot's amusement a dull flush spread over his face.

Chelsea, who hadn't caught what her mother had said, muttered, "Daddy, would you please remove this lecherous maniac? I will decide what to do and tell you later."

"*L'amour sans…*" Mimi searched frantically, shrugged, smiled charmingly and added, "*Sans le* or *la* recognition."

Chelsea stared up at her mother. "Mother, have you slipped a cog? Do you have jet lag?"

"Why do you call this nice man a lecher, Cookie?" Mimi asked. "A maniac I can understand, but a lecher?"

George said, "Chelsea is very modest, Mimi. As I well know, in the emergency room nothing is sacred."

"You're right, of course, George," Mimi said. "That wouldn't be at all romantic, now would it?"

"Mother!" Chelsea wailed.

David said firmly, "I think it's time for Chelsea to rest a bit. Why don't you all come back this afternoon?"

"George and I will drop you off at the Fairmont," Elliot said to Dr. and Mrs. Lattimer. "That's where you're staying, right?"

"Always, dear boy," Mimi said. "When Chelsea visits us there, her plotting brain goes haywire. It's that grand, ornate lobby, you know, all that—"

"Mother!"

"*Oui, oui, ma chère.*" Mimi patted her daughter's cheek. "You do what Dr. Winter tells you, all right? Your papa and I will come back later. And don't excite yourself."

Harold Lattimer said thoughtfully, "I believe that in French it would translate much differently, my love."

"Daddy!"

There was dead silence in the room. David couldn't think of a thing to say, and Chelsea looked as though she were ready to spit nails.

"All right, Cookie, we're off now. Do as you're told, all right?"

"Ha!"

The door closed behind the Lattimers and the Mallorys. David shook himself. "All right, Chelsea, time for you to walk at least to the bathroom."

She did have to go, Chelsea thought, and a bedpan was the most humiliating idea imaginable. She tried to sit up, felt a tugging pain and gasped. "My stitches!"

"It's okay. Let me help you." David eased her upright, then swung her legs over the side of the bed.

"I don't think this is such a good idea."

"Yes, it is," he said firmly. "Come on now."

Chelsea became aware that her nightgown was open in the back and muttered, "This is disgusting."

David, whose attention was entirely on helping her negotiate her way across the room, didn't respond. She was bent over like a very old person, and the top of her head came to his shoulder. He tightened his arm around her. "You're doing great, Chelsea. Can you manage in the bathroom by yourself?"

Chelsea drew a deep breath, turned to face him and said in the meanest voice she could manufacture. "If you think you're going to hold my hand in there you're not only a lecher, you're weird!"

"I wish," David said, now thoroughly irritated, "that you would stop behaving like an idiot. I am a doctor, *your* doctor, and you're a patient. Can't you get that through your silly head?"

Chelsea tried to pull away from him, felt a searing pain twist in her belly and gasped. She lowered her head, trying not to cry.

To David's combined chagrin and relief Dr. Dennis Madson opened the door at that moment. He stood quietly, his eyes widening at the sight of Dr. Winter holding his patient very closely in the open bathroom doorway.

"I'll be back in about five minutes," he said, and backed out of the room.

"Are you all right, Chelsea?" David asked.

She nodded. "I want to go to the bathroom."

He helped her inside the door, then closed it. He leaned against the wood for a moment, his eyes closed. What a bizarre mess, he thought, his jaw tightening. All that manufactured foolery Elliot had let slip was just that: foolery. From the short time he'd been with Chelsea's parents he could see—any idiot could see—that they were nuts, but loved her to distraction. And Chelsea loved them. Then what about poor Chelsea starving? He remembered his worry about her surviving on leftover salad from the Alta Mira and ground his teeth. He couldn't wait to get his hands on Elliot Mallory.

David eyed the bathroom door, aware that his entire body was tense with worry. Come on out, Chelsea. I want you back in bed where I can keep an eye on you. I don't want you falling in there.

The door opened just an instant before he was prepared to go in and bring her out.

"You okay?"

She nodded, not looking at him.

"Let's walk back to the bed." He didn't support her this time, merely walked beside her, his arms ready if she faltered.

He tucked her in, then straightened. "You're awfully quiet all of a sudden," he said.

"Yes," she said. "David, I've got a TV show in a week and a half, then a trip for a promotion back to New York. Will I be all right by then?"

TV? A promotion in New York? For sure she was starving!

"You should be." He couldn't help himself, and added, "Who's paying for all this?"

"My publishing house. Why?"

"I just wondered, that's all." He planned to kill Elliot Mallory. He glanced down at his watch. "Time for a pill and a nap. I'll see you later."

David quietly opened her door and peered in. He heard her say to George, "You should have seen Mother when she got back from Germany. I had to goose-step for her to get her to stop with her *danke*'s, darling."

"Hi, George, Chelsea," he said. "How do you feel?"

"Fine," Chelsea said. "I want out of here, David."

"In a couple of days," he said. "Not before."

"She's feeling much better," George said, smiling fondly at Chelsea. "She's already been arguing with me."

"She argued with me, screamed at me and said she was feeling like the proverbial something the cat dragged in. I don't think that's a particularly significant sign, George."

George smiled her dazzling, beautiful smile and rose. "I'll let you talk to your doctor a bit, love. I'll go to the third floor and bug Elliot."

"She is so exquisite," Chelsea said, sighing.

"Who? George? Yes, I suppose so."

Chelsea frowned at him, but he was looking at her chart. "You were polite to Dr. Madson, weren't you?" he asked, looking up.

"No, I threw my water bottle at him."

"Chels!"

"He didn't make me take my clothes off. Of course I was polite."

"He didn't have to," David said. "He already saw everything he needed to see. Besides, your clothes are already off."

Chelsea growled, then winced.

David very carefully moved any possible weapon and said, "Now be just as polite to me, if you please." He took her pulse, then placed the stethoscope against her heart. Chelsea found herself staring at his thick chestnut hair and the small curls at his nape. She quickly looked away, furious with herself.

"Sounds good," David said.

"You really do look silly in that white coat," Chelsea said.

"Would you trust me more as a doctor if I were wearing jeans and a sweatshirt?"

"No."

David drew a deep breath and said, "I need to change the bandage on your belly now. Are you going to cooperate?"

She just stared at him, color creeping over her cheeks.

"Chelsea, I'm not going to call the nurse until I have your assurance that you won't throw a fit."

She licked her lower lip. "I don't want you to," she said.

Irritated, he said, "Look, lady, I've already seen you in great detail. I assure you I won't be driven crazy with lust."

She looked at him, her lips a thin line.

"How can you have been raised by a father who's a doctor and be so ridiculous about this? You are a patient, utterly sexless, and that's it."

She was being silly; she knew it. "I'm sorry. Go ahead."

He stared at her suspiciously for a moment, then nodded. He called the nurse.

Chelsea lay rigidly, her eyes tightly closed, as David bared her stomach and gently peeled off the bandage. He spoke to the nurse, a very different voice from the one he used to her, she thought. She winced a bit, and he said, "Sorry about that, Chelsea. Just a moment longer. You look great."

Yeah, I just bet I do, she thought. She felt lousy, her head ached and she didn't think her stomach would ever feel normal again.

She heard David giving instructions to the nurse. "Now," he said, after he'd pulled her nightgown back down, "I don't think you need that IV any longer." He gently pulled the needle out of the vein in her arm and rubbed her skin.

"Ah," he said straightening, "here are your parents. I'll see you later, Chelsea."

"Much later," Chelsea said, but very softly.

"Ma chère!"

While her mother enthusiastically embraced her, Chelsea saw her dad speaking to David. Her dad nodded, smiled and shook David's hand. Ratty men, she thought. They stick together like a herd, or a gaggle, or a crash, or...a murder of ravens. Could that possibly be right? It sounded awfully silly.

David heard Dr. Lattimer say in a loud stage whisper to Chelsea, "Obvious hero material, Cookie."

He quickly eased out of the room. He didn't want to hear what Chelsea would say to that.

You miss her, you stupid bastard. David sighed, dropped to the floor of his living room and did twenty-five fast push-ups.

He checked the clock, set up his VCR and inserted a tape. He turned on a talk show, a local San Francisco show, and some ten minutes later Chelsea came on. He stared. He hadn't seen her for nearly a week now. The couple of times he'd called, she'd told him she was busy. It was George who had told him when Chelsea would be on TV.

She was wearing a dark blue silk dress, very nearly the color of her sparkling eyes, very high heels and a big, infectious grin.

She looked sleek, very sophisticated and very beautiful.

Poor starving Chelsea, indeed.

He sat back, at first nervous for her. He shouldn't have bothered, he thought some five minutes later. She was very articulate, fielding impertinent questions with marvelous aplomb. She oozed self-confidence. And, of course, the host and hostess talked about her success.

When the show was over David wandered out onto his deck and stared toward the Bay. Elliot had definitely done a number on him. But why? He had a chilling thought. If they had distorted things about Chelsea, what had they told her about him? He intended to find out—now.

He grabbed his jacket, roared Nancy into life and sped toward the Mallorys' house in Pacific Heights.

Chapter 7

David pulled into the Mallorys' driveway, grimly relieved to see Elliot's Jaguar beside George's infamous Porsche, Esmerelda. He bounded out of the car and strode to the front door.

He didn't bother with the doorbell, just pounded the wood with his fist. He heard a distant "Just a minute!"

George opened the door. "David!"

He didn't pause, didn't at first notice that George, beautiful George, looked like a frazzled wreck. "Where's Elliot?"

"I'll get him," she said, eyeing him a moment. She waved toward the living room. "Have a seat, David."

He was pacing about when Elliot said from the doorway. "What's up, David?"

George, on his heels, said sharply, "Did you hear from Chelsea? Is she all right?"

"Of course she's all right. I just saw her charming self on TV. That isn't what I wanted. Damn it, you two, why the hell did you tell me that Chelsea was a poor, starving little waif, ignored by her parents? And it *was* 'tell.' At least, you did more than intimate. Well?"

George jerked about at the piercing sound of Alex screaming.

"Anna is away with her sick sister," Elliot said, rubbing his forehead with a tired hand. "You stay here, love, and try to calm this infant down and I'll see to the other infant upstairs."

"What did you say you wanted, David?" George asked, obviously distracted by the rising cries.

David saw the weariness on her face and drew up short, feeling guilt mix with his righteous ire.

"Alex is colicky," George said. She swiped her hair away from her face, searched her hair for a bobby pin and, not finding one, looked as if she'd burst into tears. "Oh, rats," she said. "Everything comes in threes. This should all be amusing, I suppose. Now you've come to rant, so get on with it."

"I'm sorry," David said. "This will just take a minute, and then I'll be out of your hair." Poor reference, he thought, but for the moment he held his ground.

"What?"

"Why did you guys lie to me about Chelsea?"

George glared at him.

"Well?"

She turned when Elliot trotted down the stairs, Alex in his arms. The baby was red faced from yelling. Now he was hiccuping, his head on his father's shoulder, Elliot's large hand moving in gentle circles over his back.

"What's up?" Elliot asked.

"This man," George said to her husband as she waved a hand toward David, "is accusing us of lying to him about Chelsea."

Elliot cocked a black brow. "Yeah? So?"

Alex gave a particularly loud hiccup.

George, tired, at the end of her tether, snapped, "I'll tell you why, you ridiculous eastern idiot! You're so confounded uptight, unreasonable and just plain stupid...you don't deserve anybody as lively and intelligent and successful as Chelsea! Oh, yes, she earns rings around you, Doctor! I thought maybe you two would be good for each other, but obviously I was wrong! She doesn't deserve a man as opposite as you are!"

David was suddenly squirming. He'd never before heard George raise her voice, much less rake anyone down as she'd just done him. "Oh, hell, look, George, Elliot, I didn't mean—"

"I know," Elliot said. "We did do a number on both you and Chelsea. I guess people shouldn't try to matchmake." He added ruefully, "You two are so bloody different. George is right. Forgive us for interfering. It would never work between you, in any case."

"What did you tell Chelsea about me?"

George gave him a nasty look. "I told her you'd been impotent with your wife, and that she had laughed at you, and that's why you turned weird on her that night and insulted her about never being serious."

David was momentarily speechless. "You *what*?"

Elliot handed Alex to his mother. "Let me show you out, David," he said. "I think that about covers it. Excuse us now."

"Oh, no," David muttered. "George didn't. She wouldn't!" He looked hopefully at Elliot, praying George had made up that awful bit of horror.

"She did," Elliot said, trying to control the grin that was fighting to appear. "What I found amazing was the fact that Chelsea would buy such a story. After all, what man would go around telling people how he couldn't perform and his wife had laughed at him? But Chelsea didn't question it. She just wanted to take care of you, get you over your hurt and all that. Now, David, why don't you go away? Both George and I are ready to drop. I swear to you that we'll leave you alone—you and your love life, that is—from now on.''

David left and drove around for an hour. He ran out of gas near St. Francis Wood. He looked stupidly at his gas gauge, then began to laugh.

Chelsea loved New York. Her publishing house had not only paid for her appearance at the yearly conference, but also, in a spate of good will, offered her a limo to the airport. To all her business meals she wore her favorite gray fedora and her gray alpaca cloak. They made her feel confident and jaunty, sharpened her step, in short, made her feel like the neatest thing to hit the city. She saw old friends, made new ones, was feted until she was ready to drop. Writing was a lonely business, just you and your computer. That was why, she knew, that writers, when they were released into the world, danced and laughed and talked until they were dizzy. And it felt so good to hear the people who came to the autograph session tell her how much they enjoyed her novels.

But she tired so easily and quickly. The wretched surgery, she thought, angry at her body's betrayal.

She dropped into bed each night feeling like a wrung-out sponge. Then she thought of David and squirmed with embarrassment.

You lecher, go away and leave me alone! But he didn't, and despite her attempts to control her wayward memories, she found herself playing and replaying their last meeting.

''Ah,'' he'd said, grinning as he came into her hospital room, ''you're wearing lipstick. Ready to rejoin the world? I told you, didn't I, that I really like that peachy shade? Looks good with your flushed face.''

''Shouldn't you be somewhere saving lives and stomping out disease?'' she'd asked in a bitchy voice.

The jerk had the gall to grin at her. ''Bear your belly for me and I'll start stomping.''

''You are incredibly thick-skinned,'' Chelsea had said, wishing she could smack that grin off his face. ''Doesn't anything get through to you?''

''And you look incredibly sexy,'' David responded, seemingly oblivious of her snit.

She sucked in her breath. ''You're a doctor and I'm a sexless patient. Remember your sermon, Dr. Winter?''

''As of this afternoon you're no longer a sexless patient, Chelsea. Your parents are at this very moment downstairs clearing away all the details with administration. You'll shortly be a free woman.''

She said nothing, and he added, his voice suddenly very serious, "Your folks are going to stay with you for a couple of days, aren't they?"

"Yes, I couldn't get rid of them even if I threatened to move back in with them."

David felt immense relief to hear that. "Good," he said. "Get as much exercise as you can, but don't go overboard. And force yourself to straighten up. The stitches won't pull out. One last thing, Chelsea, come in next Tuesday to get the stitches out."

"Who's going to have the pleasure of doing the snipping?"

"You want me to?" he asked, moving closer and taking her unwilling hand.

She tried to jerk it away, but he wouldn't let her go. "No! As a matter of fact, if I never again see the backs of your ears I'll be eternally grateful!"

"All this drama because I took care of you?" His voice was teasing, and she readily jumped to the bait.

"You treated me like a slab of meat, you lecher, and you *looked* at me!"

"Yes, all of you, as a matter of fact. Very nice."

She growled and hissed, and he continued to smile. She remembered all too clearly that he'd examined every inch of her. It was too much. She closed her eyes tightly, willing away that very clear image.

"But you know," he continued thoughtfully after a moment, "as I recall, you do have a major flaw—a corn on the second toe of your left foot."

Her eyes flew open. "Get out!" She managed this time to jerk her hand out of his grasp.

"You know something, Chelsea?" he said in a mild, nearly disinterested voice. "You irritate me more than any woman I've ever known. You are silly and ignorant, and I hope to heaven that the next time you get smacked by a moped it will be near another hospital. Oh, yeah, you write trash."

She threw her water carafe at him.

"Be certain not to get your bandage wet," he said, retrieving the carafe and tossing it onto the bed. He watched the remaining water soak through the sheet.

He gave her a mock salute and left.

"Obnoxious jerk!" she yelled after him.

"Oh, damn and blast!" Chelsea said now into the darkness of her hotel room. Wretched, miserable man! I will not think of you anymore, except to congratulate myself on never having to see you again.

David buried himself at the hospital, and Elsa, eyeing him with renewed hope, tried to make herself indispensable. But he wouldn't bite.

Nothing. There was still a lot of gossip going around about that Lattimer woman and the scene she'd caused. And Dr. Winter's reaction. And the way he'd haunted her hospital room until she'd left. Even now, Elsa heard him being teased by administrators and other doctors.

David found himself one late afternoon near a bookstore and wandered in. He didn't mean to, but he found himself studying titles and books in the romance section. Sure enough, they had four different books of Chelsea's. He winced at the outrageous covers and the ridiculous come-on write-ups on the back. Surely she couldn't have anything to do with all that nonsense. Of course she didn't. He remembered her moaning and telling him that the covers were getting more and more dreadful—not at all romantic, just more and more skin, and fake rapturous looks—and the write-ups, "Argh!" He smiled as he read the back of one of her novels. *He was hot-blooded, handsome—and American. And now she was his property, bought and paid for.*

He shook his head, but picked up all four titles, presenting them with great panache to the clerk at the counter. To his utter astonishment he found that he couldn't put the first novel down. He was thrown into Victorian England in the early 1850s, and he could practically taste the food they were eating, almost picture the carriages and the clothing and feel the London fog. The characters were real, complex and sympathetic, and he couldn't wait to turn the next page.

He read until three o'clock in the morning. He set the book on his nightstand, lay back in bed and thought about it. He'd enjoyed the hell out of the story, laughed at the continuous, very amusing repartee between the hero—that hot-blooded American—and the heroine. He found himself wondering about the sex scenes. Her hot-blooded hero was also an excellent lover. And a marvelous mixture of Chelsea's Mark I and Mark II heroes. It was odd, he reflected, on the edge of sleep, to read about sex from a woman's perspective. It was honest, but, of course, the heroine adored sex with the hero. What if she hadn't? What if the hot-blooded hero had botched the entire affair?

Not in a novel. Especially not in a romantic novel. What had Chelsea said once? Oh, yes, she wrote escapist literature, fantasy to a certain extent, because what woman would want to escape to a beer-gutted hero who was clumsy and selfish? That, he thought, smacked of disappointment.

He found himself wondering about her sexual experience. She certainly seemed to know what she was talking about. Had she had many lovers? For all he knew her very intricate love scenes could have been taken from her own experiences with men.

He shook his head in the dark. That didn't make sense. He remembered all too clearly her unbelievable reaction to him in the emergency room. He pictured her slender, very white body in his mind, and felt his body respond instantly. She did, he now knew from firsthand experience, have a very nice bottom.

Damn her silly eyes, he wanted to see her again. He closed his eyes in excruciating embarrassment. He still couldn't believe George had told Chelsea he'd been impotent.

The days passed quickly as David immersed himself in one crisis after another. He decided finally, his misery having reached its saturation point, that if she wanted a Mark I hero, like her hot-blooded American, she'd get it. With a dash of Mark II thrown in for good measure.

Chelsea kicked off her shoes and plopped down on her sofa. She was exhausted, but also exhilarated. She'd had a ball in New York, accomplished a good deal of business, and even had lunch with the chairman of the board of her publishing house, a charming man, handsome and very articulate. Now, she thought, she had to get to work. Her mind had obligingly plotted during every free moment she'd had—when David hadn't intruded—and now her fingers were itching to get to the keyboard.

If only she weren't so blasted tired. Her eyes closed, and she drifted off.

She was awakened by the doorbell. She cocked a half-closed eye toward the obnoxious sound, forcing herself to rise. It was a delivery boy carrying a box of flowers.

"What?"

"Miss Lattimer?"

"Yes, but—"

"For you, ma'am."

And he was gone before she could even try to tip him. She stood barefoot in her entryway staring down at the box. No one had ever before sent her flowers. She opened the box slowly and gasped at the two dozen long-stemmed red roses.

She knew who had sent them, but nonetheless she very quickly opened the card. She read, "Welcome home, Chelsea. I'll pick you up at seven o'clock Friday night. Wear something long and sexy." And it was signed simply, "David."

"I wouldn't go to a wake with you," she said aloud, but she very carefully arranged the beautiful roses in her one vase and set it on her coffee table.

It was all very unexpected, she thought a while later as she slowly drank a glass of white wine. She clearly remembered his saying that she irritated him more than any woman he had ever known. Then why did he want to see her again? Something long and sexy, huh?

She was dozing on her sofa, half her attention on the TV, when it suddenly occurred to her. The realization, in fact, hit her squarely between the eyes. *No man would admit to having failed in bed. No man, even if he'd had a problem, would admit to having his wife laugh at him.*

George! Oh, no!

"I've got to be the most gullible, silly woman alive!" she nearly shouted to her empty living room. "Just you wait, George Mallory!"

It was close to nine o'clock in the evening when she pulled into the Mallorys' driveway. Thank God both their cars were there.

She slammed the car door loudly and marched to the front door. She lifted her hand to press the doorbell.

Was that a giggle she heard?

She frowned and pressed the buzzer.

Was that a curse? From Elliot?

She heard a "Just a moment," spoken in an oddly breathless voice, and the sound of pattering bare feet. The door opened, reluctantly.

"Chelsea!"

She looked at George, breathtakingly beautiful and disheveled in one of Elliot's shirts, and gulped. Her hair was tousled, and her mouth looked a bit swollen, as if she'd been kissed a good dozen times with great enthusiasm.

"I, ah..." Deep, embarrassed gulp. "Did I come at a bad time, George?"

"Get rid of whoever it is!" she heard Elliot call from the living room. Then a nasty laugh, and another shout. "I know it's Chelsea. Be rude! Send her to David. Let the two of them fight it out."

George laughed at Chelsea's expression. "I would suggest that you call first before you come over, Chels, unless, that is, you want to see my gorgeous husband in the buff on the living room rug."

"But...oh, damn! I wanted to talk to you about David. George, he couldn't ever have *talked about* what he, well, couldn't do in bed. It's ridiculous. No man would—"

"True, and David's already attacked us. Now, my dear friend, call me tomorrow. Goodbye."

"Go see David, Chelsea," Elliot called from the living room. "I imagine that he's dying to see you!"

"This is awful," Chelsea said. "I'm sorry, George." And she fled.

The following evening, Friday, Chelsea stared at the clock, then down at her ratty blue jeans and frumpy sweatshirt. My rendition of long and sexy, she thought. She should have left, but somehow she hadn't been able to make herself do so.

The doorbell rang promptly at seven.

"Go away!" she shouted through the door.

"Open the door, Chelsea, or I'll kick it in."

David was saying that? What the devil was going on, anyway?

She opened the door. "Hi," she said in a very inadequate voice. He'd gotten her again, she thought, her eyes roving over his body. He was wearing jeans as old as hers and a flannel shirt that had seen better days a decade ago.

"Hello, yourself," David said, grinning down at her. He stepped inside, grabbed her before she could move and swept her up against him. He kissed her very thoroughly.

Chelsea was too startled to react. When he finally eased the pressure on her mouth she gasped out, "You idiot! Put me down! You shouldn't be here! What are you doing?"

David gave her another tight squeeze, then set her away from him. He was beaming. "I read several of your books. Right now I'm your hot-blooded American who swept into the heroine's life and knocked her socks off."

"You're an idiot!"

"You're repeating your insults," he said. At her continued outraged expression, David managed a wounded look. "But, Chels, isn't that what your heroines like? To find a man who's as strong as they are, who will give them both heaven and hell? Who will master them despite what they think they want?"

"This is real life, David Winter!"

"Aha, so you agree that your novels are sheer nonsense."

Chelsea slammed her fist into his stomach.

He obligingly grunted and continued smiling down at her.

"You are the most ignorant, stupid, ridiculous man—"

"I like what you're wearing. It isn't particularly the kind of long I had in mind, but that sweatshirt's sexy, as well, something out of my mother's attic."

She frowned at him, turned on her bare heel and marched into the living room. He followed her, smiling at the rigid set of her shoulders and the very nice swing of her bottom. She turned abruptly and said, "I shouldn't have hit you. A writer is much too articulate to resort to violence. Now—"

"Can I have a glass of wine before you do me in?"

Chelsea disappeared into the kitchen, returning a few minutes later with two glasses of wine. "Here," she said, thrusting one at him.

"Thank you, you're a marvelous hostess, all warm and caring and—"

"Can it, David. Now what I was saying before you rudely interrupted me is that if you have indeed read some of my novels, the heroines are closer to eighteen than to twenty-eight, and virgins. I simply arrange circumstances so that they meet the *right* man for them. I might add, Dr. Winter, that men today are incompetent jerks, arrogant, still chauvinistic—"

"You've never been to bed with me, Chelsea. How do you know I'm incompetent?"

He spoke mildly, looking at her with a modicum of interest. She wanted to growl at him, but stopped herself.

Get a hold of yourself, idiot! He's just trying to pile you, make you say ridiculous things and lose your temper.

"Thank you for the roses," she said, tilting up her chin. "They're beautiful."

"Thank you. My pleasure."

"As I said, David," she continued calmly, but with a definite glint in her eyes, "I am twenty-eight years old. I have a lot of women friends. Some of those who are married find themselves resorting to technology—"

"Technology? What does that mean?"

"I refuse to get more specific!" She flushed, wanted to kick herself, but forced herself onward. "Now those who aren't married, tell me that the guys they meet all want to hop in the sack. That's all, nothing more. And that is why my heroes are tender, talented—"

"Tasteful? Torpid? Torpedoes?"

Chelsea closed her eyes a moment. "I'm going to belt you again if you don't shut up!"

"All right," he said agreeably, but she heard the amusement in his voice. "Now tell me, what is your experience?"

"Another thing," she continued, ignoring him and speaking in the most evil voice she could manage. "You men all get your jollies—reaffirm your macho virility and all that nonsense—through violent movies and your stupid Westerns!"

"You've got a point," he said.

Chelsea blinked at him, totally taken aback. "What game are you playing now, David?"

He shrugged and sat down on her sofa. "No game. Now what is your experience with men?"

She stood in front of him, her hands on her hips. Well, one hand on her hip; the other was holding the remnants of her wine. She set down the glass with a thwap.

"You've never been married, have you, Chelsea?"

"No, I haven't, and I don't think I ever will. As for my experience, Doctor, let us say that I, too, very much enjoy reading about a hero who can not only enjoy himself but also the heroine, and vice versa. It's a marvelous fantasy," she added, trying for sarcasm.

David looked at her for a long, thoughtful moment. "I see," he said finally. "Have you ever been in love, Chelsea? Ever wanted a man?"

"No! And tell me, Doctor, what does *want* mean in your marvelous lexicon?"

"As in desire, lust after, sigh over, make cute little noises, yell when—"

"Stop it! The answer is no, and frankly, as Rhett would say, 'I don't give a damn.'"

"Do you plan to spend your life experiencing pleasure vicariously? Through made-up characters?"

That drew her up short. Dear heavens, she thought blankly, is that what I'm doing? "That smacks of voyeurism," she said aloud, her voice thin and high.

He grinned at her. "I've got a wager for you, Chelsea."

"The Friday night poker game isn't until next week," she said.

"Not that kind of wager. Do you want to hear it?"

"I think I'll get another glass of wine first," she said, and left the living room.

He said very softly, "The Mark I hero has become cunning. You'd best make it a very large glass of wine, sweetheart."

Chapter 8

"Well, what is this wager of yours?"

"Drink a bit more of that wine and I'll tell you."

She did, set the glass on the coffee table and sank to the floor, tucking her bare feet under her. "Well?"

"You seem to have had crummy experiences with men," David said matter-of-factly.

"No, not crummy, probably just the same kind of experiences that many women have had, I guess."

"Ah, yes, the proverbial wham, bam, rolling over and deep snores."

"Don't be crude." She dropped her eyes a moment, knowing that she wasn't being honest. Two men did not a statistical analysis make. And they'd been young and inexperienced, just as she had been. She sighed. At the tender ages of twenty-one and twenty-four she'd been willing and eager to fall in love. Indeed, she'd believed for a while that she had been in love. But now she knew she hadn't.

"Your wager, David?"

"I want to make love to and with you."

She stared at him. This, she thought blankly, from a stuffed shirt, uptight doctor from Boston who'd once accused her of not being serious enough?

"Why?" she blurted out.

"Damned if I know," he said thoughtfully, but she saw that gleam of amusement in his eyes.

"Does this go along with being a doctor and wanting to save lives and stomp out disease? As in, see this poor confused woman who needs a man?"

"I don't think being a doctor necessarily equates to being a good lover. But if it pleases you to think so—"

"It doesn't, and this is ridiculous!"

"I've always thought that every woman needed a good man."

"And you're applying?"

"For part of it, anyway. The wager is this, Chelsea. Make love with me. If you don't like it, I'll order every male resident at the hospital to read every one of your books. Look at it this way," he continued quickly, seeing that she was probably on the brink of colorfully describing his antecedents, "even if you found the experience a total and complete bore, you'd probably save a good half-dozen guys from continuing in their doubtless selfish and egocentric ways with women. I doubt that any of them, myself included, have ever read about sex from a woman's perspective. An eye-opener, I promise you."

She thought about some of her love scenes, spun from an ideal model, so to speak. She looked at him thoughtfully. He was a beautiful man, no doubt about that. His jaw, she noticed for the first time, was as stubborn as hers. And she did like him when she wasn't furious with him. She probably liked him a lot more than he deserved. And he'd already seen her in the buff, so she wouldn't have to be too embarrassed.

"I don't know," she said finally, fiddling with her wineglass.

David, who had expected to be castigated to the fullest utility of her powers of speech, felt a jolt of very intense desire. "You could," David said, trying to sound like a detached scientist, "consider it an experiment, I suppose." He shrugged. "Who knows? The sky might fall. The earth might move. You might like it."

"Are you talking about tonight?"

He gave her a wicked smile. "What better time than the present? I have this awful feeling that even if you agreed to our wager now, you would chicken out by tomorrow."

That was a definite maybe! She shifted her weight, stretching her legs out in front of her, leaning back and balancing herself on her hands. She eyed him again, very searchingly. "Why do you want to make love to me? I seem to remember that I'm the most irritating woman you've ever met. And don't you dare say 'damned if you know' again!"

"Okay, I won't." And he said nothing more.

"Well? Why?"

"I find myself thinking at very odd moments that you're incredibly adorable. Like your heroes, I want to take you and love you until you yell with pleasure."

"A nice fantasy," she said.

"We'll see."

"I haven't agreed yet," she said sharply.

"What about George and Elliot? Do you think George resorts to technology and Elliot rolls over and snores like a pig?"

"Of course not. They're...different."

"I don't consider either of us particularly run-of-the-mill."

Chelsea fell silent, her mind skipping from one objection to another. He was also, she decided, a very good talker. She said in a rush, "What if I like it, and you?"

"Ah," David said, leaning forward, his hands clasped between his knees. "Then I would imagine we would be constrained to continue the experiment, to verify and recheck, of course." What the hell was he getting himself into? he wondered. What if she agreed and it was a fiasco? He came out of his fog at the sound of her voice. "What did you say? I'm sorry."

"I said yes."

Now, David thought frantically, what would a Mark I hero do? Grab her and carry her into the bedroom? Show triumph with a demonic laugh? Think about submission and surrender? He grinned at his thoughts, rose and stretched. No, he thought, he'd just have to be himself and hope it was good enough. After all, he was a *good* man, wasn't he?

"Well?" Chelsea asked, her eyes staring at his sneakered feet and moving upward. His thighs were thick, she saw, doubtless from jogging and swimming. She wondered if...

"Well, what?"

"The wager, David!"

"Actually, the wager is quite one-sided at the moment. What will you give me if I—we—turn out to be the greatest thing since sliced bread?"

"I will die of shock."

"That's a start, I guess," he said. "Come here, Chelsea. I want to make love with you in the bedroom. Your carpet doesn't look too thick and soft."

Chelsea gulped and slowly got to her feet. Standing in her bare feet, she didn't even come to his chin. "Oh, dear," she said, then stopped as he gently pulled her against him.

"A nice fit," he said, breathing in the sweet scent of her hair. He rubbed his large hands very lightly up and down her back, forcing himself to stay away from her bottom, for the moment at least. It occurred to him as he leaned down and gently began to nuzzle her ear that he had changed. Changed profoundly. This small, very mouthy woman made him laugh, made him see life from a slightly skewed angle, or maybe, he added silently, he'd lived most of his life according to rules that no longer fit him. It was certain that all signs of his incipient ulcer had disappeared. He wondered how that could be possible when she also made him want to wring her neck. And love her until they were both too weary even to snipe at each other.

He felt her stand on her tiptoes, and he sucked in his breath. Her breasts slid up his chest, and her belly was pressed firmly against him. Very slowly he brought his right hand around and cupped her chin. For someone who hadn't slept with a woman in a good many months, he was pleased at his restraint. Very lightly he kissed her pursed lips, not demanding, not forcing her in any way.

"You taste like shrimp salad," he said between nibbles on her throat.

"Sarah's shrimp salad is yummy. I'm not sure about this," Chelsea added in a very worried voice.

"Just relax. Isn't that what your heroes tell their heroines? Trust me? Give yourself to me?"

"Yes, sometimes, but—"

"But nothing. Stop worrying and kiss me again."

She did, with more enthusiasm this time. He tasted very good himself, she thought, and she liked what his hands were doing on her back. She pressed closer, sliding her arms over his shoulders. She was feeling warm, and very interested.

He slipped his hands beneath her sweatshirt, and she stiffened. Stop being an idiot, she told herself. You are not one of your heroines, nor are you a coy eighteen-year-old. You are also letting him control everything just as if you were a silly, helpless twit.

"You feel good, David," she said against his mouth. "Your body feels nice." To her immense delight she felt his entire body shudder with reaction. She also felt him hard and pressing against her stomach. She blinked. That felt very nice, too. It would stop, she thought, when he got down to basics.

"I'm not wearing a white coat now, Chelsea," he said, smiling down at her.

"No," she said. "No, you're not."

To her surprise he lifted her into his arms. She felt so good, David thought. When she nestled her face against his throat he began to believe that this was one of his finest ideas.

Her bed wasn't made, and David smiled, his gaze falling on a wispy pair of bikini panties tossed onto a chair. He guessed that this had been one of Sarah's days off.

He deposited her on the bed, then sat down beside her. He didn't touch her, simply smiled down at her. She looked expectant, a bit wary, but her eyes gleamed.

"When I first met you at the Mallorys'," he said, taking her hand in his, "I thought, now there is a very cute woman. I've since changed my mind. You are intelligent, warm, unpredictable and very sexy. I like your hair. It's irrepressible, like you." He tangled his fingers into the black curls over her left ear.

Think of something witty to say, idiot, she told herself, but she couldn't. She moved her head so that her cheek was against his open palm.

"I always wanted to be blond, like George. Most of my heroines have light hair," she said.

"Oh, no," David said. "Don't you realize how enticing you are? The black hair and the very white skin?"

He moved his palm against her cheek, smiling. "I'd like to see more of that beautiful white skin, Chelsea." Before she could even think of objecting, he grasped her sweatshirt and pulled it over her head.

Chelsea felt dreadfully exposed, and her hands flew to cover her breasts.

"No, don't," David said, gently drawing her hands away. She found herself watching him as he looked at her. He looked very intent, and she realized that she wanted him to touch her. She squirmed just a bit.

David very lightly laid his open hand over her breast. He closed his eyes a moment, savoring the incredible softness and the tautening of her nipple. He could feel her heartbeat speed up. "Very beautiful," he said. "Very white." He began to trace the tip of his finger around each breast.

Chelsea was taken by surprise at her own reaction. She arched her back upward, wanting him to fondle her. Instead his hand roved downward to her jeans. "I don't like one course at a time," he explained, seeing that she might protest. "I like to see everything at once. Hold still, Chelsea."

He pulled her jeans down, her panties with them. He looked up the length of her body. Her legs were as white as the rest of her, long and straight, and sleekly muscled from jogging. He realized that his own heart was pounding.

"What are you looking at?" Chelsea asked, feeling nervous, embarrassed and exhilarated all at the same time. "You've already looked at every inch of me."

"It wasn't the same thing," David said. He traced the small scar on her belly. "Any more pain?"

"No, just an occasional pulling feeling."

"That will continue for a couple months more. Dr. Madson did an excellent job."

Chelsea didn't care a bit about Dr. Madson. She realized that she was lying naked, and David, the wretched man, was fully dressed. Very unfair, she thought.

"No, don't move, let me enjoy you just a bit more, Chelsea," he said, his eyes caressing her face.

"As I said, you've already seen me," Chelsea said, her voice sharp and breathless.

"Understand, Chelsea," he said, his eyes on the small triangle of black curls, "that when I first saw you in the emergency room I was scared out of my mind. I was completely in my doctor mode until I was certain you weren't dying. Then my reaction was very natural. I did look at you—in a subliminal sort of way, of course. You're very beautiful, you know." He lightly pressed his palm over her, his fingers searching, and Chelsea lurched up, gasping.

She said rather wildly, "I refuse to lie here any longer being examined. I would like to see you, and there's nothing at all subliminal about it!"

He grinned at her and rose. Never before had a man stripped for *her*. Her heroes did for her heroines, of course, but that wasn't anything like this, like real life. She loved it. He unbuttoned his shirt and shrugged out of it. "Very nice," she said, wanting to ape him, but she couldn't quite bring it off. His chest was muscular, but not muscle-bound, and she couldn't wait to sift her fingers through the tufts of chestnut hair. She discovered that she was holding her breath when he unzipped his jeans and pulled them off. His shorts and sneakers quickly followed. Then he simply stood in front of her, beautifully naked. Chelsea gulped. "You look like one of my heroes," she said.

"Do I now?"

Her eyes moved lower, and she felt her face begin to warm and flush. He was large, thrusting outward.... She unconsciously licked her lower lip.

David couldn't stand it anymore. He moaned at that very sensuous gesture and moved down onto the bed beside her.

"Let's neck," he said, and pulled her against him.

"Do I have to be serious?"

"Not a bit, just moan to let me know what you're feeling."

"You're a good kisser," she managed after several minutes.

He muttered something, and she felt his large hand cup her bottom. "This has got to be heaven," he said.

"Close to it," Chelsea said, her own hand stroking down his back to knead his buttocks.

David was in bad shape, and he knew it. It had been a long time, and he wanted to enter her, but, he thought, grinning to himself, despite his own state he wasn't a selfish pig, and the thought of bringing Chelsea pleasure, watching her face while she experienced pleasure with him, was a heady feeling. A powerful feeling.

When his fingers found her, she was moist and delightfully soft. "Heaven, indeed," he whispered, pressing more closely against her.

Chelsea forgot the wager, forgot everything but him and his deft fingers. "It's been a very long time," she said.

"How long, sweetheart?" he asked, moving above her and looking down into her eyes. His fingers continued their gentle foraging.

"About four years. I think I've atrophied."

"*Four years!*" He simply couldn't imagine such a thing.

"Yes, I really thought that I wouldn't be able...ah, David, that feels so...please!"

Her hand closed over him, and he winced at her enthusiasm. It was probably just as well, for it gave him a bit more control.

He slipped his finger inside her and gasped at her incredible warmth. "No, not at all atrophied," he said. "Chels, hold still, all right?"

But she couldn't, and it surprised her. "David," she whispered, and felt his fingers deepen their pressure. She whimpered at the taut, convulsive feelings rampaging through her body. "I don't believe this!" Then she threw back her head and cried out.

David watched her face, watched her eyes blink with astonishment, then close, watched the arch of her throat as she threw her head back.

"That's it," he said, his voice harsh and raw in his own ears.

When he eased down Chelsea wanted nothing more than to experience him, all of him. She heard him moan, felt him thrust into her, very carefully and slowly, and clasped her arms about his back.

"Chelsea," David said, and that was his last word. It was her turn, and her pleasure to watch his face at the moment of his climax.

"You feel so good," she said when he was pressed full-length against her.

David concentrated on returning to life as he knew it. Damn. That had been unbelievable, but over with too quickly. She was so soft and small and yielding to him. He felt like shouting with pleasure, so he kissed her, deeply.

"If you dare to move," she said with great conviction, "I will never speak to you again."

He didn't. "The light," he said.

"Just don't move," Chelsea said, and reached out to switch off the lamp beside her bed. There was only the faint light coming from the living room.

"I'm too heavy for you, Chelsea. I don't want to hurt you."

"Move and I'll do something awful to you."

"Tell you what," he began, and before she could protest he brought her with him onto her side.

"I don't believe this," Chelsea said, and fell asleep, her face nestled against his chest, her leg wedged between his, her fingers splayed in his hair.

"I don't think I do, either," David said, feeling somewhat bewildered. He'd known that he would enjoy making love with her, but this overwhelming sense of well-being, of belonging, of warmth, shook him a bit. He fell asleep, too, his hand possessively on her bottom.

It was Chelsea who woke him during the night. She wanted him, and though she didn't understand it, she accepted it. "Hold still," she whispered into the darkness when he started to move over her. "I want to examine you."

He laughed, then moaned.

And when he rose over her, lifting her, and loved her with exquisite care, her protests died in her throat.

She could only stare into the darkness as the intense sensations swamped her, flinging her into a maelstrom of pleasure.

When Chelsea awoke the following morning she blinked at the sound of a rich baritone coming from the shower.

"Oh, dear," she observed to her empty bedroom, "I think I lost that damned wager of his."

She began to laugh.

Chapter 9

Chelsea looked up to see David standing in the bathroom doorway, one of her towels knotted low around his hips.

"Hi," she said, her laughter dying in her throat. What would one of her heroines do if the marauder came into the bedroom after a night of pleasure wearing only a lavender towel?

"I have good news for you, Chelsea," he said, coming toward the bed.

"What?" she asked, burrowing down under the covers.

"You don't have to worry about atrophy, not anymore, at least."

He laughed deeply, a laugh rich with satisfaction.

She threw a pillow at him.

"Weak, Chels, very weak. Didn't you tell me that you never resorted to physical violence? That you always used wit to carry you through?"

He picked up the pillow and strode to the bed. "I like the covers-to-the-chin bit," he said.

"I hope you didn't use all my hot water while you were butchering *Madame Butterfly*."

David sat down beside her and very lightly laid his open hand on her cheek. "Are you sore?"

"David!"

"Make you speechless, do I? That's what happens when a poor, confused woman finally has a good man take over. Now about our wager..."

Chelsea gave him a brooding look. "It was an accident, a freak of nature, a mistake, an aberration, a—"

"All that?" David whistled. "My, I guess I'll just have to keep convincing you, then." He leaned down to kiss her. "You wouldn't say I'm—we're—the greatest thing since sliced bread?"

"That really pleases your male ego, doesn't it?"

"Forget ego. You pleased other things much more. Do you have any idea how astonished you looked when you, shall we say, let go? Or when I made you let go, I guess.''

"An aberration," Chelsea said, eyeing him with deliberate dislike.

He sighed, his deft fingers gently stroking over her blanketed breast. "In that case, and in the interest of pure science—''

"I'm not using any birth control," Chelsea said.

David jerked back and frowned down at her. "I should have realized that, but I was too far gone on you last night. Do you want me to pay a visit to your friendly neighborhood pharmacy?''

Chelsea looked thoughtful. "I don't know. I remember overhearing one of my father's friends joking about wearing socks in the shower, and the guys he was talking to all groaned. Is it that bad?''

"No, not really, but I would prefer feeling you and just you, and me and just me.''

His words evoked very specific images in her mind, and she was appalled to feel a spurt of warmth.

"I guess I would, too," she said in a low voice.

"Do you want me to go through the alternatives? With pros and cons?''

"No, I'll go see my gynecologist.''

"Who is he?''

"He? No way. Maggie Smith is definitely a she. She's also George's doctor. Don't you remember? She delivered the Mallorys' perfect baby?''

"I remember. Forgive the brief short circuit.'' David arched a thick brow. "A woman doctor, huh? You mean you would have blown a fit in the emergency room if just any man had been there?''

"Probably not," she said honestly. "But you! That was very different, and you know it.''

"Do you know that the gossip at the hospital is still rampant? I'll walk by doctors I barely know and they'll poke each other in the ribs and talk just loud enough for me to hear about The Lecher in the ER. You've made me a legend in my own time.''

"Well, I think you proved it was true last night.''

"As in a Mark I lecher?''

She felt his hand drift over her shoulders to stop just above her breast. "No," she said, smiling shyly up at him, "as in a David I lecher.''

He felt absurdly pleased. "Will you describe my very manly technique in one of your novels?''

She tried to look uncertain, but couldn't quite manage it. She giggled. "Not until I'm certain it wasn't all a fluke.''

He sighed deeply. "When can you get in to see Maggie?''

"Well, I suppose that if we must continue with the experiment, it had better be soon.''

David sent devout thanks upward. "How about socks in the shower until then?"

"Do I have a choice?"

"Nope, not one. But you've got me."

"Did I ask for this?" Chelsea asked her bedroom.

"Well you did moan quite a bit, and make those cute little pleading sounds."

"Why don't you practice verbal abstinence for a bit?"

"Where's the nearest pharmacy?"

Chelsea moaned when his fingers finally stroked her. "You're a wretched tease," she gasped. "Men aren't supposed to tease."

"You're easy," David said, grinning even as he kissed her. "And here I thought men would be replaced by technology."

"Not yet," Chelsea said, and glided her own hand down over his stomach. When she felt his muscles tighten she said, "I might be easy, but I'm not simple."

He entered her powerfully, fully, and she watched the myriad expressions on his face as he moved over her. "You are so beautiful, David," she said, lurching more closely against him when his fingers found her.

"Moan for me, Chelsea," he said, and she did.

Chelsea found herself stunned three more times that weekend. In her novels lovemaking between the hero and heroine always got better, but she'd sincerely doubted that that was true in real life.

But it certainly seemed to be. It had to be the lost weekend, she thought.

"I love your belly," David said. "Almost as much as your bottom."

"You ain't so bad yourself, Doctor," she said, gazing at him pointedly.

Under her fond gaze he became quite enthusiastic. "You *are* a lecher," Chelsea said, laughing.

"I don't think that *lecher* fits my uptight, stuffed-shirt Bostonian image."

"You're becoming more Californian by the day. What an improvement!"

Suddenly David cursed.

"What's wrong with you?" Chelsea asked, her fingers busily kneading his shoulders.

"I'm out of socks," he said in a very mournful voice. "And I suppose I should get myself home. I'm on duty early tomorrow morning, and I definitely need to recharge my batteries with some uninterrupted sleep. I've got a staff meeting, and I've got to be brilliant."

"Want me to write a script for you?"

"As in how to cure atrophy and not through surgery?"

"How about acupuncture?"

"As in insertion of a needle or something a trifle more dramatic into a prescribed point in the body?"

"You're terrible, and not at all serious. I do think, Dr. Winter, that I could nibble your neck right now and talk Transylvanian, and you wouldn't mind at all."

"You want me to be laid back, do you?"

He kissed her goodbye for the dozenth time. "Try to see Maggie tomorrow, okay?"

"I certainly don't want to be responsible for impeding a scientific study," she said, shooting him an impish smile.

David discovered during the following weeks that he had, miraculously, become a toucher. If he was driving he held her hand. If they were watching TV he could never remember the plots because his hands were busily doing their own plotting.

"I need my Chelsea fix," he announced to himself one afternoon at the hospital. He hadn't seen her for two days. He wondered if he were going off the deep end. If he was, he decided, it was the greatest thing that had ever happened to him. Boston winters, very competitive professional people, stuffy parties—all seemed light-years away. But he missed his kids and worried about them. Damn, he didn't want them developing ulcers, and with the none-too-subtle pressure doubtless exerted on them, it could happen. He wanted them to be happy. He wanted them to be as carefree as their dear old dad was now.

He and Chelsea were dining out, David holding Chelsea's hand, his thumb stroking her palm, when he told her of his concern.

Chelsea was pleased, because David rarely spoke of his life in Boston. "There's competition out here, too, David. It's just that it's difficult to be totally immersed, as it were, when the weather is so enticing, and the ocean is at your back door, and everywhere you look it's like a postcard."

"And the pace of things is slower. Even sick people don't seem quite as sick in the emergency room. A lot of the residents are uptight, of course, but they've got boards to worry about and higher ups to impress."

"Tell me about medical school."

David groaned. "I worked my butt off."

"The original overachiever, huh?"

"That was just part of it."

"But there are rewards to being a doctor."

"True, and I firmly believe that after four years of university, four years of medical school, a year of internship and up to five years of residency, there should be something. Hell, Chels, the long hours don't magically stop after residency. They never stop. Most doctors I know deserve their income, and they really care about their profession and doing the right thing for their patients. I shudder to think about socialized medicine taking hold here in the U.S.''

"I agree that the foundation of our society—work hard, excel, and there's a payoff—shouldn't be tampered with. I suspect if the reward weren't there, the quality of service would fall.''

"Brilliantly put," David said, beaming at her. Of course, she'd spoken aloud his own thoughts on the subject. "Now that we've resolved that problem, what was that you were saying about dinner with the boys?"

"Not just Angelo, Maurice and Delbert. One of my writer friends from Sacramento, Cindy Wright, is coming. She used to live here in Sausalito, then moved. She breaks into wild sobs and deep sighs every time she comes back for a visit. She needs her Marin fix about every two weeks."

"Is that as dramatic as my Chelsea fix?"

"Yes, but not in the same way."

"Does she have a mouth like yours?"

"You can count on that, Doctor!"

"Does she look like you too?"

"Well, as a matter of fact, a writer friend of Cynthia's told me back in New York that we looked like sisters. I was astounded, and so was Cynthia. We quickly realized that we'd just insulted each other and decided that sisters it would be."

"Ah, but her bottom? No one's bottom could be as delicious as yours."

"I don't think I'd be quite that specific with Cindy. She just might give you some socks for your birthday. Knitted."

Cindy, David quickly discovered, was a whirlwind who gave him a disconcerting look and thrust a champagne bottle at him. She was small, like Chelsea, with dark hair and sparkling eyes. He thought her delightful, and waited for the coming of the inevitable bedlam.

It started when he heard her say to Chelsea, "I never should have left! Do you think I should hang out at the hospitals in Sacramento? He's a hunk, Chels." He moved a bit closer when she lowered her voice. All he could make out was something about thick fingers and big toes...

Then Chelsea broke into merry laughter.

"All right, Cindy, time to check the board and carry out Sarah's instructions for dinner."

"This time," Cindy said firmly, "I'm going to make certain everything gets to the table at the same time, and hot. Remember that one banquet where you forgot to put in the main course?"

Besides Angelo, Maurice and Delbert, another man showed up, a journalist named John Sanchez. "He's into crime and erotic Marin scandals," Cindy told David by way of introduction. "He's usually harmless and reasonable, except for his refusal to wear the beautiful yellow sweater I bought him for Christmas last year."

"Hi," said John Sanchez, shaking David's hand. "I've got this problem and Chelsea told me I should ask you about it. Do you play chess?"

David, who had thought he'd be doling out medical advice, grinned. "I was pretty good until my brain cells started dying off."

John concentrated for a long moment on stuffing his pipe. "Chelsea gave me a beginners' chess book for my birthday, so I guess you must be better."

"Come on, boys and girls," Maurice called from the dining room table. "Let's get with it. We're allowing forty-five minutes for dinner. Then onward to poker. Delbert needs money for his gambling debts." He turned to Chelsea and continued without pause, "Well, sweetie, you look like a woman who's finally met her match."

"I don't smoke," Chelsea said.

"Lord that was bad," John said, sucking on his already dead pipe.

"Does he like racing?" Delbert asked. "I don't remember."

"He looks tired, Chelsea," Angelo said. "You're not overextending him, are you, dear?"

"More beer?" Chelsea asked the table at large.

"Champagne," Cindy said.

John Sanchez looked up and said, as he tapped his pipe into an ashtray, "Make that a Chi Chi, Chelsea. I want to drink to my mother."

"John!" Cynthia said, punching him in the arm. "Your mother's going to smack you if you keep accusing her of hanging out at the Polo Lounge!"

"She loves it," John said, eyeing Cynthia's bust swathed in a new yellow sweater with black swirls on it.

"Ah, lust at the dinner table," Maurice said.

Cynthia and John disappeared into the kitchen to get dessert. When they came out, Cindy called out, "Get the camera, Chels. This is our new routine."

"Sunglasses?" David said.

"Absolutely," Cindy said.

Chelsea got her camera and snapped some corker photos.

Maurice said to John, "You know, I've never met a Sanchez with blond hair before."

John stuffed his pipe and took three matches to light it. He said in a bland voice, between puffs, "It's in the genes. Actually, I used to be a bullfighter."

"Ha," said Cindy. "Actually, guys, Sanchez was only a cow fighter. And still is."

"Come on, John, tell the truth," Chelsea said. "All you ever did was try to kill your dog with a rake."

"Unjust, unfair," said John. He turned to David. "You wanna play chess while these thugs try to kill each other at poker?"

"No way," said Delbert firmly. "I want to win the doc's money. With David eyeing Chelsea like your raked dog with a meaty bone, he doesn't stand a prayer."

"John doesn't either," Cindy said. "Now, you guys, before the slaughter begins, we've got to write down our ratings for dinner on Sarah's board in the kitchen." The average rating for a delicious meal of chicken enchiladas, tacos, homemade salsa and refried beans, was a nine point five.

David, true to Delbert's prediction, got wiped out by ten o'clock. John was wiped out by eleven, and his pipe was nearly chewed through. He mumbled every once in a while that he preferred humiliation by chess. Cindy and Chelsea were attacking a bottle of white wine, and only laughed when Delbert showed a full house, reducing them to quarter chips.

"I thought Cindy was staying with you," David said when everyone trooped out thirty minutes later.

"And you were depressed, weren't you?"

"You got it, lady."

"Well, you're saved by John Sanchez. The two of them tape every movie in the world and spend hours in front of the tube, watching."

David pulled her into his arms and kissed the tip of her nose. "Is that all they do in front of the tube?"

"That, Doctor, you will have to ask them! My lips are sealed."

"I'll just have to take care of that, won't I?" David said, and began kissing her.

"You look like a very smug man," Elliot said to David one afternoon at the swimming pool. It was a week before Christmas, sixty-five degrees outside and sunny.

"Chelsea is the most unaccountable female," David said. "I swear, we argue as much as we love. At least it's never boring."

Elliot grinned. "George told me that Maggie called you with a full report on Chelsea when she went in for an exam."

"Yes," David said. "I've never been more embarrassed. That wouldn't happen in Boston."

"That's a pity," Elliot said. "She did the same thing to me when I sent George to her. When are you flying out?"

"In three days. Back to snow and ice and wind-chill factors. I think my blood's thinned out. I don't know if this poor body will be able to tolerate building a snowman with the kids this year."

But there was no snowman that year. One day before David planned to leave, he got a phone call at the hospital.

"I can't believe the hospital is the only place I can reach you, David."

David stared at the phone as if it were a piece of rare steak that had just walked off his plate. "Margaret?"

"Who else, darling? Is that laughter I hear in the background? In your precious, very serious hospital?"

"This is California, Margaret," he said to his ex-wife in a very tense voice. "Did you call for my flight schedule? The kids are okay, aren't they? And Mom and Dad?"

"No, dear, yes, and the same as ever. Merry Christmas, David. The kids and I are here, at your apartment. Your security guard let us in. When are you coming home?"

David closed his eyes for a moment, visions of utter disaster clashing in his numbed brain.

"David?"

"Tell the kids I'll be there in a couple of hours. I assume you've made yourself at home?"

"Certainly, David."

"Give the kids my love." He sat as still as a pet rock for several minutes after he hung up the phone.

"Are you all right, Dr. Winter?"

David stared silently at Elsa. "What? Oh, yeah, just fine. I feel like a termite on his way to extermination. I feel like the dog that John tried to rake. What's up?"

"Got a little girl with a severe laceration on her leg. Fell off her bike. The kid's being taken care of. It's the mother Dr. Fellson needs you for. The woman's an unholy terror and needs your diplomatic touch."

David wasn't free to call Chelsea for another two hours. When he did, there was no answer. He cursed at the ringing phone. He was supposed to have dinner at her house at seven o'clock. Their last night together until he got back from Boston. He thought of the 1935 *Debrett's* he'd found in the dirty recesses of a used-book store, what he had lovingly thought of as her eight-pound Christmas present.

It was wrapped in bright red paper at home, he realized, sitting in full sight of anyone who cared to look on his coffee table.

Chapter 10

"Hello, Father."

"Hi, Dad."

The two young voices were restrained, and their owners stood at nervous attention, watching him. David felt an overflowing of intense love as he looked at his children. God, they'd grown, changed, and it had only been six months since he'd seen them. "Hi, guys," he said, his voice shaking just a bit. "How about a hug for dear old Dad?"

Taylor bounded toward him, snuck a look at her mother, slowed and allowed herself to be hugged heartily. She had just turned seven, and Mark, David knew, was wild to turn nine to keep a full two years between him and his sister. Taylor was tall, nearly as tall as her brother, and she looked like her father, bless her. Mark was more like Margaret, small boned, with light brown hair and blue eyes.

"Hello, son," David said, looking over Taylor's head. He enfolded the boy in his arms. For the first time in their lives he found himself noticing his children's lack of spontaneity, their lack of enthusiasm. Well, maybe it was natural. After all, he'd been out of their lives for a while now.

"You guys like the flight here?"

"Yes, Dad," Taylor said. "The flight attendant gave me three packets of peanuts."

"She gave two back, of course," Margaret Winter said. She nodded toward David. "You're looking fit. Children, go sit down. One shouldn't make noise in an apartment. It disturbs the other tenants."

"Yes, Mother," Mark said. "Come along, Taylor."

"It's a flat and the penthouse, Margaret. You make it sound like a tenement," David said, watching his two children march like little troopers into the living room. He frowned, already foreseeing those ulcers.

"Well, it isn't exactly a brownstone in Beacon Hill, is it?" She smiled brightly up at him, cleansing away the insult in her words.

He'd loved that house, but of course it had gone to her in the divorce settlement. He said nothing, merely shook his head, wanting to keep the peace. "Why did you come here with no warning, Margaret?"

"All their friends' parents decided to go to the south of France for Christmas. I thought it would be nice to see what all this is about."

"This? You mean beautiful California?"

"Why, yes. You're looking quite well, David."

"So are you, Margaret. That's a very becoming dress."

"You always were partial to clingy wool."

That was a conversation stopper for sure, and David merely nodded and walked into the living room.

"Dad," Taylor said, "this is a very heavy present. It's a book, isn't it? Who's it for?"

"For someone named Chelsea," Margaret said. "How bizarre."

"Bizarre? How's that?"

"As in a section of London. I've never known a Chelsea."

How could she make it sound like chopped liver? David wondered.

"*Is* it a book, Father?" Taylor asked again.

"Yes, punkin, it is. Actually, it's a book on British peerages and such."

"You mean like dukes and earls and Prince Charles?"

"Exactly. Would you guys like a soda?"

"They would prefer some hot chocolate, perhaps, but I couldn't find any of the ingredients," Margaret said.

"There's no sugar in the soda, Margaret. Let's keep their teeth healthy. Come along, guys, and let's see what I've got."

Taylor and Mark followed him sedately into the kitchen. They were dressed like little preppies, he saw, and winced. Taylor didn't drink soda out of a can. It had to be in a glass, with three ice cubes.

"Tell me what you've been up to the past six months," David said, seating himself at the kitchen table. For God's sake, he shouldn't be so ill at ease around his own children.

For the next ten minutes both children stumbled through a recital of events. "Of course," Mark concluded, "Mother didn't allow me to be in that play. It was far too plebeian."

Merciful heavens, David thought, he even pronounced the word correctly. He glanced up at the kitchen clock. Six.

"I would like to hear more," he said, rising. "We'll all go out to dinner at the Cliff House. It's a great place and you can see lots of seals from the window. Why don't you go get cleaned up? We'll leave in fifteen minutes."

"It sounds interesting, Father," Mark said.

No, David wanted to correct him, it sounded neat. "Interesting" was the response to a boring comment.

The only one left was Margaret. He said bluntly, as he walked into the living room, "I have one guest room, Margaret. Are you planning on sleeping with the kids?"

"No, I'll take the sofa."

"Why not a hotel? I can call if you like."

"No, here will be just fine."

He nodded, defeated, and said, "I've got a phone call to make and plans to break. Excuse me."

He listened to the third ring, then the fourth.... Then, "Hello!"

"Hi, Chels, David. Bad news, wretched news, ghastly and all that, except for my kids."

"All right, give."

"Margaret flew in with the children this afternoon. They're all here at my place, and I'm tied up. I can't make tonight. I'm sorry."

Chelsea looked at her romantically set table. "Me, too," she said on a sigh. "Well, at least you won't be going out of town, and I'll be able to meet your kids."

"Well, yes. Let me see what I can work out."

"David?"

"Yes?"

"You won't believe your Christmas present." She giggled.

"Well, you won't be able to lift yours!"

"A big red bow around your middle? Maybe an apple in your mouth?"

He laughed. "Not this year, maybe next. Or your birthday. I'll talk to you tomorrow, Chels."

Chelsea hung up the phone, a thoughtful expression on her face. Unexpected. She found herself wondering why Margaret had come out without warning. Refusing to follow that train of thought, Chelsea finally snuggled up with a Dorothy Garlock novel, remembering how she'd joked with Dorothy in New York about the second word of her two-word title— Lash! Ah, what marvelous images that evoked. Great novel, she thought, finishing about midnight. Because she didn't want to brood, she dove into the history of medicine she'd found for her doctor, Saint, in her San Francisco novel.

The evening wasn't exactly a bust, David told himself as he settled down to sleep. The kids hadn't loosened up, but he knew he had to be patient. It occurred to him that their formal behavior had been the acceptable norm during his marriage to Margaret. Had he really been such a stuffed shirt? So cold and...rigid? As for Margaret, she'd been pleasant, quite pleasant, in fact. Still, it was going to be difficult living with her until—until when? He hadn't asked her how long she intended to stay.

Indeed, his thinking continued, it would be quite nice if she could take herself back to Boston and leave the kids with him for the remainder of their vacation. He decided to discuss it with her in the morning.

He didn't have the chance.

Margaret announced over a delicious breakfast that she herself had prepared, "David, you will have the children to yourself today. I have errands to run. Will that be all right with you?"

What errands? he wondered, but said nothing. "Certainly."

David thoughtfully finished his pancakes, making his decision just as Margaret emerged from the bathroom, looking exquisitely lovely.

"Well," she said, "I'll be off now. I rented a car, David, so you don't have to worry about driving me about. Now, children, I expect you to do as your father says. All right?"

"Yes, Mother."

"Yes, ma'am."

She kissed them both, nodded to David and left.

David looked at his children. He believed at that moment that he could count the number of days on his left hand that he'd spent with them, alone, just the three of them. He realized that he had no idea what to do with them. Well, it was time he learned how to be a father.

He took his two little Bostonian preppies to the De Young Museum in Golden Gate Park. He decided, after three hours, that he was enjoying it more than they were. The children didn't eat junk food, as they succinctly informed him, so he trotted them to Fisherman's Wharf for some fresh seafood.

He stared out over the Bay as he ate his shrimp salad, his eyes resting on the sailboats. That's it! He'd take them sailing.

"Kids," he said, "how would you like to go out on my sailboat this afternoon?"

Taylor looked at Mark, a silent message passing between them. "That would be very pleasant, Father," Taylor said.

Yeah, David thought. You sound about as excited as if I'd offered you a live squid.

Chelsea, he thought, and smiled. She loved to sail. He kept his fingers crossed that she'd be free and willing as he excused himself and phoned her.

The outing sounded great to Chelsea, so David was driving over the Golden Gate Bridge some thirty minutes later.

Chelsea, dressed in her grubby sailing togs, answered the doorbell, a wide smile on her face. The smile cracked when she observed the two children flanking David. Sailing, she thought. Is he out of his mind? Both children were dressed like little fashion plates.

"Hello," she said, stepping back. "Come in. I'm Chelsea." The children filed in, stopped and turned.

"I'm Taylor."

"I'm Mark."

"And I'm David."

"And I'm overwhelmed! Come on in and sit down. What can I get you guys to drink?"

"A club soda," Taylor said.

"A root beer," Mark said.

"A stiff scotch," David said.

Chelsea shot him a wicked look and went into the kitchen. As she was making up the order she heard Taylor say, "Father, she's got a patch on her jeans!"

"A patch on her bottom," Mark said, a fiend for specificity.

David wanted to groan. He looked at his kids, really looked at them, and realized that the last thing they could do was go sailing in the ridiculous outfits they were wearing. And he wasn't much better, for God's sake. Slacks and a sport jacket!

"Her jeans are very tight," Taylor said. "Mother says that girls should never wear clothes that are too tight. They're not—"

She broke off as Chelsea came back into the living room.

I should have waited, Chelsea thought, smiling to herself. She would have liked to hear about too tight clothes and what the great Margaret had to say about them. And, she thought, my jeans aren't too tight.

"You know my father?" Mark asked, sipping his root beer, eyeing this woman whose black hair was bouncing all over her head.

Chelsea's eyes twinkled. "Yes," she said, "I guess I do know him, a bit."

"How long have you known my father?" Taylor asked.

"Not as long as I've known Torquemada," Chelsea said.

"Torque-who?" Mark asked.

"He was a very famous fellow who loved to ask people questions," Chelsea said.

"Oh," Mark said.

If the preceding minutes could have been called a conversation, there was a definite pregnant silence now.

Chelsea continued after a pained moment to Mark. "This fellow, Torquemada, if he didn't like the answers he got to his questions, he pulled out the person's fingernails." She splayed her fingers. "He wouldn't have had much luck with me, as you can see."

"Do you bite your fingernails?" Taylor asked, her voice a mixture of distaste and fascination.

"Only if I get mad at them," Chelsea said. "Actually, I type a lot and have to keep them short."

"You're a secretary?" Taylor asked, obviously horrified.

Chelsea cocked her head. Bloody little snob, she thought. David looked embarrassed. "And if I were, Taylor?"

Taylor realized she'd insulted an Adult and quickly retrenched. "Mother says that ladies don't work."

"And how about gentlemen?" Chelsea asked.

"That's different," Mark said.

"Why?"

David cleared his throat, wishing he'd never come up with this doomed idea. Before he could extricate everyone from this morass, Taylor said primly, "Grandmother Winter says that a lady is best served by allowing her husband to take care of her."

Dear heavens, Chelsea thought, that sounded like a recording! How ghastly! "How old is Grandmother Winter?"

"Old," said Mark.

"Her hair is silver," said Taylor.

"I suppose that's a step up from blue," Chelsea said.

"It is bluish," Taylor said.

Chelsea wanted a glass of white wine.

"Are you a secretary?" Taylor asked again.

"Tenacious, aren't you?" Chelsea replied.

"It's too bad you don't have a gentleman to take care of you," Mark said. "But your house is nice."

It's time to intervene, David decided at that last note of childish candor. "Chelsea is a lady, kids, and she isn't a secretary, she's a novelist. She writes books. Is that acceptable?" he added, his voice just a bit sharp.

Round, astonished eyes regarded Chelsea.

"Real books?" Taylor said.

"With covers and pictures?" Mark said.

"With sexy plots?" David said.

"Even with words and titles," Chelsea said, and burst into laughter.

"So that's why Dad bought you—"

"That's a surprise, Mark," David said quickly.

Children, Chelsea thought a moment later. What an odd experience, for sure. She rose. "Now, you guys, neither of you would last three minutes on a sailboat. You'd skitter off the deck with those shoes. Your father isn't in much better shape, either. Tell you what let's do, instead. Sausalito is a marvelous place to explore. We can do some shopping and feed the sea gulls and stuff ourselves with cookies."

Their eyes turned toward David.

"Sounds great to me."

They watched the ferry dock, wandered through the touristy shops and fed the sea gulls. "All right, sport," Chelsea said, turning to David. "Give me one of your credit cards. Taylor and I are going in this boutique and you, my dear, can take Mark shopping. This will be expensive, but, after all, you *are* a gentleman, and all of us are in need of care.''

Both children looked dubious.

''David,'' Chelsea added just before they split up, ''grubby stuff, okay?'' She added to Mark, ''Sailing is a messy business, but somebody has to do it.''

''Now, Taylor, come with me. Meet you all back here in one hour!''

Taylor giggled at her image in the mirror. She was wearing prewashed jeans and a Sausalito sweatshirt. Pink sneakers were on her small feet.

The immense cost of looking casually grubby, Chelsea thought as she signed David's name to the credit card slip.

''What do you think, Taylor?''

''I think,'' Taylor said, her young voice suddenly very serious, ''that Mother wouldn't like it.''

''In that case,'' Chelsea said, ''you can leave your things at my house. You ready to do a cartwheel for your dad?''

Margaret dropped her bomb the following afternoon. They'd just returned from Chinatown, and the kids' feet hurt from walking up and down all the hills. David wished he'd brought their sneakers home from Chelsea's house for them. Margaret looked as unmussed and immaculate as usual. ''Children,'' Margaret said, ''I want you to go into your room and play with the puzzle I bought you.''

''Regular little soldiers, Margaret,'' David said.

''They mind,'' Margaret said. ''And so should all children.''

''I suppose so,'' David said wearily. ''It's just that they don't seem to have as much life in them as before.''

''How would you know about that? Did you expect them to hang about your neck with joy? You were home so rarely, after all.''

He wanted to retort with something suitably snide, but there was a lot of truth to what she said. He'd wanted to avoid her, and thus had also avoided his children.

Margaret continued after a moment, her voice very matter-of-fact. ''I'm delighted your attitude had become more parental—''

''What the hell do you expect? I love them, Margaret!''

''Yes, of course you do,'' she said in a surprisingly gentle voice.

He stared at her, then frowned. ''All right. What's up?''

''He's a general in the army and I want to fly to Honolulu to see him.''
''*What?*''

''His name is General Nathan Monroe, and I met him at a party in Boston. He's a very nice man, a widower, and I want to spend some time with him. That's why I brought the children here, to you.''

She's acting like a child who needs her parents' permission, David thought blankly, staring at his ex-wife. Did she believe he would have refused her if she'd called with her plans before flying out?

"That's great," he said for want of anything better. A general, for God's sake! He pictured his children goose-stepping, then chided himself for being ridiculous.

"How long do you plan to stay in Honolulu?"

He watched, fascinated, as a flush spread over her cheeks. It brought back an ancient memory. Before they were married, he'd asked her to spend the weekend with him at the Cape. Hadn't she flushed then, just as now? And she'd said yes then, too.

"Actually," Margaret said calmly, "Nathan and I plan to spend a week in Honolulu, then a couple of days on Maui. Then we play to fly to Washington to spend a couple of days with his daughter and son. I was hoping you wouldn't mind if the children accompanied us to Washington."

"I see," David said. "That will be fine, of course."

"If it's all right with you, David," she continued, "I should like to meet this Chelsea person. Mark mentioned that he'd never met a lady like her before. Taylor said she wrote books. Is she a proper person for them to know? Or is she very...California?"

"What exactly does that mean?" he said.

Margaret shrugged. "Well, I'm not really certain. Being from California brings a certain *image* to mind, I suppose. Hippies and drugs and all that."

"Margaret, that was back in the sixties."

"No need to raise your voice, David. If you aren't concerned about the type of person you introduce our children to, I am. It's important that they aren't exposed to any bad influences."

He could only stare at her. He said finally, "Chelsea Lattimer isn't a type, Margaret. She is, as a matter of fact, a very loving, warm person, who also just happens to be very talented."

"What type of books does she write?" Margaret asked.

"Long historical novels," David said absently. Then he smiled. "They're the ones with the wild covers, filled with adventure, romance and intrigue."

"Good heavens," Margaret said suddenly, "I thought her name sounded familiar! I've seen her books, if one could call them books!" She shuddered. "Not exactly biographies of Winston Churchill, are they?"

"No, and I imagine that she sells a good deal better," David retorted. "Her novels are not only well written and historically accurate, they're excellent escapism, just downright fun, as a matter of fact."

"Yes, certainly you're right." Margaret turned toward the window, saying over her shoulder, "As I recall, you don't approve of women who

are, shall we say, independent, out on their own, without male protection.
It surprises me that you would see a woman who is that way.''

There was a brief, pained silence. Was I really such a jerk? David was
asking himself. Out of self-protection, he didn't decide at that moment
on an answer.

"I gather she makes a good deal of money?"

"I don't know what she makes. It's none of my business, but I should
say that she does quite well.''

Where the hell is all this leading? David wondered. All too soon he
discovered the circuitous direction of Margaret's thinking.

Chapter 11

"Have you met the Winston-Barnetts?" Margaret asked, turning from the window to face him.

"Certainly," David said. "Mr. Winston-Barnett—Andrew, I believe—is a broker on Wall Street, isn't he?" At Margaret's nod he said, "And he has a son and daughter. Why do you ask?"

"His daughter, Andrea, is now living here, in San Francisco."

"So?"

"As you know, she and I went to school together, at Vassar. She's a widow now, but her husband left her quite well off. I thought it would be...kind of you to see her."

David pictured an Andrea of nearly ten years before. Tall, very Nordic-looking, with pale blond hair and light blue eyes. He said only, "I seem to remember her."

"She, of course, doesn't write books or anything like that, but she has our—your—background, David. She admitted to me a few months ago that she would very much like to see you. After her husband's death she went back to her maiden name."

"Must take up a lot of space on a check," David said.

"She is a very well-bred, lovely lady," Margaret said, keeping her temper in check. One could never tell with David. Particularly since he'd left Boston. She did not appreciate unpredictability. It was, in fact, rather annoying. Thank heaven Nathan was enchantingly predictable.

"I'm certain she is," David said. "Honestly, Margaret, this sounds perilously close to wife swapping!"

"Her husband died in a plane crash," Margaret said. "There is no swapping involved, David."

"Why the devil is she interested in seeing me?"

"She has always admired you," Margaret said, her voice cool now, her tone denying that she approved of this idea. "As I said, she is also financially independent, just as your...friend is."

"Can it, Margaret," David said. "I have no interest in Andrea. I never did. If I recall correctly, she appeared about as warm as a fish that had been on ice for six months."

"She doesn't wallow in things like that," Margaret said, her cheeks flushing just a bit, not with embarrassment, but with anger. "If sex is what you're referring to."

David grinned; he couldn't help himself. Then he laughed. "I don't suppose you told her that I was a sex fiend?"

"I expected that you'd gotten over that some years ago. At least, you did with me."

"It isn't that I got over it," David said, still chuckling. "It's just that I gave up on you. Incidentally, just how old is this general fellow? Perhaps he's given up on sex?"

"Nathan," Margaret said stiffly, "is a gentleman. He is very concerned for *my* feelings, and he isn't old, David."

Oh, Margaret, David thought, looking at his ex-wife. We certainly didn't do things right, did we? He said abruptly, closing the subject, "I wish you luck with your gentleman general, Margaret. And I am sorry, but Andrea Winston-Barnett will have to fend for herself." He added, lightly touching her arm, "You've done your duty, but I'm really not at all interested."

"I suppose this Chelsea woman gives you all the sex you want?"

"Didn't you see the gray hairs?" he asked, trying to keep things light.

"I thought as much," Margaret said distastefully, moving away from him. "Since she doesn't appear to be after you for your money, she must be one of those loose individuals that sleep from pillar to post."

"What an odd phrase," David said, but he felt his hands clenching at his sides. He saw that she was revved up for more insults and said quickly, "Let's drop it, all right, Margaret? I imagine the children have done the puzzle, probably two times over by now."

"Very well," Margaret said stiffly, and walked toward the door.

"Margaret," he called after her quietly. She turned. "Did you ever think I was sexy? Did you ever enjoy making love with me?"

"Yes," she said just as quietly. "And yes." She turned again and left the living room.

Life, he thought, staring after her, is bloody strange.

Dr. Harold Lattimer put down the phone and looked at his wife. "It appears that our little girl has gotten herself into it this time," he said, shaking his head.

"David Winter is a fine man," Mimi said. "I wish the lot of them could come here for Christmas. This will be the first year Chelsea hasn't been home."

"I wonder if she would have come if his children hadn't been dropped on his doorstep?"

Mimi tried for a Gaelic shrug, her memory of Paris still warm. *"Qui sait?"* she asked. She frowned a moment, wondering if that was correct, then shrugged again. It sounded good, and it sounded French.

Dr. Lattimer reached for the phone.

"Who are you calling, Harry?"

"A catering company in Marin," he said. "I'll have them make up a big Christmas feast for Chelsea and her brood. I don't think Chelsea would know the front end of a turkey from its pope's nose."

"I say, Harry," Mimi said after he'd made the catering arrangements, "I could get us two tickets for, say, London."

"Look," he grumbled, "they do speak English there, but it just isn't proper English."

"I have it, then," Mimi announced. "Hawaii!"

Harry Lattimer knew when he'd lost. He had no hope at all that there wouldn't be reservations available, even at this late date. Mimi *always* got reservations.

Chelsea placed the phone back into its cradle and stared for a moment at absolutely nothing. Her first exposure to David's children hadn't been a particularly startling success. Christmas was, for Chelsea, a time of laughter and fun, not two blank-faced kids sitting on the edge of the sofa, staring at her as if she were the wicked witch of the West, bent on hexing their father.

When a messenger had delivered a cuckoo clock later that afternoon, wrapped in a huge red bow, and a notice that her Christmas meal for four people would be catered, she laughed so hard it took a rude noise from the messenger to get his tip.

"George," she said into the phone a few minutes later, "you're simply not going to believe what my folks have done now!"

"Knowing your parents, Chels, it has to be outrageous," George said, rearranging Alex on her shoulder. "Come on, give."

"A cuckoo clock and a catered Christmas meal for me, David and his kids! I do wonder what they meant by the cuckoo clock, though."

George dutifully laughed, then said, "That takes care of Christmas Day. How 'bout the group of you coming here for dinner on Christmas Eve? I swear Elliot will do most of the cooking."

"You're not going to see your parents this year?"

"January will be our month for pilgrimages."

"It will be a madhouse," Elliot said later that evening after George gave him the news. "No," he amended thoughtfully, "probably not."

"Why not?"

"David's kids. They're so uptight, so very careful, you wonder if they ever fight, even between themselves."

"You've met them?"

"Yep. David brought them to the hospital for a tour. They were dressed like two little models, and so polite it made you nervous."

"What about their mother? Margaret, isn't that it?"

"The ex-Mrs. Winter has taken off for Honolulu to vacation with a general, so David said. Three stars. Most interesting."

George looked thoughtfully at the overly large serving Elliot had dished up for her dinner. "Chelsea is the unknown factor here, isn't she?"

"Eat," Elliot said automatically. "Do you wonder if those kids of David's can maintain their formal pose around her?"

"It is an interesting thought," said George.

Chelsea drove over the Golden Gate Bridge late on the afternoon of Christmas Eve, the passenger seat loaded with presents.

For once she wasn't plotting. She'd left her hero, Saint, blinded by an explosion at a foundry, and her heroine, Juliana, holding his head in her lap.

She stopped gnawing on her thumbnail long enough to pay her dollar toll.

"Merry Christmas," the fellow at the tollgate said.

"Yeah, Christmas," she said toward the presents beside her. She hadn't seen David or his children since that afternoon two days before, and she wondered how he was making out. On the phone he sounded quite chipper, particularly since Margaret had left for Hawaii. And, she thought, smiling a bit wickedly, he missed her; that had been expressed in the most mournful voice she'd ever heard from him.

She missed him, too. I think I've become addicted to him, she admitted to herself as she turned her car onto Lombard Street. She'd never been addicted to anything before, certainly not a man, and it was a disturbing thing to have happen.

She pulled into the driveway, noticed David's Lancia, Nancy, already parked on the sidewalk and checked her face in the mirror. She was dressed to the teeth, and was even wearing her lucky gray fedora. At least it smashed down her hair a bit. "I look great," she told herself, "and there isn't a patch on my bottom."

David's eyes agreed with her own assessment. As for her, she wanted to throw her arms around him and kiss him until he was unconscious. Instead she said, "Hi."

"Hi, yourself, gorgeous," he said, and lightly kissed her lips. "Lord, you smell good enough to eat," he added.

She slanted him a look that made his body react instantly. "Chels," he said, and quickly turned away.

Taylor and Mark were seated just as she'd expected them to be, stiff as little sticks on the edge of the sofa. They greeted her politely, and that was that.

"White wine, please, Elliot," she whispered as he hugged her. "A glass followed by a jug, probably."

"They'll loosen up, Chels," Elliot said. "Just be yourself. No one can be immune to that."

Chelsea, fortified with a glass of white wine, joined David and the kids.

"Dad took us to the hospital," Mark said.

"It smelled," Taylor said. "Very funny."

"I agree," Chelsea said. "I was there not too long ago and your dad took care of me. In a manner of speaking," she added, smiling crookedly at David.

"She was a lousy patient," David said. "Wouldn't do a thing I said, fought with me, yelled at me—"

"Goodness," Taylor said, wide-eyed. "You did that to Father?"

"He really isn't the pope, Taylor," Chelsea said. "There is bull involved, but there's nothing papal about it."

"You've been wrong before, Chels," David said, giving her an intimate look. "Remember?"

Chelsea sighed deeply. "No, not really. It's been too long."

"When were you wrong, Chelsea?" Mark asked.

"Well," Chelsea said confidentially, leaning toward Mark, "your father made me a wager. He took great advantage of me, I fear, but the results are still far from conclusive."

"I don't know about that," David began, only to leap to his feet when George, her timing always exquisite, came into the living room, carrying Alex.

"Oh," Taylor gasped, staring at the vision. "You're so beautiful!"

And what am I? Chelsea wondered. A witch with spinach between her teeth?

"Thank you," George said, smiling at the young girl. "You're Taylor, right? Mark? Welcome to our home. My name is George."

"That's a funny name," Mark said.

"Yes, very true. And this is Alex." She lowered the baby for inspection.

"He's awfully small," Taylor said. Alex, demonstrating a sudden burst of showmanship, grabbed her finger and gave her a blurred baby's smile.

"Yes, he is," George said. "It scares the wits out of me—you know, I'm afraid of dropping him on his head or something equally awful."

"Mother must have dropped you on your head," Mark said to his sister.

Excellent, Chelsea thought, they aren't always so saintly. She said to Taylor, "Do you know that George is a very famous model? She's also on TV."

"Really?" Taylor breathed reverently.

"Really," George said. "Would you like to hold Alex, Taylor?"

"You can pretend you're one of the Three Wise...women," Chelsea said.

George laughed. "He is perfect, Chels, but even I wouldn't go that far!"

"Dinner," Elliot said, coming into the living room. "I've done my best, guys. Hope you like everything."

Mark looked at Taylor, then blurted out, "You cooked dinner, sir?"

"Yes, indeed, Mark," Elliot said.

"But men don't do things like that," Taylor said.

"Are we going to have another truism from Grandmother Winter?" Chelsea asked.

"Yes," Taylor said firmly. "It is a woman's job to make the house pleasant and to manage the servants."

Elliot sent David a wicked, crooked grin, and David, wishing he could stuff cotton into Taylor's small mouth, hastily said, "Things are different in California, kids. Here men and women both do everything. It's...well, it's more fun that way."

"And we don't starve," George added. "Come into the dining room now. I'll put Alex to bed and join you shortly."

"Do you believe that, David?" Chelsea asked as they walked behind the kids into the dining room.

"I'm trying to figure out just what I believe," he said. "Odd, but I don't remember my mother being so very ironclad in her notions."

"You were a boy," Chelsea said, "not a girl."

He looked thoughtful at that. "I'll have to look after Taylor," he said. "Maybe it's not such a bad idea to have a woman bringing in the bread."

"Half a loaf," Chelsea said. "Less pressure on the husband, I expect."

"As in no ulcers?"

She merely smiled up at him, and he wanted at that instant to throw her to the floor and make love to her. He groaned softly, his hand on her back drifting lower for a moment.

His hand was just about to curve around her bottom, when he cursed softly and helped her into her chair. She heard Elliot chuckle.

Mark was uncertain whether he should compliment a man on his cooking. He was saved possible embarrassment when his dad said, "Great, Elliot. That dressing had cranberries and walnuts in it, right?"

Mark decided to be impressed. His dad knew the ingredients, so it must be all right, a manly thing, in fact. "Yes," he added, "and the gravy was wonderful."

"Thank you all," Elliot said. "Taylor, you want some more lemonade?"

"No, sir," Taylor said, sleepy from all the food.

George said, "Then why don't we all adjourn to the living room, drink some of Elliot's famous egg nog—two varieties—and open our presents?"

The adults' egg nog had enough whiskey to make an elephant dance, Chelsea thought after one mug. She looked at the children and saw their eyes fastened on the presents.

"My thought exactly," she said, and fished out a wrapped package addressed to Taylor. "It's from me," she said. "And here's yours, Mark."

She saw Taylor start to rip open the paper, then pause and, as if through sheer willpower, sedately begin to untie the ribbon.

I've got to do something about that, she thought. She found she was holding her breath as Taylor opened her box first.

"Oh!" Taylor said. She held up a huge panda bear and stared at it. There was a white bow around the bear's neck and an envelope attached. Taylor looked toward Chelsea, a question in her eyes.

"They're tickets to the zoo to see the pandas next week. They're here on loan from China."

To Chelsea's surprise, Taylor rose from her chair, walked to where Chelsea sat and kissed her cheek. "I've never had a bear before. Thank you."

"You're most welcome, Taylor. Now you, Mark."

Mark squealed; there was no other word for it. He gazed in reverent awe at the baseball and mitt, autographed by Tod Hathaway, George's brother. "Oh, Dad! Oh, goodness! Look!"

"My brother Tod," George said, "is the pitcher for the Oakland A's. He told me to tell you hello and to get out there and play."

The children's faces were lit up almost as brightly as the Christmas tree, and Chelsea felt David's eyes on her. She turned to see a very tender look and swallowed a bit.

"You hit the jackpot, Chels," he said, reaching out his hand to her. She took it, and he pulled her down beside him on the floor.

David gave Chelsea her *Debrett's*, and she squealed as loudly as Mark had. "I've always had to go to the library and breathe in endless amounts of dust," she said, so delighted that she kissed him on the mouth. She heard Taylor make a distressed sound and released him. "Thank you, David. It's a marvelous present. As for yours," she continued, lowering her voice a bit, "you'll have to wait until we're alone."

David groaned.

"The evening was quite a hit," David told her later as he walked her to her car. "Thanks for thinking of the kids."

"My pleasure," she said, looking up at him.

"Sometime soon, I hope," he said, and pulled her into his arms. "Your pleasure, that is." He kissed her deeply and sighed with his own pleasure at the feel of her bottom in his hands. He held her very close, then, with a sigh of regret, released her. "You sober enough to get home in one piece?"

"If I don't make it, it will be because of my lascivious thoughts and not the egg nog."

"Just hold those thoughts, sweetheart." He kissed her again and helped her into her car.

"Tomorrow, at about one o'clock, for our catered dinner," Chelsea said. "Starve the kids. There'll probably be enough goodies for an entire battalion."

David drove his very contented children home some minutes later. When he tucked them in Taylor gazed up at him with her owlish, candid look and said, "I saw you kissing Chelsea, Dad."

"Me, too," said Mark from the other bed.

"It is Christmas," David said, looking from one of his children to the other. "Goodwill and cheer and all that."

"You kissed her hard, Dad," Taylor said.

"And I saw your hands on her bottom before George yanked me away from the window."

"Just checking for patches?"

"Dad!"

"All right, you two, yes, I was kissing Chelsea. I like her very much."

"Are you going to marry her Dad?" Mark asked, adjusting the baseball and mitt on the pillow beside him.

David blinked at that.

"I sure like my panda," Taylor said.

If the two little devils could be bought, David thought, Chelsea had made a fine beginning. He said finally, his voice thoughtful, "You know, I doubt that Chelsea would want to marry me."

"Impossible!"

"Dad, you're the best in the world!"

Best at what? he wondered, kissing his daughter good-night.

He rose, then bent down to kiss Mark. When he straightened he said only, "Let's not discuss heavy stuff like that, okay? To be honest, guys, I have no idea what's going to happen."

As he walked out of the darkened bedroom he heard Taylor mutter to Mark, "I wonder if Mom is going to marry the general."

"I don't like it," Mark said.

Like which? David wondered as he quietly shut the door. The general or Chelsea?

Chapter 12

"That was delicious prime rib, Chelsea," David said, sitting back in his chair, his hands on his stomach. "Death from pigdom is imminent."

"Me, too," Chelsea said. "How 'bout you guys?"

"That was as good as Dr. Mallory's dinner," Taylor said. "Thank you."

"Did men make this dinner, too," asked Mark.

"No, sir," Chelsea said. "This was the proud result of women's work. Not bad, huh?"

"Yummy," said Taylor. She'd brought her panda, and it was seated in its own chair. Its name was MacEnroe.

Chelsea regarded her stuffed guests with a smile that turned to a frown as she gazed out the window. It was raining in Marin on Christmas Day. All her plans for sailing, well...

"Housebound, I fear," David said, following her thinking. Then he gave her the most lecherous look she'd ever seen, and she threw up her hands, giggling.

"Was that a joke, Dad?" Mark asked, looking from one adult to the other.

David gave a wrenching sigh. "Actually not, Mark. Tell you what, kids, why don't I show a movie for you guys on Chelsea's VCR?"

"We don't watch TV during the day, Dad," Taylor said, her voice just a bit mournful.

"This is Christmas. You can do anything you want."

After settling the kids in front of the TV, David joined Chelsea in the kitchen. He stood in the doorway a moment, watching her. She was wearing gray wool slacks and a matching cashmere sweater. The slacks slithered delightfully over her bottom. "Well," he said, coming up behind her and kissing the back of her neck, "one should be able to do anything one wants on Christmas."

Chelsea felt a surge of warmth at the touch of his mouth, and frowned at the leftover green beans. He'd just kissed her neck, for heaven's sake, and here she was ready to attack him. She turned slowly, carefully set down the green beans and hugged him. "Merry Christmas, David," she said, and stood on her tiptoes to be kissed.

"You would make a turnip horny," he said after a moment.

"You are so romantic."

"I am right now in transition between a Mark I hero and a Mark II. It sometimes leads to misinterpretations of my deepest, most sincere thoughts and desires."

"That, David Winter, makes no sense at all. And there's not much to misinterpret about a turnip."

He kissed the tip of her nose, then held her against him a moment, just savoring her closeness, her warmth. "My kids informed me last night that they saw me kissing you *hard* before George yanked them away from the window."

"How did you slither out of that one?"

"It was tough, particularly when they pointed out that I was touching your bottom, too."

"Oh, dear," Chelsea said, pulling back from him just a bit. "If I recall correctly, that was my fault. I can't seem to keep my hands off you. Or stop encouraging you. Our scientific research and all that."

"I didn't keep any notes," David said, kissing her ear. "I think I've forgotten all the groundwork we laid."

"Laid? Really, doctor! Ah, but you still have the greatest enthusiasm," she said, feeling him hard against her belly.

He moaned deep in his throat, cupped her bottom in his hands and drew her up against him.

"Dad, do you think I—"

He released her very slowly before turning to his son. "Yes, Mark?"

"I—I'm sorry," Mark stammered. "I just wanted a glass of soda." His eyes went from his father's face to Chelsea's. "You were kissing again," he said.

"Yes," David said. "Yes, we were. A soda you say? Does Taylor want anything to drink?"

"No," Mark said, looking guilty. Chelsea wondered just how long the boy had been watching them before saying anything. She pulled herself together and said brightly, "You don't want to miss any of the movie, Mark. Go back in the living room and I'll bring you some root beer, okay?"

Mark nodded, but his gaze was searching and uncertain. Chelsea sighed. Play it light, she said to herself. You have no idea what David thinks or wants. She reminded herself to tell him how coincidental it was that her hero designations had the same name as his son. Maybe in the year 2000 his son would be a Mark III.

It wasn't difficult to be light and amusing during their late afternoon game of Trivial Pursuit. David had bought them the children's edition, and they switched back and forth from the children's to the adults'. Chelsea and Taylor were partners against the *men*.

Taylor, it turned out, was fantastic with the entertainment questions, Chelsea's inevitable Waterloo. They won, leading to the men's grousing and complaining about hard questions and general unluckiness with the dice.

"You're pretty smart," Taylor said as they prepared to leave that evening.

"That sounds like a judgment call," Chelsea said, ruffling Taylor's hair. "And oh, so true. You ain't bad yourself, kiddo."

"Mark said you and Dad were kissing again in the kitchen."

"Yes, your father is a very nice and kissable man."

"Mark also said Dad was holding your bottom again."

"That's possible, I guess."

"Are you going to marry my father?"

"That, Taylor, is a question I have no answer to, or to which I have no answer. Interesting syntax. Hmm. And actually, I haven't the foggiest notion! Now you don't need that Boston coat or those ghastly boots. Just your sweater. The weather person said sun tomorrow. You want to go sailing?"

Marry David, Chelsea thought some thirty minutes later as she sat alone on her sofa, staring at the blank TV screen. Chelsea Lattimer Winter. CLW. Stop it, idiot! Just because you want to attack him physically every time you're around him—well, maybe that will go away. Most likely it will go away. Or hang around, like fungus or mold.

I am not a slice of bread!

"Oh, this is ridiculous!" Chelsea said, and went to bed.

She picked up one of Laura Parker's novels, *Rose of the Mists*, and reread it until three o'clock in the morning.

They made it to the sailboat, got the lunch stowed below and the sails ready to raise, when David's beeper went off.

Chelsea jumped.

She knew David wanted to curse but restrained himself in front of the kids. He smiled, a forced motion of muscles, and said, "Let me go call in. It's probably nothing. I'll be right back."

"This wouldn't happen if he was visiting in Boston," Mark said.

"Yeah," Taylor said. "They couldn't beep him that far away."

Both Taylor and Mark were dressed in their casual togs David and

Chelsea had bought them in Sausalito. Now they both looked utterly disconsolate.

Chelsea cleared her throat. "Mark, go below and get some bread. We'll feed the gulls until your father gets back."

This occupation hadn't paled by the time David returned, but the look on his face paled everything.

He said tersely, "There's been a huge accident on 101. I've got to go in now."

Actually, Chelsea had already made up her mind, given this contingency. "Give me the boat keys, David. I'll take the kids out."

David looked uncertain. Two children who could fall overboard in two seconds and one very small woman whose skill at sailing was undoubtedly excellent, but still...

"Key, please, David," Chelsea said. "It will be all right."

"Please, Dad!"

"Chelsea knows everything, Dad."

"No, she only knows all the yellows and browns in Trivial Pursuit," he said, but he handed her the keys.

"Don't worry," Chelsea said, smiling up at him. She gave him a quick kiss.

As David strode down the dock away from his boat, the *Paramour*, a name chosen by the previous owner, he heard Chelsea say, "All right, guys. Sit down and we're going to go over the ground rules."

He smiled.

When he came up for air some five hours later there was a message from Chelsea. They'd had a ball, everyone was safe and sound and they were at his place. She would stay with the kids until he got home.

He arrived home at one o'clock in the morning, exhausted. He let himself in as quietly as possible. Chelsea wasn't in the living room. Despite his weariness, he felt himself smile. He forced himself to check on the kids first, saw that they were soundly sleeping, then went to his bedroom. Chelsea was sleeping in the middle of the bed, fully dressed, the comforter over her.

He had a strong feeling of well-being at the sight of her. He supposed it was a throwback to the male coming home to his waiting female. He wanted very much to make love to her, but frankly doubted he could manage it even if the kids weren't down the hall.

He stripped off his clothes and climbed in next to her. Just for a little while, he thought; then he'd move to the living room. She muttered something in her sleep when he cuddled against her bottom. He lightly kissed the back of her neck, still thinking that in just five minutes he'd leave.

He was asleep in two minutes.

And didn't wake up.

* * *

"Oh, my God! No, Mark, Taylor, go in the living room. Now!"

David forced an eye open to see Margaret, red faced, standing in the bedroom door, hands on hips, with the expression of a hanging judge.

"What are you doing here?" he asked, shaking his head to clear his brain.

"What is *she* doing here?" Out came a pointing finger. "In bed with you, and your children here!"

For a brief moment David didn't know what she was talking about, then he felt Chelsea beside him, stirring now, and froze. He cursed.

Chelsea came awake suddenly, with all her faculties alert, as was her habit. She was first aware of David, beautifully naked, lying beside her, then Margaret standing rigid in the doorway, in a Parent-Catching-Teenagers pose.

This is a farce and therefore funny, she told herself.

"Hello, Margaret," she said, pushing her hair off her forehead. She yawned. "Hello, David. When did you come home?"

He felt like a complete and utter fool. "Late," he said abruptly. He started to jump out of bed, realized he was naked, and said to Margaret, "I'll be out in a few minutes. Kindly remove yourself."

"We had a great time sailing, David," Chelsea said, her eyes on his body as he strode across the bedroom. "Of course, we missed you. David, I hesitate to mention this, but you don't have any clothes on."

"I know," he said, not facing her. He grabbed shorts and jeans, pulling them on as fast as he could.

She saw that he was upset and said reasonably, "David, I'm completely dressed. There is nothing to be perturbed over. Just because Margaret—that was Margaret, wasn't it?"

"Yes, and the bathroom is through there," he said. The rest of his words were muffled as he pulled a turtleneck over his head.

Chelsea frowned. She'd done nothing remotely questionable and neither had David. Why was he acting like this—guilty and angry? Angry at her! "Don't forget your deodorant," she said in the nastiest voice she could dredge up.

"Look, Chels," he said. "Oh, forget it. Stay put, it might be better. I'll handle this."

"There is no *this*," Chelsea called after him, but he paid no attention. "To handle," she ended on a mumble.

I'm supposed to stay in his bedroom like some sort of paid hooker? You're being redundant, turkey! Of course hookers are paid. Stop laughing at this situation, she told the small interior voice that persisted in seeing the entire morning as a farce.

She threw off the comforter and took herself to the bathroom. When she emerged with clean teeth, clean face and wrinkled clothes some ten minutes later, there were very civilized voices coming from the living room.

A masculine voice that wasn't David's. Aha, she thought, the general. She strolled in. "Good morning."

"How dare you—" Margaret said in the calmest voice, but her teeth were gritted.

"That's enough!" David roared.

"I agree. Hello, sir. I'm Chelsea Lattimer."

A very straight, slender gentleman with crisp gray hair rose and took her hand. "My name is Nathan Monroe. A pleasure."

Chelsea heard Margaret begin to fuel up again and quickly said, "All right, I think this has gone on long enough. If you're not aware of it, Margaret, your children are standing in the kitchen, all ears. Your attitude is absurd, and I resent you giving David grief for sleeping in his own bed, despite whoever else might be in it. It would have served your nosiness right if we'd been doing all sorts of perverse, kinky things. As it was, if you'd bothered to open your eyes and close your mouth, you would have seen that I was fully dressed. Now I want my morning coffee. A pleasure to meet you, sir."

She made her exit, chin up, back straight.

Mark and Taylor stood like two rigid puppets in the middle of the kitchen. "Hi, guys," Chelsea said, making a straight line toward the coffeepot.

"Mother's angry," Mark said.

"She said you were a loose woman," Taylor said.

"The general told her to be quiet," Mark said.

"And I don't want to hear anymore until I've drunk half a cup. All right?"

Chelsea sat at the kitchen table and drank her coffee. Her mind was in high gear, and she was furious at Margaret for upsetting the children for no reason at all. After all, what had she been doing with the general, anyway? Playing gin rummy?

David came into the kitchen looking utterly distracted.

"Is it safe to come out yet?" Chelsea asked, a grin on her face.

"Is Mother still mad?" Mark asked.

"I'll take you home, Chels," David said wearily.

"Want to escape, huh?"

His eyes narrowed on her face. He was tired, angry at the absurd situation, and here was Chelsea being a pain in the butt along with Margaret.

"Yes, if you wish to be flippant about it."

Chelsea very carefully set down her coffee mug. "David," she said carefully, "I apologize for being flippant, but I simply can't take all this brouhaha seriously. You can't take me home, because if you do, you'll just have to take a taxi back. I drove the kids back here, remember?''

He felt even more like a fool than he had five minutes before.

Chelsea softened a bit. "Why is Margaret back early?''

"We met your parents in Honolulu, Chelsea," said the general from the kitchen door. "They send their love.''

The light dawned very clearly. Chelsea threw back her head and laughed heartily. "Oh, dear, you poor man! You look all right. You survived?''

The general smiled, a nice smile, Chelsea noted. "Oh, yes.'' He gave David a commiserating look. "I'm sorry about this, Dr. Winter. Margaret insisted that we come. She's suffering from jet lag, I think. I'm going to take her back to the hotel now. I think you folks need some peace for a while. Please, Chelsea, don't leave. We will.''

He added as he left the kitchen, "I think it would be nice if all of us went to dinner this evening. Can you get a sitter for the children?''

"Yes," Chelsea said. "I'll call George, David. She's bound to know of someone.''

"But—'' Mark said.

"You need to calm Mother down," Taylor said with appallingly candid insight to her father. "Chelsea's right. This is a brou-ha-ha.''

The general laughed.

Chelsea grinned.

David sighed deeply.

The general said, "Incidentally, Chelsea, your folks flew back with us. They're staying at the Fairmont.''

"Merciful heavens," Chelsea said.

"Oh, hell," David said.

"Dad!''

"Father!''

"I think I'll take up practice in Little America," David said.

"Where's that, Dad?'' Mark said.

"The Antarctic. Trivial Pursuit, blue, geography.''

Chelsea sat back in her chair and stretched out her legs in front of her. "Merciful heavens, David, I am impressed. I never would have gotten that one right.''

"I looked through some of the questions before we started playing.''

"Dad," Taylor said, "you look awful tired.''

"I am. I think I'll go back to bed for a while.''

"With Chelsea, Dad?'' Mark said.

"Look, guys," David began, his brow furrowing, "would you all please just leave dear old Dad alone for a while?''

Chelsea laughed.

Chapter 13

I will forget this evening eventually, Chelsea thought, trying to concentrate on the delicious *sole meunière* and parsley potatoes. They were dining at the Carnelian Room high atop the Bank of America. The view was unbelievable, as usual, the service perfection itself, and the conversation, dominated by Margaret, was so civilized that Chelsea thought she would come down with lockjaw from gritting her teeth to keep silent. As for Mark's earlier comment that David needed to calm down Margaret, well, no one could be more calm than Margaret.

Chelsea didn't realize until the end of the meal that the general, bless his socks, had been steering Margaret skillfully into unexceptionable shoals, away from deep water. Then, unfortunately, the general excused himself for a moment. Chelsea looked after him wistfully, even as Margaret's voice, still civilized, but now with a layer of ice, said, "The children, you understand, Miss Lattimer, are terribly impressionable."

"And will continue to be so until they're eighteen, I imagine," Chelsea said. "Then they will magically know everything." She tossed a smile toward David. "Ah, that freshman year in college, the height of one's mental powers."

"Yes, well, it is important that they have the right *influences*, don't you agree?"

"I believe I see a roomful of probable good influences," Chelsea said.

"Perhaps," Margaret said, her cultured voice becoming a bit shrill. "It is simply different from what they're used to. David understands what I mean."

David arched a thick brow. "What I understand, Margaret, is that the world is full of people and children adapt marvelously well."

The general returned, but the spigot was open now, full blast, and

Margaret continued without pause, her coffee cup jingling a bit. "I met the Lattimers, Chelsea's parents," she said, as if clinching the matter.

"Margaret," the general said in his calm deep voice, closing his hand over hers, "Harold and Mimi are delightful people."

"*He* wears gold chains and half *her* sentences are in high school French!"

"Oh, no," Chelsea said, laughing. "Mother never had high school French. She picked that up when she was in Paris. After she visits Vienna this summer it will be fractured German again. I have always found it most amusing. As for my father," Chelsea added, her voice losing a bit of its lightness, "he enjoys life, gold chains and all, and he doesn't hurt other people."

"They are very caring people, Margaret," David said. "I met them when Chelsea had to have emergency surgery."

This elicited an odd look from Margaret, who suddenly announced, "I believe I shall go to the ladies' room."

The general, an officer and a gentleman, rose to help her.

"Won't you come with me, Miss Lattimer?" Margaret asked from her new commanding height.

Chelsea winked at David. She leaned down and whispered in his ear as she passed his chair, "She's going to bring out the heavy guns now. This ought to be fun."

"Be serious, Chelsea," David said.

She looked at him for a long, steady moment. "I'd hoped we were beyond that," she said, and left.

David cursed softly into his coffee cup. A waiter hovered, and David waved him away. The general said in his deep, pleasant voice, "Chelsea is a charming young woman. Her parents are also charming. Margaret is charming when she doesn't feel threatened and manages to forget that she's a snob. She does forget it more and more now, David."

"Yes, of course, certainly. Did you enjoy Honolulu?" David asked, striving for a little charm himself. But he felt abused and a bit angry. Damn Chelsea, anyway! This was serious, and she was treating the entire situation as if it were an amusing part of one of her novels.

"Yes, certainly. It's difficult, I think, to change one's attitudes. To view life, if you will, from more than one angle. Incidentally, I am going to marry Margaret. We will live in Washington. She will enjoy it."

David's eyes fastened on the general's face. "The kids," he said, swallowing.

"I'm delighted that Margaret, despite her motives, left us alone for a while. Don't worry about Chelsea. That young woman can certainly handle Margaret at her most...well, in her Mrs. Full Charge mode. I have three grown children, David, and I find yours delightful. I am not their father—you are. I will convince Margaret that half their time should be spent with you.''

''Good luck,'' David said, now staring at the dregs in the bottom of his cup.

''No, I don't believe luck is involved.'' He paused a moment. ''You never knew how to handle Margaret, or you were simply too busy with your medical studies, and then you didn't care, because both of you grew in different directions. I assume that you do want to see more of your children?''

''Certainly,'' he snapped, then sighed deeply. ''Life is never simple or clear-cut, is it?''

''No, but that would be boring,'' said the general.

''You should have been in World War II. We would have won much sooner, I suspect.''

The general laughed.

''What a lovely shade of lipstick,'' Chelsea was saying to Margaret at that moment. She'd spent an unconscionable amount of time in the stall, not to annoy Margaret, but to get herself under control. Damn David, anyway! Reverting to being a stuffed shirt again, without a bit of humor!

Margaret said nothing, merely continued outlining her mouth with a shade Chelsea had to admire.

Chelsea sat in a stool beside her and gazed into the mirror. ''Oh, dear, my hair always informs me when it's damp outside.'' She began pulling a comb through her bouncing curls.

Margaret said abruptly, ''I know you're sleeping with David.''

''It's all a wager,'' Chelsea said. ''A scientific study, as it were. Since you arrived, however, our lab work has been severely curtailed. Actually,'' she added with a mournful voice, ''it's been nonexistent.'' She heard David's voice telling her to be serious. Dratted man, she was serious when it was warranted, wasn't she?

''I assume you enjoy sleeping with him.''

There was no cattiness in Margaret's voice, and Chelsea frowned. Perhaps, she thought, she should be just a bit less flighty and flippant. ''Yes,'' she said, her voice softening involuntarily as she met Margaret's eyes in the mirror. ''Yes, I do. He is a very sexy man and a very nice man.''

''David, unlike most men,'' Margaret said after a brief pause, ''doesn't sleep around. He did not leave me for another woman. To the best of my knowledge he was faithful to me until the divorce. He left me because we no longer cared about our life together.''

''I don't think I'll ever marry,'' Chelsea said. She added quickly, ''Not that I'm criticizing, by any means. Commitments are tough, and I, for one, don't think I care to try one so binding as marriage.''

Margaret gave her a funny look, then fished in her makeup bag for her compact. "I am worried about my children," she said after a long pause. "It's not that I don't believe what you just said. It's just that if David decides he wants you, he will win, don't doubt it. He's very forceful. Do you know this is the first time that he's spent so much time with his children?"

"I suspected that."

"During the last two years of our marriage he spent more and more time at the hospital—to avoid me, of course. Unfortunately, it also meant not seeing his children."

"That must have been difficult," Chelsea said.

"David has changed," Margaret said, frowning a bit. "The children don't realize it, of course. They tell me that Father said this and that, and I stare at them. Perhaps it's the California air, or more likely it's knowing someone like you." Margaret turned and faced Chelsea straightly. "I've been something of a bitch to you, and I apologize. The children like you very much."

"I like them," Chelsea said. "I will try to loosen them up, Margaret, if I spend time with them. But I don't believe that involves corrupting their young minds."

"No, I guess not. Taylor showed me what she called her Marin sailing togs. Those pink sneakers are too much."

"Taylor is already showing signs of being a good sailor. Mark, too, for that matter."

"I'm pleased about that. I do want my children to enjoy themselves. May I call you 'Chelsea'?" At Chelsea's pleased nod Margaret continued, saying unexpectedly, "David told me the kind of novels you wrote, and I shuddered and made disapproving noises, which, of course, he expected me to. Actually, I enjoy reading long historicals, and I've read several of yours. They take one to a different time, away from all the complexities of the modern age, and make one, well, feel that there can be an ideal relationship between a man and a woman. Am I making any sense at all?"

"Oh, goodness, yes," Chelsea said. She added thoughtfully, "You know something, Margaret? I think I've been wearing blinders. I spouted off once to David that women didn't want to read about men like their husbands—you know, beer bellies and all that—but that isn't true at all. Maybe that's true sometimes, but I think it's just as you said. Romance is a hard quality to maintain when you're surrounded by the daily demands of work and family and fixing leaky faucets. Perhaps reading a novel, or seeing a romantic movie simply brings romance to the fore again and improves things. Ah, tell me to shut up." Chelsea grinned. "Once I get going, it's like the Rough Riders going full charge up that hill."

"Not at all. I've never met an author before. Perhaps, between us, we've made the definitive statement."

"Sounds reasonable to me."

"You really didn't make love to David last night, did you?"

Chelsea laughed. "I slept like a log. Poor man, he probably didn't get home until very late and was dead on his feet. There'd been a major emergency, a wreck on 101. It was on the news." Her voice became very sober, and as serious as David could have wished. "Margaret, I had told him that I would stay with the kids until he got back from the hospital. I did, and I eventually went to sleep. I would not have made loud and passionate love with your children down the hall."

Margaret laughed. She rose and smoothed down her dark blue silk dress. "You know something?"

Chelsea cocked her head.

"I think I shall make loud and passionate love tonight."

"Go for it," Chelsea said.

"Bizarre," David said. "I felt like I'd been put through an experience warp."

Margaret, the general and the kids had gone to the zoo, and David and Chelsea were at a hamburger joint, south of Market Street nearly shouting to be heard over the din.

"I had the same feeling. You know something else, David? I think everything is going to work out for you. And for Mark and Taylor. And for Margaret and the general."

David took a big bite out of his hamburger, chewed thoughtfully, then said, "I had consigned the evening to perdition when Margaret started on you."

"Well, we've still got this evening to go. Mom and Dad, you know. Drinks at the Hyatt."

David, diverted, said, "If they like the Hyatt so much, why don't they stay there? It's quite a taxi ride from the Fairmont to the Embarcadero."

Chelsea said primly, her eyes sparkling, "The Hyatt is too *moderne. Très chic, naturellement, mais trop*—Gallic shrug—*je ne sais pas quoi.* Another Gallic shrug."

"This is terrible. I understood you!" He sat forward suddenly and clasped her hands between his. "You're a brick, Chels."

Chelsea ran her tongue over her lower lip. "Do bricks get horny, David? Like turnips?"

His hands tightened on hers. "When do we have to see your parents?"

"Not for another three hours," she said, trying for a seductive look. She succeeded, and David sucked in his breath.

They arrived at David's flat twenty minutes later, and three minutes later than that they were in the bedroom, their clothing in a straight line from the entrance hall.

"David," she gasped as he tossed her onto her back and pulled her legs over his shoulders, "this isn't at all scientific!"

He lowered his head and began to caress her and love her. "David, I—" She had no idea what she would have said, for at that moment she felt her body go haywire. She tugged at his hair, gasping at the intense sensations washing through her. "I don't believe this," she moaned; then her body arched upward as he thrust deeply into her. She felt him moving in her, felt his fingers find her, and she was gone.

But David held back. He didn't know how he did it, but he did. He brought her to pleasure two more times, reveling in the look of utter astonishment on her face. Reveling in the feel of her, the intense heat of her body. He arched his back and exploded deep inside her, and she thought him the most beautiful sight in the universe—his neck muscles corded, his arms flexing, his eyes closed tightly.

"Is there still life in this male body?" she said after long moments of regaining breath and voice.

"No, not even an ounce." David raised himself a bit so he could see her face. "Chelsea," he said, his voice uncertain, even wary, "I've never felt anything like that before."

"You're complaining?"

"No, it scares me." He stopped and blinked, and she wondered what he would have said. He grinned now. "Do you know how great you just were, lady?"

She flushed, and David laughed. "I finally got you, huh? It's about time. I watched you and felt you—three times. It was great."

"I've never done that before," she said in a surprisingly shy voice. "I thought it was only in novels, like mine."

"So you think we're ready to publish the results of our study? Woman Succumbs to Superlover? Woman Gives All? Woman Admits Existence of Passion?"

"All right, all right, you win," Chelsea said. "But you know, David, it could simply have been the result of...deprivation!"

"Do you still feel deprived?"

"No, not at all. I feel on the brink of terminal satiation."

"You writers—what kind of a word is that?"

She was trying to find another retort, when he began kissing her. She felt his smooth, deft fingers glide over her breasts, pausing to gently fondle her nipples. To her utter shock, her body responded.

And responded.

"Some satiation," he murmured against her breast.

Shadows were lengthening, casting the bedroom into dimness.

"Oh, my God!" Chelsea nearly shouted. "We've got to meet my parents in thirty minutes!"

They were late, of course. David whispered in her ear as they entered the hotel, "They're going to know what we've been doing. Your eyes look so soft they'd melt a knife."

"Mac the knife or David the knife?"

"Cookie!" Harold Lattimer embraced his daughter, eyed her for a long moment and said, "So that's why you're late. Mimi, you need to speak to this daughter of yours!"

Chelsea groaned, and David had the grace to look a bit embarrassed.

"*Bonjour*, David," said Mimi, kissing him on his cheek. "Do sit down and tell us about Chelsea's scar. *Entre nous*, of course!"

"Mother?"

"Cookie, you're sounding like a prude, and life is too short for that. What do you want to drink? More of that wimpy white wine? Waiter!"

David sat back and watched the wildly volleying jokes. When it was his turn, which it was very quickly, he said seriously, "The scar is only about four inches long, she can still wear a bikini and the scar tissue is minimal. I scarcely notice it."

"David!"

"Now, Cookie, don't be so serious." Harold Lattimer beamed at David and said, "When are you two getting hitched? Mind you, David, I didn't think my little girl would ever find a man to suit her, but it appears that you're suiting her just fine. What do you think, Mimi?"

"It sounds as if he is keeping a close eye on her scar, *je crois*," said Mimi.

Chelsea choked on her white wine. "Never, never again," she declared, "will you guys go to Hawaii. You've become outrageous and decadent! You're embarrassing David. Now let's talk about your vacation. Censored, of course." There was a brief pause, a knowing look between her parents, and Chelsea said, "Just look at those elevators. It's like Buck Rogers in the twenty-fifth century, isn't it—"

"Chelsea," David said, taking her hand. "Shut up."

"Merciful heavens," Harold said after a long moment. "She did. What do you think about that, Mimi?"

"I hope, *j'espère*, that she isn't pregnant before the wedding."

David choked on his scotch. He hadn't used anything, nor had Chelsea. He felt an awful sense of fate descending on his head. Then he felt something he'd never felt before: a sense of well-being, a sense of rightness. He shot Chelsea a look, but she was looking frantic and nearly shouting, "Waiter! I want another glass of white wine!"

"*Mon Dieu*," said Mimi. "Another margarita!"

* * *

"I feel battered, bruised, bent and otherwise mutilated," Chelsea said, slouching in the passenger seat of David's car.

"I didn't use anything, Chelsea," David said, studiously watching traffic before he pulled out of their parking spot.

"Join the club," Chelsea said. And she started praying in Latin.

"Chelsea, could we have—"

"David, please. I don't know. I'm very erratic, oh, forget it!"

She slouched even farther down, her knees against the dash. "Please forget what my parents said—they were off the wall. Marriage is ridiculous. Out of the question."

David finally got himself into the heavy traffic on Market Street. He said blandly, not looking at her, "Lots of people do it."

"Yeah, and lots of people don't make it."

"Yes, true enough." He thought glumly that she'd just experienced first-secondhand what a divorce was like. Well, it wasn't that bad. But he saw that she was scared, skittish, and he didn't know what to say. What if he *had* gotten her pregnant? He swallowed. He decided, his scientific persona coming to the fore, that he would monitor the situation closely in the upcoming weeks.

Why not get married? He rather hoped suddenly that he had gotten her pregnant.

No, that wasn't fair. Nothing seemed particularly fair at the moment, or particularly clear. He felt a surge of desire for her, followed by a spurt of impatience. For heaven's sake, she wasn't exactly *young*. One would think that he was something of a good catch, wouldn't one? He wasn't fat, he wasn't bald, he was a good lover, damn it. What woman wouldn't want him?

Stupid sod.

Chapter 14

David paused a moment at his front door, momentarily nonplussed. Raucous laughter, squeals and general hilarity were coming from inside.

When he strolled into his living room he saw Chelsea, Mark and Taylor all sitting on the floor in front of a blazing fire, playing, of all things, chess.

Chelsea was saying, "Now, Mark, the rook doesn't go in a diagonal, the bishop does. Look!"

"Check, Chelsea!" Taylor shouted.

"All right, you guys, this isn't fair! We put your ages together and you still don't come near to me, and therefore you can't beat me. Aha! See, my knight goes here in front of my poor king."

"He's pinned!" Mark announced with great glee.

"You got that right, kiddo," Chelsea said. "What are you going to do about it? I'm awfully devious, so be careful."

"Dad!" Taylor jumped to her feet and then ran into his arms.

David wrapped his arms around his daughter and squeezed. "What is going on here?" he asked over Taylor's head.

Mark took his turn to be hugged by his father. "We're tromping Chelsea, Dad."

"If you know what a pin is you obviously are," David said, smiling at Chelsea over his son's head.

Both kids were wearing jeans and baggy shirts. All three *kids* were barefoot.

It was at that precise moment that David made up his mind to marry Chelsea Lattimer. He didn't question his decision. He just let it flow through him, making him feel pleasantly warm, making his world expand by two continents.

"Come on, Dad, Chelsea needs help—bad!"

"Hi, dear old Dad," Chelsea said, rising. She hugged him, resting her cheek against his shoulder for a moment.

"You still alive with these little devils?"

"We're fine. You look tired. You okay?"

He tightened his arms around her, leaned down and whispered in her ear, "I'm just fine, but I am feeling a bit...deprived."

"Dad, you're kissing Chelsea again!"

"At least," Mark said to his sister, disgust in his young voice, "he's not touching her bottom."

"Yeck," Taylor said.

"Just wait until she's eleven or twelve," Chelsea said. "Yeck will turn to wow."

"Boys are stupid," Taylor said.

"What about silly girls?" Mark began, and David groaned.

"I'm going to get a beer. How about you, Chels?"

"A beer, Dad?" Taylor's eyes widened. "You never used to drink that stuff."

"It's the working man's drink, and I am a working man," David said.

"White wine for me," Chelsea said. "That, you guys, is the working woman's drink."

The kids were so wound up that it wasn't until eleven o'clock that they were finally tucked into bed. David dropped onto the sofa beside Chelsea. "Lord, what an evening."

"Lots of fun," Chelsea said. "I'll give you chess lessons, too, David," she added provocatively.

"Let's neck, instead," he said, and pulled her onto his lap.

David saw movement from the corner of his eye and said without turning his head, "Get back to bed or I'm going to turn into a monster. It's my turn to have Chelsea's attention. Scoot!"

"Yes, Dad."

"Yes, Father."

David leaned his head back against the sofa pillows. "They've certainly changed," he said.

Chelsea stiffened just a bit. "What do you mean?"

"They're...children, I guess, not little regimented soldiers."

"Don't let the general hear you say that." She wrapped her arms around his neck and nestled closer. "I missed you."

"Me, too," he said, his eyes closed, his entire body relaxed. It occurred to him suddenly that Chelsea had acted like a glorified baby-sitter for him. "Chels," he began, his hand rubbing up and down her back, "I appreciate all the time you've spent with the kids."

"My pleasure," she said. "I've never been around children before. It's been fun. Truly."

"I just don't want you to think that I've, well, that I've been using you."

"I think there probably are things you could feel guilty about, Dr. Winter, but the kids aren't one of them." She added thoughtfully, after nibbling at his earlobe, "I've learned a lot from them. And something else neat—they're already very socialized, but they still blurt out what they're thinking, and it usually knocks my socks off."

"I don't think they used to blurt out anything," David said.

Chelsea squirmed a bit to get more comfortable, and David groaned. "I'm in bad shape," he said.

"Unfortunately there's nothing to be done about it, Dr. Winter."

"Then hold your bottom still, or I'll fling you on the floor and ravish you."

She laughed and pressed her breasts against him. "I need to get myself home and get some sleep. I promised Mark and Taylor that I'd help them pack all their San Francisco goodies. What time is their flight to Washington?"

"Just before noon. Thank God they like the general. Mark's all excited about visiting the space museum, or whatever it's called."

Chelsea realized that she would miss them and asked very carefully, "When will they be coming out here again?"

"In April, for a week. Then I'll have them for about six weeks this summer."

"That's not too long to wait," she said, squirmed a bit, then jumped to her feet. "Now where did I put my sneakers?"

He hadn't meant to do it, but the words just came out without his permission. In the middle of the San Francisco airport. With hundreds of people nearby. They'd just deposited the kids with Margaret and the general, said their goodbyes and waved again as Mark and Taylor disappeared down the corridor to the plane.

Chelsea stared at him. "What did you say, David?"

He looked away from her, wishing he could retract the words, to save them for an intimate moment, but it was too late. He said, his teeth gritted, "I said that I want you to marry me, Chelsea."

"That's what I thought you said," she said, and kept walking toward the escalator.

David looked at her back and got angry. He caught up with her in a moment and grabbed her arm. "What the hell kind of an answer is that?"

"That, David," Chelsea said, "wasn't an answer. It was just a bunch of words that didn't mean anything to fill in time while I tried to figure out why you asked me what you did in the first place."

"I didn't mean it...that is, I didn't mean to do it here, just after we saw the kids off with Margaret and the general...in the most unromantic place—"

"I understand," said Chelsea, who didn't understand at all. "Please, David, let's wait. Really, I don't think—"

It was his turn to cut her off. "I would have expected you to say something a bit more...loving."

A harried businessman bumped her with his clothes bag, apologized and rushed on.

Chelsea felt as though the world had tilted and she was going to fall off. Marriage! He couldn't mean it, not really. It had been brought on by the fact that she got along so well with his children. He saw her as their surrogate mother, saw them all together in a blissful, utterly fictionalized future, where all was sweetness and light and good fun. David was merely confused.

She said, "Let's go have a toothsome Mexican dinner."

"What?"

"I'm hungry, and I want my dinner."

He clamped down on what he'd intended to say. He'd give her two glasses of white wine, then trot out his good qualities for her inspection and obvious approval.

He managed a smile and said, "Onward. To Mill Valley? The Cantina?"

"Yes," said Chelsea, not looking at him.

The Cantina was crowded, and they had to wait twenty minutes for a table. David made certain she drank two glasses of wine during that time. He spoke only of things at the hospital, to which she responded with an appropriate positive or negative. He wished he knew what she was thinking.

He ordered a third glass of white wine for her over her taco salad. She raised an eyebrow at him, but said nothing. David didn't drink a thing.

"Chelsea," he began, "about what I said at the airport—"

"I will think about what you said, David, if you're certain you still feel the same."

"I still feel the same. I want to marry you."

"I will think—"

"Damn it! Just listen to me a minute. Chelsea, I'm not a pauper. My income is reasonable. I can support you—" He swallowed on that faux pas and shook his head. "What I meant to say is that I'm not a pauper. You enjoy making love with me. We have fun together." He stopped, thinking it ridiculous that he should have to be selling himself to her. She either knew all that already or she didn't. She either wanted to marry him or she didn't. He said nothing more, merely speared a bite of his enchilada and chewed.

"You're from Boston," Chelsea said, not looking up from her meal.

"That certainly is a profound statement," he said.

"What I mean is that I...well, I want to think about it, David. Please, give me some time."

And that was that, he thought. She gave him a rather curious, puzzled look when he walked her to her front door, but didn't invite him in, just sent him on his way at ten o'clock at night. It didn't occur to him until much later that he hadn't told her that he loved her. He smacked his palm against his forehead. Dumb!

It was Elsa who told him that a lady wanted to speak to him on the phone. David, in the middle of stitching up a six-year-old's head, grunted and asked Elsa to take a message. Elsa hadn't told him it was Chelsea Lattimer.

It was close to six o'clock in the evening when he finally broke free. When he saw Chelsea's name on the message slip he frowned and quickly dialed her number. Three rings, and then her damned answering machine.

"If this is David," a subdued voice said, "the answer is no. I'm sorry. This is, ah, Chelsea."

David stared at the phone as if it were something alien and quite distasteful. He heard the buzz. Damn it, she hadn't even said enough to fill up the free time between buzzes.

He rang her up every thirty minutes until midnight. Same message. By the time he dragged himself to bed his silent fury with her had changed to outraged anger. He cursed her until he fell asleep.

The next morning he called again. Her regular message was on the machine, not the special one she'd left for him. He cursed her through his shower, breakfast and drive to the hospital.

By afternoon he was back to silent fury.

By evening he wanted to cry in his beer.

"Chels, where the devil are you?"

"Up at the Heritage House in Mendocino," Chelsea said to George. "Look, George, I just wanted to get away for a while."

George looked thoughtfully out the window, then back to the phone. "It's been nearly a week. Have you been there all that time?"

"Yes."

"You really didn't have to run away, Chelsea."

Chelsea chewed on her lower lip. "Is David all right?"

"If you mean by that is he still acting like a human being, the answer is mostly. He finally fessed up to Elliot yesterday. I think he'd like to beat you silly, Chels. You really didn't explain anything to him, did you?"

There was a deep sigh on the line. "No, not really, I guess."

"Do you love him?"

"Well, yes. No. I'm not really certain, George. How 'bout I'm miserable and leave it at that?"

George was silent for a moment, then said crisply, "I think I'll drive up to see you today. How does that sound?"

"Just promise not to tell David, all right?"

"You got it."

At two o'clock that afternoon George found Chelsea in the beautiful restored Victorian sitting room-bar at the Heritage House. She looks awful, George thought, staring at her friend before Chelsea was aware of her presence. There were shadows beneath her eyes, testifying to sleepless nights, and her fingers were nervously plucking at her slacks. What a mess, George thought, planted a smile on her face and strode forward.

"Hi," Chelsea said.

"Hi, yourself," George said, then sat down on the old sofa beside her friend. "You look like a reject from—"

"Don't say it. Too true. A silly, weak woman is always supposed to look like this. George, I blew it!"

George saw the tears swimming in her friend's eyes and quickly rose. "Let's go for a walk along the cliffs."

A stiff breeze was blowing up from the ocean, but the sun was bright overhead. "It's so beautiful here," George said, taking a deep breath. "When I was last here with Elliot, I didn't get to see much of the scenery. Thank heavens the cottages are interesting in themselves."

Chelsea didn't say anything, merely leaned down, picked up a pebble and flung it with precision out into the water.

"You want to tell me about it, Chels?"

"He asked me to marry him at the airport. I was so taken aback that I didn't say one sensible thing. Then at dinner he started telling me all about his...prospects, I guess the word is."

To Chelsea's surprise and disgruntlement, George laughed. "I'm sorry, Chels, but I did the exact same thing to Elliot, only we were thirty-five thousand feet in the air. I told him all about my investments, how I'd pull my own weight and all that stuff. He looked at me as if I'd lost my marbles."

"What happened?"

"He put me off, just as you did David. Eventually he told me no. He'd prepared this damned speech, all about my growing career and his ancient years and how it couldn't work. I wanted to kill him, as I recall."

"You never told me that," Chelsea said.

"Well, I'm telling you now. Actually, I didn't tell anybody. It hurt too much at the time."

"Does David hurt, do you think?"

"For heaven's sake, Chels, he asked you to marry him, didn't he?"

George gave her a fond, exasperated look. "Of course he loves you. How can you doubt that?"

"He didn't say anything about love."

"Goodness, you must really have had him going!"

"George, look, I think he asked me to marry him because we'd had such fun with his kids, and he saw me as being the perfect surrogate mother for them. You know, all sweetness and light. At least, that's what I thought."

"I never realized David was such a shallow person," George said. "But, then again, I suppose you know him best."

"Shallow! He isn't shallow!"

"But, Chelsea," George said reasonably, "you just said that he didn't love you, he just wanted a glorified baby-sitter."

"George, why don't you just leave and smile up at me from a cover on a magazine!"

"Can't take the heat, huh, Chels? All right, I'll stop ragging you. Now you can't stay up here for the rest of your life. What do you intend to do?"

"Go home and see him, I guess," Chelsea said, her voice more resigned than glum.

"And what will you tell him?"

Chelsea stopped, sat down on an outcropping of rock and dangled her legs. She said after a moment, "George, will you please stop pacing in front of me? You look so bloody beautiful, it makes me feel like a toad."

Obligingly George sat down beside her. "Now we're two toads sunning ourselves on a warm rock. Talk, toad."

Three minutes of dead silence followed.

"I know you've been spending hours thinking, Chels. Why don't you just think out loud?"

"Oh, all right. David is from Boston."

"Good grief, a capital offense!"

"That's not exactly what I mean. I mean that he and I couldn't be more different. He's got to think I'm a flake, George, even though he's probably forced himself not to believe it right now. You know, a good-time girl who's never serious. A person who makes his kids face up to being kids and not little stuffed shirts. And he's still got to be a stuffed shirt. People don't really change, George, you know that, even though his ex-wife told me he had. He'd be at me within six months to stop joking around and running off at the mouth."

"Hmmmm."

"And he said nothing at all about loving me. I think he's lonely and sex starved, that's all."

"And you make him laugh, right?"

"Yeah."

"And you enjoy each other in bed, right?"

"Yeah. He won that wager. I kept thinking that the next time we'd make love I'd yawn and want to read."

"Hmmmm."

"It just kept getting better," Chelsea added in a mournful voice.

"That certainly sounds suspicious. I agree with you, Chels. I'm so bored with Elliot now that I've read everything on the bestseller list just to keep myself going."

"You are not! Elliot can't keep his hands off you, and you're always draped all over him!"

George arched a perfect eyebrow. "Really?" she said in a drawling voice.

"You're a rat, George, or a rattess."

"And you, Chelsea Lattimer, are an idiot. Do you love David?"

"Damn it, yes, but I'm not going to marry him. George, just imagine all the problems we'd have. It just wouldn't work."

"What problems?"

"Well," Chelsea said finally, "lots of problems. I just can't think of any right now. He'd turn back into a stuffed shirt within six months."

"Actually, I only see David as a stuffed shirt when he turns seventy."

"Maybe, maybe not. I just wish he didn't look and act like one of my heroes most of the time."

George fell silent, and Chelsea didn't see the wicked gleam in her eyes. She said, "I wonder what a hero would do with you, the heroine?"

"Something outrageous, doubtless. David isn't ever outrageous. He's too dignified."

"Even in bed?"

"Well, not usually. Well, never, actually."

"Hmmm."

"I guess what it boils down to, George, is that I'm just scared. Marriage is something that makes me start shaking. It's the heaviest commitment a person can make. What if I blow it?"

"Why would you blow it?"

"Well, just look at David and Margaret. They didn't make it, and they appear to have had everything in common. David and I are as different as…I can't think of anything original, and I don't want to be trite. Writers don't want to say the expected thing."

"Can you imagine two people any more different than Elliot and me? A doctor and a model? Lord, Chelsea, it's the differences that make life interesting. I carry on passionately about something, Elliot laughs, and we each end up seeing the other's point."

Chelsea was wearing her mulish look, George saw. "So what are you going to do?"

"I'm going home, and if he wants to hear it, I'll tell him that I want more time. Like a year or six. I don't want to be scared when we get married.''

"That sounds like a plan," George said.

"What do you mean by that snide remark?"

"Snide? *Moi?* Chelsea, you're beginning to lose your sense of humor. Come on, let's go home.'' I've got things to do and miles to go before I sleep, she added silently.

And George, who looked angelic and didn't believe that people should stick their oars in, was prepared to launch a boat. She smiled lovingly and with great understanding at Chelsea, helped her check out of the Heritage House and followed her back to San Francisco.

Chapter 15

Elliot tried his most nonchalant voice. "So, David, what did Chelsea have to say?"

David shook himself like a mongrel dog and sat down beside Elliot at the poolside. "She said she wanted time to think about it, dithered around and hung up."

"Sounds reasonable, I suppose," Elliot said.

David cursed, drawing a disapproving glance from an older woman whose bulk should have prohibited the wearing of her bilious green swimsuit.

"Actually," David continued, "I felt like flinging her over my shoulder and carting her off someplace."

"As a matter of fact, perhaps that's the way to go," Elliot said, so relieved that David himself had gotten with George's program that every tense muscle in his body relaxed.

But David was on a roll and didn't hear him. "She's being so stubborn, so damned obtuse. She won't even let me see her, much less make love to her." He cursed again the moment the disapproving woman had moved away.

"I've got a plan," Elliot said.

David arched a thick dark brow. "Yes?"

"Well, actually, it's more George's plan than mine, all based on the fact that Chelsea loves you."

David looked inordinately pleased at that. "She told George that? That she loved me? You promise, Elliot, she really said that?"

"Yes, indeed. I also gather that she's convinced that you guys are going to continue to be dynamite in bed. She's just scared because, according to her, the two of you are so different. She's afraid that you're going to turn back into the stuffed shirt Mr. Hyde after six months."

David looked honestly surprised. "That's the stupidest thing I've ever heard!"

"Yes, I agree, but she's quite serious about it. That and wanting more time. I think she's also worried about making a commitment of such magnitude." Elliot stretched a bit, then said in an offhand voice, "As I said, George has a plan. As far as I can tell, it's foolproof."

"Tell me. Lord knows I'm ready to try anything."

"There's a poker game at Chelsea's house this Friday with the boys."

"I wasn't invited," David said.

"You'll be having lunch with Delbert, Angelo and Maurice on Union Street tomorrow."

"Why? Not that I don't like the *boys*, but what's the purpose? Do they want to borrow money?"

"No money involved. The *boys* are behind you one hundred percent. You'll work out the details of the plan with them tomorrow."

"It's not illegal, is it?"

"Oh, no," Elliot said as he slipped back into the water. "As a matter of fact, you're going to become a Mark I hero. Now, supermacho stud, how about a ten-lap race?"

"You ain't got a prayer!"

"What's the matter, Sweet Lips?" Delbert asked as he hugged Chelsea.

"Nothing," Chelsea said. "Why do you think anything's the matter?"

"You look like an onion whose skin has been peeled away."

"That's disgusting! Angelo, come take this fool away. You, Maurice, come help me with the goodies in the kitchen."

"What did perfect Sarah come up with this time?" Maurice asked, following her out of the room.

"She certainly appears to have it bad," Angelo said to Delbert. "We *are* doing the right thing."

"I hope so," Delbert said, scratching his head. "David better work everything out."

"Yeah, if he doesn't, there'll be no more poker games with Chelsea." This brought forth a worried look and a doleful sigh from the both of them.

It was nine o'clock, and Chelsea had lost nearly fifty dollars. She didn't care. She was still working on her first glass of white wine. When the doorbell rang she sloshed her glass onto the poker table.

"Go answer it, honey," Delbert told her. The moment she left the living room he poured her another glass of white wine and sprinkled a bit of white powder into it. He stirred it with his finger. "No turning back now," he said.

"She's miserable for sure," Angelo said. "Have you ever seen her lose so much money so soon?"

"And not give a damn," added Delbert.

"David!"

"Good to see you, old man!"

"Come sit down. I'll get you a beer."

Chelsea looked shell-shocked. She'd answered the door and seen him standing there, gorgeous, smiling and sexy. She'd backed up. Now, with her three friends behind her, she said, "What are you doing here? You weren't invited."

"Delbert asked me," David said with his most engaging smile. "Said he was broke and needed to win, thus my invitation. You don't mind, do you?"

"He's already won a great deal off me," Chelsea said. She felt wrung out and wanted to belt David and kiss his face at the same time. Instead she bumped into the table and her wineglass tipped over. She stared stupidly at the wine spreading over the cards and poker chips.

The four men stared at the empty glass, then shot comic looks at each other.

Angelo said, "Chels, honey, go get a dishcloth or something. I'll pour you another glass."

"Keep her in the kitchen for a bit," Angelo said, motioning to Delbert.

"No plan is perfect," Maurice said easily as he poured another glass of white wine and added his white powder. "You can use *your* finger to stir it this time, Doc."

For a long moment David didn't move. What he was doing was dishonest, ruthless, unfair, outrageous...*Mark I*. He stirred the wine with his finger.

He raised her glass out of the way while she and Delbert cleaned up the mess.

"Well," Chelsea said to David, "I suppose that since you're here you might as well play." She stomped out of the room and returned with another chair. "Sit and lose."

Chelsea was too miserable to realize that every sip of her wine was to the accompaniment of four interested pairs of eyes. She gambled wildly, and won. "You guys aren't paying attention," she said finally.

"Oh, yes, we are," Maurice said. "You just got lucky, Sweet Lips."

Chelsea won the next hand with a pair of threes, and she giggled. "I must be drinking too much," she remarked to her newly filled glass of wine. "I think I'll switch to soda water."

Everything was so funny. She no longer felt nervous with David sitting next to her at the table. She thought he was the finest thing she'd ever seen, and said so.

"Finest thing?" David said, grinning at her.

"Yes," Chelsea said, and tried to focus on his face. "And you've got the most beautiful teeth."

"Very white," Delbert agreed.

"I like it when you smile like that," Chelsea said, ignoring Delbert.

"I promise to smile like this for the next fifty years," David said. He gently covered her hand with his.

Chelsea stared down at his hand. "I feel odd," she said. David caught her as she fell forward.

"Step two coming up," said Angelo.

"Stay with her while I pack her bag," David said, and took himself to her bedroom.

Ten minutes later, after congratulations and at least a half-dozen rounds of good luck, David eased Chelsea into the passenger seat, fastened her seat belt and sped out of Sausalito.

Thirty minutes later he carried her on board a small charter plane.

"Too much to drink," he told the pilot.

"She's a little thing," the pilot observed. "You'll make sure she's well strapped in?"

"You got it," David said.

Just before they landed in Las Vegas, David slipped the gold band on her finger.

He kept humming under his breath, "I'm a Mark I hero, yours all the way...I'm a Mark I hero, here to stay...."

The motel was easy. David simply left her in the car and signed the register as Dr. and Mrs. David Winter.

He gazed at her hungrily after he'd taken off her clothes.

"You've lost weight," he told her, and she grunted softly in her sleep and rolled over. "Your bottom is still the greatest-looking behind I've ever seen."

It was nearly two o'clock in the morning when he slipped into bed beside her, curving spoon-fashion against her back.

He thought he'd go out of his mind with her beautifully naked beside him, but instead he fell asleep very quickly—the sleep of the ruthless, he thought.

Chelsea turned in her sleep and flowed into a large, very warm male body. It was nice, and she wrapped her arms around the warm, hairy chest.

She came awake on a sneeze. She opened her eyes slowly, saw that a tuft of hair was responsible for the tickling nose, blinked like an owl and squeaked.

David closed his arms around her and pulled her closer.

"David!"

The sound of her own voice sent shards of hangover through her head.

David opened his eyes, looked up into her shocked face and smiled. "Good morning, love," he said.

Chelsea's mouth felt as if it were stuffed with damp cotton. "I don't feel well," she gasped. "This is a miserable nightmare.... I need some aspirin."

She pulled away from him, and he let her go. She managed to stand beside the bed, saw that she was naked, and gasped.

"Aspirin in the bathroom," David said.

She stumbled into the small bathroom, found the aspirin bottle beside her toothpaste and popped three of them down. She looked at her face, groaned at the dreadful apparition staring back at her and brushed her teeth. For want of anything better she wrapped a towel around herself and staggered back into the bedroom.

"I don't understand," she managed, staring at David, who was now sitting up in bed, the covers coming only to his middle.

"Come back to bed, Chels," he said in a very loving voice. "You'll feel better in no time at all, I promise." He was telling the truth. It wasn't aspirin in the bottle, it was something stronger, designed to relieve any ache, pain or hangover in the animal world.

"All right," she said. She slipped in beside him, lying on her back, the towel still firmly around her. "I don't understand," she said again. "Where are we? What are you doing here?"

Now it begins, David thought. He turned on his side toward her, balancing himself on his elbow. "We're in Las Vegas," he said.

"Las Vegas! But..." She looked desperate. "We were at my house! Where are Delbert and—"

"They're home, of course. They did see us off, however. They send their congratulations." He allowed a few moments to show her his disappointment. "Don't you remember, Chels?"

She grew very still. The pain in her head was only a dull throbbing now, and her brain and mouth felt as if they were working in concert again. "I didn't have any clothes on," she said. She turned to look at him. "You don't have any clothes on, either."

"No, love. It was great between us. Don't you agree?"

"We...we made love?"

"Chelsea," he said, trying to sound hurt, "did you drink all that much?"

"No! That is, I remember the white wine and then..." Her voice trailed off, and she pressed her palms against the sides of her head.

"Chelsea, are you serious? You really don't remember what we did?"

She shook her head.

"You insisted that we get married right away. Nevada seemed like the best place. I managed to buy you that wedding band."

Slowly, as if her hand belonged to someone else, Chelsea lowered it and stared at the simple gold band. She started shaking her head. "No, it can't be true...."

She sounded so bewildered and so frightened that he was ready to confess everything. He opened his mouth, but she forestalled him.

"I asked you to marry me?"

He made a noncommittal gesture that she took for an affirmative.

"And you did? Here in Las Vegas?"

"You don't remember the preacher?" he asked, unwilling to lie directly anymore.

She shook her head, looking even more miserable.

I'm simply not a Mark I hero who's ruthless and outrageous, he decided, and said, "Chelsea—"

Chelsea turned toward him at that moment and pressed herself against him. She rested her cheek against his shoulder. He stared down at her tousled head and very tentatively closed his arms around her back.

"I remember now," Chelsea said, frowning against his throat. "At least, I think I do. Didn't you tell me that you loved me, David?"

I've just fallen down the rabbit hole, David thought. "Yes," he said. "I love you. I will love you in six months and in thirty years."

"Will you make love to me again?" She raised her face, and David very willingly began kissing her. "You're not too tired?"

He groaned softly against her mouth. "It's been too bloody long," he said. "I've missed you, Chelsea."

She giggled. "Too long? Have you already forgotten last night, husband?"

"Yes," he said with great honesty. "I guess I have. It's a sign that I can't get enough of you. Come here, you crazy woman."

He pulled the towel away and smiled. She felt so damned good against him. He decided not to think about any consequences that he was certain would eventually plague him to perdition. "I've missed your bottom."

"And I've missed your—" She smiled, closing her fingers around him. "My, my," she said, giving him nipping kisses on his chin, "such enthusiasm! I'm glad you didn't drink as much as I did."

"Never," he said, his hand moving from her bottom to caress her belly. "I love you, Chelsea, and I don't ever want you to forget it."

"Why should I? You're such a gentleman, David. If another drunk woman asks you to marry her in the future, I'll just have to make certain that you're too exhausted to carry through."

He laughed softly against her temple. "Fair enough. Now, wife, let me show you the depths of my enthusiasm."

She quivered at the mental image of him on top of her, deep inside her. "David," she whispered, "I think we'll only be able to *feel* the depths of your enthusiasm."

How, he wondered as he tried to gain a modicum of control, was he not to fall on her and ravish her in a minute flat? It had been so long, so bloody long. He pulled her very inquisitive hand away and pushed her onto her back. "Lie still a moment. I want to see what I've got for the next fifty years."

He lightly held her wrists together above her head. "Very nice," he said, his eyes traveling over her body. "Very nice, indeed." He lowered his head and gently nipped at her breast. "Warm velvet. Is that what one of your heroes would say?"

"Yes," Chelsea gasped. "With maybe a soft and a pink thrown in."

"And wet?" he asked, his tongue gently lapping over her.

"Probably just damp. Wet sounds almost too explicit, more realistic than romantic."

"Let me check that out," he said. "In a romantic way, of course." He released her wrists, moved on top of her and slid down her body. Her legs parted for him, and he eased comfortably between them, resting his head on her soft belly for a moment. She felt his mouth caressing her scar, what she called her moped memento.

Chelsea felt his marvelous fingers stroking up her thigh and discovered that she was holding her breath. She expelled it when she felt him touching her. "Wet," he said, great satisfaction in his voice. "And soft and inviting and—"

He felt her hands tugging at his hair. "More evidence is needed," he said, and moved down.

Chelsea jerked upward when his warm mouth closed over her. She felt his fingers splayed over her stomach, pressing her back. "And very sweet," he said against her, and she quivered wildly.

She felt his finger ease inside her, felt his mouth warm and demanding, and she cried out. She shouted his name as her legs stiffened. Pleasure crashed through her. Small gasps of feeling continued, and when he entered her, slow and deep, she lifted her hips, tugging at his shoulders.

"David," she said, her voice trembling, "I'm so glad I asked you to marry me. It was the best idea I've ever had in my life." Then she moaned as his fingers slipped between them and found her. "I was so stupid not to grab you by the hair and drag you to my cave when you first asked…ah, David…me."

"Once again, Chelsea," he said, and she willingly obeyed him.

With great enthusiasm.

"What would a Mark I hero say about that gorgeous, sexy bottom of yours?" he asked some minutes later. He was lying on his back now, and Chelsea was covering him like his own personal blanket.

"Impudent? Sedentary?"

His hands kneaded her buttocks. "Hmmmm," he said. "How about gorgeous and sexy?"

"My heroes would never have to use the same words twice."

"Even when they're close to death from satiation?"

She giggled, raised her face and looked down at him. "You're the gorgeous one, David."

"Are you talking about my bottom? How about soft and white and a marvelous handful?"

"You or me?"

"You, turkey. I'm lean and muscled and virile. And I don't have a bottom. I have hard, sculpted buttocks."

"You read too much," she said, tugging on his earlobe. "Now if you really want to get crazy and euphemistic, how about hard and pulsing and throbbing?"

"Lord, not now, lady. Behold a limp being."

"I'll keep you, limp and everything. David, thank you for marrying me. If I hadn't gotten a tad tipsy I might not have had the courage to ask you."

He refused to think about the century's greatest lie, at least not now, on his...honeymoon.

"Then why didn't you want to talk to me, Chels? I was the world's most miserable bastard."

She ducked her face down and buried it in the hollow of his neck. "I was scared."

"Of me?"

"Of marriage. And me."

His hands moved again over her bottom. "I need a bit of explanation for that one."

"I'm twenty-eight, David. I was really beginning to think that marriage wasn't for me. And you and I haven't always gotten along, you know."

He chewed that over a bit, then said, "But your heroes and heroines don't get along right away, do they? No, I know they don't. As a member of Chelsea Lattimer's fan club I know for a fact that they fight like wombats and hummingbirds."

"That's...different. I've always had the niggling suspicion that women tend to equate sexual satisfaction with love. After all, we're not simple like you men are. I was afraid that I was talking myself right into my own theory."

"And what do you think now?" Oddly, he was tense as he asked her that question.

"I think that I'm the luckiest woman alive. If you continue to make love with me, say, twice a day for the next fifty years I probably won't give it much more thought."

"Fair enough," he said. "How many times a night?"

She laughed, hugged him, kissed his chin. "I'm so glad I asked you to marry me!" She arched back and picked up his left hand.

Frowning, she said, "Where's your wedding ring?"

Oh damn! Well, if one had to commit perjury, one might as well do it with panache. "You were in too much of a hurry. Don't you remember? You grabbed this wedding band, then yanked me out of the pawnshop. I think I remember the owner muttering about poor beleaguered men and insatiable women."

"You're lying!"

"Well, maybe just a bit, a tad, a veritable diddling amount."

She kissed him, thoroughly. "This," she said, giving him a very sexy look, "is our honeymoon."

"Yes," he said, his eyes darkening with pleasure, "it most certainly is. Do you want to gamble?"

"You've already won the wager, Dr. Winter!"

"Yes," he said. "Yes, I have, haven't I?"

The consequences of their marriage didn't occur to Chelsea until they were seated cross-legged on the bed, eating a delayed breakfast.

"The children!" she said. "My parents. Your parents. George and Elliot. Cynthia and John. The world."

He chewed on a piece of bacon, gaining great satisfaction from watching the curve of her breasts beneath the pale violet camisole. He managed to pull himself from his fond contemplation. "That sounds like a whole bunch of folks," he said.

"David! No one knows we're married!"

"True enough," he said. He grinned at the thought of Delbert, Angelo and Maurice.

"What will your children think?" She groaned.

"They love you." That was something else to feel guilty about, he thought. "Chelsea," he began slowly, "you do like Mark and Taylor, don't you?"

"Of course I do. It's not me I'm worried about."

"You don't mind being a stepmother to those two little hellions?"

"Not at all. Don't you remember Evangeline, one of my Regency heroines? She adored the hero's little boy, Edward. And don't forget Giana, who became Leah's stepmother."

"Well, that settles it, doesn't it?"

"Yes," she said, smiling, "I suppose it does. As for my parents, they'll be dancing for joy. I can't understand why they thought you, of all men, practically walked on water."

"But they do," David said smoothly. He suddenly paled. "Chels, birth control." He smacked his palm against his forehead. "I'm not using anything and you were...well, you were so excited about getting me to the preacher, you didn't use anything, either."

She was silent for a long moment. "We're married, right?"

"Yes," he said, watching her with a fascinated eye.

"Then I can say whatever is in my head, right?"

"Yes," he said again, his fascination growing by leaps and bounds.

"I mean, even if something was embarrassing to me before, now that we're married I shouldn't be reluctant about saying anything I want to?"

"Absolutely."

"All right. I told you I was erratic. Well, I'm not, not usually at any rate. I'm probably due before the end of our honeymoon."

"Bummer," he said.

"Finish your toast, David," she said, wriggling out of her camisole. "Time's awasting."

Chapter 16

It occurred to Chelsea only after she'd fastened her seat belt on the flight from Las Vegas back to San Francisco. "David?"

"Yes, love?"

"How did we get to Las Vegas?"

She wasn't certain, but she thought he flushed just a bit. No, she thought, smiling, that was silly. Perhaps he was just one of those people who were white-knuckled until after the plane was in the air.

"Actually," he said, his brain going into overdrive, "you were so anxious to get me to Nevada and married that I got a friend of mine who owns a private plane to fly us. Don't you remember at all?" Lawyers, he thought, had the right idea about getting themselves off uncomfortable hooks. Ask a question back. Chelsea was looking thoughtful.

"I do remember a loud burring sound and some bumping around. I guess it was the engines of a small plane, huh?"

"Sounds like it was," he said smoothly, and quickly added, "Since we're in first class, we'll get free champagne. You want to indulge in something other than white wine?"

"Fine with me," Chelsea said.

"You know what we can do during the flight?"

She shot him a sexy look, and he shook his head. "Get your one-track mind on different appetites. We need to discuss where we want to go on our real honeymoon."

"Hawaii," she said firmly. "Maui, to be precise. I haven't been there yet."

"You got it. I've never been to Hawaii."

"I go visit Tom Selleck on the tube every week, but it's not exactly the same thing."

"No lusting after other men now, Chelsea."

"I won't have the time or the energy," she said, and accepted a glass of champagne from the flight attendant.

They toasted each other, then David said, "When will you be free, as in between books?"

"In a couple of months. I'm on the last third of the San Francisco trilogy. And guess what, David?"

"Hmm?"

"My hero is a doctor and his nickname is Saint. He's wonderful, needless to say."

"Mark I or Mark II?"

"Definitely Mark II. Well," she added on a wicked grin, "maybe there's a little dash of Mark I in him. But, as I said, he won't be tucked away for about two months yet."

"I'll set up my time, then. Do you have a good travel agency?"

They continued mundane talk, then Chelsea grew silent. David waited a moment, then said, "What's up, honey? You getting post-cold feet?"

She gave him a dazzling smile and shook her head vehemently. "Oh no, husband. I was just thinking about all my writer friends. What Dorothy Garlock, for example, will say about my runaway elopement to Las Vegas is nearly beyond my imagination. Much less Linda Howard and Fayrene Preston and Ann Maxwell—she's Elizabeth Lowell, too, you know—and Laura Parker and Candy Camp and Iris—"

"My God," he said, interrupting her seemingly endless list. "How many phone calls are there going to be?"

"I can't forget my friends Marilyn Staggs and Jean Weisner in Houston. They own bookstores." She moaned. "I think announcements will be the best way to go. I don't think I could take all the verbal abuse I'd get over the phone."

"That's another thing, Chels," he said. "Whose phone?"

She gave him a blank look.

"I mean, where are we going to live?"

"Oh," She looked at him helplessly. "Marriage leads to more consequences than my poor brain can manage."

"My commute from Sausalito to the hospital is only thirty minutes. If you'd feel better about staying at your condo, that's fine with me."

"I love the city, too, and your place." She sat thoughtfully silent for a while, then announced in a firm voice, "I have the most portable profession in the world. All I need is my computer and I'm set. There's no need for you to be driving an hour a day."

"Are you thinking of what we could, ah, accomplish in that hour?"

"You got it," she said, grinning. Her hand roved slowly up his thigh.

He clasped her hand, halting her upward motion. "I can take tomorrow off and we'll move you to the city. All right?"

She nodded, but he could tell she wasn't terribly excited by the prospect.

"Would you like to sell your condo or rent it out?"

"Sell, I guess. Then why don't we buy a house in San Francisco? Maybe an old Victorian in Pacific Heights or Sea Cliff, though I'm not very handy. Are you?"

"No," he said firmly, "not at all handy."

"We'll have to pool our resources and see what we can come up with."

They made the necessary phone calls that evening from David's apartment. It became obvious to Chelsea after her talk with her parents that her dad was disappointed. She said after setting down the receiver, "I've got to think about this." She clasped and unclasped her hands in her lap. "David," she blurted out suddenly, "would you mind if we got married again, for my parents' sake?"

If he could have yelled for joy, he would have. For a moment he simply couldn't believe that she, bless her innocent heart, had suggested the solution to the problem, and so quickly. He'd planned to speak to her parents, as a matter of fact, say in two or three weeks, and have them request another ceremony. He'd dreaded it, just imagining their reaction to what he'd done. He swooped down on her, lifted her bodily off the floor and swung her around. "Do you know how marvelous you are?"

"Well, maybe," she said, looking down into his smiling face. She added, frowning a bit, "You look like a Cheshire cat." That gave him a moment's pause, but her mind was in high gear, and she quickly went on. "There won't be a problem with our marriage license, will there? As in having two of them?"

"Not a single one," he said smoothly, removing that Cheshire cat look, whatever that was.

"And you, you gorgeous man, must have a wedding band. I'm not letting you out of the house without one."

"You're right," he said. "I have to fight the women off all the time. A wedding band might protect me."

"Harrumph," said Chelsea.

"Let's go make love," David said, swinging her up into his arms.

"More controlled experiments for science?"

"You got it, Cookie, although I prefer uncontrolled."

"Let's hear it for science," Chelsea said later, so exhausted she could scarcely move. "I think we can submit this paper now with conclusive proof."

"Proof that women are as easy as men?"

"Proof that you, David Winter, are the sexiest, most talented, neatest... luckiest man on this continent."

"I'll drink to that," David said, and pulled her closer. He said a few moments later in a blurred voice, "Oh, damn, we'd better set the alarm clock. We need to be up and out of here early to get everything done."

Chelsea groaned. "The honeymoon's over."

"Not by a long shot, lady."

"I just wonder how long a shot you're talking about?"

He groaned. "There goes your one-track mind again."

They moved Chelsea the next day in a quickly rented U-Haul. David's apartment looked like a disaster area by the evening. He looked about ruefully. He had believed his place was large and airy.

Chelsea sat down on a packed box. "I can't believe you're going to leave me alone with all this tomorrow."

"Remember your vows. For better and worse." He grinned down at her and ruffled her curly hair. "You'll never walk alone," he said, and made a phone call, arranging for two very strong, healthy young men to arrive in the morning. "All you have to do is supervise, sweetheart."

Chelsea did, with great verve. David came home at about five in the afternoon to a very tidy apartment and a study that was no longer his.

Her computer looked quite at home on *his* antique desk, and the room was lined with bookshelves, filled with her books.

Funny about marriage, he mused. He'd pictured Chelsea in his apartment with great anticipation, but he hadn't quite gotten past that delightful fantasy to the reality of her possessions.

Chelsea saw that he was looking somewhat shell-shocked and said, "I put up temporary shelves in that closet for all your medical journals and books. I'm sorry about being such a space pig, but you work at the hospital and I work at home, and I can't do it in the closet."

"Fair enough," he said with a fond farewell to his formerly very neatly organized things as she shut the closet door.

It did please him inordinately to see her panties next to his shorts in the dresser drawer. He picked up the violet camisole and rubbed it against his cheek. "I shall always have salacious memories about this garment."

"That, David," she said, "is a three-dollar word. I didn't think you doctors were all that well educated."

"I must have read it in one of your books."

She hugged him. "I am so happy," she said, rubbing her nose against his chest, "that I almost hurt. I wish I'd seduced you to Las Vegas a long time ago."

He felt the familiar stab of guilt. "I don't know how much longer I can live with this," he said.

"What?" she asked, looking up at him. "Live with what?"

He looked startled, then realized that he'd spoken aloud. "That is," he said, improvising with quick desperation, "I don't know how much longer I can go without flinging you on the bed."

"Well, I tried my hand at some cooking. Wanna be brave and give it a fling?"

"Before we indulge in our other appetites?"

"Hamburger Happiness," she said. "I don't know what that will lead to, if anything. That reminds me, I've got to talk to Sarah. I'm not at all certain that she'd want to drive to the city all the way from Corte Madera."

"Offer her the moon. If that doesn't work, offer her my poor body."

"Forget that, Champ. Hamburger Happiness. Ugh!"

He grinned at her doleful tone and followed her to the kitchen. She said over her shoulder, on a happier note, "George and Elliot invited us over to dinner tomorrow night. They send their congratulations, by the way."

"Yeah," David said. "I saw Elliot today at the pool. He was grinning from ear to ear." Indeed he was, David thought, feeling that dreadful guilt wash over him again. Delbert, Angelo and Maurice had all called him today, demanding details and chortling like comrades in arms who had just pulled off the most fantastic coup. He added over his third bite of Hamburger Happiness, which wasn't at all bad, "All the folk at the hospital want to give us a party."

"Life isn't going to be simple for a while, is it?"

"What about all your writer friends?"

"I guess I'd best go somewhere and get some announcements. I haven't the foggiest idea of where, though."

"Call George."

"No, I'll call Neff. She'll know. Lord, she lives right here in the city. I'll invite her over and rack her brain."

"Neff who?"

"Well, it's Neff Rotter, also known as Laura Matthews, Elizabeth Neff Walker—"

"How do you guys keep yourselves straight?"

"That, my husband, is a question I should ask you."

He sat back in his chair and crossed his arms over his chest. "I'm beginning to believe that this honeymoon is going to last a good thirty years."

"Well, if I went to all the trouble of getting you to Las Vegas, it better!"

He ducked his head down, feeling a guilty flush wash over his face.

"David?"

"Can I have some more Hamburger Happiness, Chels?"

"Brave, aren't you?"

Yeah, he thought, about as brave as a mushroom.

* * *

During the next week, he played over and over in his mind what Chelsea's reaction would be to his confession. No, sweetheart, his mind said, we're not actually married, but we will be soon, or we are now—confession time after the ceremony—so what difference does it make? I did it because I love you and you love me. I just had to get you over your nervousness about it, that's all. You jerk! You made a fool of me! Oh, David it doesn't matter. I love you. You did the right thing. *Damnation!*

Phone calls came in from all over the country from other writers. He happened to pick up the phone one evening and heard, "Is this the gorgeous hunk that finally caught Chelsea?"

"Uh, yes, I guess so," he said to the laughing voice on the other end.

"I can't wait to read her love scenes from now on! You, dear man, are now raw material, buff research."

"Uh, well, let me get Chelsea!" He dropped the phone and sent an agonized look toward his *wife*.

"Hi, Barbara! Is Beth on the other line?" Chelsea asked, and then was silent, a wide grin on her face. "Yes, oh boy, you're right about that! Yes, that's *moi*! You got it. Thanks for calling."

"Well," Chelsea said, grinning wickedly at him, "you just got your second dose of writer wit. Keenan and Rowe aren't writers but they're close enough—they publish a magazine. Remember Cynthia Wright? She, my dear, was merely your first dose. Hefty, wasn't it?"

"Articulate, to-the-point bunch, aren't you?"

"Yes indeed, but you just wait until Tom Huff finds out. Lordie! Ain't it great?"

He supposed so. His kids had been a bit less articulate, but Mark had asked him quite clearly on the phone if he was kissing Chelsea more now and patting her bottom still. Margaret hadn't been at all surprised, and the general sent his best wishes. As for his parents, they'd sent a telegram from the south of France, a very noncommittal telegram.

The only snake in the garden appeared a week and a half later when Chelsea, dancing around when he got home from the hospital, handed him an article from the *Examiner*. It was all about the two of them, and he, the most romantic doctor in the world, had gotten fifty percent of the billing. He continued reading about their whirlwind romance and elopement to Las Vegas. He moaned. "Who," he said, "is responsible for this?"

"I think Barbara called a journalist friend and he called me. What's the matter, David? Don't you like it? There are only a couple of inaccuracies, and they're not anything major."

He said the first thing that popped into his mind, "Hell no! For God's sake, Chelsea, I'm a physician! This...ridiculous exposè will make my colleagues think I'm nothing more than a—"

"A what, David?"

Menacing tone, he thought, and quickly retrenched. He managed a deep sigh and said, "Please, in the future, Chels, just ask me, all right?"

"Ask you what? If you feel too above all us ordinary mortals to appear in print? Ask you if it's all right the next time I'm interviewed or on TV to speak about us?"

"No, damn it! Well, maybe. I just feel like I'm on parade, that's all. I don't enjoy feeling like a fool."

"Feeling like a fool because you eloped with me? Feeling like a fool because you married a writer who just happens to write *that* kind of thing? Lord, should I switch to Westerns? How about sci-fi? Ah, mysteries. That's manly, isn't it, with so much more credibility. You wouldn't be so embarrassed and ashamed."

"Stop turning your agile mouth on me, lady!"

"You usually enjoy my agile mouth!"

"I should have said agile tongue!"

"You enjoy that especially!"

"Damn it, keep to the point!"

"There *is* no point, except that I never should have asked you to marry me! You're becoming an uptight Easterner before my very eyes. You didn't even have to go into a phone booth to change into your stuffed shirt!"

"There's no reasoning with you!"

"Yeck!"

And she stomped out, grabbing her purse from the hall stand.

"Chelsea!" he yelled after her. The front door slammed.

He thought suddenly that it was the man who was supposed to slam out. He heard her car rev up and take off, tires screeching.

What, he thought, walking slowly to the window, had the argument been about in the first place? He saw the accursed newspaper article on the floor. Stuffed shirt, was he! Just because he didn't want to appear like some sort of...what?

A real life hero?

Marrying a creator of heroes?

Using him for subject matter?

Dumb jerk!

He knew she'd gone back to Sausalito, to her condo. It wasn't rented out yet. What to do? There wasn't any phone service.

He was at the point of driving like a bat out of hell to Sausalito, when the phone rang. It was the hospital, not his "wife." An emergency. He cursed, knowing there was no hope for it, and went in. He was in emergency surgery until two o'clock in the morning.

When he got out of surgery there was a message for him from Chelsea. She was home, *their* home, thank God.

She was asleep when he arrived, for which he was profoundly thankful. He didn't think he was up to apologizing with the proper finesse in his current state of fatigue.

She was still sleeping when he left the next morning. He didn't awaken her. Instead he had red roses delivered.

"It's something a hero would do," she said when he walked in the door that evening. "A hero who feels guilty and doesn't want to talk about it. A Mark I hero who's more macho than sensitive and believes organic matter will save his hide."

"Hi, sweetheart," he said, and pulled her into his arms. He felt so much relief just to have her close to him. "Please, Chelsea, don't walk out on me again. Let's fight until we can't think of any more words, all right? Just don't leave me."

"I didn't mean what I just said. It was awful of me. I'm a dreadful person. You're not a Mark I, except in bed. I'm sorry."

"I love this spate of apologies from both of us," he said, and gently lifted her face. "You're beautiful, I'm proud of you, I'm crazy about you."

"I guess that about covers what I wanted to say, too." She sniffed. It had been a dreadful day, filled with silent pacing, recriminations, a trotting out of all her insecurities.

"Tell you what, love. Let's have a phone booth installed here. Then, if I turn stuffy, you can shove me into it and hand in a starchy white shirt."

"Okay," she said, giving him a wan smile. "And I'll watch my mouth."

"No, let me watch your mouth, or feel your mouth, as the case may be."

"Are we still on our honeymoon, David?"

"I'm not sure. When is the wedding?"

"Next week, at George's house."

"Good, we'll start all over then."

"David?"

"Yes, sweetheart?" He was busily nuzzling her throat.

"The wedding will be very private."

"Hmmm."

"It's the reception."

"Hmmm?"

"It's going to be, well, just a bit larger than anticipated."

He drew back and looked down into her beloved face, which expressed guilt and wariness. "No," he said softly, placing a fingertip over her lips. "Don't tell me. I don't want to know. All I want right now is for you to make love with me."

She felt that marvelous warmth curling through her. "How can I turn down an offer like that?"

"You can't," he said, tossing her, laughing, over his shoulder and patting the most beautiful bottom in the world.

Chapter 17

David couldn't believe it. He stared down at the pair of leopard-print underwear and the funny note that accompanied it. He might have known. It was from Cynthia and John-blond-haired-Sanchez who had tried to kill his dog with a rake. George peered over his shoulder, burst into laughter, grabbed the appalling wedding present out of his hands and tossed it to an emergency room nurse.

David managed to slither out of the living room under cover of the roars of laughter from the guests. He continued slithering like a shadow against the wall until he found the safety of the Mallorys' kitchen. It was filled to bursting with people chopping and cooking, and people hefting up trays of food to serve the guests. He found the back door and kept slithering until he reached an isolated part of their small garden.

He sat down on the lone stone bench and leaned back, closing his eyes. You're about ready for the phone booth, he told himself. So what's the big deal about a pair of leopard jockey shorts? A good half the presents they'd received were gag gifts. Lord, he just wanted it all to be over with, all resolved, he and Chelsea finally married—for the second time, of course.

It was nice of the Mallorys to have gone to so much trouble—this party followed by the wedding and the reception afterward. Just three more days, he told himself.

Tomorrow he and Chelsea would go out and buy him a wedding ring, and, he'd insisted, an engagement ring for her. He suddenly remembered the engagement parties and the wedding reception he and Margaret had been given. They had, he decided, perking up, been very formal, very tasteful and very boring. He remembered now that he'd never seen so much silver in his life. He wondered what had happened to all those teapots and serving trays.

"Hi. What's up, Doc?"

He looked up to see Chelsea smiling down at him. "I was just counting my blessings," he said, then added, grinning, "and my leopard shorts."

"You feeling overwhelmed?" Chelsea asked, having seen him slink out of the living room.

He patted the bench beside him, and she eased down. "I love you," he said, and pulled her into his arms. "And I wish we were alone, doing crazy, wonderful things to each other."

"That's a plan I second," Chelsea said, and leaned against his shoulder, sighing. "Everyone is so kind and so much fun, and really, so marvelous—"

"But?"

"I just wish this were the wedding reception and that would spell the end of all the festivities."

"I do like that sexy nightwear you got, though. Who was that from?"

"I honestly don't remember," she said.

"Well, I think that sinful red cutout nightgown will spell the beginning of our festivities."

She giggled, feeling suddenly relaxed for the first time in days. The novel was going exceedingly slowly. Her doctor hero Saint was definitely taking a back seat to her doctor hero David. There was just so much to do, so much to occupy her mind. She ran her hand over his chest. "All mine," she said.

"Yes, ma'am. You've got a fifty-year lease on this property."

"Is there oil in these here hills?"

David was feeling punch-drunk and couldn't think of a retort. Her mind never slowed down, never. Well, maybe when she was in bed with him. He seemed now to recall once when he'd had the last word. She'd just lain there, staring up at him with blurred, vague eyes, a silly smile on her face.

"Three more days to go, sweetheart, then we'll hole up. Okay?"

She nodded against his shoulder.

"When are your parents coming in?"

"Tomorrow." She gave a shudder. "I can't imagine what they're going to give us for a wedding present."

"Let me shudder with you."

Actually, the Lattimers' wedding present, presented the following evening at their apartment, was their trip to Hawaii, including the honeymoon suite at Kapalua Bay and a Mercedes to drive around the island. It was an incredibly generous gift.

"What do you think, Cookie?"

"Oh, Dad!" Chelsea threw her arms around her father, kissed him soundly, then dove for her mother. "You guys are too much!"

Mimi Lattimer gave her daughter a fond, teary look and pressed a long, narrow box into her hands. "Just a little something for you, dear."

Chelsea shot a look at David, then opened the wrapping and the jeweler's box. Inside was a diamond-and-emerald necklace, exquisitely fashioned. Chelsea simply stared at it. Then she looked up at David and burst into tears.

"Cookie!"

"Lovey!"

"It's so beautiful," Chelsea sobbed against David's chest.

"It is, indeed," David said, smiling at Chelsea's parents over her head. "Come on, sweetheart, you're going to take all the starch out of my white shirt."

He stroked her hair for a moment, then said, "I'd like a drink. How about you guys?"

"A margarita," said Mimi.

"White wine, like my little girl. Come on, Cookie, we couldn't give you gold. You might outshine your old man."

David grinned ruefully as Harold Lattimer ran his fingers over his gold necklace.

"First," David said, "I want to see Chelsea in the necklace. Go blow your nose, sweetheart, then get back here."

The necklace looked exquisite, and David took back every snobbish thought he'd ever entertained about her parents. He wished suddenly that his own parents could show their love so openly and warmly.

After the Lattimers left for the evening David took himself off to the shower. Chelsea went to the other bathroom and took off the incredible necklace. "Well," she told her image in the mirror, "if you ever run out of ideas, you won't starve for at least six months." She lovingly laid the necklace back in its box. Her gold band caught on the clasp and she gasped, terrified that she'd hurt the necklace. Slowly, carefully, she pulled the clasp free of the ring, and in the process scratched her wedding band.

"Oh, no," she wailed. For the first time she tugged off her ring and examined it under the light. Just a very slight scratch. She held it in her palm for a moment, wondering suddenly what woman had sold the ring. She hadn't felt at all strange about wearing another woman's wedding ring until now. Had she been an obsessive gambler? How sad if it were true. She held the ring up to the light again, closely examining the inside of the band. She realized that it was old, very old. She squinted.

There was writing. She rubbed the inside with a tissue and looked again.

She froze.

                                    * * *

David was tired when he emerged from the shower, but not that tired, and he was surprised and disappointed to see Chelsea curled up on her side, her back to him, sound asleep.

He didn't wake her. She must be exhausted. He quietly got into bed beside her and turned off the bedside lamp. He lay on his back, his head pillowed on his arms, and stared up at the dark ceiling. Day after tomorrow and it would all be over. Of course, that thought led to his inevitable confession. He groaned to himself. He should be up for the Chicken of the Year award. What the hell should he do now? What if he told her before the wedding and she freaked out and told him to go to hell? What if she just looked at him, her wonderful, expressive eyes wounded? Would she ever trust him again? What if? What if? He was making himself crazy. He couldn't go on like this. He had to come clean.

"No, David. No way. Just forget it."

"I can't, Elliot," David said miserably. "I love her, and what I did was—"

"What you did was give Chelsea what she wanted," Elliot said, interrupting him firmly. "Besides, it's a little late, isn't it? The wedding's tomorrow."

David cursed.

"Hasn't she been saying continuously that she wished she'd asked you to marry her sooner? Isn't she happy as a pie-eyed clam? Doesn't she love you to distraction?"

"Yes and yes and yes, but—"

"Fine, tell her, or better yet, go talk to her parents."

"You think it would be a good idea? Get their opinion and all that? What if they look at me like I'm some sort of fiend straight up from Hades?"

Elliot studied his friend closely. David was suffering, and here Elliot was being glib and a know-it-all. David felt guilty, and Elliot didn't blame him, but it *had* seemed the best thing to do at the time. They were all guilty, guilty as hell. But what to do? He couldn't begin to imagine Chelsea's reaction if David confessed prior to the wedding. She would laugh and forgive him—that's what she'd do. At least it sounded good, he thought. Elliot sighed. Why wasn't life ever simple?

The matter was taken out of David's hands. The night before their wedding Chelsea's parents insisted she stay at the Fairmont with them. Chelsea, who had agreed to her parents' request with more enthusiasm than he liked, smiled up at him and gave him a subdued goodbye kiss. He thought indulgently that she had a super case of nerves. In all honesty, though, he was feeling subdued himself.

He spent a lonely night in the empty expanse of the bed. It was nearly two o'clock in the morning when he made his decision. He would tell her on their honeymoon. He felt like an Atlas who no longer carried the world on his shoulders.

The wedding, at the Mallorys' house, was as private as David and Chelsea wanted, and it went quite smoothly, with only the Mallorys and Chelsea's parents present. Chelsea, to David's chagrin, whispered to him after the Reverend MacPherson had pronounced them husband and wife, "Did our ceremony in Las Vegas go as quickly?"

"I don't remember," David said, his stomach curdling.

She looked so perfect, he thought, dressed in a soft cream silk dress, the beautiful necklace at her throat. She was now wearing both an engagement ring and her wedding band.

They had an hour before the reception to unwind a bit. George, a bird of such glorious plumage that it almost hurt to look at her, sidled up to her husband and whispered, "'All's well that ends well,' I've decided."

"Yes," Elliot said. "Yes, indeed. And Alex kept decently quiet through the whole thing."

"A perfect child," George said.

"I'd best go upstairs and see if his nurse had to gag him."

George crossed the living room to hug Chelsea. She watched her friend for a moment. Chelsea was holding her marriage license. The expression on her face made George frown a bit. It was an odd look. She tried to remember if she had stared with a bemused expression at her own marriage license. She didn't think she had.

Well, no accounting for people's reactions. She heard her small son's lusty cries from upstairs and grinned. He probably had been gagged during the ceremony.

"Every time I marry you I buckle up," Chelsea said, fastening her seat belt on the plane that would take them directly to Maui.

"Ah, yes, it seems so," David said.

They were silent until the plane was in the air.

"You happy, sweetheart?"

She turned to face him, and he felt himself melt. "You're so very beautiful," he said, and kissed her. They separated at a slight cough from the flight attendant.

"Honeymooners?"

"Yes," they said together.

"Well, a present was sent on board for you." The woman lifted a bottle of Dom Perignon for their inspection, a huge red bow around its neck.

"From my publisher," Chelsea said, carefully pulling away the card from the bow. "Just look at this list of names, David!"

He did and was impressed. He was married to a very successful woman, and it pleased him inordinately. It occurred to him that even a year ago he would probably have been threatened by his wife's independent success. No, he corrected himself, he would never have been such a stuffed shirt as all that.

"Will you support me in the manner to which I'm accustomed?" he asked as the flight attendant poured them two glasses of the champagne.

"Well," Chelsea said quite seriously as she toasted him, "my income has steadily increased with each contract. Who knows? Maybe in five years you'll be eating bonbons on the beach, giving lewd looks to underage girls in scanty bikinis."

"Now that sounds like a plan," he said, and felt the champagne bubbles tickle his nose as he drank.

The flight passed pleasantly, and they weren't too conked out by the time they reached the Kapalua Bay Hotel on Maui. The drive from the airport took a good hour, but the scenery was beautiful, and David, who had never been to paradise before, was duly impressed.

They spent the rest of the afternoon in bed, emerging only at seven in the evening for dinner. A walk on the beach in the moonlight, David was thinking. Tonight was D-Day. Or D-Night, as it were.

Yes, he repeated grimly to himself as he forked down a delicious bite of lobster, tonight it would be. He watched his wife down two glasses of white wine. I'm a cunning, devious bastard, he thought as he offered her another.

Chelsea slipped off her panty hose behind a tree and stuffed them into one of her shoes. It was idyllic. Moonlight, the crashing ocean waves, the balmy evening.

"Chelsea," David said finally, the word barely emerging from his tight throat.

"Yes, love?"

Dreamy voice, he thought. Onward. "There's something I need to tell you."

She stopped a moment and turned to face him. She had a sweet smile on her face. "Yes?"

He loosened his tie. "It's about Las Vegas."

"Yes?"

More interest in her voice now. But still dreamy.

"Well, you remember how we were playing poker that evening with Delbert, Maurice and Angelo?"

"How could I forget? I lost over fifty bucks."

Voice smooth, unsuspecting—loving, in fact.

He blurted out, "I slipped you a Mickey!"

She didn't say a word, merely stared up at him, her shoes dangling in her hand.

"Well, actually, it was one of the guys who slipped it in your glass. Then you spilled the wine and we did it again."

"Hmmm," she said. "So that's what made my mouth feel like a drought had hit."

He stared at her, not believing her calm, matter-of-fact voice.

"Chelsea," he said, his voice desperate now, his confession almost finished, "we really didn't get married in Las Vegas. I lied to you. I wanted you so much and I knew you wanted me and so...well, I did it."

Silence.

She said, very softly, "Did you regret doing it, David? Pretending to marry me, I mean."

"God, no! But I've felt so guilty, like a damned worm. I was too chicken to tell you sooner."

The moonlight fell over his face, and the gentle breeze ruffled his hair. She slowly raised her hand and smoothed it back from his forehead.

"Say something, damn it!"

"All right," she said agreeably. "I know."

"Know what?" he said, stiffening.

"A lot of things, actually," Chelsea said, teasing him just a bit.

"Chelsea—"

"Here, David, hold this for a minute."

He watched silently as she slipped off her engagement ring. He took it from her, feeling edgy, wary and bewildered.

She worked off the wedding band and held it up in the moonlight. "I don't think you can see anything out here. The light isn't bright enough, but I'll tell you. There's an inscription inside the ring. It says, *Rebecca Winter, 1915*. Your grandmother, David?"

"Yes," he said. "I loved her very much."

Another couple strolled past them, hand in hand.

"When did you find out?" he asked finally.

"Does it matter?" she said, a small smile playing about her mouth.

"You don't want to send me to the castration center in Sacramento?"

"Perhaps, but for just a little while. It was a marvelous Mark I thing to do, I decided. Forgive me for letting you suffer, but I thought you deserved it for just a little while."

"You wouldn't have said anything?"

"Not until you did."

"I was thinking at one point that I'd wait until our tenth wedding anniversary."

"Then," Chelsea said in a serene voice, "that's when I would have said something. Who knows? Maybe our kids would have overheard."

"Put the ring back on, Chelsea."

She did, then the engagement ring.

Afterglow

He pulled her into his arms. "Is this as romantic as one of your novels?"

"More so," Chelsea said, pulling his head down so she could kiss him. "This is real."

"You truly forgive me for what I did?" he said, nuzzling his mouth against her hair.

"I'll probably use it in a novel," she said. "Now, David, how's your energy level?"

"You want a moonlight swim?"

"That's a start, I suppose."

"What would a Mark I hero do?"

"You tell me, and that will go in the novel, too," she said, and leaned back in the circle of his arms, waiting for him to speak.

"I guess I'm feeling so happy and so sinfully relieved that I'll just have to sit here on the beach and contemplate my incredible good fortune."

She laughed.

David said, "Have I had the last word for once?"

"Don't hold your breath, Doctor," Chelsea said, and wrapped herself around him.

* * * * *

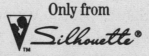

Bestselling author

JOAN JOHNSTON

continues her wildly popular miniseries with an
all-new, longer-length novel

The Virgin Groom

HAWK'S WAY

One minute, Mac Macready was a living legend in
Texas—every kid's idol, every man's envy, every
woman's fantasy. The next, his fiancée dumped him, his
career was hanging in the balance and his future was
looking mighty uncertain. Then there was the matter
of his scandalous secret, which didn't stand a chance
of staying a secret. So would he succumb to
Jewel Whitelaw's shocking proposal—or take cold
showers for the rest of the long, hot summer...?

Available August 1997
wherever Silhouette books are sold.

Silhouette®

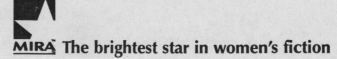

This summer, the legend
continues in Jacobsville

A LONG, TALL
TEXAN SUMMER

Three **BRAND-NEW** short stories

This summer, Silhouette brings readers a special
collection for Diana Palmer's LONG, TALL TEXANS
fans. Diana has rounded up three **BRAND-NEW**
stories of love Texas-style, all set in Jacobsville, Texas.
Featuring the men you've grown to love from this
wonderful town, this collection is a must-have
for all fans!

*They grow 'em tall in the saddle in Texas—and they've
got love and marriage on their minds!*

Don't miss this collection of original Long, Tall Texans
stories...available in June at your favorite retail outlet.

Look us up on-line at: http://www.romance.net

LTTST-T